ALL THE RIVERS RUN

ALL THE RIVERS RUN

Nancy Cato

NEW ENGLISH LIBRARY

First published in the USA in 1978 by
St Martin's Press

First published in Great Britain in 1978 by
New English Library
© 1958, 1959, 1962 by Nancy Cato

First NEL Paperback edition November 1979
Reprinted January 1981
New edition December 1981

NEL Books are published by
New English Library from
Barnard's Inn, Holborn,
London EC1N 2JR,
a division of Hodder and Stoughton Ltd.
Printed and bound in Great Britain by
©ollins, Glasgow

0 450 05424 1

All the rivers run into the sea; yet the sea is not full: unto the place from whence the rivers come, thither they return again.

ECCLESIASTES, 1:7

Contents

Prologue

High in the Australian Alps a little stream, just born, moves
invisibly beneath the snow, or can be glimpsed through a blue-
shadowed hole between the melting snow-bridges. Grown wider
and deeper, it swirls round boulders, foams through rapids and
leaps over waterfalls, until at last it flows out upon the plains as
a broad and noble river.

By now it has been joined by tributaries from the south, from
the east, and from the north, draining an enormous watershed.
Samples of every mineral and organic substance in the world, it
is said, can be found in the waters of the Murray. Gold and clay,
coal and limestone, dead men and dead fish, fallen trees and
rotting boats: all are carried in solution or suspension in that
placid stream.

It is like life dissolved in time: always passing away, yet endlessly renewed; forever changing, yet eternally the same. Growing
more complex the further it travels, the river has become old and
sluggish by the time it nears the sea. Scarcely flowing, the current
meanders through wide lakes and sandy channels towards the
breakers of Goolwa Beach, the league-long rollers of the Southern
Ocean.

The little town of Goolwa grew up on the last bend of the great,
slow, weary river. The old buildings, made of the local limestone,
have weathered to the same colour as the low sunburnt hills behind. In front, the river stretches beyond the broken and deserted
wharf. A few old paddle-boats are tied up as houseboats, or rest

on the mud at a crazy angle.

You might visit the town of Goolwa a dozen times and not
know the sea was near, nor the mouth of the Murray lost in its
maze of sandhills. Then, on a day of south wind, or a still night
of midsummer, you will become aware of a tenuous thunder, a
faint booming roar just within the bounds of hearing. It is the
voice of the sea.

The river may be calm and glassy, reflecting the bright shape
of the Cross in its dark waters; but always that thunder of the surf
underlines the quiet, pervading the stillness with its deathless
sound.

Now all has become one, the trickle under the snow, the waterfall, the mountain torrent and the gliding stream; and the river,
already within sound of its final dissolution, seems to say: 'There
is no death: in my end is my beginning.'

a river not yet tamed

Stars sweep and question not. This is enough,
That life and death and joy and woe abide;
And cause and sequence, and the course of Time,
And Being's ceaseless tide
Which, ever changing, runs, lined like a river . . .

Edward Arnold: *The Light of Asia*

ONE

Thin white smoke was drifting upward, to be lost in an expanse of pale and exquisite blue. Incense, she thought. This must be heaven, this infinite blueness.

Yet she still seemed to have a body. Something was hurting – the back of her nose and throat – and there was a memory of someone – was it herself? – coughing and retching. Her chest was sore.

She turned her head and into her line of vision came a man, a giant of a man who towered up into the sky. He had a beard, but he didn't look much like God. His round, red, kindly face was half-obscured by this whiskery growth, dark but sprinkled with grey. His chest was covered with hair too, above a pair of faded blue dungarees rolled up to the knee.

'Feelin' better, love?' The red face bent over her and smiled, showing stained and broken teeth.

She tried to smile back. 'Yes, thank you.' As she heard her own voice, the memory of what had happened swept over her like an icy wave, like the wave that had swept her into the sea.

She had got up very early, before dawn, because it was their last night on board. Tomorrow they would reach Melbourne and land in Australia for the first time. She longed to see the country her father had talked so much about, where her mother's sister had come to live years ago.

Yesterday she had seen its coastline to the north-west, low, blue and mysterious. She had smelt the faint, warm, spicy breath of the land breeze at evening. Her father had said it was the trees, the eucalyptus scrub, that scented the wind.

She had woken early this morning and dressed quietly, to go up on deck alone and feel for the last time the ship lifting beneath her feet over the long southern rollers, like a great gallant horse that cantered over the plains of the sea.

It was so dark that she could see only the white water hissing along the side, and a few stars that were being swiftly blotted out by a bank of cloud moving silently, inexorably across the sky. Full sails arched above her, wind shrilled in the rigging.

By the ghostly glow of the binnacle-lamp she could see the helmsman, and behind him the officer of the watch. No one else was on deck but the lookout man away in the bows.

The dark surface of the sea flashed in lines of white as the swelling wave-crests rose. Suddenly there came a frantic cry from the lookout: 'Breakers! Breakers ahead!'

Even as the officer roared an order and the helmsman wrenched the wheel hard over, the ship struck with a splintering crash. The masts bent like trees in a gale, the stays parted with a bang. A great foam-crested wave reared up astern and fell upon the stricken ship.

And she, Delie Gordon, the only passenger on deck, had been buried deep in icy water and swept overboard.

TWO

With a jolt and a hiss of escaping steam the little train pulled up at the dark station. It was a very slow train. It had bumped and swayed along for half the day and part of the night to reach its destination. It stood now, panting with contented achievement; the line went no further.

The guard flung open the door. Exactly as if the one small passenger who remained had been a compartment full of people, he shouted: 'Cooma! Cooma! Change 'ere for the mountain coach!'

She began gathering her scattered things: her gloves, the bulging carpet-bag full of spare stockings, hankies, petticoats, and a change of shoes, the box of fruit and the *Ladies' Home Journal*, and put on the new straw hat with black ribbons which the kindly solicitor, a perfect stranger, had insisted on buying for her in Melbourne. 'That's all right, my dear, you can pay me back from your father's estate when your affairs are all fixed up, if you want to,' and he added a pair of gloves and some shoes.

Everyone had been so kind, so wonderfully kind. Here she was with a bagful of things thrust upon her by Mrs Brownlow, the lady in whose care she had travelled all the way to Goulburn

14

where she changed trains: even one of her dresses (much too large) and a travelling-cloak. Mrs Brownlow's sympathy had been well-meant but rather overpowering. She had been glad to find herself alone at last. Now she was beginning to feel nervous. All was dark and strange; she hoped her uncle would be waiting at the station.

The guard, looking at the small white face of his last passenger, dropped the official manner and became fatherly. 'Give us yer ticket, love,' he said. 'And hand over that there bag. Got everythink? Looked under the seat? Right-oh.'

She followed him out into an icy wind. The small station was dimly lit by two square lamps. A tall man with a drooping moustache and dark beard stepped towards her. He wore an overcoat reaching almost to his heels and a wide-brimmed felt hat.

'Is this Miss Philadelphia Gordon?' he asked.

'You her uncle?' said the guard. 'I was told to 'and her over to a Mr Charles Jamieson, of Kiandra.'

'That's right. Here you are, and thanks.' The guard received something unobtrusively in his palm.

'How are you, child?' The tall man bent and kissed her cheek; the whiskers tickled. She smiled up at him shyly. He was only her uncle by marriage, but he was the first relative she had met, almost her only relative, in this strange new land.

He looked down at her in mild surprise. 'So you are Philadelphia! I had expected a – a *little* girl.' And he indicated a height not much above his knee.

'Oh, but I'm nearly thirteen, Uncle! And I'm tall for my age. Mother says – ' She faltered, while the tears which excitement had kept back began pricking behind her eyes. 'M-mother use to say I shot up too fast.'

He put the bag down, drew her hand through his arm and patted it with his other hand. 'I hope that Auntie Hester will be a new mother to you, my dear. I – we're looking forward very much to having you. We'll have to fatten you up a bit, though. Your aunt is a very good cook.'

She was glad he had not said anything about the wreck, a subject about which she would not yet speak without breaking down. As they walked to the hotel she told him about the trip from the south coast by wagon-team to Melbourne, and her friend the seaman who had rescued her, the only passenger to survive; but she did not mention the dreadful days they had spent on the beach, not the dark shapes bobbing sluggishly in the waves that she still saw in dreams.

15

As they came out of the shelter of the station the wind swooped on them. The air was cold, dry and thin; it pierced straight through the borrowed cloak. The name of the hotel was The Australian Arms, she noted with a little thrill of strangeness.

'We'd better get some sleep, because the Adaminaby coach leaves at six tomorrow morning,' said her uncle.

She was called while it was still dark and stumbled into her clothes by the light of the candle. Breakfast consisted of tea, too hot for her to drink, and burnt toast with great lumps of salty, unmelted butter. She was still half-asleep as they went out to the lighted coach.

Stars still showed in patches in the cloudy sky. Huge shapes seemed to rise up all round the horizon. There was a feeling of height in the very atmosphere, and the windless air was piercingly cold.

The coach started with a sudden forward rush. Wakened by the cold fresh air, she suddenly felt excitement well up in her throat like a bubble. How she loved to be setting off for somewhere, anywhere, in the mysterious light of dawn!

'Tell me about your gold-mine, Uncle Charles,' she said, feeling the necessity to be companionable.

'We-ell . . .' He looked suspiciously at the three other passengers, rugged-featured, wild-whiskered men wrapped in layers of shapeless clothing. Then he said loudly, 'You couldn't call it a mine. I'm just fossicking in the old Kiandra lead. All the good stuff was taken out years ago. Get a bit of colour now and then – not worth the time I put into it.' Then he turned and gave her a long, slow wink.

She didn't quite know what to make of this, so she said, 'What about the mountains? Are there big huge snow-peaks all around, like in Switzerland?'

'Why, have you been to Switzerland?'

'No. But Father sent me a postcard of the Jungfrau after he had been to the top. It is 13,677 feet high. My father used to take us climbing in the north of England. He promised to take us . . .' She faltered, and tears sprang to her eyes. There was no 'us' any more; just herself alone.

He patted her hand. 'I'll take you up a mountain one day, but they're a good way from Kiandra – that's just hills, though it's five thousand feet up. But you'll see Mount Kosciusko this morning.'

16

She squeezed his hand, inarticulately grateful that he had not tried to offer her any spoken sympathy for her loss. He looked down at her carefully. 'I didn't get a chance to see you properly last night. Blue eyes, eh, and black hair! Just the sort of little girl I always wanted.'

'It isn't really black, it's a very dark brown. Haven't you any girls of your own?'

'No, we only have one boy, and he's nearly fifteen. I – we always wanted a girl, but none came. Your auntie suffers in her health, as your mother will have told you. I was very glad when I heard you were coming to us, Philadelphia.'

'I'm – I'm usually called Delie, you know. My name is such a mouthful.' (Her mother had called her by her full name only when she was naughty.)

'Well, Delie then. Were you named after the city in America? Adam, of course, gets his from the Bible.'

'Yes, Father was always planning to go to the States, before he ever thought of Australia. Is Adam big for his age? Is he very brainy? I'm no good at arithmetic.'

'Yes, he's a big boy. He gets fairly good reports, but they all say he has the ability to do better if he tried. He's inclined to be a bit dreamy and forgetful; and his nose is always buried in a book.'

'That's just what they say about me.' She flashed him an amused glance from her blue eyes beneath their cleanly-marked brows. Her eyes were large and deeply blue, too large for her thin, pale face, with its finely-cut, sensitive features. She turned to look out of the misted coach window, rubbing it with the palm of her glove. Behind them the sky was lighted with a clear yellow sun just risen below a bank of indigo cloud. The sunlight fell cold and clear upon a great sea of ranges, darkly blue, tumbling in waves back towards the north and east. Close to the road the hills sloped up and up, and then beyond them appeared a mountain shrouded in snow.

'There's Kosciusko! There he is,' said Uncle Charles, as though welcoming an old friend.

She sat silent and entranced until the mountain was lost again behind the shouldering hills. The clear, golden light on the horizon, the dark blue of the distant ranges, their rolling, rhythmical shapes, all filled her with a sweet unrest, an obscure desire to create . . . something, she did not know what; and gave her a sudden inward surge of fierce joy.

17

It was late in the day when they reached Adaminaby. At the hotel she went straight through a dinner of thick potato soup, braised steak and onions, roast beef and trifle. Then she sat back and beamed at her uncle, who was staring at her with simulated amazement.

'Well!' he said. 'Well, I never. If anyone had told me – if any-one had told me, I wouldn't have believed it. If they'd said, "Charles, that slim little fairy of a thing can eat like a horse," I'd probably have said, "Nonsense – she lives on honeydew and acorns." But seeing is believing. Do you feel better?'

'I feel lovely, Uncle Charles. I hope you didn't think I'm greedy. It's the first time I've felt hungry for ages.'

He smiled. 'I like to see you eat, my dear. Now shall we go and sit by the fire? And how about a liqueur to finish with?'

'Oh, er – yes, I'd love one,' she said not quite sure what a 'liqueur' was.

'Right. Only don't tell your aunt,' he said with a wink. Uncle Charles put a tiny glass, in which gleamed an emerald liquid, into her hand.

'Oh, thank you!' she said, and immediately her mind began a silent, exotic commentary:

Oh, thank you, she said, taking the crystal goblet from Sir Mordred's hand. To the Lady Delie, said the knight, and looking deep in her eyes he quaffed his drink, then dashed the glass to the floor where it shattered into a thousand fragments . . .

The fire was warm, warm and red. The drink was warm and green, like green fire. She was warm and comfortable, inside and outside. Inside . . . inside a warm nest of . . .

'Oh!' she said, as the empty glass slipped from her fingers and rolled on the rug, and her neck jerked painfully. 'I fell asleep.'

Uncle Charles was regarding her mournfully from his rather weak, drooping eyes, set too close on each side of his big generous nose. 'Yes, go to bed now. Eat, drink and sleep, for tomorrow – we go home! It'll be tongue pie for both of us then, for breakfast, dinner and tea.'

Danny the mailman came out of the bar in a glow of rum and good humour. 'Looks like the last trip through for the season, Chas,' he said. 'More snow comin'.'

The wagonette which provided the only transport to Kiandra

18

waited at the steps of the Adaminaby Post Office. It was loaded with provisions that must last the gold-mining outpost through the winter, for once the roads were blocked with drifts Kiandra would be cut off.

Danny threw in the mailbag, climbed up and took the reins. 'Mail's leavin'!' he yelled. 'All aboard!' He flicked the whip over the horses' backs and they moved off uphill.

The early morning sunlight was shining upon Adaminaby from a clear blue sky. They came over the crest, and Delie jumped from her seat with a cry which startled even the most rum-soaked of the passengers into wakefulness. Beside the road a deep valley dropped away, and rose on the far side into low hills covered in grass still brown from the dry summer. Beyond them rose, tier on tier, a range of blue mountains barred and veined and capped with snow. In that clear atmosphere they seemed near, yet purely, unattainably, remote.

'The Snowy Mountains,' said her uncle.

Delie stared wordlessly, until they entered a forest of tall mountain ash and the mountains were lost to sight.

After a pause for a picnic lunch and to rest the horses, they wound on through deepening snow. At last in the late afternoon they came to Kiandra, the shell of an old mining town with that desolate, melancholy air given by roofless houses and smokeless chimneys.

Her uncle took the mailbag from Danny and helped a cold, stiff-limbed Delie down into the snow. He led the way to a small wooden house – almost a hut, thought Delie – set behind a picket fence. He pushed open the front door and dropped the mailbag and Delie's carpet-bag inside. 'Hester! We're home!' he called.

In a moment a middle-aged, middle-sized woman with thick, dark skirts came gliding swiftly down the passage which divided the house.

'Didn't you hear the coach arrive?' asked Charles, rather offended.

'Well, and what if I did? I can't let the dinner burn, can I? And the child half-starved, I suppose?'

He pecked her rather coldly on the cheek. 'Your niece,' he said formally. 'Miss Philadelphia Gordon.'

'Philadelphia! How Charlotte could choose such an outlandish name I don't know –'

'My father chose it!'

' – but anyway, welcome to Kiandra, dear – cold, miserable,

19

drink-ridden spot that it is!' She leaned over and kissed Delie's cheek. The end of her nose was cold and pointy.

I don't like her, thought Delie at once. She shows all the inside of her lips when she smiles, and her nose is horrid; the point of it is cold and wet.

Her aunt was looking at her with small, sharp black eyes. Could this really be the sister of her fair, pretty mother? Delie looked in vain for some family resemblance, and realised, in the silence, that she must say something.

'Thank you, Aunt Hester. It is very good of you to take me in. I will t-try – ' and then to her own surprise she burst into tears.

'There, there, child; you're overtired. Come in by the fire.'

After dinner Delie went to put her few things away in the little box of a room opening off the kitchen. A narrow stretcher was made up with spotless bed-linen and a white honeycomb quilt. A chest of drawers stood in one corner, supporting with an air of shame a small, damp-speckled mirror.

As she peered at her reflection, her eyes grew wide and fixed. There had been too many changes in a short time. Was this girl in the mirror, with the big, shadowed eyes, really herself – Philadelphia Gordon – somewhere in the high mountains in a strange country?

Her aunt's voice, brisk and cheerful in spite of its usual grating tone, recalled her.

'No doubt you've been used to something smarter than this,' said Hester, bustling in with a hot brick wrapped in flannel to warm the bed. 'You don't need to tell me that Lottie married better than I did. It's my work at the Post Office keeps the boy at school; if it was left to his father – pottering about looking for gold that isn't there – we'd all starve.'

She finished this speech with a sharp sniff, which removed the bead of moisture forming at the end of her high-coloured nose. Her cheeks were florid too, and covered with a network of fine red veins. Delie felt a physical relief when the metallic voice stopped.

Her aunt added in a softer tone, 'Poor Lottie! And you, poor child – an orphan, and only twelve years old! Well, dear, they're asleep in the arms of Jesus. We must remember that, and not be sad.'

Delie recoiled a little from the bony arm put around her shoulders. Her mother was asleep in the cold green sea; her father

20

and all her brothers and sisters were buried on a lonely cliff-top, lulled forever by the sound of the sea. How should she not be sad? And all the passengers, and nice Captain Johannsen, and her friend the bos'n, had drowned like rats in a barrel.

She made no reply. Edging away from Aunt Hester, she took up the straw hat with black ribbons from the bed and put it on the dresser.

'A pity your dress is brown, dear – but of course you wouldn't have known you'd need a black. Oh well, you can wear a crepe band on your arm for the time being. For of course you can't go out of mourning yet.'

'I thought you said we should not be sad, Aunt?'

Aunt Hester looked at her sharply. 'Are you being pert, child? Mourning is *always* worn for close relatives, as you surely know. Now, there's something I want you to tell me.'

She paused and looked searchingly at Delie. 'Er – there were just the two of you, yourself and this – this sailor survived the wreck, I understand from the letter I received from your father's bankers. You were marooned on a beach for two days. Ah – where did you sleep?'

'In a cave. You see there was this cave half-way up the cliffs –'

'In the *same* cave?'

'Of course. There was only one.' Delie looked uncomfortable. She wished her aunt wouldn't go on.

'H'm.' Aunt Hester brushed an imaginary speck of dust from the chest-of-drawers. Not looking at Delie, carefully inspecting the top of the chest, she said, 'Did this man – you mustn't be afraid to tell me, my dear – did he – interfere with you in any way?'

'Interfere?' she echoed uncomprehendingly. Then something in her aunt's embarrassment gave her a clue. Her father had been a doctor with advanced ideas about education for girls, and she had some knowledge of biological facts. 'Aunt Hester, Tom was the nicest person . . . He was terribly good to me and as kind as could be and a real gentleman. He looked awful, with big black whiskers and broken teeth and tattoo marks and everything. But he was gentle as a lamb. If it hadn't been for him I'd be dead too.'

Her lip began to tremble again. She bit it fiercely.

Hester said briskly, 'Well, that's a relief. And I may say you were very fortunate that he was like that. *Some* men –' she added darkly. 'Now, I'll leave you to get to bed. The chamber-pot is underneath if you need it. If you want to go out the back, you'll have to use the gum-boots by the back door.'

'Thank you, Auntie. Good night.'

She went out and Delie sat on the bed, overwhelmed with loneliness and strangeness. If only her cousin Adam had been home! If only one of her brothers and sisters, just one, had been spared to share this strange new life! She would try to be very good and make her aunt like her. In Uncle Charles she knew she had an ally.

THREE

CRASH!

'Philadelphia! What have you broken now?'

'Just a – just that old yellow mixing-bowl, Auntie.'

Hester came hurrying down the passage from the Post Office, her black eyes snapping angrily. 'That's the third thing you've broken this week, Miss. That good white cup and saucer, and now my favourite bowl. Really!'

'The second thing, Aunt Hester. What was the third thing?'

'The cup AND the saucer AND the mixing-bowl. A cup and a saucer are two things.' Her eyes dared her niece to disagree. 'I've had that bowl since I was married.'

'I'm awfully sorry. My hands were wet and it just seemed to slip out of them.'

'Everything "just slips out of" your hands. I've never seen such a butter-fingers. In future you had better not wash up at all; you can help me more with the cooking.'

Delie was delighted. She didn't like washing up, and cooking was more interesting. Her aunt was a marvellous cook, using home-frozen meat and vegetables to turn out appetising meals, with occasional rabbit stew. Delie had remarked innocently that they hadn't yet had tongue pie, and wondered why her uncle winked furiously and shook his head at her while Aunt Hester asked sharply where she thought an ox tongue was coming from!

One evening her uncle brought her back some pretty stones, yellow, red and orange, that he had picked out of the clay when he was puddling for gold. They were what she called 'chalk-stones', soft enough to draw with, and after the kitchen table was

22

clear she begged a sheet of brown paper from Hester and began drawing a gorgeous sunset. She was quite absorbed; the room was quiet, the others were sitting in by the fire, but it was still warm here from the stove. The paper was not big enough for her idea; she turned it over and began to draw on the opposite side. Sometimes the stones went over the edge of the paper and made a mark on the white deal table. For a time she was perfectly happy.

She was quite unprepared for the storm that broke in the morning. Hester was livid when she saw the 'dreadful state' of her table, whose snowy whiteness was the pride of her kitchen. Delie scrubbed and rubbed at the coloured smudges, her head down. She couldn't in the least see what all the fuss was about, but she was upset too. She hated the feeling of people being cross with her, and it seemed that she was always doing something to annoy her aunt.

The wagonette had ceased to run from Adaminaby. Instead, Danny arrived once a week on skis, cheerful and round-faced in his woollen cap, and brought the mail-sack with its seal of red wax in by the fire, where it had to thaw before they could loosen the drawstrings and open the stiffened canvas.

At mid-term a letter came from Adam in the frozen sack. Hester seemed to thaw visibly as she read it, even as the sack had thawed by the fire, all its hard angles smoothing out and slumping down.

Dear Mother,

I am quite well and school is much the same as usual. We have had some hail and it is very cold in the mornings, but no snow, worse luck! Have you had many falls yet? I can just see the slopes all white and smooth about the house, and Father getting out the skis and waxing them . . . By the way, don't let that new cousin of mine use my best skis, she's sure to wreck them . . .

'He writes such a good letter,' said his mother fondly, not noticing Delie's scowl as she read out the uncomplimentary reference to the 'new cousin'.

Delie was determined to go to school again; when she came into her inheritance she would be independent, even though she was not of age. Already she was building castles in the air. She saw herself transferred to the great metropolis of Sydney, there to dazzle everyone with her accomplishments; whether as a great dancer or a tragic actress she had not yet made up her mind, but she spent a great deal of time posing and twirling in front of the speckled mirror.

She saw herself quite clearly in these scenes of splendour, even as she trudged through the snow to empty the slop-bucket. If only she could, at least, go skiing over the hills! She went to ask her uncle about it.

Charles smoothed his drooping moustache. 'Tell you what. I'll make you a pair of skis of your own. I've got some seasoned wood here. I'll do it next week.'

'Oh, thank you, dear Uncle Charles!' She clasped her hands under her chin in a dramatic gesture of gratitude, then did a pirouette and banged her hip on the corner of the table.

But when next week came, Charles put off making the skis till the week after. He was always inclined to put things off; Hester had to nag him to keep the wood-box full.

'Next week will do,' he said mildly, when she suggested a trip into the hills for more wood.

'Next week will *not* do,' snapped his wife, rounding on him from where she was hanging the great black kettle in the fireplace. He hastily turned over the page of the *Gazetteer of the World*, in which he had been studying a woodcut of some Polynesian belles clad in nothing but grass skirts.

'Oh well, I'll go this afternoon. Delie can come with me.'

'I want Delie to help me get dinner ready,' said Hester instantly. She had noticed Charles look at the child appreciatively – of course she *was* only a child, but she would be something of a beauty when her contours filled out, with that pale and delicate skin and those deep blue eyes contrasting with her dark hair. And there was just a hint of passion about the full lips, and of determination in the level dark brows, which made Hester uneasy. Perhaps it was a pity Adam was coming home for the spring holidays.

Adam would come with the first wagon through after the winter, and everything the town was running short of: fresh vegetables, wax candles, kerosene, red-tipped lucifer matches, knitting wool, needles, rolls of flannel and wincey, new pick-handles and shovels – each year it was like the raising of a siege.

Delie helped Hester to turn out her son's room. It opened opposite the living-room from the central passage. The two front rooms were the main bedroom and the Post Office. At the back, the kitchen opened into Delie's little room and the bathroom, where hot water for the family baths was carried in to the hip-bath once a week.

In her day-dreams about her cousin she treated him with aloofness and scorn, while he was dazzled by her cleverness and prettiness. For she had a fixed picture of him as a male edition of Aunt Hester – hopelessly ordinary-looking, with coarse black hair and a ruddy complexion, unprepossessing features and an ugly voice.

Before he arrived Hester gave her a lecture on the fact that she was 'getting a big girl now'.

'And remember – no getting undressed by the stove any more for your bath when Adam comes home.'

'No, Aunt Hester.'

'You will be a young lady soon; we will have to be letting your skirts down and putting your hair up. And remember that young ladies must be well-behaved and modest. I saw you climbing the pine tree the other day; that's being a tomboy.'

'But Father used to take me rock-climbing in the mountains –'

'No buts, please. That's quite different. And another thing; you are approaching a change in your life, a certain change in – er – your body.'

The last word came out with an effort and was followed by a sharp sniff. Delie realised with horror that her aunt was embarrassed, and she felt hot all over.

'This change – it is nothing you need be alarmed about, all girls go through it at about your age –'

'Aunt Hester, are you trying to tell me about menstruation?' In her effort to put her aunt at ease she spoke loud and clear.

Aunt Hester started visibly. 'Really, Philadelphia! It is not a thing –'

'Oh, but I know all about it,' she went on airily. 'Father used to lend me his medical books. I've done physiology with him. I know all about the female anatomy, the uterus, the pelvis, the ovaries and all. Why, he did an ovariectomy on a bitch of ours that was always having puppies, and he let me watch. And –'

'PHILadelphia Gordon! Don't ever let me hear you mentioning such things again!'

'But, Auntie, why ever not? Father said that the sooner a girl realised what was in store for her the better. He said that if nature had had any sense she would have made women lay eggs like birds, and that –'

'That's enough, Miss! I don't want to hear your father's blasphemous opinions, and I am surprised at Charlotte allowing you to discuss such things. A girl of twelve! Never in my life – !' She stopped as though words failed her. There were two bright red spots in her cheeks.

Delie closed her lips mutinously. She had thought her father the cleverest man in the world; and her mother, though she pretended to be shocked by his outspokenness, had thought so too.

The next day Hester spent lying close to the fire in the living-room. Her 'old trouble', some mysterious female complaint, had come back and she had been moaning all the morning about her back. Charles lighted the stove for her and put a pile of wood ready by the fire, and said he'd be on his way to the workings, and 'leave her quiet'.

'Quiet! As if it isn't too quiet in this outlandish place!' The harsh voice went up a note. 'But don't think of me; you'll have me in my grave soon enough, which is what you want.'

'Come now, Hester, the winter's nearly over and soon Adam will be home –'

'It's this awful, continual cold . . . If only we could go somewhere to live where it's warm!'

'Just you stick it a bit longer, my dear. I'm on a good alluvial patch right now, and any day I might be lucky. This field has never been worked properly since the early days, except at the Four Mile diggings. If I stumble on something good, I'll sell out for a lump sum. No more prospecting then.'

Hester's only reply was a sniff. It sounded to Delie as though he had said the same thing many times, and no longer had much belief in it himself.

It *was* a dreadfully cold place. The thermometer, which Hester read every day as part of her Post Office duties, sometimes stood at eighteen degrees below freezing well into the morning. The one hotel did a brisk trade in rum, taken 'to keep out the cold'.

At night, Delie would undress by the stove in the warm kitchen, fill a big stone bottle with hot water and take it with her to warm the icy bed. Then she used the water for washing in the morning, for often the water in her bedroom jug would be frozen solid.

When, at last, the skis were made, Delie swept up the already clean floor of the kitchen, sliced onions and peeled potatoes and turnips, scrubbed the table-top and set off with her uncle for Newchum Hill.

She wore the scarlet woollen cap with a pom-pom which Aunt Hester had knitted, unwillingly, because it was the only wool she had; it should really have been black. Her thick blue sweater was a shrunken one of her uncle's, and her divided skirt was cut down from Hester's old navy blue serge suit. Under it were the red turkey-twill drawers her aunt insisted on, both for warmth and decency.

She looked bright as a mountain lory against the white snow, in her blue and red that intensified her hair to blackness and made her eyes more blue. Charles smiled at her.

'Well, when I saw that drab little thing on the Cooma station, in a brown dress and with great dark circles under her eyes, I never thought she'd turn out pretty as a princess.'

Delie glowed. Pretty as a princess, pretty as a princess, she sang under her breath as they trudged to the plateau-like, gentle undulations beyond the town. All the contours of the earth were rounded and smoothed by the snow; the hills were moulded into flesh-like contours with bands and fringes of snowgums like dark hair. The sky was blue, the sun drenched down through sparkling air to the dazzling, gleaming snow.

Melted by midday suns and frozen again at night, the snow had reached the consistency almost of ice on the surface. Charles was carrying their skis over his shoulder. At the top he stooped and strapped Delie's on her feet, then told her to walk about and get the feel of them, while he set off in a swooping series of turns towards the bottom of the hill.

Two hours later, bruised, breathless and almost in tears, Delie trailed back behind him to the town.

'Oh, I'll never be any good!' she wailed. 'And it looks so easy.'

'Of course you will; you have a good sense of balance, but the snow is very slippery at present. Soft snow is much easier to learn in than this crystalline stuff.'

There was a new fall in the next week, great soft flakes that settled like feathers and made deep drifts over the cleared paths.

On her next lesson she learned to stop at the bottom of a slope without sitting down, and to control her direction by shifting her weight. She felt a magnificent sense of power, exhilaration and achievement at the end of a successful run.

This time they skied all the way back to the house in one glorious skimming flight. Welcoming smoke rose from the chimney of the little wooden Post Office; yellow lamplight gleamed a welcome from its windows. For the first time she looked on it as home.

FOUR

The family sat about the table in the living-room. The soft white glow of the hanging kerosene lamp fell upon shining silverware and glass and snowy linen, for Hester strove to keep 'some of the little elegancies of life in this uncivilised place'.

There had been roast beef and Yorkshire pudding, and now there were treacle dumplings swimming in syrup, so light that they melted in the mouth.

Delie could scarcely eat for excitement; she could not take her eyes off Adam at the other side of the table with his bright hair shining in the lamplight. How, she kept asking herself, had these two managed to have such a son? What about the theories of heredity her father had taught her? Adam was like neither of his parents.

He was tall and strong, with a clear brown skin through which the red blood showed in his cheeks, golden-brown eyes, and light brown hair, straight and thick, that grew low on his wide forehead. The whites of his eyes were clear with health, and his boyish mouth looked as if it might be as easily sulky as laughing.

He was laughing now, and he looked extraordinarily attractive.

'Come on, Del!' he cried. 'Aren't you going to have another dumpling? She needs fattening up a bit, doesn't she, Mother?'

Delie passed up her plate in a dream. Adam awed her with his careless good looks, and his air of knowing that the life of the house revolved around him – as it did, in the next fortnight.

Later in the evening she went with him to get wood from the lean-to shed to replenish the box by the fire. They each carried an armful. Delie stopped a moment to look up at the splendid stars, snapping with frost. Strange constellations swung up over the hills. There was the Southern Cross, sweeping low towards the horizon and somehow far bigger and brighter than it had looked at sea.

'You can't see the Cross in England, can you?' said Adam, following her gaze.

'No. When I first saw it I was a bit disappointed, but it looks splendid tonight.'

They went into the kitchen, stamping snow from their shoes. Adam stooped to set the fire in the stove for the morning.

'Your ship was wrecked, Mother told me.' He was banging wood into the stove with unnecessary force, and Delie noticed that his ears were pink. She realised he wanted to say some word of sympathy about the loss of her family. Her heart beat fast; she had the sick feeling of panic that came when she felt someone was going to intrude on the private place of her grief.

'Yes; I was – the only survivor except for one of the crew,' she said with an effort. 'But I don't want to talk about it – you know?'

'Yes, I know, kiddie.' His voice was so gentle that she could not believe this was the spoilt, arrogant boy she had been watching across the table. Her heart warmed to him as he picked up the rest of the wood and carried it to the living-room.

Under the warm winds and clear sunshine of early spring, the snow began slowly to melt away. At the same time Hester softened, became less prickly and demanding, and allowed Delie to go out skiing with Charles and Adam, who carried her skis up the hill for her.

When he went back to Sydney after ten days, the house seemed darker and quieter. Delie and her aunt sat in the lamplight, both feeling forlorn but less antagonistic.

The snow began to lose its whiteness and translucency, to become heavy and dead-looking as it clotted in sheltered corners or on the southern side of walls. Blowflies appeared from nowhere, buzzing maddeningly about the ceilings at night, bumping blindly against the windows by day.

Charles was out all day, chasing those elusive nuggets that were always hiding in the next alluvial patch. The bottoms of his working trousers were stained yellow with clay, his boots were thick with it. He would take them off on the veranda and pad through to the kitchen in his socks to get some hot water for washing. Then, opening the neck of his flannel shirt, he would sit down by the fire and stretch out his legs, leaning back with his pipe between his bearded lips while the steam curled slowly from his socks.

Sometimes he let Delie hold the little jar of gold-dust that he had washed in many months of work, or his one small nugget, no more than a ragged twig of gold. Its dull yellow gleam allured him like the smile of a woman. He was convinced that a fortune still lay hidden out there among the hills.

Before the last of the snow went, he took Delie up the slopes and pointed out the little creeklets that had begun to flow beneath the hollow snow-bridges.

'There are hundreds like this all over the mountains,' he said, 'all slipping down to join the bigger streams and the rivers like the Ovens and the Tumut. This snow we're standing on will flow away down the Murrumbidgee to the Murray River.'

'The Murray?' She vaguely remembered it from her geography lessons on the Empire. 'That's the biggest river in Australia, isn't it?'

'That's right. Big enough to run paddle-steamers on, right from the mouth up into New South Wales. I travelled on one once, from Swan Hill to Morgan, and there was something about it . . . Warm and sunny enough even for your aunt.'

They glanced at each other, sighed and looked out over the slopes, where the afternoon sun was turning the snow to gold, with the delicacy of tint of sunlit clouds. In the level light each grain threw a tiny blue shadow.

There was still plenty of daylight, but Hester had relapsed into her soured invalidism and they dared not stay out any longer. Silently they turned back towards the town.

FIVE

After Delie was declared the heiress of her father's modest fortune, a new kindness came into Hester's manner towards her niece. For why should not Delie help them to get away from this dreadful place and buy a property, perhaps, in some civilised district?

She had never got over the uprooting from the prosperous country district where they had lived when she first met Charles in England. But the restlessness that had brought him to England as a young man, and then sent him back to Australia again still in search of his fortune, had at last washed them up in this outpost on the edge of nothing.

She and Charlotte had been the eligible daughters of a well-off farmer, brought up to be decorative as well as useful. Lottie, the pretty one, had always preferred arranging flowers and sewing, which she did with a certain artistry, to the more practical arts of the dairy and the kitchen.

Hester's dowry had long been used up in their travels from place to place, and in rescuing Charles from several wildcat ventures. She had quite given up hope of seeing the tall young man with the impressive beard, who had wooed and won her, make a success of life. All her hopes and ambitions were now concentrated in her son.

Perhaps their luck would change at last. Charles had found two small nuggets washed out of the soil by the spring freshets, and they were planning a holiday trip to Melbourne for Delie to buy clothes and see the banking firm to which Dr Gordon had transferred his capital for a start in the new country.

Hester was a great believer in good and bad luck. She kept a lucky rabbit's foot in her drawer, and would not wear green, nor walk under a ladder, nor open an umbrella indoors. She pounced upon pins lurking in the rugs, chanting:

> See a pin and pick it up,
> All the day you ll have good luck.
> See a pin and let it lie,
> You will want before you die.

She always looked in her teacup for 'strangers' floating on the surface, and punched them between her fists to see if they were soft or hard, indicating a man or a woman visitor – though any visitor at all was a rarity in Kiandra. She would undertake nothing, not even the making of preserves, on Friday the thirteenth of the month.

It was a Friday, as it happened, when Charles came rushing in without his hat, long before his usual time for returning. He went straight up the passage to the living-room in his muddy boots, Hester following the trail of them with her voice rising in protest. She stopped in the door with her mouth open at the sight of him shaking, as it seemed, a bag full of dirt over her best green plush tablecloth.

Then, with a clunk that nearly went through the table, out fell a large, nobbly rock.

'Charles! Whatever has come over you? Dirt all down the passage, clay on my best – '

'Hester, Hester, Hester!' His usual air of calm melancholy was transformed; he was actually grinning. Delie came in to find him waltzing her aunt round the table. 'Dirt!' he shouted. 'Look at it! It's gold, solid gold, every blessed ounce of it.'

31

He rushed to the table, took out a penknife and scratched at the rock. A gleam of yellow appeared.

'Now who says my "scraping in the dirt" was a waste of time? What have you to say to that, Mrs J.?'

For once Hester was speechless, though her mouth remained open as she sank into a chair.

'It's gold! gold! gold!' chanted Delie, jumping round the table.

'There's an American chap come through since the thaw, with some money. He'd pay for an option on my claim, I believe, after this; and then it's down to the plains for us.'

Hester began to sob. 'Oh, Charles – oh, Charles! Everything good seems to be happening at once; Philadelphia has brought us luck, I do declare.' She jumped up and kissed Delie spontaneously for the first time. That night they celebrated with a bottle of wine Hester had kept hidden 'for an emergency', and planned their trip to the city of Melbourne.

It was nearly the end of November, and Melbourne was sunny and pleasantly warm. They stayed in a big hotel near a green park, where Adam was to join them from Sydney as soon as the school term ended. They all felt rather flat and lethargic – even Hester, who stoutly denied that she missed the mountains, was feeling the change to a staler and less rarefied air.

Excitement counteracted the effect of loss of altitude for Delie, who was already woman enough to take a delight in visiting the bank (in shiny new boots, tight leather gloves and a mushroom straw hat with black ribbons) and then the shops.

The court had made her uncle guardian of herself and the money until she should reach the age of twenty-one. The money, some eight thousand pounds, was to be left in the bank for the time, the interest being enough for her present needs. It was still tied up in legal red tape, but the bank was quite ready to advance a sum on such security.

The ribbons on her hat, and the bow which tied back her long hair, were the only black she wore. Aunt Hester had agreed rather dubiously that six months' mourning was enough for a child, though perhaps not for a child who had lost *so many* . . .

'Why remind her of things?' Charles had asked. 'This is a time of rejoicing for us, and she belongs to us now.' Part of his delight came from the fact that in actually striking gold he had proved himself right and his wife wrong.

While the women spent their money in the shops, Charles pondered how to invest his in a home and a living. He thought he would like to try sheep-farming, as he'd had some experience as a jackaroo in his wandering life. But a paddle-steamer captain finally decided him on looking for some land on the Murray River. Captain Johnston was staying at the same hotel in Melbourne and sat at their table. He was a big man with a grey beard and eyes with that far-gazing look of seamen, or bushmen from the wide inland plains. It turned out that he was skipper of a wool-boat trading between Echuca and the stations on the Darling; he had come down, he said, to pick up a new steamer built in Melbourne, and pilot her back to Echuca, though most riverboats were built of red-gum in the town.

'But I thought the mouth of the Murray had been proved unsafe?' said Charles.

'Unsafe, aye; unnavigable, no. Ye have to bide y'r time, till the tide's right, and the wind offshore to quiet the surf. Man, it's a grand sight, that: ninety miles of beach, low white sandhills with never a break, and always a mist of white spume hiding them. The mouth is just a small opening that the first explorers failed to find – nearly two thousand river miles from its source. And I know every bend of yon weary-winding river.'

Charles soon worked out that it would take the skipper weeks to get to Echuca by boat, but that by taking the train he could be there himself tomorrow. The riverman's stories of the thriving town Echuca had become, handling two million pounds' worth of wool in a year, convinced him that Echuca was the place. There was land to be taken up along the river, and a market in Echuca and Melbourne for all they could produce, whether it was wool or wheat.

It was enough; Charles was off. He did not consult his wife about the purchase of a property. The following week a letter arrived, simply announcing that he had purchased one:

A delightful farming property situated in a bend of the river some fifteen miles above Echuca – away from the sound of the sawmills and the smell of the boiling-down works at Moama. Some of the finest red-gum timber in Australia grows about here.

Not isolated, either, for many of the paddle-steamers, particularly the smaller ones that trade up to Albury, go past the house; but of course in summer the river falls and navigation is difficult if not impossible. The Cobb & Co. coach also passes near by.

Windmills pump water from the river, so we will not be dependent on the rainfall, which is not high; it is hot and sunny enough even for you, my dear. You will be glad to know we are not leaving the mother Colony of New South Wales, as the property is on the northern bank of the river, though of course our nearest big centre is Echuca over the border. Moama, on our side of the river, is a very small township. But there is a good bridge and no obstruction save for the trifling one of the Customs.

What a letter! thought Hester in despair, feeling her head begin to ache. How like a man; wouldn't he leave the great drawback to the end and then try to gloss it over? Everything they bought in town, everything they took in for sale, would be subject to inspection and duty.

And not a word about the house! Not one word about whether it had a good kitchen, or a chimney that smoked, or damp in the walls.

She sniffed and put the letter back in its envelope. They would have to catch a train as soon as Adam arrived, and travel due north for a hundred and fifty miles to the river. Echuca was a thousand river miles upstream from the mouth, but it was the nearest town on the whole river to the port of Melbourne.

SIX

While Hester lay recovering from the heat and fatigue of the journey in the Palace Hotel, Echuca, the two cousins went out to explore the town. They found it a busy, noisy place, with a vista along nearly every street of gum trees and church spires; and on almost every corner was a hotel.

From up-river came the scream and whine of circular saws biting into red-gum logs at Mackintosh's mill. Beyond the row of warehouses and Customs buildings they could hear the bustle of the wharf – the shunting of trains, rattle of winches, scream of whistles, hiss of steam.

The wharf was twenty feet above the river's surface, for at present the water was low. They ran along reading aloud the names of the steamers tied up there: *Rothbury, Alert, Nile, Success, Adelaide, Lancashire Lass, Invincible, Enterprise* – large and small, side-wheelers and stern-wheelers, smart and dowdy. The wide sweep of water was clear and green, reflecting the dazzling sun from its smooth surface. They followed along the banks towards the big iron bridge into New South Wales, Delie dancing along through the short underbrush, a small white figure under the tremendous trees, with sunlight and shade dappling her light dress and dark hair; for her sailor-hat fell back on her shoulders and was held only by the ribbons under her chin.

She looked at the smooth sliding water and thought of the little creeks under the snow away up in the mountains she had come from. Was this water cold in the heat of the blazing summer day? She would have liked to take her stockings off and paddle on the edge, but Adam strode on without stopping.

Delie closed her eyes and breathed again and again the exciting scent of the eucalyptus scrub, leafy, pungent and warm. Out from the banks a group of graceful birds swam in convoy – black, with long necks and bright red bills.

'Are they really swans?' cried Delie, thinking what a strange country this was, where it snowed in June, and trees were never bare in winter nor green in summer, but always blue-grey or olive, sometimes almost mauve, and their trunks even paler than their leaves.

When they got back they found Hester in a fret.

'I was certain you'd fallen in the river and been drowned. How you could *want* to stay out in this awful heat I don't know, apart from worrying me almost to death. Children nowadays have *no* consideration. When *I* was a girl – ' and so on for some five minutes. Delie and Adam looked at each other over her head. They were allies against the grown-up world.

Charles had arrived in town from the property too late to meet the train, and had hurried to the hotel to find his wife prostrated by the heat, but not too prostrated to complain. He omitted to mention how she had always been carping about the cold at Kiandra, but sat fanning her till she felt recovered.

The next morning they all set off for the new home. The purchase had been made on a walk-in, walk-out basis, so that every-

35

thing changed hands down to the knives and forks and the fire-irons. Even the servants remained – a general handy-man who could kill a pig and dress a sheep and look after the vegetable garden and the fowls; one part-aboriginal stockman; and the two kitchen lubras and their families.

As the river was low, they could take the shorter route over the river flats, grey and grassless between the huge straight trees. A cloud of white cockatoos rose, shrieking like lost souls, from a dead branch. The horse's hooves went quietly over the carpet of pale dry leaves, and kangaroos bounded away ahead of the cart.

They came at last out of the forest of flooded gums into open sandy country with low rolling ridges topped with native pine. There ahead, fitted snugly into a bend of the river and high enough to be above the reach of floods, stood the homestead: a cluster of buildings of solid timber with shingle roofs, the main house facing the river.

The shady veranda was covered with white jasmine, starred with blossom and breathing perfume. Smoke rose into the still air from a chimney in one of the outbuildings at the back. Hester sat up-right, staring, all her pains forgotten. Her face wore the gentle look with which she had welcomed Adam home.

As they pulled up near the back door there was a flash of a coloured dress behind the tank and a sound of much giggling, but no one came forward. Hester demanded to see the kitchen first. It was in a separate building at the back, large and airy, its stone floor strewn with clean river sand. A bunch of herbs and another of everlasting daisies hung from the ceiling, and a picture of Queen Victoria with her family about her, rather brown and fly-spotted, was pasted on one wall.

Delie chose her own room on the west side of the house, with an oblique view of the river-bank, and a large flowering gum out-side the sash window. She found Hester in the front bedroom, looking doubtful.

'I don't know that I'll sleep easy with that so close,' she said, indicating a little cemetery at the foot of a sandhill beyond the garden. Three little head-boards surrounded three sandy mounds, each bordered by a strong picket-fence.

Delie was checked in her boisterous explorations.

'We can grow a tree between,' said Charles soothingly. 'I sup-pose the mother liked to feel they were close. But after the little girl was found in the river they wanted to leave the place. The first two died as infants.'

36

Delie's eyes became wide and fixed. Death . . . The little girl who had slept in her room . . . Her own sisters, all drowned.

She felt a warm, firm grip on her arm. 'Come and explore the garden, Del,' said Adam.

There was unspoken sympathy in his eyes.

Hester returned to the kitchen, rounded up the gigglers from behind the tank and began instructing them in how she wanted the kitchen kept: clean sand on the floor every week, three rinsing waters when washing the deal table, plenty of blacklead on the stove. But her precise English and unfamiliar voice only brought on more uncomprehending giggles, though she learned the names – Lucy and Minna – of the two girls from the part-aboriginal cook, Bella.

Charles came to the rescue with pidgin English.

'You, Bella, Lucy, Minna, this new Missus belong you. Missus savvy plenty bime-by; this time you show her all-about, you cookem dinner quick-time, or me cross-feller prop'ly.'

In spite of their soft dark eyes and perfect white teeth, Hester thought the lubras very ugly in their cotton dresses – also immoral, for quite a lot of their legs showed as they scuffed in embarrassment with their bare toes in the sanded floor.

The youngest, Minna, was not very much older than Delie, but she must be old enough for long skirts, and the others must certainly be given proper dresses and taught to cover their limbs in a modest manner.

Outside, the children had explored all the outbuildings, then raced round to the front garden where there grew one large pine tree, a trellised vine with grapes yet green and hard, and almonds, limes and willows. Near the river-banks was a tract of bare sandy soil, strewn with bark and twigs and dead leaves from the great red-gums which grew right in the steep bank.

Delie and Adam stood looking down at the river, which had cut successive lines in the bank at various levels. It came round a bend from the left and swept out of sight again round a bend to the right, slipping smoothly and without a ripple, and so clear that they could see far down into its depths.

Across the river the scrub grew thickly. Dark trees leaned above their own reflections. The clouds looked softer, the sky a deeper blue in that reflected world. It did not look far to the other side; simultaneously they longed for a boat. As if in answer to the thought, two native bark canoes came silently round the upstream bend. In each a dark figure stood upright, punting with a long

37

gum sapling, in a pose as ancient and primitive as the river itself: two of the first inhabitants of this last-discovered land.

A short stumpy figure emerged from a hut further along the banks while they watched. He came over to them, a weathered grey-beard in flannel shirt and moleskins, who regarded them from faded blue eyes which yet danced with a lively curiosity.

'Hullo,' said Adam. 'Is that your place? Aren't you afraid the river might flood and wash it away?' For it stood on the extreme edge of the crumbling bank.

'Tain't my place, young feller, belongs to them at the big 'ouse. But it carn't last – it's "a 'ouse builded upon the sand". But where in 'ell did you spring from? Don't say the new fambly's came, and I never hearn 'em!'

'Yes, we've came,' said Adam, unconsciously adopting the old man's grammar. 'Just came now, this morning.'

'Well now, what in 'ell – if you'll pardin the language – will the Boss and the Missus think of me, not a-welcomin' 'em even? I'm gettin' deaf, you know, never hearn a thing. "He that has ears to 'ear, let 'im 'ear," ' he added biblically. 'I'm Elijah, the "general". Just call me Lige.'

'How do you do, Lige,' said Adam, shaking hands. The little man had a firm grip in his calloused hand, and his eyes twinkled shrewdly from their enfolding lines.

'Those blacks over there wouldn't be wild ones, would they?' asked Delie nervously.

Lige gave a hoot of laughter. 'Naw, they're on'y wild when they can't get any baccy. Ain't no wild blacks left round these parts. Thanks be to Gawd – as if snakes wasn't enough!'

Lige took them round the farm to meet the animals, and in the stables they found Jacky, Bella's husband, rubbing down Barney and giving him a feed after unharnessing him from the spring-cart.

Lige carried a long stick with him. He seemed nervous and inclined to get behind the others as they walked over the bleached summer grass. In a corner of the horse-paddock stood an old, square iron tank, rusted and full of holes. There was a drinking-trough filled by a pipe from the windmill which pumped water up from the river.

Delie stamped her leg and brushed at her ankle. 'Mosquitoes biting in daylight!' she said. 'Do you get many here? They were bad in Echuca last night.'

'Bad in Echuca!' Lige cackled. 'Just wait till you see the size o' the mozzies here. See that there tank? The mozzies carried it there. Used ter be down by the river-bank.'

Delie looked puzzled, Adam sceptical. 'How could they carry it?'

'They carried it with me inside, what's more. I was down there fixin' up some pipin' when these big blokes come at me in a swarm. I just got inside the tank – it was empty fortunitly – an' pulled the lid shut in the nick o' time. Well, they wus that fierce for blood, they stuck their stings right through the iron; but I 'ad me 'ammer in me 'and, and fast as one pokes through I bend it flat. Was they wild! They buzzed away, tank an' all, but it was too 'eavy to carry far and they come down in the 'orse-paddock. I climbed out and left 'em there to die of starvation.'

There was a stunned silence at the end of this story; then Adam laughed and said, 'That's a tall one.'

Lige's face remained quite straight. 'Well, if yer'll excoose me I'll go and smarten meself up and go up to the 'ouse,' he said.

Hester had not expected to walk into a fully furnished home, and many treasures had of course been brought with them on the long journey from the mountains – the solid silver soup spoons that had belonged to Delie's grandmother and were now worn wafer-thin and dangerously sharp on the edges; the red Mary Gregory water-jug, the painted lampshade – as well as a great many valueless things, such as old photographs, postcards, letters and Adam's first tooth.

Delie got into trouble on the first evening by breaking the painted glass lampshade while helping with the unpacking. Hester sent her to bed, saying that she didn't want anyone 'barging about among my precious china, who was born clumsy and with two left hands'.

She wept a little in her room, and then took up the candle to visit the outhouse before getting undressed. Outside, a light fell from the kitchen door, and there was quick talk and laughter, the cheerful rattle of crockery and saucepans, the shuffle of bare feet on the floor. Delie went past to the little building with its draping of convolvulus, and pushed open the wooden door. Her candle revealed a spider-web thick in one corner. In the silence she became aware of the malignant shrilling of hundreds of mosquitoes in the confined space with her.

When she came out she blew out the candle and waited for her eyes to become accustomed to the darkness.

The night was calm and mild. The sky was soft with stars, so that it was not really dark at all. The long path of the Milky Way shed a pale radiance.

Taking off her shoes and stockings, she put them beside the candlestick at the back step, and turned to walk down to the river. As she passed the sitting-room window at the side (there were also French windows opening on to the front veranda) she heard the voices of the others within. She peeped inside, from the great silent night into the lighted box of the room. It looked unreal; the lamplight seemed part of the lighting of a stage. At once her mind began to dramatise the situation:

> *She looked indifferently through the window, from the cold night outside she looked at those comfortable and warm within. What do I care, she said, though they turn me out into the cold and darkness? I will not ask for mercy, she said, no, I will go on my lonely way to the end . . .*

Keeping her head below the level of the window-sill, she went on her lonely way as far as the river-bank. The earth was still giving off the day's heat, and under her bare feet it felt like something alive. The white jasmine, its flowers glimmering like faint stars, shed its perfume heavily on the air.

When the sandy river-bank opened out before her, she seemed to be able to see better by the light thrown up from the river surface. She climbed cautiously down to the water. It felt silky and cool about her ankles; the sand was firm and there were no weeds. The reflection of a star quivered and broke into diamond splinters as the ripples moved outwards.

The gum trees on the opposite bank made a black wall, which could not be distinguished from the solid bank. Between her feet and that blackness the river flowed, bearing the stars like jewels on the smooth breast of a woman. Purposeful, unending, the river moved from its distant source towards the unknown sea. For the first time she felt the full magic of its timeless flow.

It was very still. Then there came a sound that was scarcely sound, dropping from the air and the deeps of the sky like the audible spirit of night.

She strained her eyes upward and felt rather than saw, sensed rather than heard, a blotting out of the stars and a rushing of great wings . . . Black swans! Black swans, flying towards some hidden backwater, some secret billabong.

When that strange cry dropping from the stars was gone, she still stood rooted like a tree in the river-bank.

I will remember this night as long as I live, she thought. *When I am an old woman I will remember this night.*

SEVEN

The year ended in a blaze of heat. The house became so hot that Hester had a table carried out under the vine-trellis and the mid-day meal was taken there. Hester could see the advantage of having the kitchen in a separate building, with its wood stove.

Delie got on better with her aunt now that she was relieved of kitchen duties. But Hester would remark, 'That child is a butter-fingers, for all her hands are so big,' as the bang of something falling came from Delie's room.

'She's not well, if you ask me,' said Charles. 'She's got so leggy lately, and her eyes like two burnt holes in a blanket.'

'It's to be expected at her time of life,' said Hester meaning-fully.

The heat of that first Australian summer, at a time when the physical change her aunt had hinted at was beginning, seemed to sap Delie's energy; and they all felt the change of altitude from the mountains.

When Christmas Day came its summer colours seemed all wrong to her, the only illusion of snow in the pure white of a few streaks of cloud. But Hester insisted on a traditional roast dinner. The three kitchen girls had been given new dresses for Christmas; Bella's bright blue, Minna's yellow, and Lucy's a violent magenta. Within a week they had torn out the long, tight sleeves, and Delie saw Minna coming up from the river with a catch of crayfish tied up in hers. She had been diving, and the sky was reflected in blue highlights from her glistening body. Freed of her shapeless clothes, Minna was beautiful, slender, with satiny skin of the deepest brown.

Hester did not understand her dark-skinned helpers, and was scandalised at the easy way they shed their clothes.

41

On a day of clear, burning heat Adam and Delie wandered down to the river after the hot midday dinner, and lay among the green wild mint which grew where water leaked from a faulty connection in the windmill pipe. The river slipped by, mesmerising the senses.

Giggles and rapid, liquid-flowing talk disturbed their peace. Lucy and Minna, the washing-up done, were going for a 'bogee' in the river. Minna squatted in the bark canoe while Lucy punted it to midstream. Then there was a splash, and they saw brown arms flashing in the sun as Minna swam to a sandbank opposite and walked from the water, the yellow dress left behind. Delie sat up and stared, feeling her fingers tingle with the longing for pencil or crayon to put that perfect form down on paper: the free, graceful walk, the straight back, the firm breasts and long slim flanks, all glowing with the gloss of life. She was aware of Adam, very still, beside her.

Adam, she knew, went swimming without any clothes at the down-stream bend. Delie longed to learn but felt it was useless to ask her aunt. How stupid to be a girl, not supposed to swim, or climb trees, or ride astride, or do anything interesting! Adam was now fifteen, straight, sturdy and almost as good-looking a boy as his mother believed him to be. And he always beat Delie at running, jumping, or even marbles, which she sometimes played with him. Lately he had taken to walking alone by the evening river, when the afterglow tinted the calm surface with luminous tones of apricot and pale green. She never knew what he was thinking as he stood rapt by the river's brim. If she ran after him she felt an instant reserve go up like a wall between them. She learned to respect his moods of silence and solitariness.

His mother never learned. She would go out and put an arm through his where he stood under the scented jasmine on the veranda, staring into the night where a mopoke's intermittent call sounded like the dark voice of woods and trees.

Her 'What are you thinking about, dear?' and 'All alone out here? Why don't you come and have a game of cribbage with me?' brought an angry jerk of the arm and, 'Can't you leave a fellow alone, Mother?' She would retire with a sharp word to cover her hurt, but the next time he lapsed into one of his moods she did exactly the same.

Adam never criticised his mother in words, but by a look, a pressure on an elbow, a touch of the foot beneath the table, he told Delie when he disagreed with her narrow judgements. Poor

Hester, bitter and self-pitying from habit, though somewhat mellowed by the pleasure she took in the farmhouse and garden, was without an ally.

Even the easy-going Lige she had managed to rub up the wrong way. It was his job to carry buckets of hot water from the kitchen to the bathroom. She complained:

'Elijah, there was chaff floating in my bath last night.'

'Yairs, Missus . . . well, y'see, I 'as to feed the cows with that there bucket.'

'With a whole river at the door, there is surely enough water to rinse a bucket?'

'Yairs, but y'see, chaff is mighty sticky stuff, and even if y' rinses the ruddy bucket –'

'That will do. Don't let it occur again.'

With the dry weather the river fell steadily. A whitish line several feet up on the trees beyond the bend showed the level of last year's flood-waters. Below the Goulburn junction some bad reefs and shallows were exposed, and the steamer traffic was at a standstill.

Feed became scarce in the paddocks and had to be supplemented with oats and hay. The former owner had left some rather indifferent horses. Charles, who was a natural horseman as he was a natural skier, took over the bony chestnut mare Firefly, while Adam had to put up with Barney, who was broken to harness, or the fat, round pony Leo. Jacky, a superb stockman, rode an unmanageable roan colt he had broken in himself. Delie begged to be allowed to ride but was told she must wait until they had acquired a side-saddle.

Beyond the horse-paddock were the pig-pens, well away from the house because of their smell, and the gallows where Lige killed and hung, once a week, a pig or a sheep.

There were two sheep-dogs, but they were aloof and morose: a yellow-eyed kelpie and an elderly Border collie that seemed to acknowledge no master but Lige; and who, if Lige could be believed, could herd a blowfly into a bottle unaided. Shep, the collie, was a rather repulsive-looking animal with all the hair missing from a bare patch in the middle of his back.

'What happened to the dog's coat?' asked Adam, caressing its ears while it rolled its eyes at him suspiciously.

'That there dog,' said Lige, scratching his neck, 'that there dog had a wunnerful thick coat, but 'e used to get too 'ot, runnin' round in the summer. One very 'ot day 'e was out after sheep. I

43

could just about see the steam risin' orf him. We come to the dam, and before I could stop 'im 'e jumped in. Well, wouldyer believe it,' said Lige impressively, fixing Adam with an innocent stare from his faded blue eyes, 'but that dog was *so 'ot* that the water boiled all round 'im, and cooked 'is coat orf. It all grew again except that there patch in the middle of 'is back. Spoiled 'is appearance a bit.'

When Adam repeated this story at dinner his mother snorted and called Lige 'and outrageous old liar'.

'But it isn't really lying, Mother. He doesn't do it to gain any advantage. It's a kind of artistic exaggeration. That fellow's a real artist.'

Beyond Lige's hut was a vegetable garden irrigated from the river by an elaborate series of channels. Here he spent most of his time, hoeing the 'turmits' and 'taties' and setting out tomatoes in beautifully symmetrical lines; or wielding the scythe in the irrigated lucerne patch. He had two fears in life: snakes and women. 'Put not thy faith in women!' he was fond of quoting from the Bible.

In his hut he had a five-foot-high wooden bed with a ladder up to it. At each side of his door were two big sticks 'ready for snakes'. He had once woken up after a flood when the high land was crawling with snakes, to find one curled up asleep on his chest. He had never slept on a low stretcher since.

Charles, who had shaved off his beard and looked years younger without it, spoke of going to town to pick up 'a really good ram' at the sales. Delie asked him if at the same time he would advertise for someone to help her with her long-neglected studies; perhaps she and Adam could share a governess or a tutor. She would pay for it with the money from her father's estate.

'A governess! Another mouth to feed,' said Hester, but the thought of another white woman to talk to in this household of men and children appealed to her. She went on complaining from habit rather than conviction. 'All the extra work will fall on me, of course, and though my back's been so much better lately, my old trouble will likely come back with the winter. Not that I expect any consideration, of course. Nobody knows what I suffer . . .'

Charles put in mildly, 'Since Delie is willing to bear the expense from her own income, we can have no objection. I'd be glad for Adam to get some final polishing too, since for all the interest he takes in farming he might as well be at school. He always has his nose stuck in a book.'

Adam's lips turned down. It was not often that he was openly criticised by his easy-going father, and to his mother he was perfect.

'Thanks, but there's more in life than hog-wash and sheep-dip. If I can't go to the university, or travel or do any of the things I want to, why shouldn't I read? You ride about in your fancy wide hat looking like a farmer, but you know as well as I do that Lige does all the real work. If this governess is any good I don't mind having lessons, but she probably won't be able to teach me anything I didn't learn at school.'

'That sort of arrogant talk usually comes before a fall,' said his father, with a sudden heightened colour. 'And let me tell you, young man, that you really know very little, about life or anything else. And how do you propose to support yourself, may I ask? Because I don't intend to keep you in idleness.'

'I mean to be a writer,' said Adam in a low voice.

'A writer! What makes you think you could earn anything in that way?'

'Of course he could, if he sets his mind to it,' said Hester briskly. 'Charles, we must see about getting someone; but not one of these over-refined, helpless bluestockings who will expect to be waited on hand and foot.'

EIGHT

A new dinghy had been bought in Echuca to supplement Lige's leaky old duck-punt, and now Delie was allowed to go out rowing with Adam. They crossed the river for the first time on a sunny afternoon when its smooth surface was alight with the reflections of gold-green trees and gold-suffused clouds. She trailed a hand in the water, feeling that this, to be done with Adam on the sunsparkling river, was the very summit of happiness.

They beached the dinghy on the opposite bank in a lignum swamp, paved with dried grey mud. In the shade of the coolibahs on its edge was a deserted camp, empty bark *mia-mias* and the ashes of old fires.

'Race you to that big gum,' cried Adam, running off without waiting for her.

'No! Wait for me! Wa-it!' She panted along behind him, not wanting to be left alone on this side of the river. But Adam had disappeared among the thick scrub. She came up with him at last, sitting on an exposed root of the big tree which grew right on the river-bank. He was gazing intently across the water.

'Why didn't you wait?' she said reproachfully. 'You know I can't race you.'

'Yes,' said Adam. He looked at her, unsmiling, his eyes far away. She knew at once that he had wanted to be alone, had deliberately tried to shake her off, so that he could feel through all his bones the solitude of this lonely corner of Victoria.

Further along they came to the camp, where Old Sarah sat by her fire, smoking a clay pipe, while the goanna oil dressing her greasy locks dripped to her bare thighs. She was an ancient lubra who crossed the river sometimes to beg for 'bacca' at the house.

Delie had brought her sketching things but they were back in the dinghy: she promised Old Sarah a stick of 'bacca' if she would come over in her bark canoe one morning for a 'sitting'. They went back and rowed upstream a little, then floated down with the current. The farmhouse and its attendant buildings looked small and insignificant among the miles of brooding bush. Adam praised her sketch of them but it left her dissatisfied. She longed for a big canvas and masses of pure colour; failing that, the lessons in watercolour she hoped to get from the new governess.

The reply to the advertisement in the *Riverine Herald* had come from Melbourne. A Miss Barrett had had the cutting sent on to her by friends in the Riverina; and as she would be visiting them shortly, she could come to Echuca for a personal interview.

Miss Barrett at once became a subject of speculation. Charles dared to hope she might be young and pretty. Delie felt sure, from some mental impression the name gave her, that she would be tall and gaunt and she would not like her.

With the low river they could take the short road to town, and the whole family went, leaving Lige in charge. The spring-cart had made several trips with produce, for with the low river there were no passing steamers as customers for eggs and sides of ham. The mail, too, had to come by road, being picked up by Lige in the dinghy on the far side of the river.

Miss Dorothy Barrett, MA, had arranged to meet Mrs Jamieson in the parlour of the Palace Hotel where she was staying, at eleven in the forenoon. At five minutes to the hour Hester sat waiting for her with all her prejudices bristling.

46

She sent Adam and Delie off with her husband to 'look at the shops'. She wanted, in case the governess should be young and pretty, to deal with her alone.

A mannish step outside the door, a deep voice saying, 'I am so sorry if you have been waiting,' and a tall young woman strode into the room. She held out a large, pink, well-manicured hand.

Hester blinked, and took the hand.

'Miss – er – Miss Barrett?'

'Yes.' The young woman – well, not so young, she must certainly be thirty, decided Hester – drew up a chair with a twist of her powerful wrist, and sat down. She planted her flat-heeled shoes firmly on the floor. Her white blouse, with its high collar and tight cuffs, was impeccable, as was her long blue-serge skirt; her straw boater sat squarely on her light brown curls. But what an unfeminine way of shaking hands!

'You are Mrs Jamieson? I understand from the letter I received in reply to my application that you have a girl of thirteen and a boy of fifteen. He sounds rather old for a governess. Oh – I brought my references. I've been at a private girls' school in Melbourne up till this year, you will see. But one gets bored with a lot of girls.'

She smiled so charmingly, with a crinkling about her clear grey eyes, that Hester found herself smiling back; but she said rather stiffly:

'I haven't had very much experience of girls. My niece Philadelphia has been living with me for not quite a year, and I have only the one boy. Adam – ' her voice became softer – 'is a clever boy, and has been at school in Sydney until recently. I don't know that he needs much more schooling, but I would wish you to teach him to be a gentleman, and to foster his talent for writing, as he hopes to make a career in that way. He'd like to go on to university, but his father is against it.'

'If he wants to write he should certainly continue with Latin,' said Miss Barrett in her deep voice. 'There is no better training in the feeling for words. French too, so that he may read the great French novelists in their own language – '

'French novelists!' sniffed Hester. 'From what I've seen of their writings, they should all be burnt.'

' – English literature, of course; mathematics to help in lucid thinking; geography and geology, to give perspective in time and space. Unless he has a particular affection for Greek, I think he might drop it; it is not my strong point. Now for the girl, I think

47

we might let her choose her subjects according to her bent, though it would be simpler, of course, if they both did the same ones.

'She is the one who is anxious to learn to paint, I believe? Then she won't like mathematics.'

Hester sat helplessly while the deep, calm voice went on. She felt as though she were caught in a rapid; she went with the stream. There was no doubt that Miss Barrett was capable, from her large hands to her firm wide mouth and clean-cut, flaring nostrils. To have her would be a relief, when she had been the only capable one for so long.

' – So that's arranged, is it? I'm sure I can manage the children and that you'll find my references satisfactory. When would you like me to start?'

'Oh – er, at once, as soon as you can.'

'I will have to get my things, and my books from Melbourne. I think next week can be arranged.'

As Hester rose to accompany Miss Barrett to the door, Adam and Delie came into the dark, lofty hall from the street, having left Charles 'to see a man about a dog'.

'Miss Barrett, this is Philadelphia Gordon, my niece. This is your new governess, child.'

'Oh!' said Delie, and went pink, 'Oh, how – how do you do?'

She held out her thin hand and made an awkward bob. The firm grip made her wince, the smile in the warm grey eyes dazzled her. Miss Barrett had curly hair! She was tall, but not a bit like a lamp-post. She was lovely!

'Adam! Come here. This is my boy, Miss Barrett. Miss Barrett comes from Melbourne, and has many qualifications – '

Adam stepped forward smartly, shook hands with an air of assured indifference, and stepped backward. He crashed into a small table in the hall, which bore a dingy pot-plant of doubtful age and healthiness.

Miss Barrett laughed merrily. Adam flushed.

'Oh, mind the aspidistra,' she cried. 'It's probably a family heirloom. It looks old enough.' Still laughing, she stepped out into the sun.

NINE

Late in March, Charles drove into town with the buggy to fetch Miss Barrett. Jacky travelled with him to help unload the dressed turkeys and other produce which was packed under the seat. On the way home again he listened uncomprehendingly to a geological discussion of gold-mining, for with Miss Barrett's command of theory and Charles's practical knowledge, they developed an interesting discussion on 'fault planes', 'alluvial deposits', 'mother lodes' and so on.

'Them two all-a-time yabber about nothin',' as he told Bella.

Miss Barrett was certainly handsome, Charles was thinking, but not in a way that appealed to him. And she was such a terribly accomplished young lady, and very self-assured.

'Well, I found her all right, and here she is, safe and sound,' he said, ushering her into the drawing-room.

'Why ever shouldn't she be safe?' asked Hester sharply, for she took all her husband's remarks literally. 'Miss Barrett, sit down, you must be famished. Some tea? It's just made. A piece of cake?'

'Thank you, but I'm not hungry. I'll have a cup of tea since it's made, but I really prefer to drink nothing but water.'

'How strange!' said Hester, who had spent a lot of time on the sponge cake and had brought out her best teapot.

'Here you are, my dear. I thought you might like this,' said Charles, handing his wife a parcel.

'A present? For me?' Hester looked blank.

'Yes. Aren't you going to open it?'

Hester undid the parcel, carefully unravelling the knots and smoothing out the paper before she looked at her present. Then she merely said, 'Oh.'

'How very pretty!' said Miss Barrett.

It was a black silk blouse, embroidered elaborately with coloured beads, a bright sea-green predominating.

'Oh Charles!' cried Hester. 'You know I can't wear green. It's dreadfully unlucky.'

That night she sat up late, carefully unpicking every green bead from the pattern until it had a rather moth-eaten look, but was no longer a direct flouting of the fates.

Delie sat in the schoolroom, which became the dining-room at meal-times, in a daze, listening to Miss Barrett's deep, calm voice. She was hopelessly in love. Her world had a new centre.

She learned avidly, taking in as well as her own work the more advanced lessons given to Adam. Before she could conjugate her Latin verbs properly she had absorbed the thundering periods of Horace, and *Odi profanum vulgus et arceo!* haunted her ears with majestic music, though she had but a dim idea of the sense of the words.

She hurried to help Lucy and Minna clear the table after breakfast, and to set out the inkwells and the geographical globe on the green plush cloth, which Hester had brought all the way from Kiandra with her. (Green she did not regard as dangerous unless worn on the person; and the plush was of a yellowish olive-green which she felt to be safe, associating in her illogical mind the more brilliant greens with the more virulent forms of bad luck.)

Sometimes when she had risen early, before she began her piano practice, Delie would walk away from the house to the railings round the little graves on the first sandhill.

She felt almost an affection for the three dead children who had once slept in her room, as though they too had been members of her lost family. Their names were Clifford, aged eight days; Mary Jane, six months; and Elizabeth Ann, five years.

The pale yellow sunlight, striking across the water in a dazzling pathway from the furthest bend, threw long, cold blue shadows from the little wooden crosses. She half-closed her eyes and admired the contrast of gold and blue, while thinking about the dead children and her own brothers and sisters. Had they all met in some heaven up above? She looked at the serene blue sky, soft and fathomless, her eyes plunging deep in its softness but finding no point on which to rest.

At night there were the stars, and those terrible black spaces between them where the eye could find no boundary and the mind no limit. No, she could not imagine a heaven in the sky.

It was all very puzzling. She went reluctantly back to the house and entered the drawing-room through the long french windows on the veranda. She sat on the piano stool, twirled it up to its fullest height and down again, and fiddled with a strip of melted wax that had dripped from one of the candles down its brass holder. Each of the candlesticks had a shade of yellow pleated silk. She hated practising and was not eager to begin. At last she began on her scales, when a high, long-sustained note from down by the river made her pause and listen. It was Minna, singing in a cadence of strange half-tones that made her spine tingle:

> *Kutchinurringa nurringa na*
> *Kutchinurringa na . . .*

She shut the piano lid. Scales were more meaningless than ever this morning. She much preferred her swimming lessons.

Miss Barrett was a strong swimmer and soon overcame Hester's objections. She had brought her neck-to-knee costume of dark blue, and improvised one for Delie, who began learning in the shallow water above a sandbank. At the edge the water dropped suddenly down into the main channel; soon she was dog-paddling out into deep water, with a sense of danger and daring. At last came the great day when she swam, with Miss Barrett beside her, to the other side of the river.

Then the river began to rise in a 'fresh', and the mornings grew colder. Delie and Adam marked the rising level each day with a stick. Miss Barrett was as energetic and enthusiastic about boating as she was about everything else, and took them rowing instead of swimming.

One morning, while working in the schoolroom, they heard a regular beat like the pulsing of a heart, slowly coming nearer. Then what looked like a white wooden house moved into view beyond the trees.

'Steamer! It's a paddle-steamer!' yelled Adam, rushing outside. Miss Barrett and Delie followed. It was the first boat they had seen pass.

Smoke puffed lightly from her funnel as she made good time downstream. *Chuff CHUFF chuff chuff* went the engines softly, and *pukkiter-pukkiter* went the two side-paddles, churning the water into foam on each side, while from the stern the water rolled back in glassy curves, folded but unbroken. Two loaded barges swung behind the steamer on long tow-ropes.

The captain, standing in white shirt-sleeves and waistcoat in the wheelhouse, waved as the steamer passed. It rounded the downstream bend, followed by the first barge; the second barge

barge swung wide and grounded on a sandbank. The tow-rope parted, and the barge was left wedged upon the sand, listing dangerously.

Soon the steamer came back again upstream, made a wide turn with the other barge in tow and came down abreast of the grounded barge. The children were delighted and ran down the bank until they were opposite.

Miss Barrett did not seem disturbed by the oaths that floated over the water as the captain and the bargemaster shouted at each other. 'Let's get the dinghy and see if we can help,' she said.

The dinghy rocked violently in the wake, but they pushed off, Miss Barrett rowing. The big, red-faced captain leant out of the wheel-house.

'Well Miss, can you take a tow-rope over to the bank there, and loop it round a tree for us? That's the ticket.'

A heavy rope with pulleys was paid out, and with Adam holding it they rowed to the bank, took a turn round the tree and rowed back to the barge. The bargemaster made it fast and signalled to the steamer, which went cautiously ahead until the rope took the strain. Then the paddles thrashed furiously while the steamer stayed put.

But the barge's bows were swinging round to the pull from the tree. As the three in the dinghy watched eagerly, it slid off into deep water.

Delie saw the danger first. 'The rope!' she screamed. 'Mind the rope!'

'Lie flat!' shouted Miss Barrett.

They flung themselves down, but Adam, with his back to the danger, did not move fast enough. The taut tope passed over the top of the dinghy, caught Adam in the shoulders and knocked him out of the boat.

The others waited in stunned surprise for Adam's head to appear; but tipped out upstream of the boat, he had come up beneath it. The second time he rose he did the same thing, and when at last he appeared just below them Miss Barrett leaned over the side and managed to haul him on board, dazed and half-drowned.

The bargemaster, as soon as he saw Adam safe, cast off the rope. Before Miss Barrett had rowed back to the house they had the barge coupled up and were on their way downstream again.

Delie looked at Adam's wet head on her shoulder, at his pinched nostrils, closed eyes and sodden clothes, and felt a wave of delayed shock. He had coughed and vomited just as she had done when brought ashore from the sunken windjammer; he had nearly drowned.

'How ever would I have told his mother?' muttered Miss Barrett with compressed lips. 'I should have seen the danger . . .'

But by the time they landed, Adam had recovered enough to walk up to the house, and though Hester clucked like a disturbed hen she did not realise how nearly there had been a tragedy.

TEN

The pale summer grasses, bleached with heat, were as luminous under the moon as fields of snow. Gradually they turned grey and old, like a shaggy coat. The first rains of autumn fell, and beneath the grey the soft new grass appeared.

It was lambing time and Charles was out half the night in the lambing paddocks, for there were foxes about, and crows. The morning dew was so heavy that a lambing ewe could not get up again for the weight of her dew-drenched fleeces, once she was down. The crows would peck out the uppermost eye from its living socket, and attack the weakest lambs.

Even with care some of the ewes were lost, so a number of little white bundles appeared in the kitchen by the warm stove, where the bread-dough was set to rise each evening. Delie helped to feed the lambs from a bottle, and later taught them to drink from a bucket. She would go down to the sheds and get a warm bucket of milk from Lige, straight from the cows as he milked them.

Then winter came with its sharp frosts, so that the big, warm, bustling kitchen was a delightful place in the mornings. A red fire would be dancing in the stove, the kettle-lid hopping merrily: 'Water bin corroboree!' sang Minna to Bella, who was cutting bread at the snowy deal table. Jokes flew about the kitchen. Work was an incomprehensible game invented by the white people, who 'all-a-time worry too much 'bout nothing.'

Lucy shuffled in on bare feet, her arms full of cut lengths of wood. Delie liked all the house natives, but Minna best of all, with her shy brown eyes and wide smile. But Hester found their

53

casualness irritating. What if a pudding went off the boil and was not cooked for midday dinner? It would do all-a-same for supper.

Charles would crack jokes with the lubras when going past the kitchen or with Minna, who brought his shaving-water in the mornings. 'Boss, him funny feller! Him funny too much!' they would gasp, stamping their feet and rolling their eyes with mirth.

Sometimes Old Sarah would come across from her camp on the far bank of the river, and King Charlie, tall and muscular, with an opossum skin cloak falling gracefully from shoulder to ankle. They were the last of the old people; their tribe was dying out. Charles would give them tobacco for their pipes, for they often brought him a cod from the river or a tasty callop. While Charlie sat quietly on the ground, puffing at his pipe, Delie sketched him in charcoal and listened to his stories of the Dreamtime when the great river and all the features of the land were created:

Long, long ago, before man had been much walkabout, that Great One, the spirit Byamee, lived in the great Rock. That was his place. He say to his lubra, who properly old ... 'Now you go walkabout long-time from this place. Keep on till you come to the flat plain. Then go till you come to the big water, then sit down.' ... The lubra took her yam-stick and her dog. She travelled till she came to a crack in the Rock. She came out on the flat desert country below.

From a sand patch at the foot of the Rock a big snake came and looked at her. She started to walk on, along a sandy track, in and out and all-about, drawing a line in the sand with her stick; and behind her followed the snake.

Many moons went by. That old woman was tired of walking. A voice inside her said, 'Old woman! Look at the black clouds about the Rock. Hear the big thunder! It is the voice of old Byamee talking.'

Then the rain came. Water began to trickle along the track the snake had made.

By now she was very weary and wanting rest. The voice inside her said, 'Go on till you find the big water, then sleep.'

At last she found a cave in the rocks. At first she heard the noise of the wind. Then she heard the sound of the big water. Then she saw it. This was her place.

Today that old woman still sleeps in her cave, for Byamee sent her to that place. The boom of the sea is her voice as she sleeps. When the wind is high the roar of the waves is her corroboree as she sings in her sleep.

Delie was fascinated by this story, wondering how the River people, a thousand miles from the sea, knew how it ended on a distant coast. Uncle Charles told her that they had ambassadors, travelling men who carried message-sticks and trade goods, passing through hostile territory with some kind of special pass, and covering long distances.

Delie had told Adam that she never wanted to go near the sea again, but she dreamt more than once of the old woman trudging on her long and weary journey to the coast. She remembered the river captain's description of that great southern beach, ninety miles long, white with the drifting spume of breakers, and resounding with their hoarse, hollow roar.

She added a sketch of Minna to her gallery of portraits (wishing she might ask her to pose in the nude) and one of Old Sarah, but most of the pictures were of Miss Barrett. She had sketched her surreptitiously many times, her firm nose and flaring nostrils, wide brow and curly hair; in profile, full face and from the back, with a few delightful tendrils escaping from her coiled-up hair.

Miss Barrett noticed that her schoolwork was deteriorating, and that she started and flushed when spoken to. For Delie was living in a world of daydreams in which she saved her idol from all sorts of untimely deaths; she was becoming as dreamy and lacking in concentration as Adam.

Only her drawing and painting lessons took all her attention. Even these had so far been a disappointment. She was expected to practise object drawing, perspective, balance and composition, all in black and white or in sepia washes, while thinking of nothing but those lovely tubes and pans of colour in her paint-box.

It was during a spell of brilliant sunny weather in the midst of winter that the family went to Echuca to see the launching of a new paddle-steamer, the *William Davies*, built at the local yards. They found the shops closed, the town congregated on the bank for the ceremony, the steamer waiting in glory on the slips with her superstructure adorned with wreaths of flowers and coloured flags. The mayor made a speech and cracked a bottle of champagne over her, and as she slipped into the water every steamer in port blew its whistle loudly.

As they drove home in the late afternoon they were all silent, a little tired. Adam gazed straight ahead, his lips moving slightly.

55

Delie sat trying to register in her memory the colour of the shadows; she had suddenly discovered that they were not black, or grey. In the distant trees they were indigo, in the nearer ones a deep cobalt; while the shadows of individual trees spread across the white road like cloths of dark blue lace.

When they came out in the sandy paddock before the house the clear sky was almost drained of blue, shading down through pearl to a clear gold where the sun had just dipped out of sight. As the buggy pulled up in the yard this was deepening to a pure tea-rose colour. Without a word to anyone Delie rushed inside, got a piece of heavy paper, already mounted, a glass jar and her box of water colours. Here was something she must try to paint.

The colours were deepening before her eyes where the river bent round again towards the north-west; the smooth, silken water took on every hue of the sky in exact yet purer tones, the trees were reflected in perfect detail.

It was not until the light was failing that she became conscious all at once of a hundred burning mosquito stings, and of her aunt's voice calling crossly for her to come to tea. The brief sunset and the brief ecstasy of creation were over. She peered at the picture critically and almost indifferently. When she looked at it in the lamplight afterwards she was conscious of how far it fell short of the breathtaking purity of water and sky, and Miss Barrett's words of praise went over her head. But Miss Barrett added that she thought Delie was ready for colour now; she could start practising washes tomorrow.

Outside, the sky presented a great wash of light; brilliant blue-green at the zenith, shading down by imperceptible gradations to the palest green at the horizon, with a suggestion of faded red in it, like clear water in which a trace of blood has been dissolved.

ELEVEN

Adam got up from the breakfast table and looked gloomily out between the green plush curtains, twisting a piece of gold fringe in restless fingers. Grey clouds were flying across the sky from the south, and the garden shrubs, the pepper trees and the limes had that intense green which presages rain. Miss Barrett came behind him and gently removed the twisted fringe. At her touch he flushed, withdrew his hand abruptly and spoke to Delie.

'Coming down to the river before school, Del?' He tweaked the black bow at the back of her long hair. 'I've got a set-line out for cod.'

Delie looked at her aunt for permission. Hester nodded. Miss Barrett went to her room for some books, and when the two of them were alone Hester looked at Charles significantly.

'Do you think Adam's getting serious?' she asked softly.

'Serious?' Charles looked blank. 'What do you mean, my dear? I wish he'd take a serious interest in farming, so I'd have a son to leave the property to. He wouldn't help with the haystack because wheat gives him hay-fever; now he objects to helping with the sheep, just when we need him, because the smell of the dip makes him sick!'

'He has his schoolwork to do –'

'That's right, make excuses for him! You're ruining that boy and you'll be sorry one day. He knows you'll always take his part and he defies me right and left. By the time he is twenty he'll be a good-for-nothing loafer.'

'You're making my headache worse.' (This was the first mention of the headache, which she had just discovered.) 'If you'd listen to what I was going to say . . . Haven't you thought that if he and Philadelphia made a match – and what more natural, growing up together as they are? – with her money he could settle down to being a gentleman farmer, live in Melbourne if he wanted to and put a manager in here. I mean when *we're* gone, of course. She'll have twelve thousand pounds – it will have grown to that – by the time she turns twenty-one.'

Charles stared at her. Such an idea had never entered his mind. 'But – but they're only children yet. And I don't know – cousins marrying, and all that. I think of her as his sister.'

But Hester only smiled again, with a maddening assumption of superior wisdom.

Spring came with a dusting of gold among the thick scrub on the far bank, and the velvety, subtle scent of wattle-blossom. The river rose steadily. Water began to spread up the overflow creeks. Frogs filled the night with their joyous chorus. Undaunted by the cold mornings, Miss Barrett stepped each day into the tingling snow-water, gasping as she pushed aside the rime of frost at its

57

edge. Delie was afraid she would get cramp, but Miss Barrett continued to swim.

She said that it was a wonderful feeling when she came out again, for she was etherealised, light-headed with cold; her body glowed but did not seem to belong to her.

The river looked wider as it filled its banks to the brim. Steamers became almost a daily excitement, but their fascination never palled. At the faint beat of approaching paddles, Delie and Adam would rush to the water's edge to await the first glimpse of the steamer's name. If she brought mail up from Echuca, the boat would usually tie up and take on fresh eggs and milk. Most were going upstream, labouring against the current, with two or three barges strung out behind. These would be left at the logging-camps above the Moira Lakes, to float down again loaded with red-gum logs, while the steamers returned for another train of barges.

One Saturday morning a small stern-wheeler tied up below the house. Adam and Delie came tearing up to get Hester, for it was a floating store stocking everything from darning-needles to rabbit-traps.

Hester enjoyed herself, and so did the hawker. It was surprising how many things were needed: Silver Star starch, Nurse's corn-flour, cinnamon, a new sort of eggbeater – 'Just the thing for sponge cakes, though yours are always light as a feather, I'll bet' – and a length of cretonne for curtains.

'Of course you pay through the nose by dealing with these travelling hawkers,' said Charles when the boat had gone.

'Not at all. I know how to drive a bargain. Surely you're not going to begrudge me spending a little of my egg-money!'

'Oh, no, no; throw it all down the drain, by all means. You realise that we may not have two pennies to rub together soon, if the financial slump goes on. The bottom is falling out of the market, and soon it won't be worth taking our produce in to Echuca. If you persist in extravagance it will end by my having to go back to fossicking; just remember that.'

Hester picked up an armful of chintz and flounced inside. She didn't believe a word of it; he was just trying to humiliate her. She snapped at him at dinner. That night Delie, lying awake, heard voices arguing interminably in the front bedroom, rising now and then in anger.

The quarrel over the hawker's visit was small enough in itself, but it was apparent to everyone in the house that there was a deeper cause of discontent between the two. The breach became open now. A single bed was set up in the office; other comforts were added and it became Charles's bedroom, while Hester occupied alone the grander room at the front of the house.

With each mail Charles became more gloomy. He would sit with the week's copies of the Echuca paper, the *Riverine Herald*, spread out before him. Whenever Delie looked over his shoulder (and Charles was one of the few men who could bear someone reading the paper he was reading) he was always studying an article under the heading: FINANCIAL CRISIS.

One day she read the words:

> In less than one month six leading banks thought to be thoroughly sound and proof against runs by ordinary panic have suspended business. It is, however, no ordinary panic that prevails. The Government, realising that desperate measures were needed, has closed all banks for five days to give managers time to breathe.

'Does it mean you can't get any money out of the bank even if you need it, Uncle?'

'Yes, dear. If they didn't do this, there would soon be no money left in the banks.'

TWELVE

Swollen with melted snow, the river flowed with a visible current, its surface dimpled into whirlpools and strung with beaded bubbles. Outrigger barges, with loads of heavy red-gum logs chained to a cross-piece so that they could not sink, slipped silently past with the current, the bargeman keeping a lonely watch while his mate slept. A long chain trailing over the stern and dragging on the river-bed kept the barge's nose downstream.

Adam and Delie were intrigued to see two mounted police officers come riding up from Echuca. They stayed to lunch and it was learned that they had come to search for a body. A barge coming past at night had lost a man overboard. The other man was asleep; he had felt the barge bump against a shoal and stop. When he came out from the forepeak to see what had happened, his mate was gone.

It had been dark and late, but the bargemaster smelled flowers and knew that a garden was near. The farm was the only place for many miles along the banks where flowers were grown. The police expected to find the body downstream, at the next bend.

For two days they had no success. They camped at the bend and came in for a meal at night, making a welcome change of company. The younger of the two, a red-complexioned officer with a waxed moustache, seemed impressed by Dorothy Barrett. He would stand stiffly beside the piano, turning over her music while she played.

'He looks as if he might break if he bends,' said Adam.

Delie, watching jealously, saw that Miss Barrett gave him a warm and intimate smile, while the young officer stared fascinated at the little curls escaping at the nape of her graceful neck.

On the third day there was sudden excitement down at the bend. Charles, hurrying past and seeing Adam and Delie by the end of the garden, told them sharply to 'keep away'. They retired into the shrubbery; but Adam, grasping Delie's hand, led her down to the big hollow gum where they hid, peeping between the chinks, while a long form in dripping wet dungarees was laid out on a plank. The bargeman's face – or what had been left of it by the crayfish and shrimps – stared unseeingly at the smiling blue sky . . .

Hester did not believe in food fads and it always put her in a bad humour if her meals were not eaten. As Miss Barrett had an appetite to match her pupils', there was rarely any trouble on this score. But one night, soon after the home blacks had been on one of their hunting walkabouts, Hester decided to have a special feast. It began with cold crayfish salad.

'No crayfish for me, thanks,' said Adam.

'Delie?'

'No, thank you. I've gone off crayfish.'

Charles said quickly, with a sharp look at them both, 'Crayfish at night are inclined to cause dreams, I believe. I won't have any myself. What else is there?'

Hester began to look exasperated. However, when she rang for the next course she smiled complacently. 'We're having a special treat tonight,' she said.

60

'What is it?'

'Wait and see.'

Bell brought in a big bird, golden-brown and magnificent, which filled the best platter, and Charles began to carve. Delie looked at the splendid curve of the breast, built for flying. A sudden conviction of what it was they were about to eat dried up her mouth. 'I won't have any, thank you. Just vegetables.'

'Won't have any?' Her aunt's voice was hard and grating. 'Won't have any of the lovely roast? Charles, give her a bit of the breast and wing.'

'NO!' she said violently. Her face was pink. 'I won't eat black swan.'

Adam, who had been looking at her in surprise, stared at the roasted bird.

'It's delicious,' said his mother. 'Everyone says so. The blacks brought some in and they've been hanging in the meat-house. I cooked it myself and it's done to a turn.'

Adam flung himself back in his chair. 'I don't want any either.'

Hester laid down the spoon with which she had been serving the vegetables, with a clatter. 'What has got into you children tonight? Charles, are you going to let them behave in this finicky fashion?'

'Er, no, of course not. If you children don't like the taste that's a different matter, but you will both try a small piece, and no nonsense. Now: a leg or a wing?'

'Nothing.'

'And none for me, either.'

'Then you will both leave the table!' cried Hester in a passion. 'And you can go to bed without any dinner. At once.'

Outside the door, they heard Miss Barrett pouring oil: 'Never mind, Mrs Jamieson, it looks delicious, and I will endeavour to do justice to it. A magnificent bird.' They went to their rooms without a word.

Delie was reading in bed, a big volume of the *Chatterbox* annual with small print and dark woodcuts, when there came a light tap on the door and Miss Barrett glided in. Her long alpaca skirts swept the polished linoleum as she turned to close the door. She sat down on the edge of the bed and brought a bread-and-butter sandwich and a piece of cake out of her roomy pocket.

'Here, child, you'll sleep better with something in your stomach. Now tell me,' as Delie ate shyly, exalted by having her idol actually sitting on her bed, 'why did you object to the roast?'

Delie looked down and blushed, but did not reply.

'I think I understand. Because swans are beautiful, because they fly, and it seems a sacrilege to eat them: something like that?'

Delie looked obstinately at the quilt, munching the now tasteless cake. Not for the world would she admit to the feeling she had for swans.

'Yes, I see. But when you are as old as I am you will be less idealistic. We are all so much dead meat in the end.' She rose. 'Well, I must take Adam his contraband supper too. Was he sticking up for you, I wonder, or acting off his own bat?'

'Both,' mumbled Delie.

'Well, good night, dear. Better blow the candle out soon.' She touched Delie's face lightly with a long, cool finger. Delie snuggled down in the crumby bed. She was beginning to feel drowsy when the door opened again and a voice said quietly, 'Are you asleep, child?'

'No, Aunt Hester.' She sat up.

Her aunt walked briskly across the room, holding a cup and saucer. 'Here, I brought you some hot cocoa and some buttered biscuits. I don't think a growing boy should go to bed without his supper, so I made some for you too.'

Delie sipped the hot, sweet cocoa. It was delicious, the nicest she had ever tasted. 'It was very kind of you, Auntie,' she said, feeling sorry for the first time. 'I put Adam off his dinner, it was my fault. You shouldn't have brought me any.'

'I like to be fair.' Hester took back the cup and saucer, and Delie felt a light kiss on her forehead. Surprised, she lay down again with a warmth inside her that was not all from the hot milk.

It was now late spring and the river was in spate. Logs and tiger-snakes came floating downstream, making Lige jumpy and irritable. Even Miss Barrett ceased to swim in the icy current. The billabongs and backwaters began to fill; here the black swans gathered in hundreds, with broods of fluffy cygnets swimming behind their parents.

Steamers going upriver laboured against the current. The gallant *Hero*, the little *Julia* with trippers aboard on her way to the Moira Lakes, the *Edwards*, the *Cato* and the *Lancashire Lass* went past by day with paddles threshing the water, by night with the brilliance of comets passing.

Delie and Adam would go out on the veranda to watch. First came a lighting of the trees near the lower bend; the brilliant acetylene lamps swung round in a great fan of light till the trees seemed incandescent. Then, with cabin windows glowing and sparks flying from her funnel, the steamer would pass upstream, drawing a curtain of darkness behind her, and leaving a feeling of excitement and unrest in two young hearts.

As the nights became milder with late spring, Delie's restlessness grew. Crickets chirred in the sand, the flowering pittosporum made the air heavy with its orange-like perfume. A wakeful magpie called melodiously; a willy-wagtail repeated his five notes in the moonlit garden, so that she could not sleep. His song was like a cascade of broken glass, sharp and clear.

Even her fantasies lost their charm as she lay, on a night of full moon, listening to the quiet, monotonous, yet somehow disturbing chant of the crickets. They seemed to be saying something . . . something, timeless and ultimately important, which she was always on the verge of understanding.

At last she flung back the covers and went to the window. Beyond lay a mysterious landscape of moonlight and shadow. She could see the satiny trunk of the flowering gum, its leaves glinting like polished metal. She put one leg over the sill and climbed out.

Her feet were bare, the sandy earth felt cool and caressingly soft. She was quite warm in her long-sleeved nightgown. Excited by a sense of her own daring, she walked down the shadowed side of the house, past the front veranda starred with white jasmine, and stepped into a pool of clear and brilliant light. It was near midnight, the moon was almost overhead, the sky cloudless. Through the trees she could see the river brimming with its own mysterious life. Slowly, timelessly, the crickets chirred. She felt life brimming within her, seeking new outlets.

In a flash on her inward eye, she saw Minna walking up the bank, the sun gleaming on her naked body. How did the night air feel on your skin – that air which Aunt Hester said was poisonous, and should be shut out of the house? It would be like bathing, bathing in moonlight.

She slipped off her one garment and pranced in the night, danced in front of her own shadow. She had become a part of the night; she felt herself less solid and real than the misty, light-charged air. The stars, small and far away, wheeled in the pale cold blue of the sky.

She did not know how long she danced there, drunk with the beauty of the night. But she thought suddenly of Aunt Hester: what if she should be looking out of her window! She picked up her discarded gown.

Just then came a sound from beyond the garden enclosure: *mo-poke*! She waited and it came again, *mo-poke*! An owl hooting from a dark tree: it was the final touch of magic. She ran through the garden and out to the first clump of Murray pines, then stopped and listened. She moved forward quietly on her bare feet. From the ground there came a low, chuckling laugh, the murmur of a man's voice

She froze. Beneath the dark trees there was a darker mass, but a shaft of moonlight shone through on Minna's laughing white teeth and glistening eyes. Delie held her breath. The moonlight fell on Minna's old yellow dress, open to the waist, and on the round globe of her dark breast. There, startlingly white against the black skin, showed the long fingers of Uncle Charles.

Delie stepped stiffly backward, the blood drumming in her ears so loudly that she thought they must hear it. She reached the gate, raced back to the house and buried her burning face in the pillow. The scene was etched in black and white in her mind; she had this faculty of exact visual memory. For a long time she could not sleep. At breakfast next morning she avoided her uncle's eyes, and ate so little that Hester was again sharp with her.

THIRTEEN

About a month after she had gone into the garden at midnight, Delie went into the cool dairy one morning and found Minna, the always cheerful Minna, with swollen eyes and sullen lips. As she helped skim the cream that had risen on the wide bowls overnight, she gathered that Minna was to be utterly banished, that she was not to set foot on the property again. The others from the kitchen were to leave their humpies and live across the river, coming over by day to help with the work.

Delie was sorry. She had always liked Minna. She had wanted to ask her to pose before she went, without her clothes, so that she could transfer that lithe and slim figure to paper. But it seemed to be thickening at the waist lately. Was Minna going to have a baby? Her mind shied away from the possibilities; but she felt that her aunt was behind the order of banishment.

Aunt Hester had gone about lately with the air of a martyr, her mouth shut in a straight line and a danger-flag of dull red in each veined cheek. She had never condescended to joke with the girls, as Charles would, but now she'd hardly speak to them. Even the half-white Bella was to leave her little room behind the kitchen and go back to the camp.

Delie was called into the drawing-room after the mail arrived. Her uncle had the newspapers spread out before him. He was smoothing his moustache in a worried way. But his words conveyed very little: something about the collapse of the land boom . . . slump in the markets . . . panic . . .

There was a run on the banks, and in Melbourne they had closed their doors. He showed her a black heading: ECHUCA BRANCH SUSPENDS PAYMENT.

'But I thought banks were such safe places to keep money!' cried Delie.

'Alas, so did everyone. We must go to Echuca and find out the worst.'

They had to go into Echuca anyway to find a new maid to replace Minna. Charles drove them round the long road, past the sandhills where white everlastings and yellow billy-buttons covered the sandy soil in sheets of white and gold. He and Hester did not exchange a word.

Delie had not yet realised the disaster to her fortunes. She sat in the buggy with Adam while Hester sought out the employment agency and Charles went in to see the manager by a side door in the bank. When he came out his face was grave. He patted Delie's hand.

'My dear, the worst has happened. Your money is gone – or as nearly as makes no difference.'

She sat staring at the sunlight shining on the silken rump of the brown gelding, and at a cloud of little black flies hovering about a lump of yellow dung in the road. Years afterwards she could recall the yellow dung, the blue sky, the long vista of Hare Street with its rows of shops, and her uncle's voice saying, '*Your money is gone.*' It all seemed rather unreal at the time. She had been told there was money in the bank; now she was told that there was none – or anyway, no more than fifty pounds. It was not until they told Aunt Hester that she began to realise that it was going to make a difference. Though the first words Hester spoke were, 'Of course it makes no difference, dear.'

Delie was silent with astonishment.

'You are my own sister's child, and we mean to support you. But I don't know about a governess.'

'Really, Hester, surely that can wait.'

'Charles, we might as well discuss things at once; and I don't see how we can afford Miss Barrett. You must have lost money yourself, and then there's Annie's salary and board . . . for I've engaged an excellent girl, no nonsense about her. She will be ready to return with us this afternoon.'

'As a matter of fact I've been very lucky, having sunk all my capital in the property and in buying that good ram. And then I hadn't sold the wool clip. I'm sorry, Delie; I didn't like to ask you to invest money in the farm, yet it would have been far better; such a solid asset. . . .'

The full sense of her loss began to sweep over her. Hester would nag until Miss Barrett went, and with Miss Barrett would go her painting lessons, and she would not be able to study at the School of Arts in Echuca, or go to Melbourne as she had dreamed.

On the way home from Echuca she was diverted by studying the new maid, Annie, who sat opposite beside her round, yellow tin trunk, and looked down her long nose with pale goat-like eyes. Her hair, dark and lank, escaped in strands from beneath her hat, which sat high upon an invisible bun. She was thin and bony, with very big feet; but it was not until she had been in the house some time that they realised how quietly she could move on those feet. Adam and Delie called her Creeping Annie.

Delie would be practising scales before breakfast in the parlour, or sitting dreaming at the piano as she gazed sideways out the French windows, when she would become aware of someone behind her. When she turned, startled, there was Annie sliding noiselessly about with a duster, and whether she was looking at you or not you couldn't tell, her eyes were so blank.

She soon fell foul of Lige. Delie saw him come bounding up from the hut, brandishing one of his snake-sticks and driving Annie before him like a gaunt, ungainly sheep. She moved swiftly without appearing to hurry, and kept muttering as she went, 'Just tidyin' the place up a bit, I wor. Just tidyin' the place up.'

'I'll tidy YOU up,' roared Lige. 'I won't have no women creepin' about my hut, pokin' their long noses and messin' things up. Women! Worse than ruddy snakes, they are. "Give not thy strength to women!" '

When told of the disaster to Delie's fortunes, Miss Barrett offered at once to stay on without salary, because she was

interested in her pupil and enjoyed life on the river. She said that
Delie had talent and should study later under a master, but at
present she would guide her painting and drawing as well. 'The
trouble is, I'm saving up for a trip abroad, and I'll be getting too
old.'

'You're not old!' cried Delie passionately.

Miss Barrett smiled with that delightful crinkling at the corners
of her eyes. 'I don't *feel* old, certainly; but the years are passing.'
She said she would wait to advertise for another place until after
Christmas – and even then it might take her six months to find
such a congenial place again.

She went back to Melbourne for the Christmas holidays. Delie
and Adam swam (at different places), rowed on the river, fished
and watched the quiet summer stream slipping by in its unending
flow. The river was a refuge, for there was space now to walk on
the edge of the water at the bottom of the steep banks which were
covered at times of high water. Here the roots of the big gum
trees, submerged for half the year, clung with twisted wooden
fingers of giant hands.

When she wanted to get away from the sound of Hester's voice,
which seemed to be always nagging her into some activity, Delie
would climb to the top of the gold-tipped cypress pine in the front
garden. Reclining on the springy aromatic boughs, with the sun
beating down on her limbs, she was at peace. The universe
narrowed to a golden ring of which her being was the centre.

As she sat with Adam overlooking the far bend of the river, and
the sound of Hester's voice calling came from the front veranda,
she said, 'Your mother doesn't seem to like me any more since I
lost my money.'

Adam looked uncomfortable. 'Oh, I'm sure that wouldn't make
any difference. You're just imagining it.'

'But she's always wanting me to do some job for her which
Annie could do perfectly well. She seems to want to keep me away
from you.'

'Rot! I don't believe it.'

But it was true. When Charles and Adam were planning a trip
to Echuca, Delie was always wanted at home. 'I'm going to run
up that cretonne into curtains today,' her aunt would say, 'and
you can help me with the rings.' Or, 'I'm making jam tomorrow,
and today I want you to go down the cellar and get all the empty
jars. Annie's feet are so big, she'll fall on those narrow steps and
break the lot; whereas you will only break one or two.'

Delie choked back the hot arguments in her throat; she was a dependant who must earn her keep.

So she sat sewing on brass rings till her fingers were sore – and she hated sewing – and saw in her mind's eye the little buggy turning and twisting under the huge straight trees, and the sky blue and far away above the branches, and the carpet of pale fawn leaves shaped like knives and sickle moons . . .

The next day Adam had to ride round inspecting sheep with his father; Delie, who liked to ride, though she had to be content with old Barney or the fat pony Leo, planned to ride out to meet them with a picnic lunch. But Hester vetoed the plan. She said, 'I'm making another lot of apricot tomorrow, Philadelphia, and I need your help.'

Delie had to stay inside cutting out double rounds of tissue paper, dipping them in milk and smoothing them down over the hot jars of jam. When the paper was sealed and taut like parchment, she took the blunt quill pen that was kept for the purpose and wrote on each drum-like top in ink: APRICOT, '93. For of course there was no need to write 1893; it had been the 1800s for so long that no one could imagine any other century being the present.

FOURTEEN

Once more the green paddocks were dotted with the white of new lambs and autumn mushrooms. Adam, who had refused to do any lamb-marking the year before, kept well away from the paddocks. Charles remonstrated with him, with the hectoring tones of a weak man trying to assert his authority. Adam set his firm chin and went his own way, while his mother tacitly supported him.

Big and solidly built, he looked more than his age. There was a manliness and assurance about him already, though he was not yet seventeen. He was now a shade taller than Miss Barrett, with whom he would enter into deep discussions of life and poetry. Every spare moment he spent in reading, shut in his room.

Looking for him after school one day, Delie tapped on the door of his room, then put her head round the door. He looked up with such a ferocious scowl that she was frightened. There was a new twist of melancholy about his brows, of determination about his soft boy's mouth. Sheets of paper were scattered over the bed, and a much bitten pencil was in his hand. He gathered up the papers defensively with an ungracious 'What do *you* want?'

'Noth-nothing,' she stammered. 'I thought I'd go with Lige and help to get the cows in.'

'Well, why don't you?'

She went slowly away, wondering how her merry companion of the first summer had turned into this self-absorbed stranger.

When they all met round the fire in the drawing-room after dinner, there were frequent tensions and arguments, mostly between Adam and Charles.

Miss Barrett was teaching Delie embroidery, at which she was endlessly clumsy. But as she sat on a low stool, her head on a level with Miss Barrett's knee, and watched those smooth, well-kept fingers with their almond-shaped nails working among the bright threads, she was filled with a sense of utter peace and contentment.

Charles was reading yesterday's *Riverine Herald*, Adam was deep in a volume of poems Miss Barrett had lent him, and Hester was setting out her second game of patience on a low table by the fire.

Charles gave the paper a jerk and a rustle, an indication that he had read something interesting. 'It says here that some hotheads among the shearers are going up and down the country, inciting union men to come out on strike. H'm. Looks as if we might have to do our own shearing this year. D'you hear that, Adam? Adam! I'm speaking to you.'

Adam looked up vaguely.

'Didn't you hear me? I said we might have to shear our own sheep this year. Though if they disrupt the industry with their strikes it won't be tolerated.'

Adam's lips twisted. 'Won't be tolerated? Who's to stop them? Or do you believe we should shoot down free men like they did at Eureka? After all they do have a grievance.'

'You sound as if you're on their side! You won't be so pleased when you have to learn to shear, let me tell you.'

'I'm not going to shear. I loathe sheep.'

'You'll do what you're told, or get out of this house!'

'Suits me!' They glared at each other.

Hester intervened quickly. 'The necessity might not arise, anyway,' she said. 'And I'm sure Adam will help if we're really short-handed.' Adam opened his mouth to retort, but Miss Barrett gave him a look across the room and he subsided. Charles, with a few irritable jerks of the paper, went back to his reading.

Quiet reigned again, except for the click of Hester's cards which she always put down on the table with a bending motion, so that the end of the card flipped against the wood. Suddenly Adam gave an exclamation, his eyes fixed on his book, his mouth working as he read a passage over to himself. Still holding the book in front of his eyes, he got up and flung himself down on the floor by Miss Barrett's low chair and put the open book in her lap.

'Look, isn't that just – It's just what I'm trying to express, it says it *exactly* . . .'

'Yes, I thought you would feel Omar Khayyám as a kindred spirit. "And that inverted bowl we call the sky . . ." You must read Schopenhauer later on.'

Delie irritably snatched her unheeded work back. He had broken the magic circle of intimacy. Dorothy Barrett was staring dreamily into the fire, while Adam gazed up at her as at a prophetess. Hester's voice, sharp and harsh, cut across the room.

'Adam, I can't get this old patience out. Just look, there's nothing but black! Can *you* see anything I can do?'

Adam shook his head rebelliously, but his mother's black eyes were compelling. He got up and leaned over the table, flicked a red Jack out of the pack and placed it on a black Queen, then went back to the couch with his book.

'Ah! That's it. Your young eyes are sharper than mine.'

Whenever Adam and Miss Barrett got into a discussion, Delie noticed, his mother was sure to need help with something.

Meanwhile Hester and Charles were excessively, chillingly polite to each other, and Charles continued to sleep in the back room.

When the mail was brought in each week and the wax seal broken, Delie held her breath in case there should be a letter in the bag for Miss Barrett; but by the next winter she had still not found a new position to her liking. In the schoolroom there was some rivalry between Delie and Adam. She outstripped him in drawing and geography, while his essays were held up to her as examples.

'This is an unusually good piece of work, Adam,' she said one morning when correcting their compositions.

A slight flush crept up in Adam's clear forehead, and he looked down at the table and then up under his brows, but his mouth remained sullen. 'Oh, I know I can write. But what's the use? That sort of stuff would never get published.'

'Yes, you *can* write. This is very well done.'

Adam remained silent, absorbed in drawing circles inside the cover of a Latin textbook.

'Listen to this, Delie,' and Miss Barrett read in her deep voice from Adam's exercise book. While she listened, Delie looked out the window at long white clouds which divided the sky horizontally into three bands of colour: deep blue at the zenith, almost purple; then a band of soft, cold blue; and below that the palest colour suffused with gold, neither blue nor green. As she noted the blues mentally, she was aware of Miss Barrett's voice saying, 'an allegory of a blind artist; but it means more than that: a poet who cannot express himself. Well, Adam?'

Adam was looking up from under his fine brows, scowling, and thrusting forward his chin and bottom lip. He gave no other reply. Delie looked at him wonderingly: he behaved so strangely these days. Miss Barrett affected not to notice his expression. 'Have you tried you hand at poetry, Adam?' she asked. 'Have you any other composition to show me?'

Adam tossed an open exercise book almost rudely down in front of her. 'Only this.'

Miss Barrett shut the book abruptly. 'I don't mean Latin verses, exercises. I mean your own compositions.'

'No. Nothing.' But colour was burning in his clear brown cheeks, even his ears became pink. Dorothy Barrett wished she had not pressed him. Oh the sufferings of youth, the dreadful self-consciousness! She did not wish to be young again, not painfully young and exposed; she had her own private carapace, grown with the years.

'Well, go on translating that passage of Virgil, will you? And Delie, come and sit by me while we go through these verbs.'

She turned the pages of the grammar rather jerkily. Really, Adam was far too big a boy for a woman to teach. And far too handsome. She had forgotten, in her years of teaching at a girls' school, how disturbing was the proximity of a handsome male.

Delie was sauntering along the bank of the river, throwing pieces of bark into the water, carefully not looking at Adam who was standing contemplating the river's flow. He looked up and saw her. 'Come for a walk, Del?' he called.

Happily she ran to join him. She did not slip her hand into his, as she would have done naturally six months ago. They walked soberly side by side, over the sandy knoll at the bend and then down the other side to the clump of she-oaks on the flat.

A light, cool breeze was blowing across the river. It sang with a melancholy sound through the long drooping fronds. Adam paused to pick a round, rough-coated cone from a twig. He stood looking at it, deep in thought.

'Oh come *on*, if we're going for a walk!'

Adam 'came on', looking at her curiously. 'Why don't you like staying back there?'

'Because of the she-oaks.'

' "She-oaks"? I prefer "casuarina". What's wrong with them, anyway? They look like dark girls with long, drooping hair.'

'Because . . . because they sound like the sea.'

'Oh. Oh, of course. Sorry.'

It was blessed to talk with Adam, she thought. You never had to explain in detail. He had never travelled in a sailing ship, but he guessed that the sighing, soughing wind in the thin-leaved trees was like wind in rigging, that at a distance it was like the sound of the waves below the cliff-top where her family lay.

The first time she had passed through the flat of the singing trees she had been startled into tears. The illusion, when she closed her eyes, was complete.

She had dreamed that night of the long white beach which Captain Johnston had described, where the Murray met the sea. She was walking below a line of sandhills, and in front stretched row upon row of waves; waves of water in front, of sand like frozen foam behind. And on this beach she was utterly alone: no cry of gull, no movement of bird, nothing but a low thunder of surf. And as she realised her aloneness in this inhuman place she was seized with such a sense of beauty and terror that she woke.

Now, as she walked behind Adam to the next bend where they were sheltered a little from the wind, he suddenly put his hand in his breast-pocket and drew out a piece of paper.

'Look at this, Del.'

She took it and saw the regular lines of metrical verse. Adam turned his back and began digging in the sand with one foot.

> All things to you, my love,
> All things to you
> From the white light of the moon
> To the sky's soft blue . . .

There were five verses, and when Delie had read them she gazed at him with awe. 'It's lovely, Adam. Did you write it?'

'Yes. I've written lots more.'

'I wish you'd show them to me.'

'I might. What d'you think, er, think of it?'

'I told you, it's lovely.'

'That's not criticism. I mean – what's wrong with it?'

'We-ell . . . I don't think "shiningness of the stars" is quite – *Is* there such a word?'

'Probably not. But you wouldn't have me say "shininess". It sounds like polished boots.'

'No, but there must be a word . . . "glittering" . . . ?'

'Not one that would fit.' He took the paper back rather brusquely and Delie discerned that he did not want her criticism, only the relief of showing his work to someone.

'Have you any more with you?' He gave her another sheet. When she read it, she cried, 'But they're good, Adam. Why don't you show them to Miss Barrett? This one, say.' She read aloud:

> . . . But now the Scorpion rules
> And you are further away than the belt of Orion
> Whose fiery jewels are quenched in the cold sea.

'How could I, you little goose? They're written for her – all of them.'

'Oh, Adam!' She clasped her hands in delight. 'You mean you're in love with her?'

'Yes.' He set his jaw and gazed over the river. 'God, how I love her.'

Delie sat down in the sand to absorb this news. Adam was in love with Miss Barrett! It was terribly romantic. He was writing poems to her, he was pining away, and only she knew his secret. She looked sideways at his sturdy figure, his clear, healthy cheeks. No, he didn't exactly look as if he were pining away. Aunt Hester's cooking and his youthful appetite were counteracting the effects of unrequited love.

'I'm glad you told me, Adam. It's so exciting.'

'Exciting! It's hell,' he said gloomily.

'She's wonderful, isn't she?'

'Wonderful.'

They both sighed heavily and stared across the water. Adam stood with his feet planted wide, his head thrust forward a little. Delie sat with her weight supported on one thin little arm. They were unconscious of the picture they made there, of youth pausing by the edge of the flowing river. The sun gleamed on their bright, shining hair, hers almost black, his a light golden-brown. Then the sun went behind a thick cloud. Both looked up and shivered.

'Someone walking over my grave,' said Adam with a smile, quoting his mother's favourite remark when she felt a shiver pass over her. But Delie looked at him seriously. Since the wreck she was conscious always of the impartial power of death to strike down the young and healthy as well as the old and infirm.

They walked back to the house in a renewed intimacy, bound by their common object of worship, like the devotees of a new religion.

The Government snagging-boat *Melbourne* tied up to a tree root below the house. A long-drawn whistle from her engine, a wild and thrilling sound, brought Lige hurrying from his hut, with his grey hair standing on end and his eyes rheumy with sleep. A bag of mail was handed over, and Lige went to pack some fresh eggs for the steamer to take on board.

The cousins went down to talk to the captain, a huge man with a grey bushy beard, who invited them on board. It was only a matter of stepping from the jutting tree root to the low deck, a foot above the waterline. They inspected the wheel-house with its great steering wheel, higher than Adam's head, peeped into the neat galley, and inside the paddle-boxes with their fourteen-foot wheels, and saw on the after-deck the steam winch and block and tackle for hauling dead logs out of the river – logs which could hole a steamer's bottom and send her to the river-bed.

By now Lige was back with the eggs – 'Straight from the 'en to you, these heggs is. I 'ad to wait while the 'en laid the larst one,' he declared, bending to pick up the mailbag.

'I'll carry the bag up to the house,' said Adam.

' 'Ere, take the hegg-money up to the Missus as well, will yez?' said Lige. 'I gotta mix up the feed for them fowls.'

Adam might have dropped the mailbag in the river if he had realised what it held. There was a letter for Miss Barrett, offering her a position as governess on a cattle-station in the far north-west, a part of Australia she had long wanted to see.

She told Hester she would wait another month, which would bring them almost to the September holidays, before leaving. After that it would be too hot for travelling in the north.

When the news was broken to Adam, he got up and left the room precipitately. This was the end! Seeing the *Melbourne* today had crystallised his vague notions of getting away, perhaps with a job as a deckhand. And once Miss Barrett had gone life here would be unbearable. The whole business of running sheep nauseated him. They were fools of things, he told himself, with their blank agate eyes and mob instinct; but this did not make him feel any better when he found a ewe with its eyes pecked out by crows, its breech a crawling mass of maggots from blowfly-strike.

And the shearing season was nearly upon them, when the rounded bodies with their creamy-brown fleeces would be reduced to a mob of skinny, blood-and-tar-marked, angular shapes. He hated it all – the foolish terror of the sheep, the spasmodic kicking when an inexperienced hand took a red gash of flesh along with the wool, the smell of sheep-dung and lanolin. He meant to leave before shearing began.

He wandered along the river-bank alone, listening to the joyous mating songs of the frogs which filled the nights with throaty music; deep bass of the bull-frogs, treble of the small frogs, and the liquid accompaniment of flowing water. In two days Miss Barrett – Dorothy – would be gone. Dorothy! He cried her name to the stars, in a fierce subdued shout. For once they did not seem to be indifferent, those cold, flickering fires, but to pulse in time with his own fevered heartbeats.

> Under the stars, half-drunk with love,
> I shout your lovely name
> And at that sound the skies rebound
> And stars flash out with flame . . .

Words came to him so easily when he was alone, they flowed into place almost without his guiding or volition. And yet, if he tried to tell her of his love he would become tongue-tied, a stumbling schoolboy. Dorothy, Dorothy! How could he let her go without telling her how he felt? Yet she knew already, she must have seen how his face flamed when their fingers happened to touch over an exercise book.

Like a moth to a lamp, he drifted towards her window, where a steady light showed that she was perhaps reading by lamplight, or packing. Packing ready to leave, to go out of his life forever!

He gave a deep groan, leaning there against the house wall.

The curtains moved. A soft voice said, 'Who is there? Adam? Is that you?'

'Yes.'

'Why aren't you in bed asleep at this hour? I've been packing . . .'

'How could I sleep, when you are going tomorrow?'

As she leaned on the sill, looking out, her face was on a level with his, framed in the long curling hair she had just let down for the night. In the glow of the kerosene lamp behind her the fine lines round her eyes were invisible; she looked like a young girl with the soft hair falling about her shoulders.

She stared at him without replying, startled out of the pupil-teacher relationship by his words, the blind adoration on his young face. She had seen it before, but never so unguarded.

'You look like Juliet,' he said. " 'Tis Juliet, and her window is the sun".'

She laughed lightly, trying to regain her ascendancy, lost in those few minutes of staring into his eyes. 'I'm afraid I'm not young enough for the part.'

He put his lips to the hand resting on the sill, and now turned it over and pressed the palm against his hot face.

'You know how I feel about you,' he mumbled. (Ah, where were all the rich and golden words in his manuscript books?) 'I can't bear you to go. Everything I write is written for you. I'll never write another line.'

'Then there *are* some poems?'

'For you. Only for you.'

'Silly boy. Do you know how old I am?'

'I don't care. You're beautiful. And with your hair like that, shining in the lamplight –'

'Wait. I have a book for you. A little Omar Khayyám. It's my own copy, but I want you to have it.'

She turned away and began rummaging through a pile of books on the floor beside an open case. 'Ah, here it is. You –' She stopped with a little gasp, her hand unconsciously closing the silk

76

dressing-gown over her bosom. Adam, resting his hands on the sill, had jumped up lightly and swung inside the window. He sat there between the curtains, his hands braced each side of him, his bright eyes burningly upon her.

'Here – here is the book. Now you must really go.' She advanced, holding it out like a placating tit-bit to a large and dangerous dog. Adam took it, put it in his pocket without looking at it, and grasped her hands. 'Dorothy! I've never called you that, have I?' he murmured.

'Adam! This is ridiculous.' She stood stiffly while his arms went round her, but suddenly he felt her relax with a sigh. He felt all of her tall and slender form through the silk stuff of the gown, and buried his face in her neck, against the cool scented skin. 'Help me . . . teach me,' he said against her hair.

'I can't teach you to write, Adam. Only practice can teach you that.' She was grasping at normality, but her voice trembled.

'I don't mean that. You know what I mean.'

She laughed uncertainly. 'My dear boy – !' Her hand played in his hair, gently, rhythmically. Half-carrying her, he stumbled towards the bed, blowing out the lamp as he passed, so that all the stars seemed to come into the room.

Adam walked for miles along the river-bank that night. He stared up at the familiar constellations, still only half-believing what had happened. He was delirious with achievement and pride: he, Adam Jamieson, had proved himself a man. And Dorothy; how lovely she was, how sweet! Yet already he was looking at her from a slightly different angle, no longer as a goddess on a pedestal. She had been his. The goddess had stepped down into his arms. And, half-acknowledged in the background, was a feeling that she should not have done so, or at least not so easily.

It had been a wonderful experience, but really not quite all he had been led to expect from books. Soon over, and leaving a kind of melancholy reaction. *Foeda est in coitu et brevis voluptas* . . . No, no, he mustn't think that. There had been a wonderful feeling of peace, at first.

Dorothy . . . With her grey eyes with the little gold flecks in them, like sunlight on a winter's day; with her mind like a man's, her body so incredibly soft. And soon she would be gone. He'd never see her again!

77

FIFTEEN

'It is tempting Providence to travel by the low road at present,' said Hester. 'I, for one, shan't go if you're taking that route. It's bad enough to be making a journey on an unlucky day like a Friday, without subjecting Miss Barrett – '

'Oh, I'm not frightened of the water, Mrs Jamieson.'

Charles maintained that the low road was still usable. Old Barney knew the track, and it was perfectly safe.

'Well, Adam, there is no need for you to go, surely.'

'Yes, Mother. I *particularly* want to go.' And he set his jaw in the new way he had which made Hester give in at once.

Delie sat quiet, fearful of antagonising her aunt and being told to stop home. She was afraid, she had heard that the creeks which crossed the track were dangerous in floodtime, but she would face them to be with Miss Barrett for the last time.

'Philadelphia, if you are not nervous of the drive I'd like you to go and match some sewing-silk for me. It is useless to ask a man to match silk.'

'Yes, Auntie.' She rushed to her room to lay out gloves, shoes and hat ready for an early start in the morning. Outside the door she collided with someone in the passage. It was Creeping Annie, who glided away on her big feet without a sound. She had been listening at the door.

The next morning they were off at sunrise. Adam managed to sit beside Miss Barrett, so that the sleeve of her long-skirted costume of black-and-white shepherd's plaid brushed against his arm; this was heaven enough for him.

Delie sat where she could study her idol's smart grey toque with its two wings of silver-grey feathers, and the little light-brown tendrils which curled so delightfully at the back of her neck. Miss Barrett's cool features were a little flushed this morning.

Barney took them across the paddocks to the flooded gum forest, where he picked his way carefully along the inundated track, marked with blazed trees. (Lige declared that Barney could follow the marks intelligently; in fact, he could feel the track firm

78

beneath his hooves even though it was covered with water.) At the first creek crossing the water rose almost to the floorboards.

Twenty steamers were tied up at Echuca, taking advantage of the high river, and there was great activity at the wharf. Adam carried Miss Barrett's bag into the station while Charles took the horse to a stable for a rub-down.

Adam and Delie walked silently on either side of their teacher as she strode with her long, mannish stride to the ticket office. Misery was beginning to overwhelm them. On the train, she talked cheerfully through the window, but received very few words in reply.

'I'm going to enjoy this trip,' she said, with a glance round at the leather seats, so far unoccupied, and the framed views of Victorian State beauty spots. Then she looked back with quick compunction at the two glum faces outside the window.

'Cheer up, Delie, we'll meet again – perhaps when you are famous, with pictures on the line at the Royal Academy. I'm counting on you two to tear the world down. Never stop writing, Adam. And never be content with anything that isn't as good as you can possibly make it – '

'*All aboard' please. All-a-bo-oard!*'

'Good-bye, my dears, good-bye! Don't forget to write!'

Doors slammed. The train was slowly, imperceptibly almost, edging along the platform. Charles came hurrying up, just in time to wave.

'*Gone!*' thought Adam and Delie, feeling still the strong grip of her warm, vital fingers. Delie, who had not said a word, blinked hard and stared straight ahead, willing herself not to cry. Adam's face was white.

Charles put an arm affectionately through hers. 'Well, girlie, where shall we have lunch? I thought we'd all go to Stacy's and have a real blowout, with chocolate ices to finish with. Eh, Adam?'

'It's a matter of indifference to me what I eat,' said Adam distantly. His jaw was set in obstinate misery. Why would Father imagine one was still a schoolboy? Chocolate ices! When a man's heart was breaking. Unbidden, the lines leaped into his mind, clear, finished, as though written upon a slate:

> My heart which beat for her alone
> Is now for evermore
> Stilled by sorrow, cold as stone . . .

79

Delie felt sick, and not at all hungry, but her natural kindness made her soften Adam's rebuff. 'That would be lovely, Uncle dear,' she said. Adam came with them, but he ate little and spoke not at all, listening to some inward voice.

Charles, who wanted to look at some merino ewes advertised at the sale-yards that afternoon, stood up and put a half-crown on the table. 'Here, buy yourselves anything else you want. I'll meet you down at the wharf at half-past two.' He took his wide felt hat from a peg and went out.

Adam's hand closed over the money. 'Listen, kiddie; I need this. I'll make it up to you one day. Look, I have to see a chap – fellow I was at school with, just saw him going into a hotel as we came up here. I can't take you there with me. Would you like to go to the park? You'll be all right for a while, won't you?'

His voice was urgent, his eyes looked bright and feverish.

'Ye-es, I suppose so. But don't be too long.'

'I'll meet you at quarter-past two. Then we can go back to the wharf together, so the old man won't know we weren't together all the time. D'you want a chocolate bar, or anything?'

'No.' She looked at him with troubled eyes. This deception was not like him. But he was propelling her out of the shop, into the clear winter sunshine. They went down High Street to the western end of the town, where Adam left her at the James Macintosh memorial, an arch of red-gum in memory of an early timber-mill proprietor. She left him and walked down a track among the native trees till her way was barred by the Campaspe River between its steep banks of clay. Where it flowed into the Murray she sat down to watch the quiet meeting of the waters, the snow-waters from the mountains of New South Wales, and the rain-waters from the flat Victorian plains. Lulled by the distant whine of sawmills and the flow of water, she fell asleep.

When she woke the sun had moved behind a big tree; shadows were lengthening across the river. She began hurrying back up the track, when she saw a man's figure slip out of sight round a tree.

'Adam!' she called. He was teasing her, playing hide and seek. She ran lightly towards the tree, rounded it – and stopped dead. For a moment she was petrified, unable to move. Then she was running, running for the track. She looked back once and the man, half-naked and pressed against the tree, was beckoning her, an idiot smile on his face. Oh, where was Adam?

She did not dare look round again, but fancied she heard drumming feet. Only when she was through the arch and back in the streets of town did she look round. No one was following. But her day was spoilt. That vile, hateful . . . creature! She walked on towards the wharf where, looking nervously over her shoulder, she ran slap into Uncle Charles.

'Why, Delie my child, you're quite out of breath, and you look terrified. What happened? And where is Adam? I've been waiting –'

He breathed a mild odour of rum, and Delie noted thankfully that he was at the mellow stage.

'Hullo, hullo, sorry I'm late!'

Charles put Delie aside and turned to look at his son, struck by a certain strange heartiness in his tone. Adam was flushed and his thick, light-brown hair was tousled.

'And where have you been, may I ask?'

'Had to see a fellow – fellow was at school with. Staying at the pub.'

'You mean you left your cousin alone and unchaperoned in the streets?'

'No – no! – Cer'nly not. Del wanted to have a look at the magnificent park, so I took her there. Thassorl.'

'Adam, have you been drinking?' A long, derisive steamer whistle seemed to underline the question.

'Drinking? Well, I had to be sociable. Met this fellow – fellow was at school with –'

'Yes, we've heard all about that. Where did you get the money to buy drink with? I suppose you spent the half-crown I gave you. It's the last spending money you'll get from me.'

'You told us to buy anything we wanted. Well, I wanted a drink.' He squared his jaw and started to look truculent.

'Keep your voice down, please. Now get in the buggy. I'll have something more to say to you when we get home. As it is we'll be lucky to get through the flooded forest before dark.'

'Sorry I didn't come back for you, Del,' Adam whispered in her ear as they climbed into the buggy. But she recoiled from his wine-laden breath, looking with distaste at this new Adam with flushed face and bloodshot eyes. He had left her alone, and that horrid man might have come upon her while she was asleep. Her admiration of Adam as someone older than herself had begun to waver.

It was a silent drive homeward. Charles shut his mind to the fact of Adam's behaviour, until he should get home and discuss it with Hester. For, of course, she must be told. It was her idolising of the boy, spoiling him and fussing over him from infancy, that had caused him to grow up to be such a disappointment.

Gradually the pleasant jogging of Barney's shining rump, the smell of horse-sweat and leather, the feel of the reins in his hands, soothed him into a better mood. He was almost dozing when recalled by a shriek from Delie.

'Whatever is it, child?'

'OH – ! The sewing silk – I forgot to match it. Aunt Hester will be so cross. I simply didn't think . . . Whatever shall I do?'

'You can't really do anything now. And it really doesn't matter. Your aunt will have more important things to worry about than sewing silks. It will be dark by the time we get home, and she will be frantic.'

They turned into the low-lying flats beside the river. Soon there was no sound but the turning of the high buggy wheels in the water. It was already gloomy under the great trees, though gold light was visible on the topmost boughs away overhead. Barney went mechanically on. Adam slept heavily.

Suddenly the buggy stopped with a jerk that woke Adam abruptly.

'Now, what the dickens – ' exclaimed Charles, urging Barney on cautiously. 'It's not bogged, we stopped too suddenly for that.' But though Barney pulled, the buggy would not move.

'Go on, Adam! Get out and see what's wrong.'

'Get out?' Adam blinked stupidly over the side, as if he thought he was in a boat. 'But it's wet.'

'Get out!' roared Charles, all his irritation with his son coming to a head. 'Feel around the wheels and see what's holding us.'

Adam took off his shoes, rolled up his trouser legs and climbed down into the water, which came up to the hubs and was milky and opaque with clay. He groped around in the water without success.

'Try the other side.'

He waded round and at the first plunge felt something caught in the spokes: a springy bough with one end dug deep in the clay. He struggled with it and pulled it free.

The buggy moved on easily. Adam swung on board, wide awake and sobered by the cold water. He shivered and put on his coat, socks and boots.

'Any damage to the spokes?' asked Charles.

'Apparently not.'

'Lucky thing. If we broke a wheel it would mean wading all the way home, or spending the night in a tree. We'll have to take it slowly.'

The gold light intensified on the highest leaves, turned fiery, then faded. The whole forest became dim. Barney, knowing the track, knowing he was on the way home, tried to hurry. He became restive at being held back to a slower pace. Suddenly, for no apparent reason, he stopped dead. A long break in the trees showed one of the creek-crossings ahead.

Charles flicked him with the whip. Too late he remembered that the former owner had warned him never to whip Barney, that it only made him obstinate. The horse began to back steadily. The front wheels turned on the lock and the buggy began a circular movement. In a moment it would leave the track and tip over. Adam, not waiting to take his boots off, jumped down and held Barney's head. Then he coaxed him forward, and soon they were safely across the creek. Adam climbed aboard with water streaming from his clothes and squelching boots. Delie edged away from his wetness.

No one spoke until they came out in the sandy home paddock, above the flood-waters. Then Charles sighed with relief. Adam was cold, Delie cramped and tired. Lige came out with a lantern to meet them, his dog barking a welcome.

'The Missus thought you was all drownded,' he said cheerfully. 'We wus just goin' out to look for yez. But I told 'er Barney knows that track better'n any man.'

Hester was waiting at the back door, her face pale in the beam of light from the lamp she held.

'Thank God you are safe! Adam, my boy, are you all right?'

'As right as rain, Mother,' said Adam, putting his arms round her. 'And wet as rain, too.'

She felt his clothes and screamed. 'Adam, you're soaking wet! Have you been in the river? I knew it, I knew it wasn't safe, but you wouldn't listen to me . . . Travelling on a Friday and all.' She bustled him inside to get changed.

Delie, tired and chilled, followed slowly. Straight after dinner, which Hester had kept hot on the wood range, she announced that she was going to bed. Adam said carelessly, 'I think I'll go along, too. I still feel a bit chilled.'

'You'll do nothing of the sort! Your mother and I want to have a talk with you first.'

Delie escaped quietly. A row was brewing, and she didn't want to be in it.

Hester's eyes snapped. 'What nonsense, Charles. The boy must go straight to bed with a hot brick at his feet.'

Creeping Annie glided in and began removing plates from the table.

'We'll go to the other room,' said Charles, motioning to Adam. 'There's a fire in there, I suppose? Come, my dear.' For Hester had turned her back on him, and was angrily moving things from the table to the cedar sideboard.

Delie could hear for some time the sound of raised voices coming down the passage from the front room. Then a thought struck her and she slipped out of bed and walked along the passage in her bare feet. As she had expected, there was a gaunt figure motionless outside the drawing-room door, which was closed.

'Is that you, Annie? What do you want?'

'I thought they rung the bell, Miss 'Delphia, just goin' in, I wor.' Her pale, protuberant eyes gleamed in the dim light from under the door. Words filtered out:

'Do you want to bring me in sorrow to my grave?'

'Oh, stop it, Mother. You'll probably outlive me.'

Delie said, 'I'm sure they didn't ring the bell, Annie. If you've finished in the dining-room, you'd better go to bed.'

She watched Annie as she glided down the passage and out the back door. Then she tapped, waited a moment and walked in on a scene of domestic drama: Hester on the sofa with a damp handkerchief to her nose; Charles with his back to the fireplace, hands clasped behind him, his face stern; and Adam standing nervously and defiantly behind a chair, gripping the back.

Delie felt impelled to say something in Adam's defence. She wanted to say, 'He loved her, he couldn't bear her going away, he only drank to forget his sorrow.' But the fact that Adam had been in love with the governess would be regarded as another crime; so she said instead, 'Uncle, Adam wanted to spend the money on chocolates for me, but I didn't want any, I was feeling a bit sick and had a little sleep by the Campaspe. I told him to leave me there – '

'You needn't try to shield him, Delie! That doesn't excuse him for getting drunk – a boy only just seventeen – and making us late and worrying your aunt nearly to death.'

Hester gave a sniff of self-pity. Adam flashed Delie a look of gratitude, before she opened the door and slipped out. There was no sign of Annie. She latched the back door and went to bed, keeping her ears open for sounds of violence from the front room.

Would her uncle try to thrash Adam? And would Adam let him? She heard Charles begin to shout, always a bad sign.

There came a scuffling noise, a door crashed open.

Delie jumped out of bed and opened her door a crack.

'That settles it!' cried Adam passionately. 'I'm not living here any longer to be treated like a school kid. You'll see!'

She caught a glimpse of his dishevelled hair, his face white with anger, as he dragged open his bedroom door opposite and banged it behind him.

'There, you see – !' came Hester's voice on an accusing note.

'Bah! Young whipper-snapper. Always has to be dramatising himself. He'll get over it.'

The door of the front bedroom closed sharply; then there was quiet.

SIXTEEN

A week later, Delie was awakened by a light tap on her door. Round the door came a flickering candle, followed by Adam, fully dressed. She sat half-upright, blinking. 'Adam! Why are you up in the middle of the night?'

'Sh! It's nearly morning. I'm doing a flit, littl'un.'

'You're *what*?'

'I'm running away. Now. Tonight.'

He sat on the edge of the bed and leaned back, raising the candle to study the effect of his news. Her open mouth and wide eyes seemed to please him. His cheeks were flushed and his eyes shone.

Delie clawed back the dark tangled hair from her eyes. 'But . . . but . . . how? Where?'

'How? I'm going to take the dinghy and go down-river with the current. You can tell Father where it will be tomorrow morning – tied up below the Echuca wharf.'

'Are you going to take the train to Melbourne?'

'No-o.' He looked rather dashed, as though he'd have liked to announce that Melbourne or even the other side of the world was his destination. 'No, only Echuca. I've got a job there.'

'Have you, Adam? Oh, I wish I could come too. I'll miss you terribly. What are you going to do?'

'Be a cub reporter on the *Riverine Herald*. Saw the editor the other day; that's why I was so long. I had to have a couple of drinks first to give me Dutch courage, and then another to celebrate afterwards. It's just as well the editor didn't smell the liquor on my breath. He's a strict teetotaller, it seems. His name is Angus McPhee.'

'But why haven't you told Uncle and Aunt?'

'They'd only try to stop me. Mother wants me tied to her apron-strings, and the old man wants to turn me into a farm rouseabout. But when they see I've really got a good job, and I show them my first pay, they'll calm down.'

'But where will you live?'

'I'll get lodgings in town. But I won't have much cash over, after paying the rent.'

'Auntie will be in a state.'

'I know. But I'll be able to come home on week-ends sometimes – Listen! A steamer. If we can hail her I might get a lift down to Echuca. Come on, help me carry my things.'

Hurrying into her dressing-gown and unlaced shoes, Delie followed him outside. He carried a grip-bag and a hurricane lantern for signalling the boat. He had thrust a bundle of books into her arms.

'Chuff-*chuff*-chuff-chuff,' came swiftly and smoothly from the engines turning freely with the current. (Adam declared that steamers going downstream chanted, 'Well *done* Mac-intosh! Well *done* Mac-intosh!' – the name of the timber-mill owner.)

As they hurried down to the bank, the trees at the end of the garden were already ablaze with light, a great white fan which preceded her and left a deeper blackness behind. Too late!

'I'll have to take the dinghy after all.'

'Well, be careful, a steamer might run you down.'

Adam, in tweed coat and cap, dropped his bag in the dinghy, took the books from her and handed her the lantern.

'You should take the light – '

'No. I'll be all right. Good-bye, Del.' He squeezed her elbow in farewell. The current took the little dinghy at once; he had only to guide it with the oars.

Delie looked back at the dark and silent house. There was no moon, but a break in the thin clouds showed half a sky of stars. She could just make out the dinghy on the river's pale gleam, dropping swiftly down with the current. The silent rushing river, the trees leaning above it, the mysterious half-veiled sky, all oppressed her with a sense of foreboding. As the boat disappeared round the bend she was seized with a premonition that she would never see Adam again.

Next morning, on discovery of a note from Adam and his bed unslept in, Hester became hysterical and had recourse to her silver-topped bottle of smelling-salts to calm her nerves. She said that Charles must drive in to Echuca and bring the boy home at once, if he had not been drowned at the bottom of the river.

But Charles was unexpectedly firm. He said that he was glad Adam had enough gumption to get a position in these difficult times. It would do him good to be independent financially. After much bitter argument she gave in, on condition that he make a trip to Echuca next day to inspect his son's lodgings and inquire about his laundry, 'for I couldn't face the journey myself,' she said, 'in my state of nerves. You'll have to go for me, Delie. My back is catching me again with this cold weather. But to think – to think that he should leave home without telling me!'

On the long drive round the sandhills, Delie strained her eyes ahead, expecting to see a trooper coming with news of Adam's death. But they reached Echuca without meeting anyone on the lonely road but a drover with a mob of sheep.

They went to the *Riverine Herald* office, with its name on the windows in gold lettering. Delie followed shyly behind her uncle, who after a short wait was shown into the editor's small room, where under a pendulum clock a big man sat writing at a desk. The floor was strewn with rolled-up balls of copy paper.

In his grey-blue eyes lurked a friendly twinkle. He took a pipe from within his large grey beard and said, 'Well? And whut can I do for ye?'

'I'm looking for my son, Adam Jamieson,' said Charles, looking in the corners, up at the clock, then back at the editor, as if he expected Adam to be hiding somewhere in the room. 'He left home without consulting me, you understand.'

Mr McPhee stood up and shook hands over the desk. 'Mr Jamieson. And is this bonnie lass his sister?'

'His cousin, Miss Philadelphia Gordon.'

'Och, aye – yon's a braw big name for sic a wee lass ... Are ye there, Adam?' he roared suddenly in such a tremendous voice that it made Delie jump.

A figure appeared at the doorway in a smudged leather apron.

Adam came forward with an air of defiance, rather spoilt by a smear of black ink on his forehead, which with his thick bright hair falling over one eye gave him a ridiculous, defenceless air of youth.

'Adam, me lad . . .' (he pronounced it Ah'dm), 'so ye didna tell me that ye hadna your father's consent to take this poseetion.'

'I did not ask his consent, because I didn't want to risk a refusal. That would have meant coming against his express orders.' As he spoke, he looked defiantly under his brows at Charles.

'Why didn't you speak to me?' said his father. 'I'm only too pleased that you've found something congenial, since it's obvious I'll never make a farmer of you. But – you said you had a reporter's job.' He indicated the dirty tradesman's apron.

Adam flushed. 'So I have! But I'm learning to set up type too.'

'Aye, he's lairnin' all branches o' the worrk. A newspaper mon needs tae ken somethin' o' typefaces and printing. He's a reporter, forbye, and will mak' a good one.'

Adam looked self-conscious. 'May I show them the press, sir?'

Mr McPhee stuck his pipe back among his whiskers and waved a hand in assent. They went along a narrow passage to a high-ceilinged room lit by skylights, where two aproned men looked up from the bench where they were at work.

'This is my family, Alf,' he said off-handedly, leading them into the room. (He told Delie afterwards that both were called Alf, but the red-headed one was called Red Alf, and the other Black Alf, to distinguish them.)

Charles, who distrusted machinery, peered at the inky press, the founts of type and the forms filled with metal pages. Delie sniffed happily. The room smelled like a book.

'Adam, there's a great smudge of ink on your forehead,' said Charles in a low voice. 'I don't know what your mother would say.'

'What she doesn't see won't harm her,' said Adam, taking out a handkerchief and rubbing the wrong side of his forehead. Delie took it from him and wiped at the ink, which still remained faintly. Adam said: 'I'm sorry I ran away now, but I couldn't face another scene; and you know what Mother is.'

Charles was silent. He knew what Mother was.

As Adam escorted them to the outer door they met the editor's wife coming in. She was a charming little woman, with a round face under a fashionable hat, softly spoken as her husband was gruff. Delie explained to her that she had been sent by her aunt to inspect Adam's rooms, a mission she dreaded. 'I'll come with you, me dear, and we'll beard the landlady together,' said Mrs McPhee. 'Adam, you didn't tell us you were hiding such a pretty cousin away in the bush. And tell your wife not to worry, Mr Jamieson. I always keep a motherly eye on the new boys in the office.'

SEVENTEEN

'Tell me the worst. The poor boy is homesick and unhappy, and not getting enough to eat?' Hester brought out her handkerchief.

'No, really, Aunt, he loves the work and he's quite happy.' She saw that this news was not as welcome as it should have been. She added tactfully, 'Of course, he misses your cooking, but he's too busy to fret. His landlady looks after his laundry personally. And the editor's wife, who is a dear, is kind to him. You know how Adam can always get round people.'

Hester smiled. 'But you know he will never remember to change his socks. And does she realise a growing boy needs a great deal of food?'

'He's much better fed there than he was at boarding school, Auntie.'

Hester relaxed. It was certainly better than having him away at school in Sydney, or alone in the big bad city of Melbourne. 'Well, we must thank God that he arrived safely after that mad trip down the river in the darkness. When I realised afterwards that it was the thirteenth of the month, I wondered that he had ever got through. It just goes to show that a good Providence looks after us all.' And with this rather illogical conclusion she began to crochet medallions for a new antimacassar from scraps of coloured thread.

The first time Adam came home with a present for her out of his pay, she brought out the handkerchief again, but after a few tears became quite cheerful. She listened to his stories and looked at his cutting book where he proudly pasted his first efforts: accounts of paddle-steamer launchings, sinkings and snaggings; social notes about leading identities; police court news.

The court cases were mostly the result of drunken brawls, for

Echuca in the season of high river was a port full of idle sailors, many of them deserted from salt-water ships.

Many townspeople, among them the editor, were shocked at the prevailing drunkenness, but in spite of their efforts one of the town's main industries remained the emptying of bottles at the forty licensed hotels.

Adam had come home with one of the Cobb & Co. coaches which ran along the Victorian side of the river, and dropped the mailbag each week, when Lige would row across to get it.

Delie had received a letter from Miss Barrett, all the way from Katherine in the Northern Territory:

> The Katherine River runs almost at our front door, so it is not so different from my old place. Except that the house is shaded with mango and tamarind trees, and flowering bougainvillea and blue jacarandas. You would love it all . . . I am very happy here and find a real companion in the children's mother, though she feels the heat and is not very strong . . .

Adam showed only a polite interest in the letter; he seemed to have got over his unhappy love affair. But Delie gave herself up to visions: she saw herself by that great palm-fringed river, under a perpetually blue sky, with parrots swooping over her head and blue butterflies playing among the flowers. This frail mother would die and Miss Barrett would marry the children's father and ask her to come there and help her bring them up, and she would paint all that tropical brilliance in magnificent pictures . . .

Delie pored over all the reproductions of works of art she could find. She had one treasure, a print of Constable's *Haywain* in colour, which had come from the Christmas supplement of a Melbourne paper. And Aunt Hester lent her a volume of religious paintings she'd kept packed away. Delie longed to see them in colour, but she could lose herself in the flowing lines and sweet faces of the Raphael Madonnas, in the old master Assumptions and Annunciations, in Holbein's *Appearance of Christ to Mary Magdalene*, with its luminous pale sky of dawn-lit clouds and the dark tomb giving out light like a lamp.

Every day she walked by the river, throwing sticks and pieces of bark and watching them borne swiftly away on the dimpling, rippling flood. The unresting water slipped through her consciousness and made a background for her dreams.

One night she found herself walking alone on the bank. A big barge, without lights, was lying tied up to a tree. Curious, she ran along the bank and across a narrow board to the deck. All on board was dark and silent. Then she saw someone coming towards her, and knew it was her father. She ran to him and leaned her head on his breast. She was filled with a calm joy. 'You were not dead at all, were you?' she murmured. 'I knew it wasn't real.'

'Of course not.' He stroked her hair.

'And where are the others?'

He motioned behind him, and round his shoulder she saw the superstructure on the barge's deck, glowing with an inner light which grew steadily brighter. The light became incandescent, and she seemed to see figures moving in the dazzling glow. The square structure reminded her of something – yes, of the tomb in the dark garden, filled with angels and unearthly light.

At once she was filled with superstitious dread, and started away.

Her father said sadly, 'We are leaving now. Are you coming with us?'

'But where?'

'To the mouth, and out to sea.'

'No, no!' She turned and ran ashore. There was no movement on deck, no rattle of steering chains, but the barge moved into midstream and went quietly down with the current. The strange light had faded; there was only a dark mass disappearing down the dark stream. She felt herself standing alone in the universe.

She never forgot, though she struggled back into waking, the dread she had felt at the mystery of that pulsing light which seemed, though she dared not raise her eyes to it, to be forcing its way beneath her eyelids.

When Hester felt sufficiently recovered with the warmth of returning summer, she decided to make a trip to town to see for herself how Adam was looked after, though his bright hair and clear complexion were sure signs of health. There was an added manliness and independence about him; he had left adolescence behind and looked more like twenty-two than seventeen.

But Delie continued to look a child, with her long dark hair, immature breasts and short skirts, from which her black-stockinged legs protruded like two sticks. She still had a child's freedom. When the snagging-boat *Melbourne*, on her way down-stream again, pulled an undermined tree from the bend below the house, she went and watched the operation from the bank, jigging up and down and shouting advice to the men.

'Captain Nash, are you going back to Echuca?' she called.

'Aye; tomorrow, most likely. The channel's fairly clear below.'

'Oh! Could I come with you? I've never – ever – been on a paddle-steamer.'

'Well, I'd let you, lass. It's more a matter of whether your Ma'll let you. And how would y' get back?'

'With the buggy. They're driving in tomorrow. It's my aunt,' she shouted back from where she was already running up to the house. There she persuaded Hester to let her go, with Annie for chaperone, for it was months since Annie had been to town on her day off.

Delie was up with the dawn and racing down to the river to make sure the *Melbourne* was still there. She felt sick with excitement, and made so many trips 'out the back' that Hester demanded whether she were ill.

At last they were on board, and actually moving downriver. There followed hours of enchantment for Delie. She raced all over the boat from stem to stern, where she stood to watch the double wake bending away from the side-wheels; saw the great shaft that turned the paddle-wheels in their boxes, sending a spray over her face as she looked inside; and was allowed to hold the big steering-wheel and watch the steering-pole come round under her control.

Tired at last, she went up on the roof where the skipper kept his garden. There she lay on her back in the sun, while the engine chuffed quietly far below and the trees on each bank slid past in a moving dream.

Poor Annie hated the boat. She sat huddled in a chair which had been put on the upper deck for her, and stared straight ahead at the blank wall of the Captain's cabin. She had found the narrow steps up over the paddle-box terrifying, and once in the chair she would not move, declaring morosely, 'I feel seaoy-sick, I do.' Her hair being drawn into a bun at the top, Annie's black hat sat high above her forehead with no visible means of support.

When they arrived at the Echuca wharf, Delie coaxed her downstairs and across the gangplank, after thanking the captain who refused to charge her passage-money. The wharf was noisy and bustling; Adam, watching a bale of wool being swung high to a waiting railway-truck, had not noticed the *Melbourne* tie up.

Delie danced up to him and pinched his elbow, her blue eyes sparkling with excitement under her wide-brimmed 'straw'. (She had only two hats, a straw for summer, a felt for winter.)

'Well, you are a trimmer,' he said with a broad grin. 'However did you get Ma to let you come?'

'Oh, Adam, it was wonderful. One day I want to go all the way to the mouth. One day I'll buy a paddle-steamer, I'll—'

'Girls can't be ship-owners, silly!'

'I don't see why not!' she scowled.

'You won't get *me* on one of them things again, not never,' said Annie. 'I still feel seaoy-sick, I do.'

She went off to visit her 'pore old father', while Adam squired Delie about the town. Hester had already arrived and told him to meet the boat; she was busy inspecting his quarters.

As they left the wharf Delie felt the sun burning her shoulders through the thin white muslin of her blouse. She looked sideways at Adam, in his new straw boater with a riband and a two-inch collar mounting firmly beneath his firm chin. How grown up he was, how assured! His lips, still with a boyish fullness about them, met in a slightly self-satisfied smile.

'You and Mother are asked to Mrs McPhee's for afternoon tea. Did you have any lunch on board?'

'No, Annie wouldn't budge, and I didn't like to go down alone with the men. I wish I'd been born a boy. I'd love to be a deck-hand.'

'What about a mess-girl? That would just suit you. You could make a mess in the galley, helping the cook.'

She kicked his ankle playfully. Oh, she loved Adam, she missed him all the time.

'Look!' He pinched her arm suddenly.

An old swagman was crossing the street to their side. A perfectly round felt hat was pulled low over his ears; they could see little of his face, but an Old Testament beard flowed in silver-grey waves over his chest. His knot of blankets was slung crossways from his shoulders, with a blackened billycan hanging from it and the handles of other cooking utensils showing. His hobnailed boots and the frayed ends of his trousers were white with dust; so one might see the wheels of a wagon coated with the dust of the back roads, and think, He's come a long way.

'I bet there's a story in him,' said Adam. 'But you'd never get it out of him.'

Just ahead were the offices of the Bendigo Trustees, Executors and Agency Company. As the swaggie came opposite them he flung his swag on the ground, struck an attitude and began shaking his fist at the building.

'I'll show y', you blunny bastards!' he roared. 'Takin' a man's inheritance, you thievin', barefaced, blunny robbers. Take the bread from a beggar's mouth, you would, and the money out of a blind man's box. I'll make y' pay for it, you lot o' —s!'

And quickly pulling a black frying-pan from his swag and brandishing it by the handle, he rushed at the windows of the Bendigo Trustees, Executors and Agency Company, Ltd, and began smashing right and left. The glass went with a glorious crash and splinters flew and tinkled on the foot-path.

Passers-by rushed up at the noise; two indignant officers of the company came out and grabbed the bearded one, who stood with uplifted frying-pan and flashing eyes, like a prophet of the Lord surveying his just retribution.

As a policeman summoned by somebody came hurrying up, Adam abandoned Delie and pushed his way to the centre of the half-amused crowd. Here was a good story. The old chap had quietened down and was surveying the damage with satisfaction, but there was still a fierce gleam in his bright blue eyes. He became excited again as the policeman took his arm and suggested he should 'come on', and he shouted abuse at the half-scared clerks in the doorway. The manager stepped forward.

'I think I know the cause of the trouble, officer,' he said. 'We've had trouble with this old fellow before, over an estate of which he is a beneficiary. Apparently he thinks he didn't get a fair deal, and nurses a grievance against the company as executors of the will.'

'You're blunny right I didn't get a fair deal. Left to hump me bluey on the track while me brother-in-law rides in a carriage an' four. Blunny, blarsted robbers –'

'Here, that's enough of that language. Come along to the station now. Come on!' And the policeman, picking up the dusty swag and grabbing the frying-pan, with which the old chap seemed inclined to take a swing at someone, hustled him away towards the lock-up.

Adam got the man's name and something of the history from the manager, and came back to Delie. Already he saw his story in print in tomorrow's paper, set in minion with large Grotesque heading. Phrases were forming in his head. He took his leave of Hester and Delie and hurried back to the office.

Delie thought a lot about the old swaggie on the drive home. She hoped he wouldn't be fined much, because he certainly wouldn't be able to pay the fine, and that would mean a prison term. There had been something wild and free in his brilliant, independent gaze – something gained on the track; he had the air of a free-flying bird that would droop and die in captivity.

'Hullo, Mother. Now, don't get excited, it's all right. I'm *quite all right*. Just a bit wet, that's all.'

Adam stood just inside the back door of the farmhouse, dripping water on the passage linoleum from his streaming clothes. Bella and Lucy, who had seen his state from the kitchen door, stood just outside, discussing it in a high-pitched flow of aboriginal language, quick rippling words that had something of affinity with the flow of the river.

They were soon interrupted by the harsh voice of Hester, calling for hot water, hot tea, hot bricks all at once for her son, whose blue lips and chattering teeth alarmed her.

When he had removed his wet things and was seated by the dining-room fireplace in a warm dressing gown, sipping the brandy Hester kept hidden for an emergency, he told them what had happened. He had come home as usual with the Cobb & Co. coach; and finding an old native canoe on the far bank, and not seeing Lige anywhere on the other side, he had propelled himself more than half-way over, when the flimsy craft sank beneath him.

'I'd have been all right but for the mailbag, but it was no fun towing that in the present current.'

'Oh! Oh!' His mother began to moan. 'You might have been drowned. I saw disaster in the tea-leaves this morning. Why didn't you let the bag go, you naughty boy.'

'I didn't want to lose your letters. Besides, there's something in the paper I wanted you to see.'

He did not add that, for a moment, weighed down by his clothes and almost numbed by the icy snow-waters, he had panicked, but could not undo the drawstring of the bag he had tied to his wrist. His shivering had been caused as much by reaction from fright as cold. The current had swept him away below the house, so no one had seen his plight. Delie saw that he had not told everything.

'I'll watch for you next week and row over,' she said.

'Nonsense, Philadelphia. Lige can go and get him.'

'But I'd like to, Aunt.' Her full bottom lip began to stick out.

'That's enough. I don't like you rowing alone, with the current and all. Lige will get him.'

Adam said tactfully, 'Look what I've got to show you.' He

broke the wax seal and drew out the letters and papers, still fairly dry. He spread out the four sheets of the *Herald*. 'They have featured my story about the mad old swaggie.'

'What mad old swaggie?' asked his mother with a sniff.

On the main news page he read out:

> A man named James Allchurch Fitzroy, of no fixed address, today pleaded guilty to disorderly conduct, wilful damage to private property, and using insulting language. Accused said he did not remember the conduct leading to the charge, but was a very quiet-tempered man.
>
> Damages and a fine, amounting to ten pounds in all, were imposed, in default two months' imprisonment.

On the next page was a long article, signed by Adam Jamieson. It outlined the old fellow's wanderings in the bush, his sense of persecution, and ended with an appeal to the citizens of Echuca to pay the fine for the old man, who was in poor health and would probably languish and die in prison.

The paper led the way with a donation.

'Of course that mostly came out of my pocket,' said Adam.

'I don't know that you are in a position to be a philanthropist,' said Hester. 'But of course I will make a donation to your cause.'

'Thanks, Ma.' He kissed the top of her thin black hair, an unusual demonstration for him. Her eyes softened.

'How soon must you go back, dear?'

'I have to be back tomorrow night to get Monday's paper ready.'

'I don't approve of this working on the Sabbath.'

'Oh, the Sabbath's over by the time we get the paper to bed.'

Two weeks later Adam stepped out of the dinghy looking downcast and morose. He said little as Delie walked with him up to the house; then he thrust a folded newspaper into her hand.

She saw an item savagely marked in black ink. The heading was, MAN DROWNED AT CAMPASPE JUNCTION. The story went on to say that James Allchurch Fitzroy, aged 69, had been found dead, his body tangled in a set-line; and

> ... a large collection of empty whisky bottles suggested the deceased had been on a drinking spree; and falling in the river while attending his set-line, had been too fuddled to pull himself out again ... Fitzroy, of no fixed place of abode, was

the man who recently damaged the windows of the Trustee
Company in Echuca's main street.

'Oh Adam!'
'Old Mac made me go and see the body. He said it would
dampen my enthusiasm for indiscriminate good deeds.'
'But it wasn't your fault he fell in the river. And no doubt he
enjoyed the whisky bender.'
'But he bought the whisky with the money over-subscribed
because of my appeal. Otherwise he'd be safe in jail at this
moment.'
'You mustn't blame yourself. He'd have pined away in jail,
anyway.'
But he looked so miserable, so young and uncertain again, after
his assured manner of late, that she felt a rush of protective
tenderness; she felt older than Adam. On the veranda he turned
to look back over the river, his hands on the weathered wooden
rail.
She looked down at his long brown hands clasping the rail with
nervous tension, and noted the little golden hairs on the backs of
his wrists, gleaming in the sunlight. Those strong golden hairs,
erect in the sun! They moved her strangely. For the first time she
felt strongly aware of his masculinity, his mysterious apartness.
She looked at the round column of his neck and the pink whorls
of the ear next to her. It was all new and strange, exciting and
disturbing. She would never be able to look at him in the old
uncomplicated way again.

EIGHTEEN

Bushfires, burning south of the river, seemed to intensify the heat
that summer. Emus and kangaroos, driven by hunger and thirst,
came in to the river; large goannas ate the fowls' food at night,
and a plague of grasshoppers invaded the garden.
Delie began to revel in the heat which had sapped her strength
the year before. It was such a clean, clear, burning heat, it purified
the air and filled it with aromatic scents of eucalyptus and wild

mint, distilled in the sky's blue cup.

She could feel the paddocks burning tinder-dry, baking to brown and gold like some vast loaf. Their colour against the blue was more satisfying that the green of autumn and winter. She got out her paints and made water-colour sketches in the open air, though her paper dried too fast and the metal of the black-japanned box burnt her hand. Soon there were deep hollows in the pans of yellow ochre and ultramarine.

Hester, as usual, complained. 'This awful heat! Will it never end?' she moaned. The temperature had been over a hundred degrees for five days.

'I seem to have heard you make the same remarks about the cold at Kiandra,' said Charles.

'Yes, but this heat passes all bounds. What a country! Nothing but extremes; either a drought or a flood, a heat-wave or a temperature below freezing. There is no moderation in it.'

'Pooh! This is nothing. In the far inland they have a hundred and twenty degrees in the shade for months on end, and have to live in holes in the ground to escape being shrivelled by the sun. The water boils in the tanks. *You* don't know what hot is.' The quiet wink he turned upon Delie was lost on Hester.

'Well, let's hope you won't take it into your head to go and live there. I never know what outlandish place I'll find myself in next.'

In fact, she rather dreaded being dragged away from the farm, which was all her interest now that Adam was away. She loved the abundance of raw materials calling for her housewifely arts: the cream to be skimmed and made into butter, the fruit to be preserved in season, the mutton fat to be made into tallow candles in their long moulds of twisted brown paper. She even made her own soap.

The pungent smoke of fires drifted in on the dry winds. The bushfires had brought more birds to the river. White cockatoos, rainbow coloured rosellas, Major Mitchells with crests like setting suns, clustered in the treetops. Cockatiels and budgerigars in veering flocks filled the air with colour and shrill sound. Ibis, herons, swans and ducks came in from the dried-out swamps among the burning forest.

Lige knew the names of all the birds, their cries and nesting habits. 'You ever see a swan's nest, Miss Delie? Just a flat nest of reeds, but them birds is so clever they lay three-cornered heggs to stop 'em rolling off into the water.'

Delie laughed, and his faded eyes twinkled. 'Ah, Lige, you can't pull my leg any more.'

She was not a newchum any more; and she was no longer a child, now that she had passed her fifteenth birthday. Too thin, she yet carried the promise of loveliness in her long throat and young shoulders, budding breasts and pale skin. Her large eyes were a deep dark blue, and her lips glowed with the natural red of health. She began to be conscious of her appearance, washing her dark hair till it glowed with coppery lights, taking buttermilk from the dairy to bathe her face. She had read somewhere that plain water was bad for the complexion. She wanted to put her hair up and let down her dress-hems, but Hester would not hear of it.

Adam came home with news of a ball to be held in Echuca at the beginning of the winter season, a 'coming-out ball' for some of the local girls. He brought a note from Mrs McPhee, the editor's wife, who offered to present Delie at the ball.

> If you will entrust your charming little niece to me, she is welcome to stay here and go to the ball with us; or perhaps you may come yourself if your health permits.
> Please let me know if you would like me to look out a suitable dressmaker for Delie's gown. With her slight figure and dark hair she will make a delightful debutante . . .

Hester made several objections: that the expense of a new frock was not warranted for one ball; that the weather would be too cold, that she could never drag herself to town . . .

'Oh *please*, Aunt Hester.'

'Go on, Mother,' said Charles good-naturedly. 'Remember how you looked forward to your first ball.'

Hester looked as if she were remembering a good deal, and none of it pleasant.

'There's no need for you to go, my dear. Mrs McPhee will see to everything, and Adam will write up in the *Herald* that the bee-yootiful Miss Gordon made her debut in a ravishing creation and was the belle of the ball – '

'Don't be absurd, Charles. Philadelphia, do you know how to curtsy?'

'Of course. We learnt in dancing-lessons at school.'

'Well . . . We had better take your measurements then, and send them to Mrs McPhee. And I shall tell her to get nothing extravagant.'

'But I may have a *long* dress?'

'I suppose so. Down to your ankles, anyway. Not a train, of course.'

'And may I put my hair up for the ball?'

'Certainly not. You're only a child.'

'But all the others will have their hair up, I know they will.'

'They will be girls like yourself and they will wear their hair long, with ribbons.' Hester spoke with as much assurance as if she had lived in society constantly, instead of in isolated communities, for the last twenty years.

'Oh, *please*, Auntie.'

'Oh, let her put it up for the occasion. She will look quite a young lady.' Charles picked up her heavy, almost straight hair and piled it on top of her head. She smiled and blushed and looked so pretty that Hester said instantly, 'Allow me to know what is best, please. Philadelphia, go and get the tape-measure from my work-basket.'

When Delie was out of hearing she turned on him and said in a violent undertone, 'You idiot, Charles! You can't see beyond your nose, big as it is. If we let her grow up too soon, before Adam gets interested in someone else, there's no hope for him!'

Charles, staggered by this feminine long-sightedness, was still meditating a reply when Delie came back with the tape-measure. She was mutinously resolved about the hair, but willing to let it pass for the present, as she had gained the point about the ball, and the new gown.

'Oh, it's lovely, it's lovely!' cried Delie, standing rapt in front of the long glass in Mrs McPhee's bedroom. She had almost said, 'I am lovely,' for she was delighted with her own reflection. She had not seen herself at full length for years, except once or twice in Aunt Hester's wardrobe mirror; she did not like going into her aunt's room, which always had closed windows and a queer musty smell compounded of old papers, scent and the commode in the corner.

She turned and swayed and the white nun's veiling billowed out around her. This fairy-like creature was herself, Philadelphia Gordon: dark hair, wide eyes, tiny waist, pearly shoulders showing through the filmy fichu, skirt spreading like a foamy cloud. The top layer was caught up here and there with a blue bow, and a sprig of velvet forget-me-knots was fastened in the centre of tne fichu.

'You do look pretty in it, 'Delphia dear! And it's a perfect fit.' Mrs McPhee gave a little pull to the skirt. 'Your arms are a bit thin and your hands a bit brown, but the long gloves will hide that.' She paused and looked uncertainly at the mane of hair drawn back into a broad black bow, and hanging almost to the waist. 'And perhaps we could curl your hair into ringlets.'

'But I can wear it up, can't I?' Delie gathered her hair in both hands and rolled it into a low knot on her neck. The good bone contours of her face became more noticeable, and her delicate features at once seemed more mature.

'I'm afraid not, dear. Your aunt was very definite in her note. She wishes you to wear it long at present.'

The straight dark brows drew down; the full lips trembled. Delie flung herself face downward on the bed, heedless of crushing the new skirt. 'Oh! She spoils everything!' she sobbed.

'Dear, the gown! Be careful. You'll be surprised how nice your hair will look, with a blue bow to hold the ringlets together.'

'But I don't want to look like a child at its first party.'

'Tut! There will be others almost as young as you.'

'With their hair down?'

'Probably,' said Mrs McPhee evasively.

On the great day Adam arrived with a posy of forget-me-nots and hyacinths; she had her hair in white curl rags, and looked dreadfully plain. But when at last she was dressed she looked at herself with approval. She had white stockings and satin slippers. Her hair was in shining ringlets tied back so that from a front view one could scarcely tell that it was still 'down'. Her eyes were big and dark blue with excitement. When Mrs McPhee had added a dash of perfume to her shoulders, she began to feel like Cleopatra.

Arriving at the glittering ball, where gaslights shone through the chandeliers, she was dazzled and overcome. The little piping notes of the string band tuning up, the pale, flowing gowns of the women, the important pushing through the crowd of some official – all filled her with a dizzy expectation. She studied with delight her little programme card with its tiny pink pencil and silk tassel.

Mrs McPhee established herself with other leading matrons of the town and introduced her protégée. Delie bobbed shyly and sat down thankfully. She felt the others were studying her with surprise and amusement; the other gowns all swept the floor, while hers showed her shoes and even her ankles.

Mr McPhee claimed the first dance – his wife had given up dancing – and Adam came and asked her for the supper dance and several others. He had plenty of young men acquaintances, several of whom asked to be introduced to 'the little dark one'. Soon Delie's programme was full. The band struck up, and Mr McPhee whirled her off in a circular waltz. The dance warmed her and made her cheeks glow, so that Adam when he came to claim her for the polka said sincerely, 'You look stunning, Del.' She was acutely conscious of his strong arm about her, of his manly chin almost touching the top of her head. Her feet seemed to float somewhere above the floor.

But when it was time to be presented to the visiting Lady, she became aware of the other girls' glances at her hair, her short frock, the posy she had carelessly sat on; and self-confidence deserted her with a rush.

She looked at the others, at their sculptured satins and sweeping trains, their coiled-up hair and swan-like necks, and felt her own short, billowing skirts and drooping curls to be the depth of childishness. To crown it all, she felt sure that one of the petticoats Mrs McPhee had fastened round her waist in layers was slipping, and would soon fall in an accusing ring at her feet. Also, she had a sick conviction that she was the only one in the whole room with her hair 'down'.

The other girls all knew each other. They whispered together and ignored her. It seemed an hour before they moved up to the grand Lady's beflowered box. As she tried to grip the slipping petticoat through her skirt, Delie made an awkward bob of her curtsy. Trying to shrink out of sight behind Mrs McPhee's plump little figure, she went back to her seat and buried her burning face in the squashed posy. She would never forgive Aunt Hester, never, for making her look a freak with short skirts and long hair.

Mrs McPhee was talking to her neighbour, a large, majestic blonde woman with a fair, elegant daughter who eyed Delie without friendliness. Delie determined not to dance again; she told Adam she was sitting out the next dance. Disregarding her refusal, he pulled her up and whirled her on to the floor.

'Adam!' she cried in a voice of tragedy. 'My petticoat!'

'Well, what about your petticoat?'

'It's slipping – it will fall right off in a moment!'

'Well, what if it does? I suppose you have plenty more on.'

'Adam, you fool! Do something. Oh help! It's going.'

Adam, sweeping her close to the row of seats that surrounded the walls, at the exact moment when the petticoat wrinkled to the floor lifted her over it and gave it a deft kick which sent it out of sight under a seat. In the crowd no one had noticed.

The next was a square-dance, with Adam across the corner from her. As they joined hands and whirled madly round, her spirits rose. She laughed aloud, breathless and bright-eyed. Dance followed dance, the night expanded into a magic ring. Her dress, her posy, her qualms about her hair, were all forgotten. With eyes and cheeks brilliant with excitement, she floated about the room feeling as though her feet never touched anything so prosaic as a floor.

Home in bed at last, feeling still too stimulated for sleep, she repeated to herself her first compliment as a woman.

'You have no need of these, Miss Gordon,' A young dandy had said, touching the blue forget-me-nots on her young bosom. 'Your eyes are far bluer, and no one who has seen them could ever forget them.'

NINETEEN

During the morning there arrived the fair, elegant young lady of the night before and her mama, to call. Her name was Bessie Griggs, not at all an elegant name, thought Delie. Her mother was large and fair, with an air of sleepy majesty. Bessie gave promise of being large too, though as yet there was only a certain solidity about her figure. Her complexion was flawlessly pink and white, her eyes were like blue china. Delie thought she looked almost unreal, with her smooth golden hair as though moulded to her head.

It turned out that Bessie was only a year older than Delie, who felt, nevertheless, looking at Bessie's costume of dark blue gaberdine and pale blue blouse with crystal buttons, that there was a great gulf between them. A large blue hat was poised becomingly on Bessie's fair hair.

Mrs McPhee, welcoming her visitors, murmured something

about the girls becoming 'great friends' while the girls themselves examined one another guardedly. Delie saw Bessie note inwardly her rather shiny blue serge skirt and home-knitted jumper.

Mrs McPhee, round, quick and bright-eyed as a small bird, chirruped about the success of the ball. Mrs Griggs, whose eyes were of the same pale china-blue as Bessie's, but always half-closed where Bessie's were very wide open, replied in her sleepy, ponderous way. The girls exchanged questions and answers, but found no subject of mutual interest. Bessie seemed a little absent-minded. She turned her head frequently to study her small, regular features in a wall-mirror, moistened her lips, touched her hair and moved her neck with a little self-satisfied gesture like a preening bird.

Delie decided that she did not like her much, but she admired her and wished that she could look half as elegant.

'Why don't you put your hair up?' Bessie was asking. 'I've had mine up ever since I was fourteen.'

'My aunt won't let me.' Delie felt herself blushing.

'Pooh! No one would stop me if I wanted to.'

How explain her dependence, her aunt's implacable nature? But Bessie would get her own way with anyone, she thought, looking at the straight little nose, the firm, obstinate jaw, the thin but perfectly shaped lips, and row of even teeth.

Mrs Griggs was suggesting that she should accompany them down the street for an ice-cream soda, so Delie went upstairs to change. She had nothing but her best woollen afternoon frock, of plain brown with beads trimming the high collar. She looked with loathing at its half-mast skirt, and felt that the beads were unsuitable, but she could cover them with a scarf. Putting on her hat and gloves, she went reluctantly downstairs.

Once again she endured the appraising flicker of those cool blue eyes before the three of them stepped out into the street.

Over the ice-cream soda she felt a need to assert herself. She announced suddenly, 'I've been in a shipwreck.'

At once Bessie was all flattering attention. To her own faint surprise Delie heard herself chattering about how she had gone up to look at the stars on that last night on board, and at the low, mysterious coast of Australia.

'That's how I came to be saved, I suppose,' she said. 'Only the helmsman and the look-out men were on deck, and the officer of the watch. Anyway, only the helmsman and I got ashore. Everyone else was asleep; and they all went down with the ship.'

'Yes, I remember reading about the *Loch Tay* disaster,' said Mrs Griggs.

Delie looked down at her clouded glass. Here she was, admitting off-handedly the loss of her whole family, the things of which she had never been able to speak even to Adam. Perhaps she had felt instinctively that here was no imagination likely to fill in the details, no danger of being overwhelmed with sympathy.

'No one knows how it happened,' she said. 'It was a calm night, and we were only half a day out from Melbourne. Somehow we must have been sailing off course to have run aground where we did.'

She remembered as clearly as yesterday the narrow cove shut in by cliffs of yellow sandstone, the small curve of beach, the brilliant blue-green of the Southern Ocean beyond. 'Fortunately, there was a cave which we found –'

'You mean you slept all night in a cave, with a *man*?' said Bessie.

'*I* slept in the cave,' said Delie delicately. She was beginning to learn when the truth was not acceptable. 'Tom, that was the helmsman, was wonderful. He found cockles and things for us to eat, and looked after me like a father. Then we had to climb the cliffs.'

She paused for breath and saw even Mrs Griggs's sleepy eyes open with interest.

'I was scared, but Tom was used to climbing in the rigging, and he helped me up. Then we had to go across the headlands till we came to a farm, and I nearly trod on a snake –' (this was an embellishment added now for the first time) ' – and I thought there might be wild blacks, but there aren't any left there except in the Framlingham Mission. We found a house and the people took us up to Melbourne.'

She sucked at the froth in the bottom of her glass and the straw made a loud, embarrassing noise. But Bessie and Mrs Griggs were looking at her with new interest.

As they walked along High Street, Bessie took her arm and squeezed it, promising to call and see her every day till she went back, asking when she would be coming to town again. Delie glowed at this social success. She found that both Bessie and Mrs Griggs had been impressed by the fact that her father was a doctor of medicine. In country towns in Australia the doctor was always 'somebody'.

They crossed the road and began to walk on the sunny sidewalk towards the McPhees' home. At the corner Delie saw a familiar face. She hesitated, stopped, looked back. 'Excuse me a moment,' she said, and broke away from her companions to cry joyfully, 'Minna!'

The dark face of the woman on the street corner broke into a wide white grin. It was the same gentle face, with heavy brows shading soft dark eyes, but all was broadened and coarsened. The shapeless figure was no longer that of a girl. On one hip Minna carried a small baby. She held by the hand a boy of the toddling stage, who looked with solemn dark eyes from a pale creamy-brown face. His nose was filthy. Minna's pink dress was discoloured down the front, drawn tight over her large breasts.

After the first happy moment of discovering a known face, Delie was struck dumb. Minna, this was Minna, the lovely girl she had longed to paint! She looked at the half-white child and then at the baby; it was light-coloured too.

She looked down at the ground. She saw again the outline of white, moonlit fingers against a black breast.

Minna was full of questions. 'How the boss? The missus? Bella and Lucy still longa kitchen? Old Sarah, she dead-feller yet?'

Delie answered in a dream, watching a fly crawl unheeded into the corner of Minna's soft dark eye.

'Hello dear,' she said falsely to the filthy-nosed child. 'Are they both yours, Minna?'

'My word, Miss Delie, him both belong me.' She smiled proudly, and then as though conscious of something amiss, picked up the hem of her dress and wiped the child's nose.

'And you don't live in camp any more?'

'No-more. Me likem town more better.'

'Well . . . My friends are waiting, I must be going.' For she had become aware of Mrs Griggs's eyes, no longer sleepy, fixed upon her in an outraged stare. 'Good-bye Minna, and good luck. I expect I'll see you again.'

But she didn't want to see her again, not ever. The lithe, beautiful girl who had first given her an idea of the dignity of the human body was travestied in this shapeless bulk in the pink dress.

Bessie, curious, made a move to join her, but her mother drew her back as from a burning fiery furnace. They stood waiting at the edge of the road. Mrs Griggs's 'Really! Do you *know* that creature?' informed Delie that her social standing had dropped again. She explained that Minna was an old friend, that she had worked in the farm kitchen and she hadn't seen her for two years.

106

'Poor Minna! Town life has not improved her. She used to be really beautiful.'

Mrs Griggs sniffed. 'These people are ugly and depraved by nature. The sooner they die out the better.'

'That's not true!' flashed Delie. But seeing Bessie's look of alarmed amazement, she said no more, only sticking out her full bottom lip and walking on with a mutinous expression.

'Adam! I saw Minna today,' she said, meeting him at the McPhees' front gate that evening. He had been invited to dinner.

'Good old Minna!' he said with an ironical inflection, leaning back against the gate as he closed it.

'She's living in Echuca, she has two children. Do you think she has enough money – I mean, that the children get enough to eat? She didn't look too well off.'

'Oh, Minna's all right.'

'What does her husband do?'

'She hasn't one, that I know of. Minna supports herself in the only profession she knows. She is on the town: black, white or brindled, it's all the same to Minna.'

'But Adam –'

'Don't look so tragic. It's what usually happens once they have a half-caste baby. She's lived in the white man's kitchen and got used to their food and tobacco. You can't expect her to go back to the camp.'

She looked at him carefully. Did he guess who had fathered Minna's first half-white baby? But there was no knowledge in his eyes, no consciousness of a personal implication in Minna's sordid story – the story of thousands of detribalised women, little more than girls, who a hundred years ago would have been living an ordered existence under the marriage laws established by their race for uncounted centuries.

TWENTY

With the spring the river seemed to leap into life. The thaw had
come early this year: in the mountains the matted brown grass
was already appearing from beneath the snow like the fur of some
great draggled animal, and little streams moved beneath the
melting snow-bridges. Down the Ovens and the Indi and the
Eucumbene, the Molonglo and the Mitta Mitta, the waters flowed
on their blind journey into the Murray basin. Endless and un-
returning as time, inexorable as the force of life, the rivers ran
towards the sea.

Each day, Delie marked a level on the water-ringed bank with a
stick, and each day it was covered by the rising waters. They rose
above the roots of the big trees in the bank, whispering and gurg-
ling in hollows, plucking at the dinghy's rope. Fallen trees, re-
floated snags, sticks, snakes or drowned sheep, all floated past the
homestead at an increasing pace.

Soon the overflow creeks were flooding in the red-gum forest,
and the joyous croaking of frogs filled the night with vibrating
music. Delie liked to climb the pine tree in front of the house to
think about Adam and the way the hair grew in a peak at the back
of his neck, or simply to stare at the rushing river in a dream.
How long before she went with the river, out into a wider world?
For she never doubted that life on an outback farm was not for
her; some splendid future, shadowy but uncertain, waited out of
sight beyond the bend.

If spring made her dreamy, it had the effect on Annie of making
her play on the accordion she had brought with her, sitting on the
back steps on moonlit nights. She also began to pursue Lige.

She began by gliding silently down to his hut with a few biscuits
or a cake which she had just taken from the oven. Before he could
open his mouth to roar at her, the delectable scent of the food
made it water. Thus, with masterly strategy Annie began her
assault on the old bachelor's most vulnerable spot, his stomach.

Though Hester was a careful housekeeper she never begrudged
anyone a taste of good food, so she watched with a tolerant eye

the removal of an occasional delicacy to the table of Lige, who 'did' for himself on an open fireplace cooker.

He no longer chased Creeping Annie from his hut with insulting words. Her pale, goat-like eyes kept watch from the kitchen door, so that she knew when he was at work in the vegetable garden or collecting 'heggs' or feeding the fowls. She would time an excursion to pick parsley or mint accordingly, or go down with a plate of scraps to the fowl-run when he was there.

But what finished him was the episode of the snake.

It was a windy, warm spring morning with air full of the velvety scent of wattle bloom. Delie was on the front veranda drying her hair in the sun when she heard Lige's voice, high and wobbly with fear: 'Sna-ake! Snake!' He was down by the vegetable enclosure, which was near the river and irrigated from it, facing an angry tiger-snake which had flattened its neck dangerously. He grabbed one of the strong sticks he had always ready, and edged doubtfully towards the snake. But the stick was taken swiftly out of his hand. Annie, streaking down from the kitchen, had come to his aid. With one good blow she broke the snake's back. She turned on him a look as near to triumph as her peculiarly expressionless face would allow.

Lige's faded blue eyes popped. His jaw with its straggly grey beard dropped open. 'Gawd!' he said. 'Gawd! Wot a woman.'

'I ain't afraid of snakes I ain't,' said Annie.

'Broke 'is back with one 'it!'

'Killed 'undreds in me time,' said Annie.

' 'Undreds!'

'All sorts. Tigers, blacks, browns, death-adders. Don't scare me none, they don't.'

On the next night of full moon her accordion was silent; but two figures sat side by side on the front step of Lige's hut, facing the moonlit river. Delie, wandering outside in the moonlight, heard some wakeful magpies warbling at the sky – oigly-goiglies he had called them when he was little, Adam told her once. As she listened, she heard another sound nearer at hand:

'Think I'd be game to sit out 'ere at night by meself?' came Lige's voice. 'Not me. But I feel sorter safe with you, Annie.'

'Aw, go on with yer!' was Annie's coy reply.

Adam came home at the week-end, bearing a note from Mrs McPhee. Hester came out with it in her hand to where he and

Delie sat talking on the veranda steps. She looked pleased and somehow excited.

'Mrs McPhee says you've found a new friend, Philadelphia; a Miss Griggs. Why didn't you tell me?'

'She's not a friend yet.'

'Well, acquaintance then; of your own age almost. Her father owns the biggest store in Echuca; they are terribly well off.' She paused expectantly. 'Well, what is she like?'

'Ask Adam. He danced with her all the time at the ball.'

'I like that! Twice, at the most.'

Hester gave a sniff, like a dog on a scent. 'Is she pretty, Adam?'

'Oh, stunning! A beautiful blonde, with a complexion like a wax doll's.' (And about the same amount of brains, he added to himself.)

'I suppose you see her quite often?'

'Oh, I run into her here and there.'

Hester was too shrewd to press her point, but turned to Delie, who was apparently absorbed in watching the river.

'Why don't you ask Miss Griggs to come and stay for a week-end, Philadelphia? You need a companion of your own age, as Mrs McPhee says.'

'You can ask her if you like,' said Delie, without turning her head.

However, some wintry weather set in, with bitter southerlies driving up from the coast, rain lashing the river till its surface seemed to boil. Hester put a pad of warmed flannel to her back and a thick shawl round her shoulders, and moved complainingly about the house.

'It's the Change coming on me,' she said to Delie, whom she now considered old enough for such confidences. 'Not but that I welcome it, mind. My periods have hardly ever stopped, not for a week even, for years. It was the cold, and getting run down when Adam was born.'

She gave up all idea of entertaining until the weather improved. As the steamers had started moving on the river again, perhaps Miss Griggs might come up later by boat.

Adam did not come home for three week-ends in a row. Hester had her own ideas about this, and thought it a good omen; but Delie crouched over the fire, imagining Adam and Bessie meeting in cosy parlours, and felt utterly miserable.

But Mrs McPhee came to her rescue with an invitation to stay. It was arranged that after she had spent a week in Echuca, Bessie

110

should come back with her and spend a week-end at the farm.

Mrs McPhee's letter also suggested that she should help Delie choose some new spring and summer clothes, with a delicate hint that Echuca was full of eligible young men who were susceptible to summer finery. Here she did Delie a great service; for Hester, with Adam already betrothed to Bessie in her mind, suddenly saw the advantage of letting Philadelphia make herself attractive. The sooner she was married and off their hands the better. She was worse than useless in the home, with her dreamy ways and clumsy fingers.

'Is that a new hat?' Bessie was openly inspecting her this time.

'Yes,' said Delie defensively. It had come, in fact, from Bessie's father's store; and until a moment ago she had felt the wide yellow straw, trimmed with white velvet daisies and imitation wheat, to be the height of fashion. But at the first sight of Bessie, she had felt less pleased with her own simple costume of pearl-grey gaberdine. Bessie had called for her in a blue-striped galatea the exact shade of her eyes, with large sleeves and a wide belt. And Bessie's hat – a mere trifle of stiffened lace, utterly useless for protecting her from the weather – made her own seem large and over-decorated. Bessie carried a frilled white parasol to shield her rosy complexion from the spring sunshine.

'It's a nice straw,' said Bessie patronisingly, leading the way into Hare Street. They walked to the corner and turned into High Street, where buggies, sulkies, gigs and drays lined each kerb. Bessie met a girl-friend and her mother and stopped to chat with them without introducing Delie. At last they went on, and Bessie became affable to Delie once more, taking her arm. She bowed distantly to a pale, thin young man with a dark moustache. She giggled and looked over her shoulder after he had passed.

'Who was that?'

'Oh, he works in the store . . . in the Men's Wear. He's terribly romantic-looking, don't you think?' She heaved a sigh, caught her bottom lip between her perfect little teeth and turned to look in a shop-window at her own reflection.

Delie began to feel elated. Here she was, walking with this very fashionable young lady who knew everybody; she had on a brand-new outfit down to her shoes and gloves, and she wanted to be seen. Only a year ago she would have preferred idling along the river-bank or watching steamers from the wharf. Now, as she walked under shop-awnings or sat sucking soda-squash through a straw and gazing down at her own shining, pointed shoes, she felt urban to the tip of her toes, and entirely grown up. She had been allowed to put her hair up at last.

Passing again by the end of Hare Street, where the windows of the *Riverine Herald* office could be seen, Bessie said artlessly, 'Let's see if Mr McPhee is in his office.'

Delie, who was rather in awe of the editor and had already seen him at breakfast, demurred, but Bessie had her way. They entered the little front office where a boy was filing copies of the *Herald*, and peeped into the editor's room. Mr McPhee sat under the clock, surrounded by a sea of galley proofs. His beard was awry, his grey hair was ruffled like a cockatoo's crest and a cold pipe was clamped between his teeth. Not even Bessie dared disturb him. But just then he looked up and saw them. He spiked a proof and picked up another sheaf. 'Well, gels!' he called. 'Ye're a sicht to be seen in your finery. If Adam sees ye, we'll ha'e no mair wurrk the day.' He blinked his eyes as though dazzled.

'Oh, Mr McPhee!' said Bessie archly, 'You are a tease. I wanted to see the type being set up, and Delie said you might let me.'

Delie, who had said nothing of the sort, blushed scarlet. 'May we?' she asked shyly.

'Oh aye, off ye go! He micht as weel be lost soon as later.'

In the composing room they found Adam alone, adjusting type in a frame on the long stone. The busy time did not begin until later in the day, when the two Alfs would join him. His fingers and apron were grey, and a lock of hair fell untidily over his brow.

At Bessie's affectation of interest he took up a line of type, separating the letters for her to see.

'Don't touch them!' he cried, looking at her snowy gloves as Bessie put out an inquiring finger. She bent over the stone, leaning prettily on her parasol, and he saw a tiny wisp of golden hair that had escaped from its coil trailing down her white neck. To his own surprise he felt an impulse to lean over and press his lips to her snowy nape, just where the fine straight hair began.

'Look out of the way,' he said brusquely, 'and I'll pull a page proof to show you.'

Delie had her gloves off and was setting up her name in type. 'Come over here, Bessie,' she said. 'You wanted to see how type was set.'

Bessie pouted, but strolled over. She found such things boring unless the demonstrator was masculine. Delie's long fingers, so

112

clumsy with housework, moved expertly among the tricky little letters, for Adam had let her help him set up an article one morning.

He came over with the wet page dangling from his thumbs and first fingers. 'See, Miss Griggs? That's what a page proof looks like.'

'Oh, but how *interesting*. But do call me Bessie. I hate my surname, it is so unromantic.'

Adam smiled rather ironically, holding the page at arm's length by its top corners. 'No doubt that will be changed before too long.'

'Oh Adam . . . Mr Jamieson . . . I mean –'

'Adam, of course,' he said indifferently. Somehow the page slipped from his fingers, and smudged the blue-striped dress with ink. 'Oh heavens! Your pretty dress! I'm sorry –'

Bessie laughed gaily. 'This old thing! It doesn't matter a bit.'

Delie tried to wipe the stain with her handkerchief, but Bessie squealed, 'Don't touch it, silly! Your fingers are *black*.'

Worried and contrite, Adam followed them to the door. He ran a hand through his hair and left a dark smudge on his forehead. 'I'm afraid you'll never come again, Bessie!'

'Ah, yes I will,' she said roguishly, shaking her head at him.

'I'll be out of the composing room soon. They're getting two linotype machines up from the Bendigo *Advertiser*, and I'm to go regularly on the reporting staff.'

'Good for you!' said Delie. But Bessie was showing signs of impatience, so she followed her down the narrow passage. As they went out the front door Bessie examined her skirt, while Delie pulled her yellow gloves over her grimy fingers.

'What a careless idiot,' said Bessie crossly. 'I've never worn this dress before, either.'

Delie was relieved. It did not sound as though Bessie were in love with Adam. They turned down towards the wharves. Delie found herself watching intently a burly stranger walking in front. Dark hair, peppered with grey, beneath a sort of seaman's cap, bare feet, a rolling giant, a tattoo-mark showing beneath a rolled-up sleeve, proclaimed that he was a sailor. Many deserting seamen found their way overland to the river, and never left it again.

She began to hurry to keep up, a mounting excitement almost choking her. Then she ran forward and grasped his right arm. Below the picture of a ship were the words, 'Loch Tay'.

Bessie, left behind and almost fainting with shock and curiosity, heard her cry, 'Tom! Oh, Tom, it's really you,' while flinging her arms round the sailor's neck.

It did not need the tattoo-mark to tell Delie that this was her rescuer and friend. Here were the same bright blue eyes, the same large beard, the same broken teeth now showing in an uncertain smile. Tom seemed inclined to bolt, but she held him by the arm and pumped it up and down.

'Tom, don't you remember me? Have I grown so much? Delphia Gordon! That you saved from the wreck when the *Loch Tay* went down. Have you given up the sea? Are you a riverman now?'

Tom, who had been looking embarrassed at being accosted by this very attractive and smart young lady, gradually let his face broaden into a more natural grin. It was possible to see the workings of his brain in his broad, good-humoured, but not very intelligent face: surprise, a lurking leer, doubt, dawning recognition and finally unalloyed pleasure. He grasped Delie's hand in a great paw and crushed it painfully.

'Miss Philadelphia! Fancy meeting you agen! And growed into a fine young leddy. Never would've knowed ye.'

'I'd have knowed – known you anywhere, Tom. Just by your walk, I think, and your bare feet.'

Tom looked down shyly. 'I never could get used to them there boots. Just popped off the boat for a jiffy to get some baccy, and never thought I'd meet no-one. Least of all you. '

'Are you on a steamer? Is she tied up at the wharf?'

'Aye! I'm the owner and skipper,' said Tom with quiet pride.

'Tom, how wonderful.'

Delie, suddenly remembering Bessie, saw her leaning on her parasol and trying not to stare. She introduced Tom ('Just call me Cap'n Tom,' he said) and explained that he was the sailor who had saved her life in the wreck. They must go and see his vessel.

Bessie looked doubtful. For once she seemed bereft of words. But Delie gripped her hand and led her along the wharf, where Tom pointed out a trim little side-wheeler, with *Jane Eliza* painted on the wheel-house in black letters. She was unloading barley from the *Riverina*, and was of such shallow draught that she went right up the Walgett on the Darling River. Besides, she 'knew the rivers backwards'.

'These new craft'll run on a snag or a sandbank before ye can say "knife",' he said seriously. He explained that the boat was

114

not all his yet. He had borrowed money to make up the purchase price, with a bill of sale over the steamer. But he'd been stuck on a falling river last year and missed a whole season's trade, and there was fifty pounds still owing. His creditors wanted to sell her up. Tom's brow folded into worried wrinkles. 'An' it might as well be fifty thousand, for all the 'ope I got of gettin' it.'

'Let's have a look at her?' said Delie.

'Thank you, I will stay here,' said Bessie frigidly.

He led the way down the wooden steps in the wharf to the next staging, and across a plank to the *Jane Eliza*'s deck. Delie noted that the deck was clean-scrubbed with a seaman's thoroughness, and the paint-work was gleaming.

'While we was stuck in that billabong we give her a good going-over,' said Tom. 'She's in good nick.'

Delie cast an unprofessional eye at the big boiler, and stepped over the shaft that turned the paddles. She was more interested in the upper structure, the neat cabins and the glassed-in wheelhouse. She was a much more compact craft that the *Melbourne*. How she would love to own a boat like this!

As Delie said good-bye to her old friend, a plan was forming in her mind. She found Bessie still on the upper wharf, digging angrily at holes in the planking with her parasol. She had been the butt of sly comments, whistles and waves from the wharf-labourers, and her cheeks were rosier than usual. She led the way back to the street in hostile silence, saying only in her mother's manner, 'Really! What extraordinary people you know.'

TWENTY-ONE

On the day Delie was to leave for home with Bessie, the pain came upon her. As she lay rolling from side to side with the cramping spasms, she wondered if she could tell Mrs McPhee. She was never allowed to mention it to Aunt Hester; it was a shameful pain, and must be ignored however much her pinched face and shadowed eyes proclaimed it.

But, oh! it was particularly bad this time. A short groan escaped her. Dear God, was it possible that she had to bear this every month, every month for half of her life? As Mrs McPhee came bustling in, she looked up with the dumb appeal of a sick animal.

'Poor lamb!' Mrs McPhee understood her mumbled explanations at once. 'I'll bring you something to make you more comfortable.'

She soon brought a hot brick wrapped in flannel, and something in the bottom of a glass. 'Now lie with the warmth against your tummy, and drink this drop of brandy and hot water.'

Delie took one sniff at it and shuddered.

'I couldn't swallow that, Mrs Mac!'

'Come, it's got sugar in it. It's quite nice, dear.'

She screwed up her face and gulped it down; it burned in her stomach and warmed her like fire. The taste was nauseating, but she soon felt better and able to get ready for the journey home.

The girls were to travel in the steamer *Success*, squired by Adam. The little side-wheeler had to battle hard against the current, for the river was sweeping down in a fresh spate.

Bessie talked vivaciously as she leant beside Adam on the railing of the top deck. Delie, still suffering from cramps, sat thinking about how she was to convince her uncle that the little *Jane Eliza* would be a good investment for her last fifty pounds.

'We won't be able to take you rowing and fishing in this current,' Adam was saying to Bessie. 'We can go riding instead.'

'I haven't a riding habit,' said Bessie nervously.

Delie, listening, felt a moment of triumph. Bessie's scared of horses, she thought.

'Neither have I,' she said, joining the others at the rail. 'But there are two side-saddles, and you can have old Leo who's as quiet as a rocking-horse. I'd rather ride astride, but Auntie won't let me.'

Bessie, not looking very pleased at having her tête-à-tête with Adam interrupted, began pointing out a flight of pelicans moving in formation overhead; and in the most natural-seeming manner managed to insert her solid form between Adam and Delie, giving Delie the benefit of her plump back.

As the steamer edged into the bank and tied up below the farm, Annie came down with a pot of jam for the captain, 'with the Missus' compliments'. Delie, preparing to walk ashore carrying her bag, had it twitched out of her hand by Adam, with 'What's

116

the hurry, little 'un?'

'I'm NOT little, and I wasn't hurrying,' she flashed at him. She had an unhappy feeling about this week-end. But Hester welcomed Bessie effusively. Bessie turned on all her not inconsiderable charm for Adam's mother, so they got on famously. A special afternoon tea followed, and a walk round the spring-flowered garden. Delie, feeling superfluous, made an excuse to go inside; she wanted to find her uncle and ask him about the fifty pounds. On the way she picked some red geraniums, and before dinner she scrubbed the crushed petals on her pale cheeks to give a semblance of Bessie's rosy complexion.

It took a long time to convince Charles that a paddle-steamer, or at least part of a paddle-steamer, was a good investment; they were always burning or getting sunk, he said. But at last he agreed, so that when she went into dinner a real flush of excitement supplemented the flower dye.

Hester looked rather sharply at her glowing cheeks, which intensified the blueness of her eyes and the white purity of her forehead under the dark turned-up hair.

'You have a high colour tonight, Philadelphia.'

Delie looked at her plate, but her uncle came to the rescue.

'Yes, I noticed that the holiday had done her good. Miss Griggs, we must send her to Echuca more often, if the air produces such complexions as yours.'

Charles was gay tonight, with a twinkle in his grey eyes above the melancholy moustache; his wife noticed it, but did not let it worry her. Miss Griggs would never notice Charles's old-fashioned gallantry while Adam was there, so handsome and assured, yet with that endearing boyishness about his mouth which made all women long to mother him.

After dinner they had a gay time with charades. Then Bessie played two pieces, very correctly, on the piano while Adam turned the music for her. Charles accompanied himself in 'Way Down Upon the Swanee River', which he sang in a good tenor voice.

Delie glanced across at Adam and Bessie, their heads bent intimately over an album – Bessie in a flounced gown of white silk, her smooth golden head shining in the lamplight. Claiming that she had 'the appetite of a bird', she yet managed to make an excellent supper, with both men waiting on her. Delie ate almost nothing.

She was glad she didn't have to share a room with Bessie. She

117

was beginning to hate her heartily.

The next morning was one of those perfect days of spring when it seems almost a crime to stay indoors. The sun had a languorous warmth, bees hummed about the blossoming fruit trees, the sky was soft and delicately blue as a flower. A faint mist pervaded the air, as though the sunlight had become palpable in a dusting of fine gold over everything. Even the sombre gum trees had put forth a halo of tiny red-gold leaves, so that the outlines of trees towards the sun were as soft and rounded as clouds.

After breakfast and morning prayers, the young people went out to get the horses. In the horse-paddock the grass was already turning to its summer tint, as though a wash of yellow ochre had been laid over the ground. Bessie walked behind, looking nervously for snakes.

Barney, who knew quite well that this was Sunday, was difficult to catch. Charles had decreed that only Delie could ride his mare Firefly, the others were too heavy, so Adam had to be content with Barney. He caught the quiet Leo and saddled him for Bessie.

'I don't like the look in his eye,' said Bessie. 'He's showing the white.'

'He's quiet as a lamb,' said Adam, patting his shaggy neck. 'Now, do you want a leg up?'

As she only stared at him wide-eyed, he said, 'You *can* ride, can't you?'

'Oh yes, I've ridden before, lots of times.' She ignored the reins and clutched a handful of Leo's mane as she put her foot in the stirrup. Adam put his hand under her other foot and heaved her into the saddle, while Leo stood stolidly.

Delie was already up and cantering round the paddock on Firefly, with her dark hair flying. She had been too impatient to stop and put it up with the yet unfamiliar hairpins.

'Oh, she's lovely after old Leo!' she cried.

Jacky opened the gate for them as they rode out into the back paddock where sheep streamed away from them in a grey-brown, moving mass, bleating mournfully. As he got down to open the second gate Adam noticed that the last hinge had gone and the gate was now only wired in place. Charles had been going to fix it a season ago. The fence-wires were sagging, and as soon as this paddock was eaten out the sheep would break through into the lucerne patch, with serious results after the almost dry feed they had been used to. There were rabbit burrows everywhere too. The

118

place was going back.

Over the red sandhills crested with dark Murray pines they rode in single file. Bessie seemed content to stay at a walk; but Leo, seeing his companions getting too far ahead, kept breaking into a jogging trot. Bessie showed signs of discomfort.

'Here, I'll make the lazy little beast move,' said Adam, turning back. He took hold of Leo's bridle and urged him on beside Barney at a comfortable canter.

'Oh, I feel so safe with you, Adam,' breathed Bessie.

'Most people find Leo a bit too safe,' he said rather shortly.

He looked ahead to where Delie, emerged from the pines, was galloping Firefly over the edge of the flats yet left unflooded. The wind of movement whipped her long hair out behind her. She closed her eyes and breathed in the magical smell of horse-sweat and leather, and felt the sun on her bare head. Well-being filled her like a flood.

Beyond the furthest boundary of the property was a thicket where the big red-gums had all been felled for timber, and a new forest of saplings had grown up. Here they stopped to have lunch, leaving the horses to graze in a clearing. Bessie arranged herself gracefully on a stump, and allowed Adam to wait on her, with the good things Hester had packed in his saddle-bag. Then they all lay back, replete. Wild bees hummed among the billy-buttons and everlasting daisies.

'Oh, smell it, isn't it gorgeous?' cried Delie, taking great breaths.

'What, the flowers? It isn't very strong.'

'Oh, everything – the bush smell . . . There, that's the essence of the Australian bush.' She crumbled a dry, fawn leaf and held it to Bessie's nose. 'A most exciting, eucalyptus-y smell . . .'

'Aromatic,' said Adam, 'is the word.'

Bessie wrinkled her nose and looked uncomprehending.

They crossed a little creek now half-filled with still floodwaters, by means of a fallen tree. Bessie was very nervous; Adam had to hold her hand and lead her across step by step. She declared once more that he made her feel safe. When she came to a second clearing among the saplings she flung herself down, saying she felt exhausted.

Delie looked at the stump of a great red-gum where the sleeper-cutters had been working recently. The stump and the scattered chips of wood were almost as red as blood. She thought that when that tree was a sapling, the white man and his axe had never been heard in this forest, and no one moved among the trees but the land's own dark inhabitants. She suddenly felt an intruder.

'It's certainly quiet here,' said Bessie, and gave a little shiver. As if to contradict her, a honeyeater set up a shrill piping; but when it ceased they felt the age-old hush upon their spirits. Adam lay on his back, staring abstractedly at the sky. His lips moved very slightly. Delie knew better than to speak.

It was Adam who moved first, leaping up to brush ants and gum leaves from his riding trousers. He looked extremely handsome with his white stock folded under under his firm chin. Looking from one to the other, Delie had to admit that he and Bessie made a handsome pair. For all Leo's jogging, not a hair of her golden head was out of place. She looked as elegant as she had done at the ball.

As they walked back towards the horses, with a slight but adroit shove she placed herself between Adam and Delie, who were examining some silken gum tips between them. Bessie stumbled over fall boughs and put a hand on his arm to save herself. When he helped her back over the fallen tree at the creek she thanked him with a significant flutter of her eyelashes.

'Let's have a ride on Firefly, will you Del?' asked Adam. 'The old man will never know, and I'm sick of that old carthorse.'

Delie hesitated for just a second, then said, 'Of course.' It would give her a chance to ride astride without Hester knowing.

Adam began to lengthen Firefly's stirrup. Delie looked sidelong at Bessie and saw her eyes widen as she flung a leg over Barney's back and kilted up her brown gingham skirts.

'Wait on, while I shorten the stirrups for you,' said Adam, but Barney, with his head towards home, refused to wait. He set off at a flying canter which soon became a gallop, back to the river and the edge of a billabong where logs lay half-buried in still waters, like sleeping crocodiles. One log lay high and dry. Delie, forgetting that Barney was no jumper, put him straight at it.

He stopped suddenly just in front of the log. Delie, with an insecure grip in the long stirrups, went flying over his head. She landed almost unhurt in soft red sand, but for a long bough ending in a jagged point which struck her a heavy blow on the temple.

Adam galloped up on Firefly and flung himself down beside her. She was unconscious, with blood streaming down her white face. He knelt in the damp sand and touched her tenderly, then wet his handkerchief and bathed the wound. The bleeding stopped almost at once; it was only a graze, but a lump like a pigeon's egg was rapidly forming. He could hear Bessie's voice asking, 'What is it? Whatever happened? Is she hurt?' But it was no more to him than the piping of a bird.

He gazed in a passion of tenderness at the closed, pale lids. Then they opened. Her deep blue eyes, wide and strained, were gazing into his.

'Adam!' She raised her arms in a bemused way and put them slowly round his neck. She saw Leo's little black head come into her range of vision, and above him Bessie's worried face. Why, there's Bessie Griggs! she thought wonderingly. What is she doing here, and riding on old Leo? Did we bring Leo into Echuca? Where are we? Anyway, Adam is here; but it's probably all a dream. She snuggled her head down against his arm, feeling calm and happy.

'Help me get her up on the saddle in front of me,' he said, feeling he would like to push the stolid Bessie. 'We must get her home quickly, I may have to go to Echuca for a doctor. Oh God, the low road is flooded and that means thirty miles round! Hurry!'

He caught Barney's trailing bridle and brought him over. 'Here, you'll have to lead Firefly, she'll follow all right.'

Bessie's sturdy shoulders had made light work of the small-boned Delie. Leaving Bessie to make her own way home, Adam cantered away. He gazed down at the white face against his heart. 'Delie darling, don't faint again, it frightens me. We're nearly home. We're nearly there, darling. You must hold on, now, while I open the gate. Are you all right?'

Still with a dreaming air, she put up a hand to feel his mouth, as though to take in the meaning of the words by touch. He pressed her fingers against his lips, steadying her in front of the saddle with one arm.

Late in the afternoon Delie woke to find a beam of sunlight slanting across her room at home. She lay still, watching the motes turning and moving in an intricate dance, each one a speck of living light. Their movement was somehow mysteriously important, requiring all her concentration.

Gradually other things began to crowd into her mind. Her head was aching and she put up a hand and felt the bandage. She now remembered the fall and the sense of unreality after it. Then she thought of Adam, closed her eyes and smiled. Would he come to see her before he went? He had to be in time to hail the coach on the other side of the river, unless a steamer happened past.

She remembered his lips against her hand, the look of stricken tenderness in his eyes, his murmured endearments.

The beam of sun was turning to a ruddy gold when the door opened quietly and Adam tiptoed in. He stood by the bed looking down into her eyes for a long minute, while she lay and smiled at him dreamily. He sat down suddenly on the edge of the bed and raised her left hand to his cheek.

'Are you feeling better, dear? You did give me a fright.'

'I'm all right.'

'You look terribly pale.'

'My head aches a bit.'

They were not listening to their own words. They were drowning in each other's eyes, reading there all that had not been said.

'Oh, dearest.' He put one finger to the damp, dark hair on her forehead, where the wet compress had made it cling heavily. He bent his head slowly and kissed her long on the lips. Something seemed to rise and turn right over in her breast, leaving her weak and shaken. Tears welled out of her closed eyes and slid down the side of her cheeks.

'Darling, darling, don't cry. I shouldn't have kissed you like that when you're not well.'

'It's not that. I thought you were in love with her.'

'Who? Bessie? You silly rabbit. It was seeing her there, so out of place in the bush, that made me realise I loved *you*. I made up a poem about you this morning, with your long hair flying in the sun: '*Girl of the golden September* . . .' But I'm talking too much; you must rest . . . Delie! You're so lovely, so little, so sweet –'

'Dear Adam.'

'I want to kiss you and kiss you. Do you love me?'

'Yes.' She nodded serenely, then put a hand quickly to her head.

'Your poor head is aching. Mother will be bringing your tea. Good-bye.'

He bent his head again and their mouths seemed to melt and fuse into one, while a searing warmth ran through their young bodies. He rose, trembling, and made blindly for the door.

Delie lay in the dusk, hugging to herself the joy that kept rising within her like a bubble. She felt again his lips upon hers, and the strange sleeping thing rose and turned over inside her.

Bessie came in to see how she was. Delie smiled at her drowsily. Dear Bessie! Dear Aunt Hester, even . . . She felt that she loved the whole world.

122

TWENTY-TWO

There followed a mild month, a succession of balmy days and velvet nights.

The passionate, throaty music of the frogs reached a frenzy of sound, the stars pulsed with light, birds mated noisily in the trees; and Lige and Creeping Annie announced that they wanted to get married.

Hester was amazed at anyone as middle-aged and apparently sensible as Annie wanting to enter such a state. Marriage to her had been a disappointing and distasteful business, from which she had received only one lasting benefit, her son Adam. Now here was Annie wanting to take a man into her bed, a nuisance she herself had been only too glad to dispense with; and Annie was past the age when she could hope for a son.

'I think you should both wait until you are quite certain it is a wise step,' she said.

'Wait!' cried Annie. ' 'E won't wait, that's just it. Won't take no for an answer, he won't. 'E's that impyetient!' And she rolled her pale sheep's-eyes up to the ceiling.

Since nothing could be done, Hester made the most of it. She helped Annie sew a wedding-dress; ransacked her cupboards for second-best linen to give the happy pair; and began making the bridal cake.

Lige constructed a second high bunk, with its own ladder, beside his own, tacked a piece of bright oil-baize that the Missus had given him over the slab table, and fixed a stove in the lean-to kitchen that he had never used.

The date was set, the banns were called. The minister was away, but the curate, a thin young man with a large Adam's apple, arrived by coach from Echuca for the ceremony. It was so hot that Hester decided they would hold it in the open air, much to Lige's relief. He was sweating profusely in his 'good' suit of blue serge, his face scarlet with determination to see the day through: jaw set, eyes protruding. 'Enough to make a feller feel he's at 'is own funeral – all them flowers, and everythin' shinin'!' he muttered, after glancing in at the decorated drawing-room where Annie had scoured and polished the brass fender, the copper jug and the silver teapot till they gleamed again; and Hester had arranged white hyacinths and rambler roses – more in honour of the clergyman's visit than of the bride. For her it was a rare social occasion.

It was a strange ceremony in the shade of the great gum trees at the bottom of the garden. Jacky and Lucy watched the odd customs of the whitefeller marriage with as much interest as any anthropologist might have shown in their lost tribal customs. They saw the ungainly bride draped in her white net, symbolical of an utter ignorance of her own body, standing beside the scared-looking old man, while strange words like 'procreation' were chanted over them by the man in the funny collar.

While Mr Polson prayed, Delie stared at the grassless, ant-teeming, sun-dappled ground. She did not close her eyes. A flock of sulphur-crested cockatoos went screeching past down the river. The sound of a dog fight floated across from the blacks' camp on the far bank. She felt the miles of grey bush brooding round the little space where they stood, and heard the river flowing, flowing. Old Johnnie's 'Byamee' seemed nearer than the God Mr Polson was invoking with an English accent.

After the wedding breakfast was over, which was a great success though the jellies had melted a little in the heat, Lige and Annie escaped to their hut while Charles took a glass of port with the minister. Mr Polson was staying the night, so they had some music in the flower-stuffed drawing-room after dinner. Delie, in white-spotted muslin with a blue sash, played for Mr Polson while he turned the pages for her, and sang in a rather wobbly baritone, 'The Arab's Farewell to His Steed'.

Delie, looking down at her rather large, long-fingered hands with a secret smile, thought of Adam's strictures on 'sentimental balladry', which he called, rather shockingly, sentimental bastardry. She was unaware that the curate was leaning on the piano and studying the fine bones of her face, with its clear pallor and finely marked brows, until he heaved a deep sigh.

'You're so *ethereal*, Miss Gordon!' he murmured.

She darted him one glance from her deep blue eyes, then looked demurely down to hide the flash of laughter in them. She had eaten nearly half a chicken, two pasties and a slice of wedding cake that afternoon, and had made a good dinner as well.

Mr Polson's interest was not lost upon Hester, who began

124

making heroic resolves to travel in to Echuca for Sunday service as soon as the low road was open. She saw that Delie, young as she was, had made a conquest. What she did not see, and could not guess, was that it was love which had made her blossom into this new and attractive maturity.

Adam, who had not been able to come home for the event, had been promoted to the cable page. The *Riverine Herald* carried a line stated that all its overseas news came by 'electric cable', and the paper prided itself on giving a complete news coverage of world events. Adam hoped that some momentous news might pass through his hands, such as the death of Queen Victoria; rumours of this event filtered through now and then and were immediately denied, thus making two news items. Instead there came the tragic news of the sinking of the *Clyde* in the North Sea. She had struck an uncharted rock and gone down in a few minutes, with the loss of all on board.

Knowing Delie's story, Adam had an insight into the human tragedies behind the news, and his imagination was stirred. He gave it a larger headline than usual.

The next morning a storm burst over his head. As he arrived at the office he heard Mr McPhee's great voice roaring for him from the editor's room. He thumped the morning's paper with his fist as Adam came in.

'Do ye wish tae mak' us the laughing-stock o' the whole town, do ye? An "oncharted rock", forbye! How do ye spell yon worrd?'

'U-N-C-H-A-R-T-E-D, Sir,' said Adam.

'Then for what, in the de'il's name, do ye spell it with anither R, E?' roared Mr McPhee, clasping his grey beard wildly. 'All the steamer captains will be in, tae ask us do we wish t' charter the Bitch an' Pups or the Fairy Rocks. Luke at yon headin!'

He waved the paper close under Adam's nose; who managed to see, in large bold type:

SHIP HITS UNCHARTERED ROCK

Sinks in Seven
Minutes

'Oncharterr-ed for on-charrted! Canna ye hear the deeference?'

'I can when a Scotsman says it, Sir. But I know the difference, of course. The mistake must be in the composing-room.'

'The mistake is here! Here's your copy, in ye're ain handwritin'. I checked it before I accused ye.'

Adam took the sheets of copy-paper. There was no explaining how he had made such a slip, but he had.

'Ye hadna noticed it, eh? Hae' ye read the paper the morn's morn?'

Adam coloured. 'Well, no, Sir. I was running late, and –'

'Ah! Ye hadna read it. The furst job o' a newspapermon is tae read his own paper, aye, even the advairtisements. Mony a gude story has come frae the advairtisements. Ye should read it before ever ye come tae the office.'

He stuck his cold pipe in his beard to indicate that the interview was finished. Drawing a pile of blank papers towards him, he began a stinging article on intemperance and the demon drink. Nearly a column a day was given up to his pet subjects, temperance and punctuality.

Adam settled gradually into his new reporting job, and became known in the town as 'young Jamieson of the *Herald*'. It was not until later that his special articles, verses and nature notes made him better known, so that a bright future was predicted for him as a writer.

Charles was reading his copy of the *Bulletin Weekly* – he liked its Man on the Land articles, its stories, and the verses it printed each week – when he gave an exclamation and stared as if he could not believe his eyes. He appealed to Delie: 'Look at this! Do you think it could be our boy?'

Delie looked over his shoulder. There was a poem signed 'A. Jamieson', beginning:

> Girl of the golden September,
>   Fair as the wattle's gold!
> Will you and I remember
>   When both of us are old . . .

'Yes, that's Adam's poem! I remember that first line, he quoted it to me.' Then her pleasure evaporated. 'Fair as the wattle's gold!' That didn't sound like her, it sounded more as if it were written for Bessie.

'You know,' said her uncle, putting the pink-covered journal down on his knee while he filled his pipe, 'I always thought Adam would make a writer. Must be good for them to print it, eh?'

'I think it's good, yes.' But she frowned slightly.

Charles was scrabbling in the corner of his nearly empty tobacco-pouch. He tamped the rich, dark shreds of tobacco down in the bowl with his middle finger, lit a match and sucked the flame down into the bowl. He waved the match quickly to put it out, brushed a few crumbs of tobacco from his trousers and leaned back, crossing his knees. He drew strongly on the pipe and it made a little sharp bubbling sound.

'It's from me that he gets it, of course,' he said complacently. 'I've always written a very good letter. Even tried my hand at poetry when I was younger.' He watched the wreathing smoke drift upward in the lamplight. 'You know, there's something of the artist in me. I sometimes think I might have made a great singer if only I'd had the training.'

Delie blinked in surprise. Charles had a pleasant voice, but she doubted very much it was in world class. She only said, 'Why didn't you, then?'

'Ah, money was very short by the time I grew up. My brothers had all the advantages. I had to leave school and start work straight away. And my father was a hard man; hadn't a note of music in him. Sometimes I wonder if I haven't been too easy with Adam, when I think how my father treated me. I don't expect him to contribute anything to the home out of his earnings.'

'But Adam doesn't live at home, Uncle! And what he really wanted to do was go to the university.'

'Just as well he didn't. Journalism and real life are a better school for a writer than academic seclusion.'

Delie sighed. Her uncle would always justify himself, always be wise after the event ('I knew there was gold in that creek'), and sit dreaming about an irrecoverable past or an impossible future, while the fences fell down and the burr spread in the paddocks.

Hester was extremely proud of the poem – she also thought it referred to Bessie – and cut it out to paste in her scrapbook. But Adam was offhand about it.

'It's only a ballad – the sort of thing they like.'

Delie was not very pleased at his speaking so lightly of what he had written for her – 'Though I don't believe it was for me at all; it's all about a fair-haired girl like Bessie Griggs!'

He explained loftily that that was called poetic licence, and she mustn't be so literal. It led to their first lovers' quarrel.

TWENTY-THREE

'Coo-oo-ee!'

Adam's long-drawn call across the river, or the whistle of the passenger steamer if he comes from Echuca by boat, make the loveliest music Delie has ever heard. While the echoes are still ringing along the reach, she races down the front steps with her hair flying – he likes it down, after all her fretting to be grown up for him! – and flits through the garden, past the pine tree where she has often climbed to dream of him, through the shrubs and across the sandy slope to the river's brim.

Lige is there too, so their hands just touch for an instant; but an electric spark runs from finger-tip to finger-tip and sends a shock of love to their hearts, and their eyes speak worlds.

Then back to the house where Hester waits on the veranda watching anxiously for any cloud on her favourite's brow, any sign of thinness or under-feeding. But seeing his face clear and happy, his figure sturdy as ever, she puts up a hand to his bright hair and kisses him on the cheek.

'Have you had a good week, son?'

'Same as usual, Mother.'

Delie behaves like a tomboy, leaping up the two wooden steps in one jump, twirling on her toes on the veranda and chanting:

> The *Adelaide*
> Is very staid.
> The *Lancashire Lass*
> Will surely pass,
> The *Elizabeth* –

'Oh, I can't think of a rhyme for Elizabeth.

> Eliza, Liza, 'Lizabeth,
> Now I'm really out-of-breath.

'Philadelphia, child, don't be such a madcap.' But Hester smiled quite indulgently. In spite of that odd look of maturity

128

sometimes, Philadelphia was still just a child. To Adam, she was just his little cousin, no doubt, whose hair he liked to pull, but who could never mean anything serious.

The cousins usually had from about midday on Saturday until Sunday afternoon before Adam had to go back – a whole twenty-four hours and more under the same roof.

When the yellow billy-buttons were out in the sandy paddocks, the stiff white everlastings and acres of yellow buttercups and purple pea, they walked hand in hand through a sea of flowers. Stopping in a golden paddock, Delie picked a bunch of gleaming, lacquered buttercups.

'Do you like butter?' asked Adam, and held the bunch against her white throat. 'Yes, she likes butter!' as the sun reflected a glowing patch of yellow under her chin. He bent and kissed the spot. In a moment they were clasped in a long embrace, the flowers fallen and forgotten. She laid her head on his shoulder and seemed almost to sleep. All was a strange harmony: the beating of their hearts, the flow of their blood, the streaming sunshine, the warmth of their young limbs, the golden sea of flowers in which they stood.

When they walked on again, hand in hand, Adam said, 'I've got a pleasant surprise for you.'

'Oh, what is it?'

'You'll see; don't be in such a hurry.'

'Oh, please give it to me now.'

'Don't be so impatient. It isn't anything to eat, it's something to tell. About Minna.'

'Poor Minna! What about her?'

'I ran into her in the street and she touched me for the price of a meal. She's got another baby coming and it's rather spoiled her means of livelihood. So-o, we had this missionary bloke in from up the river, wanted some publicity for his mission, and as I was talking to him I mentioned Minna. She's gone back with him, kids and all.'

'But was she happy to go?'

'Yes, the mission is in her own country where she lived as a little girl, up near the Moira Lakes. She's of the Moira tribe, and a few of them are still left. She was glad to go.'

'Adam, you are good!'

She stopped to hug him. The words of the article he meant to write on the unfortunate and dispossessed race were already forming in his mind: 'Outcasts in the land they once owned . . .'

By common consent, whenever they had time they walked towards the scene of their Sunday morning picnic with Bessie. The little thicket of gum saplings, cut off by the branching creek, was the theatre where they played their ancient parts. Here Adam had first known that he loved her; here he told her so again and again.

The ground in the Australian bush is nowhere very inviting for lovers, but at least it is not usually damp. They lay on the hard, dry ground among prickly undergrowth, while ants crawled over their arms and legs, and pale fawn leaves became entangled in their hair; for the gums shed them at every season.

He held her close, close, and she surrendered to a great flooding peace and lay utterly quiet while he kissed her closed eyelids, which she saw as a red darkness shot with gold. For her, un-awakened and unthinking, it was only peace. For him it was a sweet and terrible unrest.

He kissed her softly, quietly, chastely, keeping in check the hot tide that threatened to rise and engulf them both if he once let go. Against her soft dark hair he murmured:

> *Sed sic' sic' sine fine feriati*
> *et tecum iaceamus osculantes . . .*
> *hoc non deficit, incipitque semper.*

'What's that – Latin?' she murmured vaguely.

'Can't you construe?' he teased.

'No – All the Latin I construe is "*amo* – I love".'

'Then I'll tell you. It's from Petronius: "But thus, thus without end let us lie/Exchanging kisses with each other/Here is no end but always a beginning." Now if they'd only let us learn things like that at school the fellows would have got on a lot faster. But of course the first two lines – I didn't tell you them – would be considered unfit for boyish ears. Miss Barrett was amazingly broad-minded.'

She turned her head to look at him, appraising the impersonal tone. 'You were in love with her, you know.'

He picked up her hand and kissed it. 'Yes. Calf-love. I got that out of my system early. Miss Barrett . . . Dorothy . . .' he said thoughtfully. He turned on his back, squinting at the blue sky and chewing a bitter leaf. 'She knew all the time, you know. That night when we wouldn't eat the black swan, remember? She came in and sat on my bed and I went scarlet and couldn't say a word.'

'How funny! So did I.'

'Yes, she enjoyed feeling her power. Vain, like all you women.'
He threw the leaf into her hair. Should he tell her about Dorothy
Barrett and that last night? And about the other adventure that
had befallen him when he was going home from work in Echuca
in the early hours of the morning? No; she was too young. He
could not destroy her innocence. He pushed the soft hair back
behind her ear, tracing its outline with one finger. 'This is different,
darling. This is for always.'

'I wish we could stay here for always.'

'This is forever. Time is only relative. The eternal moment . . .'
As he spoke the earth turned imperceptibly, the trees moved and
the sun left the clearing.

'But you still have to go back to Echuca tomorrow!'

'Eve, the ever practical. Even in paradise!'

'Oh, Adam! I wish I could stay with you all the time. All day,
all night.'

'You know we can't get married for ages, or at least until I earn
a bit more. And you know what the family will say, about
cousins marrying – '

'Marriage . . . I wasn't thinking about marriage. I just want to
be with you. And I *would* like to have your child, he'd be so
beautiful.'

'Delie, don't talk like that! Do you know what you're doing to
me?'

'But I mean it, Adam. If there was a baby I wouldn't care. I
can't see that it's wrong. I love you.'

'Delie, for God's sake! You don't know what you're talking
about. You're only a child yourself.'

He stared down tenderly at the small-boned face and the deep
blue eyes. With one finger he traced the dark line of her level
brows. She grasped the hand and kissed it passionately, and with
closed eyes strained against him. For a moment he tightened his
embrace. Then he got up abruptly, flicked an ant off his trouser
leg and brushed leaves out of his hair.

'Time we were getting back, darling. The sun is going.' His
voice was husky and shook a little.

She opened her eyes in a dazed fashion, like a sleepwalker
suddenly wakened, and saw that the sun was now behind the
saplings, outlining leaves in pale fire. She stood up. He picked the
leaves out of her hair, tenderly, one by one.

'Oh, what a heavenly afternoon it's been! So lovely, so golden. And the little leaves against the sun; look, they're as soft as auburn hair, and the saplings as smooth and white as – as –'

'As you are, darling.'

'Come, let's get back to the river before the sun gets too low. This is the best time of day for the water.'

With a sudden change of mood she was dancing off between the saplings, eager to be gone out of the dim clearing where mosquitoes were beginning to come out of the undergrowth, fierce for blood.

They raced back over the fallen log across the deep-carved creek, oblivious of any danger in its well-known surface, though it was beginning to get slippery with dew. They came out on the river flats where the water lay in mirror-like sheets, burnished with the late gold light. The river, for all its steady flow, lay flawless as the pure, pale sky. Gum trees on the opposite bank leaned above their reflections. A blue wisp of camp-fire smoke rose straight into the air.

Delie felt none of the old restless urge to capture the scene in colour and line. Her paints had been neglected for some time; her whole being was absorbed by Adam.

They passed a big red-gum which still bore the scar of bark canoe removed long ago by a stone axe. And down the river, slipping with the current and guided by an occasional dip of the pole, came a canoe which might have been cut yesterday. In the stern there burnt a small fire of twigs on a bed of clay, and the smell of baking cod was wafted to the two young people on the bank. The lubra and her little boy did not wave; they simply ignored the white people as if they had been trees.

Love and beauty were both forgotten as Delie and Adam realised that they were hungry. They crossed the paddocks in the level light. Delie stopped to strew her buttercups on the three little graves. The bell was ringing for tea as they hurried indoors with excellent appetites.

'Delie, my child, we won't have to send you to Echuca to gain a complexion after all,' said Charles, carving the cold roast mutton. 'I declare your cheeks look good enough to eat – eh, Hester?'

Hester only said sharply, 'Philadelphia, did you do your hair for tea? It looks a positive sight.'

Adam was always very big-cousinly with Delie when his mother

132

was there, and teased her as he used to do when he'd first come home from school. Whenever they could they slipped away; and as summer advanced and the water went down they found a refuge below the steep bank of the river.

There they walked in the early twilight after dinner, dropping twigs in the water to see the ripples widen outwards on its glassy surface. Delie stood within the curve of his arm and looked along the reach towards the west, where a great glowing planet hung low down. She thought of the night when she had watched his little boat gliding with the current, and of her strange dream of the dark barge. A shiver of foreboding shook her. She turned and pressed her face against him.

'Darling, I wish you didn't have to travel on the river.'

'There won't be any more steamers this season, anyway. But perhaps I shouldn't come home so often! I'd better stay in town next week-end, for instance. Bessie wants me to go on a picnic.'

'You dare!' She shook him fiercely.

He laughed and stroked her hair. 'I'll be home, little 'un.'

'The week-end after, we are coming to town on Sunday. Aunt Hester wants to go to church.'

'Thirty miles to go to church and back! There's religious fervour for you.'

'I don't think it's all religious fervour. You see – I think Aunt Hester imagines . . . That is, it's silly, but the fact is . . .'

'What on earth are you trying to say?'

'That – that Aunt Hester thinks Mr Polson is rather keen on me.'

'Mr Polson? Who, the curate? Good God!'

'Yes, the pale young curate. He *is* rather pale and interesting. He told me I was "ethereal".'

He grasped her hard by the shoulders. 'Do you find him interesting?'

'Of course not, silly. Oh, you're hurting my shoulder! You should just have seen his face when he thought he had to cross the river in a bark canoe to get the coach! He was scared stiff.' She chuckled. 'He has strange eyes, rather fanatical-looking. And a large Adam's apple. Where is your Adam's apple? You should have an e-normous one,' she said in a deep voice, caressing his throat. He grasped her fingers and bent his head to kiss them and she put her lips to his hair.

'He'd better not cast his fanatical eyes at you.'

'Why, would you knock him down and stand on him, like the

133

Indian on the Viceroy Tea packet does to the Chinaman? I'd love to be fought over! But you mustn't really truly hurt him. He doesn't look very strong.' Adam was staring abstractedly over her head. 'Do you love me, Adam?'

'Mm?'

'Do you really love me. You haven't said so once tonight.'

'Yes, I am yours truly, sincerely, faithfully, willingly, lovingly, for ever and ever and ever.'

As their mouths met they became one being, sharing one breath, one heartbeat; and it was with a shock at the returning consciousness of their separate selves that they heard, as if from another world, Hester's voice calling from the front veranda. Delie gave a deep sigh.

'I'll run and touch home one-two-three on the veranda post, and you come after as if we were playing hide and seek,' she said.

TWENTY-FOUR

There passed a happy year for Delie, seeing Adam every week-end, for though he did not always come home she went several times to Echuca to stay with Mrs McPhee, and Hester took her to church about once a month while the summer track was open.

She had not been to church for a long time. She tried earnestly to regain something of the peaceful, religious feeling she had known as a little girl kneeling on a hassock covered with red carpeting at her mother's side, at the old county church. Instead she found her attention straying to a smart toque in front, or to Bessie's new hat across the aisle, and to the young men who occupied the back pews and to whom, she well knew, she was an object of interest. The service went over her head as empty words. When the minister was away and Mr Polson took the service, she was aware of him waiting palely in the vestry to shake hands, and of how he held her hand a little longer than necessary.

'Such devotion, Mrs Jamieson, to travel so far in your state of health. You will have your reward in heaven!' he told her aunt.

Hester smiled enigmatically. Already there were several young men showing a marked interest in her attractive niece. There would be no trouble in marrying her off. She took Adam's regular visits home as a tribute to herself and her cooking.

Delie had given up hope that her aunt would ever like her. She knew how bitterly Hester would resent any sign of intimacy between herself and Adam. At home, when Adam was there, she exaggerated her natural tomboyishness and teased him like a younger sister. But in Echuca there was no need to act, and Adam and Delie had been accepted as partners for tennis or dancing, walking home from parties, or excursions on the river by steamer.

When the river began to rise after the months of low water, Delie waited and watched for Captain Tom. He had been so moved by her generosity in putting her last fifty pounds into the boat that he had re-named her the *Philadelphia*.

When she asked other skippers for news of the *Philadelphia*, they would look blank till she mentioned the old name.

'Oh, you mean the *Jane Eliza*? She's on her way down from the Darling, probably unload at Swan Hill.'

For the glory of Echuca as a river port was fading. The railway to Swan Hill from Melbourne had cut the waterway at a nearer point to the wool stations on the Darling.

The *Philadelphia* did unload at Swan Hill that year, but a letter came from Tom, written by a friend, and enclosing ten pounds. The letter said that Delie might expect a similar share in the profits of each voyage. Charles was impressed by the man's integrity, for there was no way of knowing if the boat had made a profit or a loss, though he knew their income varied with the seasons.

'You may have made a good investment after all,' he said. 'I thought myself it was a far better way to invest your money than in land.'

Delie said nothing, remembering how gloomy he had been about steamers sinking, and catching fire, and striking snags.

Adam, who passed his nineteenth birthday in October, was given more and more of the sort of work he liked – descriptive articles, nature notes, topical verse and occasionally fictitious 'letters to the editor'. But though his position had improved, his salary had not. The after-effects of the great financial panic were still being felt. The land-boom had burst and Australia was suffering an economic depression. The paper had to write off some bad debts from advertisers, and could not afford high wages.

Because the soft folds hid the thinness of her young neck, Delie usually wore a fichu of lace or chiffon about the shoulders of her gowns; they were also fashionable. One gusty winter night when she had been sitting up by the fire reading, she took a candle with her to visit the 'little house' out the back. Everyone else was in bed.

The sky was overcast, the night black and formless. The oppression of the low clouds, the lack of a single distant point of light on which to fix her eyes, made her uneasy. As she stepped out of the building on the way back, a gust blew the candle flame against the filmy fichu.

In a moment she was alight. With her mouth still opened for a useless scream, she flung herself down and rolled on the ground, still damp from a shower that had fallen earlier. She smelt her own singed hair and felt the smarting of her scorched neck; but the flames were out.

The candle had gone out where it fell, the candlestick had rolled away. Trembling with shock, she fumbled her way to the back door and roused her uncle. When he had lit his candle and come out in his dressing-gown from the 'office', he stared at her in alarm.

'You look like a ghost, child! What's happened?'

When she had told him he led her into the outdoor kitchen, raked the coals together in the stove and made her a hot, sweet drink, while she gingerly dabbed butter on her reddened skin.

'Fools of clothes young girls wear. If you knew the number of young women burnt to death every year – You take the hurricane lamp if you want to go outside, do you hear?'

'Yes, Uncle.'

'You showed some sense, anyway. The mistake most of them make is to scream and run. If you hadn't kept your head . . . Well, I leave it to your imagination.'

Her imagination had already been at work. She turned so faint and sick that she swayed, putting a hand blindly in front of her. Charles jumped forward and steadied her with his arm. As he was lowering her into a kitchen chair Hester came in, her black hair in a thin plait, her wrapper caught hastily about her.

'What's going on here? I heard a noise, and got up –'

'Delie set herself on fire; put herself out too, the sensible girl. But she's a bit shaken, naturally. She lost her candle, and called for me to help. *She'd* never wake.' He indicated the little room that opened off the kitchen, whence Bella's snores could be heard. She had been restored to the house since Annie left for Lige's hut.

'H'm. Let's see the burn. You go and look for the candlestick, Charles,' she said sharply, as she drew aside the blackened wisps of chiffon from the white shoulders, and examined the reddened patches of skin. 'I would have put carb. soda myself, but the butter will have to stay now. Come, I'll help you back to bed.'

She took the retrieved candlestick rather brusquely from Charles, and led Delie to her room.

TWENTY-FIVE

Slowly the waters went down, the shrimps and yabbies which had played among the submerged roots retired to lower caves in the mud. The river sucked and gurgled among the clutching fingers of wood. Long wedges of pelicans flew in formation up-river, nesting magpies swooped in the paddocks, and the willy-wagtail kept up his silvery, monotonous *sweet-pretty-creature* all through the moonlit nights.

As the flats dried out and the small creeks emptied back into the main stream, leaving only a chain of waterholes; as jasmine and pittosporum scented the air in the warm evenings of late spring, Adam became irritable and moody. He was more abstracted when in one of his 'fits', as Hester called them, than ever.

'For goodness' sake stop fussing over me like a broody hen, or I won't come at all,' he growled at her when she suggested he ought to see a doctor. Hester thought that perhaps all was not going well in the Bessie affair.

Alone with Delie, Adam would often drop his arms abruptly from an embrace, or answer impatiently some childish question. She knew that something was very wrong.

One night when he had been particularly morose and difficult, she felt too worried to sleep. It wanted a few nights to full moon and Annie, who had taken to the concertina again, could be heard practising outside Lige's hut.

Delie got out of bed and put her head out the open window. The leaves of the flowering gum were glinting like wet metal in the moonlight. A faint, cool breeze from the river carried the acrid

137

tang of cow-dung mosquito fires past her window. She reached for her dressing-gown. There would be no mosquitoes on the veranda, and she could see the moon-track on the water from there.

She opened the front door quietly and crept out on the jarrah boards, feeling them rough under her bare feet. In the shadow of the overhanging jasmine something moved. She caught her breath, swallowing down a cry.

'Is that you, Del?' came Adam's whisper.

'Yes. Oh! I couldn't sleep.'

'Neither could I. It's such a waste to sleep on a night like this. And when you're only a couple of walls away! I willed you to come out.'

'How?'

'I spoke to you with my mind.'

'Oh! Do you think that's possible?'

'I'm sure of it. Why, in fifty years' time, people will be able to speak to each other across the sea, just as the cable speaks now, but they'll hear without any wires. That is, people who are in tune. It's only a matter of cultivating a latent power. The natives can communicate without words. We've become so clever that we've forgotten to use the power, and almost lost it.'

The effect of holding forth in a whisper was too much for him, and the last words were spoken in his normal deep voice.

'Hush!' cried Delie in a flutter of alarm. She looked over her shoulder at the windows beyond the front door.

'Don't worry, darling, she won't hear us. How your little heart is beating.' He had put his arms round her from behind as she stood half-turned away from him, and his hand locked over her small breast and fluttering heart. She melted at his touch.

'Darling, darling, darling!' He began to tremble as he parted the soft hair and kissed the back of her neck. Then he let her go abruptly and turned to lean on the veranda rail, staring at the moon-sparkling curve of the river.

'What's wrong?' She slipped one hand into his. It was the first time she had asked.

'Nothing's wrong. Only . . . you tempt me.'

'Tempt you?'

'To . . . sin.'

Sin! The word seemed to shudder along her nerves, with all its weight of biblical-association and word-association: Adam, Eve, sin, Serpent, sinister . . . She could find nothing to say. She was

138

cold with a delicious fear. At last she whispered timidly,

'Would you rather I went in now?'

'Yes, you'd better go. No! Wait. Stand there in the moonlight, where I can see you face.'

He bent over her tenderly, gazing at the pale cheeks etherealised by the moon's light, the shadowed eyes looking darker and larger than by day.

'Your eyes are so soft; but those straight brows contradict them, and that firm little chin, and that sweet rebellious mouth. You are like – like a white moth, come out to visit the jasmine flowers – Philadelphia, Delie, Della, Del! What a fool of a name! It doesn't suit you, any way you say it. "Delphine" would be better – yes, that has an elfin sound about it. I shall call you Delphine.'

Without touching her with his hands, he bent over and kissed her lips. Then, with a light slap, he sent her off to bed like a child.

She went in a daze, her mind full of glinting lights and scented darkness, of moonlight and shadow.

After that night they always slipped out for a few minutes on Adam's week-ends home. To make sure of not being heard, Delie would climb over her windowsill when she had heard the last sounds of Charles settling down in his 'office' and Hester in the front bedroom.

One night they stood peacefully by the bank of the river, Adam with his cheek resting on her dark hair, watching a strangely swollen moon rise behind the trees. It looked for once what it was – a lump of barren rock, old, scarred and dead. Delie shivered slightly and looked away – and stiffened in his arms.

'Adam! What's that?' She had seen a dark shape move in the shade of the big red-gum that grew on the bank and was hollow inside from an old bushfire.

Adam dropped his arms and, swearing softly, dived into the shadow. In a moment Delie saw Creeping Annie's gaunt form outlined against the moonlit river, with her hands held firmly behind her back. Adam's voice, vibrant with anger, said quietly: 'Don't you come spying on me, you long-nosed, creeping misery – or, by God! I'll break your skinny neck. D'you hear?'

'Only comin' down to look at the set-line, I wor,' came Annie's whining voice. 'Don't you want no nice cod for yer breakfuss, Mister Adam? Just lookin at the set-line, I wor.'

'You can look at the line in the morning. Now get off to bed.'

139

Annie crept away towards the cottage and Adam came back.

'Do you think she saw me, Adam? Will she tell your mother?'

'Not her! She's too scared for her miserable skin. Sneaking old sticky-beak! I should have pulled her long nose for her.'

'Poor Annie! You sounded dreadfully violent.'

'Poor Annie, my foot. She's always given me the creeps.'

'Me too.'

For the next two weeks Adam was busy and could not come home. Hester sent a letter by the coach telling him not to come the next week, as they would be coming to Echuca. But the Sunday morning dawned wet and cold, and Hester decided she would not go to church after all; while Charles bemoaned the damage this unseasonable rain would do to his hay.

Adam, who had dressed himself up and dragged himself to church, sat fuming through an insipid sermon by Mr Polson. He watched the door, expecting every moment to meet those lovely, lively, dancing blue eyes that would flood the grey building with light for him. Bessie Griggs and her mamma were there, but as he saw them bearing down on him after the service like a battleship and an attendant destroyer, he bowed frostily and tacked carefully round them.

'Well! That young man may be handsome, but he has no manners,' said Mrs Griggs in offended majesty.

Adam went home to the landlady's roast dinner, and brooded over his wasted week-end. The longer he was away from Delie the more desirable she seemed. Her reckless, impetuous words of a year ago came back and set him on fire. The orange tree in the garden, scented like the pittosporum at home, seemed to bring her before him: pale, fragile, dark-haired, with the deep blue eyes he loved.

The result was that before leaving the following week-end for home, he made a speech to Mr McPhee that he had been rehearsing for some time: He told the editor that he was in love, and wanted to get married; he realised he might have to wait till he was twenty-one, but he would like to know . . .

'It's the uncertainty you see, and not knowing if it will be ten years before we can afford to marry –' (Good Lord, I'd be twenty-nine, he thought, aghast at such a colossal age) 'so if you could promise me, sir, that in two years you could guarantee me a salary – er – commensurate with my capabilities . . .'

Here he bogged down in the swamp of polysyllables, and waited for Mr McPhee to rescue him with the promise of a raise at once.

'Harrk at the laddie!' said Mr McPhee in mock amazement, taking the pipe from his mouth and looking up at the ceiling. 'Do ye ken,' he said, suddenly bringing his sharp blue gaze down to meet Adam's, 'whut age I was when I got marrit? Thurrty-fower years! Aye, tak' your time, and choose weel, as I did.'

'I couldn't make a better choice, sir, if I lived to be a hundred.'

'Aye, so ye think the noo. But these are harrd times; I canna promise muckle increase as yet. But ye'll no' be stayin' on a wee country paper; ye maun wurrk hard, and save your bawbees, and ye'll be stairtin ye're ain paper before ye ken it.' He pointed the stem of his pipe at Adam for emphasis. 'Ye're a writer, a braw writer; dinna go an' get marrit an' saddled with two-three bairns. Ye're but a lad yet. I can make nae promises; bide with me a twelvemonth, and we'll see.'

He put the pipe between his lips and puffed placidly to show that he had no more to say.

Adam knew that Scottish determination too well to argue. In a black mood he went out and walked along the wharf. For the first time he saw all the waning activity of the once great river port as a pollution of the age-old stream. Papers and peelings floated in the water in corners sheltered from the current. The rattle of winches and trains drowned the lonely bird-notes of the bush. Smoke stained the clear blue sky.

Take his time! Bide a twelvemonth! Did the old buzzard think he could wait fifteen years, or solace himself with someone like Minna –'

He caught the coach with the mood still on him. When he arrived his mother fluttered round with cups of tea and hot scones in an effort to dispel the lowering look from his brow. But he knew better than to confide in her the cause of his discontent.

Delie knew that something was wrong when she suggested, after he finished his tea and told his mother all the news of the last three weeks, that they should take the dinghy out on the river.

'What's the use?' he said gloomily.

Delie went pink with surprise and stared at him silently.

'He's tired, Philadelphia, and doesn't want to go fishing after that long journey up the river – all those bends! They'd make me quite giddy, I'm sure –'

141

'I came by road, Mother.'

'Well anyway, why don't you walk down to see the horses, and get an appetite for tea? I've made your favourite pudding; treacle dumplings!' she said on a note of triumph.

Adam's full, boyish lips twisted cynically. 'Isn't it funny,' he remarked to the empty grate, 'how women are so loath to let a man grow up. You two always succeed, as soon as I get here, in making a schoolboy of me, with a world bounded by food and active sports. Fill his belly and keep him active, and he'll be happy.'

Delie set her mouth and looked at her hands. This mood would explain itself in time. Meanwhile, did he have to lump her with Hester as a blundering female? She hated to be classed as part of 'women' in general.

Hester looked hurt and at a loss. She couldn't understand what had got into the boy lately – for of course he was a boy still, even if he was earning a man's wage. She sighed and went out to the kitchen.

Delie looked at him expectantly, waiting for him to come and kiss her. A whole three weeks, and he had hardly looked in her direction! He made no move, but sat slumped in his chair, gnawing at the side of his thumb.

Charles came in, radiating good humour. He had a record clip this year, and was expecting a good wool cheque. Adam knew that he had hurt his mother's feelings, and was a little ashamed of himself. He replied shortly to his father's unusually warm greeting.

'I wanted to talk to you, son,' said Charles.

Delie made a move to leave the room, but he added, 'Nothing I can't say before you. Sit down and drink your tea . . . Adam, my boy, I suppose you don't get much chance to save, on your salary?'

'You're right. I save practically nothing.'

'No, I suppose not.' His father glanced at the tight-fitting new suit and modish high collar and silk tie. 'Well, I've had a very good year, and I'm in a position to help you.' He paused impressively.

Adam sat slowly forward, the skin stretched over his knuckles that grasped the arms of his chair. 'Yes?' he said hoarsely.

'Yes; I thought I might give you some pocket money. Now what do you say to five shillings a week – that is to say, a pound a month? That should keep you in silk ties and pocket handkerchiefs, eh?'

Adam let out his breath slowly, then flung himself back in the chair.

'In handkerchiefs, anyway,' he said dryly. And added, 'Thank you, Father.'

TWENTY-SIX

'Would you like a game of cribbage with me, or shall we take a hand at euchre?'

Hester was sitting at the walnut table shuffling the well-used pack of cards that had a butterfly design on the back in blue and red.

Adam was lying back in the same chair as before dinner, in the same attitude, with his legs stretched in front, his hands in his pockets, his chin sunk on his chest, staring moodily in front of him.

'Adam! Your mother's speaking to you,' said Charles sharply.

'What about a hand of cards?' said Hester again.

'Cards? Whatever for? Cards are just like a drug with you, Mother, the same as cups of tea. You can't leave them alone.'

'What nonsense!' Hester hitched herself round with an irritable movement and began setting out a hand of patience, putting each card down with a sharp little click.

'Shall I play something for you?' asked Delie uncertainly. Adam merely shrugged, and thrust out his bottom lip.

'That's right, Delie!' said Charles heartily, rubbing his hands together. 'I believe I'm in good voice tonight.' He went over to the piano and set up the *Globe Song Book*. Delie began to play his favourites. Adam made no move to come near the piano, but Delie heard him mutter, 'Sentimental bastardry!'

Charles sang with rich feeling in his good tenor:

> O Genevieve, I'd give the world
> To live again the love-ly past!
> The rose of youth is dew-impearl'd . . .

'Funny how old people are sentimental over the "lovely past",' came from the depths of Adam's chair as he finished. 'Yet if they could be young again they'd be damned sorry. They forget what it's like to be young.'

'Adam!' cried Hester, scandalised at the easy swear-word.

Charles, who didn't like the reference to 'old people' (why, his moustache was as dark as ever, just a few grey hairs!) replied with some heat that he had always been active and happy when *he* was young, not forever brooding over a book and being surly with his family.

Delie closed the piano gently and said she believed she would go to bed early. Hester asked her to make some cocoa for them all, and Adam had better take some opening medicine; 'and it's to be hoped you won't get out of the wrong side of your bed tomorrow, my boy,' she added tartly.

When she finally went to her room, Delie did not light the candle at once but sat down fully dressed on the edge of the bed and looked out into the chequered light and shade of the garden. It was the last moon before Christmas; soon she would be seventeen. What a strange look Adam had given her just now in the drawing-room: cynical, almost angry, yet somehow humble, as if he were imploring her to understand. Should she go out tonight or not? He had almost seemed to want to avoid her. No! better go to bed, and see him in the morning. She unbuttoned the neck of her dress and was about to pull it over her head when there came a faint call: *Mo-poke! . . . Mo-poke! . . .* It was repeated at intervals so regular it might have been made by a machine.

She went to the window to listen, as one might listen to the chimes of a slow-striking clock, or the regular dripping of a tap. The night was calling, calling, the crickets sang monotonously, mysteriously in the drying grass. Slowly, almost unwillingly, she slipped over the sill.

The pittosporum flowers with their heavy orange scent had all fallen by now, but the air smelt fresh and sweet, of dew-damp grass and breathing trees. As she moved out from the side of the house the moon struck full on her upturned face. The white floor of cloud, mottled and broken like curds, did not impede its light, but, moving softly northward, drew an amber ring about its growing disc.

She came round the front of the house where the jasmine hung over the veranda. Adam's figure appeared silently beside her. He

144

drew her into the shadow of the jasmine and kissed her fiercely. She clung to him, startled and shaken, feeling the wild thudding of his heart through his thin shirt.

'Oh, I wasn't – wasn't sure if you'd be waiting for me. You've been so queer and cross.'

'Have I? I haven't seen you for a whole month, I was bitterly disappointed when you didn't come to church last Sunday.'

'I couldn't help it, darling. It was so wet. But this afternoon –'

'Oh, stop talking,' he said roughly, pulling her arm through his and leading her out of the garden enclosure and down by the river that gleamed through the glinting trees.

When he looked down at her his eyes seemed to have a tortured, blind darkness in them. His hand upon her arm was burning hot. He said, lightly enough, looking at the moon:

'You shouldn't talk on a night like this except to quote Shelley:

That orbéd maiden, with white fire laden
Whom mortals call the moon,
Glides glimmering o'er my fleece-like floor,
By the midnight breezes strewn . . .

'Or – to come from the sublime to the pathetic – Adam Jamieson:

When nights are heavy with the scent of pittosporum
My love comes forth like a white moth to me . . .'

'Adam, that's beautiful!'

'So are you beautiful.'

He bent and kissed her ear and his burning breath sent strong shudders, half of fear, half of delight, down her spine. She felt that she was walking with a stranger, and turned anxiously to reassure herself that this was really Adam. He looked back at her with a strange smile, his eyes half-closed, and led her along the river-bank, towards the banded light and shade of the native pines, where she had pursued the mopoke on that unforgotten night two years ago.

He led her in under the shade of a tree and leant hard against her, pressing her back into the tree-trunk. His eyes searched her face, on which a beam of moonlight fell, lighting her wide eyes and pale skin.

'Delphine. Did you mean what you said that time? About

145

wanting to be all mine?' His voice was husky and shaking.

'Yes! Oh yes!'

And all her mind concurred, but her body was stiffening into an instinctive resistance. The tree reminded her of that horrible man by the Campaspe, embracing his tree and beckoning her with a wild grin.

Adam's mouth came down on hers. His hand entered the open neck of her dress and found a small, pointed breast; but she twisted her head away and glared down at his brown hand in the moonlight against her white skin. . . . Long brown fingers, shaped like those other fingers she had seen, white against a black breast.

With a stifled 'Don't!' she grasped the hand in both her own and flung it from her.

Adam stood perfectly still and made no attempt to touch her again. He only looked at her with a hateful mocking smile which said, 'So much for brave words!' How could she tell him she had seen his father with the kitchen lubra under those very trees? And how explain all that was flooding through her at that moment? She could only grasp feverishly the hand she had spurned, and cover it with kisses. But it pushed her away with a cold hard pressure. He turned on his heel and began walking along the river-bank. She followed him, stumbling over tussocks, sobbing and begging him to wait. He walked rigidly on, away from the house. At last he turned on her. 'Be quiet, or you'll have Creeping Annie following us. Now go to bed. I'm going for a walk.'

'But Adam . . .!'

'*Will* you go?'

Before the concentrated bitterness of his voice she was dumb. She turned and made her way back through the softly moonlit garden, trying to cry quietly until she could fling herself on her bed and bury her face in the pillow. At first an angry pride sustained her. He was cruel, he was unfair. She had meant what she said; it was just that she was unprepared to meet this mood tonight. But pride faded and she began to feel a chill desolation. She had failed him. He would not love her any more.

She lay there in a stupor of misery, unconscious of the mosquitoes feeding on her exposed neck and breast. All the house was still. It seemed that hours had passed; he must have come back by now.

With a sudden resolution she got up and began to undress, and then, in her long-sleeved nightgown, crept to the door and opened it. She would go to his room and stay with him. Aunt Hester

146

could find her there in the morning for all she cared. She would show him she was not afraid. She tip-toed across the passage and turned the handle of his door. The room was dark. The faint reflections of moonlight showed his bed empty and unruffled.

Feeling deflated, she went back to bed, sitting up and hugging her knees as she listened for the creak of the back door. Her lids became heavy. Several times she dozed, and caught her head upright with a painful jerk. At last, worn out with emotion, she fell into a heavy sleep, with the candle still burning.

When she woke it was with a sense of unexplained dread. The candle was guttering in a bath of melted fat, sending great bloated shadows dancing over the walls. Then she heard the voice, seeming close to her ears: *Delphine!*

She rushed to the window, thrusting her head far out. The moon was setting behind the flowering gum, its light yellow and dull. The sky was clear of cloud.

'Adam!' she whispered, but only the monotonous chirring of the crickets answered her. She opened her door, but the passage was empty; so was his room, the bed still unslept in. Crossing back to her own room, she heard her aunt cough in the front bedroom and her heart jumped. She did not sleep again. The sense of dread still troubled her.

No one but Adam ever called her Delphine. She wrapped herself in her dressing-gown and sat by the window, looking at the stars. The moon's glow was gone, and Orion's belt showed brilliantly against the paling sky of dawn, low in the west.

She got up stiffly and washed her face in the cold water from the blue-patterned jug. Her large eyes peering back from the dressing-table mirror were shadowed with weariness, the lids still puffy from crying.

The smell of bacon in the dining-room seemed revolting this morning, but she strove to appear normal at breakfast. There was no sign of Adam; no doubt he would sleep late, and wake in a better mood.

'Adam's late,' said Hester, knitting her black brows. 'Poor boy! He didn't seem at all well yesterday, Charles.'

'Poor boy! H'mph. Lazy young shaver.'

Hester went to Adam's room, and came back with a more worried air. 'He hasn't been in all night! His bed's not slept in.'

'Perhaps he's made his own bed for once, and gone for a walk.'

Hester sat down and began abstractedly on her bacon and eggs. Adam couldn't make a bed as tidily as that to save his life. Her

147

mind began reviewing the black staff. Like father, like son! But Bella – too old and too fat. Lucy, fat and married. But what could have kept him out all night? She shot a glance at Delie, who, head bowed, was forcing a mouthful of food down her throat.

'Philadelphia! Is this another of his wild escapades? Do you know anything of it this time?'

She raised her white face and shadowed eyes. 'No, Aunt.'

'How should Delie know? I suppose he's gone off shooting possums or native bears.'

'He wouldn't – ' Delie began to protest.

'Hullo, girlie, you're looking a bit peaky today. You'd better have a lie-down after prayers. We won't wait for Adam for the service, he may not turn up till lunch time.'

Charles chose a passage from Ecclesiastes, one that Delie had always liked for its sonorous rhythms, but today the words seemed grim and portentous:

'Remember now thy Creator in the days of thy youth . . . Or ever the silver cord be loosed, or the golden bowl be broken . . .

'Then shall the dust return to the earth as it was; and the spirit shall return unto God who gave it.'

Delie stared hard at the conventional pattern on the brown carpet. Was this the secret? The dust returned to earth, but the spirit returned to – to wherever it came from. But this body that was her living, breathing, sentient self, was the seat and home of her spirit; her eyes took in colour and form, her brain told her when they were beautiful. This world was wonderful enough; she did not want any other.

'. . . and the peace that passeth understanding, be with us all. Amen.'

She started. Service was over. Bella, Lige and the rest were filing out. Creeping Annie gave her a peculiar look, she thought. Had she been watching last night? And where was Adam? Perhaps he was lost in the bush.

'Uncle Charles,' she said in a low voice, 'don't you think we should send Jacky out to look for Adam? He may have got lost.'

'Yes, I thought of that; but he's old enough to look after himself. If he's not in to dinner we'll organise a search-party.'

Delie said no more, but the sense of foreboding would not leave her. Adam did not appear for midday dinner. Hester, serving vegetables, dropped the tablespoon with a clatter.

'Charles, I insist that you send Jacky and the others out to search for Adam. There's such a big area where he might be lost,

148

and they're such good trackers. He could have fallen in the river –'

'He's an excellent swimmer.'

'– or been bitten by a snake. Oh, Adam, my boy!' Her lips began to tremble, and she fumbled for her handkerchief.

'Very well, my dear. Perhaps we should get the camp blacks to help as well. Now don't work yourself up.'

In front of her, as in front of Delie, lay a plate of untouched food. Annie silently removed them and glided from the room.

It was Jacky, Lucy's husband, who picked up the track along the riverbank, where it parted from Delie's, and followed it to its conclusion. It crossed the sandhills, skirted the swamps, passed two fences and came out at the creek with the fallen log which led across to the clearing of the picnic.

Jacky, following almost imperceptible signs on the dry ground, saw that the tracks crossed the log. He was about to follow when something between the steep banks of the dry creek-bed caught his eye. There was a mark on the edge of the log where a booted foot had slipped.

Face down in one of the stagnant pools lay Adam, his eyes closed, with a slight abrasion and bruise on one temple. Jacky lifted the limp head from the water, and coo-eed wildly for the others.

The women, waiting in growing apprehension at home, saw the little procession coming back over the sandhills, past the three children's graves. Charles and Lige, with their hands linked, formed a carriage between them. Looking from the side window, where she had been praying for his safe return, his mother saw the lifeless swing of Adam's arms, and screamed.

TWENTY-SEVEN

Delie hovered in the room where Adam lay, keeping away from the bed. She did not want to go near or touch him; while she just looked there was an illusion of natural sleep. Her uncle, gentle as a woman, bathed the dead face and put back the wet hair from the fine, wide brow. Adam's face was peaceful, faintly smiling with closed lips, as if he had just been initiated into some great mystery that had puzzled him, and was amused to find the answer so unexpectedly simple.

At last Charles looked up and became aware of her dead-white face and shadowed eyes, which seemed sunken in with suppressed suffering.

'Go to your aunt, child. Get her to pray with you if she can . . . The Lord giveth, and the Lord taketh away.'

'Then the Lord is cruel!' she burst out. She looked at Adam's mouth that would never laugh, speak, kiss again; silent, locked forever in irrevocable death. The tears welled up from her bursting heart, but a fire behind her eyes seemed to dry them before they could fall.

She went and knocked at her aunt's door. There was no response. She went in. The blinds were down and the room was dim. Hester was lying on the bed, her face turned to the wall, a sodden handkerchief gripped in her hand. Her eyes were closed and a continuous quiet, keening wail issued from her clenched teeth, seemingly without volition and without pause for breath.

'Auntie, it's me, Delie. Is there anything I can do?'

'Go away. Go away.'

Delie took a handkerchief from the top drawer of the chest, and dipping it in lavender water, placed it on Hester's forehead. She tried gently to ease the wet handkerchief out of her convulsive grasp, but she would not give it up. Delie laid another clean handkerchief on the pillow. The quiet keening sound continued. She went out the french windows and stood by the rail of the veranda where she had waited, so often, for Adam to arrive by river.

She gripped the rail and glared through dry, burning eyes at the curve of the downstream bend. She had feared the river – and Adam had been drowned in a puddle! Uncle said he had fallen while crossing back over the creek; had hit his head on the log, and lain unconscious with his face under water. A few more weeks and the creek would have dried right out, with not enough water to drown so much as a field-mouse. But Adam had been crossing it last night, in the dark of the setting moon, when the log was slippery with dew. And she had sent him there.

She ran down the steps and over the sandhills the way they had carried him home, through the she-oak grove and the native pines, round the dry swamps, towards the place where he had died.

The perfect afternoon enclosed her in its mocking peace and

beauty: the placid river, the flakes of silvery cloud intensifying the blue of the sky, the motionless trees, the yellow grass. She raced on unseeing, her mind bent on one picture: Adam lying unconscious in the treacherous creek.

But when she reached the fallen log she could not bear the sight of the place but veered away and crossed the creek-bed near where it joined the river.

She could feel the unshed tears burning behind her eyes. They were there, in a hard, twisted knot that hurt her forehead. She went on, making her way blindly round logs and through scratchy lignum patches. Once she fell into some mud that had not yet dried out, and wished that she might drown and die there and be at peace. But the mosquitoes biting savagely at her hands and neck spurred her up and onward.

The sun was already out of sight behind the trees. At first she had the vague idea of putting the scene of death as far as possible behind her. At last thought became numbed, and she went on mechanically. The undergrowth thinned and disappeared, and she was walking through a forest of red-gums on a vast flood-plain. There was no sign of the river nor any gleam of water. She was burning with a fever and increasingly thirsty.

Suddenly weary, she rested on a grey fallen log. All was so silent that she might have been under the sea. Then a pair of kookaburras laughed sardonically.

It grew dark under the trees. She began to shiver all over. She had slept very little in the past twenty-four hours, but she was not conscious of anything but cold and thirst. She must keep moving. She stumbled on, forgetting to look up at the patches of sky for familiar stars. She must come to the river soon.

'Ay, I'm full o' sleeper-cuttin', Joe. What say we cut and stack some small wood for steamers tomorrer?'

'Won't be 'ardly any more steamers with the low river, fathead. There's good money in sleeper-cuttin'. What's wrong with yer?'

'Ar, I'm sick of it, thassorl. Reckon I've cut enough red-gum to lay a railway line from 'ere to London. What about a bloody fencin' contract –'

'Well, I'll be jiggered! Shut up, Joe. There's ladies present.' A pale figure, with white face and staring eyes, had appeared on the edge of the clearing where the sleeper-cutters had their camp. Delie, worn out with emotion and lack of food or sleep, pitched down senseless just within the circle of firelight.

151

' ''Old 'er 'ead up!'

'No, y' hold it *down* when they faint, stoopid.'

'Throw some water on 'er. Not too much, don't go and drown the girl. Look, 'er clothes is all damp and muddy. Wonder where she comes from?'

'Dunno, but she's burning with a fever. Better keep 'er away from the fire and wrap 'er in a blanket.'

'A nip of rum ud bring 'er round. There's a bit left in the bottle. Now put some water in it. Don't want to choke 'er.'

The burning liquid trickling down her throat made Delie cough and open her eyes. She only knew that a male arm was supporting her; she thought she had just fallen from Barney again. She put her arms round the neck of the vague shape beside her and whispered, 'Adam.'

'Adam! Gawd, it must be Eve 'erself,' said the whiskered Joe to hide his embarrassment. Delie put up a hand and wonderingly felt his bushy beard.

'But you're not Adam! Take me home, I must see him, must see . . . He's going away today, tomorrow . . . What time is it?' She sat up to ask with fierce intensity, her eyes wild.

'There now, it's Saturdee I think . . . no, Sundee. Why now, where's your 'ome? Is it far from Echuca?'

'Echuca . . . Yes, they'll take him to Echuca, and put him in the ground. Oh, take me home!'

'We will, lass, we will. But where is 'ome? Is it on the river?'

'Yes, above Echuca.'

'Below the Bamah punt crossing?'

'Yes, yes. Let's go!'

Joe looked at his mate and whispered, 'She's come a long way . . . Whose place is it, Miss?'

'Jamieson's. That's my uncle. Why don't we go?'

'Orlright, we'll go when you've got this inter yer. Shivering like I dunno what.'

He handed her a thick enamel mug of hot, sweet black tea. She felt the rough chipped edge under her lips, but the sweet hotness sickened her. 'Water, please, water.'

Joe brought her canvas-tasting water from the bag hanging under a tree. She could see the white tent in the firelight, the clean swept space in front, and empty jam-tins and bottles arranged in a neat pile, glinting back the fire. It was like a dream, yet the details were vividly, painfully real.

'Now, Miss,' when she had thirstily gulped the water, 'just put

152

yer arm round Joe's neck again ('e's frightened of girls, but 'e'll 'ave to put up with it this time) and the other round mine, and up we go.'

They chaired her on their crossed hands and carried her between them until she saw the light, wide expanse of the river, gleaming beneath the moon. Then she found herself in a boat, shivering and burning inside a roll of blankets, her head propped on Joe's folded best coat.

She watched the dark tree-tops glide by in a strange unearthly motion. As the boat followed the river's bends the moon changed its position and the stars moved with her, marching steadily on behind the backward-flowing trees. She felt she was the core of stillness, the centre of some great spinning movement. It was very peaceful there. She wanted it to go on forever.

It was with a shock, an agonising wrench, that she felt the flattie grind on the sand and heard Joe's voice: 'Lights burnin' everywhere. I bet they're worried stiff.'

The voice seemed to come muffled from the other side of a thick black wall. Then the wall collapsed on top of her and she could see nothing but blackness, lit by wheels and flashes of lurid colour.

TWENTY-EIGHT

'It was the best thing that could have happened, dear,' said Charles, sitting by Delie's bedside and holding her thin hand. 'I think it saved your aunt's reason, having you to nurse at such a time. She was still lying there with her face to the wall, when it was time to take him to Echuca for the coroner's inquiry and the funeral . . . No, don't try to talk.

'When I sent the doctor back ahead of me, I told him he'd have two patients on his hands. But he made Hester realise how ill you were, with this Murray Valley en-encephalitis, and how everything depended on careful nursing . . . They think it's carried by mosquitoes.'

'How . . . how long – ?'

'Since you've been ill? It's nearly three weeks. You've had this fever, but you're going to be all right. Hester got up, and nursed you night and day. When you turned the corner, she collapsed – simply worn out. She slept for nearly two days. Annie is nursing her, and she will be herself in a day or two.'

The empty words echoed inside her head. Hester would be herself in a day or two, and Delie had turned the corner . . . She could see herself turning a corner of a high, grey paling fence, and all ahead stretched a long grey street, empty of life, empty of Adam.

'Don't want to get well.'

'You are getting well, whether you want to or not. And one day you will look back on all this and wonder how you could ever have felt that way. Believe me, I know how you feel.'

When he had gone she lay and watched the beam of late afternoon sun slanting in the window, and the brilliant motes turning and twinkling in a leisurely dance. Motes in a beam of light – without that light they would be invisible, yet there just the same.

The slanting sunbeam took her back to that other afternoon when Adam had come in and kissed her for the first time. She turned her head on the pillow, half expecting him to come through the door. But no; his shape was lost in darkness forever.

When Charles came in again the following morning, he carried a sheaf of manuscript in a folder.

'Here, you might like to have these; Adam's writings . . . you feature in them quite a lot: For Philadelphia . . . Delie . . . Delphine – all sorts of variations on your name.' He gave the ghost of a melancholy smile and put them down by her hand lying listlessly on the cover. 'Don't read too much and tire yourself. The doctor is coming today, so try to look as well as you can and he may let you get up.'

'I'm feeling much better.'

'That's the girl. Annie and Bella giving you enough to eat?'

'Too much. Bella looks so worried when I don't eat that I feel I have to even though I'm not hungry.'

'That's the girl. You must get strong.'

She lay and waited for him to go, exhausted by talking. Three weeks. Three weeks she had lain here in the red-streaked, wavering darkness, which had sometimes cleared to show the figure of Aunt Hester or Creeping Annie, bending over with a cup or a wet cloth.

There were times when it had been so silent that she had wondered if she were dead, and others when the accusing voices started to shout at her again with a terrifying clamour: *'You failed him! You killed him!'*

154

She had a recurring nightmare of the long white beach, endless and lonely, with its pounding breakers and sandhills stretching out of sight. One wave would tower up in the sky, like a hill, while she waited for it to crash and sweep her to destruction.

Now she lay with closed eyes, thinking of this dream. Charles left and she opened her eyes and moved one hand tenderly, experimentally, over the surface of the thin sheets of paper. Adam's handwriting seemed to give her strength. She turned the sheets and held one languidly up to her eyes. She read:

> . . . And through uncounted years this sun will burn
> Through the blue air, and the short springtime die;
> When you are long forgotten, and when I
> Am scattered dust, the summers will return.

Then she was weeping, helplessly, dropping floods of hot tears over the crumpled sheets of paper. At last she had no tears left, but dry sobs shook her until she fell into a deep sleep from which she woke refreshed and renewed. They were the first tears she had shed since Adam died.

On the day when she was to get up, Charles came and sat on the edge of the bed. He seemed to be searching for words.

'Er – When you see Aunt Hester –'

'Oh, can I go to her room?'

'She's up. You'll see her in the dining-room.'

'But I thought – She's all right again, then? Why hasn't she been in to see me?'

Charles looked down and picked an imaginary thread from his trouser leg. 'Philadelphia, you will find your aunt . . . er, you will find her changed. She is quite normal except . . . except in one direction. You mustn't be upset if she seems strange and hostile.'

Delie looked at him silently.

'The doctor says, delayed shock. She seemed all right at first, but now she has certain . . . hallucinations. And she feels rather bitter towards you.'

'But you said she nursed me night and day!'

'So she did; that just shows her present mood is not normal. I suppose she has always felt that her sister had the best of everything; and now perhaps she feels that her child has been unfairly taken while her sister's is spared. It's a perfectly unreasonable resentment.'

'She has something my mother hasn't – life.'

'That's quite true. You must try to ignore her attitude, or to bear with it as patiently as you can, and remember what she has suffered.'

Delie wanted to cry out, 'What about what I have suffered? For the second time, the whole basis of my life swept away. What about me?' She swallowed the words and nodded dumbly.

When she got up, she felt strangely altered and aged. It was Annie who helped her into her dressing-gown and supported her along the passage to the dining-room. She found herself so weak and shaky that after taking a few steps on the numb, wooden feet that did not seem to belong to her, she was glad to lean on Annie's bony shoulder.

She found her aunt sitting in one of the deep leather armchairs with her back to the green plush drapes at the window. A dark wicker sewing-basket was beside her on a stand, and a piece of crochet worked jerkily in her fingers. She did not look up or cease to work as Delie came slowly into the room. Annie tried to lower her into a chair near the door, but she went on and stood beside Hester.

'Auntie, I'm glad you are better.' She put out her thin hand, but it was not taken. Hester looked up briefly, coldly, and continued to crochet furiously.

'Uncle has told me how you nursed me when I was so ill . . . Thank you.'

The words fell into a flat silence. Delie felt her weak legs beginning to tremble with the effort of standing. At last Hester looked up again and said, 'I did nothing but what anyone would do. It was my duty to try to save your life.'

The cold words were like a slap in the face. Delie turned and flopped into a chair with hot tears stinging her eyes. Hester began to discuss the arrangements for lunch with Annie; they both ignored Delie.

She did not speak another word until lunch was on the table, but when her uncle came in with his dolorous moustache and his pathetic efforts to lighten the atmosphere, she felt the strength of an ally. As he tried to encourage her to eat, and answered his wife's sharp or querulous tones with unfailing good humour, she felt that she had never loved him so much, since the days when he had been her only companion among the snowy wastes of Kiandra.

But her eyes did not seem to be focusing properly because a terrible pain had started in her right temple. A red-hot knife seemed to be twisting there. She pushed her plate away and buried her face in her arms.

Alarmed, Charles put down his knife and fork and came round the table. 'Are you feeling faint, child?'

'It's only histrionics, Charles. Sniff! The doctor said she was well enough to get up.'

'What nonsense, Hester! Look, she's white as a sheet. Would you like to go back to bed, dear?'

'Yes.' To get back to the haven of her bed, to close her eyes and cover them against the light that seemed to pierce her brain with needles; all her will was concentrated on this. Charles helped her to her room, gave her one of the sedative powders the doctor had prescribed and a wet cloth for her forehead, and left her.

In the next few weeks these appalling frontal headaches recurred every day. She learnt to weather them, to ride them out like a storm. The doctor gave her a stronger sedative and she would lie utterly still in the darkened room, not daring to move her head as the pain gradually quieted and receded. She was afraid to move, to speak, lest the raging beast woke again.

Christmas passed almost without her being aware of it. The headaches gradually became less frequent and ceased to trouble her. She went out again into the garden and felt, as she had never felt before, the terrible and wonderful power of the sun. It woke her young body into vigorous life again almost against her will.

A letter came from the north from Miss Barrett, with a message for Adam. Friends in such distant places had not heard of the tragedy, though Adam's end had been recorded in the *Riverine Herald* in the type he used to set up. Miss Barrett was leaving Australia soon, for the family was travelling to England and she was to take charge of the children on the sea trip. Then she would go on her own to see all the places in Europe she had long wanted to see.

It meant little to Delie. Her former idol had long been fading into the mists of time and distance. And would Adam, too, gradually fade from her mind and heart? She couldn't believe it.

Miss Barrett had sent her a book for Christmas, a modern novel – *Tess of the d'Urbervilles*, by Thomas Hardy. It made a profound impression on her at this time. The final words seemed to echo something half-formed in her brain: 'The play was over; the gods had finished their sport with Tess.'

For her wavering faith had died when Adam died. The senseless waste of that promising young life meant more to her than all she had read of disasters far away; of ten thousand Japanese dying of earthquake and fire, of a million Chinese dying of famine, of praying children trapped in a burning church, even cases nearer home of blameless hard-working families losing all in a bushfire.

She had a malicious desire to say to her aunt, who spent a lot of time in prayer and was tearful over anything that reminded her of Adam, 'Why do you cry? Isn't he asleep in the arms of Jesus?' In her hard bitterness she wanted to destroy the simple faith of others.

She avoided Hester as much as possible, not speaking to her if she could help it, and being careful not to be left alone in the same room with her. She had seen Hester look at her in such a way that a kind of sickness came over her, and she had to go out of sight of those sharp black eyes.

As soon as she was strong enough, she began to climb the gold-tipped pine, lying along its feathery, springy branches, with the sharp hot scent of the sunwarmed fronds eveloping her. It was only in the top of the tree, or shut in her own room, that she felt free of those black, brooding glances. But though she climbed up with a book or a pad and pencil, she read little and never sketched anything. It was enough to lie in the sun and absorb its light through her pores like a leaf, like a flower. It was a time of drifting, as strips of fallen bark drifted on the river without aim or volition: carried forward on the dark stream of time which bears all living things from birth to death.

It was the evening beauty of the river, with a soft mist rising from its glassy surface, which first stirred Delie out of her state of suspended animation. Beyond the bend the stubble of the hay-paddock shone with a white, unearthly radiance, and a full moon was rising in a honeyed light. The bands of delicate rose and pearl at the horizon were like the inside of a shell, and all was reflected in the river's nacreous expanse.

The old familiar unrest, the urge to capture this transient beauty in a timeless form, rose strongly within her. She crushed it down and walked quietly up the front veranda steps, to where Charles was sitting in a canvas chair, smoking his pipe. The fumes of the cow-dung mosquito fires drifted off with the blue wreaths of tobacco.

Delie leant on the veranda rail, watching the first stars in a sky now brilliantly banded with amber and blue-green, against which the gum trees showed in black silhouette their supple forms. She watched them intently, her mind recording each smooth shape.

Charles got up and leant beside her, resting his forearms on the rail. He looked up at the brightening stars.

'I wish I'd learnt astronomy when I was young,' he said musingly. 'I don't seem to be able to take in new things nowadays, but it's struck me what worlds of things I know nothing about.' He puffed out some smoke and removed his pipe the better to talk. 'You know, it's only when you're getting old that you realise how short even the longest life is. It's short, it's terribly short. Why, a man could spend a lifetime just studying the habits of bees! Then there's physiology, and botany, and chemistry, and astronomy, and all this new theory of evolution, and electricity ... They'll do wonders when they harness electricity. Some of the new steamers have electric lights, you know; light at the push of a button.'

Delie turned to look at him. Good old Uncle! He had some ideas in his head, though he rarely expressed them. She was about to answer when the noise of something falling on the wooden veranda made her turn.

It was Hester, dimly outlined in the twilight, her eternal crochet in her hands. The crochet-hook had fallen; Delie went politely to pick it up for her, but Hester bent quickly and snatched it up, with a look of such bitter aversion that Delie shivered and went inside. As if she would pollute the thing by touching it! She heard Hester's voice raised angrily, then Charles too came inside and banged the door of his room behind him.

The next day was mail day. There was nothing for Delie in the bag, but as she went out to the veranda after lunch, Hester followed her.

'I have a letter here,' she began gratingly, 'from Mrs McPhee, who suggests, *if I can spare you*, that you should go into Echuca to stay with them. Charles thinks you need a holiday; and I can't say that you're much use around the house.'

Delie turned with her back to the veranda rail, gripping it for support.

'Aunt Hester, why do you hate me?'

Her aunt's face set like a stone. 'Hate you?'

'I know you never used to like me, but now it almost seems as if you couldn't bear the sight of me. Why? What have I done?'

'Why? Shall I tell you why? Yes, I hate the sight of you.' Her loose lips were trembling with passion, her black eyes snapped. 'You killed him. You killed my boy. Why weren't you drowned with the others?'

159

Delie went white. She leant hard on the rail for support.

'I didn't kill him! I loved him.'

'You loved him! Ah, now we're hearing something of the truth. You met him by the river bank at night, didn't you? It was you lured him out of the house when he should have been asleep. Men – they're all alike when it comes to a pretty face or a pretty figure. And Adam was a man. Why was he spared for me to lose him now? I prayed that he should live through that night when he had croup, and the doctor said he couldn't last till morning. Better if he had died then, in his innocence. Oh yes, Annie has told me of your meetings and kissings in the dark.'

She had come close and thrust her face at Delie, who bent back over the rail before the working mouth and mad eyes of her aunt.

'You don't understand –' she said faintly.

'Oh yes, I understand well enough! I know what women are like, and girls just feeling their power. Do you think I haven't seen you making eyes at Charles? Like father, like son! Of course he's no blood relation, he's not really your uncle –'

'Aunt Hester! How can you be so – so utterly foul-minded?'

'Ah, I see more than you think, young lady. But why did you do it? Of course you pushed him off the log. Was it jealousy? Because of that wealthy girl in Echuca I wanted him to marry? But you didn't have to kill him. My boy! My only son.'

Her voice and her face crumpled up together and she was crying, noisily and grotesquely. Creeping Annie appeared silently and with a peculiar, pallid, half-triumphant look at Delie, led Hester away to her room.

Delie stood, white and stunned, and went over in her mind the incredible scene that had just passed. She trembled violently. She couldn't, wouldn't stay here another day. The doctor had said she was cured of the 'river fever', as it was known locally. There was nothing to stop her leaving. But she had no money except her interest in the *Philadelphia*, somewhere away up the Darling after wool.

She was filled with a wild longing to get away, to catch the first steamer that came past. She was young enough to believe that her life was ended; she would never love anyone again, but would live as a hermit on some quiet reach beside the river's endless flow.

She found her uncle in the horse-paddock about to mount Firefly. After one glance at her face, he hitched the mare to the fence and walked with Delie towards the river-bank.

'Uncle, I can't live here any longer!' He did not seem surprised.

'Where else could you go?'

'To Echuca, for a start. Mrs McPhee will have me for an indefinite visit. Perhaps I could get a job as a nurse at the hospital.'

'I doubt if you are strong enough for that sort of work, even if they would take you at seventeen. But your face was white just now. What's the matter? Has your aunt – ?'

'Yes! Oh Uncle Charles, she hates me like poison. And there's something so – so strange about her, she frightens me.'

He sighed deeply and kicked a small stone into the water. 'Yes, I know. The doctor . . . I don't think he realises just how queer she is. He said it would pass as the shock wore off. She hasn't offered you any violence?'

'Only words. She accused me of, of murder and . . .' She could not bring herself to utter the other poisonous accusation. Already she felt a constraint with her uncle.

Charles's mouth formed a silent whistle of surprise. 'Poor Hester! I'm afraid she really went over the edge when Adam died. She poured out some rigmarole to me, but I wouldn't listen to it and I thought she'd forgotten it. Though her hostility has been obvious.'

'The terrible part of it is that it's true.'

'Now what do yo you mean?' He took her gently by the shoulders and turned her towards him. 'Don't tell me *you* are starting to imagine things. He was in love with you, was that it? And you with him?'

'Yes. And I did meet him outside that night. We quarrelled; it was my fault, and I *have* felt to blame. She doesn't hate me more than I hate myself.'

It was a tremendous relief to accuse herself like this, to tell what had been pressing on her mind like a dull weight.

'You blamed yourself! You foolish child, why didn't you tell me all this before? Adam died accidentally, the coroner didn't even find it necessary to hold an inquest. If Adam went roaming about in the dark, well, that was due to his own wild nature as much as to anything . . . It happened that he met with an accident. He'd had other accidents. He might just as well have been drowned on that mad escapade down the river at night, or when the tow-rope swept him out of the dinghy, or when the bark canoe sank beneath him that time.'

'Yes, I know. I ask myself, why, why, why? Why did it happen as it did? A few weeks earlier, and the creek would have been full enough to break his fall without doing him any harm. A week or two later, and the last pool would have dried out. He might have been knocked unconscious, but he wouldn't have drowned. It does seem like fate.'

'Yes, fate; blind fate.' Charles bent and picked up a piece of fallen bark, thin, curved and smooth. He ran his long, sensitive fingers over the pale inner surface. 'We are carried blindly into acts which lead inevitably to other acts, that set up a train of circumstance beyond our comprehension or control. If I had not found that gold at Kiandra, Adam would not have died on the Murray at the age of nineteen. Yet perhaps an early death was somehow inherent in his character. Who knows?'

Delie trod thoughtfully on a piece of curled bark, feeling it crunch crisply beneath her shoe. Her uncle had evidently been brooding on this subject. He went on:

'I don't know all the circumstances that put Adam into the particular mood he was in that night. I remember how moody he was at dinner, and after. I'm not surprised you quarrelled. We are all caught in the stream of our own acts and we can't go against our natures.'

He sent the piece of bark spinning into the river. It went steadily floating down with the current. 'We can no more order our own fate than that piece of bark can turn and swim upstream.'

'But Uncle, it was you who said "The Lord giveth . . ." and read out the piece about not a sparrow falling –'

'Yes. Words can comfort sometimes, even when they have ceased to have any meaning. I was brought up on those words, and they still create an illusion for me. But at night, when I look at the silent stars and those black, terrible voids in the Milky Way, they all fall away to nothing.'

Delie stared at him. Here was a new side to Charles, who read the prayers and lessons on Sunday mornings almost like a minister.

'I didn't tell you about Old Sarah,' he said. 'She came up from her camp that day to ask if anyone had died. She said the Spirit Bird passed over her camp in the early morning, about moon-sit-down, she said. I hadn't much hope after that.'

Delie looked down at the endless flow of water, thinking of the blacks and their strange beliefs: the Bunyip, the great Snake, and the Death Bird, that nameless one which was felt but not seen as it passed over the camp when someone had died. Sarah had known; she herself had heard something, a warning voice, just as the moon was setting.

162

'Anyway, you can see I can't stay here any longer,' she said at last. 'Aunt Hester suggested herself that I should go and visit Mrs Mac. She need not know that it's to be more than a visit.'

'I hope it may not be more than a visit. Hester may recover her balance soon, and ask to have you back. She'll miss you.'

Delie said nothing, but she was inwardly resolved never to return.

'Don't do anything rash, dear. Go to Mrs McPhee for a month, and we'll see. As the banks recover they may be able to pay their clients back in part. Meanwhile I'll advance you whatever you need. But don't forget I'm still your guardian, and you can't dash off anywhere without my permission.'

A gentle smile removed the threat from his last words. 'Well, I'd better get out to the sheep. We'll all drive into town tomorrow. Hester wants to visit the grave.'

Delie had no wish to go to the cemetery. She never wanted to see the place where Adam was buried.

In the morning she rose early, having finished her packing the night before, and went round the place saying good-bye to five years of her life. The morning was windless and clear. The hens clucked contentedly, the dogs lay dozing or snapping at flies. She went down to Lige's hut with one of her landscapes of the river as a farewell gift. As she walked back along the river-bank the sun glittered back from the perfect surface. Two magpies sat on the garden fence, warbling a morning concert.

After breakfast the buggy was harnessed up and Delie's expanding wicker basket was placed beneath the seat, with some hams and dressed poultry for market. Delie had not told Bella that she was leaving for good, yet as though she guessed, Bella stood at the gate, waving good-bye as they left.

As Delie got down to shut the outermost gate before they entered the low road through the forest, she looked back at the house, smoke rising lazily from a chimney at the back as when she first saw it. Jacky, in a bright blue shirt and wide hat, was riding out behind a mob of wethers being moved to the back paddock. She climbed up again, sitting with her back to Hester who had not addressed a word to her this morning.

As they wound along the track beneath the great trees, she looked up at the patches of blue sky between the smooth trunks, and wondered if she would ever pass this way again.

When they stopped to be checked by Customs at the bridge, she got down again and walked on to the footway to gaze at the dwindled summer current, clear and smooth as glass, slipping between the stone pillars. She watched the endless movement of water, flowing onward and downward until it reached the sea. And yet the river did not end there. When this body of water arrived at its destination there would still be a river; it was never destroyed but only changed as it moved in the great cycle of distillation and descent. It was as endless and self-renewing as life itself.

She looked towards the upstream bend. It was lost in dark, leaning trees. Downstream the high wharf could be seen, the boats lying idle beneath it and the river curving on and out of sight.

That must be her direction now, downstream, out into life. She must follow where the river went, and travel the unknown landscape towards the distant sea. Pausing on the bridge between the dead past and the relentless future, she knew that there could be no standing still. Life beckoned her from beyond the furthest bend.

time,
flow softly

The river, the dark and secret river,
full of strange time, is for ever flowing
by us to the sea.

Thomas Wolfe: *Of Time and the River*

TWENTY-NINE

'The River's coming down!'

The word passed joyously from mouth to mouth, the *Riverine Herald* printed it, and the river itself proclaimed it, eddying past the wharf with increasing speed and volume. The clear summer water was beginning to be stained with the brown sediment of winter streams.

Rain had fallen away in the high mountains of New South Wales and Victoria; and now the Murray and the Goulburn and the Campaspe were bringing their separate streams to the Meeting-of-the-Waters, Echuca.

This year there would be a good river before the snows started to melt in September. A 'good' river, to a town that depended on its steamer trade, was a full river; even if it overdid its goodness and spread into the streets, no one complained. Only a drought was to be feared.

Steamers for up-river, which had been lying at the wharf all summer, suddenly became active. Barges were tied to towing-poles, steam was raised, and with triumphant blasts on their whistles the *Adelaide* and the *Edwards*, the *Elizabeth* and the *Success*, each with three empty barges trailing behind, set off to begin the logging season. Some of the barges would be dropped off at the logging camps and then floated down with loads of red-gum; others would return with the steamers, loaded with flour from Albury, Howlong and Corowa.

The Government snagging boat *Melbourne* had left to free a jam of logs and debris at Stewart's Bridge on the Goulburn. Soon the Darling and Murrumbidgee traders, caught on a falling river last year, would begin to arrive back at their home port.

Seated in her small back room cluttered with frames and mounts at Hamilton's Photographic Studio in the main street, Delie Gordon could see nothing of all this; of how the awakened river sparkled in the sun, and the shadows moved under the great red-gum trees on its banks.

There was no rain in Echuca. The lovely sunny days of autumn passed over in calm progression; the gold and silver fleets of cumulus cloud sailed from west to east; but by the time she was free at six o'clock the sun would be setting.

Sounds of the life beyond filtered into her room: the life of a busy country town that was also an inland port. She could hear the clop-clop of horses' hooves in the street, the whine of a steam-saw down by the river, the rattle of cart-wheels and the shunting of trains. And, cutting across them all, the shrill, exciting note of a paddle-steamer blowing off at the Campaspe Junction.

She looked out at a glimpse of dusty back yard, and next to it the back yard of the Shamrock Hotel beyond a grey paling fence. Sighing, she turned back to tinting a picture of the Echuca wharf, lined with paddle-steamers unloading bales of wool. It was her first day at the studio and she wanted to do well, but her heart wasn't in the work. The long, lovely, disturbing note of the steamer's whistle had set her foot tapping restlessly.

Little Mr Hamilton, thin and worried-looking in rimless glasses, came bustling in with a handful of tinted postcards she had done that morning.

He put them down on her table, took off his glasses and tapped the cards with them.

'Very delicate work, very creditable, Miss Gordon.' His mouth was thin, straight and unsmiling; she had not yet seen it relax. 'Yes, yes; but – ahem, unfortunately not what people want. They like plenty of Antwerp blue.'

'You mean the sky? I didn't want to make it look unreal.'

'Yes, yes; but it's not reality they want, only a pretty picture to send to their friends. The river in this one, now; looks a bit drab, doesn't it?'

'But the Murray isn't the least bit blue, Mr Hamilton!'

'True, true; it's either green or brown, usually. But then people have fixed ideas. The sea is blue; the sea is water; therefore all water should be blue. Something like that their minds work. Believe me, I know what will sell. Now try and see what you can do with these.'

Delie's full bottom lip stuck out as she drew the bottle of Antwerp blue towards her. She had been delighted when her old friend Angus McPhee had found this job for her, but already she knew she was not going to like it. All her artistic instincts were in revolt against the requirements of Public Taste.

Still, at least she'd be independent. She'd rather scrub floors

168

than go back to being dependent on Aunt Hester, to being the 'orphan child', the 'helpless nuisance'. 'I'll never go back to the farm, never,' she said aloud.

It was no good Mrs Mac wanting her to stay with them indefinitely as a kind of adopted daughter; she had insisted on paying board, because she was really not much help in the home and anyway she wanted to be free to put all her time into studying at the Echuca School of Arts. And now the McPhees were going to Bendigo, and she was really alone in the world. Alone in the world. It sounded pathetic, but also rather exciting, when she said it to herself like that.

And all her money was gone, though the bank had made some small reparations after the '93 crash. She had been living on her capital for two years now. And though Aunt Hester was only really about fifteen miles away up-river, she never saw her. She had gone out to the buggy and exchanged a few words with her the last time Uncle Charles was in town. They had been polite and stiff. I wouldn't go back, she said to herself, with her old childhood habit of dramatising a situation, if she asked me on her bended knees.

No, Echuca was her home. This was the place where she had gone to her first ball, and to picnics and parties with Adam. Though she still played tennis with Bessie Griggs, walked with her to church with a group of other young people, and joined her in boating excursions on the river, she had drifted away from her since Adam died.

She thought of Bessie's hurt tones when she had accused her of being sentimental: 'You're so unfeeling these days, Delie! I'm sure I cried more over Adam than you did; and you never go to the cemetery. Your own cousin! And such a handsome boy . . .'

Of course she couldn't explain to Bessie how she felt about the cemetery, how it filled her with an oppressive horror of the physical fact of death. She had not felt like this over the lonely boards that marked the far southern cliff-top where her family was buried; yet the cemetery had nothing to do with her memory of Adam's warm and vital flesh. He lay in the large community cemetery on the outskirts of the town, where all denominations were buried in marked sections, keeping up among the dead the artificial divisions of the living. There was no graveyard at the church where Delie went each Sunday, from a kind of social habit rather than for any spiritual solace she received there.

169

The incumbent was the Reverend William Polson, who had been a curate of the same parish when she had first met him, out at the farm.

How he had gazed into her eyes then, over the piano (How old was she? Not more than fifteen, surely!), and he did it still, every Sunday morning, as he shook hands with the congregation in the porch. Like a mesmerised hen, thought Delie irreverently. And surely he held her hand a trifle longer than was necessary, while inquiring after her aunt?

He had funny pale eyes, set so deeply beneath his light eyebrows as to give him a fanatical look at times. Oh, bother Mr Polson! She dabbed irritably at the sky in a view of Echuca, making it a brilliant blue. She remembered his last visit to Mrs McPhee's.

He had balanced his tea-cup delicately and crooked his little finger with killing elegance, while talking fashionable nothings and a little politics.

'Federation must come, of course; the year nineteen hundred will see us all one nation. The present system of the various states cutting each other's throats is uneconomic and foolish; and border restrictions . . .'

Delie had looked at him, at his pale, thin, bony face and deep-set eyes, his prominent Adam's apple (Adam, and his strong brown throat! Adam, drowned and dead . . .). This was a spiritual leader of men, God's anointed, behind him all the dignity of the Church. She heard him saying in an affected voice, 'Yes, I will have another of those delicious little cakes, I believe. Is your light hand responsible, Miss Gordon?'

'Oh no, my cakes always flop, or else they burn. Mrs McPhee won't let me in the kitchen, will you, Mrs Mac? How many things did I break in the first fortnight?'

'Now, Delie child, you're not as bad as all that. It takes all sorts to make a world; we can't all be domesticated types, can we, Mr Polson? Didn't the Lord himself say that Mary had chosen "the better part", while Martha was "cumbered with much doing"?'

'True, Mrs McPhee. Though I hardly feel – '

'And even if she can't bake cakes, Delie can paint like an angel.' And she glanced proudly at two small water-colour sketches over the mantelpiece.

Delie looked at the floor while Mr Polson paid them an extravagant tribute of praise.

She knew that they were competent, passable sketches such as

170

any 'accomplished' young woman could turn out by the hundred. But she longed to paint great rich canvases that would hold all the remoteness, the subtle colour harmonies of this strange land where the trees were amber, olive, mauve, blue, but rarely green; where the skies were so pure that it seemed impossible they could ever be set down in the medium of heavy oil paint.

There was no limit to her ambition; but she writhed inwardly at these ill-informed praises of her present work, and the remarks: 'Philadelphia is *so* artistic. How beautifully she tints postcards!'

When Mr Polson had gone, Mrs McPhee chided her gently: 'Dear child, you shouldn't go out of your way to announce your shortcomings as a housekeeper. I do believe that young man is getting close to the point of making a declaration, the way he looks at you! But you must remember that your face is your fortune, and act accordingly.'

'Good heavens, Mrs Mac! The way you and Aunt Hester talk you'd think there was no career open to a woman but marriage and having babies! I intend to make a career as an artist; I won't get married for ages, if ever; and as for him, I can't stand his languishing looks and his pale eyelashes. I'll say something really outrageous one day, and frighten him off for good.'

Mrs McPhee sighed, thinking that if Delie had no other fortune than her looks, she had still been well endowed. She wore her hair in the latest top-knot syle that seemed to add height and grace to her figure. From its piled dark mass little ends escaped, to fall in tendrils over her neck and soften the outline of her white forehead. And besides her large blue eyes, she had a beauty that would last; it was built into the fine bone-structure of her face.

'Anyway,' said Delie, who had been following her own train of thought, 'you forget that I'm part-owner of a paddle-steamer, which might be making me a fortune up the Darling, for all we know.'

'Part-owner! What part, may I ask? A twenty-fifth! No doubt you owed Captain Tom a debt of gratitude, but I still think your fifty pounds could have been better invested. The sooner you ask him to pay you back, the better.' Mrs McPhee's sandy, frizzy grey hair stood out indignantly about her small face. 'He should have known better, taking the money from a mere child, as you were then.'

'I knew what I was doing, Mrs Mac. And Uncle Charles gave his consent.'

171

'Yes, but your guardian is a little – well, impractical, I think, dear.'

'Anyway, Tom will offer me the money back as soon as he's paid off the interest, I know. Then I could keep on at the School of Arts for another year, instead of taking a job. Or perhaps I could do both.'

Now, in the studio, looking at the row of postcards with impossibly green trees and bright blue water that she had finished tinting, Delie thought of the same problem: how could she do both? She had meant to ask Mr Hamilton at once for time off for art lessons, but so far his unsmiling face and severe demeanour had rather intimidated her.

He came hurrying in again – he was always in a hurry – and looked over her shoulder critically. Then he straightened up and rocked complacently on his heels, his mouth as straight and unsmiling as usual. Delie's heart beat uncomfortably.

'Now we're getting it,' he said at last, with surprising enthusiasm considering his expression. '*Now* you've got the idea. McPhee told me I'd be getting a very artistic young lady, a real gem. H'm, yes. Pity McPhee's leaving the town. A loss to the community.'

'And to me personally; I'll miss them both terribly. They were my first friends in Echuca. They wanted me to go to Bendigo with them, but – I didn't want to leave the river.'

'They both think very highly of you, I know that.'

'Well, I hope I won't be a disappointment, Mr Hamilton. I was going to ask you –'

'I'm sure you won't, my dear, sure you won't. Just remember, plenty of Antwerp blue. These are excellent.'

The bell in the outer studio rang sharply, and he bustled out. Delie took up her brushes with a sigh.

THIRTY

As a parting gift Mrs McPhee had given Delie a new afternoon gown; or rather she had bought ten yards of pale blue bombazine, patterned with dainty pink rose-wreaths.

Together they had fashioned a gown with the new simple princess-skirt, with a slight train at the back and rows of frills about the wide hem. When she first put it on, and tied the blue sash about her waist, Delie felt a new poise, a sensation of being taller and more graceful. As she held the soft folds of the train in one hand to descend the stairs, she formed a deep feminine plan. First she must ask Mr Hamilton to take her portrait in the new dress.

It was her job each morning, before beginning work at tinting, to check the appointment book and dust the fittings – a carved wood and horsehair sofa, a potted palm, a backdrop with a painted staircase and marble balustrade, and a plush arm-chair.

Mr. Hamilton didn't like taking children, but she was a great help with them. She would sit a fractious infant on the fur rug, removing its boots so that it could feel the delightful tickle on its toes. Little girls with wide, frightened eyes and enormous sashes round their middles would stand on one black-stockinged leg and slip their hands into hers. Little boys, mutinous in best knicker-bockers and lace collars, would cease to glare when they saw her smiling at them like a conspirator from behind their mothers' backs.

She had also learned the art of retouching, or making sitters appear more like their own flattering idea of themselves: erasing blemishes, darkening pale eyebrows, adding highlights to hair and teeth.

Mr Hamilton was very pleased with her (though he said little) and wondered how he had ever managed with the rather dim-witted lad who had been his assistant before. But he didn't let her overwork. He was impressed with her fragile appearance, and on days when she looked tired and pale, would send her home early to rest.

173

But the pallor was natural, the tiredness was only boredom, and as soon as she was free she rushed to get her sketching materials and would be out drawing and painting until the last of the light.

She had the gown packed in a cardboard box in her work-room. She hurried away when she had made sure the appointment book was empty for this morning, changed from her high-necked blouse and fitted skirt of blue serge, and slipped on the lovely soft folds. At once she felt a different person. Taking out brush and comb, she softened her hair a little with a few wisps of curls on the forehead. Then, with head up and skirts trailing gracefully, she swept into the studio.

Mr Hamilton, who was pulling the sofa into a better light, stopped and blinked at her. The excitement of dressing-up had put a delicate colour in her clear cheeks and deepened her eyes to an intense blue, while between the dark hair and the level dark brows her forehead seemed white as marble.

'We-ell!' said Mr Hamilton, staring. Delie smiled in triumph. 'Here, this isn't wanted.' He gave the sofa an impatient push. 'This calls for the staircase and the Italian balustrade. I only wish,' he said, bowing with what was almost a smile, 'that I had a background worthy of the subject.'

Delie stood calmly while Mr Hamilton, the artist in him aroused, fussed over arranging her pose in front of the painted staircase. He fetched a cushion and spread her train over it on the floor. He went back to the camera, looked through, and emerged again, putting his head on one side.

'Er – your hands, Miss Gordon. I think they would be better behind your back. No, not jammed out of sight like that, just clasped lightly behind . . . that's better.'

Her flush deepened a little. Her hands were much too big, she knew, and in a photograph they always looked worse – bony, long-fingered, too large for her slender wrists.

'A little more cheerful, please. No, I don't want teeth; just the hint of a smile. That's it – hold it!'

And her image as she was at that second of time, and would never be again, was transferred to the sensitive plate.

Before changing she fetched two pictures that had been packed at the bottom of the cardboard box – a canvas stretched on a frame, and a water-colour mounted on board. The first was a view of the town from the far bank, with its spires and water-tower

174

rising among trees.

'Good, very good! I must get a photograph from that angle.
Make a good postcard,' said Mr Hamilton. 'H'm! These both
your work? Very nice indeed.' He picked up the sketch of a
dinghy under a group of red-gums, reflected softly in green water.

This was her opportunity. She clasped the paintings to her and
begged him to let her go two afternoons a week to the School of
Arts landscape class. Still life she was already doing at night; but
painting was more important to her than anything . . .

'Tch, tch! You'll soon be marrying and having a family, my
dear, and you'll forget all this nonsense. You won't stay single
long, if the young men of today are not stone blind. Er – how many
lessons a week?'

'Only two, Mr Hamilton. On Tuesdays and Thursdays, from
three o'clock. I'll come back and work at night, if you like.' She
was very lovely and appealing, leaning forward in the soft blue
dress with lips trembling with eagerness.

'No; I don't want you working back at night.' He sounded
quite gruff. 'But you could start earlier in the morning, I suppose.
All right. But don't go taking up portrait painting and putting me
out of business.'

The landscape class, with stools and easels and sketch-boxes,
tramped off twice a week to some vantage point to indulge in
plein-air painting, with all its delights and difficulties, from midges
landing in wet paint to the worse hazards of tiger-snakes and irate
bulls.

Daniel Wise, the principal, was a landscapist at heart, and expanded in the open air. Striding about behind his students, in an
old velvet jacket stained with colours like a paint-rag, he would
tell stories of his early student days in Melbourne, and of artists'
camps he had joined in the Dandenongs.

He had been a friend of Tom Roberts, and had stayed with him
and 'that clever young chap, Arthur Streeton', on the hilltop above
Heidelberg, where they had a hut overlooking the Yarra basin and
the long blue folds of the ranges.

'More than ten years ago . . . Ah, those were golden days,' he
would sigh, his greying beard ruffled wildly, his rather prominent
eyes staring at nothing. 'I'll never forget the hill of sunburnt grass,
and the view of the long Divide to the north-east, all dreaming
and remote . . . Great days, great days!'

And the students were careful not to look at him, for they knew that his eyes were moist with a facile emotion. Those others had dedicated themselves to art; he had married early, and had a large family, and now spent his time teaching in a small town while his own artistic fire dwindled away.

In her usual impulsive way Delie was ready to worship him, because he was her master, because he was older, and because he wore for her an almost visible aura as a man who talked to Roberts and Streeton. She was intrigued to learn that, like her, Roberts had come from England as a child and, like her, had worked for a photographer.

When Daniel Wise passed behind her easel the blood began to pound in her ears, she gripped the brush tightly and put on tiny, self-conscious brush-strokes until he had passed on. A brief word of praise made her glow with pleasure. He never said much before a picture was finished, except to indicate some fault in composition or drawing in the original sketch. Sometimes he took a brush and with a few deft touches of deep-toned colour transformed a pallid muddle into a picture.

He began to stop more often behind Delie, sometimes with an approving grunt, and to walk beside her when they were returning from an outdoor class. Gradually, as her awe grew less, they developed into friends; and the three other young women in the class showed that they resented this.

Delie didn't care; she was bored by their two subjects, clothes and boys, and preferred to talk to the men. She knew that they had labelled her as 'fast', but she was happy and absorbed in her work.

Her lonely and discouraged times came at night, when she sat in her cold bedroom sketching or reading, rather than join the stuffy types in the boarding-house parlour. If the night was mild, she opened her window and hung far out, when she could see past the side of the building the thick dark mass of trees that marked the river.

Why hadn't she done this earlier, come to Echuca to live while Adam was still here? Why had she failed him, why did he have to die? They still went round in her head, the old, unanswerable questions and regrets.

Her small collection of books, a print of Streeton's *Golden Summer* taken from a calendar, some geraniums on the window-sill, could not disguise the bare ugliness of the room. Beside the bed there was a rickety washstand, and a yellow-varnished duchess chest with a swinging mirror that would not stay in place unless a piece of cardboard was jammed in the side. Over this was draped a vivid striped silk scarf that she went without lunch for a week to buy. Bright canvases and painted boards, some unfinished, stood round the walls.

Colour was now a passion with her, colour more than form. She took less time and care than she should have done over her drawing, because she couldn't wait to squeeze out the lovely colours, so pure, so soft and delightful in texture, so exciting in their smell of oil.

This smell was more pleasing to her than the sweetest perfume; and Bessie Griggs declared that 'she always smelt like a paint-shop'. But canvas and paints were expensive. She begged cigar-box lids and other smooth pieces of wood from her friends to practise on.

Walking down High Street at lunch-time, she met her Uncle Charles in the buggy. He pulled in to the gutter, and she stood and patted Barney's glossy neck while she talked to him. Barney lifted his tail and dropped three spherical lumps of yellow dung on to the road.

At once she was thirteen years old again; she sat in the buggy staring at a heap of yellow dung about which the flies hovered, while her uncle told her that all her money was gone in the bank crash.

She shook off the memory and smiled up at Charles. 'I'm going to paint a picture of the *Philadelphia* when she comes in. The *Pride of the Murray* and the *Invincible* came in yesterday from the Darling. She shouldn't be long now.'

Delie was hatless. Her dark hair gleamed in the sun, glossy as the horse's coat, with rich amber lights in its sheen. He smiled down at her, but the melancholy droop of his eyes, the dispirited curve of his moustache, were accented by a sagging of his whole tall frame. Since Adam's death he had aged noticeably.

'Don't forget to show it to me, then. I'm bringing your auntie in to see the doctor again next week. She's got painfully thin, you know. I thought it was just with moping over Adam, but that pain in her back and side is worse, and the doctor seems to think it's something serious.'

'Poor Aunt Hester!' said Delie dutifully, but she thought to herself that her aunt would really be pleased to have a doctor's sanction for the self-pity she had indulged in for years. Now I'm

177

being malicious, she thought . . . But it was hard to forgive old injuries, to feel a Christian sympathy with someone like her aunt.

'I think she's better in other ways, though,' said Charles, looking at her anxiously. 'That last time when you came out to the buggy – I mean, she seemed quite glad to see you, none of that strangeness, that open hostility she showed when Adam died.'

'No-o. But I felt the antagonism there still, under the surface. She hasn't forgiven me, for whatever she imagined I did; but she seemed quite normal, if that's what you mean.'

'Yes, yes. Quite normal. Just what I think,' said Charles, relieved.

THIRTY-ONE

At lunch-time Delie would go every day down to the wharf to see what new steamers had come in. She greeted old friends among the captains, and asked for news of the *Philadelphia*.

Steamers were arriving from the Darling every day now. The wharf was alive with shunting trucks and swinging cranes and the rattle of steam winches, as the square bales of wool bearing the stamp of far western stations were transferred for their train journey to Melbourne. Not only the barges, but the flat decks of the steamers were piled high with wool; as much as two million pounds' worth had crossed this wharf in a single year.

On a clear day in June, when the slanting sun shone with a golden light that gave an illusion of warmth in the midst of winter, Delie saw the *Clyde* and the *Rothbury* tying up, the little *Bantam* beyond, and then another small side-wheeler, painted white. She couldn't see the name yet, but surely . . . Yes! It was the *Philadelphia*, her namesake, back from a thousand-mile trip into the far west of New South Wales.

She dodged under the iron rails that fenced off the working area of the wharf, and began to run, skipping over obstacles like thick mooring ropes and iron hooks. She went down the wooden stairs to the lower levels, and came out opposite the *Philadelphia*'s gangplank.

'To-om! Hi, Tom!' she called, but there was no answer. The

steamer appeared to be deserted.

Delie kilted up her serge skirt to her calves, crossed the gang-plank and climbed the narrow steps over the nearside paddle-box, intending to knock on the door of the main cabin, where she thought the captain might be dozing. She was nearly at the top when she heard a low, appreciative whistle.

She turned on the narrow steps, and dropped her skirts instantly. A large young man, with crisp, red-gold curls, was leaning against the housing of the boiler with his arms folded. He wasn't actually grinning, but there was a certain light in his eyes.

'Oh!' said Delie, with a slight flush. 'I was looking for Captain Tom. Is he aboard?'

'Not at the moment, no. Won't I do instead?'

There was a lazy insolence in his attitude as he leant there, with an old cap pushed to the back of his head; yet his voice was pleasant.

'I'm afraid not.' She lifted her chin and stalked down the steps. Her dignified descent was spoilt by a stumble on the second-to-last one. The stranger leapt forward and caught her arm under the elbow in a grip so strong that the bone tingled. 'Careful!' he said.

She disengaged her arm with some difficulty, and moved to the side. 'Are you a new member of the crew?' she asked distantly.

'Yes. I'm the mate. Any objections?'

'Oh, then you're an employee of mine. I'm part-owner of this steamer.'

'Then *you're* the original Philadelphia? She certainly is a trim craft.'

This could be taken two ways. Delie was silent.

'But I'm not exactly an employee. You see, I'm a part-owner too.'

'So Captain Tom has sold another share?'

'That's right. A half-share, to be exact.'

'Oh.' Delie felt herself growing pink again. Her miserable twenty-fifth share was known to this horrid man, and he was laughing at her. She hastened to escape. 'Would you please give Captain Tom a message for me? He's probably gone to look for me at my old address. Would you tell him I can be found at Hamilton's Studio, in High Street? Thank you.'

'Hamilton's, High Street. I won't forget, Miss Philadelphia.' He raised the cap from his shining curls. But she hastened across the gangplank (raising her skirt only the minimum necessary for safety) and up the dark steps, with a sense of discomfort.

Did the conceited beast think she wanted him to know her address? For of course he was far too handsome, in a rather burly fashion, to be anything but conceited; and what cheek, the way he had looked at her! She hoped she wouldn't see him again.

'Capital was needed, y'see; she needed a over'aul. That's why I've took on a partner, like.' Tom's big, awkward frame seemed to fill the little back room, as he balanced on a packing-case just inside the door. Delie wondered how he and the mate could both fit in the wheel-house. 'This young chap was left money by 'is gran'pa, an' wanted to put it into a steamer, so I sold 'im an arf-share. We could pay you back your fifty, Miss 'Delphia, if you was wantin' it.'

'Oh no, Tom! I love to think I own even a tiny little bit of her. I'd like to have a steamer of my own one day, and travel up and down the Murray and the Murrumbidgee and the Darling. Did you get up as far as Bourke this time? Walgett! Oh, I wish, I wish I could come on the next trip!'

'Well, Miss, you know 'ow it is . . .' Tom scratched his greying beard. His tanned forehead was wrinkled with the effort of expressing himself. 'You bein' a young leddy, and all. If ony the mate was married, now, we could take 'is wife along too as – as a sort of a, what d'you call it?'

'Chaperone? Oh yes, we have to remember the proprieties! Not that I'd care, but Uncle Charles is still my guardian. Oh, why did I have to be born a girl? It's not fair.'

Now why did I say that just now, about not wanting my fifty pounds back, she asked herself wonderingly. With that money I could have gone to Melbourne and the Gallery School for a year . . . But she was proud of the steamer, if only that wretched mate –

'What's his name?' she asked abruptly.

' 'Oose name?'

'That mate – your partner. I saw him down at the boat today.'

'Brenton Edwards, if y'll believe it. But 'e's known as Teddy Edwards on the river. Shaping as a good riverman, 'e is.'

Tom was fumbling in his waistcoat pocket (he was more smartly dressed than she had ever seen him, with a complete dark suit, a bowler hat he had forgotten to remove, and even boots on his feet). He now brought out five one-pound notes, which he counted on to her table. Delie stared. She had not expected any such return. Now she could lay in a lovely stock of paints and canvas.

On Saturday afternoon she gave up a picnic trip to Stewart's Bridge, so as to paint a picture of the *Philadelphia*. Tom had promised to move her down below the wharf and tie up against a background of trees as soon as the stores for down-river – flour, tea, rabbit-traps, sugar, bullets, chaff-bags, machinery – had been loaded.

She took her painting things, and an old, loose dress she used as a painting-smock, and went down to the river's edge. The boat was tied beneath a steep bank, but there was a path going down and a level place where she could set up her easel.

She did so in some excitement and haste. The light was just right, but it would not last. The steamer was partly shaded by an enormous gum tree that dappled the superstructure with a pattern of leaves.

She had no stool; she preferred to stand, and step back frequently to see the effect as she proceeded. With eyes half-closed she planned the balance of lights and darks, fixed the boundaries of her picture, and sketched in the contours and the darkest tones. Then came the delightful moment of sqeezing out the pure, new colours on to her palette.

Time passed unnoticed as she felt the picture begin to 'come'. Though the shadows had moved, and the light was becoming yellower with the declining sun, she had its final form fixed in her mind's eye.

With a new power and certainty she had not felt before, she worked surely and swiftly, every brush-stroke seeming to fall unerringly into place.

She added a highlight to the sparkling water beyond the shadow of the boat, and stepped quickly back to see the effect. She bumped hard into a sturdy someone who did not stagger or yield and inch.

Her mouth open to apologise, she turned quickly, a long hog's-hair brush in one hand, the palette and spare brushes in the other. A wisp of hair was falling in her eyes. There was a smear of viridian green on one cheek, and the faded painting-dress, daubed with many colours, hung in shapeless folds about her.

The blood rose in her clear cheeks as she saw who it was, and became conscious that Brenton Edwards was holding her at arm's length and looking at her – well, in the strangest fashion.

181

The next moment he was kissing her. She might have dropped her best, biggest brush into the sandy dirt, perhaps; she might even have jettisoned the palette, with its fresh and carefully mixed colours. Instead she submitted, stiffly at first, holding her cumbered hands at rigid right-angles. Then she sagged against him, lost, bewildered, given up to a new sensation.

Devoured by tigers, she thought confusedly. I shall die. I shall die . . . But now he was kissing her gently and more gently, a series of soft kisses that seemed to be taking farewell of her outraged lips. When at last he let her go she swayed, dizzy as if she had stood up too quickly after a long sleep.

He put out his arms to steady her; but as his head bowed above her again she woke to reaction. Rage filled her at this insolent stranger who had made her forget time, place, self, until her personality seemed to be dissolving in his.

She gripped the palette firmly and brought it down hard on his red-gold curls. 'You beast!'

He laughed with the surprise of it, a loud roar of uninhibited laughter that woke the echoes like a chorus of kookaburras. This, and the loss of the good oil-paint now decorating his hair with streaks of flake-white, cobalt, crimson and yellow ochre, enraged her further.

'Oh, you – you – you – !' she stammered. Tears of rage stood in her eyes. She dashed them away with the back of her wrist.

'Come now, don't tell me you've never been kissed before,' he said, clawing some of the paint out of his hair and stooping to wipe his fingers on a tuft of grass.

'Yes, but not like that! You know very well – '

'I thought – I didn't mean – '

'You thought I wouldn't mind! If a woman chooses to paint, or become and actress, or do anything unusual, you regard her as fair game!'

'No, really.' The mocking smile went out of his eyes, and they looked at her seriously and intently. She noticed for the first time that they were a clear, vivid blue-green, the colour of the sea on the south coast. 'I didn't mean any disrespect. I didn't think at all. I'm sorry. It was just that you crashed against me, and then you looked so sweet, with that funny old dress, and your hair coming down, and a smear of paint on your cheek . . .'

She looked down at the 'funny old dress' to hide the softening in her face; she looked up under her straight brows, and suddenly she began to smile. 'Do you know your hair is all the colours of the rainbow?'

'It was worth it.' He smiled; she scowled, and turned her back on him. She began gathering up her things, packing paints back into her box, folding her easel and slipping the wet canvas into the special carrying attachment.

'Can I see the picture?'

'No. It's not finished. I'll have to try to finish it at home, and now the colours are all spoilt on the palette, I'll have the trouble of mixing them again.' Her temper began to rise once more at the thought. 'Oh, *why* did you have to come blundering down here and interrupting me when I'd nearly finished?'

'Well, after all, the *Philadelphia* is my home. I was just coming on board quietly when *you* blundered into *me*.'

'Oh – !' She dipped a brush in a dipper of turpentine and wiped it vigorously on a rag.

'I wonder would you lend me a little of that? I don't believe there's any left on board.'

She looked at his parti-coloured hair, hesitated, and poured some turpentine on to a piece of rag. 'Here.'

'Thanks.' He took it and rubbed his hair while she cleaned the other brushes. The curls darkened, turned into ringlets, and glistened in the sun. She was conscious of an absurd wish to touch them, to run her fingers through them.

'Is that all right?'

'No, there's a large patch of cobalt over your left ear.'

He rubbed ineffectually. She reflected that it would be embarrassing for her if anyone saw the paint in his hair. He was quite capable of explaining how he came by it.

'Here, let me.' She poured some more turps on to a clean piece of rag. 'Bend you head!' The worst of the colour came off, and she gave a good tweak to the tuft of hair.

'Ouch!'

'That didn't hurt.'

'Not really, no.' He smiled at her with shut mouth, his brilliant but rather small eyes half-closed: a considering look. She didn't like it.

As if I were a picture and he was considering my tonal values, she thought, instantly upon her dignity again. She hastily finished packing up. 'Turn you back, please,' she ordered.

He obediently swung round and contemplated the bank. She

dragged off the painting-dress, disarranging her hair still more, and stuffed the dress into her satchel.

'Now good-bye, Mr Edwards.'

'But of course I'll carry your easel for you, Miss Gordon.'

'No! I absolutely forbid it.' And she marched off.

With a very slight shrug, he looked after her. Then he turned and crossed the gangplank to the *Philadelphia*'s deck.

THIRTY-TWO

Charles ordered his second rum and stood looking unseeingly at the rows of bottles in the dim bar of the Shamrock Hotel. He would have to go next door to Hamilton's in a minute and break the news to Delie; but at present he needed the fortifying warmth of spirits.

So Hester was dying! The doctor had made his diagnosis, and it was as bad as could be. Cancer in an advanced stage; no use to operate.

He thought with remorse of his old attitude to Hester's confirmed invalidism, the feeling that her aches and pains and headaches were convenient ones that came on only when she was crossed, or wanted sympathy.

He dreaded the thought of sick-room duties, the last hours, the suffering he would be forced to watch . . . Their marriage had ceased in all but name years ago, and yet she had once been his bride. And Hester flatly refused to go to hospital.

Delie – ? No, she would be useless as a nurse, even if Hester would have her. He would get a trained nurse to live in. And Bella, old Bella was wonderful, so gentle and kind. Better than that sly Annie who had given notice, like a rat sensing trouble on a sinking ship, more than a month ago.

Delie fixed her eyes on the slow turning of the windmill, the glint and quiver of gum leaves beyond the window. Her uncle had just left, and she was trying to take in his news. Aunt Hester dying! And she had not been able to shed a tear.

It was as though some petrifying process had taken place in her

184

emotions since Adam died. She felt nothing.

She hadn't even offered to give up her job, to go and nurse her aunt. What had she said? 'I'll come and see her if you like.'

Oh, generous offer! Her aunt had taken her in when she was an orphan in a strange land. She was her own mother's sister.

Yet Delie knew she would be useless as a nurse. And what if Aunt Hester, in spite of her more friendly manner, still held the same fantastic suspicions about herself and Uncle Charles? No, she could never go back to the farm to live.

The little steamer *Julia* was struggling up-river, keeping close against the bank to avoid the current. The steady movement, the regular chuffing of the funnel and the *chunk, chunk, chunk* of the paddles lulled Delie into a peaceful state.

She watched in a dream the pale grey trunks of the big trees, the forests of saplings and the fallen logs slip by, and the shallow, steeply sloping banks tiger-striped with sun and shadow.

The sand of the banks, gripped by the hand-like roots of great flooded gums, was a warm yellow; the shadows were indigo. Half-closing her eyes to appreciate the tones, she saw a ghostly fence, as of pale wire-netting, in front of the trees. On opening them again, she found that it was the high-water mark from last year's flood, showing at the same level on all the trunks.

Suddenly a grassy clearing swam into sight, then the grey posts and rails of the sheepyards. They had arrived.

Here she was back in the landscape of her past, as if she had travelled in time as well as space. Every tree and bush, the curve of the river sweeping round the bend, the angle of the trees leaning above it, spoke of a happiness that was gone.

Going up through the garden, she welcomed old friends: the vine-arbour where they used to have dinner on hot days, the pine tree she used to climb to get away from her aunt, the scented jasmine burdening the veranda with a mass of fragile stems and trailing white stars.

And there was the veranda rail, worn and grey, that was so mixed into her most tender and painful memories that she swerved away, thinking, No, I can't bear any more just now. She went instead down the side of the house to the back door.

The dogs greeted her with wild barking. Old Bella, fat and comfortable-looking as ever, burst out of the kitchen with her brown hands outstretched, her dark eyes alight with pleasure.

'Craikey, Miss 'Delphia, you all-a-same grown-up young lady!'

'Well, it's been nearly three years, Bella.' Holding the cook's hands in a warm clasp, she thought how Bella looked exactly the same; but she guessed that the kitchen did not shine as before now that Hester was not in charge. She had made the trip specially to oversee the cooking of dinner next day in honour of the minister, who was coming out to give her aunt Holy Communion.

'And how is Jacky and everybody? And Lucy – is she still about?'

'No more. Juss plurry black fella, that one,' said Bella with scorn. 'Her live all-a-time longa camp, longa river!'

'And Minna? You hear how Minna is lately?'

'No good, Miss 'Delphia. Her close-up finish, longa mission. Pewmonia, Jacky say.'

A young lubra, about the age Minna had been when they first came to the farm, with the same bright dark eyes and attractive figure, came to the kitchen door and shyly withdrew again.

'Delie! There you are!' cried Charles from the house door. 'Come in, child, your aunt has been getting worked up in case you'd missed the steamer.'

Delie followed down the familiar passage with a sick feeling in the pit of her stomach. She had to face Hester in the front bedroom which she had not entered since the day Adam died. She feared and hated illness; and how was she to greet her former enemy, doomed to incurable illness and a lingering death? How would Hester greet her?

But she need not have worried. Hester fell naturally into her old style: 'Come in, come in, child, it's ages since I heard the steamer at the landing, where on earth have you been? I told Charles to see if you'd arrived, but he would fuss about putting my bed-jacket on and moving the pillows and the flowers and goodness knows what . . . Where that nurse is or what she's doing with herself is beyond me – '

'She's getting your lunch ready in the kitchen,' Charles interposed quietly.

'They're all the same, there's Annie that I trained to do everything just as I like goes and leaves me when I need her, because she was restless after old 'Lijah died, but what did she expect but to be left a widow, marrying an old fellow like that, I'd like to know? Now, I've got the minister coming out tomorrow to give me Holy Communion, and I know you don't like housework, but at least I taught you how things should be done. Will you watch over Bella for me, and see that the meal is dished up properly?

For of course we'll have to ask him to midday dinner after that long drive.'

'Yes, Aunt,' said Delie. She felt as if she were twelve years old again, and all that had passed since had never been. Hester did not seem so very changed. Her voice seemed strong, her face was still ruddy with its network of red veins, though the cheeks had sunken in a little, and the once piercing black eyes were lack-lustre and filmed at the edges of the iris.

Only a trace of grey showed in the straight black hair. Delie felt cheered. This did not look like a doomed person; the doctor must be mistaken.

'Have you much pain?' she asked. 'I was so sorry to – hear – that it has become worse . . . That is, to – to find you in bed – ' she floundered.

'Yes, it's worse; much worse,' said Hester, with a half-pleased, triumphant air. 'I knew there was something there. Nobody knows what I've suffered.' But the old fretful whine had gone out of the phrase; Hester, in becoming the centre of anxious attention, had achieved some kind of happiness at last.

That afternoon, in a fit of remorse over her laziness and un-helfulness in the old days, Delie organised Bella in a thorough house-cleaning, down to the brass candle-brackets on the piano. A duck was already dressed for the next day's dinner, and Bella was instructed to make golden pudding, which she could be trusted to turn out perfectly.

The nostalgic sound of clucking hens, the clank of the windmill pumping water up from the river, woke Delie with a sense of contentment in her old room.

Then she realised with dismay that she had dreamt not of Adam, but of Brenton Edwards. She had not seen him since the day by the river-bank; she had kept away from the *Philadelphia*, though she had seen Tom several times in the town, and she tried not to think of Brenton. But although she banished him from her conscious mind, the mate would appear in dreams; always larger than life, gay, golden-haired, vital and disturbing. When Mr Polson arrived in the house sulky, half an hour late for one o'clock dinner, he seemed a pallid spectre beside the vivid dream-Brenton.

He was nervous and apologetic and voluble. The floods were so bad on the low road that he had been forced to come the long way round, and he feared he had kept the poor patient sufferer waiting.

187

Hester in fact had had no breakfast or lunch, so that no profane food should pass her lips before the symbolic body and blood of her Saviour; but as she had little appetite it was no hardship.

At the same time she had felt she should refuse her usual sedative, and the nagging pain (getting a little worse with each week that passed) had begun to worry her.

Hearing of this fortitude from the nurse, Mr Polson cried, 'I will administer the Sacrament to this brave sufferer at once; but by all means let her take a sedative first, that she may be in a state of grace to receive it.'

'It won't take effect immediately,' said Hester, taking the powder gratefully, 'so please go and have your dinner. I don't want mine yet, anyway. It will distress me far more to think of my good roast duck spoiling in the oven, than to wait while you eat. Go on, do.'

Delie, coming in with some freshly picked jasmine in a crystal vase, heard for the first time a note of weariness, of weakness in the harsh voice. 'Yes, it's already dished up,' she said, noticing that Mr Polson showed signs of interest at the mention of roast duck. 'Not cooked as perfectly as Auntie would have done it, but as good as may be. Do come on.' And at her smile the minister's pale face flushed to the roots of his pale hair. Hester lay back and closed her eyes, a faint smile on her lips.

The duck was all that Hester could have wished. Charles, stimulated by all this unusual company, conversed and carved with a flourish. But when the steamed pudding was brought in a hush fell on them all. The outside edges looked light and appetising, but the middle had caved in. Raw pudding was oozing over the plate in a gluey yellow mass.

'Oh, Bella!' cried Delie as the cook made hastily for the door. 'The pudding – did it go off the boil?'

'No more, Miss 'Delphia. Him boil too-much, boil all-a-time. Mine tink too much pflour longa belly that one puddin. Mine tink Mr Polson likem big-pfella puddin.'

'Very well, Bella; never mind. Bring some jam and the loaf of new bread.'

She looked at the minister, ready to catch his eye and laugh at this simple tribute to his supposed appetite for pudding. But he was gazing pointedly out the window; his ears were pink. The word 'belly' not in a biblical context was scarcely fit for mixed company. These natives were really very crude, he thought.

Charles and Delie exchanged an understanding grin. The nurse stolidly ate bread and butter. 'Scrape me a bit off the outside, I like 'em soggy,' said Charles.

'Don't breathe a word about it to Aunt Hester, will you?'

'I won't.' He gave her a conspirator's wink.

The nurse was a taciturn person, middle-aged, heavy-faced, with circles under her eyes and a tightly compressed mouth. She seemed to bear some secret grudge against life. Delie would not, she felt, like to be helpless in her hands. But Charles had said she was an excellent nurse.

She said little at table, only showing a flash of life when Mr Polson mentioned the church choir. 'I used to sing in a choir in Melbourne, once. I had a good contralto voice,' she said, and lapsed into silence again.

Charles looked at her with new interest. 'Mine is a tenor,' he said. 'I've been told it's quite good; if only I had had the training . . .'

While Delie helped to clear away the profane repast, the minister took out the symbols of the ritual feast, the consecrated bread and wine, the holy chalice; and donned the white surplice and embroidered stole of his office.

He suddenly took on the ancient dignity of the Church, and became impressive. He really looked distinguished, she thought, with his pale, fine hair and thin features above the white robe, and his deep-set, fanatical eyes.

A small table covered with a clean white cloth was carried into the sick-room, with the paraphernalia of the ritual set out upon it.

Delie knelt in the room and took a physical part in the service, but her mind strayed. She noticed that the minister had well-shaped hands and the nails were beautifully kept, but the high, nasal sing-song he adopted when praying meant no more to her than the singing of the crickets outside the window, as he began the Prayer for the Sick:

'O Father of mercies, and God of all comfort, our only help in time of need: We fly unto Thee for succour in behalf of this Thy servant, here lying . . . in great weakness of body . . .'

After the service, Hester was left alone with her spiritual adviser. Delie went out to the kitchen and helped to butter some hot scones. She came back to ask Mr Polson if he would take a cup of tea before starting on the long drive.

'Your aunt is a brave sufferer, Miss Gordon,' he said, accepting one of Bella's rather heavy scones with home-made butter.

'Yes,' said Delie shortly. 'She has told you that – she is dying?'

'Ah, yes.' He swallowed a piece of scone, and coughed. 'But she is truly resigned; a thoroughly Christian woman. She looks forward to meeting her son again in Heaven.'

Delie stared at the teapot. 'I wish I could be as sure as that.'

'Ah, you have Doubts, Miss Gordon?'

He said it as though Doubts were an infectious disease, like mumps or measles.

'Sometimes I have no doubts at all. On the contrary, I feel quite sure . . . that there is nothing beyond.'

'Ah, Miss Gordon, you do not know what you are saying! All doubts are resolved in the light of faith. It shall all be made clear to us one day, by the One who knows all things.'

This seemed both wordy and vague to her. She looked out the window at the pale, distant sky, at the glimpse of curving river. 'You mean,' she said, 'that God knows about disease and suffering yet does nothing about it? Or that He *can* do nothing?'

'There is a mighty plan which we mortals cannot comprehend. We can only pray.'

But she thought obstinately, Pray to what? And how do we know our prayers are heard?

THIRTY-THREE

When the South African War broke out, it was just something in the paper, like an earthquake in Japan or an uprising in Bolivia; not of the first importance to the pleasure-loving young people with whom Delie now spent her week-ends.

She played tennis, went on dray picnics and steamer excursions and to balls and tea-parties. She knew that she was considered 'fast', and that the mammas of eligible young men did not approve of her.

Among Bessie's set her position was unusual. First, she earned her own living. Then she lived alone, which was not quite 'nice', she was an orphan, and she did not have much money. In the eyes of Society she was trebly damned.

It was partly her own fault, for she cared little for conventions. The two young men who vied with each other to be her escort were not slow to take advantage of this; and when one of them managed to kiss her in a quiet corner, he boasted of it to the other, and embroidered the extent of his conquest, so that each became progressively a little more daring.

Delie accepted all this with a detached amusement. Neither of them could rouse in her the flood of feeling that Adam had, or even stir her to anger as Brenton Edwards had done . . . Coolly she noted their growing excitement and enslavement. It was a game to which she could call a halt whenever she felt inclined.

Her highest moments came when she was alone, or when she was painting; yet she loved company and could be as gay and foolish as any young thing. She flung herself into picnics and balls with thoughtless enjoyment, until suddenly it would all fall away from her. She would stand apart and stare as the whirling figures on the dance floor became as unreal as puppets in a marionette-show, while a terrible sadness descended upon her, objectless and profound. Or she would slip away from a noisy picnic to stand on the brink of the river, whose endless onward glide filled her with melancholy while it yet harmonised with something unresting in her own spirit.

The delicate sky-colours reflected in the still water, the very shape of the soft dark trees against the skyline, filled her with an emotion she could not express. She wanted to expand through all the visible world; she was the river, and the endless flow, and the soft, limitless sky.

It was the river, more than any person, that bound her to Echuca; the ancient river of the blackfellows' legend that came down out of the high places after the old woman and her magic Snake, and followed its winding course across half a continent, to end on a far away coast.

There was not a soul in the town to whom she could really talk and open her inmost thoughts. There was something hollow about Daniel Wise, and the boys she went out with she could not take seriously. It came as a shock to her to realise suddenly that they were men, about to take their part in a man's world. For Kevin Hodge, coming shyly to her office door one morning in a new khaki uniform, announced that he was having his picture taken before leaving for South Africa.

He had been in training with the militia for some time, and was to go with the next contingent from Victoria. Two others, George Barrett and Tony Wisden, were going too.

She was dismayed, shaken with apprehension for his young

191

defencelessness against those huge and horried Boers about whom she read such frightening tales. It seemed unfair that Kevin, with his smooth pink cheeks and dark eyes fringed with long lashes like a girl's, should be sent away to fight them.

She promised to give him a picture of herself to take to South Africa.

Two weeks later she was sitting in her room after dinner, making a study of her own left hand in crayon, when a tap came at her door. It was her landlady, smirking rather unpleasantly, to announce a visitor – a young man.

Surprised (for she had seen Kevin only on Sunday night, and John, the other young man, was away in Melbourne), she ran downstairs. Kevin was waiting nervously just inside the front door. The pupils of his eyes were dilated so that they looked intensely black, and his girlish cheeks were flushed.

'Delie! Can you come out for a while?'

'Out? But I'm rather tired, Kev. And I should be working at my sketches – '

'Never mind. Get a coat, and come.'

She hesitated for a moment, conscious of the disapproving stare of the landlady somewhere in the background. Then the suppressed excitement in his manner conveyed itself to her, her tiredness disappeared in a moment, and with a brief 'Wait outside for me', she flew up the stairs, slipped on a long coat and wound a filmy 'fascinator' about her throat and hair.

Kevin was waiting tensely. He came to her quickly, and took her arm in a hot, nervous grip. He was sturdy, not very tall, and they walked in perfect unison; the movement of their feet, their legs, the swing of their hips was a pleasure felt all down their sides. They walked along High Street to the end, and towards the ornate red-gum arch that marked the entrance to the park. Delie stiffened and drew back. 'Not there, Kev!'

'Where then? I want to say good-bye to you properly. Do you know why I brought you out? We're leaving almost at once, the day after tomorrow. I've brought you my picture.' He handed her the stiff cardboard print, and in the dim gaslight she could see his young, fresh face smile confidently out at her from beneath the army hat turned up at the side. She tucked it away in her sleeve.

'Let's go back the other way, along the river.'

'Towards the bridge? All right, but hurry,' he grumbled. 'I want to get away from people where I can kiss you.'

She gave his arm a little squeeze. His excitement had roused a recklessness in her. What if anyone saw her walking alone with a young man in the dark streets, towards the lonely scrub by the river? She had no reputation to lose, anyway.

They turned down beside the silent foundry, and just above the wharf, where a train with a long line of goods trucks was shunting, they came in sight of the dwindled summer river, with stars swimming on its calm expanse. Below the steep banks there was a wide space for walking which would be under water when the floods came down.

There was no sound but the echoing call of a wild duck or water-hen in the reeds on the far bank. The river slid by with silent, unhurried motion. Kevin held her hand and led the way until they had drawn well away from the town, and passed beneath the big cement pillars of the bridge; then he led her back a little from the water's edge, took off his coat and spread it over the springy bushes, and sat her gently upon it. He knelt before her and gazed at her dim, pale face in the double starlight reflected from the water and sky.

'You'll be cold!' she protested.

'No, I'm burning. Give me you little hands to hold.'

'They're not little.' She felt inclined to giggle. 'They're large and clumsy.'

He took her hands and pressed them against his thin shirt, so that she could feel the strong beating of his heart.

'I wish I could make your heart beat like that.'

'Perhaps you could.' Oh, why did she say these stupid, meaningless, coquettish things? Her heart was dead, and buried in Adam's grave.

'Could I? . . . Could I?' he whispered, his breath hot on her ear. She kept her head averted, but his lips came seeking softly after hers, his young soft mouth enclosed her own, and she sighed with dreamy pleasure; yet her pulse kept up its even beat.

As in a dream she felt his hands explore her softness and warmth. She had never seemed so beautiful to herself, it was as if she had never known she had a body before; it was revealed only under his delicately searching fingers. At last she thrust him away and sat up, the scarf falling about her shoulders, her hair slipping from its knot.

'Delie! Delie! I love you.' She was touched by the eager trembling of his voice, but she moved further away from him.

'But I don't love you, Kevin.'

'But you must, you must, just a little! Why did you come?'

'I'm sorry you're going away, and you wanted to say good-bye. Now I must really get back, or I'll be locked out.'

'You won't let me say good-bye to you properly.' His mouth was sulky, he flung himself down and buried his face in his arms.

She was moved by his small boy's attitude, and in the dim light the shape of his head, the thick hair, looked like Adam's. She was sharply reminded of that moonlit night when she had refused Adam, and sent him to his death.

And this boy, too, was probably going to his death . . . She put out a hand and stroked the thick dark hair. He grasped it and kissed the fingers, palm and wrist. When he drew her down again beside him she did not resist.

They were both very young, very inexperienced; but Delie had enough knowledge to realise that little had really happened, that she did not need to fear a fate like Minna's. They walked back almost in silence, his arm close about her, their bodies moving in unison down the quiet street.

He kissed her long and insistently outside the door. 'Let me come up with you,' he murmured. 'Let me stay with you all night.'

She shook her head firmly. She was beginning to feel rather amazed at herself. It had all been unimportant, almost as if happening to someone else. 'It's impossible, Kev. I'm sorry.'

But as she went up to bed she felt warm and molten, as if some hard shield of metal about her heart had softened and run.

She sat down on the edge of the bed, unwinding the fascinator thoughtfully from her disarranged hair. Then she went to the drawer and took out a small print she'd had made from the large portrait in the blue gown. (Mr Hamilton had asked her to tint one of these; and it was such a success that it now stood in the studio window to attract customers.)

She put the picture Kevin had given her carefully away in the drawer, and wrapped the other to give him. Then she flung herself down on the bed and stared at the ceiling. Would she ever really love anyone again? She would write Kevin long letters at the front, she would knit him khaki socks and send him books; she would be a sister to him, but that was all.

Before the dwindled summer river stopped all traffic, Delie had a letter delivered to her by one of the last paddle-steamers to get in to Echuca – and she had taken ten days to come up from Swan Hill, warping over all the bad patches. The letter came from Bourke, away in the far west of New South Wales. With a sudden inexplicable excitement, which made her tear the letter anyhow from its envelope, she turned to the rather cramped signature of a man not used to holding a pen. As she had expected: Brenton Edwards. He wrote in a careless, schoolboyish hand. She turned over the pages and felt the inked words with her fingers, as though they had a physical life of their own. She smoothed back the letter and began at the beginning.

Dear Miss Gordon,
   I am sending this letter by hand, with a mate of mine, as I don't trust the mails, but I do trust the skipper of the *Kelpie* to get through to Echuca if it's at all possible. It is bad news I have to tell you, I'm afraid.
   It's about poor old Tom. He was checking the engine when Charlie wasn't too good, and in stepping over the paddle-shaft got his trouser-leg caught in a cleat we use for winching sometimes. His leg was torn off before anyone could do anything. We just got him to Bourke in time to die in hospital.
   Well, he was always scared of ending up in an Old Men's Home where they wouldn't let him chew baccy or swear. He's safe from that, anyway.

Delie skipped ahead a few lines and saw: 'So now you are the owner of a paddle-steamer – half a steamer, anyway . . .' It seemed that Tom had always meant to leave the *Philadelphia* to her, and he'd been conscious long enough to sign a paper leaving her his share. Brenton Edwards had taken over as skipper, as he had his master's ticket. They would probably be discharging at Swan Hill this year.

   You'll be glad to know that Tom did not suffer too much at the end, he was very weak with the shock and loss of blood and just seemed to fall asleep. I made a cross out of the *Philadelphia*'s steering-pole, he was that proud of her I thought he'd like to keep a piece of her near, even though she killed him.

Before she had properly taken in the sense of the words, she had noticed unwillingly one or two spelling mistakes, a slip of grammar. She had wondered so much what sort of a letter he would write! But it was a good letter, it showed more sensibility than she would have expected of him.

Then the sense of the letter swept over her. The *Philadelphia* was hers; or half hers, anyway. And Tom – dear, kindly, rough, generous Tom – was no more.

Delie sat still in her little office, and felt a slow, hot tear fall on the hand that held the letter. Dear old Tom, to have escaped the sea, and then come to such an end! She groped for her handkerchief, that was always stained with Prussian blue, sepia and vermilion. This was only the second time she had cried in years – the other time was when the three Echuca boys left by train to join their contingent in Melbourne. And it was not for them she had wept, but for herself; the hot hissing engine, trembling with leashed power, the crowd, the flags, the stirring music of the band, had filled her with a wild discontent, a longing to be a man and setting off for the other side of the world.

When her uncle came in the next day to see her she bounded up from her table, full of the importance of her news, eager to show him that her investment of fifty pounds, which Charles had always regarded so doubtfully, had repaid her tenfold.

One look at his face made her bite back the eager words. 'What is it? Is Aunt Hester worse?'

'Yes dear. The end is – mercifully – very near. She suffers a great deal now, and she's not easy in her mind either. It's been a strain listening to her these last few weeks. It's dreadful, it's – ' His lips quivered a little out of control; he groped for the packing-case and sat down.

Delie felt ashamed; she had almost forgotten her aunt's illness. Charles had come to ask her to return to the farm and stay until the end. Hester wanted to see her, seemed anxious to make her peace before it was too late, and she needed nursing for twenty-four hours a day now. It was too much for the one nurse.

When Charles had gone Delie asked Mr Hamilton for indefinite leave.

'Your aunt, eh?' he said doubtfully, tilting back his head to look at her through his pince-nez. 'Hasn't she any daughters of her own?'

'Oh no, Mr Hamilton! I'm a sort of adopted daughter, she

brought me up since I was twelve when I lost my own mother and father, and then her only son was killed' (how easily she could say it now, without the old bitter constriction of the throat!) 'and she has no one but me. My mother was her sister, and –'

'All right, all right,' he said drily. 'Come back as soon as you can.'

THIRTY-FOUR

Beyond the half-drawn curtains at the french windows the summer sun beat down upon the land. Glassy in the heat, scarcely moving between its steep banks, the river mirrored the blue sky and leaning trees in an imaged world as perfect in detail as the real one. Though the water of which the mirror was made slowly passed away and was replaced by new water from above the bend, the reflection did not change; but like the rainbow on the waterfall remained constant, always different in its components yet always apparently the same.

Delie moved restlessly to the windows and looked out, then back at her aunt. Beside the bed the lamp now burned day and night, and meant more to the sick woman, whose whole world had narrowed to these four walls, than the rising and setting of the sun.

In the lamplight her yellow, waxen skin seemed stretched over the bones, so that nose and forehead had a new prominence, while the eyes were sunk deep in their sockets. She turned her head wearily, and asked, 'Did you say it was moonlight, dear? A lovely clear night?'

'Yes, Auntie.' The night before she had mentioned that it was full moon. Now it was broad day, the blaze of noon filled the garden, shadows were at their smallest and blackest; but of what use to say so?

'Would you like a drink?' she asked instead.

'Yes . . . I think so. When can I have my sleeping-powder?'

'You just had it, Auntie, half an hour ago. Is the pain bad?'

'Yes, it's very bad.' Her mouth, before rather loose and red-lipped, had become compressed, turned down in an expression of

197

bitter resignation, the lips a thin line. Delie held the glass to them. Her aunt's fingers, yellowish, waxen, curled weakly about the glass without being able to hold its weight.

Hester began to fling her head from side to side on the pillow, as if trying to escape. Now and then a moan came from her, or a cry: 'Oh God, have mercy!'

Delie rushed from the room to get the nurse, who had been having her morning tea. She walked briskly up the passage, her stiff apron rustling, adjusting her starched cuffs.

'It's not as bad as it sounds, you know,' she said. 'They make a lot of fuss, that's all.'

Delie looked at the small, tight mouth, the heavy jowl, the eyes deep-sunken and ringed with shadow. What had life done to this woman? She looked like one who had received no mercy, and meant to give none.

'Oh Nurse, I want my medicine. It's bad, it's very bad today.'

'You had it half an hour ago, Mrs Jamieson.'

'But give me some more, just one more. The doctor doesn't know, one doesn't help any more.'

'I couldn't take the responsibility. In three hours –'

'Three hours!' Hester began to cry weakly.

'I will take the responsibility,' said Delie, picking up the packet of opiates from the washstand.

'Give me those!' The nurse snatched them from her hand. 'I am in charge here, Miss Gordon.' She slipped the package into the pocket of her apron. Her face was stony.

Fortunately the doctor was due on one of his infrequent visits that afternoon. Blessedly soon after the injection he gave her, the tortured twisting of the features, the flinging of the head from side to side, the helpless moans had stopped, and Hester sank into a heavy-breathing sleep.

Delie spoke to him as she went with him out to his sulky, telling him what had happened that morning and asking him to leave some stronger opiate.

'I told her she would be more comfortable in hospital,' he said rather impatiently, drawing on his yellow gloves. 'She wouldn't hear of it, and now she's too weak to be moved.'

'Surely, though, the sooner it's over the better? There's no hope of recovery, is there?'

'None.'

'Then why can't you give her some help? You wouldn't let a dog suffer like that, you'd put it out of misery.'

'I've increased the dose; but if you increase it too soon it loses its power, and the only dose effective for the pain would also be lethal. And that we haven't the right to give. In the eyes of the law –'

'The law! What does the law know about suffering?'

He shrugged his heavy shoulders and climbed into the sulky. 'At least it won't be long now. She's very weak.'

For a while Hester seemed better; though so painfully thin she did not seem to be in pain, but slept easily and woke with a more tranquil expression than Delie had ever seen on her face – that detached, faraway look of one who is about to leave the world.

Towards evening she was alone in the room with her aunt when she woke, and Delie was almost startled at the mild and loving look Hester bent upon her. 'Charlotte!' she cried suddenly, loud and clear.

'What is it, Auntie? It's me Delie.'

'Oh! Child, I thought you were your mother for a moment. I've been dreaming, dreaming, dreaming . . .'

'You've had a good sleep.'

'I'll go to sleep for the last time soon. Then I'll see Lottie again, and Adam. They're waiting for me over there, on the other side of the river. It won't be long now.'

Delie looked silently at the floor.

'I wanted to say to you, it was why I asked Charles to bring you here, that I – I was wrong to accuse you of Adam's death. He was a headstrong, wilful boy, and perhaps . . . All the same, it would have been better if you had never come to us. Yes, I wish I had never seen you.'

Delie looked up, startled and shocked. In the faded black eyes was the old sparkle of anger.

'I've tried to forgive you; I've prayed; but there it is, I can't. I'm sorry, Delie, but life's been too hard on me. I can't change now. I don't hate you any more, I haven't the strength to love or hate anyone, but in my heart I haven't forgiven you.'

'Would you like me to go back to Echuca then? I only came –'

'No, no, I like to have you here. Charles is hopeless, he seems frightened of the sickroom, he hardly ever comes near me; and to tell you the truth, I don't like that nurse.'

'Neither do I . . . Sh-h, her she comes.'

The nurse came in with a cup of beef tea and began feeding it to the patient with sippets of bread; but after a few mouthfuls

Hester turned her head away.

'I don't want it. I don't want to eat. Nothing has any taste. Delie, go out and get some sunshine. She's looking very pale and peaky, isn't she, Nurse?'

'The sun has set, Mrs Jamieson.'

Delie stepped out through the french windows. There was still enough light for Charles, sitting on the end of the veranda outside the drawing-room, to read his paper. The river gleamed like polished steel between the trees, and gnats danced in little clouds against the pale sky.

'Why don't you go in and see her?' she said in a low voice. 'Her mind seems very clear tonight, yet I've a feeling she's very near the end.'

'Yes, yes, I must.' Charles folded his paper with guilty haste. 'But I sometimes think I only annoy her.'

'I used to think that about myself, but it seems she likes to see us.'

He walked, lean and stooped, along the veranda and entered his wife's room.

Two days later Hester began to cough. All that day and all night, every thirty seconds, sleeping or waking, she coughed. The next morning, Saturday, Charles set out early in the buggy to fetch the doctor; but soon after he had gone she stopped coughing and lapsed into a coma. Her jaw had fallen, her breath came stertorously and slowly. Every now and then it stopped briefly, as though the breathing mechanism had forgotten its work; then would come a few rapid breaths as though trying to catch up, then another pause. Each time it stopped Delie held her breath too, and waited . . .

Then Hester began to grow restless. Her head turned from side to side on the pillow, her brow puckered, she muttered and moaned. The head turned and turned, as though to escape from something unbearable. In desperation, Delie tried to call her back.

'Auntie, Aunt Hester, what is it? Can you hear me?' she cried, taking her hand.

The head stopped for an instant, the closed lids fluttered, struggled to rise; but only a glimpse of a white, turned-up eyeball was seen. The restless turning began again.

'Oh, God, why doesn't the doctor come?'

'She's only dreaming,' said the nurse.

'How do you know?' cried Delie, turning on her fiercely. 'How

200

can *you* know what she's suffering?'

Just then the barking of the dogs announced the return of the buggy or the doctor's arrival. Delie ran out the back door and saw with relief the doctor's bulky form descending from his trap. She wanted to kiss his hands, lifting out so carefully the little black bag that contained the magic of peaceful sleep for the weary, of sweet release from pain.

He felt Hester's pulse and at once took a syringe out of the bag and filled it. 'Are you awake, Mrs Jamieson?' he said loudly and clearly. 'I am just going to give you something to help you to rest.'

Even as they watched, the drug flowed through her veins, and floated her high above the tides of pain and torment. The brow smoothed, the mouth sagged open, the eyelids lay flat in the hollows of the cavernous eye-sockets.

The doctor began his examination, while Delie yet hovered in the door. Suddenly he gave a sharp exclamation, took out a handkerchief and held it to his nose.

'Nurse! She's had a terrific haemorrhage. I've never . . . Ugh! Will you leave the room, please?' he added sternly to Delie, who had turned deathly white as a foetid stench was wafted towards her. She fled out of doors and down to the river, breathing hard, hard, emptying her lungs of that horror and filling them with the clean, hot scent of dry grass bleaching in the sun.

It was not until she heard the doctor's trap leaving that she came slowly, unwillingly, back to the house. As she came in the front door the nurse came out of Hester's room.

'The doctor says, that to all intents and purposes she's already gone. She won't come out of this coma. It's only a matter of time.'

'Yes . . . I wonder what has kept my uncle? Is she likely to go at any time?'

'Yes. Yet she may hang on till tomorrow. Though how she can still live after what came away this afternoon – ' and she launched with a gloomy relish into details that made Delie turn faint and sick.

She sat down alone in the drawing-room. There was nothing to do but wait and listen. The pauses in the heavy, snoring breaths seemed to lengthen into minutes. She waited, with a kind of sickening excitement: was this the end? But always, with a series of jerks, the breathing began again.

Bella came in with tea on a tray; she drank a cup mechanically, and went across to call the nurse. Her aunt's face was a mask of death, the waxen skin moulded over the skull, the eyes sunken, the jaw helpless; but still the nerves carried on their useless task, the breath rasped in and out. The candles were lit, but still Charles did not come. Delie went outside and wandered about restlessly. She felt an aversion to the nurse's heavy face, a physical oppression in being alone with her.

She had not touched her painting things. She could not detach her mind, fall into the trance of observation where she was merely an instrument that recorded, in delicate vibrations, the rhythms of nature. She felt out of tune with the whole world, the familiar pattern of the stars was alien and without meaning. She came in again and suggested that the nurse go and rest while she took over. By half-past ten there was no change; the nurse came back, and she crossed to the drawing-room again.

At last, about midnight, when she was dozing in her chair, the nurse came in and announced quietly, 'She's gone, Miss Gordon.'

'What! Why didn't you call me? Is Mr Jamieson back yet?'

'No. I called you as soon as I was sure. Do you want me to do the laying out? There's an extra charge for last offices.'

'Yes, yes, of course,' she cried, feeling a spasm of disgust for the woman's cold efficiency. She went across the passage to her aunt's room, full of guilt and compunction that she had let Hester die alone with that impersonal creature. Yet death must always be a lonely business, even among troops of weeping friends.

Hester looked much the same; her mouth still open, her eyes closed, she seemed to sleep, but more deeply and peacefully than before. After the noisy breaths the room was deathly still. No sound would issue again through those lips which had been so tightly, so bitterly compressed, and now in their helpless sagging showed the complete surrender of the will.

It was nearly one, and the nurse was just finishing her task, when the sound of roused dogs announced Charles's return. Delie waited till she heard the back door open. Charles came in noisily and went straight to his room at the back. She walked along the passage and tapped at his door.

'All right, m'dear, all right. Bit late, what? How – how's m'wife?' he muttered, opening the door and lurching against it. Delie stared. She had never seen him like this.

'She's dead. An hour ago.'

'Dead? She – she's gone? Well – I s'pose I'd better go and see her.' He looked guilty and miserable.

'There's no hurry; she'll wait for you,' said Delie unkindly, and turned away. She realised now that the failure of this marriage had not been all due to Hester's nature; this, she felt sure, was not the first time Charles had failed her aunt in a crisis.

In the morning, as she went into the still room, she was conscious first that the lamp was out, the lamp which had burned day and night for weeks. The nurse had been making some sort of fumigation in the room, and Charles, to atone for his defection yesterday, had been out and picked an armful of Christmas lilies from the garden. The room smelt like a church; and the rigid form on the bed seemed no more related to life than a stone image carved upon a tomb.

Outside, an orange butterfly drifted sideways, drunk with summer, and bees hummed drowsily among the petunias which Hester had planted under the side window. The leaves of the river gums moved in the morning breeze with the glint and clash of metal.

A sound of sawing and hammering came from the back, where Charles and Jacky were constructing a coffin of Murray pine. The nurse had intimated that it was as well, in these cases, to get 'the deceased' underground as soon as possible; and the weather was warm.

But Charles showed an unexpected obstinacy when Delie suggested that Hester should be buried in the little plot by the sandhill where the three unknown children lay. 'No, she wanted to lie beside Adam, and so she shall. We can have her there by this afternoon.'

It was already noon when the cart with its long, flat burden, strewn with white jasmine and lilies, set out across the dry river-flats. Bella and the new young lubra, Jessie, who could have had no love for her dead mistress, set up a high-pitched wailing chant as the cart went out through the gates. Delie, with no black clothes in her wardrobe, was perched incongruously on a box in a frilly white muslin dress, while the nurse, dark and sombre, sat beside Charles in front.

The sun was directly overhead, the heat oppressive, until they entered the shade of the red-gum forest. Here, though the direct rays of the sun were muted, the air was breathless, and from the flowers wilting on the coffin came a strong scent, below which Delie dreaded to discern another scent, and felt sure that she did. An errant blowfly buzzed past, came back, circled, and settled on the side of the cart. She brushed it away fiercely, but it came back. Soon there were two.

By the time they came out in the avenue leading to the bridge, the flies were following like a swarm of bees, and crawling among the flowers. Charles, unconscious, drove on. Delie beat at them with a long-stemmed lily, but they always persistently returned. When they came to the bridge and the Customs officer emerged sleepily from his little enclosure, she was almost hysterical. She nearly shouted at him, 'Nothing to declare! Only a dead body. No taxable produce. Nothing but a corpse!'

At the cemetery there was an unexpected check; the sexton was not on duty, and would have to be fetched to dig the grave.

'I'll dig it myself!' cried Charles wildly. He had noticed the flies.

'The grave-digger can be fetched at once,' said the caretaker imperturbably. 'But you must produce the death certificate before th' burial.'

'I haven't it yet, the doctor wasn't there, we've just come in from the country, you understand. He didn't expect her to live above a day or two, but naturally he didn't leave a certificate in advance.'

'Then you'd better go and get it from 'im whiles I see about the grave. There's extra charges on a Sunday.'

'All right, all right. But if you don't mind we'll leave the coffin here under the trees. For obvious reasons. Nurse, will you come? The doctor may need you as a witness.'

At the doctor's there was another delay, for he was out on a call. Delie and the nurse stayed in the waiting room while Charles went to see the minister.

But Mr Polson was having a well-earned rest between services, and at first refused to see him, and then told him that he did not bury people on Sunday. When the necessity was explained to him he agreed ungraciously, but said the death certificate must be produced.

Back to the doctor's again; he had just returned. Charles felt better when he had the certificate. He had begun to feel that he was in a nightmare.

As they came out into the glare of the street again, Delie stumbled, unable to see properly. She put out a hand to steady herself on the gate, over which a square glass lamp was suspended in an iron bracket. A loud roaring had begun in her ears, and darkness came crowding in from all sides.

'I think I am going to faint,' she said, and did so.

When she came round she was back in the doctor's rooms.

'You've been under a strain, young lady,' he said sternly. 'And you've had enough for one day. You shouldn't attend the funeral in this heat, and if you have any friends in town where you can stay, I wouldn't advise that long drive back tonight.'

'Oh, I – I live here, not out at the farm.'

'Good. Then you can go to bed at once.'

'I'll take her straight home, doctor,' said Charles. 'She's had nothing to eat all day, poor child.'

'But I'm all right. Of course I must be there.' She began to protest, but she swayed on her feet as she stood up.

They left the nurse at her home on the way to the boarding-house. When she had been helped up the stairs, Delie crawled into bed with immense relief. She felt as if she had been beaten all over with sticks, and her inside was hollow.

Yet when the landlady brought her some food on a tray, she could scarcely eat it. She gulped the drink of tea, and picked at the potato salad, but she could not force herself to touch the cold chop. She felt that she would never want to eat meat again. There was a taste of death in her mouth.

THIRTY-FIVE

In the autumn there came a cheerful note from Kevin Hodge, who seemed to be enjoying the adventure of soldiering half-way round the world:

> We started to trek on January 3rd, going as far as Natal, where we met about 200 Boers, who we chased over the border, and had two of our fellows wounded. Poor old Barrett could not stand the rough roads, and died two days later.
>
> We got a mail yesterday, I had your letter and some papers father sent me. It's good to hear from you and to see the old *Riverine Herald* again. I am in a Maxim Gun Corps here, it takes five men to work it and it fires 700 shots a minute. It's

a splendid bit of mechanism . . .

There had been a memorial service in the town for George Barrett when the news came through, and emotional speeches had been made about 'giving his life for the Empire', but there was no false emotionalism in this letter. Death was mentioned casually, as an inevitable part of life and war.

The war news became more alarming; Mafeking was besieged and the defenders were known to be in a desperate plight. When the great news came through on the electric cable, the *Herald* brought out a special poster, MAFEKING RELIEVED, and the town went wild. All the church bells and the fire bell were set ringing, people fired off rifles and shotguns, and Delie raced through the boarding-house writing 'Mafeking' on all the mirrors with a piece of soap.

She had been out to the farm only once to see how Charles was getting on. The faithful Bella, still as fat and jolly as ever, was cooking adequate meals; but the house was dirty in the corners, the once spotless kitchen table had taken on a grey shade, and the sand on the kitchen floor needed changing.

When, on the first morning, Delie inadvertently lifted a corner of her breakfast fried egg, she saw that the bottom was a dark viridian green, from which she could deduce the state of the frying-pan.

The young lubra, Jessie, was cheeky and pert. Delie was puzzled at her attitude until, getting up early on the second morning of her stay, she saw the girl slipping out of Charles's room at the back of the house. Jessie was the new unofficial mistress at the farm.

Delie felt hopelessly that her uncle preferred the almost-squalor of his present life; he was too old to change now, and he would never find another white woman to take Hester's place. He had let himself go and his appearance was not prepossessing. When she had arrived there was several days' growth of stubble on his chin, his moustache was unkempt and his eyes were watery and red-rimmed. Perhaps it was only his wife who had kept a naturally indolent man spry and spruce; or was it a slow process of disintegration which had been going on for years, and which she had only just noticed after an interval?

She went back to Echuca resolved not to visit the farm again. She would always be glad to see Charles, who had once been her only ally in a strange world; but the place was full of painful memories for her.

And since Lige's death, evidences of neglect showed everywhere about the property; broken gates, sagging fences, fowls scratching where the neat vegetable plot had been, and Hester's flower-beds run to seed.

When the first fresh came down the river she welcomed it as a harbinger of the *Philadelphia* and Brenton Edwards; but it was July before she had any news of her. Hailing the *Waradgery* skipper as he was tying up during her lunch-hour, she asked about the former *Jane Eliza*, for the skippers were inclined to ignore her new name.

'The *Jane Eliza* that was? Sure, passed her back there by Dead Horse Point. She's not far behind. My oath, she's got a good boiler. Has to be, with the treatment it gets from that batty engineer. He was hopping mad when we passed her; he'd have sat on the safety valve till she blew up, if the skipper'd let 'im. Rotten luck that about poor old Tom.'

'Yes . . . I heard. He left me a half-share in her.'

'That so? Young Teddy Edwards has took over. He'll be a good riverman when he realises that he still has a lot to learn.'

'He must have had a good instructor in Captain Tom.'

'Too right. But there's some things on'y time'll teach you.'

Waiting in the sun and the cold breeze, her ears strained for the steamer's whistle, Delie suddenly became nervous. She noticed the blue paint under her finger-nails, began to wonder what her hair looked like, wished she had worn a fresh blouse this morning. She turned and almost ran back to the studio.

He would be busy berthing, she told herself, and anyway she'd rather meet him here in her own little room than on the public wharf . . .

She made a pretence of tinting a bride and her beaming maids, but the old familiar sickness, a hollow place bubbling with excitement, was forming in her stomach. She jumped up and smoothed her hair for the third time.

Yet she kept her head down and pretended to be busy when at last she heard his voice in the outer room, asking Mr Hamilton for permission to come through. When she looked up he filled the doorway.

She got up in a fluster and knocked over a jar of paint. He remained composed, smiling slightly.

'Hullo, Miss Philadelphia. Did you get my letter all right?' He was hatless, and she looked at his crisp golden curls as they shook hands, and thought of the paint and the turpentine.

'Oh, yes, thank you. It was good of you to write and let me know – about poor old Tom, and his generosity to me.' The words sounded stilted, but she could not speak naturally. 'So we're partners now?'

'That's right. Aren't you coming down to see your namesake? I thought you'd be on the wharf to welcome us.'

'Well, we're very busy here, you see – '

'Then I mustn't keep you any longer,' he said, turning to go.

'It will be my lunch-hour soon,' she said hastily. 'I'd love to come down then.'

'Good! Then you can come to lunch with me, and show me a decent place to eat. I'm sick of river fare; I'm even tired of Murray cod. Come down to the wharf when you're ready, Miss Philadelphia!'

He was the only one these days who called her by her full name. From him she rather liked it . . . There was nothing she could do about her blouse now, she thought anxiously, putting on the coat of her costume and perching a sailor-hat on her dark hair.

But her glance in the piece of mirror she kept behind the door had reassured her; it showed clear, pale skin and healthy red lips, and blue eyes fringed with dark lashes, looking back under straight brows. She wished her eyebrows had been fine and arched, like Bessie's; but at least they were dark and well-marked.

She scrubbed at the blue paint under her nails in a little bowl of water, and then sat down impatiently to wait for one o'clock.

Brenton Edwards, on the top deck, took off his cap and waved it at her. She went down the wooden steps inside the wharf to the lower levels, and found him waiting on the narrow gangplank to help her across. The river was still low and under the wharf the bank of slimy mud gave off the damp, nostalgic river smell.

The grip of his strong hand sent an electric tingle along her wrist, up her arm to her heart and brain, where a momentary panic was set up. But now they were on the deck, he had released her hand, and she was conscious of the half-shy, half-admiring glances of the crew, grouped near the paddle-box under which the galley was built.

One, she noticed, was a Chinaman with a long pigtail. Beside him was a little man in grease-stained dungarees, wearing an ancient cloth cap that was black with grease and engine oil, and under which a pair of fanatical blue eyes glared from beneath shaggy eyebrows.

'The engineer, Charlie McBean,' said Brenton. 'And this is the mate, Jim Pearce.' He indicated a dark, wiry fellow with humorous grey eyes and a weather-beaten face, brown as an old boot. 'He's a Pommy, like yourself –'

'I am not!' flashed Delie.

'An' neither am I,' said the mate.

'Anyway, this is your new boss, chaps. Miss Philadelphia Gordon.'

There was an embarrassed murmur from the men. A dark-eyed, thin-faced lad was gazing at her with his mouth slightly open.

'Say how d'ye do to the lady, Ben.'

'How d'ye do?' said Ben huskily.

'He's the deckhand and cook's offsider. And this is Ah Lee, the cook.'

'Vellee pleased, Missee,' said Ah Lee, bowing low.

'I'm delighted to meet you all, and – and to see my namesake again, looking so clean and shipshape,' she said shyly.

The engineer muttered something into his grey moustache that sounded like 'Jane Eliza' and 'ruddy women', and stumped away to his boiler.

'He's a bit surly at present, probably get drunk tonight,' said Brenton in a low voice. 'When he's sober he's the best man on the river for getting the last ounce of power out of an engine without it blowing up. But drink's his trouble. He got some rotten plonk at Louth up the Darling, and it was because he wasn't fit to be on duty that Tom was in there and got mixed up with the paddle-shaft. Charlie hasn't forgiven himself for that.'

'But shouldn't we get rid of him then, if he's not reliable?'

She had used the 'we' unthinkingly, and could have kicked herself for seeming to want to dictate already. He said rather stiffly, 'I've told you he's the best engineer along the river. He doesn't often go on a bender.'

'Oh, I see. Of course. Do show me evertyhing again.'

After they had been the round of the boat, from the neat little galley to the wheel-house and the tiny saloon, they went off to get some lunch.

'I hope you'll bring her back again, Teddy,' shouted Jim Pearce.

Delie was rather taken aback at this casual way of addressing the captain; they all seemed to call him 'Teddy' in the most friendly way. But why not, since they all knew who was boss?

I really am a Pommy still in some of my ideas, she thought impatiently.

The luncheon was a great success. Brenton ate with appetite a thick steak and three eggs with chips. She liked to see a healthy man enjoying his food, and for once she made a good lunch herself.

There was something about him so mature and assured, as of a man used to making decisions, that she found herself comparing him, to his advantage, with the boys she had gone out with lately. His sea-blue eyes, sometimes more green than blue, could be both direct and intimate in their glance, or diffused and far-seeing as though looking down a long reach of river.

And there was some subtle, electric attraction between them so that even the casual brushing of their fingers as he took the sugar bowl from her, even the vibration of the tones of his voice, made her acutely aware of him as a man.

'I see you have managed to get all the paint out of your hair,' she said demurely, half-way through the meal.

'I was wondering if you remembered our last meeting,' he said with an intent look.

But she refused to be embarrassed 'Oh, I haven't forgotten,' with a glance at his shining gold curls. She felt again the old compulsion to touch them, to twine them round her fingers.

'And have you kept up your painting?'

'Yes, I'm still studying at the School of Arts, though I feel I've learnt almost all I can here. I should go to Melbourne really, to the National Gallery school. The students here . . . they're not serious about art; there's not enough competition. Does that sound conceited?'

'No. I believe you're good, without seeing your pictures.'

'Most people here prefer Hamilton's tinted postcards.'

'You tint them very well.'

'I tint them horribly, because I'm paid to.' For the first time she felt a little out of tune with him. 'I wish my pictures would sell half as well. The pleasure of spending money is one of the minor, but more perfect pleasures of life.'

'I don't know. I suppose, for a woman it is. Money doesn't

mean much to me except in a negative way – as a – well, as a sort of sheet-anchor against want, and to save you from having to do a job you don't like.'

'You like the river, don't you?'

'Love it! But I don't want a lot of *things*.'

'Neither do I! I hadn't realised it before, but you made me see it. Of course I like pretty clothes, and new hats and smart shoes. But "things", like a little home with roses round the door, and fandangles on the mantelpiece, and vases to get broken – they just clutter you up.'

He gave his great shout of laughter, and a waitress at the end of the room jumped and stared. 'It's just as well some people like things, anyway, or they wouldn't buy your pictures.'

She laughed. 'True. And I suppose a paddle-steamer is only a very large "thing".'

'Ah, but a moving thing. They don't get cluttered up like houses. And then there are things *and* things; for instance, I like buying books.'

'So do I. And prints too, for that matter.'

'So you see we're just a pair of bower-birds after all; collectors of junk.'

'Oh, I do envy you your life on the river, waking in a new place every morning. Sometimes I feel stifled in Echuca. I suppose I'd be lonely in the city; yet I feel like going off to Melbourne, and even if I starved – '

'Don't fool yourself with romantic dreams of the city. That sort of existence, starving in a garret and so on, is all right to look back on. You kind of forget the worry about where the next meal is coming from, the poor food, the cold and the misery, afterwards. But at the time it's no fun, except in romantic books. You'd soon wish yourself back again.'

She looked at him speculatively. 'You sound as if you knew something about it.'

'I do. I ran away from home when I was little more than a kid, because I couldn't get on with my old man. I lost my mother when I was only twelve – '

'Why, so did I!' They stared at each other, struck by the coincidence. 'And you came to Melbourne?'

'Yeah, I tramped about looking for work, taking odd jobs and nearly always hungry. But I was too stubborn to go home, crawling back to my old man. There was never enough money for

211

things like new boots, and I couldn't get a steady job. I was really on me uppers when I saw an advertisement for a deckhand on a river-boat. By the time my grandfather died and left me my bit of money, I didn't want to leave the river. It sort of gets into your blood.'

'Yes, I know, but Echuca is so *far* from anywhere. It's neither Sydney nor the Bush, No one will ever hear of my work in this backwater, and I can't study properly here.'

'Then you'd better save up for a year in Melbourne. We made just over a hundred pounds clear on the trip, in spite of missing the river with that hold-up in Bourke. There's fifty pounds to begin with; you could do it on that ... Damn it! I meant to discuss business with you from the beginning, and you put it out of my mind.'

He was looking at her so intently, as though memorising every detail of her face or trying to read some answer there to a question not yet asked, that she dropped her eyes in confusion.

'It's too late now,' she said. 'I must fly.'

'Then you'll just have to come to lunch with me again. Or what about coming to tea on board? Ah Lee is off duty tonight, but I'm quite a good cook – you'd be surprised.'

She hesitated for a second, wanting to ask if the mate would be on board; but she felt sure he would not have asked her otherwise. 'Yes, I think it will be all right. You're almost certainly a better cook than I am.'

He touched her elbow lightly as he led her out in to the street. 'I'd like to see the final result of that painting – the one I so rudely interrupted. Will you bring it along, or have you sold it?'

'No. I was going to present it to Tom. Now you can have it, to hang in your – er – state-room.'

'In my saloon.'

As she hurried back to the studio Delie kept frowning and then smiling, shaking and tossing her head, as though carrying on a conversation with someone.

He's far too sure of himself, she was saying inwardly, and yet at times he can be endearingly small-boyish. But really, when you look at him, his eyes are too small and his mouth too hard. Yet there's no doubt about his charm ...

And to think I may have enough to go to Melbourne soon, and see the Art Gallery, and perhaps study there for a whole year!

She gave a skip in the air at the thought.

Just ahead of her an old woman, dressed in rusty black, with a humped back and hopelessly shaking hands and head, was shuffling along, her eyes on the ground. Delie looked at her in pity and horror.

If I can't skip when I'm seventy, she resolved, I mean to die.

THIRTY-SIX

The winter dusk settled down on the river. Wisps of steam curled up from its surface, and away behind the western trees an orange glow lingered between smoky clouds. After the noise and bustle of the day there was now quiet, though occasional shouts from boat to boat, a laugh or a sudden oath drifted over the water, to startle the wild duck and water-hens in the reeds.

Delie had put on her cherry-coloured costume and a little hat trimmed with two wide grey feathers that swept back on each side of her brow, giving her a swift, forward-moving look, like a bust of Mercury or a figurehead on a ship.

Down to the wharf she hurried, the cold air putting a delicate glow in her cheeks. She was filled with a pleasurable excitement. She was going to tea on board a boat, probably unchaperoned, with a man she scarcely knew.

He was leaning with lazy grace on the end of the paddle-box, his hands in his pockets, his golden curls uncovered, looking musingly down at the water. When he heard Delie's step on the hollow wooden wharf he looked up, bounded across the gang-plank, and came up the stairs to meet her.

Does he really think I might fall in, or is it just an excuse to hold my hand? thought Delie as he led her carefully aboard, and along to the galley next to the paddle-box.

'Now sit on that stool and don't interrupt,' he said. 'I like to concentrate when I'm cooking. But first, a snack in case you get too hungry watching me.'

He handed her a plate of dainty savouries made with several kinds of tinned fish. '*Smögäsbord* – I learnt that from a Norwegian captain. Omelettes I shall now make as my grandmother used to make them.'

'You *are* clever,' she said admiringly, crunching a crisp cheese biscuit and looking at the mixing bowls, eggs and bags of flour neatly arranged on the bench by the wood stove. 'I'm hopeless in a kitchen.'

'Then pipe down and watch.' He beat the eggs vigorously, carefully measured out milk and water, and poured the mixture into a pan of sizzling butter.

'Onions!' cried Delie, as he scooped up a pile of onion shreds. 'Whoever heard of onions in an omelette?'

'Quiet! Who's cooking this meal?'

He put on another pan with dripping, deftly rolled the omelette and divided it on to two warmed plates, then lifted a round cake of dough and slid it into the fat. 'Fried damper – you'll like it. Now grab your plate and come on.'

Delie was by now enjoying his unceremoniousness, which had put her at her ease at once. She did not even notice that the mate was nowhere to be seen, until they were seated at a table fixed under an awning on the deck.

'I should have taken you up to the saloon, but it's stuffy, rather.'

'Isn't the mate on board for tea?'

'Oh, he's got a girl-friend in the town; practically engaged to her. He's staying with her people tonight. Ben's at his married sister's place. Ah Lee has gone to some opium joint, no doubt, and poor old Charlie's on a bender . . . Christ! I forgot!'

'What?'

'I used the last onion for the omelette!'

'It's the nicest omelette I've ever tasted. What about the onion?'

'Charlie will be looking for one to help him recover in the morning.'

'An *onion*?'

'Yes, he won't eat anything but raw onion sandwiches the morning after. Says it's a cure for a hangover. The mixture of stale whisky and fresh onion is a bit overpowering if you get to windward – '

'Help!' she giggled. 'And with Ah Lee reeking of opium, and Jim Pearce of his girl's scent, you'll have an interesting atmosphere on board tomorrow. And Ben – no, somehow I can only think of Ben smelling of books. He's a clever-looking lad. He ought to be at school.'

'Yes, Ben's a bright lad but he hasn't had a chance. Farmed out as a kid – family couldn't afford to keep him – half-starved on a cocky's run where he had to get up at dawn to milk the cows and

214

didn't finish separating till eight or nine at night . . . He was half-stupid with weariness when he came to us. There are some farmers, you know, who drive themselves and their families into an early grave; just go on grafting like bullocks for a bare living until they drop.'

'Of course, ours was a fairly big farm, and well-run in those days, with irrigation from the river. And not many cows.'

She found herself telling him about their arrival at the farm, their long trek from the mountains up near the source of the Murray, about Adam and how they used to go skiing over the snowy slopes about Kiandra, and, later, boating and fishing on the river.

'We used to watch the steamers go past, and you've no idea how wonderfully exciting they seemed at night, with those great reflectors lighting up the trees and the trail of sparks from the smoke-stack. I always wanted to go on one right down the river to the sea. Tell me about the river, Mr Edwards!'

'I only know the top end, as far as Wentworth,' he said. He began to tell her about long nights at the wheel, black nights when you had to steer by instinct, and every shadow looked like a sandbank.

'When I first came up the river I was only a lad, you know; but I'd had some experience steering a steam-launch that ran trips from Williamstown on the Bay. I had a job on her for a while. The first river-steamer I was ever on, the mate said to me the second evening, "Can you steer?" I'd just brought him up a cup of tea to the wheel-house. "Yes," I said like a fool. "Well, take the wheel for a while, son. I want to go below and have a drink." '

'Well, I took over, feeling mighty pleased and proud, and looking back all the time to see how straight a wake I was leaving. But it got darker and darker and the mate didn't come back; there wasn't a soul on deck I could call out to. There was no speaking-tube to the engine or anything like that. I shouted, but no one heard, or anyway they didn't take any notice.

'For more than two hours I steered that ruddy boat along reaches I'd never seen before, not knowing where the channel was, and cursing that mate for all I was worth. At last we fetched up with a horrible jar on a sandbank.

'The skipper came out from his cabin and roared me head off. The mate had gone below and got on the plonk, leaving me to steer until someone happened along to relieve me. The skipper gave me a steering lesson after that; he was a good-hearted old bloke really; but the mate got the sack after that trip.'

'And did you get off the sandbank?'

'Oh yes, we winched her off finally. There's no waiting for the tide to lift you off in the Murray; you get off by your own efforts, or roost on the mud for perhaps six months waiting for the next rise. There was a steamer once took nearly three years to get up the Darling to Bourke.'

'Is the Darling worse than the Murray to navigate?'

'When it's a good river it's good, the channel is fairly straight-forward, while in the Murray it's shifting all the time. But in a drought the Darling is just a chain of water-holes in the bottom of a muddy ditch.'

'I'd like to go up to Bourke. Oh, there are so many places I want to go. There's so much I want to do!'

She stared out over the darkening water. A moth came flying from the darkness against the lamp, fell down on the cloth and crawled painfully in circles. 'I'll probably singe my wings, but that's no reason for not flying; or at least making the attempt.'

He put out a big finger and crushed the moth deliberately. 'You mean Melbourne?'

'Yes, I'm beginning to feel I must get away. Mr Wise, my art teacher, advises me to go to the Gallery School there.' She averted her eyes from the smudge on the cloth.

'That reminds me – the picture.'

'Oh! It's in the galley.'

He brought it and stood it where the lamplight fell on it. 'Jolly good – the highlights on the water, and that dappled shade on the awning – it's got the very breath of summer in it.'

'Do you think so?' The shyness she felt when anyone looked at her work was doubled as she thought of the circumstances in which he had last seen it. Did she want him to kiss her again like that, did she? The tingling of her veins told her that she did. He showed that he was thinking of the same thing.

'Yes; and considering the interruptions you suffered . . .' There was discreet laughter in his eyes. She looked down, trying not to smile, conscious of rising colour.

'This calls for a celebration,' he cried, jumping up. He hauled on a rope at the side, until a dripping sack came up with a clank of bottles. He took out the two bottles of beer, gleaming brown in the lamplight. The sack lay on the floor, oozing a black puddle of water.

'To the success of Miss Philadelphia Gordon! May she dazzle

216

the Melbourne critics – '

'Delphine is the name I paint under,' she said shyly, sipping her beer. It was very bitter, and she swallowed it quickly like medicine.

'Delphine? No, I like Philadelphia; I've got used to it, seeing it on the front of the wheel-house all the time. And you call me Teddy, will you? This "Mr Edwards" business sounds so stiff.'

'Well . . . I prefer Brenton, really.'

'Good. No one but my mother ever called me that, and you remind me of her. She had a fine skin like yours, fine and pale, like ivory with a tinge of life in it.' He was staring at her so hard that she blushed, a rosy wave mantling up from throat to forehead in her clear skin.

'Finish your beer and you can come and show me where to hang it,' he said, producing wire, nails and screws from his pocket. 'More damper and jam first?'

'No thank you! I feel as if I should sink like a stone if I fell overboard.'

'Good God! Was it as heavy as all that?'

'No, but I've had so much. Now I must help you wash up.'

'Nonsense, Ah Lee will do that tomorrow.'

'Oh, but that's not fair.' She stood up and began gathering their plates. She was not used to beer, and it had gone straight to her knees. One of the plates fell with a crash.

She began to apologise for the breakage, but he pointed out that the plate was half hers anyway, and persuaded her to leave the rest. He handed her the lantern and preceded her up the narrow steps over the paddle-box to the little panelled saloon beside the two cabins. He tried the picture on the limited wall-space.

'I think here is almost the only place.'

'Yes. That should be a good light, by day. Not too high – about eye-level.'

He tapped in a nail and adjusted the picture carefully, stepping back almost out of the door to get the effect.

'It really looks quite good,' said Delie, flashing the lantern.

'Here, be careful with that.'

Catching her hand in both of his, he held it while he took the lantern from her and set it carefully on the floor, so that their faces were in shadow. She could see only the gleam of his eyes as he stood over her, looking at her strangely. Her heart beat suffocatingly, but she could no more move than a bird fascinated by the eyes of a snake. In a moment she was no more, lost,

217

devoured, drawn up by his mouth to somewhere above the earth.

At last with an effort she struggled back to consciousness, but his lips would not set her free. In desperation she twined her fingers in his thick curls and dragged his head away.

'Why did you do that?' His voice was pained, his eyes looked dazed.

'I – I couldn't breathe.'

'Oh, darling! I'm sorry. I wish –' He rested his cheek on her hair, rocking her gently in his arms. His fingers traced the whorl of her ear, delicately explored the curve of her eyebrow and cheek, the outline of her quivering lips, travelled down her warm throat where a pulse was throbbing under the high collar. He followed her whole shape as if he would remember it for ever.

This was worse than his destroying kisses. She leant against him, mindless and relaxed. Nothing mattered; the rest of the world did not exist.

'Would you – ?'

His voice came huskily, he cleared his throat and began again more strongly. 'Would you like to go for a row on the river?'

Like a drowning man hit on the head with a lifebelt, she started, and grasped at the solid, unexpected words.

'Yes. Oh yes. I should like that very much.'

The world was flowing back. They were still standing, as an eternity ago, with the lantern at their feet.

He bent and lifted the lantern, and they moved out under the sky. Great cold stars were glowing brightly in the darkness, reflected in trembling points of light from the river. Warm lights from other boats further upstream fell softly on the water.

In silence they made their way to the bottom deck, where he pulled the dinghy up to the stern. A burst of laughter came from one of the boats, and then, drifting unexpectedly over the water, a baby's wail.

'I can row, you know,' said Delie, settling in the dinghy.

'I'll row, thanks,' he said rather shortly. Bending to the oars, he sent the boat leaping forward with a sudden sweep. She trailed her fingers over the stern, feeling the water, as she had expected, warmer than the night air.

'Are you warm enough?' He was turning to look over his shoulder for direction, and flung the words back at her without a glance.

'Quite, thank you. It's a lovely night.'

218

She looked up at the slanting bank of the Milky Way, and the great dark Emu that Minna had shown her, stalking over the plains of the skyland of Byamee; and the sharp bright notches of the Southern Cross by which many a Dreamtime hero had climbed up there from earth.

'We'll go and call on George Blakeney, of the *Providence*,' said Brenton. 'His wife's just had a baby, and he's like a dog with two tails over it. She lives on board, and travels up and down-river with him . . . Ahoy there!' He brought the dinghy round with a few expert sweeps of one oar to the stern of the steamer, where gay curtains hung in the lighted windows of the little saloon, and the ledges were bright with geraniums growing in boxes.

'Who's there?' cried a dark, nuggety man with a pipe between his teeth, his brown arms showing against his rolled-up shirt-sleeves.

'Edwards, of the *Philadelphia*.'

'Ah, Teddy me boy! Come aboard, come aboard! Have ye come for another look at me wonderful nipper?'

'I've seen it, thanks.'

'It! It! Listen to the man, Mabel, he's callin' our beautiful daughter an "it", Well. and who's this lovely young lady?'

'Miss Philadelphia Gordon, the new owner.'

'Part-owner, you know,' said Delie shyly.

'How do ye do, and welcome aboard the *Providence*, Miss Philadelphia. Now there's a fine-sounding name for a girl and a steamer. I wanted to call the baby after a steamer, but when it was a girl the Missus wouldn't hear of it, till I remembered there was a *Marion* down the bottom end.'

'I should think not,' said a plump, pretty woman with merry black eyes, coming forward into the lantern light. 'Mary Anne is all right, though. Won't you come into the saloon, Miss Gordon? I'm sure it's that untidy, but with a young baby and all, you know how it is . . .'

Delie didn't at all know, but she agreed enthusiastically.

In the corner of the saloon a was dark wooden crib, in which the baby played with its own fingers, with sudden, uncoordinated movements and misdirected grabs. It was making a quiet bubbling sound of pleasure.

'Would you like to hold her?' said the proud mother, as if this were the highest honour she could offer the visitor.

'Well –' said Delie, embarrassed. She knew nothing about

219

babies and was terrified she would drop it. But 'Here's the little love,' said the mother, and a warm, solid bundle was put into her arms.

'Isn't she beautiful!' said Delie, feeling foolish.

The baby looked up at the strange face with wonder – not curiosity, but simple wonder, its eyes stretched as round as they would go. A clean, sweetish, milky smell came from it. Suddenly it put both fists to its mouth and smiled, doubling up its knees. Delie looked down, with a reciprocal wonder, at the pink, crumpled hands, the perfect little feet with their nails like tiny shells. The mother, with a gentle, possessive movement, took the baby back, but as she moved with it the baby's head turned, the round eyes kept watching in complete absorption the strange face.

'She's starting to take notice of everything. Her father thinks she's that cute – '

'And so she is,' cried George Blakeney, coming in followed by Brenton, who had to bend his head to get under the low door.

Brenton went up and gave the baby a big finger to hold, looking down at it with a half-amused expression.

'She's the best baby between here and Wentworth, eh, Teddy?' said George.

'Yes, you haven't been up with her night after night, crying, like I have,' said his wife darkly, perhaps feeling that she should temper this extravagent praise a little.

'Now, what will you have to wet the baby's head?' said George.

'We won't stop for anything, thanks, old man. I'm just showing Miss Gordon some of the rival steamers, and then she has to get back.'

He looked down at her compellingly, his sea-blue eyes very bright, and for the moment it seemed that she was alone with him; there was no one else in the world. She made her good-byes mechanically.

They waved good-bye from the dinghy, and rowed on up the line of steamers, some black and deserted, others glowing with lights. The sound of singing came from one, and the wheezing wail of a concertina; from another a clatter of tin plates being washed up. A bucket of refuse was thrown overboard with a splash.

And yet the river is so clean! thought Delie, for all the pollutions of life that it receives. . . . She looked at the few soft clouds moving majestically across the stars from the south-west, and thought vaguely of the circle of water: the river flowing down to the sea, the clouds arising and drifting back over the land, to fall as snow or rain, and flow down once more to the sea. Some lines that Adam loved to quote came into her head:

> When I behold, upon the night's starr'd face,
> Huge cloudy symbols of a high romance,
> And think that I may never live to trace
> Their shadows. . . .

For the first time in many months tears rose to her eyes for Adam. Oh, what was the matter with her? She had been so happy, so unthinking, tonight. As she looked at them, the stars blurred and flashed out points of light. Oh splendid stars, oh jewelled Cross! Their splendour and indifference seemed to pierce her through.

The dinghy swung round, the sky whirled slowly about her head. They were dropping down with the current, the oars slipping effortlessly in and out of the water, silently but for the click of the rowlocks.

As they came opposite the *Philadelphia*, Brenton rowed to the centre of the river, shipped the oars and came back beside her, letting the boat drift. He wrapped his arms about her and put his cheek against hers.

'What's this? Tears?' He pretended to start back in surprise. 'Don't you think there's enough water in the Murray already?'

She smiled wanly. His solid figure and strong arms were infinitely comforting.

'You're a strange creature.' He drew her back over his knees and they stared into each other's dim faces, while the boat drifted silently on. He played with her hair until a long strand came loose. He wound it about her throat with a mock-threatening gesture; she closed her teeth gently upon his hand. Then he was kissing her, endlessly, until the dinghy went quietly aground on the bend below the Campaspe junction.

They rowed back to the steamer in silence, and all the time he looked at her. When he took her hand and helped her clamber over the rudder to the deck, he cried: 'Your hands are frozen! I must get you a hot drink.'

'No, I don't want anything. I'll just get my hat – it's under the awning, I think.'

'I'll get it.'

She was twisting ineffectually at her soft hair, which was tumbling loose from its pins, when he came back with the hat.

The lantern was burning in the stern, and she was outlined against it in an attitude of grace; he saw her small waist, her rounded bosom, the long, graceful flow of her skirt.

As they went to the side, he stooped suddenly and did something to the gangplank. Then he stood up, pulled it inboard and flung it down on the deck with a crash.

'Now we are on an island, entirely surrounded by water,' he said, and lifted her in his arms.

THIRTY-SEVEN

Mr Hamilton looked suspiciously at Delie as she came into the studio with a blithe 'good morning'. Taking off her hat before the little mirror, she stared at her face to see if it looked different, wiser and more mature. Last night she had had the strangest feeling of being possessed by the elemental force of life, ruthless, impersonal and inescapable; as if their human bodies were only the instruments of some blind power. Surely she must be changed . . .

'What's the matter with you this morning?' grumbled Mr Hamilton. 'You're looking very smug about something.'

I'm in love! she almost said. I love, I have loved, I have been loved, I shall love – She controlled herself and managed to say, 'Oh, I don't know, it's such a lovely morning.'

'Is it? I thought it was a bit cold.'

'Oh no! It's a wonderful morning.'

He pushed the sofa in front of the Italian balustrade. 'We've got Miss Griggs booked for this morning, you know. Here, will you arrange these flowers? I want to make a good job of this, she can bring us a lot of custom.'

Bessie coming this morning! Delie remembered with wonder how she used to be jealous of Bessie, when Adam first came to live in the town. Bessie Griggs, with her charming features, easy manners and unlimited means for dressing; popular with the girls, sought after by the boys, patronising to herself. This morning she suddenly felt impervious to Bessie.

She worked quietly, while physical memories of Brenton stirred her blood and every now and then made her heart turn over in her breast. She was dreaming of him when the door opened and Bessie came into the studio. She was dressed in a smart costume trimmed with fur, and a little hat on which was mounted a whole bird, its wings sweeping back on each side of her fair brow. Her golden hair was drawn back smoothly, her lips and cheeks were as fresh and rosy as when she had been a schoolgirl.

Behind her came a tall, languid girl with dark hair and long dark eyes, dressed with a careless elegance that spoke of Melbourne. Delie wanted to stare, but pretended to be busy with the engagement book.

'Hullo, Delie, do you have to be here as early as this every morning?' cried Bessie gaily. 'We could only just drag ourselves out of bed in time. Delie works for her living, Nesta. Isn't she quaint?' Her perfect little teeth showed as she laughed; her eyes were as flat as blue china.

The tall girl did not reply to the words or the laugh, but looked at Delie attentively.

'My name's Nesta Motteram, since Bessie has forgotten to introduce us.' Her voice was warm and deep, as Delie had expected.

'How do you do? I'm Philadelphia Gordon.'

'What an unusual name! Were you called after the place, or a ship, or what?'

'The place, actually. My father always wanted to go there. But there *is* a ship named after me,'

'A ship! A little old paddle-steamer,' jeered Bessie, annoyed at being left out of the conversation.

'But what fun! I love paddle-steamers. Could I see it?'

'She's in port at present, if you'd like to come down to the wharf with me at lunch-time,' said Delie, wondering at her own impulse.

'I was going to ask you to have lunch with us anyway,' said Bessie. She left them rather huffily to take up her pose on the sofa, seemed to resent the instant attraction between her two friends. But she smiled brilliantly at Mr Hamilton and the camera.

'Come and see my work-room.' Delie looked under her lashes at the girl's neat figure in its brown-and-white shepherd's plaid, trimmed with brown velvet, and the velvet toque that matched exactly the long, Egyptian brown eyes. The stranger fascinated her. She ushered her into the small back room. Nesta moved as if bored and tired, but her luminous dark eyes were quick and observant.

'What's this?' she said at once, picking up Delie's oil-painting of Echuca from the back of the table. 'Is this your work?'

'Yes. Painting's my real job. This other is my bread-and-butter.'

'Mm.' A deep note of approval. Delie flushed happily.

'I hope to get to Melbourne to study soon.'

'You should. I hope I'll still be there.'

'Don't you belong there?'

'Yes, but I'm going abroad, the end of August.'

'Oh-oh! France, Italy . . . Florence . . . the Louvre; the Uffizi, the Pitti palace –'

'I hope to write a travel book. I love writing, but I haven't the – the inventive faculty, I'm not a tale-spinner.' She sat on the edge of the table, her eyes fixed on a slowly turning windmill beyond the window. 'D'you know the trouble with me? Too much money.'

The confession was made so naturally, so humorously, it could not be taken for boasting. Delie looked astonished.

'Too much money! Impossible.'

'It's true. It takes so much will power to give up comfort. I know if I travelled steerage and second-class, I'd see more and meet more interesting people. Stevenson walked about France with a donkey, and see what a book he made of it! But there it is – I like comfort, and then being a girl is a snag.'

'Yes, isn't it?' They looked at each other and laughed.

'What are you two gossiping about in here?' cried Bessie brightly, sailing in with one hand to her hair, her neck turning in the old coquettish, swan-like movement.

'Oh – shoes, and ships, and sealing-wax,' said Nesta.

'Sealing-wax!' Bessie seized on the last word. 'I saw a *divine* violet colour in the stationer's the other day, so much more attractive than that common old red.'

'I'd like to paint you like that!' said Delie suddenly. She had been studying Nesta's carelessly graceful attitude as she sat on the edge of the table, one long hand lying palm upward in her lap, her dark eyes fixed on something far beyond the window, somewhere in the future.

Nesta turned her deep gaze upon her. 'Do you paint portraits as well?'

'Yes, but don't let Mr Hamilton hear! He doesn't like opposition from painters. I've only tried a couple of self-portraits actually, apart from exercises in class with other students for models. Oh, if only I had my things here!' She was searching feverishly for a pencil, feeling that she must catch that pose before Nesta moved.

'You've never offered to paint my portrait, Delie.'

'Oh, only the camera could do you justice, my dear Bessie. You're too perfect.' Her blue eyes were sparkling with joy and excitement. 'Will you sit for me, Nesta?'

Nesta stood up, and smoothed down her skirt. 'Why yes, I'll commission a portrait if you like.'

Delie stared at her, while the quick colour mounted her throat, flowed in a wave to the very edges of her hair. The lazy insolence of the tone stung her, more than the words. 'I don't want your money,' she said contemptuously. 'I'm only interested in your face. If I weren't, no amount would induce me to waste my time over you.'

'I'm sorry.' Nesta put out her hand with the swiftest movement she had yet made. 'That's what I mean about having too much money. It makes you suspicious of people's motives, even people of such obvious integrity as yourself.'

'Thank you!'

'No, but really! Say you forgive me. Please do my portrait.'

'Of course. When can you sit for me?'

'Couldn't you come round to our place to do it? Nesta's staying with me for a fortnight.'

'I'd have to come at night for the first sketches. Only you mustn't talk to her while she's posing, Bessie. I want to get that faraway look in the eyes.'

'Oh, all right. But do come on, Nesta. We've got all that shopping to do.' Bessie was becoming bored by a conversation in which neither men nor clothes were mentioned.

'What a perfectly sweet little steamer!' Nesta was standing on the wharf gazing down at the *Philadelphia*, neat with fresh white paint. The current slipped past her bows with a ripple of brown water, giving the illusion that she was moving upstream.

Smoke was coming from the galley chimney. The figure of Ah Lee, in blue trousers and white jacket, could be seen moving to and from the awning. Ben came to the side and dipped up a bucket of water. Brenton appeared from his cabin door and waved to them, cap in hand, the sun gleaming on his hair.

Delie wondered if the others could hear her heart thumping, as they made their way down the dark stairs to the lower wharf.

Brenton was waiting to help them aboard. 'Oh, thank you,' said Bessie archly as he took her hand. 'I was *simp*-ly *ter*-rified coming down.'

Nesta came next, and Delie, watching with eyes made aware by love, saw the long look she exchanged with Brenton. He's attracted by her, she thought with a pang. The attraction of opposites, the dark and the fair, brown eyes and blue. How could he look at anyone else this morning! Then her hand was taken in his firm grip, and she forgot everything but the warm current of feeling that flowed from his touch.

'Oh, Captain Edwards, could we see all the little wheels that go round and everything? This is my friend, Miss Nesta Motteram, from Melbourne, and she's most terribly interested in paddle-steamers.'

'Well, it's not like a watch mechanism, Miss Griggs. There's nothing much to a steam-engine; just a boiler the same as on a locomotive, but instead of driving land wheels, it drives paddle-wheels . . . Mind, step over carefully, that's greasy. This is the shaft that turns the wheels – '

They went on through the narrow space beside the boiler, and Brenton suddenly pulled Delie back and kissed her fiercely. 'Darling, I'll call for you at about eight tonight.'

'Yes . . .' she gasped.

They went on behind Nesta with her indolent walk and alive, interested eyes, and Bessie with her blank eyes and excited chatter.

'This is where the boiler is stoked.' Brenton opened the fire box door and pointed to the stacks of red-gum in four-foot lengths that made a wall behind the end of the boiler. 'That thing's the pressure gauge; if it shows over seventy-five pounds the boiler may blow up, so the safety valve is set to blow off at that pressure. But Charlie, the engineer, keeps her at about eighty; if she tries to blow off before that he puts a weight on the valve.'

'But isn't it dangerous?'

'Not very. Sometimes a boiler blows up and kills somebody, like the fireman and engineer of the old *Lady Augusta*. But all the best engineers sprag the gauges. You have to keep up your speed these days, with railways taking so much of the trade. It's a race to get what cargo is offering.'

A sound of raucous singing came from the port side, and there appeared the wild figure of Charlie McBean, his cap rakishly over one ear, wavering on the edge of the wharf.

'Oh, he'll fall in! shrieked Bessie.

'He'll be all right,' said Brenton calmly. 'He gets like this now and then.'

Charlie suddenly flopped on all fours and crawled along the gangplank, singing as he came. Arrived on deck, he pitched flat on his face, muttering 'Lee! Ah Lee! Bring me fresh onion shang-wich. Full o' vital ju-juices. Nothin' like a nonion for little – little indigeschun.'

Brenton went over to the prostrate form. 'All right, Charlie, I'll help you up to bed. We'll get some onions for you soon. There's none on board at present.'

'No *onions*! All I ask – just one li'l onion – man's last requesht –'

'All right, Charlie. Come on now.' Lifting him easily and carrying him, Brenton took him up the steps, and disappeared into the engineer's cabin.

'I must go if I'm to have time for any lunch,' said Delie, sharply reminded of how she had been carried up those same steps in those strong arms.

'Certainly, let us go,' said Bessie with an expression of disgust on her face, drawing her skirts closely round her. But Nesta looked amusedly up at Charlie's cabin, from which came muffled blasphemies.

'I like your captain, Delie. I wouldn't mind owning a steamer.'

I can see you do, thought Delie, feeling vaguely resentful. Yes, it's easy for you; you can indulge your whims, from buying steamers to trips round the world; you could study art with the greatest living masters, you could buy all the paints and canvases you wanted . . .

Brenton's interested look as he said good-bye to Nesta did not improve her temper. The luncheon was not a success. Delie had quite lost confidence in herself, and sat uneasily between her two well-dressed companions, feeling dowdy and poverty-stricken in her serge skirt and blouse.

Bessie, who had never been a tactful person, completed her discomfiture by exclaiming suddenly, in a profoundly shocked tone, 'Delie! Your nails are dirty!'

It was true; there was some of that wretched Antwerp blue beneath her nails, and in her impatient and excited state before lunch she had not scrubbed it out properly. She blushed and put her hands beneath the table. What would Nesta think of her? And had Brenton been comparing her with this beautiful, well-groomed girl from the city? She finished her lunch hastily, without tasting it.

227

THIRTY-EIGHT

Brenton, lying on a couch of scratchy but aromatic scrub, gazed up into the formless, clouded sky. It was unexpectedly warm for a winter night, which was just as well, for they were wrapped in nothing but his coat.

'I feel so peaceful, don't you?' he said.

Delie propped herself on one elbow and played with his hair. 'Yes. I'm very happy.'

It was true; she was happy that she had given him pleasure, that she had managed not to cry out, that he had no inkling of how much he had hurt her. But she'd had to bite her lip hard to keep back the tears, and tell herself that she must bear it, while he breathed endearments into her mouth. And since extreme suffering and extreme pleasure are perhaps only different forms of the same thing, they had really had some sort of consummation together.

'It must be very late,' she said, as the clouds parted low down in the east and showed a few bright stars swimming in a black sky. The once strange southern constellations had now become as familiar as the faces of friends; their endless progression across the sky was like the flow of water, the visible flow of time.

'I don't care how late it is.' As he spoke the Town Hall clock in Echuca chimed the hour of twelve. But he only laughed, and reaching upward kissed her small, firm breasts as she hung above him, while she sighed with pleasure.

'Oh, but I must go. My landlady . . . What if the door is locked?'

'That will be a good thing. Then you'll have to stay with me all night.'

'But I have to go to work tomorrow. Please darling. Let me go.'

'All right, go. I'm not stopping you,' he said, holding her tightly, while desire flooded through his veins again like a returning tide.

But she was too wise to struggle. She became limp and pathetic. 'I'm so terribly tired.'

'Of course. I'm a selfish brute.' Reluctantly they drew apart,

228

feeling the cold strike between them. A damp exhalation came from the river slipping quietly past the bank where they had lain. Its surface glimmered faintly.

'What about tomorrow night?' he asked as they neared the boarding-house.

'I'll be busy, I'm afraid. I'm starting work on a portrait of Nesta Motteram.'

'That dark girl?'

'Yes, she's only here for a couple of weeks, and –'

'Well, I won't be here much longer.'

'No, but I've promised. And she has such an interesting face.'

'All right. Saturday, then.'

'Saturday night. I'll be painting all the afternoon.'

As they stood alone in the long, deserted street outside the door, he surprised her by suddenly putting his head down on her shoulder, hiding his face like a guilty child.

'I'm sorry, Delie!' he said, in a muffled voice.

'Sorry! What for? I'm not, so why should you be?'

'You're so young! How old are you?'

'Just twenty.'

'Twenty! And I'm twenty-eight. And I can't get married just yet.'

'But I keep telling you I don't *want* to get married.'

'I'm afraid you might have a child.'

'I'd love to have your child. He'd be a boy, and perfectly beautiful. But it's all right, I did everything you told me.'

'Yes, it'll be all right But still . . .'

'Why can't I have your baby because I love you? I don't see why there have to be legal complications. Our social system's all wrong.'

'It's better than most.'

'It's all wrong. Unmarried mothers –'

'It's a matter of economics. Women can't support children by working, and bring them up as well. And there are so few jobs for women.'

'They could do anything a man can do, if they had the chance.'

'Anything but one thing,' he said, and laughed.

'Pass the beetroot to Delie, dear.'

Mrs Griggs presided over the table in sleepy majesty, her eyes, of the same china-blue as Bessie's, perpetually half-closed as if the effort of seeing beyond her vast bosom was too much for her.

229

Delie had come for the evening meal, her sketching things under her arm. She was burning to begin.

Mr Griggs passed the beetroot, and looked carefully about the table to see what might be missing. He was a small, fussy, grey-haired man with alert, sharp features. He liked to hold up a meal while he sent the knives away to be sharpened, or demanded some extra from the kitchen.

Though for years Mrs Griggs had been gradually increasing the variety of sauces, chutneys and jams on the table, he kept thinking up something new.

'My dear, where is the mushroom catsup?' he said now with a sharp, triumphant glance at his wife.

With a look of heavy despair, Mrs Griggs rang the bell. 'Susan, is there any mushroom catsup?' It was produced, rather to Mr Griggs's disappointment, and the meal was allowed to proceed.

'Delie's so busy studying Nesta that she's hardly eating a thing,' said Bessie mischievously.

Delie flushed as she felt every eye turned on her. She had been unconsciously staring; her mind full of the work ahead, she had been noting the warm olive tone of Nesta's complexion, the shadows at the corner of mouth and nose, the rather arrogant curve of nostril and lip, and the deep brown eyes.

'How shall I pose for you, Delie? Like this?' Nesta rested her elbows on the table, locked her fingers beneath her chin, and turned up her eyes in an exaggerated pose.

The others laughed. Delie did not smile; she was furious. The food seemed to choke on the solid lump of rage in her throat. For the rest of the meal she kept her eyes on her plate.

The others did not notice, or affected not to notice, her silence; but as they were leaving the dining-room Nesta took her arm in a warm grasp, and whispered, 'Don't be cross, Philadelphia dear. Come on, we'll shut ourselves away from them all, and I'll do just what you say.'

The magnetism of her touch, the words that made them allies again, melted Delie's resentment at once. She followed into the small room which had been set aside for her to work in. Nesta was as good as she had promised, and at the end of an hour she had several crayon sketches, one of which would work up into the portrait she wanted. She had caught the indolent curve of hand and wrist, the intent but dreaming expression in the dark eyes, that had first stirred her interest.

On Saturday she went without lunch so as to get the crayon

sketch transferred to the prepared canvas. Excitement moved her as she felt the whole conception grow in her mind's eye. The highest lights would be on the brow and eyes, the white hand lying in the lap, and a light-covered book thrown down on the table by the sitter's elbow.

When she arrived at Bessie's her fingers were itching for the brush, and she chafed under the necessity of being polite to Mrs Griggs. Midday dinner was just finished, and she insisted on Delie taking a cup of tea with them at the table.

'You're quite sure you've had your lunch, child?'

'Quite sure,' lied Delie firmly.

'Oh, Delie lives on the smell of a painty rag,' said Bessie. She liked her food, and was beginning to take on the same opulent curves as her mother.

Delie laughed, and took a dingy paint-rag out of her satchel. 'Ah, that smells better than a roast dinner,' she said, sniffing with closed eyes. 'Do come on, Nesta.'

They talked of many subjects while she worked, with intervals of warm and friendly silence. Delie found herself in agreement with most of Nesta's ideas; though sometimes a flash of that arrogance or intolerance that was part of Nesta's nature would antagonise her.

But there was something wrong. She could not get the pose the same. The attitude was right, but the expression of the eyes had changed. They seemed to be smouldering with some inward excitement; they would not dream.

'What's happened to you since I did the sketch?' she asked. 'Something has stirred you up and altered your face. I'll simply leave it for the present.'

'I don't know why I should look any different.' But Nesta looked down with a secretive smile about her full lips.

Delie concentrated on getting the hands right. 'Look at the hands in an Old Master,' Daniel Wise used to say, 'and then at the hands in any modern portrait. It's enough to tell you whether the man can paint.'

The portrait progressed rapidly, Delie giving up all her spare time to it. Brenton complained that she was neglecting him; he seemed so remote and changed that she became alarmed, and promised him the next day's lunch-hour, as Nesta had a luncheon engagement and she had only been going to work on the background.

'I'm engaged for lunch myself tomorrow, as a matter of fact,' said Brenton. 'So you may as well work on your picture.'

'I'm worried about it. There's a sort of suppressed excitement about her – I think myself it's a man – and I can't get the expression of the eyes right.'

'She has strange eyes,' said Brenton.

The next Thursday was the last sitting before Nesta returned to Melbourne. To Delie's joy she found what had been missing: the intent, dreaming gaze, fixed upon some vision over the horizon, had come back, and a small, involuntary smile curved the full lips.

'That's it! That's just the expression I want! Oh, I'll have to paint out half your face and start again.'

Her brush flew between palette and canvas. The power and the glory had descended upon her; she could do nothing wrong. When at last she had finished she gazed upon her work and found it good, though still far below what she had dreamed.

'It's excellent, Delie! I really would like to buy it,' said Nesta warmly.

'No. It's not for sale.'

By the time the *Philadelphia* was due to leave, Delie wished she had the time over again to spend it all with Brenton. She went aboard one night when the crew was ashore, to sign insurance papers and joint indemnity risks; and finished up, as before, in his bunk. This time it was less of an ordeal; she felt refreshed and renewed, utterly new, as if they were Adam and Eve waking on the first morning in Eden. Adam and Eve . . . Oh, Adam, she thought with compunction, how utterly I had forgotten you!

But Brenton was there, was alive, she felt beneath her ear the steady, strong thumping of his heart. She thought of that strong heart stopping, of this whole warm person, living, breathing, loving, thinking, being turned to a handful of helpless dust.

She clasped him in anguish. 'Brenton! Promise me not to die.'

'Afraid I'll have to, some time.'

'You mustn't die! You mustn't!' She began to weep, kneeling beside him and rocking back and forth, her long dark hair falling over her face, as if she already mourned over his dead body.

'You silly creature!' he said lovingly, twining a long strand about his wrist. 'I promise you not to die for at least twenty years.'

'I've been afraid you might go to this horrid war in South Africa.'

'Not me! I've woke up to just what a horrid war it is. Why should we go and help the British empire-wallahs to shoot a lot of blokes like ourselves, because they wouldn't pay unjust taxes? All the Boers wanted was freedom, to be let alone.'

'Brenton! You're a pro-Boer.'

'Too flaming right I am. *And* anti-war. I don't believe in killing my fellow-men just because a lot of politicians and high-ups tell me it's the noble thing to do.'

'Pro-Boer, anti-war,' she chanted. She had never heard such sentiments expressed, and she was rather shocked. Pro-Boers were always spoken of as the lowest type of human beings, next to the Boers themselves: 'them blasted Boojes' as she had heard the caretaker at the Institute, a veteran of Crimea, refer to them.

She realised now for the first time, that there were Boer girls in South Africa at that very moment taking leave of soldier-lovers with the same anguished cry: 'You mustn't get killed, you mustn't!'

Towards midnight there were voices on the high part of the wharf above. She leapt up, suddenly conscious of her position, of the defying of convention it implied. She saw her conduct from the point of view of her dead mother, of Mrs McPhee, even of Bessie Griggs. All of society seemed to be lined up, pointing an accusing finger at her.

'Don't get in such a panic,' said Brenton, as she hastily dressed and pinned up her hair with shaking hands. 'It's only some late revellers trying to find their boat.'

And in fact the noisy voices were dying away towards the other end of the wharf. She relaxed, and wandered about the confined space of the cabin, looking at his two neat hairbrushes in their circular leather case, picking up a book or two from the little built-in shelves. One was a small volume of selections from Shelley. Idly opening the cover, she saw inscribed on the fly-leaf in green ink, 'A farewell gift. N.'

It did not look new, but the handwriting was familiar, she had seen it when Nesta had dropped a note at her boarding-house to say that she was sorry she could not sit the next day.

'N!' she repeated aloud, while she stared at the writing, square, upright, with the letters separated almost like printing. And green ink! The blood began to drum in her ears. 'Did Nesta give you this?'

'Oh, that!' He leant over casually and took it from her hand. 'Yes, she did, as a matter of fact.'

'But, Brenton!' She stared at him, her blue eyes wide and

rou bled. 'I didn't know you'd e ven met her, except for that day when we all came on board.'

'Oh, yes, we met several times. It was her I took to lunch the other day.' He looked self-conscious, though he smiled lightly.

'But why not tell me? And why didn't she tell me? I don't understand.'

'Well, she had no idea of the relationship between you and me, unless you told her; and naturally I didn't.'

'No, of course not. But why didn't you tell me?'

'Don't know. I suppose I was afraid of a scene. Thought you might be jealous, and wild with me for taking her away from a sitting.'

'Jealous! Of course I'm not jealous. Why, you hardly know her.' She laughed, but a question remained unanswered.

Nesta was so very attractive. She had felt the attraction herself, of that warm and vital person. And Brenton too; they were of a kind.

She shook the uneasy feeling from her, determined not to show any unworthy suspicions. After all she and Brenton had been to each other, it was just impossible that he could be seriously interested in anyone else.

THIRTY-NINE

That little seed of suspicion, once planted in her mind, sprouted and grew until all her happiness was overshadowed by its dark growth. Unable to sleep, Delie rose, lit the lamp and went over to the portrait of Nesta standing on an easel against the wall.

The long dark eyes gazed out at her, dreamily intent upon some remembered vision, the full lips curved secretively. With an angry movement she turned the picture towards the wall.

Next day, unable to concentrate, she moved restlessly about her little room at the studios. At last, when the mail train from Melbourne had come in, she asked for permission to go up to the post office to get a letter she was expecting from Melbourne.

At the post office, when the Melbourne mail had been sorted, she bought some stamps and remarked casually that she was going down to the wharf, and if there was any mail for the *Philadelphia* she would take it. The clerk, who knew her and her connection with the steamer, looked through the pigeon-holes with maddening deliberation.

There were three letters, two for the mate and one for the captain. She did not let her eyes drop to them till she was out in the street. Then she saw the handwriting she had expected – unmistakable, in green ink, with a Toorak postmark.

Her first feeling was one of rage, that left her weak and shaking. She turned off to the right instead of going straight to the wharf, and went down between the bordering gum trees towards the river. She wanted to tear the letter in shreds and scatter them in the water.

She also wanted, very badly, to open and read it. But if she did so he would despise her, and her suspicions might be unfounded; while if she sealed it up again without telling him she would despise herself. Best to destroy it at once.

Putting the others under her arm, she took the letter in two hands to tear it across. No! Best to confront him with it. She could not bear this suspense of not knowing. She took her handkerchief from under her cuff and wiped her sweating palms.

At the wharf, Brenton was busy taking on stores, directing the men in placing a dangerous cargo of cartridges to be delivered to a Darling station.

He was stripped to the waist. She averted her eyes from his muscular chest and satiny skin that gleamed in the sun, very white where it was not tanned. He came towards her smiling.

Suddenly bringing the letter out from behind her back, she presented it to him with a stony look. His hands were grubby, but he did not ask her to put it in his cabin. He frowned quickly, took the letter and slipped it into his hip-pocket.

'I brought the mail, as I had to go to the post office,' she said with an effort at casualness. 'There are two for the mate as well.'

'Better put them up in his cabin. He's off duty today. I'll see you up there in a minute.'

She turned stiffly and went up the steps, and after putting the letters in the mate's little cabin went into Brenton's cabin next door. She hunted quickly for the little volume of Shelley, and found it slipped under some papers on the table.

Opening it, she looked at the inscription again, and leafed quickly through the pages. She caught sight of a line of green ink marking one verse. With the blood beginning to pound in her head until she felt as if it would burst, she read:

> When passion's trance is overpast,
> If tenderness and truth could last
> Or live, while all wild feelings keep
> Some mortal slumber, dark and deep,
> I should not weep, I should not weep!

The book fell out of her hand to the floor. She heard his step behind her.

'Brenton!' Faintness, accusation, unbelief made her voice waver uncertainly.

He sat down on the side of the bunk, his splendid shoulders naked and beautiful, and looked at her with candid blue-green eyes.

'Brenton, there is something between you!'

'No, it's over.'

'Where is the letter?'

'I tossed it overboard.'

'Without reading it?'

'No; I read it first. It was just to say good-bye.'

'There's been everything between you, hasn't there? Just as much as between you and me?'

'In a way, yes.' His vivid eyes looked puzzled and almost hurt, but not guilty.

'But . . . how *could* you?' She sat down suddenly on the bunk beside him; her legs had given way. Tears began to run down her cheeks in a scalding stream.

'Don't cry, Phil darling. It's not what you think.' He wrinkled his brows in an effort to explain. 'You couldn't be expected to understand but . . . she looks at these things almost as a man does. And . . . well, she has a terrific urge.'

'No doubt. Also a terrific amount of money,' she said wildly.

His face darkened. 'She didn't buy me, if that's what you mean. But I knew I was only another experience for her, one of many. She was no virgin.'

'And do you feel that excuses your conduct?'

'Of course it doesn't, not from your point of view. But it's quite different with you. I'd like to be married to you, I don't really want anyone else. But you stirred me up, and then left me unsatisfied. You seemed to be always busy painting, or in a hurry to get home.'

236

'That was because you hurt me so much.'

'Hurt you?' He stared at her, while she blew her nose miserably. 'Delie, why didn't you tell me? You're such a little thing.' He pulled her close to him and began caressing her taut face, smoothing the straight brows with one finger. She stiffened with resistance, but as always her bones seemed to melt at his touch. She tried feebly to push him away.

'Don't. You could go from me to her, and from her to me, as though it meant nothing. Do you even remember that I am me, Philadelphia Gordon, or do I just become woman to you, any woman?'

'Oh, help!' He groaned, and stopped her mouth with a kiss. 'Why can't you enjoy life, dear child? All this thinking and talking, and talking and thinking . . . it doesn't mean anything. This is what's real.'

'Oh, don't! Please don't.'

'You like it, you know you do.'

'Let me go!' She struggled away from him. 'I don't know if I ever want to see you again. I'm horribly mixed up.'

'You're going to see me again.'

'I don't know, I don't know!' She dabbed at her eyes, peered in the mirror, and straightened her hair. Her feelings were indeed confused. He should surely be on his knees begging her forgiveness; yet somehow he had managed to put her in the wrong. Her foot kicked something, and she stooped quickly, picked up the volume of poems, and threw it hard out of the little window. As it splashed into the river she felt better.

After a half-hearted attempt to eat tea in her room that night, Delie went to the easel and turned the portrait about. The calm, secret smile, the dreaming eyes, looked out at her with what seemed like deliberate mockery. She knew what memory those eyes were dreaming over; she knew now what that smile meant. The cat that had eaten the cream!

In a red rage, she picked up a knife and stabbed at the painted eyes. Then she slashed the face and arms, until the canvas hung in gashes and ribbons. Then, trembling, she sank on the bed, flinging the knife on the floor. She felt as if she had murdered her own child.

Later she got a pencil and writing-pad and wrote to Brenton, telling him she was going to Melbourne and that there could be nothing more between them. There were pages of it, vehemently and badly written, in a savage, careless scrawl – recriminations, soul-searchings, face-savings:

It was not that I really loved you, I took to you as some men take to drink or drugs, in order to forget someone else . . .

When he came for her two nights later she was surprised to find her heart thudding with excitement, as though she had not, quite definitely, decided that she did not love him.

His brilliant eyes searched for hers, though she tried to avoid them, and his mouth twisted into a wryly humorous grin, as though he deprecated his inability to look more guilty and downcast.

That mouth – at the thought of the other mouth, not hers, that it had so lately pressed, such a pang went through her that she gasped as with a physical pain. And all the hot, salty tears she had dropped into the book she tried to read herself to sleep with last night; great many-pointed stars of salt had been left on the pages as they dried. And he could smile!

'Did you get my letter?' she said stiffly as they walked up Hare Street.

'Yes; but I'm not going to answer it, at least not in writing. We would go on writing at cross-purposes for years, and only waste a lot of paper. Words! They muck up the real business of living.'

She thrust out her bottom lip obstinately, but did not reply.

When they were in Stacey's waiting for their order, she told him what she had decided: to sell him her share in the steamer and use the money to go to Melbourne and study art.

'Tom would have been disappointed,' said Brenton soberly, 'to think that you had no share in her. Is that what you want?'

She fingered some crumbs on the cloth, not looking at him. 'I don't know what I want, except to get away! Perhaps I could keep a quarter-share. If I had three hundred in cash I could live on it for three years.'

'Materials for painting would have to come out of that.'

'Yes, and fees for tuition. I'd get a cheap room somewhere.'

'Well, I hope you can do it on that, because three hundred is about all I could raise at present, after the outlay on stores and repairs. You know you should share in the buying of stores if you're going to share in the trading profits; but Tom didn't insist on it and I won't either.'

'Brenton!' Her cheeks were pink. 'Why didn't you tell me! It always seemed like a miracle to me, the money just coming in like that. I just didn't realise. I'm hopeless at money matters. You must take back that fifty, or half of it, anyway.'

'Rats! You're going to need all of that.'

'But I can't keep it . . . don't you see . . . after what has happened between us. It would seem as if I were being paid – '

'Don't talk like that!' he said roughly, grasping her restless fingers. 'If you say bloody silly things like that, I'll kiss you right here in front of everybody.'

The waitress came with fried Murray cod, and they began to eat mechanically, intensely conscious of each other.

'You're to write to me from Melbourne, and let me know pronto if you get into any strife. I should think that whenever we're in a Victorian port I'll be popping down to Melbourne, even if it's only for a day.'

'I'm not alone in the world, I still have my guardian. You don't have to be so protective.'

'You independent little devil!' he said. 'I believe you still love me all the same.'

She would not meet his eyes, and remained obstinately silent.

When they were in the street again he took her hand and locked his fingers through hers. He looked down at her with bright, compelling eyes. Because he was going tomorrow, his face became more clear; the way his hair grew in tight curls, the set of his ears against his head, seemed to pierce her with love.

'We'll go for a walk by the river,' he said. 'You're going to let me say good-bye to you, aren't you?'

'Yes . . . I suppose so, yes,' she sighed.

As soon as they were below the sheltering slope of the river-bank he took her in his arms. With her face pressed against his solid shoulder, she felt all the tension, misery and bitterness of the last two days fall away. Peace, she thought, this is peace, the peace that passeth understanding.

Delie went down to the wharf to see her namesake set out. The spring freshets of melted snow-water were following the winter rains, and the river was rising steadily; all was noise and bustle on the high, curving wharf.

239

Watching the endless flow of water until it was hidden by the next bend, thinking of the Southern Ocean towards which it flowed, and the clouds that rose from the sea to fall as snow or rain, she felt herself at the heart of a mystery. Time, that everlasting stream, might bear her far from this place; yet this moment would always exist, just as this point in space would still exist when she no longer occupied it; even when she stood within sound of the breakers on the final shore.

And there below lay the *Philadelphia*, with her name freshly painted on the wheel-house. Was it possible that she would never see her again? She could not believe it. The rhythm of the river had got into her blood, and one day it would draw her back.

She went on board and had a last look round. In the wheel-house she turned the wheel a little, touching the big spokes where Brenton's hands would rest. She peeped into the saloon where her picture of the boat seemed to bring the sunlit river into the dark, panelled space.

Down on the main deck again she shook hands formally with Brenton, wished him luck on his voyage, and stepped back across the gangplank.

As she was groping for the stairs up to the higher levels, her eyes misted with tears, Brenton dashed across the gangplank and kissed her in full view of the crew. They cheered loudly, all but Ah Lee and the engineer, who scowled and said, ' 'Ow much longer d'you expeck me to keep steam up in this 'eap of junk?' as he wiped his fingers on his oily cloth cap.

Standing on top of the wharf in the sunlight, Delie watched the paddles begin to churn, the milky bubbles froth against the piles, as the steamer edged out and turned downstream. With a long, echoing, infinitely moving peal from her whistle, she disappeared round the Campaspe bend.

FORTY

A slanting curtain of rain was driven along Swanston Street by the cold wind, buffeting the passengers just emerging from Flinders Street station, beating on dejected cab-horses, sweeping up the hill, and darkening the massive grey pillars of the National Gallery to almost black.

Inside, the gloomy bays were lit with artificial light, and a few dispirited visitors drifted from picture to picture, conversing in funereal whispers. The attendants, sitting aloof, looked like undertakers who had given up all hope of business.

In the lofty downstairs rooms where the students of the Gallery School worked at their drawings and canvases, a pale grey light from the sky came through the tall windows. A bell shrilled through the building; the nude model in the Life class relaxed upon the dais; students in the Still-Life room wiped their brushes and blinked their eyes, suddenly aware of tired backs, a foot that had gone to sleep, the coldness of the winter morning.

One of them, a slender girl who was remarkable for the amount of paint she had managed to get on her person as well as on to the canvas, seemed not to have heard. She continued to work with concentration through the sudden clatter as the others began to pack up satchels and sketching-boxes, and to put their easels back against the wall.

'You can leave it for now, Miss Gordon,' said the instructor, dark and dapper with his thick moustache and clean-shaven chin. 'Don't forget to put your easel back, will you?'

'No, Mr Hall.' She looked after his retreating back as though dazed, her deep blue eyes remote, still focused on the idea of the picture she had been working on. She wiped back a wisp of dark hair from her forehead, and left there a smudge of yellow alizarin.

She hated this working to a time-table, having to stop before she was ready, and to begin slowly and fumblingly again when the creative mood was not upon her. She removed her smock after cleaning her brushes with turpentine, and washed her hands and face in the little washroom with its warning notice: BRUSHES

241

ARE NOT TO BE WASHED IN HAND-BASINS.

At the front doors a plump young man, a fellow student, was waiting to relieve her of her satchel. She had no class this afternoon and was going home to lunch.

'Come up to town and I'll buy you a hot coffee, Del,' he said, looking at her pale, thin cheeks. 'You never look as if you get enough to eat.'

'Sorry, Jeremy. Imogen is expecting me; she's made one of her curries.'

'It won't hurt you to have a hot drink first,' said Jeremy obstinately.

'I suppose not.' But she did not look at him. She despised herself for accepting the drinks and lunches and afternoon teas he bought her, and which she could not have afforded herself; but she must not get ill, and she needed something hot after a chilly lesson in the studio, or a landscape class out of doors in winter.

Jeremy was fond of food, and too lazy ever to make an artist. She did not admire him, but . . . 'A girl must live,' as Imogen was fond of saying. She made a half-hearted attempt to take back her satchel, and then walked on beside him, drawing up her coat collar against the rain.

A cable-tram was coming down the hill. Jeremy took a firm grip of her elbow and they ran across the splashing street in front of a trolley drawn by a steaming pair of brown horses. Delie leaned back in the tram, coughing a little; Jeremy looked at her anxiously.

'Are you warm enough? Sure? Would you like my scarf? Melbourne is a good place to be out of in the middle of winter.'

'Oh no; I love it in all weathers. You don't know what it means to me to be here, after a country town.'

It was not quite a year since she had come to Melbourne, yet she felt as if she belonged here. When she came in by Prince's Bridge on a smoky, misty morning, and saw the reflections of trees and buildings in the calm Yarra, the tall grey spires of St. Paul's, the streams of people and traffic hurrying along, the parks so green and smooth under the dark bare trees, her heart lifted with an excitement that was always new.

This for her was the City, here she had found her spiritual home. A lively art movement had been stirring since Tom Roberts came back from Europe five years ago with first-hand experience of Impressionism; and as in an Impressionist painting the air seemed to quiver with life, the impalpable ferment of ideas.

She was not quite in sympathy with Bernard Hall, the Art School master; but she found the drawing master, Frederick McCubbin, with his big walrus moustache and bright eyes twinkling with enthusiasm and humour, a delightful person to work with.

She was happy in her work in this southern city. It was only on days like this, when the bitter wind caught in her throat, that she sometimes thought nostalgically of Echuca, with its delightful, sunny winter climate.

On New Year's Day she had joined in the city's celebration of the new Commonwealth; and later in its mourning for Queen Victoria, when she had worn a purple silk blouse for a whole week.

Echuca, which as a border town had long chafed under Customs restrictions, had apparently gone mad on Federation Day, 1901. Her uncle had sent her the cuttings from the *Riverine Herald*, a special edition printed entirely in bright blue ink . . .

But Echuca, the cramping work in the photographic shop, the seasonal life of the river, were far away to the northward, and receding daily further in time. She had just got off a tram at Little Collins Street, Melbourne . . .

It was still raining, but more lightly, in a fine drizzle. Obedient to the pressure of Jeremy's well-padded arm, she turned into an entrance and they made their way down the dark steps of a little coffee-shop.

Hurrying up the steep slope of Punt Road to the flat in South Yarra that she shared with Imogen, Delie began to cough. Bronchitis had troubled her, in successive attacks, all the winter, and now this cough began whenever she hurried or got excited.

She slowed down and forced herself to breathe evenly. Her cheeks had begun to burn with a dry flush, and in spite of the cold she felt a sensation of heat and weakness through her limbs.

She was nearly home now; the next iron gates. One advantage of the flat, which was really the gardener's lodge of one of the big houses, was the large garden where they were able to make sketches of light and shade on fine Sunday mornings. The occupants of the house were friends of Imogen's mother, so they had the freedom of the garden. It was wonderful to Delie to have shaken off the deadly trappings of respectability, of heavy roast dinners and dressing for church, and all the time-frittering conventions of Sunday in a small town.

As she stepped on to the old stone-flagged veranda of the cottage

243

there was a scuffle and a giggle from within. Treading as noisily as she could, she came into the living-room to find a young man standing by the window, pointedly looking out, and Imogen – small, black-haired, quick and yet sensuous as a cat in her movements – uncoiling herself from her divan-bed in the corner.

'I told you it's only Delie; she won't be shocked,' she said mockingly.

The young man bowed, Delie smiled hastily and hurried through to the kitchen (the only other room), taking off her tam-o'-shanter and wet coat as she went. She was getting used to Imogen's amoral ways, but at first she *had* been shocked at the rapidity with which Imogen changed lovers, as some women change hats.

She turned off the stove and began to dish up the curry. She was hungry, and she hoped the young man would not be sharing the meal, which contained very little meat bodied forth with much rice. Imogen came in with another plate. 'You won't mind if Alby stays to lunch, will you?' she said, smiling her oddly mechanical smile.

She looked hard at Delie with her pale green eyes, fringed with black lashes. 'You're looking tired out, darling. Are you very damp? Go and sit down inside while I make the tea.'

Imogen was inclined to mother her. There was something helpless about Delie Gordon in her vagueness and forgetfulness. She was always losing things, or getting lost herself, taking the wrong train and finding herself miles out of her right direction, or forgetting to get out at the right station. Even places she had visited half a dozen times she could not find again alone.

The other students regarded her with a half-irritated irony. She was late for appointments or didn't turn up at all, she broke their pet vases and tripped over their pet cats, she lost her purse and had to borrow her fare; but by now they were used to it.

Delie went back to the other room, lit the kerosene heater and crouched over its meagre warmth, breathing in its hot, oily smell. She tried to talk to Alby but she didn't know what to say to him.

He was very long and thin, pale and etiolated like a plant kept too long indoors, with a large soft moustache and eyes veiled by heavy lids. His voice was deep and drawling, which made him sound profoundly bored with life. He was not an artist, but a university student taking some vague honours course which had already taken him years.

Delie was annoyed to find him here today, when Imogen had particularly asked her to come home to lunch. Not that she was jealous, of course; that would be ridiculous; but still . . .

Alby looked out of the window in a bored way and did not try to help the conversation which Delie, out of politeness, tried to keep up. She felt faintly irritated that he seemed unaware of her as a woman; but she was too tired and cold to be piqued into an attempt to interest him. She felt suddenly, desolately lonely; and, as often happened, she imagined how different it would be if Brenton had been there instead.

Imogen came in with three steaming plates on a tray. She had divided the curry evenly, eking it out with triangles of buttered toast. It had been intended for two only, and then Alby, who never seemed to have lectures in the mornings, had turned up. She set down the tray and put up her hands to tighten the silver earring on her left ear.

Alby gave an exaggerated shudder. 'I can't *bear* to see you do that.'

'What, my angel?'

'That *cold* metal biting into your flesh.'

'Poof, it only pinches a bit. I should get my lobes pierced.'

'Don't!' Alby shuddered again. 'I shan't be able to eat a *mouthful.*'

Good thing, thought Delie, there's not enough to go round anyway. But though he eyed his food with distaste, the young man disposed of it quite rapidly.

There was some fruit for dessert, but nothing else. Delie still felt hungry. She decided to have some biscuits later. As they were sipping their claret afterwards, Alby cried dramatically, 'Stop! Don't move!'

Imogen paused with her glass at her lips. 'You see?' said Alby, throwing himself back in his chair with his long legs spread under the table. 'You see the light on her cheek, on the glass, the *je ne sais quoi* of her whole pose?' He turned to Delie earnestly. 'I have the eye, the sensibility, of an artist, but not the – er – the execution.'

Imogen set her glass down suddenly. 'I forgot, Del. There's a telegram for you. It's on the mantelpiece.'

Delie got up and tore the envelope open slowly, with the premonition of disaster which telegrams always roused. But as she read the words the flush deepened slowly in her thin cheeks, her

245

pupils dilated, her eyes seemed to grow larger. She looked up at Imogen with an intent blue stare from her shining eyes.

'I know! Brenton's coming down,' said Imogen.

'Yes. Arriving tonight.' She looked down again at the brief words: ARRIVING TONIGHT 6.30 PM TRAIN FROM ECHUCA LOVE BRENTON.

Brenton was coming! She lifted her tight skirt well above her ankles, and did an energetic *pas seul* round the table, taking a kick at a half-finished canvas leaning against the wall.

'You'll have to take me out tonight, Alby. Out *late*,' said Imogen. 'Off you go now, Delie will want to start decorating the flat. Meet you at half-past seven at the post office.'

Alby was staring. He had never seen Imogen's friend so animated.

Delie was so afraid that she would be late, or the train would be early, that at six o'clock she was already waiting outside the barrier, in a cold fever of excitement. She felt faint and sick, her mouth was dry, and her cold hands trembled. There was no torment like this last half-hour of waiting.

She should really have had something to eat. It was a long time since that unsatisfying lunch, but she could not eat in this churned-up condition. Instead she had to hurry away to the retiring-room. In the mirror over the wash-basins she stared at her own pale face. Was she very thin? Would he find her changed? The filmy scarf wound about her dark hair and tied beneath her chin framed her hollow cheeks and made them look rounder. Her lips were a healthy rose-red.

Reassured, she went back to the platform. But here her fears began again. It was a year since they had met, since she had told him she never wanted him to make love to her again. How would he greet her, what would he say?

Two letters had come from him, from somewhere up the Darling, mostly about the steamer's adventures and the state of the rivers. His letters had always come from strange and faraway places. Now he was coming himself, and would bring with him a breath of the far outback, of the sun-warm rivers and the great dry plains through which they wandered.

Above her head the platform clock showed a steady 6.30, the hour of the northern train's expected arrival. She began to feel as if time really stood still. He would never come. She would stand for ever under a stopped clock, looking at two empty rails which disappeared into the misty darkness of a winter night.

A train whistled with a shrill, echoing peal, like the *Philadelphia* blowing off at the Campaspe junction . . . Porters began to hurry up the platform, wheeling luggage-carriers; the crowd surged forward. She hung back behind the iron gates, feeling as if she might faint.

FORTY-ONE

In the restaurant, in the light of the shaded candle that burned on their table, she looked bemusedly into his sea-blue eyes. It was all strangely like a dream; she scarcely knew what they had talked of, though they had talked happily and eagerly all the way from the station.

As soon as his hand touched hers, all her fear and weakness disappeared, and she floated calmly as a ship in harbour. They had walked hand-in-hand through the crowds, and as the dark streams of people broke and eddied past them, she had felt that they were the real, the focal point in an unreal and fluid world.

Now she watched him eat with his old gusto, winding hot spaghetti round his fork and shovelling it in with speed and precision.

'You're not eating, darling.' He stopped and regarded her anxiously.

'I like to watch you.'

'But I like to see *you* eat. You're looking much thinner. Have you been to see a doctor in Melbourne?'

'No, whatever for?'

'I don't like that cough I noticed as we were walking for the tram.'

'Oh, it only starts when I get a bit out of breath. It's nothing.'

'All the same, you ought to see a doctor.'

'But I can't afford it.'

He took out a wallet and counted a pile of notes on to the table. 'Your share of this year's earnings.'

She looked at him under her straight brows. 'But I only have a quarter-interest now. Brenton, we've had this out before. I'm not

247

going to take a quarter of the profits and put nothing back into the boat. You put nearly everything back into improvements and repairs and buying stores. You spend hardly anything on yourself.'

'Well – I regard it as an investment. And I pay myself a salary of twenty pounds a month. There is one simple solution to these arguments – let's get married, and then it will adjust itself.'

She looked down at the cloth. She had unwound the filmy scarf from her hair, and let it fall back about her shoulders, and from its soft folds her slender white neck rose like the stem of a flower.

'Don't let's talk about that now,' she said almost inaudibly.

'All right.' He lifted his glass of Riesling. 'To the most beautiful eyes in Victoria.'

She smiled, then divided the pile of notes in two, without counting them, and handed half back to him. 'That's to buy stores, and paint, and so on. I regard it as an investment too.'

He scowled, but put the notes back in his wallet. 'You're the most obstinate, the most pig-headed little devil I've ever met. You're to let me know at once if you get into difficulties over money.'

'We're always in difficulties, Imogen and I, but we manage.'

'Living on dry crusts in a garret, I suppose. You artists!'

'We live, that's the main thing.'

'You might die.'

He said it so soberly that a thrill of fear went through her. Could there really be anything wrong with her lungs? That cough, and the feeling of exhaustion in the mornings . . . She pushed the lurking fear out of sight, and closed a door in her mind firmly upon it.

When they had finished the second bottle of wine she realised that she'd had more to drink than ever in her life before, in fact she was quite light-headed. When they rose to go, she needed his guiding hand under her elbow to steer her among the tables. She seemed to float down the stairs without touching more than one or two with her feet.

As the cold night air filled her lungs, a wild exuberance seized her. She danced and twirled along the street. It was not just the wine, but everything: the bright shop-fronts, the noise of traffic, the electric lights, the fact that she was twenty-one and walking with her lover at night through the streets of a great city. I'm drunk, I am drunk, she said to herself exultantly, looking up at the faint revolving stars. Drunk with wine, and happiness, and

248

youth, and hope, and love.

She savoured the new experience, recording it on that inward sensitive plate on which, as on a photograph, all the events of her life were printed indelibly, to flash upon the eye of memory long after they had seemed forgotten.

Her earliest memory was of digging moss, bright green and velvety, from between the old red bricks of a wall that towered above her head – the earthy smell, the texture of the moss, the contrast of emerald and old rose, were as real to her now as then. Experience – she welcomed it all, she wanted to explore life, that great river, to its most hidden backwaters and billabongs.

'I believe you'd enjoy having your leg amputated,' Imogen said to her once. 'You'd be sitting up, noting with interest what it felt like to have a leg cut off.'

'How early can you remember?' she asked Brenton as he checked her wild gyrations and looked about for a cab.

'Oh, I don't know; back to when I was about five, I should think. My earliest memory is of my mother sitting on the side of her bed crying, because of something my father had said or done; and of how I wished I was big enough to hurt him for hurting her.'

'I can remember much further back than that, it's a coloured memory, rose-red and green; before I was three; a wall of my grandfather's garden. Do you know, I believe I must have been born with a feeling for colour. When I was five I dipped one of our White Leghorn fowls into a bowl of pink dye. Its feathers turned a most delicate shade of pink, but they were all gummed together by the dye, and after staggering about a bit it succumbed. I cried, because I was scared of getting into trouble, but Father said it showed a scientific and enquiring mind. And then one day when Mother left us with an aunt, John and I found a tin of paint and painted her front door with red roofing paint, and I got it all in my hair . . .'

The words were bubbling out of her in a continuous flood, she would have talked all the way back to the flat, but he silenced her with kisses. When they arrived, they found the lamp alight and a well-banked, glowing fire in the grate.

Brenton pulled the divan in front of the fire and drew her down on his knees.

'I said,' she murmured drowsily, 'I said I never wanted to see you again.'

'Yes. And you said you wanted no further share in the *Philadelphia*. But you still own a quarter of her; and you still want to see me.'

'Yes.'

'And you still want me to make love to you.'

'No.'

'Yes, you do.' And he began slowly, seriously to undress her.

'We don't need the lamp,' she said, overcome with shyness.

'Yes, we do. I want to see you. There is this dear little mole here, and there are these branching blue rivers that I must explore down, down through the dark forest to the sea . . .' he said, kissing each part as it was uncovered.

'Ah, Captain Sturt!' she said, laughing, deeply content. This was not the first voyage of discovery he had embarked on, she knew; how many Nestas had there been in his life? But she felt invulnerable now; not even the thought of Nesta could hurt her. Nor was she the same person as a year ago. Time had flowed softly, imperceptibly onward, carrying her to this new point of view. Looking back at her life so far, she felt that she had died and been reborn many times, though a thread of memory joined her various selves.

It was two hours before they thought of Imogen's possible return, and reluctantly got up, drugged and weary; but even as they slowly dressed and straightened the bed, they kept drawing together to stand locked in a peaceful embrace, warmed by the memory of desire. Brenton, still intent on 'feeding her up', made toast on the sinking fire, and they ate from the same piece, exchanging buttery kisses.

The cloakroom where he had left his bag closed at eleven, but he still lingered, saying for the third time, 'We ought to get married'.

She sighed and bit her lip. 'You know it's impossible.'

'*Why* is it impossible?' Now that he had come round to the idea of marriage, her resistance filled him with impatience.

'Because . . . because I want to be a painter, and then . . . we have different ideas. I couldn't share you with a succession of Nestas.'

'I've told you that she meant nothing to me, except as a sort of challenge. I'm surprised at you being jealous of someone like that. A girl of your intelligence –'

'I can't help it, Brenton. I couldn't help being possessive with you.'

'I'm afraid you'll marry some long-haired artist bloke, and I'll never see you again.'

'I promise you I won't marry anyone. I just want to work. But . . . oh, I do want to be with you always, and travel up and down the river! And then the life here isn't quite up to what I'd expected. I mean, sometimes when we were sketching in the little back yard behind the Gallery, isolated in a sort of – of religious devotion to Art (please don't laugh, I've never tried to express this to anybody before), sometimes then I felt as if I were at the very summit of existence. But I've been disillusioned a bit since . . .

'I've found that Bernard Hall isn't God, and that most of the others haven't that high seriousness which makes priests and devotees, and perhaps I haven't it really either . . . You're not listening, are you?'

'No. All sounds like rot to me. You're a woman, and I'm asking you for the fourth time: Will you marry me?'

She only said obstinately: 'It wouldn't work.'

She longed to say yes, but some deep instinct warned her that it would be wrong. She must go on with her painting, she had to be true to something in herself.

He left in rather a surly mood, and the next day they parted at the station with stiff faces, almost like strangers. To cover the hurt to his pride he had adopted a rough, jeering tone. In his twenty-nine years he had not before encountered a woman who could resist him when he was determined to get his own way.

As soon as his train had gone she felt an overwhelming desolation, and the next day, after a sleepless night, she wanted to rush to the post office and send a wire, 'Will marry you at once.' But still that instinct held her back.

She was engaged on an interesting study in the Still-Life class, and when it was completed she received what was high praise from Mr Hall: 'H'm! I don't often get that quality of work from students.' She became fired with new ambition, to be the first woman to win the travelling scholarship, won two years ago by Max Meldrum and available every three years.

There was a tradition of good portraitists winning it; there was less sympathy with landscape at the Gallery School, and it was in landscape that she felt her true power. But she meant to try. She worked hard, keeping under her longing for Brenton.

In the Melbourne Art Gallery there were many reproductions

251

of Old Masters, for one of the conditions of the travelling scholarship was that the winner should send back copies of the masterpieces in the overseas galleries he visited.

Delie studied these with interest, but went back again and again to four Australian landscapes – Louis Buvelot's *Summer Evening* and *Waterpool at Coleraine*; David Davies's *Moonrise, Templestowe*; and *The Purple Noon's Transparent Might*, by Streeton.

Buvelot, she could see, was the first artist in this country who had painted the unique anatomy of the gum tree as it really was, and not as a kind of etiolated oak. Streeton had the native-born's appreciation of the dry grass, the burning blue and gold, of an Australian summer. And she could look for hours at Davies's lyrical impressionist study of twilight, with a sky as purely luminous as a pearl.

There was a painting of Frederick McCubbin's, *Winter Evening*, which interested her too, and she had seen works of his exhibited with the Victorian Artists' Society, that were so full of Australian atmosphere that they seemed to exhale the eucalyptus odour of the bush.

By long study of these pictures, by going close up and 'putting her nose into the paint', she learnt something of the artists' technique; it was almost as if they stood beside her, instructing and encouraging. 'See, it is done like this; those delicate gradations of colour and light can be conveyed . . .'

It was time to get ready for the spring exhibition of the Victorian Artists' Society. Several of the students who were members of the society were sorting out their best work for submission to the selection committee. Delie got out the only large canvas she had brought from Echuca, a study of a 'hatter's' camp at the Campaspe junction, with a wisp of blue smoke curling upwards against dark trees. With the money Brenton had brought her, she could now get it framed.

She entered another river picture, one that she had worked up from a sketch since coming to Melbourne, and two that she had done in class, a still life and a landscape. Of her four paintings only one was returned by the committee; the *Evening on the Campaspe*, her most ambitious canvas, was accepted. But when varnishing day came and she went along to oil out her pictures, they looked incredibly small when hung beside all the others on a large wall, compared with their appearance at home in the flat.

Before opening day she had a new worry to take her mind off the exhibition; and in spite of her brave words to Brenton about

252

not being afraid to have his child, the possibility that confronted her now filled her with terror.

She pored over the calendar and did sums in her head which would never come out right. She was vague over dates as over most things unconnected with painting, and thought perhaps there was no real cause for worry yet. But she did not feel well, and could eat nothing in the mornings.

She did not mention her worry to Imogen; to speak of what she feared would only make it more real. Her sleep was troubled. She woke several times each night in a clammy bath of sweat.

At last opening day came. Although she was only one of many, she felt sick with excitement at exposing her paintings to the public gaze for the first time. When the *Age* came the next morning she opened it at once to read the notice.

Imogen's single flower-piece was not mentioned; but half-way down the column she saw: 'Delphine Gordon is a newcomer whose work shows promising technique (especially in conveying the liquid, shifting brilliance of water) but a lack of originality. Her *Evening on the Campaspe* is strongly reminiscent of Louis Buvelot . . .'

Well! She had painted that picture in Echuca, before she had ever set eyes on a Buvelot. The river paintings were mentioned, but not the still life into which an extra year of study and knowledge had gone.

She began to wonder, as she had wondered before, whether the academic teaching of the Gallery School was damaging rather than helping her art. Smith of the *Argus*, who bitterly hated the Impressionist school, did not mention her name.

By the end of the week, when her period had still not made an appearance, she could bear the suspense no longer. She walked along Upper Collins Street reading the names of doctors on their brass plates, and chose one at random. She gave her name as Mrs Edward Brenton. She hated being examined, and her heart beat with fear of the strange doctor as well as of the condition he might find.

When she emerged on to the street again, there was a feverish colour in her cheeks, her throat was dry and her hands trembled. feeling suddenly faint, she walked into a tea-shop and sat down, while she tried to adjust herself to the shattering news of the diagnosis.

She could not believe it yet: that her career in Melbourne was finished, that she would have to leave the art school and the possibility of the European scholarship behind her for ever.

The doctor had looked at her hands, taken her temperature, sounded her chest and questioned her closely about her meals and sleeping habits; it had all seemed rather pointless to Delie, who wanted to know only one thing. And then, when he had completed his examination, he had mildly, quietly dropped the bombshell:

'I'm afraid you are suffering from tuberculosis in an early stage. Only one lung is affected. But you need rest in a warm, dry climate if the disease is to be arrested. A sputum test would be necessary to confirm the diagnosis, but I feel quite certain.'

At first she felt only relief; she was not going to have a baby. He would not advise a pregnancy in her present state of health, he said. Plenty of sun, plenty of rest, some good red wine with meals, and a tonic . . .

She ordered some coffee mechanically, and sat staring at the wall. 'I advise a move to an inland climate . . . Another winter in Melbourne may be your last . . .'

The coffee came, and she drank it without tasting it and ordered another. Her head was clearing now, but her cheeks still burned, her breath came short and quick. She felt a great longing for Brenton, to be able to look at this frightening thing from the shelter of his arms.

Brenton! What had he said? 'You might die.' And it was true, she might die, next winter might be her last. But she could not believe it. There was too much that she wanted to do, too much to be seen and known, there were too many pictures that she must paint. She couldn't die yet.

'You must move . . . Another winter in Melbourne . . . the inland would be ideal for a person with your complaint . . .'

Suddenly she felt tremendously happy. For weeks, ever since Brenton had gone back to Echuca, she had been fighting against her need for him. Now it was all decided for her. She would write at once, and tell Brenton she was coming back. Surely he would still want her even if she had only one lung, just as she would still want him if he lost a leg.

The waitress brought the second cup of coffee, and received a dazzling smile. Delie warmed her cold fingers on the cup. She had stopped trembling. She would return to the river, as she had always known she would. There, in that clean, eucalyptus-scented air, she would get well. She knew she would get well.

FORTY-TWO

Delie spent a short holiday in Bendigo with the McPhees before her wedding. Already her health was better, her cough had almost stopped. It was as if the conflict between her love and her longing for a life dedicated to art in the city had been tearing her apart.

Now that it was resolved for her she accepted the new life with happy relief. Nor would Brenton consider waiting for a year to see if the change of climate would cure her lung. He insisted that they should get married at once, that she should travel with him when the *Philadelphia* sailed again for the Darling and the dry, sunny plains of the West. He was not afraid of the disease.

She had been shocked at what two years had done to Angus McPhee. He seemed to have aged quite suddenly: it was rheumatoid arthritis, Mrs Mac. whispered. He shuffled along slowly with a stick, his big frame bent, his once powerful hands twisted and useless. Though his hair and beard were as thick as ever, his shrewd blue eyes had lost their sharp twinkle. They seemed dulled by the continuous pain from his inflamed and tortured joints.

When she was leaving, he presented Delie with a handsome cheque.

'Tae buy a wee pr-resent for yeself. Ye'll be needin' a sicht o' new furnishins ben the hoose.'

'But I'll be living on a boat, Mr McPhee. There's no room for much furniture, except for bunks.'

'Livin on a boat! Och, harrk at the lassie! Livin on a wee sma' boat, wi' oot e'en a front gairden, and the bairns aye fallin' in the river and gettin' drooned!'

Delie laughed. 'Well, there aren't any bairns yet, you know. I'll just have to teach them all to swim very young.'

'She's not going to be a good river this year,' said Brenton gloomily. 'I dunno how we'll get past the Bitch an' Pups, or even past Campbell's Island, with two barges.'

'Well, why take two barges then? You only took one last year.'

'Because now I'm a married man, with a wife to provide for.'

(He kissed her lightly.) 'I must make more money. Another barge-load of wool last year would have meant at least another five hundred pounds in freight.'

'But *we*,' said Delie, faintly stressing the joint pronoun, 'would have had to pay another bargemaster and two more hands.'

'Yes – about twenty pounds a month in wages, and look at the extra profit. No, I'm taking two.'

Delie gave up the argument. She didn't really care how many barges there were, but she had noticed already that Brenton no longer made a pretence of consulting her over the running of the steamer. His idea of sharing their worldly goods seemed to be 'What's yours is mine, but what's mine's my own.'

'Of course,' said Brenton, 'it means the load won't have any insurance cover till we get past the 'Bidgee junction. We haven't a certificate from the Underwriters' Association for towing two barges.'

'Then shouldn't we get a certificate?'

'Yes, but not for this trip. It takes too long. We should get away in a week or two. The bill of lading warranty only refers to towing downstream so we'll be covered all right on the way back.'

However he might try to exclude her, Delie was determined to take an intelligent interest in what was obviously the centre of her husband's life. She believed that he loved her, but love was not of the first importance to him. It was as well, she saw wisely, that she had her own work; and he would never be jealous of her other interest.

Brenton had given her his undivided attention for perhaps three days after their wedding. It was an impossible time to get married, of course; the *Philadelphia* had just come off 'Rotten Row', the dry dock, after an overhaul; word had come that the river was rising upstream, and Brenton was busy wiring for those of his crew who were not in the town, signing on new members, and preparing to load.

For her wedding Delie had worn a cream serge costume and a hat with huge yellow roses. Bessie was rather scandalised, saying that she 'wouldn't feel married herself' if she had no veil; but Delie had her own ideas and Brenton preferred as little fuss as possible.

She had been touched by her uncle's efforts to make himself presentable for 'giving the bride away'. Charles had evidently brushed his old-fashioned dark suit with care, his chin was freshly shaven and his hair had been cut; but there was a large hole in the heel of one of his black socks. At the wedding breakfast he drank too much whisky and became maudlin, the tears running unchecked from his red-rimmed eyes down into his moustache.

When they had first broken the news to him he did not seem pleased.

'Live on a boat!' he said dubiously. 'I had hoped, dear,' he said, taking Delie's hand in the front room, now sadly dusty and cobweb-draped, 'I had hoped and expected that you make a brilliant, er . . . With your looks, and your talents . . . However, I'm not a good one to advise anybody, I know. My own marriage . . .' He sighed.

His mournful eyes, unhealthily bloodshot, and his drooping, unkempt grey moustache moved in a melancholy smile. 'However, as long as you are happy, I suppose . . .'

She noticed that he seemed unable to finish a sentence, but would let it trail off into an indistinguishable mumble. He wore elastic-sided boots down at the heel, corded riding-trousers and a not very clean shirt. It seemed odd to hear him cavil at Brenton Edwards as a husband for his niece – Brenton who had spruced himself up to meet her relative, his shining curls flattened with much brushing, his high collar spotless beneath his hard, clean jaw.

When she called him in, Charles was quite affable, rather flusteredly producing whisky and glasses. Brenton had been warned what to expect, and did not blink an eyelid at Charles's seedy appearance. He looked with interest at the faded elegance of the room, the dusty pleated silk shading the candles on the piano, the lustre vases and threadbare gold brocade, the worn rose-flowered carpet.

Two young aboriginal women had come out of the kitchen when they arrived in a hired sulky, and fled giggling over the sandhills beyond the house. Delie remembered her first arrival here so many years ago, Lucy and Minna giggling behind the tank-stand.

Now Minna was dead, that lovely girl whose image Time had destroyed years before her death; Hester and Adam too. When Charles asked, with obvious reluctance, if she and Brenton would stay for a meal, she assured him that they must get back. Her old home was haunted by ghosts, most of all by Adam's young and troubled spirit.

Her uncle told her to choose something from the house for a wedding-present. Feeling that Hester would turn in her grave if she took any breakable treasure, she chose the tapestry-covered footstool on which she used to sit at Miss Barrett's knee in the old days. She still heard occasionally from Miss Barrett, who was now living in France; they had kept in touch, though their letters became less and less frequent.

After the wedding, the happy pair had gone to the Palace Hotel until the *Philadelphia* should be ready to leave. Brenton said he would have quite enough of sleeping with her in a narrow bunk; and the large double-bed was certainly more comfortable.

'You're looking better already,' he said after the first week, parting the long dark hair that fell over her white shoulders, and delicately feeling her vertebrae with his fingers. 'I can't count the bumps nearly so easily, and you don't look so hollow and dark around the eyes.'

Her smallness, her fragility, even her delicate health delighted him, made him feel more strong and protective. He examined her slender, fine-boned feet, her little knee-caps, with the tender absorption of a child with a new doll.

He had used to like a more voluptuous type of figure, but now he was enamoured of small, pointed breasts and transparent skin through which the blue veins showed.

'It's just as well,' he said, burying his face between her breasts, 'that we'll be sleeping in separate bunks on board. I'll be wearing you out. You know what the doctor said.'

'He said I mustn't have a baby just yet, either.'

'No. We must be very careful.'

Delie felt sure that she was going to be happy ever after. She felt only pity for Imogen, leading a restless, unsatisfying life of violent affairs that never lasted; and a new sympathy for Bessie, now married to a prim, stiff-collared, anaemic young man who had never been out of Echuca and had no ideas outside the drapery business, which he hoped to inherit from her papa.

Bessie was radiating contentment, smugly proud of her new home which her father had furnished with elaborate pieces. She was with child, and her face, that used to be always animated with chatter, had often a still, listening look, while her lovely complexion bloomed. Bessie was a fruiting tree. Almost Delie envied her the ripeness of maternity.

At night she often felt feverish. Her cheeks burned with a dry flush, symptom of the disease she had, that enhanced her looks and made her eyes bluer and more brilliant.

In the mornings she would be pale and lethargic, with her dark

258

hair spread upon the pillow still damp from the night sweats that sapped her energy. But though she often stayed in bed for breakfast, soon the longing to see Brenton, to be near him, to touch him, would become so strong that she got up and went down to the wharf.

He rarely glanced in her direction after his first greeting, but she knew he was aware of her presence as he directed the loading of farm machinery, bags of flour, piles of rabbit traps, cases of beer; himself the most active man there as he lumped bags or stacked a pile of red-gum boards for spare paddles.

She felt impelled, when he stopped for a breather, with the sweat darkening his fair curls, to stand close beside him with her arm just brushing his. With her senses roused but unsatisfied, she was intensely aware of his physical presence. She felt that the strong current of attraction that flowed between them must be visible to others, in an arc of fire between her arm and his, like the electricity which the *Gem* and the *Ellen* had to light their cabins – 'at the touch of a pretty little button, and without smoke, fuss or smell', as a delighted passenger had written.

There was a new member of the crew already in his quarters on board. The first day Delie went down to the boat, sniffing delightedly at the old, muddy, decaying river smell, watching the ripple-reflections dance in golden light on plank and beam, she was startled by a commanding voice from the wheel-house:

'Stand at . . . HEASE! Stand from under! Some of you lubbers will be getting killed down there yet!'

She looked up, expecting to see some grizzled sea captain, and saw instead the wise old eyes of a green parrot regarding her through the open windows of the wheel-house.

'*What* did you say?' she asked politely.

'Which of you devils has had the screwdriver?' replied the parrot severely.

She went up to the wheel-house and offered to shake hands or scratch his poll, but the parrot, which had a length of light chain tied to one leg, backed away with a flow of incomprehensible language.

'He's swearing at you in Danish,' Brenton called up to her. 'He can swear in three languages, English, Danish and Swedish.'

'But where did you get him?'

'From a Captain Jacobsen who's retiring from the river. He was a deep-sea man, and picked up Skipper in South America. He said

Skipper would never be happy away from a boat, and he seemed fond of me.'

'All birds seem to like you,' said Delie, thinking of the parrots he had whistled up in the red-gum forest across the river, when they picnicked there on the first day of their marriage. He wanted to make love to her in New South Wales, he said, because that was his home State. He had been born in a small bush town, but had lived in both Sydney and Melbourne before he was fifteen. He had a married sister in Queensland and a brother in Sydney; both his parents were dead. His father had been a saddler.

'We never had things flash like that,' he said after they'd visited her uncle's place. 'No carpets and pianos and things. We lived in the kitchen mostly, and had a parlour for visitors that was hardly ever used. But I was never in the house when I could help it, and I was always wagging it from school. That's why the city got me down – all these houses and walls. Out here, a man can breathe.'

She had never seen him out of the town before, except at night when they had roamed along the river-bank with the one idea of getting away from 'people'.

Now she discovered a new side to him, the bushman and naturalist with the keen, trained eyesight of a boy born and bred in the country, and a wide knowledge of native birds. She had seen Murray magpies come down to take cheese from his fingers, and he told her about the tame willy-wag that used to ride on his shoulder when he was a boy.

He never used to take more than one egg from a nest, and used to fight the other boys who wanted to take the lot. He kept boxes full of eggs under his bed.

'Sometimes I'd forget to blow one, and there'd be a row from Mum when it started to pong.'

Delie was filled with tenderness for that little fair-haired boy with his collection of birds' eggs. And he had a gentleness with small things, this tough bushman who could roll an unruly member of the crew on the deck with one blow of his fist.

He found wildflowers that she had not noticed, touching them delicately with his big fingers, naming them for her; he held a tiny lizard in his palm and stroked it till its alarm subsided; lifted her up to see the neat white eggs of a parrot in the hollow limb of a tree.

Children liked him too. When they came down to the wharf, pestering to be allowed on board, Delie noticed how he handled them, firmly and gently.

All this erased the rather unpleasant impression made by the way he had crushed the wounded moth so deliberately with his finger, when they first had tea together.

But the pleasant companion of these bush picnics became again the busy captain, and even on Sundays she had him to herself only at night. Then, at the last drowsy moment before drifting into sleep, she felt with utter content the touch of his side, the intimacy of their feet beneath the bedclothes, annulling all the loneliness of the day.

In the afternoons she rested for two hours in bed, as the doctor had ordered. She filled her time with painting and drawing, visited Bessie, and waited, almost as impatiently as Brenton did, for the expected break in the season.

At last all was ready, and the rise that was coming down the river, its progress posted every day in the town, was due in two days' time.

The extra deckhands and the new bargemaster were engaged, and a new fireman. He was a taciturn man with a dark, seamed face. Delie thought he looked rather frightening, but Brenton explained that the man couldn't help his appearance, he had once had hot ashes and cinders and even fragments of metal blown deep into his skin when a boiler exploded; he was lucky to have survived.

Ben came back, a little older and more assured than when she had seen him a year ago but with the same shy, dark, intelligent eyes. He helped her to hang new chintz curtains in the cabins and saloon, and was always eager to run messages for her.

Charlie the engineer was a surly and disobliging as ever; the mate, Jim Pearce, as friendly and jolly. Ah Lee came on board with a suitcase which he did not let out of his hands till he had it stowed away in some mysterious place in the galley.

There were not enough cabins for everybody. The mate and the engineer shared the cabin next to the captain's. The fireman and Ben had a small cabin aft. The other deckhands, the bargemaster of the first barge and the bargemen, with the Chinese cook, slept under a tarpaulin on the first barge.

Ah Lee, who complained of the others' snoring which kept him awake, decided to sleep in the forepeak which was used for paint and stores. But the mate, forgetting he was there, jumped down to get a piece of rope during the night. He landed right on top of

Ah Lee, who was not pleased.

'Jesus blunny Cli!' he yelled. 'A man no can sleepee on this blunny boa'!'

Steamers which had already been upstream for flour from Yarrawonga and Albury reported the Moira Lakes almost dry. Rivermen were gloomy about the prospects for the year's trading, for there had been little rain in Queensland either, and the Darling was low.

'We'll leave as soon as there's enough water over the Bitch an' Pups to take us,' said Brenton. 'It'll be a race to get to the Darling junction before the river falls again. If we're caught we'll just have to lie up and wait for another fresh.'

But when they finally got away, Delie had no idea that it would be nearly two years before she saw Echuca again.

Before they left, she had a letter from Kevin Hodge, just leaving South Africa to be repatriated. 'This place will do me,' he wrote. 'As soon as I've seen my people I'll be coming back here to take up land, and there's a little South African girl who will be waiting . . .'

Delie had almost forgotten him. She was glad he no longer thought of her.

FORTY-THREE

They had passed Murrumbidgee Reef while more cautious skippers were waiting to see if the rise would hold. At Clump Bend Teddy Edwards swore for the first time, long and softly, as he turned the big wheel rapidly, heaving down on the spokes.

His eyes never left the river, where the current slipped round a sharp S-bend with a large snag sticking up in the middle. He swung the boat straight at the snag, and it crunched harmlessly beneath the solid red-gum stem. Tangled in a paddle-wheel, it would have bent the iron frame and smashed the paddles.

'Come up, old girl; come up,' he muttered, heaving the wheel in the opposite direction. 'She's dropping her right shoulder,' he said to the mate, who had stood by on the other side of the wheel to give an extra heave on the spokes.

'Yair,' said Jim Pearce. 'Some of the cargo not trimmed properly?'

'Must be. We'd better see to it at the first stop to wood-up.'

(Not 'You'd better see to it,' or just 'See to it,' Delie noticed, but 'We'd better see to it.')

She was standing quietly in a corner of the wheel-house, trying not to get in the way. Watching him as he looked back at the two barges negotiating the bend after him, she saw why they said, 'Teddy Edwards is shaping as a good riverman'.

'Whee!' He let out his breath with relief as the second barge came safely round, and rubbed the back of his wrist across his sweating forehead. 'She's going to be a picnic, this trip. You'll be seeing the river just about at its worst, darling.'

For the first time since they had left he looked directly at her. The boat had taken all his thoughts and all his endearments so far; it had come alive under his hands, he talked to it as if it were a sentient being. But now he looked down at Delie in the old attitude she used to dislike, his head thrown back a little, his eyes half-closed, and her heart seemed to stop. She had never loved him so much.

She saw him now in his man's world, taking command so naturally, so easily, without the least arrogance or fuss. He was nearly ten years older, and in him she seemed to find her lost father, her dead cousin and husband all in one.

The fresh that had brought a rise of two feet had already passed on, and the river was falling again. The fantastic twisted roots of trees growing in the bank showed clear of the water once more.

For Delie – setting off at last round those unknown bends, along that mysterious channel which as a child she had so longed to explore – there was something of anticlimax in the steeply sloping banks of clay, varied with clean sandy spits of a warm yellow colour on the inside of bends. Here were the same banks, the same dark leaning trees, and behind them the endless grey forests of the flooded gums that she had known above Echuca.

The day was overcast and dull. A cool wind from their movement came in the open wheel-house, but a shaft of sunlight struck down on the sombre trees ahead, lighting their pale grey trunks, turning their leaves to olive and amber, the tiny stems to threads of scarlet silk.

Suddenly it came over Delie that she was really started on her great adventure, that she was off 'up the Darlin',' away into the outback with the man she loved.

Her happiness swelled in her breast until she felt she could not contain it, she must burst like an over-charged boiler. She seized the rope that hung at the back of the wheel-house, and blew a tremendous blast on the whistle.

'Avast and belay there!' cried the parrot, startled.

The mate looked shocked, and Brenton frowned.

'Here, don't do that. The engineer will think I'm blowing off steam so as I can pull in at a woodpile, and he'll let the pressure drop. Or the bargemaster'll think it's a signal to come alongside for his lunch.'

'Sorry,' said Delie, blushing. But she lifted her head to hear the lovely peal, wild and free, echoing back from bends far out of sight. She nearly added, in explanation, 'It was because I love you,' but the mate was standing there, leaning forward through the window, looking for the mile-tree that marked their distance in river miles from Albury.

'Is that a five?' he muttered. 'Can you see a five on that big tree in the bight of the bend there, the one with the niggerhead? I'm seeing fives in every twist of bark. Three-sixty-five's the next one.'

Delie leant in her corner and sang softly to herself. She was off at last; and the whole future beckoned her from round the next bend and the next.

If the movement was only illusory; if it was the banks that moved, while she and the boat stood still on an unflowing, un-returning stream; well, it did not matter. She was content to let life flow towards her, or carry her on, whichever it might be. She stretched out her hands to draw it all to her, up to the last experience, the final great fact of death. She heard the white waves stamp upon the shore.

Near Koondrook, where big red-gum logs were piled on the banks and the redolent blood-red sawdust lay in great heaps, they sighted the smoke of the *Success* which had left just behind them. The throttle was immediately opened, wood was thrown recklessly into the furnace, and they drew away once more.

Then for seventeen miles they churned past Campbell's Island, where kangaroos and wild black pigs stared at them from the reedy grasses. The river, being halved by the island, became ex-tremely narrow. Leaning trees swept the decks with their lower branches; leaves, twigs and birds' nests clattered aboard.

The mate was taking his six hours off duty, so Ben came up to lend a hand on the wheel round the sharp turns. Because of the way she was loaded, the *Philadelphia* came sluggishly out of the bends, sidling round them like a befuddled crab.

Ben, thin and awkward in half-mast pants, gave the skipper's wife one scared glance from his shy, dark eyes and did not look at her again. His ears tingled when he felt her eyes, so large and soft and blue, fixed upon him. He stammered some reply to her friendly greeting, and stared straight ahead.

Brenton had entered in his log that morning:

> 6 A.M.: Steamer loaded with list to starboard, also three inches down by the head, a trim in which she will scarcely steer. When through Swan Hill bridge will stop to re-stow cargo.

(In spite of his experience in Williamstown harbour, he sometimes used the terms 'left' and 'right', which were understood on the river as well as more seaman-like terms; but his journal was kept like that of a seagoing craft.)

They stopped at Falkiner's Woodpile, where six-foot logs for the furnace were 'walked' on board by a chain of men standing along the gangplank. Then, while the cargo was being moved, Delie went up to a bare little wood-and-iron farmhouse back from the river-bank, to ask for fresh milk.

A gaunt woman in a black dress, long apron and sun-bonnet came out, and rather grudgingly filled her billy-can with three-penn'orth of milk.

'How old are you?' she asked, looking curiously at Delie's slim figure in its pink cambric blouse and straight skirt, the waist emphasised by a wide belt; at her dark shining hair and beautiful complexion.

'Just twenty-one,' said Delie.

'And how old do yer think I am?'

'Oh, I don't know . . .' Delie looked at the lined brown face and leathery hands, the stringy, mousy hair straggling from under the bonnet, the mouth with a missing front tooth. She looked away again, embarrassed.

'I'm twenty-five,' said the woman, with a bitter smile. 'Yes, just four years older'n you. Wouldn't think it, would yer? But I've 'ad a hard life, yer see. 'Ad to slave amongst cows since I were about ten year old; 'ad to milk before I went to school, an' milk again at night when I were too tired almost to sit up . . . I hate cows.'

Three frowzle-haired wiry children, all under five or so years, pushed round her skirts and peeped doubtfully at the stranger. 'Why did you marry a farmer, then?' Delie was on the point of asking. But she realised that for this woman there could have been no escape. She would meet no one but cocky-farmers; she'd had no chance to educate herself for anything except marriage. Her life would be bounded by cows until she died.

'Sometimes I've cried with fright, getting the cows in from them swamps. Crawlin' with tiger-snakes, they are. And the river's that dangerous about 'ere, I don't expect the kids will live to grow up. We'll never get away,' said the woman, with a kind of pride of hopelessness.

Delie felt terribly guilty when she thought of the easy, interesting life she led; her own smooth hands and unblemished complexion made her feel ashamed.

With some obscure idea of consoling the other with her misfortune, she blurted out: 'I – I'm ill, you know. I have to rest a lot and I can't do much. But this climate is supposed to be very good for TB. The doctor said – '

The woman drew back as though a palpable cloud of germs had issued from Delie's mouth.

'Get back! Get up to the 'ouse!' she cried angrily to the children, shooing them away. 'Keep away, I tell yer. Come away when you're told,' she cried, angrily grabbing the youngest who was toddling towards the visitor, blowing bubbles from her sticky lips.

There was such disgust in her voice that Delie was stung. 'It isn't leprosy I've got, or the plague,' she called after their retreating backs. But she was shaken. What if Brenton had felt like that about the disease?

The *Success* should have caught them up while they were stopped, but there was no sign of her or even of her smoke in the distance. It was not until much later that they learned how her barge had been snagged and sunk above Campbell's Island, and her crew had taken days to rescue the cargo and refloat the barge.

Below Swan Hill the character of the river had changed. From a mysterious stream flowing between uncharted forests where strange birds called, it had become an open river winding between flat, grassy plains, with farmhouses and patches of irrigated orchard on the banks.

Delie travelled most of the way in the wheel-house, finding it all fascinating. Brenton, who was supposed to have every other six hours off duty, scarcely left the wheel-house and even had his meals brought up to him there.

266

She learned a great deal of river lore by listening to the laconic phrases dropped by skipper and mate.

Every bend, almost every tree, seemed to have its own story of collision, fire, snagging or sinking, races between rival skippers and remarkable tows.

It amazed her that Brenton always knew where he was, without referring to the long, linen chart wound on rollers that was kept in the cabin. He had every bend, bight and reef photographed in his mind, and before a punt-crossing had come in sight, would give a blast on the whistle to warn the punt-man to drop the cable to the bottom of the river.

They had passed Tooley Buc and the experimental pumping station at Goodnight, and other places whose names made a weird music in Delie's mind: Black Stump, Wood Wood, Gallows Bend, Tyntynder, Pyangil.

Then Teddy Edwards pushed the throttle in the wheel-house to dead slow, and, holding the wheel steady, rested his chin meditatively on his brown forearm.

'What is it?' she asked, seeing nothing but an innocent bend of river ahead.

'The Bitch an' Pups. Round the next bend. Can't you hear the roar?'

FORTY-FOUR

Ahead lay the large island and several small boulders, the Bitch and her snarling Pups, that barred all but a narrow, dangerous channel: the place that all rivermen liked to have behind them on a low river. At the shallowest place the water foamed and swirled like a mill-race, only three feet deep, over a bar of rock.

'We're drawing just two feet six, so that's all right,' said the skipper calmly. He blew a long blast on the whistle and swung the wheel to starboard, bringing the *Philadelphia* round in a slow sweep until she faced against the current, the two barges following until the whole convoy faced upstream.

Now they proceeded to drop the barges through the dangerous passage, by tying up the steamer and letting each barge drift slowly downstream, paying out the tow-rope as they went. Deck-hands stood ready with poles to push off from the hard clay and rocks of the islands; even the fireman and the cook stood ready to help.

When the barges were safely tied up below, Brenton began to drop the steamer through without using a rope. With the paddles just turning ahead, he let the current take her slow backwards. All hands watched anxiously as she was dragged a little sideways by the current, dropping towards the narrow race that seemed scarcely wide enough to take her.

Just then a gust of wind sprang up, caught the high super-structure, and swung her out of position. Brenton moved the throttle to Full Ahead and the boat shuddered as paddles bit into the water and took her upstream again out of danger.

He appeared cool as a cucumber; he might have been cruising somewhere in the middle of a big lake.

A second time they dropped down, inch by inch, and a second time the wind caught them. This time the port paddle-box scraped one of the Pups as they went forward. The third time they edged back into the channel, like a hermit crab with a tender behind feeling its way into a shell, the racing current took them through without damage except for a piece of wood knocked off the paddle-housing.

The *Philadelphia* turned downstream again, with her two barges attached, at her full speed of eight knots increased by the current to twelve. They all felt a slackening of the tension with that hazard behind. There was nothing to worry about now before Jeremiah Lump and the Boundary Rocks, above Euston.

Brenton took out a handkerchief and wiped his sweating palms, the only outward sign of the strain he had been under.

The banks became closely timbered again; then the Wakool came in sharply on the right, and the river widened out. Delie refused to go into the cabin for her rest, because they were soon to pass the Murrumbidgee junction. The banks were higher here, with ridges of red sand topped by dark Murray pines.

Clouds came up and the wind blew cold. Brenton shut the windows, so that it was snug and companiable inside the wheel-house. He pointed out to her the nankeen herons flying out of the trees just ahead of the boat, the light shining through their coppery wings.

'See them birds?' he said. 'There's one in a tree quite close, see? See his blue crest? And the long white plumes at the back?

They're night-herons really, they only feed at night, but the boat flushes 'em out of the trees.'

'Where, where?' she cried, unable to see. She was used by now to his occasional slips in grammar when he was excited, and scarcely noticed them.

He left the wheel and walked over to her, turning her head between his two hands until she was looking in the right direction. But she did not see the birds; she closed her eyes and leant against his hands, marvelling again at the magic of their touch.

A pair of black swans, after much beating of their white-tipped wings, took off and sped down the reach. A kookaburra flew silently across the river.

'Those damn' birds,' said the mate meditatively. 'Whenever I see them, or hear 'em in the mornings and at sunset, I remember how they laughed at me when I first come to Australia.'

'They frightened *me* the first time I heard them,' said Delie.

'Well, you know what I was when I first arrived; a real Pommy, dark blue suit, tweed cap, black shoes and all. I deserted off a merchantman at Port Adelaide, got a lift to Murray Bridge, and set off to walk to Morgan, where they said there was plenty of steamers and I could get a berth.

'I walked through the bush, following more or less the line of the river. Hot! I've never bin so hot. I took off me coat and tied it round me neck; I took off me waistcoat and chucked it away. I was dead scared of snakes, and lots of times I had to cut across dry swamps full of reeds . . .

'And whenever I got into the shade of some big tree, those damn' birds'd start laughing at me. Mocking. You never heard such heartless laughter. What a bee of a country, I thought. I'll never set foot on it again (me feet was blistered by this time). And I never did, neither, except to cross the road from a steamer to a pub.'

'But you like the river, even if you don't like the country?'

'Don't like the country? Who says I don't like it? I wouldn't live nowhere else, certainly not back in damp old England. She's a beaut country, and a bonzer river, and no one better call *me* a Pommy.'

'Same here,' said Delie enthusiastically.

'There's the 'Bidgee coming in,' said Brenton casually.

'Where? Where?' She flew across the wheel-house, and pressed her nose to the glass on the starboard side.

'All right, it won't fly away.'

269

'Is *that* it?' She was disappointed; the Murrumbidgee, which brought the snow-waters down from Kiandra where she had lived as a child, which was a navigable river for half its length, came into the Murray as tamely as any small creek. But below the junction the main stream widened; it was now a river of noble proportions, but still very circuitous. They were coming to a cutting, where the main stream had cut through a narrow neck of land, leaving a six-mile bend to silt up gradually until it should become a billabong, no longer connected with the river. Through the narrow cutting, which was only a hundred yards long, the current raced. There was quick consultation between skipper and mate.

'I think I'll take her through, Jim.'

'I dunno, Teddy. The current's pretty stiff.'

'The old channel's silting up, though, and there's not much water. Yes, I'll take her through.'

There was a tap on the wheel-house door, and Ben put his head in, about level with their knees as he stood on the bottom step.

'Message from the engineer, Skipper. He says if you're going through Wilson's cutting you'd better take her dead slow.'

Teddy Edwards put his head back and looked down at Ben through half-closed blue eyes. He leant comfortably on the wheel, holding it in position with the weight of his big frame.

'Oh, he does, does he? You just wait here a while, my lad.'

He left the wheel a moment, stepped down to the deck and walked over to the side. He stood with both hands on the rail looking down towards the cutting, estimating the speed of the current. Then he stepped back, took the wheel, and set his jaw hard.

In a moment they were racing in the grip of the current. There was a shout of alarm from the barge behind, the steamer and barges rushed through, dragged sideways against one bank until the port wheel was churning up reeds and mud. The skipper looked back as the last barge hit the bank and cannoned off safely.

'Now Ben, my boy,' he said, 'you can go down and tell that interfering blanky engineer that I took her through full steam ahead.'

'Y-yes, sir.' He disappeared, still pop-eyed.

'We saved about six mile there,' said Brenton.

'And might have lost six hundred pounds' worth of cargo and barge,' said the mate darkly.

But the skipper only smiled, a small self-satisfied smile.

270

FORTY-FIVE

Below the Devil's Racecourse, the *Philadelphia* was held up for repairs. One paddle-wheel had been dismantled and its iron frame straightened, and two split paddles had been replaced.

Teddy Edwards, turned carpenter, was on the bank planing a young tree to replace a smashed deck stanchion. He was an expert axeman, and had felled the tree with a few well-aimed blows.

The parrot hopped out of the wheel-house, flew on to Delie's shoulder where she was leaning on the rail of the top deck to watch, and looked down at the carpentering with knowing eyes.

'Which of you devils has had the screwdriver?' he asked sternly.

As the mate came up on the way to his cabin, Delie stopped him. 'Jim,' she said in a low voice, 'I heard you advise the skipper to warp over that bad reef back there – what is it, MacFarlane's Reef? – and to drop through at the Racecourse. Isn't he being a bit foolhardy? It almost seems as if he goes directly against advice.'

'Ah, Miss Philadelphia, a man can only learn through experience. Us older chaps can't teach him. He'll be a good river man, but he's young yet. He'll learn what can and what can't be done with two barges, on this trip.'

At MacFarlane's Reef they had scraped and bumped, but got across safely; at the Racecourse, when Brenton slowed down and prepared to take the rapids bows first, the treacherous cross-wind, that had been blowing in gusts all day, caught them side-on. The *Philadelphia* had sailed like a great paper boat diagonally across the river, to crash into the overhanging trees and the bank of the New South Wales side. The paddle-housing crumpled like paper, deck stanchions were smashed, a long bough poked through the fly-netting window of the galley, narrowly missing Ah Lee ('Jesus blunny Cli! Tlees knock po's off of stove now!' he yelled); and there they were impaled like a bird on a thorn.

The following barges, with less wind resistance, could yet do nothing to stop themselves. The bargemen could only try to steer clear of each other and the disabled steamer, as the current caught them and swirled them down past her. The first barge brought up with a jerk at the end of its rope that almost pulled the towing-pole out; the second went aground with such a list that half the cargo was lost, and bales of hay went floating down the river. Some of these were salvaged and spread on the bank to dry, but many were gone. Meanwhile everyone shouted advice, swear-words and instructions, even the parrot joining in from the wheel-house in Danish.

The whole crew, even those who were off duty, had turned out to get the *Philadelphia* steaming down-river again. They all knew the need for haste; they had ventured out on a river yet danger-ously low to beat the other steamers to the Darling and the back-loading of wool, for it was a case of first come first served at the station landings. Brenton worked harder than any of them, cutting trees, taking a line across the river from the winch to warp off steamer and barge.

Just before the repairs were completed, the engineer came up on the top deck, wiping his fingers on his greasy cap. He gave Delie a surly nod and then lifted his nose into the wind, sniffing like a dog.

'Thought I smelled smoke,' he said. 'C'n you see anything?'

He shaded his eyes and gazed towards the east. In this part the Murray made a ninety-mile bend to the southward below Euston, and returned upon itself towards Mildura. Far across this wide neck of land appeared a faint smudge of smoke, extending in a tail along the skyline, as though a train had just passed. But it was not a train.

'Hell!' said Charlie loudly. 'The *Pride of the Murray* is on our tail.'

'You mean you know which steamer it is by the smoke?'

'I know by the way the smoke is spread out, an' the colour,' said Charlie without the flicker of an eyelash.

Delie marvelled, not knowing that Charlie had seen the *Pride of the Murray*'s engineer just before they left, and knew that she was nearly ready to leave and would do her best to race them to Wentworth and the Darling junction. She was a stern-wheeler, a faster but a bigger boat, so that she would have more trouble over the bars and rapids than the little *Philadelphia*, unless she was travelling behind a fresh.

Charlie had run down the steps over the paddle-box to the skipper, and Delie saw Brenton look briefly over his shoulder to the eastward, before raising the completed stanchion into place. Within half an hour the *Philadelphia* was under steam again, churning down-river with dark smoke curling from her funnel.

Delie thought there was a new note in the engine; the effortless churning along with the current had changed to a more urgent *chuff-chuff-chuff-chuff*, the paddles went *clunk-clunk-clunk* in a faster rhythm, and the whole boat began to tremble and shudder with effort.

She put Skipper back on his perch and went down to the bottom deck, in behind the great pile of flour-bags that darkened the opening to the boiler and engine between the paddle-boxes, bathrooms and galley. She saw the dark-faced fireman knock open the furnace door and fling another length of box into the fire. Charlie was standing with a bit of rag in his hand, looking at the pressure gauge with satisfaction.

She knew she was not welcome, but she went up and looked at the gauge. It showed nearly 80 lb. pressure. A large brick and a heavy spanner hung from the safety valve by a piece of wire.

Charlie looked at her with a fanatical gleam in his blue eyes beneath his wild, fierce-looking eyebrows.

'It ain't no use pokin' yer nose in 'ere,' he said. 'I know what I'm a-doin'. I've 'ad eighty-two on that there gauge and she never turned a hair. Them manufacturers is cautious blokes.'

'Never turned a hair! Listen to her! She sounds as if she's tearing herself to pieces.'

Charlie listened to the frantic sob of the funnel with what was almost a smile on his weather-beaten face.

'She knows! She knows the *Pride of the Murray* is after 'er. If I give 'er 'er head now we'll be at Wentworth first, you'll see.'

Delie marched up to the wheel-house and tackled Brenton.

'It's not safe! That mad engineer will blow us all up.'

'Nonsense, little 'un. I'd trust Charlie with any engine when he's sober.'

'Oh, you men! You're all the same.'

They travelled all night, with the two acetylene lamps with their big reflectors lighting up the bends ahead, making the trees gleam with a gem-like brilliance against the sky, startling the plover and the roosting cockatoos. But in the dawn, when the river reflected the trees as in a steel mirror, a dark streamer of smoke still showed to the south-east, much closer than it had been the day before.

They stopped briefly at Mildura irrigation settlement, while

273

Brenton went up to the post office to learn the latest reports on river levels in the Darling. Delie, who often felt a deadly lassitude in the mornings, lay on top of her bunk in her dressing-gown, summoning her strength for the effort of getting up. Through the cabin door she watched the remarkable red cliffs, the green vineyards and the glowing orange sandhills swim past.

At last the colour of a green willow against an ochreous sandhill, all reflected in almond-green water, stabbed her into activity. She dressed quickly, hoping they might stop again somewhere. But she managed only a quick water-colour sketch of some pink and yellow cliffs, for they did not stop; the little *Philadelphia* ploughed gallantly on her way, always with the menace of following smoke nearer in the pure, pale sky.

'We'll lick the *Pride* to Wentworth,' said Brenton with satisfaction as she joined him in the wheel-house. She gazed at his strong profile, the short, straight, determined nose and firm chin. He did not look tired in spite of sleepless nights and long hours at the wheel. A boundless vitality flowed from him, and seemed to be imparted to the eager, throbbing vessel through his hands.

When they came in sight of the Darling junction the *Pride* was only a few bends behind. They could see the other river for some time through the trees; then they rounded a long sandspit and turned into the Darling, into the milky, muddy waters of the tributary. The sloping Wentworth wharf stood well out of the water, and alongside were several 'bottom-end' boats – *Fairy*, *Pyap*, *Renmark* and *Queen* – unloading stores, while the *South Australian*, the 'flyer' of the lower river, was just casting off.

The lift-bridge was open, and with a loud whistle the *Philadelphia* steamed through without slackening speed.

'Hell!' said Charlie, who had come out to watch Wentworth go by. 'The *South Australian*'s after us now. Two barges, but the current doesn't worry her none; we're sunk for sure.'

'Don't use that word, Charlie,' admonished the fireman.

'What word? I never swore.'

' "Sunk", I mean. It's bad luck.'

'Tchah!' said Charlie, polishing his nose rapidly with the back of his hand. 'You'll 'ear some words if she goes past us. Jump to it, now! Pour some kerosene on that there wood.'

He dived into the space between the paddle-boxes, while the fireman knocked open the firebox door and slung in his choicest, dryest logs. He had used all the kerosene there was to spare in beating the *Pride* to Wentworth.

They struggled upstream against the current. But the faster *South Australian* drew nearer, drew abreast – and then, with a derisive whistle and shouted jibes from her crew, she forged past and left the *Philadelphia* in her wake.

On the bottom deck Charlie McBean danced up and down on his cap, shouting at the rival engineer: 'Yah! We could steam all round ye goin' downstream!' In his excitement he kicked at an empty bucket, as he thought; but 'the silly bucket on the deck' happened to be full of nuts and bolts the fireman had been sorting out, and it hurt his toe. A flood of lurid language accompanied the trail of smoke and sparks from the funnel as they streamed out behind.

When Delie took his lunch up to him, Brenton scowled and refused to eat anything, though he swallowed a mug full of hot tea at one gulp. He hated anything to pass him. She thought he was being rather childish in refusing to eat, but she said nothing.

Now that no steamer was in sight behind them, Brenton reduced speed a little and jumped in for a swim while they were going along.

Though the nights and mornings were bitterly cold, the inland sun blazed down from a blue sky all day long. The water, coming over a thousand miles of sun-scorched plains, was always warm. He would hand over the wheel, take off his shirt and shoes – if he had any on, for he liked to go barefoot on the boat – and dive overboard. In few moments he was on deck again, having climbed up over the rudder.

The men on the barges behind enjoyed this spectacle, especially when he did his famous trick of diving beneath a paddle-wheel.

Delie saw this terrifying performance for the first time when she had just been down to the port paddle-box for some butter which was hung there for coolness. She paused to watch the fourteen-foot wheel threshing round in its blind power.

Fascinated, she watched it hitting the water with a series of solid blows, and felt the cool mist of spray drift over her face. The wheel did not go very deep, but the wooden paddles were set at an angle to give the maximum forward thrust.

She went to the galley to butter some biscuits for Brenton's afternoon tea, arranging cheese and gherkin on them in dainty patterns. But when she came out with the plate in her hand, there was Brenton, in nothing but a pair of dungarees, standing on the edge of the deck and looking down at the milky water.

'Just going in for a dip,' he said, and dived straight in front of the churning wheel. Her mouth was still open to scream a protest when he came up in the wake. He swam diagonally to the bank, ran along its steep, mud-ringed side until he was ahead, and swam out again to the steamer.

'It's terribly dangerous!' she cried, clutching him as he came back along the deck, regardless of his dripping wet condition. 'Don't do it again, Brenton! Please!'

But he only smiled, his eyes very clear and blue-green in his brown face, and told her not to fuss.

'I've done it a hundred times. The "River Murray Spaniel" they call me. It's simple enough to go under the paddles, if you dive deep.'

'I still wish you wouldn't.'

But she knew that he would, all the same.

FORTY-SIX

Delie hated the Darling River for the rest of her life. From the time they entered that muddy stream everything seemed to go wrong. Between the close confining banks of grey mud nothing could be seen but the stretch of cloudy water ahead, and the stretch behind; the sky above, and on top of the high banks a procession of blue-grey box trees with trunks like dark, twisted iron.

'It's just like a ditch!' she cried. 'A great, muddy ditch full of drain-water.'

'Ah, you haven't seen the Darling in a good season, when the banks are brim-full or overflowing. Why, once Captain Randell picked up wool twenty miles from the main channel. You can see for miles and miles then, across the blacksoil plains,' said Brenton, 'and the only way you can get wood is to take the dinghy and cut it off the high land. Even where there's no water, the mirage glistens along the horizon with reflections in it like a lake.

'It's a tremendous country out here. Not like that little green cabbage-patch of a Victoria.'

'I prefer the Murray,' she said obstinately. 'There's nothing to

276

paint here; no distance, no colour. It's all grey and brown.'

She hated the feeling of being shut in; it was like travelling through a railway cutting hundreds of miles long.

At the small settlement of Menindie, a galvanised-orin town of one pub and many goats, they unloaded beer and flour, and then hurried on; the river was low, but the seasonal rains from Queensland had already come down, and it was not likely to get any higher.

The first misfortune overtook them below Wilcannia, at four in the morning. Smoke was seen issuing from the forepeak as they travelled along, and the steamer was hastily brought into the bank. There was a fire in the dangerous cargo for'ard. The crew, helped by the barge-hands, made a line with buckets of water. Then a case of gunpowder exploded, and cartridges began going off in all directions, luckily without injuring anyone.

Ben helped Delie ashore before this happened. The cook followed, apparently filled with Oriental calm, lugging his portmanteau from the galley. Just then there was a second explosion, which fortunately blew the fire into the river; but several bags of flour that had been stowed on top went up as well, and flour fell like snow from the sky. An empty jam-case that had been lying on top of all seemed to take an enormous time to come down, and when it did it missed Ah Lee's head by about six inches.

Oriental calm evaporated. 'My Cli'!' he yelled, and went off like an arrow, but not forgetting the portmanteau. In the dark he ran across the narrow neck of land between the river and a creek, and in he went.

Delie was meanwhile attending to burns and binding up wounds caused by falling debris. It was not until half an hour later that someone thought of the cook. After a search he was found in the creek, hanging on to a snag with his head just above water. When fished out he was still clinging firmly to the portmanteau, and though shaking all over with cold would not let it out of his convulsive grasp. He was given a hot drink and persuaded that the danger was over and hustled off to bed, still trying vainly to explain what had happened through wildly chattering teeth.

There was surprisingly little damage, except for a charred hole in the foredeck. It was found that mice nesting in a box of wax matches had set off the fire. Brenton also found that a cask of beer, destined for Louth, had been 'accidentally' broached in the excitement, but he turned a blind eye. Most crews were always thirsty, and would provide themselves with a gimlet and a few straws with which to sample a liquid cargo.

While the mate took over the wheel in a clear stretch of river next day (for the skipper would not sleep while they were travelling by night, even though it was safer going upstream than down), Brenton came to the cabin to snatch a few hours' sleep.

Delie drew the two little curtains at the cabin windows and prepared to leave him, sprawled hugely on her bunk, for he seemed too tired to climb to his. But as she drew the cover over him one of the limp hands hanging over the edge took her wrist in a grip of steel.

'Don't go yet. I never see you alone now.'

'But you want to rest.'

'Who says I want to rest? I want *you*.'

'But I thought you were tired.'

'I am; but not too tired.'

She sighed, but came to him happily. Each time she felt it to be a reavowal of his love and his need for her; though she had not yet learned to respond fully to his love-making, which was almost brutally ruthless and direct, she knew the contentment of giving herself and feeling his pleasure in her. Reason told her that he could have found it, had found it often in the past, with other women, perhaps any woman would suffice; but her unreasonable feminine heart construed it always as an act of love.

The mate tied up and did not try to negotiate the Christmas Rocks alone. He called the skipper. Brenton looked worried at the lack of water over these two ledges of rock running almost across the river. If it was like this so early in the season, what would it be like when the river began to fall? There was danger of being bottled up there for the rest of the year in some water-hole.

Just below Wilcannia they were overhauled by the *Waradgery*, a stern-wheeler from Echuca, but there were none of the usual jeers and cat-calls from the passing crew; only a serious, quiet salute which puzzled the *Philadelphia*'s men. But when they tied up beside the *Waradgery* and the *Pride of the Murray* they learned the reason.

'The *Providence* just blew up, below Kinchega,' said Captain Ritchie of the *Waradgery* to Brenton as he came aboard, accompanied by Delie. She gripped his arm as he stared back at the other captain.

'Anyone . . . killed?'

'Everyone aboard her. No one escaped but the man on the barge behind. He said she just blew to pieces. Nothing was left.'

'The baby!' said Delie, white-faced.

'George Blakeney!' said Brenton. 'Poor old George.'

'It's just as well the whole family's gone, if you ask me,' said Captain Ritchie. 'It'd be awful to be the only one left.'

The news threw a gloom over the whole port, where paddle-steamer crews made up most of the floating population, with drovers, bullockies, opal prospectors, shearers and station hands in for a 'bust'.

The town was an attractive place, Delie thought, a real Western town with lanky, casually dressed horsemen on the street corners, store windows full of saddles, boots, hobbles and Condamine bells; with its one church and thirteen hotels, big stone jail and court-house, and wide streets shaded with green pepper trees, it seemed like a metropolis after the few iron shacks and sandhills of Poincarrie and Menindie.

Delie went shopping for things she had forgotten, while beer and chaff were being unloaded from the boat, and a new load of beer was being taken on via the crew's thirsty throats. Brenton was anxious to get away before the men became drunk and quarrelsome, when a brawl with men from one of the 'bottom-end' boats would be inevitable; for there was deadly rivalry between 'top' and 'bottom-end' men. The *Pride of the Murray*, now that they were in hostile waters where enemy South Australian boats could be met, became an ally instead of a rival.

Brenton had sold the chaff he had bought for five shillings a bag in Swan Hill, for one pound a bag in Wilcannia. The upper Darling was in the grip of a drought, and fantastic prices were being paid for fodder to keep starving stock alive. He had topped-up the barges, not fully loaded before, with 1,000 bags of chaff, and these now brought him in nearly £750 profit, which more than made up for the fire damage, and the loss from the grounded barge.

When it was time to leave, Charlie the engineer was missing. Brenton finally ran him to earth in a semi-conscious state after he had searched eight hotels, and 'walked' him back to the boat;

alternately singing and protesting that his tremendous thirst was not yet slaked.

At the wharf, he refused to walk across the gangplank. He flopped to his knees and crawled aboard, muttering that 'a little onion sangwidch woulden do ush any harm.' The fireman had got steam up and Brenton took the *Philadelphia* a few miles upstream and stopped there, on the far side from the town, while the engineer and several other members of the crew sobered up a bit.

Then the steamer sidled out from the bank and hurried off upstream in the face of sand-bars, islands, rocky bars across the river, snags and sharp bends.

The fireman, at the beginning of his six-hour spell when the deckhand took over, brought out a pea-rifle and began potting at ducks from the top of the flour-bags piled in the bows. Teddy Edwards leaned out through the wheel-house window.

'Don't you go shooting at any wood-ducks,' he said warningly. A pair of tame-looking grey-and-white ducks sat quietly on the bank just ahead.

'Ar, can't a bloke have a pot at anythink?' growled the fireman.

'Not at wood-ducks. How would you pick them up if you winged 'em? It's not as if they was in the water.'

The fireman contented himself with firing harmlessly at two wedge-tailed eagles that soared and circled high in the blue, so high that they looked like black cinders rising above a fire. He was a dark, saturnine man with a jeering voice, and Delie could not get used to his ugly, pitted skin.

He hated Chinamen, and gave the cook no peace. 'Yellow scum!' he would mutter audibly as the cook came out of the galley to empty a pot overboard. 'This soup smells of the dirty Chink that made it,' he would say at meals.

The cook appeared impassive, but sometimes he was seen looking at Steve with a fierce gleam in his slits of eyes. One day the fireman went too far. He had been wiping the engine for Charlie, and came aft with a piece of filthy, oily cotton rag in his hand. The cook had just put his head out of the galley, and was squinting up at the sun to gauge the time. Steve took deliberate aim and caught Ah Lee on the side of the cheek with the oozing rag.

The cook clawed it off, then reached behind him into the galley and brandished the mallet he used for pounding tough meat.

'Yah! Come outside and put yer fists up!' jeered Steve. 'Yellow skin, yellow all through.'

'By Cli'!' yelled Ah Lee, beside himself. 'I come outsi' all li'! Outsi', insi', any blunny si', I hit 'ou in 'ou mou' an knock 'ou blunny tee' ou'!'

He rushed at the fireman, with such a murderous air that Steve decided on discretion and disappeared into the lavatory under the paddle-box until Ah Lee had cooled down a bit.

The sky was the same unbroken blue day after day, and the sun shone brilliantly in the clear dry air. Delie's chest was improved already; she slept better, and rarely became breathless. One afternoon they came to a piece of the 'high' land along the Darling, perhaps fifty feet higher than the usual flat clay plain, where the red sand of the old inland sea had not been covered by layers of black Darling silt.

The red sand, which had absorbed the sun all day, gave off heat like an oven. A few thin trees with limp, drooping leaves stood beside a solitary iron shack. Away on the horizon a low line of indigo, which was a belt of trees, wavered above the shimmer of mirage.

'We can get fresh goats' milk here,' said Brenton, blowing the whistle and pulling into the right-hand bank. 'Also I could do with a drink meself.'

He had been morose and silent since hearing the news of the *Providence*'s end. Delie noticed that the weights had been removed from the safety valve and the *Philadelphia* was allowed to proceed at her own pace; but she said nothing.

When a rope had been taken out to a tree fore and aft, and the gangplank laid across to the steep water-ringed bank, she prepared to step ashore with him, for she wanted to see everything.

'You don't want to come, do you?' said Brenton.

At once she felt that he did not want her to come, and said obstinately, 'Certainly I do. I'm tired of seeing nothing but banks of grey mud.'

It was a steep climb to the top, and Jim the mate and Brenton both helped her. An ugly, witch-like old woman and a bold-faced, dirty, handsome young one emerged from the shanty door as they came up, followed at a distance by some of the crew. Delie carried a billy-can for the milk.

She felt uncomfortable at the stares of the two women, who were taking in every detail of her dress and appearance. They greeted the captain and mate with warm, avaricious smiles.

281

'Are you gennlemen coming in for a drink?' said the old
beldame. 'I've got some nice cool lemonade and orange squash
inside,' with a hideous wink below her shaggy grey eyebrows, 'and
roast duck or roast mutton with vegies.'

'Roast cockatoo and roast goat, you mean,' said Brenton coolly.
'I'll come in and try your "orange squash" though. The lady
would like some goats' milk to take back to the boat.'

'Lily, fetch some milk,' said the old woman, snatching the billy
and handing it over. But the bold-faced, black-haired girl stood
still, swinging the billy provocatively round her hips.

'You won't be tying up for the night this time, Captain, I
suppose?' She flashed a dark look at Delie.

'I will not,' said Brenton. 'We're racing a low river and have
half the bottom-end fleet on our tail.' He scowled at the girl and
pushed past her.

She did not move aside for him, but stood her ground, swaying
forward a little so that her almost bare breast brushed his arm.
All the time she stared mockingly at Delie with her black eyes.
It was the old woman who took the billy-can and came back with
the milk. Delie snatched it from her with a mumbled word of
thanks and fled back to the boat, over the burning red sand,
through the thin patches of shade cast by the scanty belars.

That awful woman, how could he? she was thinking. She had
accepted the fact that there had been others like Nesta; but never
others like this! She would never understand men, never.

When he came aboard after dark, rather noisy and smelling of
whisky, she was already in her bunk, and pretended to be asleep.

FORTY-SEVEN

At Tilpa there was a licensed hotel, though the quality of the
liquor was little better than at the riverside shanties, with their
sly-grog disguised as 'orange squash'.

The hotel-keeper had a large lead-lined coffin on the counter
which he kept full of rum, ladling it out at threepence a nobbler.
He liked to have it ready, he said, in case he should 'pop off
sudden', and he thought the fact of its having been used as a

282

container for spirits would help to preserve him when he was buried in it.

On all sides were the same flat, barren surroundings, the same grey soil alternating with red sand, the same shimmering mirage in the indigo distance, dry roly-poly and steel-blue trees in the foreground. The primary colours of red, blue and yellow, bleached and softened by the heat, were here muted to the ghosts of themselves. Delie was reminded of a piece of potch opal she had once seen, with the colours barely showing in the milky stone.

They unloaded the beer, and received the disquieting news that there was no more water coming down the river. It was doubtful if any steamers would get through to Bourke, or even as far as Louth. A sudden fall of a foot or eighteen inches could trap them above the Yanda Rocks until next season. The *Pride* and the *Waradgery* were not going above Wilcannia; but the *Philadelphia* had a load of flour, rabbit-traps and ammunition to deliver at Dunlop Station.

Brenton expected to get a valuable back-loading of wool, as shearing would be over when they got there. Rather than sell his cargo at a loss and return to take his chance with the other steamers over a wool-loading from Tolarno and other lower Darling stations, he pushed on, travelling night and day. And the river had begun to fall.

It was an anxious time, and tempers became short. When the barge-master of the leading barge fell asleep (having been on duty twelve hours instead of the usual six) and let the barge hit the bank where it stuck fast in the mud, there was much angry shouting and slandering of ancestors. However, as the barge was not heavily loaded it was winched off successfully.

But before they got to Dunlop disaster overtook them. Teddy Edwards had gambled with the river levels, and lost. The river fell a foot overnight, and another six inches the next day. Their retreat was cut off; and soon it became impossible to go forward.

Just below the little shanty at Winwar, they scraped over a bar into a fairly deep water-hole about a quarter of a mile long, with an impassable bar of rock above; and there, in this natural dam, they were forced to stay. Tarpaulins were stretched on each side to shield the decks and paintwork from the inland sun. The crew were put on half pay, and set to painting and cleaning to give them something to do.

Charlie overhauled and polished the engine; Teddy filled in his log, though there was nothing to record, and began inking in a

283

faded and much-altered chart; Ben read all of Delie's books; and Delie painted, in the early morning and at sunset, when the colour that was lacking in the landscape during the day tinted the clear skies and calm water with hues of opal and of rose.

The landscape above the high banks of the river frightened her; it was so empty. Not just that there was nothing to be seen but a vast grey plain dotted with saltbush, and an indigo mirage on the horizon; but it conveyed such a feeling of stillness, dryness and immensity, so that you felt the desolate wastes stretching away out of sight.

She was happy there at first. It was calm and peaceful, she saw more of Brenton, and the landscape would at least stand still while she painted it. Yet she missed the strange sensation of peace that came to her always with the steady onward movement of the boat. She felt this only when her body was being moved through space by some external agency, and most particularly on the river. It was as though in that endless flow, the backward flow of trees and banks and water, some inner restlessness was annulled; or as though only in movement could she feel in harmony with the progression of time, the revolution of the earth, and the endless cycle of the stars.

But as the water ceased to flow, and became stagnant; as the steep mud banks dried out, their lower levels swarming with hopping, crawling vermin; and in the airless channel between the banks the boat sweltered in the heat, while a smell of decay rose from exposed logs and dying fish, she grew almost as discontented as the men. They had begun to mutter that the skipper should never have ventured so far on a falling river in a bad season. Become wise after the event, they said they 'knew' it would lead to this – though none had said so before. Tempers became short, and arguments were frequent.

Teddy Edwards had two alternatives: to hang on to his stores, and his crew, in the hope of a fall of rain in Queensland that would bring a substantial fresh down the river and allow them to proceed up to Dunlop and back to Wentworth; or to cut his losses, pay off all but a skeleton crew, and send a message for bullock teams to come from Bourke and lift his stores at exorbitant rates.

The sky remained a pure, deep blue. The idea of rain, even away in Queensland, seemed preposterous, but he still hung on. Solid white clouds, piled round the horizon like marble palaces, came sailing slowly across from the dry west, casting a temporary shadow so dense that it seemed to have weight. Far up in the burning blue there was always a pair of wedge-tailed eagles, endlessly circling as they rose.

One day a flock of pelicans came winging down the river with majestic, measured flight. The backwaters were drying up, and they were making for the more permanent waters of the Ana-branch and the Murray. Brenton stared at them sombrely. They were not trapped in a drying puddle; they had wings and could escape.

He whirled round as the sound of a shot came from up for'ard. The fireman, his dark face creased with disgust, took aim again, just as Brenton strode up and knocked the gun-barrel aside.

'I've told you not to shoot at pelicans,' he said furiously.

'Ar, y' can't shoot at anythink on this ruddy tub. First it's wood-ducks, then it's pelicans. Who d'yer think you are? Mother Carey?' and he raised the gun again, though the birds were almost beyond range.

In a moment the rifle clattered to the deck, knocked out of his hands by Brenton. Steve snarled and put up his fists. With one quick blow Brenton laid him on the deck beside the rifle.

The fireman got up surlily, rubbing his jaw, but did not attempt to touch the gun again. Brenton stood it against the paddle-box and marched off to his cabin. Steve, his dignity hurt, saw the cook leering at him from the galley door.

'Don't you grin at me, you yellow Chinese scum!' he snarled, 'or I'll wipe the deck with your nose.'

Ah Lee continued to grin, unperturbed. Steve gathered the spittle in his mouth and spat, accurately though at long range, so that the gob landed on the cook's arm. Ah Lee's grin disappeared. He rushed to the paddle-box, snatched up the rifle, whirled on the fireman and shot him through the chest.

At the report Brenton came striding out of his cabin with a black brow, thinking that Steve was shooting at pelicans again; but he stopped short, his hands on the rail of the upper deck, and looking down at the fireman's inert form, from under which blood was oozing.

He ran down the steps and turned the man over, felt his pulse, listened for a heart-beat. The fireman was dead. At first he thought Steve, overcome by chagrin, had shot himself; then he saw Ah Lee standing motionless by the opposite paddle-housing, the smoke still curling from the rifle he held. He stepped towards him, but Ah Lee raised the rifle and pointed it menacingly.

'No touchee!' he cried in a shrill voice. 'Ah Lee kill 'ou too, kill evlybodee.'

'Go back!' said Brenton urgently, seeing out of the corner of his eye that Delie had followed him out of the cabin and was at the top of the steps. 'Tell Jim to come down quietly. Quick! I think Ah Lee's gone off his rocker.'

Charlie came from the other end of the deck as Jim came down the steps, and Ah Lee waved the rifle from one to the other. His eyes were mad slits, his lips were drawn back to show his big teeth.

'Keep his attention while I try to get behind him,' said Brenton. But Ah Lee had his back to the superstructure, and now, keeping the rifle on the three men, he began to climb up on the crates and flour-bags piled for'ard, from there over the rail to the wheel-house, and thence to the wheel-house roof.

From this point he controlled the boat; there was nothing higher, except the funnel. For an hour the others argued, threatened and pleaded with him. Delie, terrified, heard it all from just inside her cabin door. At last she realised that Brenton, in a desperate attempt to disarm him, was climbing up after the cook.

'Kee' away! Kee' away!' Ah Lee was shrilling. 'I shoo'! I kill 'ou deadibones-dead.' Brenton came on steadily.

Delie wanted to call him to come back, but she knew she must not distract his attention for a moment. With his eyes fixed commandingly on Ah Lee's fanatical ones, he was talking all the time in a soothing voice: 'Now then, Ah Lee, we don't want to hurt you. We friends, eh? Just come down like a sensible chap. You can't stay up there all night, and besides you've got to get the tea. Come on, now. That fireman's been asking for trouble, hasn't he? We don't blame you, Ah Lee. We just want you to come down before you fall. Come on now, let's help you. . . .'

He had his foot in the wheel-house window now, his head above the roof. He stood very still, with the gun pointing straight at his head, and went on talking.

Gradually Ah Lee relaxed and lowered the rifle towards his feet.

'Lee! Ah Lee! Put that gun away now, and come down quietly. Are you listening, Ah Lee? There's no need for you to . . .' and just then he got high enough to make a grab at the gun-barrel and twist it from the cook's hand. He threw it to the men holding their breaths below, got Ah Lee by an ankle and brought him down with a thud on the wheel-house roof. In a few minutes he was over-powered and trussed to a deck stanchion on the lower deck, where he raved and gibbered and swore in Chinese and pidgin for two hours.

Someone rowed up to Winwar to ask for a message to be sent to Bourke for a mounted policeman to take him in charge. Ah Lee became quite quiet by nightfall, but they didn't dare let him in the galley in case he set fire to the boat, so they shut him in the bathroom until the trooper arrived next day.

Brenton opened the portmanteau that was hidden in the galley, and found that it contained a thousand pounds in notes. When the trooper came to take him away, with a spare horse for the prisoner Brenton handed over the money and the cloth bundle of Ah Lee's clothing, and also a written statement of all that had occurred, including the provocation the cook had received from the fireman.

Thus the crew was reduced by two, and someone else had to be found to cook the meals. All eyes turned on Delie, the only woman on board. Cooking was known to be a woman's job; all women could cook; she was a woman. There was no escaping their logic. In vain she told Brenton she had never cooked a meal in her life, except to boil an egg for Imogen and herself.

Fortunately Bessie had given her a cookery-book when she was married, and though she had scarcely glanced into it before, it now became to her a bible, its pronouncements as authoritative as Holy Writ. The pages were soon dog-eared, stained with spilt milk and coated with flour, for she referred to it at every step.

The raw materials at hand were so limited that she could not make any spectacular failures. 'Take twelve eggs, beat for twenty minutes . . .' she read, and turned the page. There were no eggs, only tinned milk and salt meat, and sometimes a duck, a rabbit or a fish that Ben cleaned for her. The only vegetables were potatoes and onions which had been among the station stores.

Remembering the wonderful meals her Aunt Hester had turned out at Kiandra with the same limited materials, she felt ashamed. There was plenty of flour to experiment with, but her first attempt at making bread was a lamentable failure.

Brenton, who was a good cook but would have considered it beneath his dignity to get the meals, took over the bread-baking. Ben became cook's offsider, peeled all the vegetables and did the washing-up.

But in spite of his help, almost every morning there was a reek

of burning toast or scorching porridge from the galley, a series of
groans and shrieks from Delie as something boiled over or burned
her hands. The crash of breaking crockery and the clatter of
falling saucepans echoed between the steep banks of the Darling.

For a week they feasted off roast mutton; for a ewe, thin and
weakened by the drought, came down the opposite bank to drink
and bogged in the mud there. They could have hauled it out but,
arguing that if they hadn't been there the station would have lost
the sheep anyway, they slaughtered it. The carcass was hung in the
shade in a muslin bag to keep the blowflies off.

The crew manfully ate Delie's soggy puddings and tough
scones; they actually seemed to like them, and asked for more.
But she knew she was a terrible cook. 'I'll learn, all the same,' she
vowed. 'Anyone with normal intelligence should be able to learn
anything from a book.'

She couldn't try things out on the dog, because there wasn't
one; but once she fed the parrot on one of the hard scones she
had just baked. Skipper held it up critically in his claw, put his
head on one side and regarded it suspiciously.

'Which of you devils has had the screwdriver?' he muttered, as
if appealing for this strong instrument to crack the scone with.
Then he began to shell it like an almond, nibbling off the outer
crust and letting the pieces fall to the deck like pebbles.

'Cocky wants a drink,' he said hoarsely when he had finished.
Delie brought him an enamel mug and put it over his head; he
wanted a cup, not a drink. He began to sing and talk to himself
inside the cup, dancing up and down on his perch in a ridiculous
fashion. Delie made a drawing of him and labelled it 'Ned Kelly
on the Darling,' and Brenton put it up in the saloon.

In the long, mild evenings, the skipper and the men used to lie
out on the deck yarning and smoking and slapping at mosquitoes.
There was magic in those far inland nights, on that quiet reach
of water undisturbed by any sound but the call of night-birds. It
made up for the heat and monotony of the day.

The stars were huge and golden in the velvet sky, or the moon
rose and turned the desolate banks and muddy water to a pattern
of black and silver. No dew fell; the air was dry and warm.

Delie wished for the hundredth time that she had been born a
boy. She would like to be lying out there smoking and yarning,
but though there was never any overt hostility, she did not often
join the men. A subtle sex antagonism excluded her from their
circle.

If she came out on deck she felt the constraint; the men sat up and watched their language, looked sideways at the glimmer of her pale face above her white frock, and looked quickly away again. She began to long for a woman's companionship.

If only I were old and ugly it would be better, she thought miserably. One day, when I'm about fifty – no, sixty – it will be all the same. But she couldn't really imagine herself as old as that.

As spring advanced into summer it became obvious that the *Philadelphia* would not move again that year. The men had become more discontented and quarrelsome, and began rowing off to Winwar and getting drunk on cheap whisky. Brenton decided to pay off all but the bargemaster, the mate, the engineer and the deckhand. Ben could steer the second barge if necessary, until they picked up a full crew again after the rise that must come.

A message was sent for bullock or horse teams to come and lift the cargo, and the crew went back to Wentworth with the first coach that came through. Some would go home to Echuca, but most were rolling stones who would take jobs in the back country until another steamer job was offering.

The pool in which the *Philadelphia* lay shrank lower and lower, but was still enough to float her once she was lightened by the removal of her cargo. This all had to be lumped by hand up the steep clay bank of the river.

As long as she floated, the boat still had the feel of a live thing, and if there was the slightest breeze the ripple-reflections danced in quivering gold over every projection.

But the water grew stagnant, and it became steadily hotter and more stifling on board. The mate grumbled that he wanted to go home to his family for Christmas. Brenton agreed to pay his fare back to Echuca, but he would get no wages until he rejoined the boat.

Delie refused to go back too, and stay with Bessie. 'This dry inland air is doing me so much good,' she said, 'that I believe my lungs are almost cured already. And anyway, I won't leave you. I couldn't bear to leave you.'

He kissed her and did not argue. He did not fancy the one woman at the Winwar shanty, who had been shared among the crew before they were paid off; and if they were going to be stuck here for months on end, a woman would be as much a necessity as food and drink. Bsides, he would miss her; she was very lovely, even if she couldn't cook.

The men did their own laundry. Delie did hers and Brenton's, taking the clothes along to the rocky reef that was keeping the water back. When she thought of all that went into that stretch of water she could scarcely drink her tea, although it was boiled.

Below the bar the river had shrunk to a channel of mud, with a few little puddles along its dry, cracked bed. In one of these she looked at the mass of water-life that swarmed in a last frenzy of activity before dying, as the pool dried out. The water seemed to boil with the frantic movement of tadpoles, water beetles, and larval shrimps and crayfish, that fought for the last of the moisture and the oxygen it contained.

She looked with horror at this meaningless, terrible struggle for survival. Why? she thought. Why? But there was no answer.

Ben still managed to get a few fish by going up or downstream to other water-holes that were not fished out. Birds were shy of the ungainly shape of the steamer, but she saw them veering past at sunset: black cockatoos, crested quarrians and cockatiels, and flocks of budgerigars, the little shrill-voiced parrots that looked like shoals of emerald-green fish, as they darted through the blue air.

Brenton could name them all for her, but it was Ben who accompanied her to the next water-hole to watch for their coming down to drink at evening. When he brought her a bright feather he had picked up or a fish he had caught, his shy, dark eyes would light up with pleasure at her happiness.

He never irritated her by looking over her shoulder when she was painting, but he always asked, diffidently, to be allowed to see the picture when it was complete. His occasional pertinent remarks surprised and pleased her, more than Brenton's indiscriminate praise of everything she did as 'jolly good'.

Ben's quiet, gentle ways made up to a certain extent for the lack of a woman's company. Brenton had given her a sewing-machine when they were married, and in the long summer months she found plenty of time to run up the lengths of material she had brought with her. Ben showed surprisingly good taste, choosing styles for her from the *Ladies' Home Journal*, dismissing some as 'too fussy' or 'too old'.

It would be nice to have a husband who was interested in your clothes, she thought wistfully. Brenton never noticed what she wore. If she appealed directly to him for an opinion on a new dress, he only replied that he liked her best in nothing . . .

290

FORTY-EIGHT

It was not until the meagre rains of the following season that enough water came down the Darling to float the *Philadelphia* and her barges over the rocky bar that had held her prisoner for nearly twelve months. They made all haste downstream, picking up a full crew as they went, and wired the mate to meet them at Wentworth.

After the long summer they all felt reinvigorated by the perfect winter climate, the cool, crisp inland nights with their frosty stars, the clear blue skies and the dry cold winds that swept across the black-soil plains.

They picked up some early wool, enough to load one barge, but the drought had decimated the flocks so that the clip was nothing like a normal year's.

No following flood came down behind the first rise. There were alarming reports too, about the Murray; not only had there been an unprecedentedly dry year in New South Wales and Queensland, but there had been scarcely any fall of snow in the highlands.

Victoria had not had its usual opening rains at the break of the season. Tributaries like the Goulburn and the Campaspe had almost ceased to flow.

As the *Philadelphia* made her way cautiously down the Darling in that black year of 1902, a man was kept in the bows continuously with a pole to sound the channel ahead. At night they tied up, for the shallows were too dangerous to negotiate in darkness when coming downstream.

Although the bare, eaten-out country (where the starving sheep had even dug the saltbush roots to eat them) was out of sight above the steep grey banks, the drought made itself felt. When they tied up, the sluggish current carried past numbers of floating things, bloated shapes with legs sticking up towards the sky. The banks became lined with pitiful shapes – exhausted, starving sheep which had come down to drink and been too weak to extricate themselves from the sticky mud. Sated crows flapped away as the steamer came past, and the rows of eyeless heads turned their bloody sockets, round which the blowflies buzzed, towards the sound of the paddles as though in mute appeal.

At first, at Delie's frantic request, they had shot the creatures to put them out of their misery, but soon there were so many that no one had time or inclination for the task. Delie shut herself in the cabin and would not come out, even for meals, though now she had the luxury of a cook again. She ate nothing but dry bread (there had been no butter for so long that she had almost forgotten its taste) and tea made with tinned milk. Even the air she breathed tasted of corruption.

When at last they steamed out again into the Murray, after their slow and difficult journey down to the junction, she felt a tremendous relief. But the once noble river was changed and dwindled; a long spit of sand ran out at the junction almost to the opposite bank, and the narrow channel wound between wide muddy flats exposed for the first time in many years. Old snags and sunken barges, covered with grey silt, were drying out in the sun.

Brenton took one look at it and swore softly. 'We won't get far on *this* river,' he said. 'As for getting above the Bitch an' Pups, there's not a hope.'

A small fresh caused by a cloudburst near the source of the Ovens, hundreds of miles away in Victoria, took them safely over MacFarlane's Reef. But the water drained rapidly away, and then it was winch and warp over the bad patches, sometimes making only a few miles in a day. But at least the cargo of wool was not perishable. At Mildura they had found the growers still gnashing their teeth over the loss of their last season's crop of fruit, which had been left to rot upon the wharf because the steamers could not get through. The railway could not be finished soon enough for them.

Their next season's crop was threatened too, for the water was so low that the pumping plant could not operate and irrigation was at a standstill. Things were so serious all along the river that an Interstate River Murray Commission had been set up to inquire into the possible locking of the river.

Boundary Rocks and the ugly-looking Jeremiah Lump were passed safely, but after the Murrumbidgee junction, where the tributary was scarcely flowing, it was obvious that they could not go much further.

They took on wood at Fraser Smith's woodpile, and learned

that above the Wakool Junction the river was no more than a series of pools. No steamer had got above the Bitch an' Pups this year.

Still Teddy Edwards would not tie up. As long as there was half an inch of water under the keel he pushed on. He had sold one of his barges back in Wentworth, as there was no loading for it and it might hold them back.

Then, round a bend, they came upon a doleful sight: the *Excelsior*, listing slightly, aground on the mud. She looked a fixture. Tarpaulins had been put out, duckboards were laid across the mud to the shore, and set-lines for cod were hanging from her decks. An ironic cheer went up from her men as the *Philadelphia* edged slowly past.

'Come to join us on "Rotten Row"?' they asked. 'You won't get no further, mate.'

Round the next bend a whole row of stranded steamers appeared – the *Oscar W.*, the *Resolute*, *Trafalgar*, *Waradgery*, and even small steamers like *Alert*, *Success*, *Cato* and *Invincible*.

Teddy Edwards, always wanting to be first, managed to make his way to the head of this forlorn group before the *Philadelphia* too shuddered to a stop with her paddles in the mud.

This was different from their lonely stranding a thousand miles up the Darling. There was something even of a picnic air about the collection of steamers, and misfortune shared was somehow lessened.

Delie liked it much better, for in the open Murray Valley – which is really a huge flood-plain through which the river meanders from one mile-wide bank to another – she had a wide prospect, and none of that shut-in feeling that seemed to confine her spirit on the Darling.

From the top deck she could see away across the monotonous flats of mallee scrub, a sea of dark-green leaves and thin branches; and among them, quite near, the clearing of a desolate, drought-stricken mallee farm. Its fences were half-buried in sand-drifts, its paddocks bore crops of white limestone pebbles.

There were no passenger steamers among the stranded group, and no women; or if there had been any they had already left by coach. At the farm, though, there would surely be a woman. A suspicion which had been growing in her mind the last few weeks made her long for another woman's advice.

Delie made her way through the brief twilight towards the glimmer of the farmhouse window.

She loitered along the river-bank, feeling how strange it was to see the water lying in a lifeless pool; the charm it had had for her was in its irresistible, endless flow onward. Looking toward the south-east, the way the river bent, she saw the delicate bands of colour reflecting the more garish hues of the west. David Davies had caught that ethereal effect of light, transcribed it on to solid canvas. If that were possible anything was possible. Tomorrow evening she would try to paint that eastern sky.

Mosquitoes were beginning to shrill about her ears as she made her way over the stony soil to the half-broken gate that led in to the farmhouse. It was only a two-roomed shanty with a lean-to at the back, yet it was softened in the evening light – with its warm glowing window, and smoke curling from the chimney – to an epitome of home.

Pausing under the low veranda, she looked through the open window at the group within. A woman sat sewing at the rough slab table, close to the lamp. Her hair was grey and drawn into an untidy bun, a deep line was creased between her brows, and her skin was leathery with exposure to sun and wind. On each side of the fireplace, where a black kettle simmered, sat a man and a young woman, evidently the daughter, for she was like him in her thin features and mousy hair.

Something in the stillness of the two by the fire caught Delie's attention. The girl stared sullenly at the glowing mallee roots; the man stared at the girl. There was no sound but the quiet singing of the kettle.

She walked across the earthen veranda and knocked at the door. There was a startled silence within; then footsteps, and the door opened a few inches. The woman, holding the lamp high in her left hand, regarded her through the crack. She seemed inclined to shut the door again, but Delie held out the billy-can she had brought as an excuse for calling.

'Please . . . I'm from one of the boats held up in the reach below. If you could let me have some fresh milk I'd be very grateful. I have not been well . . .'

This reference to her illness, which she felt reasonably sure was now cured, was perhaps not quite honest; but she had felt an odd *malaise* in the mornings lately. The woman opened the door a little wider, and as she took in Delie's fragile form and pale, delicate features the grim expression on her face softened.

'Come through to the back,' she said quickly, almost furtively.

She set the lamp down on the table as Delie followed her through the door that led straight into the living-room. The man looked at her swiftly, but did not meet her eyes. The girl still looked at the fire. The woman had lit a candle and now led the way to the lean-to kitchen.

Two wide bowls of milk were setting their cream by the back door. The woman took up a jug and half-filled Delie's billy. 'Sorry I can't let you have any more now, but I don't want to disturb the cream. I c'd let you have some butter, though.'

'Butter! I'd love some. I haven't tasted butter for – oh, for almost a year. But is this enough . . .?' She fumbled with the money she had brought. The woman took it without seeming to notice it, and put it in her apron pocket. Delie described how they had been stranded up the Darling.

'It couldn't 've been worse than this place,' said the other, standing with the wrapped butter in her hand and staring out the back window at the dark, flat land. 'The everlastin' mallee – I hate it!' She spoke of the terrible year of drought, the loss of all their sheep, their crops withering and blowing away, the paddocks full of stones.

'But you have the river.'

'Yairs; the river makes it bearable. But it makes you kind of restless, though – when it's flowing I mean, not how it is now. Never see it so low all the time we bin here; an' that's more'n thirty years.'

She turned her head. Her eyes were still wide and abstracted from staring out at the dark, and Delie saw with a shock that they were beautiful – large, china-blue, clear as a child's.

'Thirty years!' she cried, appalled. 'Have you been married all that time?'

'You're just married, aren't you? I can tell.' Her lined face softened in a child-like smile.

'Just a year ago. My only home since we've been married has been the boat. My husband's the skipper. Won't you come over and visit us tomorrow?'

'I'll see.'

Just then a wailing, snuffling noise began beyond a blanket hanging from the roof, that cut off part of the kitchen. The woman's face hardened instantly into its former bitter lines. The brows drew down, the deep angry line was like a furrow between them.

'Sarah!' she called harshly. She thrust the butter into Delie's hands, opened the back door and almost pushed her out into the night, as the girl came through from the front room.

Bewildered by this sudden dismissal, her eyes unaccustomed to the dark, Delie stumbled round the yard, falling over old wheels and bits of rusted iron lying half-buried in the sand. Then she picked up the *Philadelphia*'s lights down in the bend and made towards them.

It was so warm that she decided to have a swim, now that it was too dark for any wandering crew-members from the other boats to see her. She got into her navy-blue stockingette costume in the cabin, and enveloped herself in a towelling rob. How lovely it would have been just to step in without any clothes, as the aboriginal girls did at the farm when she was a child!

She found a sandy bank without any weeds to swim from, and launched herself into the cool embrace of the river. The current was negligible; she floated as though in a great bath. It was very different from the feeling of danger and excitement when she had been learning to swim with Miss Barrett in the upper reaches where the current was strong. And where was Miss Barrett at this moment? On the banks of some great European river, the Rhône or the Danube or the Seine? And was she grey by now? It was hard to imagine.

She floated between two skies of stars, the one above and the one reflected in the still water. She heard a cry from the *Philadelphia*: 'Look at this cod, Charlie! A beaut fifteen pounder . . .' and a splash as the set-line was thrown back. She climbed out on the bank, feeling refreshed, as though all the year of Darling drought had been washed out of her system.

As she went to cross the gangplank, Brenton hailed her from the bank: 'We're going to have a picnic supper, darling. Get dressed and come over to the fire. You've never tasted fish like this before, I'll bet.'

And it was true. She found most of the crew gathered round the fire, and Brenton superintending the cooking of the cod on a wire grill. When she was handed her portion on a piece of bread she lingered over it, for it was delicious: freshly caught, freshly cooked above a fire in the open, with billy tea to wash it down. She thought she had never tasted anything so good. There were compensations about being held up in this beautiful lagoon shaded with enormous trees.

FORTY-NINE

All next day she waited for the woman to call, but when evening came she had only seen her in the distance, carrying a bucket between the riverbank and the back door. The water supply for the house, once the rainwater tanks had run dry, was apparently of the most primitive kind.

The five cows and the horse stood listlessly waiting to be fed. There was nothing for them to do, not a blade of grass for them to crop among the stones.

Perhaps she's busy today. I'd better not worry her, thought Delie, buttering fresh-baked bread with the pale but delicious dairy butter. I'd better not worry her. I'll wait till she comes to see me.

She had wondered about the strange, almost animal noises from behind the blanket in the kitchen, the woman's obvious haste to get rid of her, the harshness of her voice when she called the girl. It had sounded like a baby; not her own, surely, she would be too old. An illegitimate child most likely – a 'bastard brat' in the local idiom; and the mother felt the daughter's shame.

As if it mattered, thought Delie. She wondered how she could convey tactfully that she had no conventional ideas about such things.

That evening on the river bank, absorbed in her painting of the sunset light, she heard the woman's voice behind her.

'So yer paint, do yer?' It was a flat statement, and held neither admiration nor censure. 'I never thought an artist'd find nothin' to paint around here.'

'But then you live here. To you it's just the "everlasting mallee", but I find those slender whip-like branches with their thin leaves extremely graceful, especially when they're silhouetted against the sky. I came from England, where the trees are dense masses of foliage for half the year, and bare skeletons the other half – no subtlety about them, you know. Now, gum trees—'

'You come from *England*?' said the woman, as if Delie had said she came from the moon. 'It must be lovely and green over there.'

'It is; green and tidy. I was only a child when I left, and now I find that a paddock of dry yellow grass pleases me more than a green meadow. By the way, my name is Delie Gor – I mean Edwards.'

The woman turned her large, beautiful, child-like eyes from the canvas and looked at Delie thoughtfully. 'I'm Mrs Slope. I've alwus thought I'd like it on a boat, to travel up and down. That's what I meant – the river makes you restless. Me four boys all went off, up or down the river.'

'I lived on a farm above Echuca, and every time a steamer went by I wanted to be on it.'

'Yair. I see the steamers passing in a good season. Never had so much comp'ny as we've had this year, though, with the low river.'

They were selling all their produce to the steamers, she said, and hardly kept even enough milk for themselves. The lucerne patch was just lasting out, with water from the river. She promised to keep some eggs for Delie the next day.

She walked back to the boat with her and was shown all over it from the saloon to the galley. Then they sat and talked about dress materials, and recipes, and illnesses and operations (though Delie, remembering the reaction of the woman at Wood Wood, did not speak of her own health); and all sorts of feminine chatter. The one subject she wanted to discuss, babies, was never mentioned by Mrs Slope, and out of delicacy Delie refrained from bringing it up either.

That night she told Brenton about the mysterious crying she had heard, and that she liked Mrs Slope but felt there was something queer about her. He was obviously not interested, but after listening indulgently with half his mind for a while, he cut short her flow of words with a kiss.

'Why, you're quite wound up, little 'un. It's a long time since you've had another woman to mag with, eh?'

'Yes, and there was something I wanted to ask her, but I didn't. You see, I think . . . I'm afraid . . . something's gone wrong with our precautions. I mean, Bessie told me her symptoms and I seem to have them all. Do you mind very much?'

'Mind! Good God, having a baby might kill you. You know what the doctor said!'

'But I'm ever so much stronger and better than I was then. In fact I think that doctor was mistaken . . . I believe I'm rather glad.' She smiled softly to herself.

298

'But it will make you ill, and a funny shape, and you won't have time for painting. I believe you actually are glad! Women are queer creatures.'

Next day when she went to get the eggs she met Mr Slope, and was not impressed. His wife's opinion of him was evident in the contemptuous way she addressed him. He was skinny, mousy-haired, thin-nosed, with reddened eyelids and almost white eye-lashes. He seemed to cringe before his wife, to be trying to placate a deep anger that he knew to be justified.

Delie saw nothing of the baby, if baby it was, and the thin, slovenly girl she saw only in the distance, as she slouched down to the river-bank for water for the hens.

'Get the eggs while yer there, yer useless lump!' her mother shouted harshly, as the girl came out of the hen-house again with the empty bucket. She turned back without looking up. 'The girl's a bit soft,' explained Mrs Slope. 'Yer have to shout at her to get anything done.'

She took a cardboard box from among the litter round the back door, and going over to the fowl-house as the girl came out again, snatched the bucket of eggs from her with a sort of bitter aversion. Delie felt uncomfortable. There was something poisonous, some corrosive hate, in the atmosphere of this drought-stricken farm.

As she paid Mrs Slope for the eggs and was turning away, a strange animal babbling and grunting came from the lean-to kitchen, making her almost stop in her tracks. She forced herself to walk on as if she had not heard.

Struggling to finish a painting in the last of the failing light, Delie heard the crunching of bark behind her, and without turning wondered if it were the step of Ben or of Mrs Slope.

It would not be Brenton, she knew; and the knowledge hurt her. He would be visiting on one of the other boats, and anyway he rarely sought her out. Sometimes it seemed as if he had no use for her except in bed, she thought rather bitterly.

The footsteps stopped behind her, and suddenly she felt her back grow cold. She turned quickly. Mr Slope stood a little way off, leering at her.

'Good evening,' she said coldly.

He put his hands in his pockets and shambled closer, chewing at a dead gum leaf that hung from his loose lips. He wore a soiled flannel singlet open at the neck, and shapeless moleskins low on his hips. She felt a revulsion from the unpleasantly reddened eyelids and pale lashes. His nearness filled her with aversion.

'Paintin', are yer? Mind if I 'ave a look?'

He was slightly above her on the river-bank; and rolling her eyes towards him uneasily, without turning her head, she saw that he was gazing intently, not at the easel, but down the front of her smock.

She stepped back abruptly, thrusting her paint brushes into the satchel, folding the easel and inserting the wet painting in the carrying attachment with trembling fingers. A late kookaburra flew straight across the river. Down in the the bend the *Philadelphia*'s lights gleamed reassuringly.

'Good night,' she said curtly, trying to move with dignity, not to break into a run.

'What's the 'urry?' said the man softly, moving after her.

She did not look back or reply, but all the way back to the boat she fancied she heard him following her.

Every day, at almost the same time, the river ran for a little, filled the lagoon where they were trapped, and flowed out the other end. Then the flow would cease entirely until the same time next day. Brenton watched this phenomenon with interest, and even timed it with his watch.

Later he announced that someone further up was damming the water and pumping it out of the river for several hours each day. Then they stopped pumping and allowed their dam to overflow for a while.

'Mighty nice of them to let us have a trickle of water once a day,' he said. 'Isn't there a law against stopping the flow of the river, Jim?'

The mate, who was something of a bush lawyer, closed his eyes and chanted rapidly: ' "Whenlandabutsuponanaturalstream – " '

'Here, hold on! Not so fast.'

' "—the owner of that land 'as a right to take an' use the water for all reasonable purposes. The lower proprietor is entitled to 'ave 'is flow of water coming down to 'im unaltered in quality subject only to the right of the upper proprietor aforesaid." The trouble is, who's to say what's reasonable in a drought?'

Two weeks later the water stopped flowing altogether. It was agreed that 'them b——s farther up are pumping the Murray dry'.

Mr Slope, though he was the main sufferer and the one whose riparian rights were being transgressed, refused to do anything about it. He 'didn't want no trouble', he said. But his wife was in distress. They had to have water for the cows.

Brenton took out his .303 and oiled it. Charlie cleaned the rifle that had belonged to the dead fireman. They set off up-river on foot, without Jim Pearce, who said 'he'd 've gone if there was enough water to float the dinghy, but he wasn't going to walk for nobody.'

The others came back in triumph, a pair of thin, starved rabbits swinging from each of their belts. Before them had arrived a trickle of water, then a substantial flow.

'It was a big place about eight mile up-river,' said Brenton. 'They was hogging the lot, eh, Charlie?'

'*Was* they! They'd a great dam right acrost the river bed, and a lagoon stretching back for ruddy miles. Paddocks of lucerne all nice an' green, and a fruit garden round the 'ouse. They don't know there's a drought on, they don't.'

'We actually found them making the dam a bit higher. It needed a bit of persuasion,' Brenton tapped the barrel of his gun, 'before they agreed that the river belongs to everybody. They'd got an underground tank full of rainwater, too.'

The flow became a trickle again the next day, but did not entirely cease.

At last Delie confided in Mrs Slope, who had come aboard with a little jar of cream, that she thought she was going to have a baby.

'Then I wish yer joy of it,' said Mrs Slope in a flat voice, looking out the cabin window.

'But . . . surely . . . your own sons! You must have been pleased about the first baby?'

'Pleased! Ah yes, I was pleased. I never knew they'd grow up to desert their mother just when she needed them! I never thought a child of mine would be the cause of me everlastin' shame.'

'You mean – your daughter?'

'Yes – her. I suppose you must've guessed by now that there's a child. That's the sort of a slut she is.'

'But it's not such a terrible thing, Mrs Slope. It's happened many times before, and will again, to all sorts of people. You shouldn't be so bitter.'

'P'r'aps I shouldn't. You can't 'ardly blame the girl, being a bit soft, like I said. But him – !' She spat the word from her.

A hateful suspicion entered Delie's mind, so hateful that she crushed it down. She jumped up in her agitation from the bunk

301

where she had been sitting, muttering something about putting the cream in the cooler. Mrs Slope followed her, and went ashore without another word being said about the baby.

The next time Delie went to the farm for eggs there was no one about outside, so she went up to the back door and knocked. Mrs Slope's voice called her to come in, and blinking in the darkness of the kitchen she saw her with her arms up to the elbows in dough.

'I came to get a few eggs if I could –'

'Gugg, ugg, gugg,' said a voice near her feet.

She jumped, and peered down. A boy of four or five was sitting under the table, arranging black saucepans in a row. He was neatly dressed in a pair of grey overalls and a faded green shirt.

'Hullo, what's your name?' she said cheerfully, bending towards him. But as her eyes became accustomed to the light the smile froze on her stiffening face. The boy was looking at her with small, animal eyes, and a leer exactly like Mr Slope's.

His head and neck were all in one, the cretinous head no wider than the neck, the ears set flat against the head and too low down. His loose jaws hung open; a dribble of saliva trailed towards the floor. His expression was one of cheerful cunning.

'Ug-gurr un agwith,' said the creature.

'Yes, that is a lady. Now take your things and run in the other room. Go on,' said Mrs Slope gently, 'you make too much noise in here.'

The boy stuck out his under-jaw in an ugly grimace, but he gathered up the saucepans and trotted off like an obedient animal, grunting to himself.

Mrs Slope looked at Delie with her large, clear, china-blue eyes. 'Now you know,' she said. 'No wonder that I'm ashamed. He was born like it, and won't never be any different.' She was almost whispering. 'I swear if there was another one I'd kill it with me own hands. I'd drown it in the river.'

Delie stared at her, appalled. The growing life within her seemed to cry out in protest.

'And do you know why he's like that? It's a judgment, that's what it is. A judgment on a unnatural monster – and on her that she let it happen.' Her voice had become harsh and strident. 'And I have to live with their shame before me eyes.'

Delie could find nothing to say. She knew now that she had expected some such revelation, but it still shocked her. Mrs Slope came to her aid. She kneaded the dough fiercely for a moment,

302

then spoke in her normal voice. 'You wanted some eggs, love? Do yer mind going and getting them from the fowl-house? You might as well have the fresh.'

'Thank you,' muttered Delie, putting her money on the table. 'I must take them to the cook in time for tea, I'd better get back.' She made her way to the hen-house, keeping her eyes straight ahead, fearful of meeting the man or his daughter.

In the nests there were fourteen eggs, warm and white and clean. So pure and symmetrical, they held within the potentiality of all sorts of horrors, double-headed chickens, birds without feet or eyes, six-legged monsters. For the first time she felt a qualm about the coming child.

FIFTY

Delie knew that there was no such thing as a pre-natal impression affecting the appearance of an unborn child, yet she felt a kind of superstitious fear. She didn't want to see that imbecile again with his face of animal cunning; she didn't want to see the girl, knowing her secret, and still less the man.

'I wish we could get away from here,' she said to Brenton without telling him the real reason. 'This place makes me nervous. Couldn't we, just you and I, go to Melbourne for a holiday?'

'And leave the boat?' He stared at her. 'You know I wouldn't leave her. No skipper worth his salt would. And what if a fresh came down, and me not here to take charge?'

Delie felt, not for the first time, a stab of jealousy of the other *Philadelphia*. 'Have you ever heard of a fresh in the middle of a drought, in summer?' she asked.

'Stranger things have happened.'

She knew that he didn't believe it, but it was clear that he had no intention of taking a holiday with her. He couldn't see the need of it. 'You go on your own,' he said. 'Go down to Melbourne and see Imogen.'

'I don't want to go alone. I want to be with you.'

For she was still physically obsessed with her husband. Through the day she made excuses to go up to the wheel-house, to stand where she could just touch him as if by accident. And then, when he came into her bunk, she became tense and unable to respond fully. It did not occur to her that a holiday from him was just what she needed.

Mrs Slope had not visited the boat again, and she had not been to the farm, though there had been the promise of some patterns of baby clothes. Mrs Slope might be regretting the impulse that had made her confide in one who was almost a stranger.

Delie felt so nervous and lonely that she took to sitting on the deck with the men in the evenings, especially when visitors called from the other boats.

Sitting with her back to the end of the starboard paddle-housing, she found herself one evening next to Charlie McBean.

There was a discussion of boilers going on – Brenton was all for designing an engine with double boilers that would drive the paddles twice as fast – but Charlie was not joining in, though it was his subject.

He seemed very nervous, hitching himself about on the deck, sniffing, clearing his throat, making sudden abrupt movements to ward off mosquitoes. Delie knew that her presence was embarrassing him, but it was too hot to retire to the saloon or her cabin.

His sniffing became louder; it was beginning to get on her nerves. Any little thing seemed to upset her these days. She took out her own handkerchief and pointedly blew her nose.

Charlie was seized with another fit of wriggling and jerking. Then he began struggling with the laces of his old canvas shoes. He removed one shoe, then a black woollen sock; blew his nose carefully upon it; replaced the sock, and then the shoe. Delie was so astounded that she didn't even laugh, until she thought about it afterwards.

Emus and kangaroos, almost tamed by their hunger, were more plentiful than rabbits. Kangaroo-tail soup was on the menu, besides wild duck roasted by the new cook, who was not a Chinese but a very fat Australian called Artie.

He had no outmoded old-world ideas about his position, but called the captain 'Teddy' like the rest of the crew, with whom he was on terms of perfect equality. But like the rest of the crew, also, he called Delie 'Mrs Edwards' or just 'Missus', with the deference due to a lone woman outback.

When Mrs Slope came to see her at last, with her great child-like eyes in her ravaged face, Delie realised how much she had missed her. Mrs Slope seemed happier and less restrained, almost as if speaking of her secret shame had helped to lift some of its burden from her. 'I suppose we must all expect our cross in life,' she said, and that was the only reference, however vague, that she made to what had passed between them.

She had brought patterns for night-gowns and dresses with tremendously long skirts, and tiny bodices and sleeves.

'But they're too small!' said Delie. 'These wouldn't fit a doll – not a good-sized doll.'

'You don't know nothing about it. How big a baby do you think a little thing like you's going to have? They don't weigh more'n seven pounds usually.'

Between them they unpicked two of Delie's white night-gowns and a full-skirted cashmere dress, for she had made up most of her material before realising that she would need it for baby clothes. The sewing-machine whirred all day. Mrs Slope had brought some white wool too, and Delie began knitting, as busy as a bird preparing a nest. It went through her mind that Aunt Hester would have liked to see her employing herself in these domesticated tasks – poor Hester who had had no grandchildren, whose only son had died without issue.

By March the small trickle from above had entirely ceased, and another expedition up-river, with rifles, revealed that there was none flowing above either. The whole great Murray had ceased to flow, and was nothing but a long chain of stagnant water-holes.

You could walk across the river under the Swan Hill bridge, they said; and down in South Australia there were thirty boats lying in the mud at Morgan, like logs in a jam. The members of the River Murray Commission, who had set off by boat last year to examine the river, had had to take to road vehicles somewhere below Renmark. The urgent need for dams and locks could not have been made more clear.

Delie looked at the dead pool in which the boat lay, still afloat; and she thought about the endless flow of time, and how often she had said, 'If only time would stand still! If only this moment could last for ever.

She saw now that this would mean stagnation, the end of all change. Would she still be the child absorbedly digging moss from between the rose-coloured bricks in her grandfather's garden – a sentient, but almost animal creature, feeling warmth, breathing the earth-tang of the moss, seeing the contrast of rose and emerald, but without thought? What had that child known of the beauty and terror of life?

Even the happy, drowsy girl standing among the golden buttercups with Adam, lying among the fallen gum leaves in the bush ... No; she preferred growth, experience, change, the soft relentless flow of time. The river that carried all away on its unreturning stream was for ever renewed and renewing, though the individual drops were lost in the great sea that waited somewhere ahead.

She was now twenty-three, and her baby would be born in May. The weeks and months had passed imperceptibly in this strange arrested life, but time was measured for her by the growing life she carried, the first faint movements of which she had felt with mingled delight and fear. If the river had not begun to move by the end of April, she would leave for Swan Hill and go down to Melbourne for the birth.

FIFTY-ONE

In April, month of new birth, month of Easter, the river began to move; first a trickle, then a muddy, swirling flow along the bottom of its bed – so small, so dirty, that it was hard to believe the stream would ever flow deep and clear again.

Wires were sent off for missing members of crews, expeditions were made to Swan Hill to pick up others, tarpaulins were taken in, and all was made ready for departure as soon as there should be enough water under the ten red-gum keels of the stranded steamers.

The *Philadelphia* was in beautiful condition after her two enforced rests, when the remaining crew-members had occupied themselves with painting, scraping and repairing until she looked like a new boat.

In the first week of May she moved off upstream. Teddy Edwards, always impatient, determined to be first, had no intention of waiting for a good river. A couple of inches under her keel was enough.

At Swan Hill there was a delay. It was so long since any steamers had been through that either the lift-bridge or its operators were rusty; they were told it would be an hour before it could be opened. While Brenton fumed, Delie went up to the town to buy some white wool and ribbons, and to see a doctor. He was pleased with her condition, said that he did not expect any complications, but as she had a rather small pelvic opening it would be better for her to have the baby in the Echuca hospital.

As for her lungs, he could find nothing whatever wrong with them. He asked her who had diagnosed tuberculosis in the first place, and remarked that even city doctors could make mistakes. 'In fact, my dear,' he said, 'I very much doubt that there was anything wrong with you beyond a chronic bronchitis.'

Mrs Slope had been terribly depressed at the departure. She had put on a freshly laundered cotton dress to come and say good-bye. Over a cup of tea in the saloon she told Delie that the farm was already mortgaged, and that there was no more credit to be had from the bank. If the drought didn't break soon they must abandon the place to the crows, and go to Melbourne to live on charity.

'It's *got* to rain,' she said doggedly, staring with her soft blue eyes at the pure, hard blue of the moistureless sky – that sky which had turned the same blue smile on many a wanderer perishing with thirst outback.

Of course it would, Delie agreed; after all it was nearly winter, wasn't it? And at least the river was flowing again.

'Yes, and that means you're going. It's been – you don't know what it's been to me, having someone to talk to after all these years. Thank you, dear, and God bless you,' and she pressed a little hand-crocheted pillow-slip into Delie's hands.

Delie caught the rough, cracked hands in both of hers. 'It's meant a lot to me, too,' she said warmly. 'And thank you for all your kindness. It seems unfair that I should be so happy, and you've got so much to bear – the drought, and – and everything,' she stammered, feeling that she could not refer more directly to what had passed between them.

'That's all right, dear. Good luck, and I hope it's a boy.'

It was a boy; but it was not born in the Echuca hospital. A week after they left they were still struggling upstream, winching and warping along past Black Stump, Funnel Bend, Kelpie's Leap, and all the difficult places in the narrow, winding, snag-filled channel that skirted Campbell's Island.

Here the black swan and wild duck were in thousands. The swamps and backwaters, the wide sheet of the Moira Lakes, were still dry; and the birds had all congregated in the tree-lined

307

channel that had not been disturbed by steamers for almost a year.

Although the spring rains had come down from the highlands to fill the channel, the weather was summery still. Charlie, who was a self-styled weather prophet of the pessimistic kind, gloomily prophesied another year of drought.

'One more year like the last two, and the river trade'll be finished, mark my words,' he said. But as for years past he had been saying every spring, 'This'll be the worst summer ever, you'll see!', no one took much notice of him now.

At Euston, Tooley Buc and Gonn Crossing, where there were punts to take traffic across the river, they heard that bridges were soon to be built.

'More difficulties put in the way of navigation,' growled Brenton. But at Koondrook they found the bridge already completed, linking it up to the New South Wales town of Barham on the other side. At their whistle crowds came running from the two towns, for this was to be the first steamer through. A cheer went up as Brenton churned through the narrow lift-section, only a few feet wider than the boat, at full speed.

Delie, who was in the wheel-house, held on nervously until they were through; the child she carried made her more anxious for her own safety than before. But Brenton only laughed, pleased by the admiration of the crowd.

He had been taking a rest in the cabin through the last fairly open section of river, only coming up to the wheel-house to take her through. His blue eyes looked bloodshot, his bright curls were rumpled and there was a short, fair stubble on his chin. He was often careless about his appearance these days, would shave when he felt like it, and slopped about the deck in old canvas shoes bursting at the toes, or barefoot.

The *Philadelphia* went on her way, not knowing that she would be the last steamer through for a fortnight. For the excited crowd, impatient for the bridge to be down again so that they could cross, jumped upon the mid-section before it was back in place. The bridge fell at once with the weight, the pulley-wheel whizzed round madly and flew to pieces with centrifugal force, just missing the two men who had been winding. It was two weeks before another wheel was cast and installed.

The day they left Barham was hot and dusty, with a north wind bringing a scorching breath from the drought-dried heart of the continent. Though their general direction was south-east, the river wound so much that sometimes the wind was behind, sometimes head-on.

It was late afternoon, and Brenton was staring with gritty, bloodshot eyes through the red haze of dust at the narrow channel. Delie was resting her heavy body and swollen legs in the cabin. The baby had moved lower and become quiet, as though gathering its strength for the great effort of birth.

Suddenly there was a confused shouting on deck, a thudding of feet, and she sat up in nameless alarm. She heard the clatter of buckets, the thumping splash of water. Surely they were not going to wash the decks at this hour? Then an acrid scent drifted in the door, a smell she had learned to know and fear – the smell of fire.

She rushed out and into the wheel-house next door. Brenton, with his jaw set, was trying to bring the *Philadelphia* round, for she was travelling straight into the roaring, hot wind; and from the forepeak flames and black smoke were climbing. The flames, fanned back by the wind, were licking already at the front of the superstructure with its new paint. Skipper, the parrot, was swearing in Danish, and excitedly demanding the screwdriver.

'Go and get in the dinghy,' said Brenton through his teeth. He swore savagely, wrenching at the wheel.

'I won't go without you.'

'Don't be a fool.' With dreadful rapidity the woodwork had caught fire, and flames were now leaping at the windows of the wheel-house.

'Leave it – we'll have to abandon her!' he shouted to the men who, in spite of all they could do, were being forced back into the waist of the steamer. Ben came rushing up the steps with white face and singed eyebrows.

'The Missus, Captain – ?'

'Take her to the dinghy – quick, lad.'

Ben took her arm, but Delie dragged away and rushed into the cabin.

She had no time to think. Her paintings were on top of the chest, her baby's clothes in a case under the bottom bunk. In a moment she had rolled up the canvases and thrust them inside the neck of her dress, and rushed out again as a swirl of black smoke puffed in the door. Ben grabbed her and began hurrying her aft, but already the paddle-box was in flames and the steps were gone.

Delie dragged back. 'Where's Brenton? I won't go –'

'He's all right. He'll have jumped overboard. We'll have to jump, too.'

She stood petrified, staring at the water that seemed such a long way down. A flame licked again her foot, and Ben gave her a swift push. Screaming, she dropped into the river and felt cold water close over her head.

When she came up after seeming to go down into endless depths, she heard, like an echo of her own cry, the steamer's whistle blowing off in a continuous peal. Brenton had tied the lever down so that the boiler could blow off steam and would not burst at the sudden cessation of motion; for, unable to turn so that the wind was behind, he brought the *Philadelphia* up as far as he could on a shoal which he knew ran out from the left-hand bank, and beached her there. Then he unchained the parrot and jumped overboard just as his clothes caught alight.

Ben had become separated from Delie in the dust and smoke, and with a dreadful feeling of aloneness she struck out for the bank with her weighted body, cumbered by its long dress and smock. She had not even stopped to unlace her shoes. Brenton would be all right, she knew. But she was beginning to be alarmed for herself, and the life within her.

Then a wet golden head appeared in front of her, a reassuring flash of white teeth.

'All right, darling, I've got you. Just relax. Lie back in the water.' And with a delicious feeling of repose she lay back in his arms and floated into unconsciousness at the same time.

She awoke from a vivid dream that she was on that far southern beach with Tom, her first rescuer. Then she saw Brenton sitting beside her, and smiled. Then a pain took her in a sudden savage grip, front and back, shook her violently as if she were a rat in the mouth of some huge terrier, and laid her down gently to recover.

But just as she was drifting off to sleep, quite relaxed, the pain seized her again. It shook her a little harder this time, and let her go again more reluctantly.

She struggled to sit up, in a swift panic.

'Brenton!'

'It's all right, dear. Just lie still.' A large hand held her down gently. 'You fainted as I was bringing you in – a perfect piece of co-operation, really. We can't be far from Torumbarry station – George has gone up-river to see how far. We can get some sort of vehicle from there, if there's any way it can be brought through the scrub. But anyway one of the other steamers can't be far behind.'

The pain had receded, and she asked calmly after the boat.

'The poor old girl's burned to the water's edge, but she's fast on a sandbank and we'll be able to rebuild her. Thank goodness the barge and the wool are safe. We'll need all our pennies after –'

'Brenton!'

This time the panic in her voice, the dark suffering in her blue eyes, really alarmed him.

'What is it? For God's sake, are you hurt somewhere?'

'Brenton, the baby's coming!'

He stared at her, the same panic reflected in his face. 'Oh, no!'

'*Yes*.' And another pain took her in its relentless grip. She clutched his hand in her extremity, but as he winced and drew in his breath she saw the hand was roughly bandaged with a torn shirt. In a moment she forgot her own pain and fear.

'You're hurt!'

'Only my hands. They got burnt while I was at the wheel, trying to get her round. I put some grease from the steering-chains on them. They're all right, just a bit sore. Darling, is the pain bad?'

'Not really, but each one is a bit worse, and – and I'm frightened.' Her pale lips quivered, and she began to shiver, for her clothes were soaked.

'Oh, God! What can I do?' Brenton stood up and clutched his damp curls in despair.

A thin figure, with wet dark hair plastered down about a white face, stopped beside him. 'Excuse me, Skipper, but I brought some dry blankets from the barge for the Missus.' He spoke above a bundle clasped in his arms. 'And one of the men had some clean underclothes, all been boiled. You'll need plenty of clean cloths, and hot water –'

'Ben! Do you know something about these things?'

'Yes, Cap'n Edwards. I helped the midwife more than once, with my mother. We must get a fire going, and some water boiling; and you had better help the Missus out of them wet things.'

The skipper hastened to do as his youngest deckhand told him. It was pathetic to see how helpless and how frightened he was. Between her pains, in the wonderful respite that came, at shorter and shorter intervals, between each one, Delie smiled to see his eager blundering. She was not frightened now, only excited.

She saw Brenton take Ben aside, and saw Ben's solemn nod of understanding, and knew that he was being told that she was delicate, that the doctor had said she should not have a baby at all.

311

But there was no room for fear. All her will, all her powers of resistance, were concentrated on bearing the present. 'Oh God, if it would only stop, oh God, if it would only stop,' she muttered over and over; but she knew that it would not stop, nothing could stop it now.

Once again, as on that first night in Brenton's bunk, she felt herself possessed by something beyond the individual, by the relentless and impersonal force of life. Like a straw tossed on a flooded river, she was borne along by the resistless pain, flinging herself from side to side in a hopeless effort to escape. She moaned regularly, and began to vomit with the pain.

Brenton clutched his head with his bandaged hands. 'I can't stand it!' he yelled wildly. 'Someone row me over the river, I'm going to Echuca for a doctor. This might go on for hours. Why doesn't another boat come? Even if Jim brings the wagon, we couldn't move her now. Ben – !'

He could not say any more, only wrung the boy's hand as he turned away.

It did go on for hours. Brenton's big-boned child, which had possession of her small and delicate frame, fought its way slowly and painfully towards the light.

The life-force took no account of the vessel that bore the new life, as the seed bursts the pod in order to be free and grow; but in the long struggle the new life suffered too.

Delie was dimly aware of Jim Pearce's return, well after dark, of men's figures moving on the edge of the circle of firelight, of Ben's soothing voice, his touch on her sweating brow as tender as a woman's. In those hours she seemed to live as long as in all her life before, as if Time had frozen to the imperceptible flow of a glacier; yet the whole experience had the quality of a dream, lived in some borderland of reality.

She asked for Brenton, but he had not returned. She felt indescribably lonely, even with Ben beside her, whispering that the doctor would soon be here. Then, with a shock that made her forget everything else for the moment, she looked straight up and saw the stars.

There were the stars! Unchanged, wheeling with majestic, unvarying pace across the sky, when she had felt that everything in the universe was contracted to the little core where she struggled to deliver her child. The Milky Way was a river of calm light, the Scorpion swung towards the west like a giant interrogation mark, a jewelled, eternal question.

It was long after midnight when the last stage began. Now she was sure that she would die, she could not endure this and live; yet it did not matter. Any end to this must be welcome, she thought, listening with detachment to the animal scream that was forced from her own throat. Then a blissful unconsciousness descended, from which she woke in perfect peace. The dreadful rapids were behind.

The mood of detachment remained. She felt no shame at the intimate things Ben had to do for her; they were like two initiates of a new religion, they were within the holy circle.

The raging north wind had stopped, and a cool southerly, gentle, with a moisture-laden breath, had blown the dust away. The early hours were clear and mild. Delie looked up and beheld, upon the night's starred face, huge cloudy symbols that mingled with her dreams. She slept the sleep of exhaustion, without noticing that she had not heard the child cry.

At last the doctor arrived with Brenton, who had brought him almost by force from his bed. They had driven to Perricoota station, and walked through uninhabited scrub from there. The doctor, alarmed by her weak pulse, administered a stimulant at once by injection. Then she asked, faintly, to see the baby.

There was a small, difficult silence. The doctor, who had kindly eyes set among wrinkles, and large grey beard, patted her hand. Delie's eyes flew open to their widest extent.

'What is wrong with the baby? Of course, I know . . . I had a feeling all along. Crippled?' she asked pitifully. But it wasn't a twisted body that she feared.

'No, my dear. A perfect male child.' The doctor cleared his throat. 'But unfortunately . . . It was a difficult birth, and it did not live.'

'It doesn't matter, darling,' said Brenton eagerly, putting his bandaged hand on hers where it lay limp on the ground beside her. 'It's you that matters. Thank God you're all right.'

'The lad did very well to bring the mother through. A very difficult birth. Some stitches will be necessary, and the sooner the better. If someone will hold the lantern, I can manage here, I think.'

The doctor directed Ben to make a rough table of three boxes, and they lifted Delie on to this. But Brenton could not bring himself to watch. It was Ben, with his thin, suffering boy's face, who held the lantern in a hand that trembled slightly.

313

Delie drifted off into unconsciousness again, to the accompaniment of a sickly smell and a fireworks display of pretty, coloured wheels. Her last conscious thought she uttered aloud, in a drowsy voice:

'A perfect male child. Perfect . . . What a waste.'

FIFTY-TWO

Delie's baby was not the only casualty of that disastrous fire. The fat cook was lost, presumably drowned; his body was never recovered. The parrot had disappeared into the bush. Charlie, who had stayed with his precious engine till the last moment, had his hands badly burned, and the burns turned septic. He was admitted to the Echuca hospital, where he stayed while the *Philadelphia* was towed to the dry dock and rebuilt.

Delie had lost all her clothes but what she wore, all her paints and brushes, and the things she had prepared for the baby; but her canvases, the record of those two years of inland drought and heat, were safe.

When she felt better she decided to hold a show in the Echuca Mechanics' Institute. Mr Hamilton put one of her pictures in his window with an advertisement of the exhibition, and Mr Wise, her former master, brought his students from the School of Arts. She collected a good return of shillings paid at the door.

Daniel Wise bought for the school one of her Darling oils. He was tremendously pleased with the progress of his former pupil. She also sold two traditional studies of sunrise and sunset reflections, painted at the lagoon in the Murray where they had been stranded.

The other pictures were mostly too 'modern' in their realistic treatment of drought and heat and despair; they were 'ugly and depressing', the visitors told each other, and besides they weren't solid enough. Some of them looked as if they were dissolving in light.

Delie did not mind. She was buoyed up by the praise of Daniel Wise, who wrote a notice of the exhibition. Her uncle came in to see it, and was so pleased that he was moved to tears of joy as he

314

shambled from picture to picture, peering short-sightedly. Delie's depression began to lift.

Brenton didn't understand or share her feelings about the child's death. He had known she did not really want it. How then could its loss mean so much? he wondered, looking at her shadowed eyes and rebellious mouth, which had lost a little of its youthful sweetness.

But Delie, whose breasts ached with the milk that was not needed now, bound a tight cloth round them and felt that the constriction was about her heart. She could not tell Brenton – it was surprising how many things she could not tell him – of her unreasoning feeling of guilt. But she had thought first of him, and then of her paintings, not of the baby she carried. If she had got to the dinghy in time . . . if she had reached a hospital where oxygen was available . . . it might have lived.

And the pictures? Were they worth it? Looking at them critically, framed and hung upon the Institute walls, she felt a little thrill of pride. She had created something, and her technique had developed. They were still not what she wanted to do, they fell far short of her dream; yet she felt that she had managed to capture that feeling of light, heat and immensity which brooded over the inland plains.

She decided to send her three best canvases to the Spring Exhibition of the Victorian Artists' Society. Imogen had written of the Society's latest activities: 'We are a strong body now, though the leading lights, Arthur Streeton and Tom Roberts, are both in London. But at least we have the principle of *practising artists* running the show, not a lot of old fuddy-duddies who paint china. . . . I'm painting hard. Did one of the Prince's Bridge, all gold light and deep blue shadows under the arches, which is one of the best things I've ever done. Do you realise I'll reach the alarming age of *twenty-two* this year? God, I feel alive . . .'

Prince's Bridge! Delie thought of Melbourne on a misty morning, its green lawns and grey streets, its delicate spires melting into the soft sky, the Yarra reflecting them all. It seemed that it must be another continent, almost another planet, from the hot, dry immensity of the inland plains.

She began to long for the green, gracious city again. When she had recovered her strength, and Brenton was established comfortably in a boarding-house while he supervised the rebuilding of the boat, she took the train to the south.

With every mile her excitement grew; she watched the blue

signs fleeting backwards: Eighty Miles To Griffiths Brothers for Teas, Coffee, Cocoa . . . Seventy Miles . . Fifty . . . Emerging from the station into the traffic that raced up and down as it had done unceasingly all the time she had been away, she felt newly young and light-hearted.

The experiences of the last two years, which had set her face in firmer lines, seemed to roll away from her; but they had left their mark in the passionate rebelliousness of her mouth, the faint line of distress that was creased between her level brows.

She stayed with Imogen, who was currently without a lover, and delighted to see her. Delie wandered round the flat, looked out the windows, admired or criticised Imogen's latest canvases, and felt again the strangeness of returning in space to the setting of a time that was past.

'You look well,' said Imogen grudgingly, 'but I'm sure it's not a suitable life for you. You're still terribly thin. You shouldn't live on a boat.'

'But why not?'

'Well, it's so far away from everything, and . . .'

'I'm not sure that isn't a good thing for an artist. I get a terrific yearning for Melbourne, and for the good talk and stimulating company of the studio days, and yet . . . everyone has to work out his own salvation, and he can probably do it best alone, away from the influence of other artists and the distraction of the city.'

'Distractions, yes! I know I don't work nearly as hard as I should.'

'Oh, *you'd* find distractions anywhere – I know your sort of distractions.'

Imogen smiled and smoothed her sleek black hair with a graceful, cat-like movement.

'There are none at the moment, truly! I got fed up with the last one. He wanted me to marry him and settle down to suburban respectability in the same house with his widowed mother. I ask you – !'

'You see, I have all the advantages of home life without the deadly dullness of the suburbs. Even a garden, in window-boxes – or I had before the fire. And everything will be new, and Brenton has promised to build a water storage tank to be filled from the engine, so we'll have hot water all the time when we're running.'

'But it isn't safe, you might have been killed in that fire. Though I suppose you're really glad about the baby. I mean, it would have

316

been a terrific tie, and if you want to paint –'

'Glad!' Delie was looking at her in horrified amazement. A flush rose slowly from her throat to her cheeks. 'I'm afraid you just don't understand, Imogen.'

'Oh, well . . .' Imogen looked uncomfortable. 'I guess I'm not the maternal type, darling.' She changed the subject hurriedly. 'I say, I must show you the new négligé I designed myself. It's white chiffon, lined with flamingo pink . . .'

Delie stayed on for the Spring Exhibition, for which her three pictures were accepted by the selection committee; but not one was sold. People bought the fresh flower-pieces, the familiar views of the Yarra, the paintings of picturesque cottages and well-known churches.

Her landscape, *Beyond Menindie*, showed an iron shanty, a few sparse iron-grey trees and a vast plain melting into mirage. 'Interesting, but I wouldn't like to live with it,' was one comment she heard from a well-dressed matron.

The second of her pictures was a study of a huge thunder-cloud in an intensely blue sky, throwing its shadow over the saltbush plain. Into the third, *Mallee Farm*, she had put some of the horror of the drought, the starving, dispirited stock, the white limestone gibbers lying in the paddocks, the drifts of sand over the fences; and something of the drought of the spirit that had seemed to pervade the place where they were marooned.

The press critics mentioned them: 'Three unusual studies by Delphine Gordon include two rather sordid, dreary interpretations of the outback scene, and a vivid, arresting cloud-study . . .'

'Her improbable blues and staring highlights . . .'

'An attempt to catch the atmosphere of desolation . . .' This last was better; it showed an appreciation of her aims. But she cared little for the critics. What mattered was the judgment and commendation of her fellow artists, and the stimulus of talk with people who could see what she was trying to do. She began to feel a new creative urge; and with it, an overwhelming desire for Brenton.

He took her in sleep, in dreams, and she woke trembling with longing for his presence. She waited only until after her appointment with the doctor, who confirmed what the doctor in Swan Hill had told her: there was nothing the matter with her lungs. She took the next train back to Echuca.

That night they slept little. The boat was nearly finished, and,

317

as Brenton said, they would soon be back in the discomfort of separate bunks; he wanted to make hay while the sun shone.

'You are certainly a most indefatigable haymaker,' she said with a drowsy chuckle when he woke her for the fourth time. Brenton leaned above her and looked at her face in the dim, filtered moonlight from outside.

'It's your fault,' he said. 'You're different altogether. What have you been up to in Melbourne?'

'Nothing. I just feel different. I feel wonderful.'

'Then why did you cry tonight, for the first time?'

'Because I was so happy.'

'Well – ! I give up.'

The next day she felt immortal, transfigured. The man-child who had invaded her body, who had almost destroyed it in getting born, had not come to perfection in vain. All the love that had been building up for the coming child now turned towards her husband; she was, mysteriously, both his mistress and his mother, and for the first time wholly content.

FIFTY-THREE

The drought had broken. The Murray and the Darling both came down in good volume in the spring of 1903. The *Philadelphia*, brand new above decks, smartly painted in white with her name in black letters on the front of the wheel-house, set out again on her travels. Her paddles seemed to turn with a gayer rhythm.

Her namesake was happy too. She wanted nothing more than to paint all day, and lie beside Brenton all night. She had accepted by now the limitation of the relationship; he spoiled her, and petted her, and ignored her when he had a man to talk to. Now she no longer minded.

He had given her a free hand in redecorating the saloon and the cabins, where she had crisp blue-and-white cotton hangings at doors and windows, with bunk-covers to match. Travelling up and down without the hazards of drought conditions, she felt that her life was one long holiday. Even the Darling River seemed a different place when it was not lined with starving stock; and seeing the box trees in creamy blossom, and banks of sand covered with the white blossoms of Darling lilies, and the carpets of wild flowers that sprang up after the rain, she realised that it could have its times of softer beauty.

But the river trade was sadly diminished. Settlers had become used to doing without the steamers in the two drought years, and railway-lines now tapped the river network in so many places that loading was scarce. Cut-throat freight charges introduced by the governments of New South Wales and Victoria, both trying to draw the rich river trade to their own capitals, made it difficult for the steamers to compete.

Brenton, who had never been satisfied with the *Philadelphia*'s performance, had included all sorts of new ideas in her design when she was rebuilt. She now had double boilers, which in theory would make her go twice as fast.

'As if *one* boiler wasn't enough trouble to keep steam up in, an' be weightin' the gauge and watchin' the pressure of,' grumbled Charlie. 'Nex' thing 'e'll be wantin two engineers; an' when another engineer walks on this 'ere boat, I walks off.'

The twin boilers did not improve her performance much, and made a lot of extra work. Brenton became gloomy; he had to recoup himself for the expense of rebuilding, but even on the Darling trade was not what it had been. In 1904, when they were tied up at Wentworth after unloading a half-empty barge, he said to Delie that the 'top-end trade seemed to be about done'. It was the new railways to Swan Hill, Mildura and Menindie that were the trouble.

The best thing these days seemed to be a floating store like the *Mannum* or the *Queen*, or to have a mail contract like Randell or Hugh King had. He'd been talking to Captain King, who wanted another small steamer for the mail run between Morgan and Wentworth.

'He's rather taken by the *Philadelphia* in her new rig,' added Brenton.

'You wouldn't *sell* her?'

'No, but we could join his fleet, the River Murray Navigation Company – he *is* the company now – under contract. Or we can go on losing money; one or the other.'

Captain King asked them on board his steamer for dinner. He was travelling as skipper on the *Gem*, the largest and most luxurious passenger steamer on the Murray, with Jim Mutchy as mate. The

319

Ellen, which was even larger, had turned out to be little use except on a high river, because of her deep draught, and was to be turned into a barge.

The little *Ruby*, with a draught of only twenty-one inches, which had carried mail and cargo for the fleet, was being extended by forty feet and made into a passenger steamer. He would like the *Philadelphia*, said Captain King, to take her place on the mail run; he would prefer to buy her outright.

Private owner-skippers, he said, would soon have to join the big firms or give up; trade was getting too uncertain for the man on his own, without big capital . . .

'Well, sir,' said Brenton, 'my wife owns a half-share in the steamer, and she has a sentimental feeling for it, as it was named after her. She wouldn't like to part with the *Philadelphia*, eh, darling?'

'Oh *no*!'

'Then we'll say no more,' said Captain King, bowing gallantly. 'A lady's wishes should always be respected.'

Delie was charmed by the large, courteous, genial captain with his big grey beard and twinkling eyes; a Father Christmas sort of man, she thought.

'Well, you have a reputation for always being the first through, my boy, and speed is what we want on the mail run. Speed and reliability. It's no use piling the boat up and not getting there at all. About these twin boilers, now –'

'I'm thinking of going back to one. I'm always trying for more speed, but I'm not sure the extra power isn't lost in the extra weight and stops for fuel. Now, I've got these new condensers –'

They went into a technical conversation that was over Delie's head. Soon they disappeared to look at the *Gem*'s engines, while Delie talked to the mate, not unaware of the admiring glances of the men passengers in the saloon.

'What a nice man Captain King is,' she said impulsively.

'Yes, he's a thorough gentleman. But he's not always so mild, don't get that idea. I remember one time when we were bringing a mob of shearers down from Avoca station. At Lake Victoria station we stopped to pick up wool, and the shearing outfit too. Just after the big strike it was, and Lake Victoria was shearing "black". You should've heard the riot when those scab shearers tried to come aboard. The shearers were yellin' blue murder at each other. Capt'n King bellowed at the Avoca men to get aft and stay there, and then he brought her bows quietly in and had

320

the wool piled up to the rails of the top deck for'ard. He made the Lake Victoria shearers, the new mob, climb up on top of the wool. Then he said that the first man that crossed the paddle-shaft he'd throw in the river.

'We had no more trouble; but we missed the train at Morgan.'

'He looks like someone who can handle men,' said Delie.

Brenton and the captain came back, and they sat yarning a while longer.

'Wonder how I'll get on below Wentworth?' asked Brenton. 'I suppose it's not as tricky as the top end – not so many bends.'

'The whole of this danged river's tricky. But the worst thing about the bottom end is the wind, when you're in a long, open reach; and the shadows of the cliffs on a dark night. Old Captain Hart, who was on the *Ellen*, ran on a bank one night, thinking it was only a reflection. He was found dead at the wheel with the shock.'

'Are there any reliable charts?'

'Yes, Captain Hart made a good one; it's on the *Marion* at present, but I could get hold of it for you. There's some awkward places you'll soon get to know, like the Devil's Elbow – some queer-looking cliffs there – and Pollard's Cutting, a cut-off with a very fast current . . . Your mate know this end of the river?'

'No; Jim Pearce is an Echuca man.'

'Then I'd advise you take someone who does know it on your first trip. There's no way to learn the channel except at first hand. And charts soon get out of date, because the channel moves after every flood. You can go aground in no time.'

'Thanks,' said Brenton, 'for those cheering words. I'll try to find some old bloke who wants a free lift down to S.A.'

When they went back to the *Philadelphia*, she seemed small and cramped after the one-hundred-passenger *Gem* with her big saloon, her red plush dining-saloon and gleaming woodwork. Delie was excited, wound up with the novelty of dining among so many people, and full of wonder at the luxuriousness of the big steamer. She had seen and admired everything, the up-to-date galley, the little bathrooms with hot and cold running water, the smart cabins with their magical buttons for turning on the electric light.

She had dressed with care, in the pale blue bombazine with the rose-wreaths, now getting a little tight in the waist; for she had put on some weight with the quiet, contented life she had been leading, and it suited her. Her white throat and smooth arms no longer showed their young bones; the ripe bosom and rounded shoulders were just suggested beneath the filmy stuff of the fichu. This year she had attained the full flowering of the flesh, after which comes the slow decline as in a tree which has passed its fruiting time.

'God, you look lovely tonight,' said Brenton sincerely, as he watched her cross the gangplank – unaided, for he no longer bounded forward to hold her elbow. 'I haven't seen you dressed up for ages, and under the electric light you fairly sparkled.'

She turned as she reached the deck, a flush of pleasure in her cheeks, her eyes intensely blue in the light of the deck-lantern.

'Do you remember the night you pulled the gangplank in, and said "Now we are on an island . . ."?'

'I should say so! And we're still entirely surrounded by water.'

As she lifted her trailing skirts and began to climb the steps to the top deck, he caught one of her slim ankles in his hand and kissed it, running his fingers up the curve of her leg. She stood still and trembled under his touch. 'Run on up to your bunk, darling. I'll be with you in a minute.'

She stumbled in her eagerness, running up the steps. In the little cabin she lit the lamp and stared for a moment in the mirror, into her own brilliant eyes. Then she undressed quickly, pulled the pins out of her dark hair and let its piled-up mass fall about her bare shoulders. She brushed it smooth, and slipped naked between the sheets.

'Come quickly, my darling,' she murmured to the pillow. She lay and trembled slightly with the cold of the sheets and the eagerness of her desire. The outing, the unexpected luxury of the dinner, the coming back with him late at night to a silent boat, had brought back vividly the early days of their love, in Echuca, before they were married.

She waited impatiently, staring at the dark oblong of the doorway, waiting for his step. He had been a long time, surely, if he was only going to the bathroom under the paddle-box. At last she got up and stood just inside the door, listening.

She cautiously put her head out. The cabin opened on the side away from the town, and she could see the dark water hurrying by to its junction with the Murray just beyond. There were voices coming up from below, Brenton's and Charlie's.

They were arguing about boilers.

She did not know how long it was before she finally heard his step on the deck, and started nervously out of a fitful doze.

322

'Not asleep are you, darling?' he said cheerfully, undoing his tie as he came in.

She was silent. She felt like a glass of champagne that has been left standing all night, flat and sour; and was almost as surprised as he when, at his first touch, she began to sob uncontrollably.

'I don't know!' said Brenton irritably. 'There's no understanding women.'

FIFTY-FOUR

Before they left Wentworth Delie enjoyed some social life, visiting other steamers, attending a local ball which was held in the Mechanics' Institute. The whole crew went, except for Charlie, who spent the night with a collection of bottles.

All the men in town, their hair unnaturally sleek, their throats enclosed with spotless neckerchiefs, gathered in a group just inside the door, for mutual support. The girls sat round the walls, waiting demurely for the music to start.

The first dance after Delie's arrival, the moment the music began, there was a concerted rushing movement as the whole male contingent descended upon her. She was someone new, and the most attractive young woman in the room; so Brenton had to fend off the would-be partners and stand up with her himself to save her from the crush.

He danced masterfully but without finesse, and became a little breathless. He was glad to hand her over to Jim after two rounds of the hall.

During the evening she danced with everyone – shearers and deck-hands, drovers and cooks, roustabouts and jackeroos from the nearest stations. Until two in the morning, still looking cool and radiant in a white muslin gown with a black velvet sash, she danced in the light of the hanging kerosene lamps that glimmered through the haze of dust under the ceiling.

She had to cope with some surprising conversation. One broad, muscular bushman, after whirling her round in a breathless waltz without once reversing, looked down at her with sympathetic concern.

'D'you sweat much, Mrs Edwards?' he asked. 'My oath, I do. I'm sweatin' like a pig.'

Another, bronzed and handsome and terribly shy, seemed to be looking round desperately for some subject of conversation, and at last brought out, with a kind of gasp:

'What 'orse do y' reckon's the best for a pack-'orse, an 'orse or a mare?'

An elderly little shearer's cook with a large paunch danced her round at arm's length in a polka, and gave her a recipe for brownie.

By two o'clock the kerosene gave out and the lanterns flickered one by one, though the accordion and the drum still sounded from a dim corner. Reluctantly, borne up by the excitement so that she felt not a vestige of tiredness, Delie was persuaded to return to the boat. It was, she thought afterwards, the last night of her youth.

On her first run as His Majesty's Royal Mail steamer, the *Philadelphia* left Wentworth on a sunny spring morning, and instead of making the wide swing round the sandspit at the junction to go upstream, went with the curve of the waters into a new part of the Murray river she had never entered before.

Rains in Queensland had brought a full head of water down the Darling, while the Murray, not yet swollen with the melted snow-waters from the mountains, ran slow and clear. At the junction, the translucent, dark-green waters of the main stream, and the yellow, cloudy Darling flowed for a while side by side, like two alien races. Gradually these mingled and intermarried, leaving patches of different colour here and there, until about three miles below the junction they became one, in the typical milky green of the lower Murray.

A grizzled old 'Murray whaler', who had been 'whalin' up the Darlin'' as a change from the Murray, drifted into the town just before they left. He didn't like the Darling, and declared that 'there was nothin' but 'ungry squatters and lousy cooks' the whole length of that accursed river, who wouldn't give a starving man a hand-out of flour. He knew the lower Murray, he said, 'like the back of me 'and', so he was given a free passage as pilot.

His name was Hairy Harry, and he wore a growth of wild grey whiskers among which the mouth was indicated by an area stained yellow with nicotine. His eyebrows were even fiercer and more luxuriant than Charlie's, and his hair looked as if it had last been cut with a pair of sheep-shears, by a very inexperienced shearer.

His old dinghy had sunk beneath him, he said, just above Wentworth. He came aboard carrying all his worldy possessions rolled up in a grey blanket, to which was tied a black billy-can and a frying-pan, and a tin pannikin. Many a hand-out of tea and sugar, and many a pannikin of flour had been carried off in these utensils; and, if the truth were told, many an illicit mutton chop had sizzled in that pan, cut from a sheep that 'prob'ly would 've died any'ow'.

'Me livin' was took from me,' said Harry grandiloquently, 'when that there boat sunk beneath me, with all me rabbit-traps and 'fishin'-lines an' gear; and now I'm carst orf in a cold world to make me way as best I can. If yer'll give me a passage down to South Oss, Skipper, yer won't regret it, and it'll be the savin' of pore old 'Arry. I'll stick in them irrigation towns till next summer, an' then snatch a few grapes for some grower till I makes enough to buy another flattie.'

('He won't get another boat, of course, if he ever had one,' said Brenton. 'If he gets a job for a while picking grapes, he'll drink all the cash as fast as he earns it.')

'Where do I put me knot?' asked Hairy Harry as he came aboard. He eyed the sleeping arrangements with some disdain, when Brenton indicated a tarpaulin stretched on the after-deck. 'Wot, I gotter sleep under there? Don't the pilot get a cabin to 'isself?' But when Brenton didn't bother to answer this one, he walked aft, muttering in his beard.

The two boilers gave trouble all the way down to Renmark. Brenton declared that Charlie wasn't looking after them properly because he'd been against them from the first. He fumed and fretted and worried about the channel, and complained of head-aches. His face had become rather high-coloured, and when he was angry it turned puplish; a vein stood out at the side of his neck, distended and blue in colour, looking as if it would burst.

In the end they had to pull into the bank to overhaul one of the boilers. It took nearly twenty-four hours by the time they had damped down the firebox, cleaned the boiler flues and got steam up again.

Delie welcomed the delay because they stopped opposite a brilliant orange sandhill, decorated with two dark Murray pines and reflected in green water. She spent all day sketching and painting.

'The scenery down this end is gorgeous,' she wrote to Imogen.

'Such colour and variety after the endless trees of the upper reaches! There are magnificent gums in the lagoons (which are sometimes nearly a mile across), and green reeds and willows and coloured cliffs, that look as though they had been carved out of pink and yellow candy, and the sandhills have the most subtle colours of orange and salmon pink and Venetian red . . .'

They passed some of the largest sheep holdings along the river: Moorna Station, that belonged to the Chaffey brothers who founded Mildura, and Ned's Corner with its eighty-mile river frontage. Kangaroos and emus were seen on the banks, and pelicans sailed in stately flotillas as they fished the lagoons.

Hairy Harry sat proudly in the wheel-house on a tall stool, giving the skipper advice. Delie, in her cabin next to the wheel-house, heard much swearing, and hands pounding on the spokes of the wheel as it was spun rapidly. She looked out and noticed that a good deal of mud had been churned up by the port paddle in negotiating a sharp, involved bend. When Brenton had got his breath back she heard him speak in rather bitter tones:

'Wasn't that the Devil's Elbow?'

'Eh? Yes, it would be, I s'pose.'

'Well, why didn't you warn me? Thought you knew this part of the river like the back of your hand.'

'So I did, boss. But the blanky channel 'as moved a good bit since I was larst through 'ere.'

'Moved a bit? When *were* you last through here?'

'Well, boss, it's about twenty year, since I was on a steamer, that is. O' course in a flattie you don't take no account of the channel.'

'Twenty years! Why, Pollard's Cutting wasn't even there, I suppose.'

'Yairs; but she wasn't used much, like. The old channel wasn't silted up much then, an' the skippers most went round – it was safer.'

'Why, you hairy old hypocrite! You won't be any use to me at all. You can have your free trip and tucker, but you can blasted well get out of my wheel-house, and stay out. Ben! BEN!' he roared. 'Come up here and lend us a hand with the wheel round these bends.'

Hairy Harry came shuffling down the three steps from the wheel-house. Delie felt sorry for his deflated self-importance as he walked past, muttering darkly in his tobacco-stained whiskers, as

326

his freckled, trembling hand felt for 'the makings' in the pocket of his worn waistcoat.

He was a real character, and she decided that she would like to paint his portrait. So Harry, deprived of his status as pilot, became a model. He posed on the foredeck, with the wind of their motion blowing his grey beard and ragged locks sideways, his old hat shading his eyes.

Delie found that he was an ardent reader of *The Bulletin* and could quote Banjo Patterson and other bush balladists by the hours. He also had a repertoire of old bush songs, and would beat out the time of 'The Old Bark Hut', or 'Whalin' in the Bend', and sing in a quavery tenor:

> With me little round flour-bag sittin' on a stump,
> Me little tea-and-sugar bag a-lookin' nice an' plump;
> With a fat little codfish just off the hook,
> And four little johnny-cakes a credit to the cook . . .

When he was not singing he entertained her with yarns and tall stories; and Delie felt that he earned his passage.

The healthy state of trade on the lower river was shown by the number of boats they passed. Apart from the passenger steamers and floating stores, they saw the *Pevensey, Undaunted, Queen of the South*, and *Little Wonder* – so called, it was said, because it was a wonder she didn't capsize. She had an incurable list to starboard, and waddled along like a drunken duck. The *Rothbury*, a small fast boat, and the *South Australian* both passed them on the downward run. After that Teddy Edwards was in a black mood.

Delie, who had been in the cabin and did not know that the second boat had just showed them her wake, unwisely went to the wheel-house to beg him to stop for a little near an inviting sandbank while he had a swim. She wanted to paint some curious cliffs on the other side, that had been carved by wind and water till they looked like the battlements of a Moorish castle.

'Stop while you paint! Stop for a swim!' He closed his mouth sharply on each word, and she noticed how hard and straight it was. He glared at the river, and the vein swelled in his neck.

'I – I just thought it was such a lovely spot – '

'I have work to do, in case you don't realise it. We happen to be running on a contract.'

'Jim Pearce says we're running ahead of schedule, and –'

'We've just been passed by the *South Australian*, and I'm going to catch her up at the next woodpile,' he said grimly. 'She wouldn't have caught us at all if they'd handled the wood a bit quicker back there at the last stop. Ben! Slip down and tell Charlie to give her everything, pour some kerosene on the wood if necessary.'

Delie sighed, and looked at the pictures slipping by on each side. What a lovely length of river this would be, with its long reaches and fringing lagoons, if you could take your time over it.

She looked speculatively at Hairy Harry, taking his ease on his back on the sun-warmed deck, his hat tilted over his eyes. He 'whaled' the rivers in a slow old dinghy, stopped when he felt like it, ate when he was hungry, slept when he was tired. No clocks or schedules in his life!

And was life meant to be lived in the endless activity of ants? She began to weary of Brenton's mania for speed, for success. The two of them could have lived comfortably on the boat, fishing, swimming, painting, lazing. But he would be bored by such a life. What use, though, to have the fastest boat on the river, to own a whole fleet of boats, and lose your health and youth over getting them?

By now the funnel was sobbing frantically, the whole boat shuddered with effort, and the steady *chunk-chunk-chunk* of the paddles blurred into a single threshing sound. She gripped a wooden stanchion, tense and nervous.

What if the twin boilers burst? What if they hit a snag at this speed, or crashed the bank at a sharp bend? Ever since she had heard of the *Providence*'s end she had been nervous; the fire had made her more so. She ventured to put an imploring hand on Brenton's arm.

He looked down at it in surprise and almost distaste. 'What is it, dear? I'm busy.' The endearment was the merest formality; his tone was cold.

'It's just – well, do you think it's quite safe, with the two boilers? I mean, can Charlie watch them both at once?'

'Look, I suppose I know my own job. I don't tell you how to paint a picture, do I?'

That silenced her, and she left the wheel-house abruptly. Three years! Was it only three years they had been married? Already

328

he had changed; what would he be like in ten years, in fifteen?

They passed Border Cliffs and the old customs House on the South Australian border, entering this State for the first time; and from here to Renmark the cliffs were so beautiful, with their glowing colours and strange conformation, that Delie tried to sketch them as they went past. This was not so difficult, for the river twisted and turned so much that sometimes they would be passing the same cliffs again an hour after they first sighted them.

The cook came up to the wheel-house to say he was out of eggs, and could they stop at the farmhouse just ahead to get some? Brenton looked at the bend of the river, and the wide flat it enclosed. 'Fetch me a string bag,' he said, 'and I'll get the eggs.'

He reduced speed slightly, handed over to the cook (who was quite handy at steering; the mate was having his six hours off duty) and dived overboard. As the *Philadelphia*, having circled the flat and negotiated two tortuous bends, steamed past half an hour later, he swam out, carrying the string bag full of eggs, and climbed up the rudder without one being broken. He dragged on a dry pullover and took the wheel again, still in his sopping sand-shoes and dungarees. Then he thrust the throttle lever to full speed again.

In Bunyip Reach, there was such a clangour from the labouring engines, echoing back from the high cliffs, that Delie came out on deck and saw, with a shudder, the blackened trees where the *Bunyip* had burned and sunk with the loss of three lives. The smoke of the *South Australian* – at least Charlie said it was the *South Australian* by the colour – could be seen now, just around the next bend.

Black smoke from the kerosene-soaked wood was now pouring out of the *Philadelphia*'s funnel, and Delie closed her eyes, imagining the figure showing on the pressure gauges. Not one boiler, but two, ready to blow them sky-high!

They rounded the bend, and there was the rival steamer, hated 'bottom-ender', in her own home waters. In ten minutes they had overhauled her, and the *Philadelphia*, with a short, insolent blast on her whistle – for Teddy Edwards wasn't going to waste steam with a peal of triumph – churned past so close that the two engineers, popping out from between the paddle-boxes, were able to glare right into each other's faces.

'Yah!' yelled Charlie. 'See yer in Renmark – if youse ever get there.'

'Guh! Two boilers! Bet yer blow up!'

But they arrived safely in the willow-lined, tranquil reach of river where the young irrigation settlement was thriving. Rows of vines, covered with the pale green of new leaves, lined the rich red earth, and the dark green of oranges, and groves of pears and apricots, made an oasis in the desert of saltbush and sand that stretched on all sides of the settlement.

Here they left Hairy Harry, who took a last admiring glance at his portrait and offered, rather diffidently, to buy it.

'Thank you for the offer, Harry,' said Delie, 'but if I could bear to part with it I'd give it to you. I think it's one of the best portraits I've ever done, though, and I want to save it for an exhibition in Melbourne.'

Harry admitted that it would be nice to have his portrait hung in 'one of them big Melbourne galleries', and he obviously had no money with which to buy it. He confided to her that he 'used to paint a bit meself, once', and this statement she took in the spirit in which it was offered, as mere conversation; as she had his earlier statements that he 'used to own a share in a paddle-steamer once', and 'used to have a bit of a property down in South Oss'.

Delie had developed a new interest in figure painting, and scouted the town for likely subjects. The second morning, while the *Philadelphia* was loading for the return trip, she got up early and walked up to the bridge, past a long lagoon where fish were leaping in a series of silver flashes. The surface of the water was like silk, spangled with silver sequins. She never saw the shape of a fish, only the dazzling flash of the sun on its side as it leaped.

Steam was curling from the still surface of the river, softening the reflections of gum tree and willow; and standing in the shallows was a buxom, comely girl, cleaning a catch of bream.

Her dress, of a faded pink material, was kilted high about her thighs. On the bank behind her was a fisherman's humpy of bags and tin, with smoke curling from the kerosene-tin chimney.

'Good morning,' said Delie, feeling the old excitement flowing through her veins, making her fingers tingle for the brush. The curve of the woman's legs, the curve of her wet arms, the silvery curve of the fish she held, contrasted with the level line of the water and the straight line of the knife; while the silvery green of water and trees made a foil for the warm tones of the figure. 'Do you mind if I sketch you while you work?'

She soon had the essentials in her sketch-book, and was hurrying back to the boat for paints and canvas. She spent a delightful morning, painting and yarning with the fisherman and his wife, who gave her a delicious lunch of fried fresh-caught bream. Then she went on working at the picture, and it was well into the afternoon when she remembered that the *Philadelphia* sailed at two.

'Oh, my goodness!' she gasped, suddenly realising the import of the series of impatient toots from a steam-whistle that she had heard vaguely for some time. She gathered up her things and ran, shouting good-byes and thanks.

Brenton greeted her with a thunderous look, his mouth set hard and straight.

'I suppose you realise we've had steam up for nearly an hour. It's nearly three o'clock. Where in God's name did you get to? Ben's been searching the town, and I've been blowing the whistle till I'm tired.'

'I'm sorry, Brenton,' she said in a small voice. 'I was painting, and I forgot the time.'

'Painting! If your painting brought in any return it wouldn't be so bad. But it's just a sheer waste of time *and* money, so far as I can see.'

Angry words rose in her throat. What about the time and money he wasted over his 'improvements' to a perfectly good steamer? And how did he know she was wasting her time? The phrase was meaningless; they did not talk the same language. She swallowed hard and managed to keep silent, but she made a fierce vow: I'll make him eat those words. And if only money will convince him that I'm any good, I will make money.

On the return trip she worked hard, finishing the cliff pictures after she had seen the subjects again and made a sort of composite of her impressions; what she called the 'cliff-ness' of the cliffs, with their primitive, aboriginal rock and ochreous colours. It was something new and, though Melbourne people mightn't like it, it must at least startle them into attention.

331

FIFTY-FIVE

'You're lucky,' said Delie, 'that you didn't marry some domesticated type who'd be always fussing about the galley annoying the cook, infuriating the engineer by dusting the boiler – sorry, boilers – and generally getting in the way.'

' *You're* lucky,' said Brenton good-humouredly. 'Nothing to do all day but sit and look at the scenery going by.'

'Oh, I know, I know I am! But I'll have to sit and do some knitting from now on. Little garments, darling. About next September they should be needed.'

He recoiled, looking at her in horror. 'My God! You've got to be careful this time. You're to get off this boat at once, do you hear, and go and stay next door to a hospital, I'm not going through *that* again.'

She gave a faint smile at that 'I'.

'Don't worry, I'm not going to take any chances. I'd like to go down to Melbourne, and have specialists and nurses and anaesthetics – particularly anaesthetics.'

'So you say now! But I know how game you are – much too game – and you'll put it off and say you're all right –'

'No, really and truly. I want to go to that nice doctor who sent me back to you, even if he did make a mistake and give me a terrible fright. He started all this, really.' She looked at his bright, ruffled curls, his sea-blue eyes for once concentrated on her with tender interest, the boat forgotten. Thankfulness for all they had had together flowed through her. 'Dearest, I'm terribly glad he did!'

Brenton held her close, caressing the soft dark hair as she buried her face against his chest. The emotion in her voice had moved him too. He felt a rare tenderness for this irritating, helpless, irrational creature, for ever smelling of turpentine and linseed oil. He had valued her less once she was his; but no other woman had ever held for him her unique charm.

Physically she had improved with marriage. He ran his hands appreciatively over the new roundness and softness of her form.

332

In spite of inland summers the skin of her neck was still like satin under his lips; only a faint, thoughtful line creasing her white forehead, a nervous drawing-down of her straight brows, marked the passage of time. And with approaching motherhood, as happens with some women, her complexion seemed to bloom.

'Why does Ben always clean your shoes for you?' he asked with apparent irrelevance. He held her away from him and looked into her deep blue eyes. 'He's not starting to make sheep's eyes at you, is he?'

She laughed gaily. 'Ben! He's only a boy.'

Brenton laughed too. He was quite sure of her really. In any relationship with women he had always been the one to tire first.

He was already fed up with his new toy, the double boiler, and Charlie never lost an opportunity of pointing out how wasteful it was in fuel. The speed gained was lost again in loading stacks of wood, for they had to stop twice as often at woodpiles.

Then he saw an old locomotive advertised, with a large boiler having three fireboxes. He became obsessed with a new idea for improving the steamer's performance. Delie worried about the expense when he bought it, and Charlie prophesied that it would use even more fuel than the double boiler. But Brenton transferred to another of the *Gem* line, the *Shannon*, while the *Philadelphia* was disembowelled, and the new boiler installed.

Delie stayed in Wentworth, buying materials for baby-clothes, and feeling a mixture of delight and dismay at the prospect of motherhood once more.

When the *Philadelphia* made her first run after the alterations, she went like a bird. She left even the fast *Rothbury* standing, and could easily show the bigger *South Australian* her wake.

Brenton seemed satisfied at last. Delie begged him to give up his dangerous practice of diving beneath the wheels, now that they went so much faster; but he only laughed at her fears.

'She knows me,' he boasted. 'She wouldn't hurt me, would you, old girl?' and he thumped the steering-wheel affectionately. 'Anyway, now that she goes faster it takes less time for the wheel to pass over me, so it's actually safer, see?'

But she didn't see it at all. She felt, not for the first time, a jealous dislike for her namesake. Jealous of a boat! It was silly, but there it was. She wished he would come to Melbourne with her; but he saw no need for it. Imogen would look after her, and she would be perfectly safe in hospital.

They were travelling up-river, and on their way were to pick up a load of wool and hides for the railhead at Mildura. Delie sat in the doorway of her cabin, for the night was hot, enjoying the breeze of their movement as she sewed by the light of the lamp behind her. Small insects danced about it in a filmy cloud, or fell in a ring of corpses at its base.

Ben was sitting on the lowest of the three wheel-house steps, playing old, plaintive Scottish airs on his mouth-organ: 'Afton Water', 'Bonnie Doone' and 'Loch Lomond'. A half-moon floated on the calm waters ahead, or danced on the ripples of the wake as they turned. The gum trees along the banks showed every drooping leaf in silhouette against the moonlit sky.

Delie felt an ineffable sadness, compounded of the wan moonlight, the calm stars, the mournful music and the steadfast onward movement of the little steamer through a dark and lonely land.

A lantern could be seen waving on the bank ahead, and the two lamps of a buggy beside it. The owner of the wool had come down to his landing to guide them in. As they tied up, Delie discerned a plump womanly figure in a light dress seated in the buggy, so she went ashore to invite her on board.

'Hosts, lassie, I'm no' a body for veesitin', ye ken.' Delie saw that her hair was white, and heard without surprise her broad Scots voice; it was as though Ben's playing had been prophetic.

'Ah, go on board, Miss Flora,' said the station-owner. 'It'll do you good to see some new faces.' He introduced her as Miss Flora Anderson, his former governess, who had stayed on at the station to become governess to his own children, now grown up with babies of their own.

The old lady got down, protesting, but obviously excited. Her wrinkled hand, twisted with rheumatism, trembled as she grasped Delie's arm to be helped over the gangplank.

'Och, it's a fine floating hame ye have,' said Miss Flora. 'And nae bairns tae be tumblin' intil the water?'

'None as yet. But in about six months' time, we hope –'

'Then ye'll wire in the decks, nae doot? Aye, a hame and bairns o' one's ain; that's ae a thing I havena' had in ma life.'

She saw Delie's painting things in the saloon, and admired some of her pictures. 'Aince,' she said wistfully, 'I did a wee bit paintin' masel'; aye, an' playing the piano forbye, and sang an' a'.

334

But it's lang syne; lang syne.'

'Could you sing to the mouth-organ? We lost our piano in a fire.'

When the wool was aboard and they were all in the saloon having a cup of tea, Delie got Ben to play 'The Bluebells of Scotland'. Miss Anderson tapped her foot, her rosy cheeks glowing and her old blue eyes bright. She joined in with a clear, thin, but sweet soprano when he began 'Annie Laurie'. But when she started on 'Bonnie Doone' and came to the lines:

> Thou mind'st me o' departed days
> When my false love, my false love was true . . .

the tears rolled down her cheeks, and she had to have another cup of tea to calm her.

She left the boat happy and garrulous. 'Ca' in comin' doon, and I'll hae some scoons for ye in the buggy!' she cried as they churned out from the bank.

Delie went up and stood beside Brenton in the wheel-house. It was late, and the moon was dropping down behind the trees in their wake; but the reach ahead of the boat was lit up by the great reflectors with their brilliant acetylene lamps, so that the trees stood out as if carved in green jade against the dark sky.

'Wilson back there told me that old girl's story,' said Brenton. 'Seems she hardly ever leaves the place, hasn't for fifty years. She was only a girl about twenty when she came out as a governess, straight from Scotland, to a place further up the river. The owner fell madly in love with her – she was a lovely girl, this chap says, and a clever pianist – and not long afterwards his wife died, very suddenly.

'There was a lot of talk about it, and in the end he was charged with poisoning her, and convicted. The sentence was commuted to life, and he died in prison long ago. Miss Anderson was quite innocent, but she was so upset by all the publicity that she hid away from people, except for this family that gave her a job on their station.'

'That old thing!' said Delie incredulously. 'You mean someone committed a murder for her sake?'

'That's the story, anyway. You forget she was young as you once. One day you'll be an "old thing" yourself.'

'No! Never!' said Delie violently.

335

But she looked back at the setting moon, smouldering darkly among black and yellow clouds, that had been so silver-bright before; and a chill feeling settled about her heart.

'Time, flow softly!' she begged of the night. 'Flow gently, you dark implacable river.'

FIFTY-SIX

In August, Delie set off by train on the long, slow journey from Mildura to Melbourne, to have what she was quite sure would be a son. Buoyed up by excitement, she didn't feel tired even after travelling all night.

Next morning, when the suburbs began with their fences and smoke-grimed back yards and chimneys, she looked down like a god on the innumerable little lives flashing past below. The hoardings on stations, the advertisements painted on walls, the motor-driven vehicles becoming more noticeable in the streets, all added to her sense of adventure.

At the Spencer Street station Imogen was waiting with a taxi. She looked, Delie thought, a little haggard and strained. She had moved to a room high in a city building, with a view over the grey roofs of Melbourne to the silvery Yarra and the cluster of shipping at the docks.

Delie sat down and let Imogen make her a cup of tea on her gas-ring. Then Imogen unpacked for her while they both talked at once of all that had happened in the past year. She never minded letting people do things for her if they liked it. She relaxed utterly, saying, 'Oh, it's heavenly to be in Melbourne again, even the shape I am! I'm going to enjoy myself; it may be the last time for years.'

She entered hospital two weeks later, rather earlier than she had expected to, and still keyed up to a point where she felt no fear. Towards the end she was allowed to breathe deeply of the blessed anaesthetic, and felt her limbs freeze and the pain whirl up into a coloured ball above her head. She woke to hear the angry crying of her son.

Weak as she was, she insisted on seeing him at once. The nurses held up a little crumpled thing with a purplish-red face and black, damp hair, whose tiny fists beat at the strange, cold air in puny rage. Yes, he was alive! She gave a deep sigh of content, and as soon as the afterbirth had passed, fell into a heavy sleep.

She wanted her son to be modern, so she travelled from the hospital to Imogen's room in a motor taxi-cab, feeling very unsafe as they bowled along at nearly twenty miles an hour. She was rather ashamed of the ugly, skinny, black-haired mite lost in long gowns and rolls of blanket. Brenton would surely expect a bigger, handsomer son than this! (She had wired Brenton at once.) She privately decided to call him Gordon after her father's family.

Imogen, watching for the cab, flew down the stairs to help her.

' 'Et me take the 'ittle doo-ums den, was he a ickle ducksy-wucksy pet?' she crooned.

Delie stiffened protectively. 'I can carry him,' she said. Her child was not to be gooed over, he was a man-child and must be treated with dignity. 'My son,' she said proudly. 'My son . . .'

Imogen, temporarily free of emotional entanglements, looked after her like a mother. Delie insisted on buying her own food; she fed the baby from the breast. Imogen minded him between feeds while she went out and had her pictures framed. She had a collection of unusual canvases, and felt they would make some impact on the Melbourne art world if she could exhibit them.

A group of artists came to a party at the flat. They sat on the floor and all talked at once, while the baby slept peacefully in his crib out in the corridor, undisturbed even when the party began to overflow out of the door. It was really a private viewing of her work. Most of the visitors were enthusiastic, and advised her to hold her first one-man show.

So Imogen helped her send out invitations to the opening of 'An exhibition of paintings by Delphine Gordon, to be held at Buxton's Art Galleries, Swanston Street, at 5 P.M. on 20th September 1906'.

It was a gamble. There was the cost of printing the invitations and the catalogues; on top of the cost of framing; plus the rent for the room, and fifteen shillings a week for the attendant. Delie crossed her fingers and waited in suspense on the results.

Her largest picture, a study of orange cliffs reflected in a billa-bong, was an art gallery piece, she hoped. She had marked it in the catalogue at 100 guineas. But though women novelists were accepted as being as good as men, women artists were under a handicap. There were very few represented in the Melbourne gallery; yet the fact that she had been a promising student in the Gallery Art School was in her favour.

The Press was invited to a private viewing, and the *Argus* critic did her the service of describing *The Fisherman's Wife* as 'daring' and 'sensual', while admiring the excellent painting of the flesh tones and the harmony of the composition. After that she took good money at the door – for it was customary to charge one shilling admittance – as a procession of staid Melburnians came to be shocked.

The *Age* admired her cliff scenes, the rich and glowing colour, the Impressionist technique with which she had captured 'this little-known part of Victoria, reminiscent of Alfred Sisley's landscapes of the Loing'.

She went to the public library and found a volume of reproductions of his work, together with some other French Impressionists. She was dazed and delighted by the 1870 canvases – even in reproduction their brilliance and vivacity, their tender lyricism, made her feel that he loved the vibrating blue of the sky, the curving river between its high cliffs. They might have been painted in Australia, on the lower Murray.

She made several heartening sales, and then came triumph. Three members of the National Gallery Board had attended her show, and now she was told that the Board wished to acquire *The Fisherman's Wife*, at forty guineas.

No one had approached her for the big picture, and she wondered what she was going to do with it. It was too big to take back to the boat, or to leave cluttering up Imogen's crowded room.

On the last day, one of the visitors was a well-dressed, brown-faced gentleman with a pointed white beard that looked startling against his brown face. He went back several times to look at the portrait of old Harry, with its red sticker showing that it was sold.

Before leaving he went up to the attendant, producing a cheque, and left before she had affixed the small red dot to the large painting, *Murray Cliffs*. Delie felt that she had seen him before; his long dark eyes were strangely familiar. Looking at the cheque he had left she saw the signature 'W. K. Motteram', and knew who it was. He must be Nesta's father.

In the midst of her rejoicing over the sale a pang went through her, surprising her with its intensity. She remembered the bitter time when she had destroyed Nesta's portrait. Where was Nesta now? Married, probably, and living on the other side of the world, and too wealthy or too busy to keep up her writing.

Did Brenton ever think of her now? A little doubt crept into her mind. Was he consoling himself, perhaps, while she was away bearing his child? She had been of little use to him for some time past, and he was not one who could happily live a celibate life. Let me never find out, that's all, she thought.

Altogether, her show cleared more than a hundred and fifty pounds, even after expenses had been deducted. For a newcomer it was quite a success; but far more important was the seal of approval which the Gallery purchase gave her. She felt that she had arrived.

She wired the news to Brenton almost as proudly as she had sent the news of her son. She would show him if she was wasting her time! Then she enjoyed the pleasure of spending her won money, buying some dainty things for the baby, a new night-dress for herself, a present for Imogen, a set of hair-brushes for Brenton. She began to long for him, and for the river, once more. She loved the city for a visit, but she did not belong there. She took the train for home.

There was no need to defend the baby from any spoiling by his father. When they arrived back at the boat and she had unwrapped his swathes of clothing, Brenton regarded the infant curiously, as if it were some strange phenomenon, gave it a large finger to hold for a moment, and then walked across the cabin, whistling. He began to examine his back teeth in the small mirror over the wash-basin.

'Don't you think he looks like you?' asked Delie, rather crest-fallen. The baby was now five weeks old and beginning to look more as she had imagined he should.

'He looks like nothing on earth,' said Brenton.

'He *is* rather small, I suppose. And I did hope he'd be fair . . . But the nurses say his hair will change later.'

She prepared to feed him, undoing the high neck of her dress. Brenton watched in some distaste the greedy guzzling of his son, his passionate attachment to the nipple. He went out until she had finished feeding him.

When he came back, Delie was playing with the baby, leaning over him while he clutched at her dark hair just within his reach. Brenton walked about the little cabin impatiently. At last he said, 'Well! Aren't you going to put him in his crib?'

'In a minute. He likes to play a little after his feed.'

339

'You'll give him indigestion, and then he'll yell all night.'

He did yell, as soon as he was put down. The milk from a tired and excited mother had disagreed with him. Some of it came up again in a small curdled mess. Delie picked him up, wiped his mouth, patted his back and put him down again. He continued to yell.

'I'm going out!' said Brenton. 'I can't stand that noise.'

Delie sat and listened to his firm footsteps receding over the wooden wharf. On her first night home, when she was bursting with talk and news! And for the first time in months she was fit to make love to; but he had gone off like that! Was he jealous of his own son?

She sat there stunned, only half-aware of the crying infant, who was working himself up into a rage. She picked him up and buried her face against his baby-smelling warmth.

At last he fell asleep in her arms – this was 'spoiling' him, but she didn't care. She put him down and shaded the lamp, then got undressed and put on the pretty night-gown with blue bows that she had bought in Melbourne. She took out the black hair-pins from her dark hair, putting them in a neat pile on the dressing-table, and brushed the soft, shining waves.

In her bunk she turned her back to the lamp and stared with wide-open eyes at her own shadow on the wooden wall: a humped mass, the edge of the sheet, the curve of her eyelashes and the hollow of her cheek. If she had a pencil . . . but she was too tired to look for one now.

Sighing, she turned back the other way. She could see the baby's head mistily through the mosquito-net that covered him. Then her eyes became wide and fixed. He was quite immobile, and she could hear no faintest sound of breathing. In a panic she leapt from her bunk and tore off the net.

His eyelids were tightly closed, his face that had been flushed with crying had faded to a clear pallor, and one tiny hand was folded beside him into a pale bud-like fist. She watched, holding her own breath, and saw the faint regular movement of the coverings which meant that he breathed. His lips began to make a small sucking motion as he slept.

Smiling at her own foolishness, she covered him again with the net and got back into her bunk.

After a while the pillow became hot and insufferable. She raised herself on one elbow and turned it over. At the head of the bunk something gleamed in the lamplight, something sticking out from the crack between the edge of the bunk and the wooden wall. She poked at it with a fingernail. It slipped down a little farther, then she managed to draw it out. It was a hairpin of golden wire. She had never used a hairpin that colour in her life.

'Did you carry some passengers on the last trip, Jim?' said Delie to the mate, as though confirming something she knew already. Brenton was off duty, asleep in the cabin, and Jim Pearce was steering the boat along the lovely Moorna reach, where the leaning trees seemed to grow out of their own still reflections.

She had not mentioned the hairpin to Brenton. Her suspicions might be unfounded, and anyway she was not going to make a jealous scene. Somehow he would manage to make her feel in the wrong.

'Yair, we had passengers,' said Jim rather sourly. 'Chap and his sister. Least, he *said* she was his sister.' He eased the wheel round by three spokes and set the steering-pole on a white-boled gum almost at the end of the reach. The *Philadelphia* began to cross to the other side of the river, following the invisible channel.

'But where did they sleep?'

'In the saloon – hung a blanket between for a curtain. But she was a menace, that one. Used to come up 'ere when I was on duty: "Oh, Mr Pearce, may Ai make a nuisance of myself for a little while? Ai do so love to see you handling that great wheel," ' he mimicked savagely. 'I was dead scared o' being alone with her.'

'I'm sure the Skipper wouldn't have been alarmed.'

'Oh, she tried it on with him, too. But he wasn't interested, you needn't worry.' Then, realising that this wasn't very tactful, he blundered on: 'She wasn't too young, though she made out she was. *He* was always playing cards – the brother. Took a couple of quid off me. I never had no luck playing with him, somehow.'

Delie folded her arms along the ledge of the wheel-house window, leaning her forehead against the glass. She said, her heart beginning to beat suffocatingly, 'Don't you know that card-sharpers always have yellow-haired accomplices?'

Jim Pearce whistled and leant on the wheel thoughtfully. 'Card-sharpers, eh? I'll bet that's what they was. She did have yellow hair – well, gold, I suppose you'd call it, though it didn't look quite real. There was something fishy about them altogether.'

'Still, they provided some – feminine company while I was away. At meals, I mean.' She spoke wildly, the first words that came into her head, and ran down the steps from the wheel-house, Not to the cabin – Brenton was there – but to the bottom deck and into the bows, where she crouched against the stem-post and watched the green water curling past on either side.

'She did have yellow hair.' She used gold hairpins, then. She had lain in the bottom bunk in the captain's cabin, *her* bunk, where . . . Delie struck her fist hard against the red-gum block, but she felt nothing. She went on staring at the endless curl of water past the bows.

FIFTY-SEVEN

How could she have known, thought Delie in despair, what it would be like to bring up a family of young children on a boat? She could not tell them to 'run and play outside'; she could never relax, unless they were asleep, for fear of their falling in the river. She had never meant to have more than one child, or perhaps two, at sensible intervals; and almost before she knew it there were three, the eldest only a toddler.

After her discovery, she had been bitterly determined that there should be no more babies. Gordon was hers – she announced flatly that this was his name, and Brenton grumbled but gave in. She decided to go to bed early and pretend to be asleep each night until he understood that she was no longer his plaything. She would not share him with every passing passenger.

She should have known that it would be no use. She still loved him, whatever he did; and his sheer physical charm for her was as strong as ever. The very night after her conversation with the mate, he came in just as she had settled the baby in his crib, and took her confidently in his arms.

She stiffened for a moment, and then relaxed against him, conquered without even a struggle. As he would have lifted her on to the bottom bunk she drew back. 'Not there!' she muttered, and climbed to the upper berth.

'You've hurt your hand, darling,' he said, noticing for the first time the swollen bruise as she gripped the edge of the bunk.

'It's nothing,' she said dully. 'I knocked it on something . . .'

She lay and stared past his head, while Brenton wondered briefly what was wrong with her tonight. He concluded that she had not properly recovered from the birth of the baby. She would come good again later. He eased on to his side and put his face in the hollow of her shoulder, and was soon contentedly asleep. Delie stayed awake, staring into the darkness until it was time for the baby's next feed.

Oh the nightmare years that followed, the sleepless nights and days filled with nappy-washing, with hushing children so that they would not annoy Brenton, with terrifying childish ailments to be cured without aid from a comforting family doctor!

'Three sons!' said Delie, folding napkins late at night on the saloon table. 'Four, if you count the one that – that didn't live. I feel as if I were Lady Macbeth, and you had said "Bring forth men children only!" Oh, I'm so tired of having babies!'

'I would like a daughter,' said Brenton obstinately. 'A daughter to look after me in my old age –'

'She'd more likely marry and go off to the other side of the world. But really, we can't have any more, there just isn't room.'

'I know, but there doesn't seem much we can do about it, does there? I mean whatever we do doesn't seem to work.'

'We could try separate cabins. *That* would be infallible.'

He looked at her quizzically, and she tried to keep a steely glint in her eye; but he put out one hand and drew her to him, and soon she felt the old delicious warmth and weakness stealing through her. It was no use.

'We'll just have to be very careful,' she said feebly.

'Mah-mee! Dordie wanna drinkawater,' came from the cabin next door which had long since become the nursery. At the same time the baby in the crib by her bunk gave an irritable coughing cry, was silent for a second, and then began a full-voiced wailing.

'There's one thing,' she said, detaching herself from Benton's arms. 'There soon won't be *time* to start another.'

She gave the baby a dummy and took a drink of water to Gordon, but by the time she got there he had fallen asleep again. Little Brenny opened his eyes at the candle, blinking his long lashes and scowling. She felt Gordon's brow under the soft silk of his fair curls. It was damp and hot. She drew off one of his blankets, kissed Brenny lightly and went out. Gordon had nightmares if he became too hot, would wake screaming and could not be soothed for half an hour. She walked to the rail and looked at the peaceful night.

They were tied up at Overland Corner, below the high lime-stone cliffs in which were the fossils of molluscs that lived in the warm Cretaceous sea that once covered the valley of the lower Murray. The run was now between Wentworth and Morgan, at the Northwest Bend, where the Murray made a great right-angled turn, its first major change of direction, and began to flow steadily southward to meet the sea.

The river was so low that it was dangerous to travel at night. The water slipped silently past below the deck, the Pointers of the Southern Cross and the bright star Canopus reflected on its calm surface. Delie stared at the dark water and then up at the great starlit sky, remembering how she had gone outside with Adam at Kiandra and see the Cross sparkling in the frosty night.

It was all the same, all unchanged, yet she was away down the river where the current began to slow; here was she, twenty-nine years old, she would be thirty in no time – thirty! And what had she done? With three little children, a baby only six months old, what could she do?

Her painting was almost at a standstill. Ideas for pictures, compositions, canvases more ambitious than she had ever at-tempted, swam all about her in the air. She felt the immense dry continent, the slow burning summer, the pure skies in all her veins, and longed to translate them into paint, to get her vision of this great southern land down on canvas before it faded and was lost. But there was no time, and there was no escape.

There were days when the promise of the morning, when the way the thin streamers of cloud were swept across the blue as though by a giant brush dipped in flake white, filled her with a sweet unrest. She felt a longing for paint and canvas that was physical in its intensity. Then came the first waking cry of the baby, and the deadening, deadly round of domestic chores began, to end only when she fell into her bunk long after sunset, too tired for anything but sleep.

Somewhere behind her she seemed to hear a giant key turning in a lock. Like so many others, like her own father perhaps, who had always longed to travel, she had gone joyfully, willingly, with wide-open eyes, into the trap so cunningly set, so deliciously baited, by Nature; and too late had heard the iron door clang shut.

The decks were now enclosed with wire-netting to a height of nearly three feet; but Gordon, now almost four, was beginning to climb everywhere. He was fair, slender, active and nervous; with Brenton's firm chin and nose showing even through the baby fat, but with his mother's eyes: larger, softer, more deeply blue than Brenton's had ever been.

Little Brenny had brown curls and eyes like his father's: bright, sea-blue, straight-gazing and unimaginative. He was very little trouble. The baby, Alex, was delicate, with a chronic cough that kept him from sleeping soundly. Delie rocked him sometimes by the hour, dozing upright from weariness. The doctors could do nothing for him. It was a congential weakness, they said.

Every month or so he developed bronchitis, ran a temperature for a week and had to be nursed night and day. Delie, dreading pneumonia, wondered if he would survive childhood, or join the little unnamed brother in a lonely riverside grave. She thought sometimes of the woman she had never known, the mother who had buried her three children in the sandhill grave above Echuca.

She had a new sympathy now for that unhappy woman. Was there anything more terrible to a mother than the death of a child?

Ben was a wonderful help. He would carry the ailing baby about, and keep young Brenny amused. Gordon followed his father everywhere, helped to hold the big wheel, and hung on so tight that he was lifted in the air by the spokes. His father had begun to take an interest in him as soon as he could walk, and was teaching him to swim.

In the mornings, Brenton came crashing down from his bunk – he never moved quietly, however tired Delie might be – and she heard the splash as he dived overboard. In a few minutes he would be calling for Gordon, and she didn't want him to wake the others. She dragged herself from her bunk and went to call Gordon. His bed was soaked; she could smell its steamy, ammoniated reek.

'Gordie!' she whispered. 'Daddy's in the river already. Are you coming for you swimming lesson?'

'Yes-es, Mummy.' Gordon sat up and looked rather scared. She lifted him down and he struggled out of his wet pyjamas. She helped him put on a little pair of drawers. His fair hair stood on end, his eyes were sleepy and one cheek was brightly flushed.

There were noises coming from the galley now. The fireman could be heard stirring the firebox, throwing in logs.

She took Gordon down to the bottom deck and lifted him over

the netting. Brenton, swimming effortlessly alongside, called, 'Jump, Gordie!'

Gordon hesitated and shrank back, shivering.

'Come on! Jump, I say.' His brows drew down as he waited, treading water. 'If you don't jump before I count three, I'll come out and throw you in. I don't like cowards. Now, one – two –'

Gordon, one fear overcoming the other, jumped. Delie let out her breath with relief. He would be quite happy by the time he came out; but he was a nervous child, and she thought his nightmares had something to do with his swimming lessons.

When young Brenny turned three, his father began to teach him too. The difference in the two children was apparent at once. Brenny took to the water like a duck.

He too had his father's chin, besides his short, determined nose. When he once made up his mind to do something, nothing would stop him. He jumped fearlessly every time, would have jumped from the top of the wheel-house if his father told him to. Soon he was like a fish in the water, and could swim faster than Gordon.

'He'll make a champion one day,' said Brenton proudly.

Their headquarters were now at Morgan, known more often as the Northwest Bend, or just The Bend. Morgan was an ugly town, with buildings of staring stone and corrugated iron strung along a bare rocky cliff; no trees, no gardens, and a hot north wind usually driving the white dust through the gritty main street in summer.

Yet the river, away from the busy wharf where the trains from Adelaide delivered and picked up goods, still kept its ancient charm. The green, translucent water flowed steadily past the yellow cliffs, while gum trees grew from the water's edge – not in a continuous wall as in the upper reaches, but in isolated majesty, each one leaning towards its reflection in an attitude of contemplation.

Jim Pearce had got his master's certificate and left to command a steamer of his own. Charlie McBean was still with them as engineer. Young Ben was reading for his mate's ticket.

He did not have to navigate by the stars, or shoot the sun to get a position; but he had to be able to carry the whole river-system like a map inside his head. He might be asked questions on more than three thousand miles of winding channels; he could be examined on the Wakool, the Edwards, the Murrumbidgee and the Darling, even though he never intended steaming out of the Murray River.

He had to know the height of the lift-bridges at high river, the shape of the Murray at Pollard's Cutting, the depth of water by the wharf at Goolwa, and the width between the pillars of the bridge at Echuca, a thousand miles upstream.

'Ben, are you sure this is what you're really meant for?' asked Delie one day, finding him wrinkling his brows over the forty-foot chart from the wheel-house. 'You've got brains, you should sit for a scholarship and you might get to the university.'

'It would be years before I was earnin' anything, Miss Delie,' said Ben, looking surprised.

'Well, what matter? You're not thinking of getting married, are you, Ben?'

He flushed. 'No, it's not that. But I don't know – I don't fancy leavin' the river, somehow.' His dark shy eyes looked at her warmly a moment.

Something of what he meant was conveyed in his look: I wouldn't think of leaving the river because it would mean leaving you.

Delie blushed slightly and bent over the baby, who was picking at the pitch between the planking of the deck. His cough had gradually improved, and he was rapidly putting on weight. She could not forget that Ben had delivered her first child; it was an intimate bond between them.

She began to crawl about the deck, growling like a bear. The baby laughed delightedly. Ben flopped down on his knees beside her. They growled and crawled and hid behind crates and barrels, while Alex crawled after them. The eight years between the two adults seemed to fall away.

Brenny came trotting along the deck, bellowing. His face was scarlet, his mouth open to its widest extent.

'What's the matter, dear?' Delie took one of the fists from his eyes and stroked it, but he struck her hand away and roared on.

'Tell me what's the matter!' She felt her own rage rise to meet his. She could not be calm and patient for more than a minute, and the noise was shattering.

Gordon came sidling along the deck against the cabins.

'Gordon, come here! Did you hurt Brenny?'

'No! He's mad.'

'Dordie hurt me. Dordie bung my yedd. Wah-wah-wah!'

Delie flew at Gordon and slapped him, venting her irritation with the roaring Brenton. Gordon yelled, and the baby, upset by the sudden change of atmosphere when he had been having a lovely time, began to scream. Ben picked him up, but Delie ran to the other side of the deck, covering her ears.

She would have liked to begin screaming too. The noise scraped her nerves, exacerbated by lack of sleep. On that side was a lovely yellow cliff – the place was known as Broken Cliffs, and three great angular boulders had crashed down and lay half out of the olive-green water. Her fingers ached for the brush; a fierce longing to paint swept over her.

She closed her eyes, took a deep breath, and went down to the galley to prepare the baby's feed. Thank God, she thought, thank God they were all getting older, and in perhaps three years she would have them all out of napkins. For once she wanted time to flow swiftly, to bear her forward out of her present bondage.

FIFTY-EIGHT

Between the high yellow cliffs the air was breathlessly still. The river drowsed in the heat, seeming not to move. Small lizards lay basking on spits of white sand, unmarked except for the tiny tracery of their feet.

Huge motionless clouds, white and solid-looking as marble, were massed round the horizon, and far up in the burning blue, directly above the *Philadelphia*'s deck, two wedge-tailed eagles circled, like cinders rising in the hot currents of air over the baking land.

Sweat poured from the crew as they 'walked' a load of firewood on board from the pile below the Lyrup village settlement. Teddy Edwards would not wait while they had a dip to cool off. They must swim in the early morning, or when the boat was moving, as he did. When they started again one of the younger deckhands, who had climbed down into the dinghy, let himself over the stern on a rope for a quick swish though the luke-warm water.

The skipper stood in the wheel-house, bare-footed, wearing only a pair of cotton-duck trousers. He wiped at his moisture-beaded upper lip with his wrist.

'Take the wheel, will you, Ben?' he said to the lad. 'I'm going in.'

The mate was off duty, resting in the little cabin that had been built aft for the mate and the engineer since the skipper's family expanded.

He throttled back the engine to half-speed, and dived neatly from the top of the paddle-box. He came up, caught the rudder as it went past, climbed up to it, and walked lightly back along the deck, cooled and exhilarated. The caress of the deep water had filled him with recklessness and daring.

He did not climb to the top of the paddle-box again, but vaulted the wire and stood poised on the deck just in front of the great wheel.

Delie, who was feeding the baby on deck to get some of the breeze of their movement, saw him and leapt to her feet. 'Wait!' she cried. She had noticed how his figure was thickening lately; he was putting on weight, there were some grey strands among his golden curls. And he still thought he could do his boyish tricks.

'Not under the wheel, darling! Please, Brenton, don't.'

With a brief wave and a flash of white teeth he turned, filling his lungs deeply, and dived clean beneath the thundering paddles. Delie closed her eyes for the space of twelve heart-beats. When she opened them again his head was bobbing in the wake.

He swam diagonally to the shore, ran swiftly along the bank, leaping roots and fallen trees, and swam out ahead of the boat to meet her and climb up the rudder as before.

Delie was furious. The reaction from her fear of a moment ago left her trembling.

'How can you!' she cried as he came past to the wheel-house steps, all dripping as he was, his eyes washed to a clear blue, almost green. 'If you don't care for my feelings, you might remember that you've a family to support. Showing off like a boy of ten! You haven't the figure for it any more,' she added unkindly, 'and if you get killed, what will become of us all?'

He stopped dead and looked down at her as she waved the baby's bottle vehemently before his face. Pride and anger sparkled in his eyes. His chin was raised in the old arrogant way, as he looked down his straight nose at her. She would have given anything to take back her words.

'Is that so?' he said distinctly. 'Well, just to show you, I'll do it again.'

Without another look at her he retreated to the bottom deck, vaulted the wire and dived in front of the wheel. There was a momentary check in the regular *chunk! chunk! chunk!* and then he was spewed out behind, to float lifelessly in the curling wake.

Delie dumped the baby on the deck and ran up the three steps to the wheel-house. In a moment the scream of the whistle was echoing the silent scream in her mind. They could not stop suddenly without letting off some steam. She helped Ben drag the wheel round. The *Philadelphia* cut her own wake, the dinghy was cast off and Brenton's inert form was hauled aboard.

He was not mangled or crushed, but there was a terrifying dent in the base of his skull. Delie put her head down against his bare, wet breast, and heard the faint beating of his heart.

'He's alive!' she cried, tears of thankfulness pouring down her bloodless face. 'Help me get him to the after-cabin – we mustn't move him more than we can help.' Gordon appeared beside her, looking scared and tearful. 'Gordie, go and see to the baby. Don't wake Brenny. Daddy's been hurt, but it's all right.'

She packed hot-water bottles around Brenton and dribbled some brandy between his bluish lips. She could only keep him warm and quiet until they reached medical aid at Renmark.

Charlie McBean came up, his fierce blue eyes under their wild eyebrows softened with the moisture of strong emotion.

'I'm givin' 'er every inch of steam I can, Missus, without blowin' up,' he said. 'Teddy was a good skipper; one of the best.'

'Not *was*; is,' she said quickly. 'He's not dead. He's not going to die.'

He's not going to die, he's not, she told herself. If she said it often enough it must come true.

While Brenton lay in the Renmark Hospital, another skipper took over the *Philadelphia*. Delie and her children had to board in the town. Whenever she could she hurried to the hospital. The land-lady, taking pity on her, offered to mind the baby while she went out.

'Leave 'im with me, love,' she said comfortably, tucking a wisp of yellowish-grey hair into place. Her skin was raddled, her eyes were pouchy with what had probably been a pretty dissolute life, but her heart was kind.

For ten days Brenton did not recover consciousness. Concussion and shock, she was told; and there might be some permanent injury to the brain. There was no way of telling until he came round.

'You must be prepared,' said the doctor, 'to find that he can't speak, or is perhaps paralysed on one side.'

On the eleventh day she found him conscious, lying quite flat and still, his head bandaged. The bright sea-blue of his eyes seemed to have clouded over; but he smiled faintly.

'Delie, Delie!' he muttered. 'I'm . . . sorry.'

'You needn't be sorry, darling!' She was on her knees by the bed, trying to keep back her tears. She smoothed his springy curls where they twined round the bandage. 'As long as you've come back to us.'

'My . . . right arm. Can't move it. I'm . . . finished.'

She gripped his good arm urgently. 'No! You're going to get better. Here's Gordon, see! And Brenny . . .'

He turned a bitter, brooding look upon his sons, and rolled his head impatiently upon the pillow. Was there a slight distortion at one side of his mouth? And his speech seemed slurred . . . But his brain was clear enough.

A starched rustling behind her, and a nurse put a hand on her arm. 'You mustn't tire him, Mrs Edwards. That will be enough for today.'

As the slow weeks went by he gradually improved. Feeling returned first to his fingers, then to the whole of his right arm. His skull had not been fractured – he must have a particularly strong one, the doctors said – but he suffered for a while from severe headaches.

Delie was beginning to get used to a life ashore. She faced the fact that Brenton might never skipper another boat. She had a new worry that she dared not tell him in his present state.

And what if Brenton never recovered fully? With a helpless, dependent husband, how was she to provide for a family of young children? She could not have another!

In her panic and loneliness she thought of the kindly but hard-faced Mrs Patchett, the landlady – a courtesy 'Mrs' surely, for there was no mention of a Mr Patchett, though a 'gentleman friend' came in three nights a week to drink gin with her and play poker.

But she could not bring herself to speak to the landlady. Mrs Patchett, she felt sure, would know something that could be done about these things, had perhaps helped plenty of other women in the same predicament. Apparently Mrs Patchett guessed her thoughts; for one day when she was in the kitchen preparing the baby's dinner, the landlady looked at her pale face, then at her figure, and said, 'Been off yer food a bit lately, love.'

Delie flushed slightly, pretending not to hear.

'Not eatin' yer breakfast, like. You weaned the baby, 'aven't yer?'

'Yes, He's eleven months old.'

'M'm.' She chopped away at some onion on a board, with swift, sharp chops, holding the knife lengthwise in her pudgy, ringed hands. 'That's the time when yer wanter watch it, when you've just weaned 'em.'

'Yes, I suppose so.'

'Don't want to go startin' no more just now, I s'pose, with yer 'usband sick, and all.'

'No,' said Delie in a choked voice.

'If yer ever want any help, like . . . as one woman to another, I've got a friend could fix you up easy. On'y cost yer a fiver.' Chop, chop, chop went the knife.

'Thank you. But I don't want any help.'

Grasping the plate of warmed food, she hurried out of the kitchen with burning cheeks.

She knew what Mrs Patchett meant by 'help', and that the 'friend' was probably the gentleman caller. At the thought of his black finger-nails and greasy collar, she shuddered.

That night she looked up an advertisement inside the pink cover of a well-known journal. It looked promising:

LADIES! WORRIED RE HEALTH

Take my special triple-strength pills for all case of irregularity. Even most obstinate cases yield to treatment. Send only One Pound.

One pound seemed a terribly large sum to Delie, but she sent off a money order and waited nervously for the parcel to arrive. The pills looked innocuous enough, but even their triple-strength action did no good. They made her feel violently ill, but had no other result than to leave her pale and exhausted.

She dragged herself to the hospital, leaving Brenny, who had a bronchial cold, in charge of Gordon in their room, and the baby with Mrs Patchett. She found Brenton so much better that he would be able to be moved the next day, and it was just as well.

She could hear the noise as soon as she opened the front door of the boarding-house. Mrs Patchett and the gentleman friend were singing, loudly and drunkenly:

> Oh don't you remember Black Alice, Ben Bolt,
> Black Alice so dusky and dark,
> That Warrego gin with a straw through her nose,
> And teeth like a Moreton Bay shark?

The baby was wailing in a drowsy, exhausted fashion, Brenny was coughing and crying as if he would choke, and Gordon was chanting loudly, 'Shut up, shut up, shut up . . .'

Delie rushed upstairs, picked up the scarlet-faced Brenny and soothed him, while scolding Gordon for not looking after him better.

'He was teasing me,' said Gordon sullenly. 'He was asking for it. I only slapped him.'

'You come with me,' she said, putting Brenny down and taking Gordon's hand firmly. 'The baby's crying, and I don't think Mrs Patchett can hear him.'

Downstairs, she knocked on the parlour door marked 'Private', but the knock was lost in the noise within. She opened the door and saw Mrs Patchett, her dirty blouse undone, her hair falling down, leaning back against the wall and singing. A half-empty gin bottle was on the table. The 'gentleman friend' was singing loudly, waving his glass in time: 'Oh, don't you remember . . .'

'Wait there, Gordon.' She shut the door quickly, leaving him outside. She snatched up the wailing baby, which seemed strangely inert and unaware of her. At the first movement it vomited slightly, and Delie smelt its spirit-laden breath.

'Mrs Patchett! You've been giving the baby gin!'

Mrs Patchett stopped singing, hiccuped solemnly and stared at her owl-eyed.

'Jus' a li'l drop, love. No 'arm in that. Lapped it up, 'e did, the li'l lamb. Makes 'im sleep better.'

'Oh, don't you remember – ' warbled the friend.

'He's not asleep; he's been crying. I could hear him from the front door.' She was so angry that her legs trembled and felt weak.

'Don't you worry, love – '

She left the room abruptly, resolving that she would leave the boarding-house too as soon as possible.

Brenton had quite recovered the use of his arm, though he walked with a slight limp, dragging his right leg. His speech was clear again, but his eyes had lost for ever a little of their youthful brilliance, and the grey was spreading in his hair.

He had put on weight while lying helpless. His waistline had thickened further, and a heavy crease ran round the back of his neck. There was a faint blurring of all his well-cut features, as in a picture out of focus.

'Ah, it's good to be back in a real bed again, with you,' he said on the first night after he left hospital. He stretched his great bulk comfortably, and looked at her with the old smile in his eyes.

'It's wonderful to have you back.' Her lips trembled. He wound a strand of her dark hair about his wrist.

'And how wonderful it'll be to get back to the river! I felt stifled in that hospital. Everything standing still. Have you noticed how a boat's always alive, even when she's tied up? The river-reflections on the woodwork, the bit of a creak as the wind or the current catches her – '

Delie sighed and bit her lip. 'The trouble is, there's really not enough room on a boat. I mean, when we have another baby . . . Oh, Brenton!' She flung herself into his arms and wept.

'So that's how it is?' He whistled tunelessly for a moment. 'Gosh, I don't know, Del. You'll have to come with me. It's much cheaper when we all live aboard.'

The baby Alex began to cry, wakened by the mosquitoes feeding on his tender cheeks. 'Can't you stop him?' cried Brenton. 'God, I can't stand that row.'

Delie started up guiltily. Since his accident Brenton had become abnormally sensitive to noise; the baby had scarcely made a sound yet. She picked him up and carried him round the room.

Brenton, who had been down at the wharf yarning with the skipper of a steamer that had just come in, came hurrying back to the boarding-house, moving his dragging right leg impatiently forward with a hand behind his thigh.

He had been talking with Captain Ritchie of the *Mannum*, the little steamer that was supposed to be built to cross a grass flat on a heavy dew. She was fitted out as a trading vessel, with a counter over which goods were sold, from dress materials to rifles, from sewing-needles to pumping-machinery. Such things were scarce along the river away from the towns, and he was doing very well.

The old River Murray Navigating Company was going to be

turned into a limited company, and Captain Hugh King was drawing out, and retiring from the rivers.

'Our contract was with the old company,' said Brenton, 'and we're pulling out too. Hughie King was such a decent old cove, and such a gentleman to deal with, that I didn't mind being under contract to him, but I don't know this new crowd. We'll turn the *Philadelphia* into a floating store, and make a fortune.'

Delie looked sceptical.

'And no deckhands needed for lumping cargo; even a mate won't be necessary when we can tie up overnight while I have a sleep. That will leave more room for the family. But you'll have to pull your weight, too. No cook –'

'No cook! Oh, Brenton! Couldn't I be deckhand or mate? I should learn to run the boat in case you got ill. I don't mind hard work, I can help you tie up and take a turn at the wheel – you said yourself I was getting quite good.' Her eyes were eager and pleading, too large in her pale face. She hadn't the blooming look that went with her first pregnancy.

He chewed his lip, looking at her down his nose. 'You aren't strong enough. And besides, in your condition, you won't be fit soon for jumping ashore and all those capers.'

'I don't intend ever to get in this condition again.'

'Well . . . I suppose it'll be different in six months. But then you'll have your hands full with the new baby. There's no harm in you studying for your mate's ticket, though. I don't know as there's ever been a woman registered as a skipper on the river, but there's no reason why you shouldn't be the first.

'Come up to the wheel-house when I'm steering, and I'll start learning you the channel. Now, what's the greatest depth of water ever found over the Christmas Rocks above Wilcannia?'

Delie looked crestfallen. 'But that's in the Darling. I don't know the Darling.'

'There's an awful lot you don't know. You'll have to be able to answer questions on any of the rivers. I'll draw you a chart of 'em later. And Ben can coach you a bit too.'

355

FIFTY-NINE

Brenton was steering, the baby slept, and Delie was in the wheel-house learning the channel; but she was not being taught much, for the *South Australian* was chasing them. Soon the bigger boat steered past them up-river, with jeers from her fireman and engineer, and derisive toots on her whistle.

Teddy Edwards seemed to see red. His jaw became rigid, his mouth set and the vein stood out in his neck in a frightening way as he clenched his teeth. His face, usually rather florid, became beetroot-coloured.

'What does it matter if they *do* pass us?' cried Delie. He looked as if he might have a fit or a stroke, and fall like a log at her feet. 'We don't need to race.'

For the *Philadelphia* was now fitted out as a floating store, and traded up-river from Morgan, through the growing irrigation settlements of Waikerie, Berri, Cobdogla and Loxton. There was enough trade for more than one boat, and a leisurely progress between lonely farms and out-stations was best for business. But Teddy and his 'batty engineer' could not at first take things quietly. The only thing he had let up on since his accident was swimming. He no longer dived in when they were going along.

Now he opened the throttle wide, and the funnel sobbed and panted with power. Charlie needed no message to tell him to throw on the last of a load of fine, straight, tinder-dry boxwood he had been saving for just such a crisis, and to weight the safety-gauge so that it couldn't blow off under eighty pounds of pressure.

'She's towing two loaded barges,' said Brenton tensely. 'We've got no barge, and she bloody well left us standing.'

They rounded a bend and began to overtake the other steamer in a long, straight reach. The river was wide here, and a strong wind was sweeping downstream, aiding the current. The much larger *South Australian* and her two barges, swinging into the wind, were slowed down at once. The *Philadelphia* soon over-hauled her. Brenton steamed cheekily all round her before leaving her his wake.

356

When the excitement was over he turned to Delie with a look of triumph; and found, to his surprise, that she was in a towering rage.

'Left him standing!' he said, giving her an uneasy sideways look as he steered. He stood always on the left of the big wheel, while she sat on a high stool beside him, unless she was helping through a stiff bend, when she would jump down and handle the spokes from the other side, neatly and with surprising strength.

She had jumped down from the stool and crossed the wheel-house, and stared at him now across the width of the big wheel.

'Will you never grow up! Racing, just for the sake of racing, and risking all our lives! If you have no thought for me, you might at least think of the children. Don't you remember what happened to the *Providence*?'

He set his mouth, scowled and gave an impatient twist of the head. 'Of course I remember. But the *Providence* wasn't racing when she blew up. She had a faulty boiler.'

'I don't care, it isn't safe! And you know what a gauge-spragger Charlie is, and you encourage him. It's not as though you had no responsibilities.'

'Oh, for God's sake!'

They were steaming up a wide reach with yellow, honey-combed cliffs on one side, a reed-bordered lagoon on the other. She knew she was being unwise, but the words kept tumbling out. 'It's so stupid! We passed a farmhouse back there, I saw the woman on the veranda, we should have stopped and let her see the dress materials. And when we do stop the *South Australian* will pass us anyway. I just can't see –'

'I don't like taking any man's wake,' he growled. 'Now shut up, and take the wheel for a bit. I'll go down and see that the gauge is all right, since you're making such a song and dance about it. Keep her on that black stump in the bight of the bend.'

She crossed over the wheel-house, and taking two spokes in her hands brought the steering-pole slowly, slowly round till it cut the black stump vertically in half. There she kept the wheel steady. Sometimes she moved out of the course she had taken up, just to feel the sensation of power that came from swinging the great boat round again, its bows cutting across the horizon.

Her anger evaporated. She loved to steer, and to be left alone in the wheel-house like this.

She let her mind fall into the dreamy, hypnotic state that the steady onward movement, the regular beat of paddles and engine

357

lulled her into whenever she had time to relax. The boat throbbed with eager life. Onward, onward, ever onward, it chanted to her ears.

The wheel-house windows were closed. Reflections, always moving, cut across other reflections which crossed again the real scene outside. It was as if there were several layers of reality: you could fix your mind on any one, and all the others became unreal.

A sparkling sheet of water, reflected from the river behind, cut at an angle across the trees that marched steadily backward outside the window; on top of these marching trees were the reflections of other trees moving just as steadily forward. Shadow-clouds crossed real clouds, behind was before, the past came towards you while the present slipped away.

Time, thought Delie confusedly, is always there, all of it; you can travel across it in any direction if you can once free your mind of the illusion that you must move continuously from an irretrievable past into an unknowable future.

And doesn't the river return upon itself in endless windings, and flow back again from the sea on the currents of air, to begin all over again, endlessly? It is all there, always, in spite of its apparent movement from a fixed beginning to an appointed end. Time is a river in which our lives are only molecules of water . . .

She could see herself faintly reflected in the windows, an insubstantial ghost through which the river gleamed and the landscape flowed. Was she real, either? Was it all an illusion, a mere arrangement of waves of light? But she felt the growing heaviness of her body, the weight of the new life within. This was real, all too real.

She was wearing the full-gathered black poplin skirt that she had worn in her last three pregnancies. It concealed the changes in her figure. A pale pink blouse set off her dark hair and delicate complexion. She could still wear pink, for she had never tanned or freckled in spite of the open-air life.

Still Brenton did not come back. She had rounded the bend, and she didn't know the channel ahead; only that deep water was usually found on the outside of bends, and shoals on the inner curve where the river flowed more slowly. Though the *Industry* kept the river snag-free, there were tricky places where the inexperienced could easily run aground.

It was nearly time to prepare the baby's vegetables and broth.

358

She always cooked the children's food, though they had a cook-deckhand who was better as a hand; he was referred to by Charlie and Ben as 'The Chief Poisoner', and they kept asking each other, 'Who called the cook a bastard?' and replying, 'Who called the bastard a cook?'

Delie was becoming tired. Her hands sweated on the wheel, and her back ached. The nervous frown that had etched three little lines between her brows became deeply marked. Surely Brenton wouldn't risk the boat just to punish her?

A step on the deck cheered her. She called out, and Ben's head appeared.

'Let me take over. You look tired,' he said tenderly. 'How long have you been steering?'

'Oh, only about half an hour. I love it really, but I don't know the channel.'

He was standing beside her, and as he put out a hand to take a spoke, she moved hers to the same one ahead of him. His hand closed over hers. It tightened at once to a painful grip, squeezing her hand into the wood, while she felt his eyes fixed upon her face. She stared straight ahead, but a pink flush began to mount in her pale cheeks.

'My hand,' she said distantly. 'You're hurting it.'

'I'm sorry.' He released his grip at once. 'But you're so beautiful! I – had to tell you.' His voice was low, almost a whisper. Slowly he bent his dark head and kissed the hand upon the wheel. Her confusion vanished. She suddenly felt very old and wise and maternal.

'Thank you! But d'you know how old I am, Ben? I'll be thirty this year; and by the time you're thirty, I'll be forty – middle-aged. Apart from the fact that I'm married.'

'I can't help it.'

By now the boat, unguided, had veered towards the left bank. Ben hastily swung the wheel up and away, while looking at her with the eyes of a sensitive dog that has been rebuked.

' "To me, fair friend, you never can be old," ' he quoted. 'I've read all of Shakespeare's sonnets to the Dark Lady in the book you gave me, and they always make me think of you:

> Shall I compare thee to a summer's day?
> Thou art more lovely and more temperate . . .

'Ben! Hush! Stop this foolishness at once.' But her voice was moved, gentle.

'It's not foolishness. It's my life. You – are – everything to me: mother, teacher, friend, sister, and . . . my only love.'

'Ben! Please!'

Now he was kissing her arm, the hollow of her elbow beneath the rolled-up sleeve. She had felt herself beginning to be moved by his passionate voice, and now a stirring of response in her deepest feminine being told her that he was no longer a boy, but a man with a man's desires. She steeled herself to hurt him.

'Ben!' she said sharply. 'I am a wife, someone else's wife, and I'm going to have another child, quite soon. His child. He's my husband, and I love him.'

Even as she said it she wondered with detachment if it were still entirely true. She loved the image of Brenton as he had been, the gay, golden-haired, irresistible lover; and since he was still the same person – he was, of course he was! – she must love him still.

Ben had dropped her arm abruptly. 'I'm sorry,' he muttered. 'I guess I forgot myself.' It was his turn to flush. He glared painfully at the river, his face averted.

'I must go down to the galley and get baby's feed ready.' And then more gently, sorry for his misery: 'I'm sorry, Ben dear. I'm immensely touched and flattered, as any woman would be. But in a few years you'll be laughing at your present state.'

'Never!' said Ben fiercely.

Delie debated with herself whether to tell Brenton, but decided against it, as long as she could avoid further scenes.

She became cool and distant with Ben, but the children loved him and sought him out, and their presence kept the atmosphere natural enough between them.

When they got down to Morgan again, and were tied up at the high wharf, Brenton told her that Ben was leaving the *Philadelphia*.

He came to her cabin to say good-bye. He stood in the door while she changed the baby's napkin, a wisp of soft dark hair falling forward over her face as she bent above the squirming, kicking child.

'Here, you might as well have them back,' he said gruffly. He was holding out the volume of sonnets. 'I know all the best ones off by heart.'

She sat Alex on the bottom bunk, and took the open book. A

black pencil line was marked by sonnet number LXXXVII:

Farewell! thou art too dear for my possessing . . .

She thought of the marked volume of Shelley she had thrown out of this window, so long ago! She put out her hand frankly, and he took it in both of his.

'It's not farewell, Ben; just *au revoir*. We'll meet again one day, when you have your own boat.'

But he was leaving the river, he told her. He had only stayed because of her; now he was going down to Port Adelaide to get a job on a deep-sea boat.

'But, Ben, you're too fine and sensitive just to be an Able Seaman. And you're so good with children, you should become a teacher. If you were to do your training –'

'Well, I might. I dunno. I've got quite a bit saved out of me pay. Never spend any on liquor or smokes.' He gave the ghost of a smile. 'Only books. It's thanks to you, and the books you've lent me, that I know as much as I do. You've opened up a whole new world for me.'

'I'm glad about that, anyway.' She withdrew her hand.

'I know I'll never forget you.' He was staring at her in a mesmerised way, at her lips, and her eyes, that were so soft, so large and lustrously blue that he seemed to drown in their clear depths. 'There's only one thing I want to ask of you, and I'll go away, and never ask another thing. Philadelphia! Let me – ? Just one kiss. Just one.'

She had meant to keep the parting brisk and business-like, but he had taken both her hands again, and was drawing her slowly towards him. Impulsively she leaned forward, and their lips met and held for a long moment. Then he turned and stumbled out on to the deck. She did not see him again.

SIXTY

Not a single tributary flowed into the Murray in all its five hundred miles of wandering through this dry corner of Australia. The river, instead, flowed out into the thirsty land; sucked up by powerful steam-pumps, it flooded the irrigation settlements and orangeries that appeared like green oases among the yellow stone and burning sand.

The vines and fruit trees were just beginning to sprout with new leaves when Delie's fifth baby was born at the Waikerie hospital – a girl. Brenton was delighted with his daughter at first. But she was a small baby and never seemed to get enough to eat, though in desperation at her endless wailing Delie got up two or three times a night to give her extra feeds.

Because of these disturbed nights she had a wonderful view of Halley's Comet, which had returned that year trailing clouds of filmy glory across the sky. Probably no one but nurses on night duty and seamen on midnight watch had such a view of it. It spread its train right across the dark inland skies, and the stars, usually so bright in that clear air, shone mistily through a cloud of light. She gazed at the mysterious and lovely visitor, which would not come back again until after she was dead.

As the new baby's fretful wailing went on night and day, Brenton's pride in the baby turned rapidly to irritation. One night he sat up in his bunk, clutching his hair wildly, and roared, 'If that kid doesn't shut up soon, I'll drop it in the river!'

He looked so mad, with the great vein swelling in his neck, his eyes distended and bloodshot, that Delie, who had slipped out of her bunk to try to hush the baby, clutched it protectively to her. He's not well, of course he doesn't mean it, she thought; but the brutal words still rang in the little cabin, in the shocked, vibrating air.

Soon the baby became more lethargic, did not cry much and slept a great deal. Its skin was waxy, its head seemed unnaturally large for its thin limbs. When they got back to Waikerie after nearly a month Delie took her to the hospital.

The doctor who had delivered the child made the examination, and looked at Delie's breasts. 'Malnutrition,' he said briefly. 'She must go on to prepared feed at once, but she may not keep it down at first. Better leave her here for a few weeks till we get her settled on the new diet.'

'Leave the baby? You mean I needn't stay to look after her?'

'No; she'll be in good hands.' He looked at her shrewdly over the top of his glasses. He was a little, tubby man with a kindly, rubicund face, more like a family doctor than the head of a public hospital. The hair had all worn off the pink crown of his head, leaving a fluffy grey fringe all round. 'You could do with a bit more weight yourself,' he said. 'You've got your hands full, eh, with bringing up three kiddies on a boat? The rest will do you good.'

She explained that they would be away at least a month, but Dr Hample waved his hand. 'That's all right; we'll look after her till you get back. You won't know her once she starts to put on weight.'

It was like a reprieve. Delie went back to the boat, to the blessed silence of undisturbed nights, to a less irritable Brenton, a happy Alex who thought his rival had been disposed of, and only half as many napkins to wash. Her maternal feelings were exhausted. She had begun to feel nothing but weary impatience with that wailing scrap of life.

For the first time in months she got out her paints. Some colours she had left on the palette, with the intention of using them up in some spare time that never came, had dried in hard lumps, rubbery at the core. She scraped them down with the palette knife and sqeezed out fresh blobs of colour all round the edge, with a large blob of white at the top.

She still didn't know what she was going to paint, but she was filled with excitement at the feel of the tubes and brushes, the smell of the oil-paint. There was a prepared canvas ready, with a smudgy charcoal drawing on it that was now meaningless. She cleaned it down with bread and looked about her for a subject.

They were tied up just out of the town because the engineer had found a fault in the working of the water gauge. Nothing met her eyes but the wide green river, with stark yellow cliffs on one side, and a monotonous grey-green flat of lignum and native willow on the other. One twisted she-oak tree, black and meagre against the blue sky, showed on top of the cliffs, beside two tin boxes that were evidently the 'conveniences' attached to the local oval. They had once been painted red, which had now faded to a chalky pink.

There was nothing for it but the cliffs. Soon Delie was painting in, with uncompromising realism, the ugly emblems of civilisation poised between the enduring rock and the infinite blue of the sky. The pink blocks, with their solid dark shadows on one side, made a satisfying pattern against the blue. She scratched the legend MEN and LADIES in the wet paint, remembering her Aunt Hester's comment on the first drawing she had done in Australia, of the 'little house' at Kiandra lost in a waste of snow: 'Not a very delicate subject for a picture, I *must* say.'

She would call it *Equality of the Sexes* in the catalogue of her next exhibition. It was a topical subject now, and its flippancy would annoy some people. She liked to annoy people who took themselves too seriously.

Before she had finished, Gordon and Brenton came crowding round with endless questions and comments, and then Alex woke, hot and uncomfortable, from his day-time sleep. 'You go to him, Gordon,' she said impatiently, and went on painting. It was only when the last brush-stroke was in place that she became fully conscious of his roars of rage or distress, which had been heard with only the very surface of her mind.

Gordon came back, saying disgustedly, 'He's mad. He won't stop.'

She threw the brushes down guiltily and rushed to him, smeared with paint as she was.

'Fuppy bite me.' wailed Alex. 'Na'ty pink fuppy . . .'

'All right; there's no nasty puppy now,' she soothed him. 'All gone, puppy.' His nightmares were always of biting things, and would rival those of a man in the D.T.s for colour and diversity. He was nearly two, his distressing cough had gone, and he had a delicate milk-and-roses complexion, with black, finely pencilled eyebrows and grey eyes. He was not really like either of his parents.

She kissed the soft, damp curls at the back of his neck, that were like a floss of fine black silk. Some tension and conflict had been resolved in her by being able to paint again, and she felt happy in her motherhood, relaxed and content.

Brenny came in and put his face down close to his brother's, tickling the pink cheeks with his eyelashes. Alex gurgled happily. Delie drew them both into her arms and relaxed in an animal happiness, gazing at their petal-soft skin, their shining hair, their long eyelashes and wide, clear eyes. They were at their most perfect now, like buds just opened in the dew. Impossible to believe that they must decline towards baldness, wrinkles, the infirmity of old age!

She had long been obsessed with time as a destructive agency, bearing every living thing away into nothingness; but now she began to see it as a quality inherent in things; they existed in time as much as in space. From now on she looked at everything with new eyes, seeing it under its aspect of time, so that people's bodies seemed to waver like flames in a draught. In every old man she saw the eager youth he had been, in the grown youth the helpless infant and in the fresh-faced girl the wrinkled wreck she might one day become.

The baby, when she saw her again, had the same tiny, delicate features and wispy black hair; but already she had changed, put on weight, her cheeks were rosy and she was full of life.

'She's putting on twelve ounces a week now,' said the matron proudly. 'You can just about see her growing.'

That was exactly what Delie could see; but she saw her growing into a little, wizened, grey-haired old woman.

She had chosen the name of Mignon for her, but Brenton objected; he wanted 'something plain'. They compromised by christening her Mignon but calling her Meg for short. Alex, now that he could hold the bottle and help with feeding her, had forgotten his former jealousy, and Brenton began to like her now that she did not cry.

I wouldn't mind having babies if they weren't such messy things, thought Delie, as she cleaned the bright yellow stain from the second dirty napkin in one day. At least there was plenty of water available, but she still shuddered at the pollution of the great river that their human life upon it involved.

Yet the river purified itself in its endless flowing, as time absorbed the events of history in its stream, but was never saturated; bearing away all the noisy complications and struggles of life into an eternal silence.

Brenton was reading the report of the Interstate Premiers' Conference of 1911. Occasionally he muttered aloud or jerked the paper irritably.

' "No river in the world lends itself so easily to locking," ' he read, ' "and only a fraction of the present flow of water would then be needed to keep the river permanently navigable." Bah! They knew all that before, but still they did nothing. If only the S.A. Government would make a beginning, the others might follow.'

The South Australian Government, he read, was prepared to act on its own in building a series of locks to make the river permanently navigable as far up as Wentworth. An interstate agreement was necessary because locks No. 7 to 11 would be over the border. The conference had ratified the 1907 agreement by which S.A. could use Lake Victoria, in New South Wales, as a storage basin. Work on this was 'to be begun at once, at an estimated cost of £200,000.'

He flung the paper away from him.

' "At once!" That's good. They still won't do anything. The first conference on locking the river was held in 1872, and now, forty years later, nothing has been done. If only they had some rivermen in Parliament!'

'Why don't you stand yourself?' asked Delie half-jokingly.

'And so I should!' Brenton got up and strode round the small saloon, kicked the paper savagely, and roared, 'By God! Do they have to wait for another drought like '02? Wasn't that enough to show them? But if there's another drought now, it won't be only the steamer-trade that'll suffer, and a few grape-growers. There're thousands of holdings depending on irrigation now, right along the lower river. They'll all be ruined; and what a howl there'll be when all the work and money that's gone into establishing orchards and vineyards is thrown down the drain. But these hot-air merchants do nothing but talk.'

Delie soothed him down, for she was frightened for him in these violent moods. The children had learned to keep away from him, or to stay very quiet, when the vein stood out in his neck and his blue eyes became bloodshot and savage. His temper was more uncertain as the months went by. At his hasty, limping step they shrank together and turned their eyes uneasily to their mother.

Only with little Meg he was always gentle, now that she no longer wailed. She was a bonny, laughing toddler now, with her mother's dark hair and Brenton's green-blue eyes.

If only she'd been born first, thought Delie, she'd have been a help to me before very long, which Gordon will never be.

Yet Gordon was her favourite; shy, dreamy Gordon, with bright golden curls like his father's had been, and large blue eyes shadowed with long lashes like a girl's.

Delie always tried to be impartial, and to hide her feeling for her eldest son; but little Meg was openly her father's favourite. She could take liberties with him that none of the others dared. She would chuckle and look up at him with her merry blue eyes, trying to climb his trouser leg as if he were a tree growing far above her head, and he would bend down and swing her up on his shoulder.

Young Brenny was his shadow, copying everything his father did with slavish admiration, mixed with awe. Alex quietly kept out of his way as much as possible. He usually had a fold of his mother's skirts in his hand, and peeped out from their safety at the big man. Gordon, shy and faintly hostile, avoided him too.

'You like Gordie better than me, don't you?' said young Brenny conversationally to his mother.

'I love you all, darling.'

'It doesn't matter, though,' said Brenny, brushing aside her red herring, 'because Daddy likes me best. I'm braver than Gordie. I can just about lick him now, and I can swim faster. I wish he'd stop growing until I was biggest.'

'Never mind, dear, you'll catch up one day. When you're eighteen you might be taller than Gordon even, and he'll have stopped growing by then.'

'*Will* he? *Then* I'll be able to fight him.'

'Oh, stop talking about fighting,' she said wearily.

Gordon was six this year, and she would have to start teaching him to write and do sums. Already he knew his letters and could read the simple primers she had bought for him. Gordon loved his lessons. He had, first of all, his mother's undivided attention; he loved the smell of her hair as she bent her head low beside his, and the feel of her fingers as she held his hand and guided the pencil. Then the colours, clear and primitive, in the first Reader were lovely too; the lovely cat sitting on a bright pink mat with yellow fringes, the red cricket ball, the yellow bat, the blue top. And he would be happy for an hour at a time with a box of coloured crayons and some shelf-paper, making up patterns or pictures of birds like curly letter V's flying over a hill.

He knew there were hills, and how to draw them, from picture-books, though he had never seen one. In his young life he had travelled thousands of miles along a river that flowed endlessly through a great plain. He had seen nothing but flat-topped cliffs or low sand-dunes. Hills were high and round, he knew, and mountains were high and pointy. He *knew* there were such things, and that somewhere there was a great spread-out water without any banks, called The Sea.

'Away up where the river begins,' Mummy would tell him, 'there are big blue mountains with their tops covered in snow. The snow melts in spring and comes down the river, and some is flowing underneath our boat now; it has taken nearly two months to get here,'

And Gordon would look over the side in the blazing summer day, at the water sliding quietly in the shadow of the boat. It was greeny-coloured, like glass, only you couldn't see through it properly; and it looked cool but he knew it wasn't really, because when Mummy or Daddy took him for a swim (and he was always afraid that Something might come up from a deep hole and grab his foot; once a weed had wrapped itself round his leg, and he had screamed) it was quite warm on top, with queer cold patches here and there. On a calm day it glittered like glass, and you could see everything double like in a mirror; but on windy days it got rough and dirty-looking, with froth like old soapsuds on the top.

He was learning to row the dinghy, which was great fun, only one oar *would* go much better than the other. If only they would both go as well as the one he would get on very fast. He always went along the set-lines in the morning, if they'd had lines out overnight, but he didn't like taking the live fish off the hooks very much; all the same, it was exciting when there was a good haul, and they could have cod or callop for breakfast.

Brenny always wanted to come too, but then he would want to row, and in the end Gordon would have to push him hard, and then he would yell and Dad would get wild. So he usually tried to sneak out early, without waking Brenny in the bunk below.

Across the river was a wide lagoon, dotted with clumps of reeds which showed that it was not very deep. Beyond the lagoon were more cliffs in which he could see mysterious caves, black and shadowed. It was very early, the sun was not even up yet, and they would not be leaving until after breakfast.

Gordon rowed as quietly as he could. He didn't want another soul to be awake, he wanted the whole great sweep of river to belong to him alone, him and the big white crane that stood fishing at the edge of the lagoon. Sky and river were bright with the dawn, but without any pink colour, for there was not a wisp of cloud anywhere. It was like sailing through a great bowl of light.

The trees upside-down in the water, standing in the still lagoon, looked as real as the ones above; and as he drew away from the boat he saw another boat upside-down below it. A fish leaped, and a spreading circle of rings cut through the boat-image, and wobbled and broke it into pieces. But the pieces began to touch, to join, and soon it was whole again. It was like magic.

He looked over his shoulder and fixed a big tree to row towards, but he kept bumping into reeds and getting his oars tangled. The sun was already up, and there was blue smoke going up from the galley chimney, before he reached the cliffs. And then the biggest cave was only a hollow in the yellow rock.

There were sounds of activity from the boat, floating across the still water: a clatter of dishes, a bucket of rubbish being emptied into the river, the clang of the firebox door. They must be getting ready to leave! He tried to row faster, dug too deeply and nearly lost an oar. Then he got wedged on a clump of reeds.

He found that it was quicker to stand up and punt with one oar. With one last wild push he sent the dinghy out into the main stream, but overbalanced and had to grab the side of the boat to save himself. He let go of the oar. It went floating gently down the river.

At first he tried to reach it with the other oar, but he was afraid he might lose that too; then he heard unintelligible yells and shouts from the *Philadelphia*, and saw his mother and father leaning over the rail, so he thought he'd better make for the boat.

It was very awkward with one oar, and he kept turning in circles, but he drew gradually nearer. Soon he was near enough to see that Daddy was furious; the vein was standing out in his neck, his face was red; while Mummy looked pale and worried. Brenny was watching too, which made it worse.

'Why didn't you get the other oar, you bloody little fool?' roared his father.

'It was floating too fast, and I thought you were calling to me to leave it.'

He splashed and floundered miserably, bringing the dinghy at last up to the stern.

'It's lucky there's no wind, or you'd never have got back at all,' said his mother. 'You must never go out like that without asking, do you hear? I've been worried to death.' Her voice, too, was sharp and angry.

'We've had steam up half an hour, waiting for you,' growled his father, as he made the dinghy's rope fast. Gordon clambered up the rudder, only to be knocked flat on the deck by a stinging blow

369

on the ear. 'And I hope that'll learn you. Now get into your bunk and stay there.'

Gordon crept up the steps, holding his ear, with a white face and tearful eyes; but he did not allow a sound to escape him until he was in his bunk in the dim cabin.

When Delie came in a little while later with some hot breakfast she had saved for him, he turned his face to the wall and would not look at it.

SIXTY-ONE

Survey work on the Lake Victoria storage brought new life to the lonely south-west corner of New South Wales, just over the border from an arid and unpopulated part of South Australia.

Set among orange sandhills and low cliffs or red clay, the shallow lake had to be built up and strengthened. It had a naturally sealed bottom of fine impervious clay, and an inlet from the Murray along Frenchman's Creek. Regulator gates were to be installed at the end of this and on Rufus Creek, the lake's outlet back into the river.

But a war was to interrupt construction so that the lake could not be used for storage for another six years.

'They haven't even begun work on the first lock yet,' said Brenton, 'and until No. 9 lock is built to divert water into the lake, and the regulator gates are finished, what's the use of surveys and embankments?'

'I suppose they've got to begin somewhere,' said Delie.

'Then they should begin with the locks. You'll see; they'll be caught by another drought before they do anything.'

There was a surveyors' camp on the south-wester shore of the lake, near the outlet of the Rufus, and Brenton had the idea of running stores and whisky to the camp. The men had nowhere to spend their money and it was burning holes in their pockets. There was no liquor at the camp.

'And no women, either,' he said meaningly. 'Don't you get off the boat while we're tied up there. We don't want any trouble.'

'I can look after myself, thank you.'

Only a small steamer like the *Philadelphia* could make its way through the narrow, wooded, winding Rufus to where the road bridge crossed it at the lake outlet, eight miles from the Murray. Wentworth was sixty miles away along a rough bush track.

The men from the camp, whose tents were set up in the angle between the creek and the lake shore, found plenty of things they needed among the stores. They crowded on board to lean over the long counter that had been built into a store-room up for'ard, where once the extra cargo used to be stacked. Fishing-tackle, matches, tobacco, lanterns, lamp-glasses, flannel shirts, tinned fruit and jam, all changed hands rapidly.

Delie was well aware that she was a centre of attraction as she moved about the store-room, handing goods to Brenton from the shelves, helping him to find things that had been stored out of sight. The men eyed her admiringly, yearningly, sentimentally or appraisingly; none of them was indifferent. In this male outpost she was Woman, a symbol of all that was lacking in their lives.

A young surveyor's assistant, lean and brown-faced, called her over to ask if she had any wool to match the pullover he wore. He twisted round to show her a large tear with unravelled edges in the shoulder.

She began looking through the skeins of royal-blue wool, glad of the occupation and the excuse for bending over that it gave her; for she felt her colour rising with his clear blue eyes upon her. She was attracted by something boyish and appealing about him; he reminded her in a way of Brenton when he was younger. Though this lad was more slender he had the same assurance, the same certainty of his own attractiveness.

'My mum knitted it for me,' he said, 'and I wouldn't like it to get wrecked for want of a few stitches.'

'It should have had a few stitches as soon as it was torn. Now it will need darning.'

'No needle; oh, a packet of darners I want too, with big eyes. I'm not much of a hand at sewing.'

'Leave your pullover here and I'll mend it for you,' she said impulsively.

'Gosh, would you? That's awfully kind of you.' His blue eyes, clear and shining with health and youth, looked at her gratefully; and though Adam's eyes had been brown it was Adam he suddenly reminded her of. Ah, youth . . . She suppressed a sigh as she took

371

the garment from him, while the men standing nearby chaffed him and complained that they had plenty of things that needed mending, too.

'Come back after lunch and it'll be ready,' she said, ignoring them.

Brenton, busy taking and counting money, took no notice. The engineer in charge, who had come to get a new razor, found that he was interested in all water-conservation schemes, and offered to take him over the site of the projected works that afternoon.

Delie sat on the top deck, outside her cabin door, darning with the blue wool. The pullover was felted under the arms a little, and from it came a scent of male sweat that was not unpleasant.

Alex and Meg were asleep, Gordon and Brenny were resting in their bunks with picture-books. This was the most peaceful time of the day for her. There was a pile of ironing waiting to be done, and plenty of her own mending; but she took time and care over making a neat darn that would have surprised her Aunt Hester.

'How's it going?'

She looked over the rail at the fair-haired young man who hailed her. He was wearing a clean, faded blue shirt and had obviously slicked down his curls with water.

'Not finished yet. Come up,' she said.

He came on board and drew up a deck-chair beside her, leaning over to look at what she had done.

'Marvellous!' he said, feeling the darn with a long finger. 'You know, it's really – '

' – Awfully kind of me!' she chimed in. They both laughed.

'Shh, the children are still asleep.'

They talked in low voices so as not to disturb them. This gave them a feeling of intimacy as they sat together in the sun. She felt instantly at ease with this young man, as if they had been friends for years.

When she had finished she patted the darn and smoothed it with the point of the needle. 'There! It should really be pressed but at least it won't run any more.'

'It's perfect.' He took the jumper from her and pulled it vigorously over his head.

'But you've got it on back to front!'

'Yes. That way the mend is over my heart,' he said with an unmistakable look.

She blushed and got up quickly. 'It's time for the children to wake up,' she said.

She peeped into the cabin where Meg was still sound asleep in her crib. Next door Alex slept peacefully. From the saloon came Gordon's voice: 'Can't we get up now, Mummy?'

'All right, dear. Can you put on your shoes by yourself?'

'I'll be going then, Ma'am. And thank you again.'

'That's quite all right,' she said coolly and formally to the young man. 'I'm sure your mother would have done it better.'

The pullover had ruffled his light curls as he dragged it over his head, and he looked so charming and so young that she was alarmed at her own feelings.

Gordon came clattering on deck with his shoes undone.

'Hullo!' he said in a friendly voice. Delie went to help Brenny with his shoes. When they came out, Gordon and the young man were deep in a discussion of fishing methods. He was telling Gordon that he would show him the proper way to rig a set-line, so that a cod could never get away, if he'd come down to where his lines were set.

'Can we, Mummy?' begged Gordon.

'Well . . . Baby will wake in a few minutes. How far is it?'

'Just a step along the bank, Ma'am.'

'Well, wait a minute, will you?' She looked again at the sleeping pair, and then put on a hat – a thing she rarely wore, but she felt that it gave her dignity, a married woman's status.

The four of them walked round the shore of the lake. She was afraid to let the boys out of sight in case they wandered away and got lost in the desolate surroundings.

When they came back she felt gay, young and light-hearted as she had not felt for years. She would never see this young man again, and the thought did not worry her, yet he had made her afternoon happy. In him she saw, made new and young again, the two loves of her life – Adam and Brenton. Because of this she felt a rare, renewed tenderness for her husband.

She had been going to tell Brenton about the walk that night; but at tea-time Gordon let fall that they had been out with one of the men from the camp, and he had been on board 'talking to Mummy'.

Delie explained how she had offered to mend the pullover; it sounded odd and unconvincing now. She could not explain the impulse, how he had reminded her of her young cousin. Brenton's brows drew down and the vein swelled in his neck. The children became silent and apprehensive. As soon as they were alone in their cabin that night, he turned on her.

'Didn't I tell you not to get off the boat without me?'

'Yes, but the boys did want to go, and he seemed such a nice young man –'

'A nice young man! And how long was he on board this afternoon? I suppose you thought you'd like a change, you little bitch.'

She stared at him, too surprised to reply. Had he really said that? The veins were standing out in his temple as well as his neck, and his face was red. She noticed with a corner of her mind the contrast of colour that it made with the sea-blue of his eyes.

'So you thought you'd like a "nice young man" as a change from your poor old husband with the gammy leg?' He limped irritably about the cabin, helping the lame leg with an impatient hand behind it.

'Brenton, for God's sake be reasonable. Nothing happened, we talked a little while as I was finishing the darn, and then walked along the bank with the children.'

'I suppose it's the one I saw as I was coming back . . . A fair-haired, skinny chap, I could break him in half with one hand. So I'm not enough for you?'

He gripped her wrist in steel-hard fingers.

'How much whisky have you had since dinner?' she asked contemptuously.

'Never mind. It takes more than a few whiskies to make Teddy Edwards drunk.' He bent her arm until she was forced to her knees on the floor. 'What else happened? Tell me!'

'Let me go! *Let* me go!' She was in a rage now, she beat at him with her free arm, trying to bite the hard brown hand that held her. He jerked it away from her and she dropped in a heap on the floor.

She realised that it was the other man's youth that had infuriated him. He hated the thought that he was getting older. She got up slowly, rubbing her arm. If only Ben were here! She thought of Ben, always so gentle, and loving her so much. It was as well she had not tried to tell Brenton about Ben.

'You're such a fool,' she said coldly. 'If I'd wanted "a change", as you call it, I'd easily have found a substitute for you before now. Don't you think I had plenty of admirers in Melbourne? You never bothered to accompany me, but I was always loyal to you. And now you make a jealous scene about a lad I have seen once, just because he makes you feel old.'

That went home; she rejoiced bitterly at his hurt look.

Brenton turned away with a strangled noise, then rounded menacingly upon her. 'Get out of my sight! Go away!'

She went with her head high, and began to pace up and down the unlighted deck on the far side from the cabin doors. For him to talk to her like that! After all she had silently put up with, the girl in the shanty, the woman with the gold hairpins, Nesta and how many more?

Her mind whirled on the edge of black depths. For the first time she understood the meaning of the phrase, 'his senses reeled'. All was over then between them; this was the end.

She went to the stern and climbed down into the dinghy, undoing the stiff rope with clumsy fingers. For hours, after passing under the low bridge, she rowed about aimlessly on the broad expanse of Lake Victoria, while the stars moved slowly westward, and danced in points of white fire on the black waters of the lake.

SIXTY-TWO

There were still plenty of craft on the lower river – trading steamers, fishermen's boats, houseboats, the dinghies of 'Murray whalers', and strange one-person boats worked by a treadle like a sewing-machine. Usually there was someone to yarn with, and Brenton stayed away night after night.

Delie had made a resolve not to share his bunk again; she had not forgiven him, and she didn't want any more children.

'Of course if I can't get what I want here I can always go elsewhere,' he said coldly one night when she repulsed him. He got dressed and went out again, and did not come back until the next morning.

He left her alone after that, but though she told herself that this was what she wanted, she was oddly discontented and unhappy. She did some drawing at night after the children were in bed, to keep her hand in; but mostly she went to her bunk soon after them.

It was a month later when Brenton came in one night earlier than usual, just after she had blown out the lamp. She lay very still in the warm, kerosene-scented darkness. A mosquito was shrilling up near the panelled ceiling. She could hear Brenton's breathing, heavy and quick, as he undressed close beside her in the small cabin, and see his broad figure against the starlit doorway. In a moment he would climb into the top bunk.

Then suddenly, treacherously, her body began to long for him. She became intensely aware of his every movement, his every breath, and she longed for him to come nearer.

I don't want him, she thought fiercely. I hate him. But when in a moment he began groping his way into her bunk, a great wave of gladness swept over her.

'No . . . I'm tired,' she muttered feebly.

He laughed confidently. 'You want me; I can tell.'

After all, he's my husband, she thought in the last moment before her conscious, reasoning self was overwhelmed. But she could not escape from the feeling, afterwards, that she had been betrayed by her senses.

It was not the first time her body had taken control and ordered her life against her will. It had betrayed her before when she had wanted with all her mind to give herself to Adam; it had let her down when she wanted to go on with her art studies rather than get married; and in its weakness it had led to the years of childbearing which were sapping her creative energy and using up the best years of her life in a round of domestic drudgery.

The saints were right to mortify the flesh, to scourge and starve their despised bodies into submission. The flesh was not weak; it was strong, with the power of the whole life-force behind it, demanding to be reproduced for ever, and always at war with the life of contemplation.

She should, she thought in despair, have belonged to some stern sect whose discipline was imposed from without: fasting, continence, solitude and silence were what she craved, having too little of any of them. Alone, her spirit would always be vanquished.

Alex was an enquiring child, with bright, alert eyes under their fine black brows. He was fascinated with everything that lived and moved, from a green caterpillar that he found in a cabbage to a beautiful moth, its gold-dust wings marked with crimson dots, that he brought to his mother in his hot little hand with 'all its powder tummin' off'.

She found him some chrysalids of the Orange Wanderer butterfly to keep in a cardboard box with a few twigs of cotton-bush.

376

He handled the beautiful pale-green cases so much that only one pupa survived.

Delie found him watching with big eyes and set face the terrible struggles of the insect to emerge – the splitting of the now transparent case, the protrusion of one crumpled wing.

'Doesn't it *hurt* it??' he kept asking.

'Getting born is a very exhausting business sometimes; but it is worth the struggle to get out into the sun.'

But is it, after all? she thought, watching the frantic movements of the butterfly, and wondering again at the ruthless, impersonal force of life. At last the new, complete individual emerged, and rested, trembling, with spread wings that were still crinkled like a leaf just out of the bud. She looked with pity at this fellow-creature that would fall into the river, or become the meal of a bird or lizard, or simply die of cold next winter.

Alex caught a little gecko lizard on a sandy spit where they had been tied up overnight. Even when he had put out his hand it remained frozen, regarding him with small, bright eyes. He picked it up by the tail – and next moment the lizard was gone, while in his hand remained a horrible, squirming stump, like a very lively worm. Alex dropped it with a yell. It rolled about on the sand like a caterpillar attacked by ants.

He went roaring to his mother. 'His tail tummed off! His tail tummed off!' he cried between sobs.

She explained that it hadn't hurt the lizard, its tail was meant to come off to distract its enemies when it was in danger; but Alex was not convinced, and didn't believe the lizard could grow a new tail. Would his own big toe grow again if it dropped off? Well, then . . .

He was fascinated with the little Welcome swallows which nested year after year beneath the overhang of the after-deck. They never went away for the winter, as Mummy said some of them did, flying all the way to Japan across the sea. They stayed with the boat winter and summer, and travelled with it up and down the river.

He liked to see them flashing round and round the boat as they steamed along, darting past the steering pole in front, round and back to their nests again. Their backs were like dark blue satin. They didn't mind people; he was sure they wouldn't object if he put his hand into one of the little mud nests and felt the young ones. But Mummy would never let him climb over the rail, and he couldn't row the dinghy and was not even allowed to climb down into it on his own, because he hadn't learned to swim properly yet.

One day when Daddy and Gordon were ashore, carrying a pile of newly bought goods up to a farmhouse, he and Brenny stood by the wire-netting of the after-deck. Two swallows came back to the nests, each with a small insect in his bill. An excited cheeping came from the young ones out of sight.

'I'm goin' to c'imb over and look,' said Alex.

'You'll get into a row,' said Brenny indifferently. He was sulking because he had not been asked to help his father.

Alex climbed up and got one chubby leg over the rail. There was a ledge outside, only a few inches wide. He clung there by one hand while he felt under the deck with the other. But his arm was too short; he couldn't reach.

Just below, the greenish water glided past, reflecting the sun dazzlingly from its silken surface. He could see tiny insects and even bits of dust floating on the water's skin. He dropped a lump of spit and saw the ripples widen outwards, their reflections dancing in golden waves across the stern-post.

He hooked a toe in the netting and hung dangerously far out over the edge. His fine dark curls hung down, the blood suffused his face. His fingers just reached the edge of one nest. He felt something warm and fluffy, and moved excitedly. His foot slipped. With a short cry and a splash he fell head-first into the river.

Delie was in the galley, stirring a mixture of mashed potato and egg-yolk for the baby; the Chief Poisoner was clattering dishes on the work-bench; when young Brenny rushed in and announced importantly, 'Alex is in the river!'

She dropped the saucepan on the floor and rushed out, while the Poisoner, who never listened to 'them kids', stared vacantly after her and then down at the mess on the floor, twisting one side of his long yellowed moustache in amazement.

Alex had fallen in on the side away from the bank. Delie saw that at any moment he might sink again in deep water. He was face down on the surface, his arms and legs moving feebly.

She tore off her shoes and jumped in beside him. The moment she came up she grabbed him and turned him over; he was semi-conscious, and she was able to tow him while swimming on one side. When she felt the soft, oozing mud of the river-bank beneath her feet she grasped with relief.

Before she was well out of the water she had held Alex upside-

378

down; water streamed out of his mouth and nostrils, and he began to cough and cry. Once, long ago, she had been rescued like this from the sea . . .

Trembling and shivering in her wet clothes, she held and soothed him. Brenton came charging down the bank, Gordon at his heels.

'What happened? Did you fall overboard?'

'Alex did,' she quavered. 'If Brenny hadn't come and told me, he'd have been gone.'

'How did you fall in, son? Did you climb over the railing?'

'Y-yes, Daddy. Alec wanted ter see ve swallows in veir nests.'

'Oh Alex, you naughty boy! You might have been –'

'Quiet a moment, Delie. Now, Alex, I want you to do it again.'

'What on earth – !'

' "Quiet," I said.' He took the shaking child from her arms and went on board, then set him down outside the netting, where he clung in terror. Taking off his own shirt and shoes, Brenton dived overboard.

'Now jump,' he said.

'I won't, I won't! Alec f'ightened of the big water.'

'Jump when I tell you! You're quite safe when I'm here. Daddy will catch you.'

Whether he lost his grip and fell, or let go on purpose, Alex dropped into the water with a thin cry. Brenton had him in his arms the moment he came up.

'Stop panicking; do as I tell you. Now turn on your back and float.'

After supporting the child's head for a while, he quietly removed his hand. 'Now, isn't that easy? Hey, don't cave in in the middle. Just lie back as if it was a bed. Now if you ever fall in again, just float till someone comes.'

By now Delie was recovering from the shock, but she snatched Alex back as soon as his father brought him to shore.

To her remonstrances he only replied, 'If he hadn't gone in straight away, he'd have been scared of the water for the rest of his life. And what's the good of a riverman who can't swim?'

Delie, fearing a chill, packed him in his cot with two whisky bottles filled with hot water. He was just getting drowsy when Brenton came in with a baby swallow, grey and downy, cradled in his big hand.

'You can keep it warm in bed for a while, but don't hurt it. I have to put it back in the nest for the mother to feed.'

Alex beamed with happiness.

'Huh!' muttered Brenny sourly. 'If *I'd* climbed over the rail I'd of got whacked.'

Delie gave the two older boys lessons on deck every morning. Gordon would try to smooth away the frown-lines that were now marked deeply between her level brows, and that showed up in the clear light.

'You look awful tired,' he said, looking up from his lesson book and seeing with the uncompromising eyes of youth his mother's sagging lips and the wrinkles which time had made in the fine skin about her eyes.

She bent over to correct his spelling, and he stared at her head near his own. 'Your hair's going grey!'

'It is not!' she started and recoiled as if she had been stung.

'It is so!' He reached up and tried to pull out one of several grey threads. His fingers could not sort it out from the brown mass, and he pulled several with a painful tweak. He held them up triumphantly before her nose.

She took the hairs irritably and sat staring at them, silent and perturbed. Four of the hairs were glistening like fine brown silk; the fifth was dead and grey, and seemed coarser in texture, more like wire.

That night she went early to her cabin and, taking the lamp, looked long and critically at the changes that had come so gradually to her face that she had not noticed them. She sat down on the lower bunk, and took off her shoes and stockings.

Her legs were white, with a few fine, brown hairs. Still shapely, but thickening, with a cluster of bluish veins knotted and contused at the back of the calves, the result of being on her feet too much during her last pregnancy. And her feet, her beautiful slim feet! The splayed toes, the pinched little toenail flattened on one side from thirty years of shoes, the corns and callouses looked back at her. They were no longer the feet of a girl.

How short a time it seemed since she was thirteen, and had walked on these same bare feet for the first time into the cool, silken waters of the Murray! She closed her eyes and remembered that night, the far, fluting call of the swans going over, the stars like jewels on the river's calm breast.

Twenty years ago! Twenty years!

The river lapped past the bows, steadily, quietly flowing

towards the sea. Softly, flow softly! she cried in her mind. But she had the sensation of being caught in a current that was relentlessly speeding up. There was no way of arresting that endless flow.

SIXTY-THREE

In the narrow world of the river, world affairs seemed far away and unimportant. Politics were local: legislation that affected navigation or the wool industry, the long-standing jealousies between States over riparian rights, the findings of interstate commissions on the river – all these were discussed knowledgeably and heatedly.

Few bothered their heads about a British pledge to defend Belgium against aggression, or the growing might and arrogance of Germany. Yet in the next four years many a riverman was to die far away from the quiet Murray, in France and Flanders and Gallipoli, defending 'little Belgium' and fighting Germany.

More important to Delie than world affairs, more terrible than the threat of war, was the knowledge that she was once again pregnant. She blamed Brenton for carelessness, but she blamed herself more for yielding to him again in spite of her resolve. Such weakness degraded her, and now she was to be punished.

He was drinking more than ever, and was little help with the children, who were rather frightened of him. Delie contemplated the future with despair. Five children! She felt that she could not bear it, that she would rather die.

It was not the discomfort to be gone through again, the shapelessness, the heaviness of her body, the sickness and indigestion, the pangs of labour and birth; but she began to feel that she was on a treadmill, year after year doing nothing but rear babies and do without sleep or rest.

And meanwhile her youth was slipping away, her creative time when she should have been painting. The coloured cliffs and long, calm reaches of the lower river, the great leaning red-gums as graceful as willows but so much more interesting in form, the lagoons with their reeds and birds, all filled her with an urge to draw and paint that was like a physical craving.

She did some crayon and charcoal sketches, made notes in her sketchbook that she could use – 'some day' – for the basis of a large picture. The longing for colour, for slapping the paint in free masses on a big canvas, had to be fought down while she washed and folded napkins, prepared baby food, sat by Alex's bed through a fresh attack of bronchitis, corrected Gordon's and Brenny's copy-books and bathed little Meg. How she missed Ben's help when the boys fought and squabbled until she felt like screaming!

Brenton seemed indifferent when she told him, and could not see why she was upset. More sons meant free labour. The older boys were already becoming useful as deckhands. He was making good money out of his trading ventures, particularly the running of whisky to Lake Victoria, where he had a monopoly, and to the officially 'dry' town of Mildura, where he could get huge prices for hard liquor.

He decided to buy a barge again to carry extra stores, and to employ two more hands. He seemed to have forgotten his mania for speed, and a new obsession had taken hold of him: to make money.

One night she came upon him emptying a little out of each whisky bottle into a tenth one which was empty. The other nine were being topped up with water.

Delie appreciated the extra money for baby-clothes and blankets, but she felt guilty about the way they were getting it. Already she had protested about the selling of whisky at Lake Victoria; one man had been killed in a drunken brawl in the engineering camp, and another had rolled into the fire in his sodden sleep and been burnt to death.

'You can't do that, Brenton!' she said now. 'It isn't honest. They pay high enough prices for the whisky –'

'What's the matter with you? Do you think they care, as long as it tastes like whisky? First you complain that I cause their drunken fights, now you complain because I'm making the whisky a bit weaker. Don't you think it's better for them to take a bit of water with it, even if they don't know?'

'I suppose it is,' she said unhappily. 'But I wish we had nothing to do with it.'

She had never been off the boat since Brenton's display of jealous rage, and had not seen the young man with the blue sweater, as since her pregnancy she had not helped in the store.

She hoped he was not drinking too much; his eyes had been so clear and healthy.

She felt no need for the company of other women, but there was a great loneliness in her spirit. She had been too busy to keep up letters, and Imogen had gradually ceased to write. It was years since she had been to Melbourne. She wanted to 'talk shop' with other artists, to engage in stimulating arguments. The two art journals she took only seemed to accentuate her isolation.

In Morgan one day when the *Philadelphia* was loading stores on to her barge, she noticed a spare, bearded figure on the wharf – a man with aquiline features and observant dark eyes, who carried a sketch-block under his arm and a painting-satchel in his hand.

She looked at his thin, rather red lips below the fine dark moustache and bony, arrogant nose, the pale face shaded by a Panama hat, the smart but casual clothes. He stood out among the wharf-labourers and river-hands and railwaymen like an orchid among potatoes.

She walked down to the wharf and past the stranger, looking deeply into his dark eyes. Here was a fellow-artist, and she longed to speak. He returned the look for what seemed a long, breathless moment; then his eyes passed over her figure, and were quickly averted. There was a spark of humour in them, a quirk of an unruly eyebrow that encouraged her. He reminded her in some indefinable way of her dead father.

He turned to walk up the white, stone slope to the main street. She followed, hovering outside a shop when she saw him go in, but she could not pluck up courage to speak.

Before he could come out again and perhaps notice that she was following him, she hurried back on board.

The next day she saw him loading his satchel and some provisions into a dinghy drawn up to the bank and laden with camping gear. He went off towards the yellow cliffs above the upstream bend, rowing deliberately and effortlessly. Not very young, she judged, at least forty. She felt absurdly desolate as she watched him go, as if she had lost a friend.

Before they left Morgan again the water began to fall. The river was flowing clear and slow, all the silt fallen to the bottom.

'Fishing pretty good, Dan?' asked Brenton in a genial roar from the wheel-house, as the *Philadelphia* pulled in by Old Dan's

383

camp, where drum-nets spread on the bank, and the twin stakes of a cross-line set in the river, showed the headquarters of a full-time fisherman.

'Aye,' growled Dan, known along the river as 'Dismal'. 'Callop and bream are bitin' well with this clear water. But the damn' river's getting so slow that the cod'll stop movin' soon. I don't like it.'

He was 'in the money', and had hailed the steamer to get in a stock of things for his camp – a new quart-pot, a couple of grey blankets and some extra hooks and lines.

' 'Ad that there quart-pot for nigh fifteen year,' said Dismal, kicking an ancient black billy lying by his neatly swept fireplace of stones. 'Now it 'as ter go on me. Leaking like a sieve.'

'D'you reckon we're in for a drought?' asked Brenton. 'Looks uncommonly like the beginning of '02 to me – the weather, I mean. I don't know about the river, I was up the top end then.'

'There'll be a bad drought next year', said Dismal Dan impressively, taking his black pipe from among his yellowed whiskers and waving it in the air. 'Yer can take it from me, mate. And it'll be wuss than the larst one, when I walked acrost the river at Morgan in me boots.'

Brenton scowled and tapped his teeth. He had faith in the weather prophecies of old-timers. And here he was with a barge in tow for the first time in years, and more goods to dispose of than he'd ever carried before!

As the dry winter was succeeded by a dry summer, the gloomy predictions of Dismal Dan were confirmed. Little or no rain had fallen in Victoria and New South Wales, and it was so warm that hardly any snow gathered on the Alps. The river continued to fall steadily.

Millions of gallons of life-giving water, urgently needed by farmers and fruit-growers for the irrigation works they had built up, flowed wastefully out to sea. By the summer of early 1914 things were desperate. At Renmark, the Irrigation Trust had built a dam in the river-bed with sandbags to hold back sufficient water to keep the pumps working until after the fruit was harvested. All along the lower river, steamers lay trapped in shallow and dwindling water-holes, or went aground and lay canted in the mud.

'One lock! Even one lock would have stopped it from all flowing away,' cried Brenton. 'I told you they'd do nothing until there was another drought! And how many millions are they wasting in running their railways at a loss to compete with the steamers? Blind, stupid fools.'

He regarded the drought as a piece of personal spite on the part of Fate, or Nature, or some such abstraction; coming as it did just when he was expanding his trade, and had sunk most of his capital in the new barge and extra cargo. Delie listened to his ranting and watched his blood-suffused face, in fear that he would have a stroke when they actually ran aground.

Brenton was not in the wheel-house when it happened. They were between Waikerie and Kingston and he had just handed over to the new mate and stepped to the side to watch how the water was sucking in from the bank as they passed – a sure sign of very low water.

'Alf!' he called to the Poisoner. 'Start taking soundings in the bows there. We haven't got more than six inches to spare, I'd say.'

He had put the engine back to slow. When they hit the sand-bank in midstream that had always been covered by many feet of water, they stopped softly, reluctantly, almost without a jolt.

The new mate had never been known to swear. He had a sanctimonious expression, and had brought three different copies of the Bible on board among his things. When the skipper rushed back to the wheel-house he found the mate on his knees, praying.

Brenton pushed him aside with an oath, put the engine astern and tried to get her off, but he only churned up some sand.

'God blast the bloody boat!' he cried, stamping round in the wheel-house. 'God blast this flaming river, and the bloody blasted Government that does nothing about it. And as for you!' he roared, rounding on the cowering mate, 'Get out of my sight! Praying!'

He had a wire rope taken round a solid red-gum tree on the bank ahead of the boat, and wound the other end on a cleat on the paddle-shaft. The *Philadelphia* slid forward a few feet, and then stuck fast again. A line was taken out astern and the paddles reversed, watched interestedly by the children; but it was no use. They were fast aground, while the barge still floated free behind them.

Before long the *Philadelphia* was isolated in a stagnant pool, as she had been years ago in the Darling; but this was worse, for she was aground on one side and as the waters fell the deck began to slant. Things slid and rolled off the table, the milk sat at an angle in the saucepan, the pans almost slid off the stove. It was like being at sea, like the steady lean of a sailing-ship driving with her lee-rail under water.

The children thought it great fun to run down the slope of the deck and bang into the railing; or to walk along with one foot higher than the other, chanting, 'I was born on the side of a hill, I was born on the side of a hill.'

'Just like '02!' groaned Brenton, as he put the crew to stretching tarpaulins from the barge over the western side to protect the paintwork from the afternoon sun. He had plenty of tins of paint on board, so the crew need not be idle but could give the upper structure two new coats of paint. He settled down to wait, helpless and frustrated, for the fresh that did not come.

To Delie it did not seem as bad as the 1902 drought, because she had not before her eyes the miseries of the dying sheep along the Darling banks, or the dreariness of the mallee farm near which they had stuck the second time. The tall gums that studded the banks retained their even olive-green foliage, the delicate colouring of their mauve and coral twigs, the amber and grey and salmon-pink of huge, smooth trunks.

On one side was what had been an island; now it was a low wooded patch among a sea of mud, where lignums grew in twisted profusion, and native willows and coolabahs drooped their blue-grey leaves. Brenton laid boards from the base of the gangplank across this mud, so that they could walk on to the island.

Across the lagoon in which they were aground was a high yellow cliff rising out of the water, very rich in its colouring against the deep blue of the sky. An irrigation-pipe ran down this, and there was a steam-pump at its base. Out of sight on top of the cliffs there must be a farmhouse.

When the river-bed had dried out sufficiently, Delie got out and walked on the bottom. It had become a mass of solid hexagonal cakes of baked mud, with fissures running down between them so deeply that they seemed to have been formed by some convulsion of the earth's surface. Where the bottom was sandy it had not cracked, but was ringed in successive layers where the water had slowly receded.

She stood in the deepest part yet uncovered, beside a little winding channel, narrow enough for her to jump over, which represented the whole of the Murray's flow. She looked round at the boat, saw that nobody was watching, and, holding her skirts high, she ran and took a flying leap across. She imagined herself telling a ring of open-mouthed grandchildren of 'the day I jumped across the Murray river'.

Looking up at the ringed banks, she saw that at the highest levels green herbage had begun to grow; but where she stood was a dead world. A few empty mussel-shells lay in the cracks, the bleached claw of a yabbie, a shrimp's thorax, a dried-up fish.

Where she stood now, the water would have been about thirty feet over her head. She thought of that huge volume of water, the amount that would be needed just to fill this reach, without flowing steadily through it at two or three miles an hour. It seemed as if the river had died, and would never flow again.

Yet she had seen it like this before; and if only the engineers' plans could be carried out instead of being left to moulder in pigeon-holes in Government Departments of Works, it need never be like this again.

Already the engineers had shown what they could do, with the construction of the huge Burrenjuck Dam on the Murrumbidgee. It was even now saving the lives of stock on irrigated Riverina holdings. Another big dam on the Murray, and a series of weirs and locks to prevent the water flowing away to the sea, were all that was needed to ensure that the river would never run dry again. Only the inability of the different state governments to agree prevented these works from being carried out.

There was even talk of building a great wall or barrage across the mouth, to be closed in time of drought so as to prevent the flowing away of fresh water and the inward flow of salt; for the whole of the lower reaches had now become saline, and a salt-water mullet had been caught at Mannum, more than a hundred miles upstream.

She looked round at the mud-caked slopes and wondered if she would ever see the mouth, the long white beach with the foaming breakers that she had heard about as a child; or if her life would end in some stagnant pool like this, fallen and dwindled from its high purpose, and ringed with the abandoned levels of old achievements.

SIXTY-FOUR

The farmhouse on top of the cliffs was a very different place from the mallee selection where Mrs Slope had led her terrible and hopeless existence. The land was irrigated from the river, and the house, cool and comfortable, built of the local limestone, was surrounded by fruit trees.

The farmer's wife, when she learned of Delie's condition, offered to take the children while she went to hospital. Mrs Melville's own children were all grown up and had left home, except for one son, Garry, who helped his father with the orangery, the lucerne paddocks and the cows. The older son, Jim, was married and lived in the irrigation settlement of the Waikerie.

The house lay well back from the cliffs, down which the only track was at some distance from where the steamer was aground. Here there was a break in the high wall of yellow rock which made a natural stair-way. Above the break, for the last fifty feet, steps had been cut in the cliff-face.

Mr Melville when he wanted to descend preferred to use the pipe, which was quicker if more dangerous; letting himself over the edge of the cliff, he would slide down in a few moments to his pump at water-level. From here a narrow track cut in the base of the cliffs led round to the steps, where he kept a dinghy moored.

Mrs Melville was delighted to have the company of another woman. She had visited the boat, though she was rather scared of the steps, and Delie and the two older children had gone back with her to the farmhouse. But it was the baby Meg who won her heart, with her cheerful friendliness and vivid colouring.

She might have been of the same colouring herself once – her eyes and her brows were still dark, though her hair was iron-grey, and her cheeks had a healthy freshness.

'I'd just love to have four children again,' she told the incredulous Delie.

'But they're so much *work*!' she cried. She had been tremendously busy lately, sewing a pile of new night-gowns for herself and the baby from material in the boat's stock, and catching up on the mending she had been putting off for months.

'That's because you're trying to bring them up in such difficult conditions. How tired you must get of living in such a poky space, and sleeping in a bunk. It must be most uncomfortable.'

'But it's not!' said Delie, watching Mrs Melville fill a kettle and take it across to the stove. 'I love it, and I wouldn't like to live in a house, now. There's just one thing I miss.'

'What's that?'

'A tap with running water.'

'You mean to say you haven't got a tap? You have to dip all your water out of the river with a bucket?'

'Not all. When the engine's running it's pumped automatically to a high tank, and feeds to the bathroom from there. But Brenton says a tap in the galley would be turned on all the time and waste too much water.'

'Well! And you manage to cook in a galley?'

'Oh yes, I learnt to cook in a galley; I taught myself from recipe books, and took lessons from our various men cooks. I was determined to become a *good* cook, and I think I am, but I'm clumsy and get things in a mess of broken eggs and spilled flour.'

'Because you haven't enough room!' said Mrs Melville triumphantly. She looked complacently round her large, tidy kitchen. 'You need more room to work in.'

'No, I don't,' said Delie obstinately. 'Big rooms mean more floor-space to keep clean. It's all so compact on the boat. Think of the time most women have to spend on washing and polishing floors, and windows, and verandas and front steps. Housework is always a waste of time; merely a process of making things clean so that they can get dirty again.'

'Well, I don't know,' said Mrs Melville with a little laugh, but looking rather shocked. 'I've never looked at it that way. And I must say I wouldn't like moving about all the time.' She poured boiling water on the tea, decisively.

'We're not moving at present, and it's terrible.'

'All the same, I think you should persuade your husband – I mean when you have five children – to take some job on dry land, or at least to establish you in a little home along the river somewhere while he travels.'

'I wouldn't think of asking him,' said Delie.

She couldn't help feeling that Mrs Melville had forgotten what four children, the eldest eight, could be like, that she didn't realise what she was letting herself in for in offering to take them for a fortnight. But it was a great relief not to have to leave them with Brenton in his present mood, especially with cases of whisky still on board.

There was a road along the top of the cliffs, but it would be a difficult job to unload the crates by dinghy and have them hoisted up the cliffs for delivery by wagon. On the other side of the river was a waste of dried swamps, lignum, reed-beds and dwindling billabongs.

The *Philadelphia* was aground on a sandspit running out from the island, on the far side from the cliffs. There were plenty of rabbits, and even a few hares on the island, and the river was alive with fish, so there was no lack of fresh meat.

Brenton paid off the engineer and Prentice the Poisoner, and stayed on morose and lonely when Delie and the children left. Winter had begun, but still there had been no rain anywhere to speak of. He felt that he was doomed to be stuck in this hole in the mud for ever; yet he would not leave the boat unguarded.

Mr Melville drove Delie into the nursing-home at Waikerie in his motor-truck, a bumpy and uncomfortable ride, slithering through drifts of sand and crossing dry creek-beds full of stones.

Delie came round after a final anæsthetic with a feeling of triumph. It was not that she had produced another child – that was nothing new now – but that for the first time she felt that she knew how to bear a child. The knowledge which the wise aboriginal women passed on to the young girls of the tribe before they brought forth their first baby upon a clean, antiseptic bed of gum leaves, she had acquired slowly and painfully, alone.

With each of her six confinements she had come nearer to that ancient knowledge, which meant, quite simply, not to fight *against* the pain but to go *with* it – to welcome each twisting, tearing spasm as a step onward, and let herself be carried along like a boulder on the bed of a flooded river.

Instead of bracing herself against the pain she yielded to it, and at once it became less. 'That's right, little one! Push! Struggle! You're getting nearer to the light,' she whispered, unconsciously echoing the songs that the ancient lubras used to hasten the coming child: 'Come! Here is your auntie waiting to see you. Come! See what a beautiful day it is . . .'

The baby was lifted up for a moment for her to see its wet black hair and screwed-up eyes. Like a little Chinese doll, she thought drowsily. The next day she waited and waited for the baby to be brought in – it was a girl, they had told her – but the light began to fade, it was evening and still she had not seen her child.

Suddenly all her old misgivings came back to her. There was something wrong. She had seen only its face last night, at midnight when the birth took place.

'Where's my baby?' she demanded of the sister-in-charge when she came in on her evening round of beds. 'Why won't you let me see her?'

'You'll see her tomorrow,' said the sister soothingly. 'You've no milk yet, anyway. We're letting her have a rest today, after the tiring business of getting born.'

'Why?' said Delie suspiciously. 'It was a normal birth, wasn't it? An easy birth, in fact.'

'Yes, it was. I must say, my dear, you're an ideal patient,' said the sister warmly. 'If they all had their babies with as little fuss as you do . . .'

'I've had plenty of practice.'

She relaxed and stopped worrying. She felt at home in this place, it seemed no time since she'd been here with Meg. And now another baby! She would soon be seeing more than enough of it; meanwhile let her sleep undisturbed while she had the chance . . .

When the baby was brought in the next morning it was awake, looking at her dully from two small, queerly shaped eyes. She gazed at it with a painful curiosity, her heart beating heavily. It seemed apathetic and uninterested in the breast, though with the nurse's help she finally got it to suck.

As soon as the nurse had gone, she examined the features in detail. The nose was a mere blob, the mouth shapeless, the ears unnaturally small and set low down on the head; and the head itself was the wrong shape, wider than it was long.

With shaking fingers she unwrapped shawl and blanket, and laid the child on the pillow. Its limbs seemed normal, if rather short. But the head, and the eyes which disappeared at the corners into puffy folds of flesh, reminded her of that queer, repulsive little boy at the mallee farm, with his small, cunning eyes and animal voice. She heard Mrs Slope's voice: 'The doctor said it could happen to anyone . . .' But she said nothing to the nurse when she came back and put the baby in a crib beside her.

When the doctor came in to see her, with his shrewd, cheerful gaze and jolly rubicund face, she felt better just at the sight of the little man. He had remembered her from the time of Meg's illness, and they were friends.

'The baby – is she all right, doctor?' she asked urgently, struggling to sit up again under the white quilt as soon as he had examined her. She felt tears of weakness and anxiety start from under her lids.

'Of course she's all right,' he said heartily, but his face was turned away as he picked up the swathed bundle from the crib. 'They all look a bit queer the first day or two, you know that.'

'Yes, I know . . . But the shape of her head?'

'H'mm . . . A bit distorted with the stresses of birth, perhaps. Often happens. It will adjust itself in a few days.'

'But it was an easy birth, and she's quite small, only seven pounds.'

'Don't you worry your head, my dear. Worry's no good for nursing mothers. And as for you, young lady, you don't want your tummy upset by milk from a worried mother,' he said, carrying the baby over to the window.

He kept his back to the bed as he examined the child in the full light, feeling the fontanelles at the top of the skull, but Delie watched him intently. He took one tiny fist and uncurled the fingers, examining the palm closely; unwrapped the feet and spread the toes with his fingers. The baby yawned, and he peered at the roof of its mouth.

As he turned to put the baby in the crib again, his back was to the light, but she thought she saw a look of suffering on his face, before it was covered by a mask of cheerfulness.

'Well, you know the formula,' he said. 'Fill 'em up and let 'em sleep. The milk's coming all right, eh? I don't think you'll have any feeding difficulties with this one, and you're in excellent condition. Ten days' rest here, and then you can take her home.'

Her lips moved soundlessly. She wanted to say, 'Is she sub-normal mentally? Will she grow up an idiot?' but the words would not come. She dared not ask.

He gave her a friendly wave from the door and went out.

She lay down and drew the sheet over her head, and gave way to a feeling of helpless horror. She knew, as clearly as if he had told her. She flung off the sheet, leant over the side of the bed and with an effort lifted the child and once more unrolled the shawl. She looked at the feet, and noticed that the big toe seemed to stand away from the others, but otherwise the feet were normally formed. Then the hands; they were certainly not artistic hands, but broader than they were long, with short, stumpy fingers and an incurved thumb. But it was the head that frightened her, the short skull, the malformed ears. In a baby it was not so bad, but this would grow into a girl, a woman . . .

She put the baby to her breast, but as it sucked she turned her face away to the wall.

The matron steadfastly refused to admit that there was anything wrong, though she could not fail to see that the mother was not happy with her child; where other mothers had to be restrained from disturbing their infants' sleep with too many displays of affection, this one hardly ever took hers into the bed except at regular feeding times, but lay with her face turned away from it, staring at the wall or out the window.

On the doctor's next visit, the last before Delie was to go home (for he had been away for a week visiting an urgent case, in the back country north of the river), the matron came in with him, looking solemn, and began:

'I'm afraid we have something to tell you, Mrs Edwards. Your baby will need special care – '

'I know, matron. Would you please let me talk to the doctor alone?'

The matron looked slightly offended, and then swept out majestically, holding her white-capped head regally erect. The doctor raised his eyebrows and gave Delie a helpless look.

'I think you know what I have to tell you, my dear.'

'Yes.' Her voice was toneless and flat. 'My baby is a congenital idiot. She will never be an adult mentally. She will always be misshapen and ugly, and the older she gets the worse she will look. I would just like to know why. My first baby was born dead, a beautiful, perfect child. And now this – this is allowed to live. Why?'

He shrugged his shoulders and spread his hands, palms outward. 'Who can tell? There seems no meaning in these things. If you want to know the clinical reasons, we are still not sure. It seems to happen without reason, yet it's thought that some prenatal condition must be responsible – an endocrine disturbance in the mother, emotional stress, tuberculosis; but we don't know. One thing is known, that the older the mother, the more chance there is of its happening. What are you – thirty-four?'

'Nearly thirty-five. But I knew a case – I saw a case along the

393

river, where the mother was only a girl.'

'More likely a case of cretinism. That has a definite cause in the child's own glands, and doesn't appear usually till the sixth month. It may be possible to cure it. But this – it's a typical case: the simian line, the incurved thumb, the formation of the skull and the feet – I'm afraid nothing can be done for the Mongolian child.'

'Nothing can be done.' But she thought, Oh yes, something can be done. Something must be done.

SIXTY-FIVE

The light-ripples danced on the cabin-roof as Delie lay looking up at it. Running in endless ripples of refracted sunlight . . . dancing, as a child dances, a little girl full of the joy of life . . .

She groaned and turned her face into the pillow. Beside her the baby lay in the crib, quietly, but moving her hands aimlessly, perhaps seeing the bright patterns crossing the ceiling. Delie clutched the pillow-case in an agonised grip.

How hatefully, meaninglessly cruel could life be? Her first child, the child of her love and joy, had not even breathed. And now, out of hate and shame, was born this healthy, breathing, growing . . . monstrosity. For the rest of her life she would have it before her eyes. She knew now how Mrs Slope must feel. Her daughter, too, had been 'a bit soft', and her grandson had been like this.

She lifted her head and looked at the crib, and her face became set like a mask. She got up and went out to the deck where Brenton was putting in set-lines.

'Brenton, could you go up to the farm in the morning and ask Mrs Melville if she'd keep the children a few more days? I know we were supposed to get them tomorrow, but she won't mind.'

'All right, but why?'

'I don't feel – I don't feel quite strong enough. And the baby isn't as well as I'd like.'

'She seems bright enough. Certainly not a beauty, though. She doesn't take after *me*.'

'Will you go, though?'

'I said all right.'

He had taken a fair-sized callop that morning, and Delie baked it with potatoes and a savoury stuffing for dinner.

'You're getting to be quite a cook,' he said grudgingly, taking another helping. 'But you're not eating any. What's wrong?'

'I told you I don't feel too good. And then, I'm worried about – Oh, stop asking me questions!' she flared hysterically.

He stared, and put down his fork. 'You're not quite yourself, are you? Well, go on to bed, if you like. I'll finish this up and wash the things.'

'Would you? I'd . . . I'd rather go for a walk, it would help me to sleep.'

'You'll tread on a tiger-snake.'

'Then I'll take the dinghy and just row round the lagoon.'

She climbed down unaided and got into the dinghy – the same dinghy into which Brenton had helped her on that fateful night so many years ago, in which he had kissed her while they drifted unheeding on the river.

A pang went through her for the inevitable change and decay of human relationships. She saw now that Adam's death had not been the tragedy it had seemed; in her memory he was always young and handsome and loving, she had not had to see him grow coarse-featured and indifferent.

She took the oars and rowed to the end of the stagnant lagoon in which they lay. It was not the same as when the river was flowing. She liked then to row upstream and ship her oars, letting the boat drift down again, slowly, slowly but inescapably borne by the current. It was then that she felt most a part of the river.

Now when she stopped rowing the dinghy stayed still, except to swing slightly in the faint breeze. She listened to the chorus of the frogs, the cry of a startled water-hen, the drip of water from the suspended oars. Time . . . her mind reverted to its obsession, yet she had a feeling that time was suspended as long as she sat there with the oars motionless above the still water.

Yet even now the baby was breathing, growing, becoming older . . . She knew with absolute certainty that this was wrong. She had only to be strong and unflinchingly do what was right, for the sake of the other children, for the sake of the child itself. No false sentiment, no cant about the sacredness of human life, must be allowed to obscure the issue.

With a decisive movement she dipped the oars, breaking the reflection of a star. Only a few bright stars were out, for the sky was still full of cold blue light. As she came under the stern and picked up the rope to tie on, she froze in horror. In the dim light she could see a red stain on the rope. She dropped it with a faint cry. There were two more stains on the dinghy's bow. Blood . . . She looked at her spotless hands, and hurried on board with a painfully beating heart. Brenton was already asleep in the top bunk.

It was a brilliantly sunny morning, and she was walking on the river-bank, on a long beach of yellow sand that sloped into the water. Someone had been digging in the sand not far from the water's edge, she noticed.

She walked towards the uneven heap. It seemed to take a long time to get there. With a curious unwillingness she looked into the hole in the sand. A child lay there, a small boy of about ten years, with smooth fair hair and closed eyes. Instantly she knew that she was looking at a grave.

But surely not this child's grave! He appeared to sleep, his skin was clear and healthy, his cheeks faintly pink, and his hair glistened in the sun. She took a step forward, feeling impelled to wake him. A little cascade of sand fell as she moved, and trickled on to the boy's bare arm.

She saw the eyelids flutter and struggle to rise. The eyes opened; and there was nothing beneath the lids but a white worm-eaten cavity.

With a scream she turned to run, but the sand gave under her feet and seemed to entrap them. She was still screaming when Brenton woke her, bending over the bunk. After that she dozed only fitfully, afraid to sleep again, until the first ray of the morning sun sent the light-ripples dancing across the ceiling.

She knew that the child of her dream was her first son, long buried in the sand of the river-bank up near Torumbarry. He would be ten – no, eleven this year. She got up and swung the bucket over the side, and dashed some cold water over her swollen eyes.

The rope on the bucket reminded her of something, and with superstitious fear she went to the stern and pulled up the dinghy. There was a blob of bright red paint on the rope, and two more on the bows . . . Under one of the thwarts was the small tin of red that Brenton must have been using yesterday to brighten up a lure for cod. She almost laughed aloud at her fears. She felt once more strong and determined.

'I'm going now,' said Brenton. Delie did not look at him, but busied herself with the dishes. The baby, fed and bathed with her usual care, was asleep in the crib. She remembered how Brenton hadn't wanted her to help with the dishes, that night when she first had tea with him on board . . . Strange, how her mind kept reverting to that time. But she knew that the events of that year had led inevitably to the present, to this particular day in her life which she would never forget.

'D'you want anything special from the farm?'

'No. Give the children my love. Mrs Melville will load you with eggs and cream anyway.'

'She'll ask about the baby.'

'Tell her . . . tell her it's all right.'

He climbed rather heavily down into the dinghy. It rocked and then steadied. He fitted the oars and balanced them a moment above the water, before making the first stroke. To Delie, watching impatiently, he seemed to be taking hours to get away.

Because she had been thinking so much of the past, the change in him seemed to strike her afresh. She looked at his thickened figure and heavy, red face, the grey curls that used to be gold as the sun, and down at her own work-stained hands with brown moth patches appearing on the backs. Oh, what has time done to us? she thought. Slowly, softly, imperceptibly making us old!

She went and finished the dishes, putting everything away tidily, sweeping the galley, but all the time going out to see how far Brenton had gone. When she saw him reach the cliffs and fix the dinghy to a boulder, she went up and looked at the baby, still fast asleep. Then she came down again and walked round the bottom deck.

He was going up to the break in the cliff now. She went up to the top deck and came down again. She couldn't stand still for an instant. Then she clenched her hands and climbed the steps again. When she looked into the cabin her heart began to hammer in her chest. Thank God! It had been taken out of her hands.

She saw at once that the sleeping child had rolled on to its face, and was lying inert in the crib. It could lift its head a little, but not for long; the neck-muscles were not strong enough. The pillow was soft and thick.

She turned and ran out of the cabin, down the steps over the paddle-box, and crossed the gangplank over the mud to the island. She had never walked far on the island, for she was afraid of tiger-snakes, but now she went on and on through the thin scrub of native willow and box tree, scarcely looking where she was going. A lignum swamp blocked her way, but she pushed straight on, blindly, through the twining, scratching stems. There would be nothing to hear, she knew; but she wanted to be far out of ear-shot of any sound from the boat.

It was a long island, though not very wide. When she had reached the channel on the other side – nothing but an expanse of mud at present, with a small water-hole in the centre – she went on down its edge and followed round until she was on the boat side of the island, and could see the cliffs, though the steamer was still out of sight.

She thought she would sit and wait till she saw the dinghy leave the cliff landing, for her legs and arms were aching and scratched and bleeding; but she could not rest. After a few minutes she got up again and started round the island in the opposite direction. She was fighting a wild desire to go back to the boat and look at the baby.

At last she came round again to a point almost opposite the boat, and then she heard the creak of oars, the click of the row-locks. She dropped flat behind a bush. Something rustled away from near her feet, a snake or a lizard, but she scarcely noticed. She strained her ears. Was that the child crying? She could never go through this again . . .

Then it came, his shout with a note of alarm in it.

'Delie! Delie! Where are you?'

She forced herself to move slowly, not to run. She must not show any anxiety.

'Delie! My God! She's gone overboard! Delie! Where are you?'

'Here I am. On the island. I was looking for –'

'Come quickly. Why did you leave her?'

'What?'

'The baby – I think she's dead. She must have rolled on to her face. She's not breathing . . .'

'Are you sure?'

He stared at her a moment, struck by the pale composure of her face contrasted with her lacerated limbs and wild hair, as she came across the gangplank.

'Why on *earth* did you go ashore? I came back – and there she was, with her face in the pillow.'

She hurried now, running up the steps. Brenton had put the baby down on the bunk, and it lay there inert, the queer eyes closed for ever. There was no movement of the tiny chest, no pulse in the arteries. Delie flung herself on her knees by the bunk and burst into sobs of relief.

When she had recovered her composure she insisted that he should go in to Waikerie and get the doctor. He wanted to take the baby with him, but she was obstinate. She wanted to face the doctor here.

When he was gone, and the sound of the rowlocks had ceased, she washed herself and did her hair very carefully, and put on her good dress of lilac poplin. Her mind was clear and calm now. She must not appear nervous, she must not act an appearance of grief, for the doctor knew that she must be relieved, not sorry at what had happened.

Then she sat down on the bunk, took the infant on her lap, and stared at it musingly. It was the first time she had looked on death without emotion. Her mind felt cold and emptied of all but simple wonder, as she stared at the little finger-nails – still growing? – and the wispy hair. What had changed, except that the heart no longer beat, the lungs no longer moved?

If somehow breath could be restored, as happened sometimes when a man appeared to be drowned, life would go on as before; and what then became of the theory that a man's soul fled at the moment of death? Soul, personality, mind, seemed to be but a manifestation of energy, much as heat was. And a child so young, without the physical equipment for a proper brain; could it be said to have a 'soul' at all?

Yes, it was death that made life so mysterious. The individual, so fragile, so complicated and delicate in his organism, could so easily die; yet the life-force was indestructible: call it energy, will, motion, rhythm, God, or what you liked.

She stared at the light-ripples in their rhythmic dance over cabin wall and ceiling; it was there, and in the faint, pulsing light of the most distant star, and in the tiniest transparent creature crawling in the river mud, and had been in this scrap of humanity, bud of her own living flesh, and now was gone from it. She saw now that it was wrong to say 'He is gone', 'He has passed away'. Rather one should say 'It has gone; it has left him; he is bereft of life.'

She was still sitting there in a kind of trance, the dead child in her lap, when Brenton returned after two hours, with the doctor. She heard their feet on the paddle-box steps, but she was so stiff and numb that she could not move. For a fleeting moment she thought, It has left me too; I am dead. Then a painful aching began in her legs and arms as the blood began to flow again, and she thought, It must be agony to be recalled to life.

Brenton bent his head under the low door, leading the way. The little doctor followed, a bag in his hand which he set down on a chest. Before glancing at the baby he took Delie's cold hand in his, and looked searchingly into her face.

'You'd better get Mrs Edwards a hot drink,' he said, his cheerful voice subdued. 'Her hands are like ice.'

'Yes, right away,' said Brenton, seeming glad of the excuse to go out again.

'And you lie down there and pull a couple of blankets over you,' said the doctor sternly to Delie. He took up the dead child and laid it on a cloth on top of the chest of drawers.

'I'm . . . all right.'

'You're chilled, and, naturally, feeling a certain amount of shock.' He began loosening the baby's clothes and making his examination. 'H'm, yes . . . asphyxia, obviously. Your husband found her lying on her face, I believe?'

'Yes.'

'How long would that be after you left the boat?'

'I don't know . . . Some time.'

'And she appeared to be all right when you left?'

Silence.

'She was breathing normally when you left?'

'Yes.'

'Why *will* mothers use these soft pillows? Dangerous things.'

The pupils of her eyes were so wide that the eyes appeared black in her pale face. She clutched the top of the blankets and stared at him over the edge. He turned his back on her and covered the baby with a cloth.

'I don't know if I told you, Mrs Edwards; but it may help you to know that few, very few Mongoloid children survive the first five years of life, and only half of those who do ever reach adulthood. Your daughter had a very small life-expectancy anyway.'

'Oh.' It was the faintest breath of sound.

'They are particularly susceptible to pulmonary infection and tuberculosis, so that with your medical history . . .'

He walked over to the cabin window and looked out at the sparse trees and tangled lignum bushes of the island. 'You often go for walks on the island, Mrs Edwards? It doesn't look particularly inviting.'

'Oh . . . I prefer rowing, but you see Brenton had the dinghy, and I thought –' Her voice trailed away. He had turned and looked at her, his bright little eyes shrewd and comprehending. In that instant she knew that he knew. The words died in her throat. There was an interminable moment of silence, in which she saw herself arrested, charged with murder, convicted, sentenced to death or life imprisonment.

'. . . Well, I must sign the death certificate. Cause of death: asphyxia. There will be no need for you to attend the inquest. I will give evidence of death by misadventure while the child was unattended.'

'Thank you, doctor.' And her large eyes said a great deal more.

Brenton came in with a cup of hot cocoa, and asked the doctor to step into the saloon for a whisky. He had brought a bottle of hot water wrapped in a towel to put at her cold feet. Delie turned her eyes away from the tiny shape under the cloth and drank the hot milk. She felt suddenly, overwhelmingly sleepy.

SIXTY-SIX

The children asked very few questions. They had not seen the baby, so for them it had scarcely existed. They came back to the boat looking healthy and happy, and Delie could not have enough of them, of their eager voices and bright, intelligent eyes. Her breasts ached with the unwanted milk, but already time had washed a silt of days over the dreadful fact that lay like a rock at the bottom of her mind.

Had the doctor said anything, hinted anything to Brenton over their whiskies, or on the way back in the dinghy? It seemed to her that he looked at her strangely. He was getting more morose as the river failed to move, and the whisky became a daily habit.

One morning, hearing the crack of the rifle, she came out to see him aiming at a formation of pelicans, flying downstream towards the nesting grounds of the Coorong, far to the south, He fired again, but the undulating flight of the birds did not change. He swore, taking new aim.

'Brenton!' She put her hand on his arm. 'You wouldn't shoot *pelicans*!'

His eyes had a dazed and clouded look, but he dropped the rifle and went inside. She heard the cork being drawn from a new bottle of whisky.

'I wish you wouldn't drink so much, Brenton,' she said to him one night, trying to keep her voice level and impersonal, to avoid nagging. 'It's bad for you, and – '

'What else is a man to do, stuck in a puddle with nothing coming in but doctors' bills and hospital accounts . . . and a wife that's no use to him.' He moved the whisky bottle irritably on the saloon table.

'If only you wouldn't sit here, drinking all alone – '

'Who else is there to drink with? You?' He laughed nastily.

'You could go over and see Jim Melville.'

'And climb up that cliff in the dark? What if I fell down and broke me neck? Where'd you be then, eh? Though I don't believe you'd care, apart from the money angle.'

'Brenton! How can you say – '

' "Brenton! How can you!" ' he mimicked. 'I don't mean you're interested in money, you haven't enough sense. I mean you'd like to be free, rid of the lot of us, and be able to spend all your time dabbing paint on canvas. You hate responsibility, don't you? Only you can't get out of it, and without me you'd be worse off than ever.'

She was struck silent. There was a grain of truth in his words, enough to startle her into a doubt of her own motives. Had she not, subconsciously, desired the baby's death before it was ever born? Had she welcomed its imbecility as a justification? She felt as if a black pit had suddenly opened just in front of her feet. Turning and pushing open the wire-screen door of the cabin, against which moths and midges flung themselves in a mad dance, she stumbled out on deck.

There were the stars, unchanged, unchanging; Orion moving towards the west, the Cross swinging low over the island. On the river they lay reflected, in the same patterns yet softer, slightly blurred. If she looked down long enough the river became a black sky, the sky a great river which flowed for ever westward. Above was below, below above, and all became unreal.

But her mind shook off the solace of the stars.

'You want to be rid of the lot of us.' Did he suspect what had happened, that she had deliberately walked off and left the baby to die? The feeling of certainty in the rightness of what she had done deserted her. She walked up and down in a torment of self-loathing.

But gradually her old ideas asserted themselves. The doctor had known, she was sure, and had tacitly approved. The child would never have been an adult mentally, and had little life-expectancy. She clung to the idea that in the infant was only the germ of a soul, which grew and developed with the body and mind. What had been destroyed was only one step further from the embryo and the seed; only a potential. And she had done nothing except by default, whatever her intentions had been . . .

And hadn't she felt the same bitter despair before the last two were born? Yet natural love had not failed her there. And she had jumped in to save Alex from the river without any hesitation. No! It was a cruel lie of Brenton's. Her courage flowed back to sustain her.

Mrs Melville came to see her, bringing fruit and flowers as to an invalid, and an overwhelming sympathy which she found hard to bear. Yet such kindness brought tears of weakness to her eyes.

There was still no break in the drought by August. One day Mr Melville came to the cliff-top, shouting and waving his arms, with some news so important that he couldn't wait to slide down the pipe and come over in the dinghy. He cupped his hands and shouted. Delie and Brenton, staring across the water, heard faintly the one word, 'War'.

They looked at each other soberly, impressed by the historic moment. There had been rumours of war, and now it had come. It would not affect Australia much, of course, and certainly not this stagnant reach of an inland river; but there was something solemn and dramatic about the thought of men, even on the other side of the world, marching out to kill each other, to conquer and destroy.

Delie remembered the Boer War, and how she had been afraid Brenton might go. Thank heaven her sons were too young for this one. It would be over in a few months, Brenton said.

He celebrated the news by opening another case of whisky As the number of full bottles steadily decreased, he began to stay up later and later at night, singing loudly to himself, beating time with a bottle on the table and keeping Delie awake.

His temper had become so uncertain that she was afraid to remonstrate with him. She kept out of his way as much as possible in such a confined space. He slept late in the mornings, and got up with a sour breath and bloodshot eyes. He still walked with a stiff leg, and she noticed lately that his voice had become blurred again, almost as it had been just after his accident.

One night when he was particularly noisy she crept to the saloon door to shut it so that he might not wake the children. Alex and Meg now slept in what had been the engineer's and mate's cabin, and the two older boys in the small cabin that had been newly built aft.

As Delie silently stretched her arm in for the handle of the door, Brenton raised his bloodshot eyes.

'Leave it alone!' he said roughly. 'I want some air.'

'But – '

'And gerrout, djer hear me? Lookin' a' me all the time with those great eyes . . .' His grey curls were on end, the vein stood out in his neck like a blue cord.

She shrank back on to the deck, and was startled by bumping into a small figure.

'Gordon! What are you doing here?' she whispered.

He grasped her hand and pulled her urgently along the deck. 'Why's he making such a noise? Is he mad?'

'Shh! No, it's just that – it's not his fault, but the drought's got him down, and he's drinking too much. He – '

She stopped short, listening rigidly to the slurred voice from the saloon:

'Murderess! Bloody murderess! You're no berrer than I am, d'you hear? Least I wouldn' leave me own flesh an' blood t'die. I oughter finish you off before y' kill any more with yer damn carelessness . . .'

Petrified, clutching each other's hands, the mother and son stood on the dim deck. They heard a chair scrape back, fall to the floor, a sound of breaking glass . . . then the click of a rifle-breech being opened and shut.

'Quick!' Delie breathed almost soundlessly into Gordon's ear. 'Run aft and get Brenny out of bed, and untie the dinghy. Get in and hold it ready till I come. Quiet, now!'

As she slipped into the cabin where the two youngest lay, and lifted a sleeping child on to each shoulder, her mind was calm and clear. Something had been happening to Brenton for weeks past; it seemed as if the old injury was having some long-delayed effect on his brain, and even now, perhaps, he was insane.

She was half-way down the steps to the lower deck when Alex began to murmur sleepily against her ear.

'Hush! Hush, darling,' she whispered in terror.

But, half-awake, he began to twist in her arms. 'No! *No!* I don't wanner!' he shouted. There was a dragging step on the deck above, and Brenton's voice:

'Whatsh goin' on there?'

She did not answer, but, reaching the bottom deck, fled aft. She handed the children down to Gordon, and as she was climbing after them she saw Brenton at the rail of the top deck, a lamp in one hand, his rifle in the other.

'Come back here!' he roared.

With trembling hands she grasped the oars and swung the dinghy round under the shelter of the paddle-box, where he could not see them. Then she rowed as hard as she could for the landing across the river.

'Come back, y' bitch!' He was on the lower deck now. There was a sharp crack, and a bullet skipped on the water close by. Thank goodness it was so dark! But her fear was not of the wildly aimed gun, but that he might jump in and swim after them, perhaps overturn the dinghy. But he remained, cursing, on the deck. A second shot, a third echoed back from the cliffs. Then there was a muffled thump, and silence.

She could not remember afterwards how she got the whimpering, frightened children up the cliff track in the darkness. Without Gordon she would never have managed it. Perhaps the darkness helped, for they could not see the steepness of the steps and how one slip could plunge them all into the river. The Melvilles' farm was in darkness, but soon there were friendly lights and voices.

'I'm afraid, I'm afraid!' she moaned. 'There was a dreadful thump, and then nothing. I think he may have shot himself.'

Mrs Melville gave the shivering, frightened boys some warm milk and popped them into the beds they had occupied a short time before, while Delie put down the two youngest. She insisted that Mr Melville, who wanted to go to the boat alone, should not do so without the local policeman and the doctor.

'If he's alive he may be dangerous,' she said. 'He has the gun, and he seemed quite mad. But please go as soon as you can. He may be wounded.'

A faint, cold dawn was breaking and the roosters were crowing in the Melvilles' yard when the farmer returned, looking tired and drawn.

'He's not dead,' he said, laying a kindly, heavy hand on Delie's shoulder and pressing her down into a chair near the glowing wood stove. 'But . . . you must be brave. The doctor says he's had a stroke, and will be paralysed for the rest of his life. He will live unless he has another stroke; that would probably be fatal. I've taken him into the Waikerie hospital.'

SIXTY-SEVEN

In 1915 the river began to flow again. Delie heard the curlews crying in the swamps and knew that the drought was ending; but by now she knew also that Brenton, who had been so strong, so active, so virile, would never move again, but was reduced to an inert lump of flesh.

Ironically, now that he was no longer capable of navigating a boat, the river reforms he had advocated for so long began to be carried out. The last drought (which had meant among other things that the Renmark fruit-growers had to transport their goods by horse and cart to the railhead at a cost of eighteen and six a ton extra) had brought the bickering States to final agreement over the locking question.

South Australia was to build nine locks between Blanchetown and Wentworth; the river would be converted into a series of great steps, each forty miles long, ensuring a depth of six feet all the year round. On 5 June 1915, Sir Henry Galway, Governor of South Australia, laid the foundation stone of the first lock at Blanchetown.

Delie read the report of the ceremony, of the cheering crowds and the Parliamentary party in the *Marion*, to the silent Brenton. He could hear what was said to him, though he did not always appear to take in the meaning of the words. He answered questions by closing his eyes, once for yes, twice for no. He had not lost any weight, and the sight of such a big, strong-looking man lying there helpless was worse than if he had looked thin and weak.

When he first came back from the hospital, he was able to articulate a little. But all he said, over and over again, was, 'I want . . . I want . . .'

Though she strained her ears in agony, bending close to his lips, and though the sweat broke out on his brow with the terrible effort he made to express his wish, he never got past those two words. She wondered if he wanted to say that he preferred to die and be done with it, or if there was some person he particularly wanted to see. But when she suggested this, and mentioned different names, he only blinked his eyes wearily in a negative.

After that he did not speak again. His mouth never moved, except to take the spout of the feeding cup. His lips were not twisted by the stroke, but had taken the line she remembered in Aunt Hester's mouth towards the end – a downward curve of bitter resignation, yielding nothing, unchanging and severe.

Mrs Melville had adopted Delie and her family. Brenton had a front room with a big bed; Delie slept on a stretcher beside him. He could call her attention by making a noise in his throat. Well, there would be no more babies, anyway, thought Delie. Instead she had a man to nurse who was helpless as a baby, and who would never grow out of it . . . a life sentence. She couldn't help feeling that she was being punished.

To repay Mrs Melville, who would not take a penny in board, Delie began to make small arty objects for her hostess. She painted a glass lampshade with a river scene, made book-covers and penholders of coloured suede, and even used her precious oil-paints for pen-painting on doilies of black silk – an art which Mrs Melville appreciated more than the finest landscape.

This gave her an idea for making money. The next time she was in Waikerie she went into the leading draper's shop and showed some of her work. The result was a commission to paint knick-knacks with local scenes for the tourists who visited the river in the summer months.

Mrs Melville asked her what she was going to do with the steamer; wouldn't it be better to sell it, and perhaps invest the money in a small shop where she could sell the things she made? But Delie shook her head obstinately. The steamer was half

Brenton's, and it was his life; without it he would not wish to live. Somehow she would get the *Philadelphia* working again.

Before the first big fresh came down the river she had sat for the Harbours Board examination and received her Master's certificate – the first woman ever to qualify as a steamboat captain on the Murray. She had completed her two years' experience as acting-mate on the *Philadelphia*, and she passed her theoretical exam with flying colours.

Luckily she had a visual memory, and she could close her eyes and see the long Moorna reach and the burnt stump you kept in line when the channel crossed over, or the treacherous point that stuck out opposite the end of Pollard's Cutting . . .

She had the certificate framed and took it proudly to show Brenton.

'Aren't you pleased? Doesn't it show you must have taught me well?'

A brief closing of the eyelids.

'Darling, the river's coming down; soon the *Philadelphia* will have enough water under her to float her again. Would you like to go back on the river?'

His lids closed long and emphatically. When they opened again his eyes, now more grey than blue yet still alive and alert in his helpless body, sought hers anxiously.

'Don't worry. I've sent a telegram for Charlie, and I know he'll come for your sake. The boys can stay here and go to school – it's not very far across the paddocks, and they can have a pony ride. I've promised Mrs Melville to let her have Meg too, for a while, but not Alex until his chest gets stronger. I'll insist on paying board for them.

'In a few years they'll make good deck-hands, but they must go to school, and meanwhile I've got a boy from the draper's in Waikerie who's mad about steamers and would pay us to let him come as crew. You'll still be the skipper –'

He closed his eyes twice.

'Well, *I'll* be the skipper, and you'll be the mate. We'll build a big window in your cabin so that you can see all that goes on. Won't that be fine?'

He closed his eyes, rather wearily, and she pressed his big, nerveless hand. Tears of sympathy started to her eyes, and she put her head down beside his. All past bitterness and wrong had been wiped out by his terrible misfortune. She could feel nothing but tenderness and love for the magnificent wreck he had become, like a once proud steamer hopelessly aground.

He, too, seemed to have forgotten his mad rage against her. His eyes would light with something like pleasure when he saw her enter the room. But the expression of his mouth never changed, though its muscles were not completely paralysed; he could still eat.

Everything else had to be done for him; he was as helpless as a new-born infant. Yet Delie hoped to act as his nurse, look after a young child, and run a paddle-steamer with the aid of a mad engineer and a boy who had never been inside a wheel-house. She would have to get a cook, she realised; he and Alex would be able to keep an eye on Brenton when she was busy at the wheel. For the rest, they would just have to tie up when she was not steering, at least until she had taught the boy to know a snag from a reef.

And her painting? There would be no time for that any more. Her youthful ambition had faded with the years; she no longer cared to set the Yarra on fire, so long as she could be left quiet to paint the truth that was in her. But there was no time now. Firmly she packed her painting things away in a locker, snapped a padlock on the latch and threw the key into the river.

Charlie McBean arrived to see Brenton. His wild eyebrows were more white than grey now, but his eyes still had a blue gleam of independence.

Though she had warned him what to expect, he became speechless with shock when he saw what time had done to his old skipper. He could only sit and press the lifeless hand, blinking his fierce old eyes rapidly, and breathing a waft of onion-laden breath across the bed.

The engine and the boiler he greeted like old friends, and went over them lovingly with a piece of cotton rag, crooning to himself. 'I know the old girl's ways, and she knows mine, Missus,' he said. 'She'll always do 'er best for me.'

'Teddy's still the skipper, you understand,' said Delie, who wondered how Charlie would react to working for a woman. 'I've got my ticket, in case of any queries from the Board; but he'll be able to see everything that goes on from his cabin, and direct things from there.'

This was a myth, and they both knew it, but Charlie nodded vigorously and polished his nose with the back of his hand.

'Teddy Edwards would rot on dry land, just like I would,'

he said. 'Even the way 'e is, 'e's a better skipper than most. Poor old Teddy – never would of believed it, if I 'adn't seen 'im with me own eyes.' He sighed windily, and Delie retreated a little from the blast of onion-laden air. Charlie had evidently been applying the onion therapy after a bender. 'You're game, Missus; I'll give you that in.'

Delie blushed like a girl, and smiled. She knew what high praise this was from the misogynist Charlie.

'There's just one thing, Charlie. No spragging the gauge. She's not as young as she was, and if anything happened I'd feel it was my fault. The skipper wouldn't stand a chance if she blew up.'

'*Me* sprag the gauge!' said Charlie as if offended at the very idea. 'What do you take me for?'

He needed this job, for he was too unreliable with his drinking-bouts for a mail steamer or a passenger boat that had to keep to a time-table; and the private trading steamers which might have employed him were getting less. The drought had been another blow to the river trade; the railways were taking more and more away from the boats.

Delie had arranged for the sale of the rest of the whisky to a hotel in Waikerie. She wanted to get rid of this cargo before Charlie disposed of it for her. She was wondering how they were ever to establish themselves as a trading vessel again without any capital for buying new stock, when an unexpected windfall solved her problems.

It was as if dear old Uncle Charles had known of her need and sent the money. A letter arrived, which had been long delayed in its journey to various towns along the river, telling of his death and her inheritance of the farm property.

In the first moment she was tempted to give up her difficult plan of running the steamer alone, and go back to the farm with her family, where at least they could live off the land and would not starve. But this would be a retrograde step and she knew it. Her courage rose again to meet the challenge of the future.

Probate would have been granted by now; she wired the Executor company in Echuca to sell, to realise what they could and send her the capital. She could depend on them to get as good a price as possible, as their commission depended upon it. Then she set about ordering stores; no whisky, but a great many small useful items which would sell readily among housewives far from the nearest shop.

The last connection with her own family in Australia was now gone, and Brenton's only relatives lived in Sydney. Yet she had new ties in her children, natives of this country as she was not, third generation Australians through their father. To them England would be but a misty country beyond the seas, learned about in geography lessons but remote from their experience. Perhaps they would return one day, but she would not. She still feared the sea.

Mr Melville, that handy man, had put a new, large window in the cabin over the bed that had been installed for Brenton, and as soon as they were ready to leave he was carried aboard.

As he lay looking up at the dancing light-ripples on the cabin ceiling, his face seemed to relax; the bitter, closed lines of his mouth looked more content, or at least resigned. Remembering how he used to show her the wild flowers in the bush when they were first married, she picked some Murray daisies to put in his cabin, the small everlastings like stiff, golden suns surrounded by white flames.

Thinking to cheer him, she put one of the papery flowers in his hand that lay lifelessly on the coverlet. There was a noise in his throat, and to her horror she saw two tears form in the eyes that looked at the flower. They ran down towards the pillow. He closed his eyes but the tears continued to force their way out. She had never seen him cry before.

She flung herself beside him, feeling shamed and desolated. All the consoling words that rose in her throat died there before they could be uttered. What could one say to a man in his plight? The flower had already said for her, 'Spring is here; life goes on just the same without you.'

He could not even raise a hand to brush away the tears. She took a handkerchief and mopped them for him, and then used it on her own eyes.

'Charlie has steam up,' she said at last. 'We're ready to cast off. You'll feel better once we're moving, you always said a boat was a live thing, and you'll feel how glad she is to be off again. You watch out the window and see if I handle her right. Brenton, can you hear me?' For his stillness frightened her.

His eyes opened and blinked once. She dropped a kiss upon his stony face and went out, feeling an angry rebellion against life which could do this to a man. Usually she loved life, but there had been times, the time of the wreck, of Adam's death, and the loss of her first baby, when its senseless cruelty revolted

411

her . . . And Brenton had been such an active, vital person.

As soon as she was in the wheel-house, her spirits rose again. This was more than just a setting out; it meant leaving behind a hateful place and moving into a future that could not be worse. It was only parting with the three children that gave her a pang. But she would be calling at the farmhouse regularly, and she knew that Mrs Melville would look after them better than she could herself. Little Meg had taken to her at once.

It was a proud and thrilling moment when, with the ropes inexpertly cast off by the new deckhand, she brought the *Philadelphia* round and headed her downstream.

The shrill, indomitable note of her whistle echoed from the cliffs as if she had not lain there useless for more than a year. The red-gum paddles bit into the water; smoke panted from the funnel and streamed out across the river.

Charlie came up from below and stood at the bottom step of the wheel-house.

'You're doin' all right, Missus,' he said. 'I never bin engineer with a woman givin' orders before, but I'll get used to it. Just go easy on that there whistle for a bit, willyer? The new 'and is a ruddy useless bandicoot as a fireman, and I'll 'ave ter 'elp 'im till 'e gets the knack of it.'

'Right-oh, Charlie. That was just for the skipper's benefit.'

But it was for herself, too; a challenge to the future, a defiant cry against fate. She closed her eyes and heard the faint echoes of that peal, so wild and free, echoing back and back from bends far out of sight.

*still glides
the stream*

And the leap of the startled fish in the river
Laps into the stillness that brims on forever.

Roland Robinson

SIXTY-EIGHT

Slowly the faint flush of pink deepened behind the willows. Smoky mist hung low on the river. A reed-warbler babbled its liquid notes from a hidden nest.

Dawn was hushed and expectant, awaiting the deeper sound which now approached: growing from a distant panting to a regular, throbbing beat as the small paddle-steamer *Philadelphia* rounded the downstream bend with her twin paddles churning the water. The hollow, painted shell of the sky seemed to be overflowing with the sound.

With a great beating of wings, a flotilla of pelicans took off from the backwater beyond: flying, their ungainly bodies became suddenly graceful. They flew round and round the steamer at a distance of half the river's width, in a silent, ghostly motion.

The woman who stood alone in the wheel-house watched them with delight as they circled low above the water, like the spirits when they flew round the ship in 'The Ancient Mariner':

Around, around, flew each sweet sound . . .

And indeed, sometimes I begin to feel like the Mariner, she said to herself, 'alone on a wide, wide sea'. Except for the banks and cliffs of course, and Charlie popping up to complain about the new fireman or the Limb o' Satan or the useless lot of wood we took on at the last woodpile.

She stopped, suddenly aware that she was talking aloud.

Talking to herself! She was beginning to get queer, like a 'hatter' in some lonely camp on a deserted billabong.

She badly needed someone else to talk to, besides children and crew and the Engineering Department labourers at the Lock works. Yet the works provided their means of livelihood, now that she had sold all her stock to provide for the children and pay doctors' bills for her husband. She hadn't enough capital to become a trader again, though fortunes were being made in that way with floating stores. And the boat was not big enough for a passenger run, while much of the wool went to Melbourne or Sydney by rail these days.

The building of the first lock and weir across the Murray was using great quantities of manpower and material. The *Philadelphia* was one of the boats commissioned by the Works Department to bring barge-loads of equipment from the railhead at Murray Bridge – iron sheet-piling for coffer-dams, pumping engines, blocks and tackle, piles and pile-driving machinery. It was certainly a change from dress-lengths and household goods, her old stock-in-trade.

Blanchetown was like a small city, with the huts of the construction camp and the stores that had grown up about them. And when this lock was completed there would be a dozen more built to harness the river into a series of still pools, each forty miles long, like the steps in a giant staircase.

She brought the wheel round and straightened out again for the seven-mile reach. Looking back over her shoulder, she watched the loaded barge following like an obedient sheep, the bargemaster spinning his own wheel away at the stern. The steering-chains rattled, the funnel panted, the paddles hit the water with regular blows. All was well; not even a complaint from Charlie. Their speed, she judged, was about eight knots. She must remember to slow down, when she approached the Lock works, to five miles an hour according to the regulations.

She smiled wryly, thinking how Brenton had stamped and stormed over the Government's do-nothing attitude when he was well. Now the great plan was actually in motion (the first stone had been laid more than a year ago, in 1915) and was well under way. It was the Lock building which provided them with a livelihood, while Brenton lay in his bunk and stared out of the window with the blue eyes which were the only live things in his great helpless body.

As he recovered from his stroke he had begun to talk again and, though it was in a halting mumble, he seemed less cut off, more like a normal man now that he could at least communicate his wants. He would watch the passing scene, the moving banks, the bustle of the Morgan wharf from his cabin, but he never spoke of the running of the steamer or showed any interest in the details of her cargo or schedule. He had resigned all that part of his life when he was struck down.

Life now – the whole exciting world of the river with its rivalries, steamers and skippers and recalcitrant crews, races and

416

brawls, fires and snaggings, beer and girls, swimming and diving and racing a falling river – all had narrowed to one small room, the ministrations of the wife he could never hold in his arms again, and the recurring interest of meals (cut up small and eaten with the aid of his left hand) breaking the monotony of the long day.

The steamer was now approaching the first bend at the end of the Long Reach, one of the few places where the river flowed straight for more than a mile or two.

'In close here. Cut the point, but don't come under too soon . . . Now keep her steady on the burnt tree till you open up the next reach.'

It was as if she heard his voice, instructing and chiding, and the map of the river unrolled in her mind as she had often unrolled the long linen chart on the wheel-house shelf, with its ominous cross-hatchings for hidden rocks and sandbars coloured yellow and its occasional warning letters: 'V.D.' for Very Dangerous, sometimes qualified with 'Bad at low water'.

Philadelphia leaned against the wheel-house windows and held her namesake steady on her course, following the invisible channel which crossed the river-bed here in a long diagonal line.

She had not cut the point, which would have meant crossing the sweep of the current at right angles and then fighting the wheel to get the steamer lined up again, because she was not strong enough to follow the time-honoured system of 'top end' skippers like Brenton Edwards, used to the short, sharp bends of the upper river; she had worked out her own system of taking them. She swung the steamer wide – a safer manoeuvre really, for shallow sandbars were usually found lying off the points – and took the current full on the bows, aiming for the bight of the next bend. Then, when it was time to swing, the current pushed the stern round for her, helping instead of hindering.

Beyond, a brilliant orange sandhill caught the first rays of the rising sun, seeming to flame with pure colour. It rose from the river's edge, its crest a curve of warm ochre against the cool pale blue of the sky. Ahead were the bare hills and cliffs about Blanchetown, lit to pink and gold by the sun, opalescent through the blue haze of morning. A few windows glittered like yellow diamonds. She watched as the escort of pelicans left to plane down to a quiet billabong behind the fringing line of gum trees. Mist was curling up from the river like wisps of steam.

Delie, who had once painted under the name of Delphine

Gordon, felt the old unrest rise in her throat as if it would choke her. Oh to stop, to rest, to be able to stay in one place long enough to stare her eyes full and then translate her vision into paint!

There were certain colour combinations as of this particular gold and orange and blue, which gave her a sensation physically painful in its intensity. But her paints were locked away and she had thrown the key in the river.

Now, as she stood rapt in contemplation of the scene, she was reminded of another time when she had looked through a window – though not the window of a wheel-house – and concentrated on the colour of the sky in its subtle gradations of blue. She had not thought of it for years, yet now she saw the whole scene of twenty years ago: the green plush tablecloth, Miss Barrett's soft brown curls, Adam's young embarrassment . . . One of those companions was removed by death and the other by distance, yet both existed somewhere in the convolutions of her brain.

She had wondered, when Adam died, if he could ever recede, his image fade from her mind and heart. Now she knew that all relationships were inexorably ended by time, yet existed in their own reality for ever. The little girl she had been, digging moss from between her grandfather's rose-coloured bricks, was for ever more a part of the fabric of life; just as the Miocene fossils in these limestone cliffs existed both now and millions of years ago when they were sentient creatures living in a warm sea.

While steering the boat she had half-consciously noticed the Works settlement approaching, without being aware of how close it was. Now she realised with a shock that she had forgotten to blow the whistle to warn the man working the 'flying-fox' to raise the cables.

They stretched in a black line across the river just ahead of the *Philadelphia*, charging upstream at eight knots. The hopper full of stone and cement was near the centre of the stream, weighing down the wires.

She grabbed the rope of the whistle and thrust the throttle back to dead slow, in the one movement. It was too late to blow a warning now, but she must let off some steam or they'd go sky-high. The whistle screamed on a desperate note. There was a loud rending noise, followed by a crash. Part of the wheel-house had been carried away with the funnel, which had fouled the lowest cable, and the funnel had crashed down on the after-deck. Smoke belched down over the engine and firebox.

Charlie McBean, the engineer, came rushing out on deck with his grey beard standing on end with surprise.

'What the flamin' hell's goin' on?'

But she was too shocked to answer him. Looking back through the gaping hole in the corner of the wheel-house, Delie saw the Works man dancing in rage on his platform, while a right-angled piece of wood still hung on the quivering cable.

Workmen were running out of tents and huts to see the cause of this commotion before breakfast. Some were hopping on one leg, dragging on their trousers as they came. She had certainly caused a sensation.

With the engine choking in its own fumes and the blow-off valves screaming out steam, the *Philadelphia* limped into the bank. Before the excited crowd reached her, her owner could hear their comments drifting on the clear morning air and her ears burned.

'Steamed straight into it. You'd think 'e never even saw it.'

'There was a woman in the wheel-house. Skipper letting 'is wife steer while 'e sleeps in –'

'No, she *is* the skipper. Geez, where you been all yer life? That's Delie Edwards, she's got 'er Master's ticket for the lower river. Takes that boat up an' down all the time, kids as deck-hands and a crazy old coot as engineer. Her old man had a stroke or something, never comes on deck.'

'They didn't orter let women have charge of a steamer.'

'Ar, they're starting to run everything these days, with so many blokes away at the war. (I'd be there meself, if it wasn't for me flat feet.) They'll be taking all the men's jobs, you'll see.'

'Cold feet, did yer say?'

'Who said that? Who was the bastard said that? I'll show yer –'

Delie felt hopeless fury, with herself and with the men. It had been a long struggle to get her ticket, to get herself recognised as a responsible, intelligent adult of the human species, not just a woman capable of doing a man's job. Because she was small and still slender, fine-boned and delicate-looking, they classed her as helpless. They could not gauge her obstinacy and her indomitable will to succeed.

Now she had played into the hands of the reactionaries

damaged Government property by straining the cable, damaged her only asset, the steamer, and her own reputation as a skipper in the eyes of her crew and the Lock workers – all, of course, men.

Still trembling from the shock of having the wheel-house roof torn from over her head, she felt tears of mortification in her eyes. Then she remembered Brenton lying helpless in his cabin, on the roof of which the funnel had fallen with such a crash; not knowing what they had hit, or what had happened. But she could not leave the wheel.

Young Alex came along the deck, pulling a jumper over his dark head.

'What happened, Mum? Gee, what *happened*?' he cried. Charlie McBean had dived back to help the fireman damp down the firebox and stop the clouds of smoke.

'Nothing much. The funnel fell off,' she said brightly. 'Go and tell Dad. Speak slowly and clearly and make sure he understands. He must be worried. Run, Alex.'

She brought the steamer into the bank with an expert sweep, so that the barge followed in line. The Limb and young Brenny tossed the ropes to the waiting men and ran out the gangplank with accustomed smoothness and speed. As soon as she had made sure Brenton was all right, Delie went to make her explanations and apologies to the head clerk of the works. Instead she met the consulting engineer in charge of construction, who was a Canadian.

An elaborate plant had been installed under his direction, with a floating quarry from which the flying-fox would carry stone and cement across the river to the great coffer-dam, whose piles were now being driven deep into the river's sandy bed. A steel tower was fixed on one bank, and on the other was a travelling head-crane which ran on wheels and rails.

'Think nothing of it, Ma'am,' said the brown-faced, solidly built Canadian when she nervously explained it to him. 'The cable didn't part – it can easily be stretched taut again. You should be more worried at the damage to your boat.'

'Oh, she's insured. And as I was travelling upstream, with only one barge in tow, the Underwriters' Association will pay up. I'm thinking more of the loss of time while we fit a new funnel. Also the possibility of a fine from the Department or the Harbours Board.'

'Now, now, Ma'am; I can guarantee they won't do anything so ungallant as to charge you. Your throttle jammed open, and there was nothing you could do. You blew the warning whistle as soon as you realised you couldn't stop in time. That's about what happened, I guess.'

Delie smiled with relief. 'You are very kind,' she said. 'The fact is, I was dreaming . . . about the past . . . and forgot that two material bodies cannot occupy the same space at the same time.'

Cyrus James looked at her with new interest, and speculated about that past. When she smiled, she was quite beautiful – not young, but womanly and appealing. And she had the loveliest blue eyes; he'd thought they were dark at first, but that was only the lashes shading them. Now that her too-taut, rather haggard features had relaxed, she was charming. How old? Thirty-five, perhaps.

She seemed an educated woman, too. It was odd. He'd heard of the woman skipper, but he'd expected someone hard and weather-beaten, with a raucous voice and muscles like a man's. Why, this little thing didn't look as if she could handle her own steamboat and a crew of men!

He looked down at her, smiling, conscious of his height beside her smallness. He said: 'Waal, Ma'am, now that we've met I sure hope you'll call again some time. Don't wait to break a cable or run into a cement pier. We don't get that much feminine company around here.'

Her smile vanished. Her chin lifted perceptibly, and her level black brows drew down.

'Thank you, but I don't make a habit of running into things. However, I'm sure my husband would be glad to entertain you aboard the *Philadelphia*, if you care to visit us. He's a – an invalid, you know.'

'Yes; I'm sorry, Ma'am – Mrs Edwards, isn't it?' His voice was serious and sympathetic; he regretted his former bantering tone. 'James is the name – Cyrus P. James.'

'How do you do, Mr James? I hope we may meet in pleasanter circumstances in the future. And now I must go and see about the repairs.'

He accompanied her along the bank a little way, reluctant to let her go, until at last she stopped, held out her hand and firmly bade him good-bye.

He stood looking after her with new respect. How she had fired up when he tried to tease her a little and how quietly and determinedly she had dismissed him! He sensed in her unexpected reserves of spirit, in spite of her delicate frame. He resolved to see more of her in the future.

SIXTY-NINE

As though it objected to the attempt at harnessing its waters, which had flowed unimpeded across nearly a sixth of the continent for so many thousands of years, the Murray rose in a mighty flood. The new coffer-dam filled with water, and work on the Lock and weir came to a standstill.

Whole haystacks came sailing down the river, besides drowned beasts and fallen trees, and innumerable tiger-snakes were washed out of hollow logs. Water filled the main street of Mannum, washing about the pillars of the hotel veranda, and barges for the first time floated level with the high Morgan wharf. It was the biggest flood yet seen, bigger than the '70 or the '90 floods remembered by old-timers.

On a low river the *Philadelphia* could easily get loadings because of her shallow draught, but now every steamer on the lower river was in action. The machinery-carting job cut out with the flooding of the Lock works and, as Delie's ticket was a limited one for the lower river only, she could not go above Wentworth seeking cargoes of wool from the Darling.

She took a load of stores up to one of the village settlements and came back with produce from the irrigated land to the railhead at Morgan. But some of the more progressive farmers like Mr Melville were beginning to transport their own goods in sturdy model T trucks and to bring back their requirements from the nearest railhead.

He was on his own again, for both the youngest boy and Jim, the married one, had gone to the front. Delie had no relatives there, but she was sickened by the news, by the appalling loss of young life recorded in the casualty lists. Yet the war conditions helped her indirectly.

She heard that because of the shortage of shipping, wool was piling up at the docks in the city. Exporters no longer had the wool railed down to the seaport, because there was nowhere to store it; and gradually the big warehouses further up the river had filled too.

She was asked to take the *Philadelphia* up to Wentworth and bring down a thousand bales to be stored in a large empty warehouse at Morgan, belonging to a man who owned stores and steamers all along the lower Murray. When his agent approached her with the contract, she nearly fainted.

The dark eyes, the pale face, the thin, rather red lips and pointed dark beard in which she now saw a few threads of grey, the fine arrogant nostrils – she had seen him before and dreamed of him for three years.

Whenever they came in to the Morgan wharf, which reminded her of Echuca with its great hydraulic cranes and bustling activity, its three trains a day shunting busily and its line of steamers and barges, she would look hopefully for the small, dark man she had once seen rowing upstream with his painting-satchel, and to whom she had longed to speak. But she had never seen him again and did not know his name.

She had thought how exotic he looked, as though coming from another, more civilised world than the rough and ready life of the river ports – as though he might be on a sketching holiday from Melbourne, perhaps. It seemed like a hundred years since she had been in Melbourne; and though Morgan was only a hundred miles from the city of Adelaide, she had never been there.

Now she found that his life was bound up with the river as closely as was hers; he was a connection of the family which owned the chain of mills and warehouses, whose name she had seen painted over doorways in so many ports of call. He explained why she had not seen him more often; he had always been stationed at Goolwa or Milang, but now the trade at the lower end of the river had dwindled so much that he had moved to Morgan. His name was Alastair Raeburn.

They discussed their business in the saloon. She noticed his eyes going more than once to one of her glowing cliffscapes which seemed to light up one wall of the little room. (The painting she had done of the *Philadelphia* for Brenton had been lost long ago in the fire.)

'I say, do you mind if I have a closer look at that picture?

I thought it was a print at first.'

'No, go ahead.'

He went close up to it, putting his fine aquiline nose nearly into the paint, examined the corners for a signature and stepped back, screwing up his eyes critically. They were brilliant eyes; dark habitually veiled with heavy lids, but capable of flying open and revealing a glance of fire.

They were wide open as he turned to her now, and she saw that the picture had excited him.

'I'm interested in Australian painting,' he said. 'I paint a bit myself – though not as well as my Scottish namesake.'

'I know you do,' said Delie. She almost laughed with excitement – her eyes were dancing; she was longing to tell him about herself.

'You do?' His eyebrows lifted a little. 'Anyway, I can't place this. Who is the artist?'

'I am. I painted it.'

'You mean – you copied it?'

'No, I didn't copy it. It's my own work entirely.'

He smiled slightly and she saw that he did not believe her. The lids had drooped again and a film seemed to have spread over his eyes, leaving them flat and cold.

'This is the work of a professional, Mrs Edwards.'

'Exactly.'

'But I thought your – profession was that of master mariner.'

'And I thought you were an artist, not a warehouse agent.'

He smiled more warmly at this. 'So I am. But I went into this business with my brother and I'm helping to run it for the benefit of his widow.'

'And I'm supporting my children by running this boat. Is that why you gave me the contract?'

'I had heard about your difficulties, yes, and thought you were very plucky –'

'I don't want charity. I've managed so far.'

'You don't let me finish. Also that you were a very good skipper. The *Cadell*'s captain told me.'

'Oh!'

'Yes. I wouldn't risk my wool otherwise . . . I'm really interested in this painting, Mrs Edwards. Is it for sale?'

She hesitated. She had sold or given away all her good things except this, and at present she could paint no more. Perhaps she would never paint again. But she needed the money, and this man could afford to pay a high price. She opened her mouth, and found herself saying 'No'.

He bowed his head slightly, accepting her decision as final. He glanced round the room, noting the absence of other paintings, of half-finished canvases, of tubes and brushes or a used palette. She saw that he still did not believe her and was suddenly angry.

'I have locked my things away and given up painting – for the present.'

'I see.' He bowed again and took his leave. She had wanted to tell him to look up Delphine Gordon in the catalogue of the Melbourne Art Gallery if he did not believe her, to tell him that this was her name. But pride held her back. Let him think what he liked, the arrogant, self-satisfied . . . She sat down and stared at the picture, fighting against tears of disappointment. It had been a very different interview from the one she had imagined taking place if ever she met the mysterious stranger.

On the way up to Wentworth she called at the farm above Waikerie where her other two children were boarding. Healthy-cheeked Mrs Melville and her placid, hard-working husband seemed not to have changed at all since the time when the steamer first went aground below their property. Now her boys were away at the war Mrs Melville was more than ever delighted to have other youngsters to fill her empty nest.

The changes in the children were more noticeable than the last time she had left them; Delie noted Gordon's new sturdiness and manliness, for at fourteen he was a big lad; while Meg was losing her baby-fat and becoming leggy and coltish.

As soon as the school year ended Gordon would have to leave and help with running the steamer. His own father had had no education beyond his thirteenth year and Brenton had determined that his eldest son was to be 'a riverman'. Gentle, dreamy Gordon – it would have been better if he had been born a girl perhaps. Brenny was the one who would make a riverman and he would have to leave the boat soon and begin his schooling in earnest. She couldn't take him any further with the limited time she had for supervising his lessons, though the Government Correspondence School was a great help.

Brenton would like to have Meg, his favourite, on board, but she did not like to leave one of the boys alone at the farm. She remembered too vividly her first months at Kiandra before Adam came home, before she had become used to the loss of her brothers and sisters. Mrs Melville was kind, but it was not the same thing as an ally of your own generation.

'Gee, Mum, when can I come back to the boat to live?' Gordon kicked at the leg of his bed, while she sat upon it unfolding the parcels of new clothes she had brought him.

'Just try this pullover, dear, and see if it's long enough in the sleeves.'

He pulled it on ungraciously, tousling his already untidy hair, much darker than it used to be. A faint greyish down showed on his upper lip. 'When can I?'

'Aren't you happy on the farm?' she hedged.

'Aw, it's all right, but I like the river better. Besides, I'm fourteen and I'm sick of school.'

She smiled and sighed. Now that his voice was deepening, he had that unexpected air of maturity, combined with a boyish freshness of complexion, which had been part of Adam's charm. It was strange, incredible, that she had a son of her own almost as old as Adam was when they first met. This could have been Adam's son: the blue eyes with their dark lashes she had given him. Brenton's were smaller, closer together and of a clear bright blue that was sometimes nearly green. It was young Brenny who was most like his father.

Alex – well, Alex was a 'sport', she decided, with his hair of black floss and his sharp, inquiring eyes. He would be a biologist or a naturalist, perhaps a doctor – yes, it was as if her own father had skipped a generation and reappeared in Alex. He was fascinated with living things and had no fear of anything that swam, crawled or flew.

'When can I, Mum?'

'At the end of the year, dear – as soon as you've got your Qualifying Certificate. You can come back to the boat and Brenny will go to school. And of course you can be with us in the next school holidays. I don't know; it seems terrible that you boys should grow up in different households, but I don't see what else I can do.'

'Why's it terrible?' said Gordon sensibly. 'We always used to fight, don't you remember? I was jealous of Brenny because he's a better swimmer and he hated me being bigger than him.'

'Bigger than he, dear . . . Yes, but he's your brother.'

'Anyway, let's go aboard and see him now. He's all right for a while but then he begins to drive me mad.

'You must come and see Dad, anyway. Brenny stayed with him.'

426

'O-oh. Do I *have* ter?'

'Of course!' she said sharply. 'He's much better, sitting up and using his left arm. There's some feeling back in the other hand as well.'

'It's so hard to understand what he says.'

'You get used to it. I can understand him quite well.'

He looked unconvinced. She went to the kitchen to look for Meg and found her helping Mrs Melville to ice a cake, while young Alex cleaned out the bowl.

'Look Mummy, I made a pretty pattern!'

'She's that clever', said Mrs Melville admiringly. 'Chops up the almonds and makes pictures in the chocolate icing with them.'

Delie admired the pattern, the more extravagantly as she was always looking and hoping for some sign of artistic talent in her children. But a woman was handicapped from the start; she hoped it would be one of the boys.

Meg, who had been lovely as a baby, was turning into rather a plain child, with a snub nose and a large mouth; but her hair was like black silk and her eyes sparkled with life and mischief. Mrs Melville declared that she wouldn't be able to bear to part with her when the time came. 'She's such a help in the kitchen, you wouldn't believe it, a real little housewife. It'll be wonderful for you to have her on board, all the same.'

'How different from me at that age!' thought Delie with rather a pang. She and her daughter were almost strangers; would they find anything in common? When she came back to the boat she would be able to supervise Meg's reading and educate her in the things that were not learnt at school. If only there were someone like Miss Barrett to help her realise her possibilities! But she must face the fact that perhaps none of her children had any remarkable talents; every mother was ambitious for her off-spring, of course. Yet she had a kind of faith in Gordon. There was something in his wide-set, thoughtful glance, in that odd look of maturity he had at times; something of Adam's promise. And of course Adam had been his second cousin, she need not be imagining the likeness. She was glad that he carried her name, her father's name.

Brenny was the practical one, the one who took after his father; active, fearless, straight-gazing and with an obstinacy and singleness of purpose when his heart was set on something which he perhaps inherited from them both. In spite of all her anxious remonstrances, he had practised diving from higher and higher points on the boat until he could go in cleanly from the wheel-house roof; but she was always terrified that he might hit a hidden snag under the water.

When during his practising he made a belly-flopper and had all the breath knocked out of him for a moment, he rested only until he could get his breath back before climbing up and trying again.

'That kid's got guts,' said Charlie with grudging admiration, for boys and deckhands were his natural enemies. 'He'll either die young or grow into one of the best skippers along the river – like 'is old man.'

SEVENTY

With her barge piled high with tiers of wool-bales, the *Philadelphia* made good time down-stream on the flooded river. Delie wanted to make a record trip, to surprise Mr Raeburn with her speed as well as her reliability.

She took no unnecessary risks; and as the landmarks were left behind which marked their rapid progress – Ned's Corner, Rufus Creek, the Border Cliffs, Isle of Man (where an absconder called Mann had once taken refuge, and been shot there by the troopers), Chowilla Big Bend, Murtho Station – she felt sure of a successful run. Then, near Ral Ral Creek just above Renmark, the barge struck a snag.

The sharp, iron-hard end of a red-gum log holed the barge just below the waterline – fortunately in shallow water, where she settled down in five feet of river, held fast by the piece of wood sticking a foot through her side. It took three days to un-load the wool and refloat the barge, but only two bales were lost.

A third was broken open at Delie's orders. The bargemaster, working in the early morning when the decks were coated with the white rime of a heavy frost, slipped and fell into the icy water. He was carried downstream by the current and by the time he was pulled out he was blue with cold.

'Strip off his wet things and cut open a bale,' ordered Delie.

'But, Missus – '

'Oh, I won't look,' she said impatiently. She had actually forgotten for the moment that she was not a man, giving orders to his crew. 'Hurry up, now, for goodness' sake, before he gets pneumonia. Now, pack him in among the wool with only his head out so that he can breathe. Never mind if he's damp – the wool will generate its own heat.'

Doubtfully, the men cut the hessian down one side, and the tight-packed wool, released from pressure, foamed creamily out. More was pulled forth to make room for the shivering bargemaster. Then he was popped into the bale as into a Turkish bath. He was given hot drinks and a swig of brandy, and his blue lips regained their normal colour.

After a while he declared that he was 'quite warm' and after getting into some dry clothes seemed none the worse for his ducking. He was full of admiration for the skipper's quick thinking: 'Even if she is only a woman.'

Delie decided that she would tell Cyrus James about it on her way back through Blanchetown. She had rehearsed the story and was quite disappointed – in spite of her hurry to make up lost time after the accident – to find that he had gone down to Adelaide for a few days. The bales of wool were insured; Alastair Raeburn was not worried by their loss and was only amused at the damage to the third one, when he heard to what use it had been put. He too was inclined to praise her quick-wittedness, not knowing of the similar incident she had read of in *Life on the Mississippi*.

She did not tell him, for his approval was sweet to her. Why did she care so much for his good opinion? She did not find him attractive, except for his mental alertness and a quality as of molten steel beneath his surface urbanity.

'Bathing in wool! What a sybaritic existence you river people enjoy!' he said teasingly. 'Asses' milk would be no softer or creamier.' His hand, white and delicate, caressed the white-gold of the scoured fleeces with sensuous delight.

Used to seeing men's hands sunbrowned and hardened by sun and rope and wheel, Delie thought it looked effeminate; but she reflected that he had much to do with wool and even tough shearers and pickers-up often had marvellously soft hands at the end of shearing, from contact with the lanolin in natural greasy wool.

'We have another big wool-store down on the Lakes,' he said

'Have you ever been across Lake Alexandrina? It's more than two hundred square miles of water, you know – almost a sea. Different thing from navigating between two river banks. You'd probably get lost.'

'I would not get lost. I know where I can get a chart, and of course I know the channel in theory. After all, there's nothing to bump into on the lake, no snags to sink one's barges.'

'No; only the bottom. Sometimes the waves are eight feet high and, since the lake is only about eight feet deep, you have to have eighteen inches of freeboard, minimum, for the Lakes, and an extra insurance cover. Often you have to wait two days for the wind to drop before you can venture out.'

'Are you trying to frighten me, Mr Raeburn?'

'I don't think that would be easy. No, I don't doubt your courage, or that it is capable of rising to any fresh demands upon it. I was thinking of your steamer. You have more to lose than some.'

'I also have more need to prove that I'm not afraid – if only to myself.'

'Then you'll bring another load down for us, to Milang?'

'Very well. When?'

'I'll send you a wire. Not till shearing is finished at Lake Victoria Station. It may be a couple of months yet.'

When they had concluded the paper work and she had given him a receipt for his cheque for £500, she asked him aboard to take a glass of wine in the saloon, hoping he would refer again to her picture.

He invited her, instead, to step into his living-quarters behind the wool-store. They passed through a heavy door into a different world, where a fire danced brightly in a wrought-iron grate and was reflected by a few pieces of good rosewood furniture, some lovely Venetian glass, and an Italian figurine, in marble, a copy of the *Dying Gladiator*.

It was the room of a connoisseur, as unexpected in this raw riverside port as coming upon a Greek temple in the middle of the Australian desert. Delie went straight to the only picture in the room and gave it a close examination. There was no signature; the painting was fairly old, dark in the corners; it was a portrait, done with assurance and insight, of a young man in the costume of a hundred years ago.

'Let me see; one of the Scottish portrait painters of last century – Raeburn? Oh no, it couldn't be. And yet the lighting . . .

the modelling of the head . . . the square brush-strokes . . .
Raeburn! But of course, that's *your* name!'

She turned, excitement making her face youthful, and found
Raeburn's bright dark eyes fixed upon her, open to their fullest
extent.

'So you do know about painting,' he said softly. 'It *was* you
who painted that brilliant, extraordinary cliff study.'

'Of course; as I told you. Do you take me for a liar?' she said
with a flash of temper.

'No, no, please don't misunderstand me. But I thought you
had perhaps been helped – influenced by –'

'I painted that picture in the intervals of producing six babies,
if you call that "help". But if anyone influenced me it was Sisley.
You know his landscapes of the Loing?'

'I've seen some of them, yes, in Paris.'

'You mean the originals? Oh!' She stared at him as if he had
just said he had seen God. 'In that picutre I was trying to get the
essence of all cliffs, all rocks, the hardness and enduringness of
rock against the fluidity of water; and yet to suggest that the
rocks are fluid too, under the aspect of time. To paint the thing-
in-itself and suggest all life, all time, in the transitory embodiment
of the thing.'

'An ambitious object. It requires perhaps too much of the
average art lover, who will see just the pleasing texture and the
feeling of life in the canvas. People are conditioned by art-
school terms – Life, Still Life, Landscape. It is all Life, equally
there in rocks and flowers and trees and people – like this very
alive man.' He nodded at the portrait of a man in a grey-green
jacket and high stock, with thin, incisive, ruddy features and a
bright mocking glance. 'There is something about his face which
appeals strongly to me. But for the accident of time, we might have
been friends.'

'You mean if he hadn't died before you were born?'

'Yes; I often think of all the delightful people we are separated
from by time as well as space. Wouldn't you have liked to meet
Leonardo in person? Or La Gioconda, for that matter?'

'Oh yes! And Rembrandt and this interesting young man – *is* it
a Raeburn?'

'No, it's by his follower John Watson Gordon and could easily
be mistaken for a Raeburn.'

'That is my name, too – Gordon was my father's name. And
yours? Are you related to the artist?'

431

'My father was a second cousin of Henry, Raeburn's son, who had a shipping business in Edinburgh. When the firm failed, my father, who was to have gone into business, came out to Australia and started a shipping business on the Murray. My brother carried it on after his death. I was only interested in art in those days, and went off to London and Europe to study.

'Then, when my brother died, I had to come back and keep things going for his widow and their children and my two old aunts who were dependent on him. Henry's widow is charming, but rather a helpless person.' He glanced at her, as if making a quick comparison in his mind's eyes. 'I can't tell you how I admire your grit and resourcefulness, in a similar situation.'

'I am not a widow.'

'No; but –' He spread his hands in a quick gesture.

'But my husband is helpless. He's fighting his way back, though. I'm only carrying on until he can take over again.' She did not really believe this, but it was a comforting myth.

'And how have you managed to find time to paint?'

'I don't paint any more, as I told you. I knew I had to put it right away from me. It was like death at first. But perhaps one day I'll have more time.' She sighed.

He raised one eyebrow comically. It was a wild, tufted, unruly feature, in contrast to his neat beard and neat figure. 'I hate family responsibilities, don't you?'

'I do.'

'They are so cramping –'

'The dullness of domesticity –'

'The monotony of monogamy!'

'You are married, then?'

'Not at present, no. My wife found it impossible to get on with her sister-in-law and my brother's children – we had none of our own – and my Scottish aunts. It's a big house, but somehow those women managed to get under each other's feet all the time. Heavens, how they bickered! Eventually my wife went off with a visiting wool-buyer from England.'

His tone was light. If he had suffered, he had evidently put it behind him.

'I've never seen any of Brenton's family; he left home when he was quite a youngster. There's a married brother living somewhere in Sydney, I believe, but he's lost track of him. In-laws would be difficult, I feel.'

'They are. Especially when they're women. The only one of the

432

family my wife really liked was poor Henry.'

There was a bitter undercurrent to his words and Delie revised her ideas a little. He had not forgiven his ex-wife, perhaps, and his light tone might cover an open wound.

'D'you know what we should do, you and I?' he said suddenly. 'We should fly together to – to South America or China or somewhere and devote our lives to Art.'

'And leave our families to sink or swim? What a wild idea! And why together? That would be only recomplicating our lives,' she said, adopting his mock-serious tone. 'I'm afraid you have too much imagination for a practical man of business, Mr Raeburn.'

'Ah, but I'm an artist as well. When you come down to Milang I shall show you some of my work. And I should dearly love to see some more of yours. I'm returning to the Lakes in a few weeks, to clear the warehouse in readiness for the Lake Victoria wool.'

Delie told him to look in the catalogue of the National Gallery of Victoria under 'Delphine Gordon' and watched for his re-action. There was none. She felt a little deflated. 'And the next time you're in Melbourne, you could pay a visit to *The Fisherman's Wife*.'

'*The Fisherman's* – ! Delphine! Of course, I know it well. One of my favourites among the moderns.' He took her hand and bowed low over it. 'Sincere homage, dear lady. You are already a greater artist than I shall ever be. And you must begin painting again.'

Delie left the wool-store, treading on clouds. His words, more than the wine, had gone to her head. He had kissed her hand, reverently, humbly; her hand that was browner and rougher than his, hardened by gripping the spokes of the big wheel in all weathers and helping to load wood when they were short-handed; she had even learned to use an axe efficiently.

And his name was Raeburn! It was the final touch to her dreams and imaginings about the dark stranger.

SEVENTY-ONE

Travelling downstream at night, there was danger of running into a new, uncharted snag; yet Delie enjoyed the excitement of it, now that she had grown out of her earlier terror at being alone in the wheel-house and responsible for the safety of all on board.

Every reef and sandbar was known to her like the back of her own hand. As the winding channel shifted, she recorded its new shape in her photographic memory. The training of an artist, she had found, was invaluable to a skipper on the Murray.

She had learnt to tell the difference between the solid-seeming reflection of a cliff and the real cliff, and on a dark night would steer calmly into the heart of a black shadow because she knew the shape of the river by heart. Her courage had grown steadily to meet the demands upon it; for they carried no mate, to save wages. Brenton was nominally the mate and she let young Brenny relieve her at the wheel in open stretches in daylight, while she attended to Brenton's needs or snatched a brief rest and a meal.

The only luxury she allowed herself was a cook. The men must be properly fed or they would leave. She could not do with less than a crew of engineer, fireman, bargemaster and deckhand, besides the two boys.

Now that the flood had gone down, they were busy carting crushed stone from the quarry at Mannum, a hundred miles downstream of the Lock site, where there was a deposit of granite close to the river.

Here the steamers loaded their barges under the quarry chute, which was built out over the water above a deep part of the channel where they could come in close. Sometimes when the quarry-workers stopped at night they would leave a hopperful of stone ready in the chute, and the first steamer along in the morning could load from this and get a start on her rivals.

The biggest and most powerful steamer on the river, the *Captain Sturt*, used to push three laden barges ahead of her, so that after she had loaded up there was often a long wait until more stone was ready. She was a stern-wheeler, a Mississippi type brought from America and assembled in the river.

They had passed the *Captain Sturt*, with Captain Johnstone at the wheel and his young family on board, just coming into Blanchetown at dusk, for she did not travel at night when loaded; she was almost as long as a goods-train and had no rails to follow.

None of the other steamers had left ahead of the *Philadelphia*, so Delie hoped to be first at the quarry in the early morning.

The two acetylene lamps with their great reflectors lit up the river ahead; the big trees shone jewel-like in the white glare, carved in detail against the dark sky. There was no moon, so she did not have to allow for the confusion of moonlight and its reflections on the river's surface. The wheel-house was in darkness, and her eyes were well accustomed to the gloom. They were just out of Blanchetown on the downward run to Mannum.

Delie hummed contentedly to herself. She was not lonely, though not a single light of human habitation showed anywhere ahead, and the cliffs and backwaters lay in primitive darkness.

Once, there would have been flickering campfires of the aborigines, the fierce Moorundi tribes who occupied the west bank of the river here. In those days the whole length of the meandering Murray had supported four natives to every mile. Now only remnants were left, living in dirty camps on the edge of settlements like Swan Reach and Mannum, where they could get white man's food and tobacco and cast-off clothing, and contract the white man's diseases.

She stopped humming and listened to the regular beat of the paddles, the soft *chow-chow-chow* of exhaust steam puffing from the funnel. A dark figure, small and spare, appeared at the wheel-house doorway and glided in beside her.

'Engine running' sweetly,' said Charlie the engineer. 'She seems to like the new set o' the funnel. Happy as an old gin puffin' at a pipe. Listen to 'er.'

'I was just listening. You have a way with her, Charlie.'

'Aw! She knows me, that's all. Well, I'll be dang-blasted for a son of a cross-bred dingo! What's that there light?'

'Where?'

'Comin' up astern – comin' fast. She be the *Cadell*, you reckon?'

'Could be. She was getting steam up when we left. I bet she's trying to beat us to the quarry chute at Mannum.'

'Beat us! By cripes, we'll see about that. I'll just –'

'Charlie! Charlie McBean!' She called him back sternly. He knew quite well how she felt about racing.

435

'Yes, Missus.' Charlie paused on the steps reluctantly.

Delie looked back over her shoulder at the steadily gaining lights. Afterwards she could never make out what had happened to her – perhaps she was 'possessed', taken over by Brenton's old competitive spirit. But 'Hurry, Charlie!' she cried. 'Give her everything we've got.'

'Yes, Missus!!'

She pulled into the centre of the river to get the full benefit of the current. The empty barge made very little difference to their speed. She heard the clang of the firebox door as the best and driest lengths of wood were flung into the furnace and as the steam pressure rose, they went racing down the river at their full speed of nine knots.

Behind, the *Cadell*'s crew stoked madly and sparks flew from the pursuing steamer's funnel with a continuous roar. Delie could hear their own funnel throbbing and panting as if in pain and was thankful that it was new and well-fitted. Down below Charlie would be 'spragging' the safety valve with a series of heavy weights.

She gripped the wheel and felt the eager vibration of the straining steamer through her hands, communicating a feeling of reckless power. Here was her chance to show the men if she could handle a boat! But the *Cadell* slowly drew level. Delie cut a point finely, her paddle-wheel housing scraping the overhanging trees, and gained a few yards. Charlie came dancing into the wheel-house, wringing his cap in his hands. She could feel the vibration of excitement in him as well as in the steamer.

'It's no use, Missus!' he yelled. 'They've got the edge on us, and if they once get past – There's that there kerosene we got in for the lamps – if I could just slip a bit to the fireman – '

'Get the kerosene!' cried Delie. 'And ask the cook for all his tins of dripping. No, don't wait to ask him, he's asleep. I'll square it with him in the morning.'

Now the *Cadell* was steaming alongside and Delie saw her crew dancing in the glare from the firebox and yelling insults. For fifteen miles they jockeyed for position, but by skilful steering she kept her advantage of a few yards.

'Hurrah! Blow up but don't slow up!' yelled Charlie somewhere below, and she felt a moment of cold sanity. She remembered the *Providence* . . . But that steamer had not been racing; she had gone up for no apparent reason. Delie stopped worrying and felt a fatalistic calm.

436

On the last bend she managed to get the 'inside running' and the few yards' lead was kept down the nine-mile reach. The two steamers thundered through the dark night, neither yielding an inch of way nor a pound of steam. The lights of Mannum grew brighter, the engineer and fireman gave a cheer, and the *Philadelphia* slipped under the quarry chute just as dawn was breaking. Steam hissed from the exhaust valves in a deafening scream and the whistle pealed in triumph.

The defeated *Cadell* gave three blasts to acknowledge defeat and went in to the bank to wait her turn.

SEVENTY-TWO

'We raced the *Cadell* from Blanchetown.'

Delie sat on the bed, where her husband's helpless bulk was propped on an arrangement of pillows, and waited in agony for some response. If there was anything left of the old Teddy Edwards, the skipper who could not bear to be beaten, who always had to have the fastest boat on the river; if one spark of the old Brenton remained, he must show some interest.

Slowly his brooding eyes opened to their fullest extent, his lips moved and the words came out, distorted but recognisable:

'That . . . old tub! I should . . . think . . . so.'

She smiled and relaxed. Taking his left hand, which had more feeling than the right, between both her own, she began to describe the thrilling contest: the two steamers racing through the night, the final spurt which brought them under the quarry chute to take the whole four hundred tons of stone ready in the bin, while the *Cadell* had to wait till a new load was ready. Even now the rumble of falling stone sounded as the barge filled from the conveyor-belt; they would be ready to leave again in less than half an hour.

'To think how I used to scold you for racing!' said Delie, pressing his hand. 'I'm amazed at myself, I must have been mad, but just this once I *had* to prove that we had the better boat – and a better man in the wheel-house. That'll teach them to sneer at women skippers!'

437

'Bes' man . . . river . . . all think that.'

'What did you say, darling? *I'm* the best man on the river? Who says so? After hitting the flying-fox cable and everything – '

'Charlie says. Best man nex' me.'

'Charlie McBean!' She put her face down on the pillow beside his grey head, to hide the triumph that she felt. Charlie, the woman-hater, had praised her. After tonight's performance he would surely be her slave.

They had left Blanchetown at eight o'clock the night before; it was already nearly dawn. By the time they reached the Lock works again and unloaded, she would have been on duty continuously for twenty-four hours. But she had to make up for the time lost while there was no loading. Now she was snatching ten minutes with Brenton while the barge was being loaded.

'Did you look at the book?' She picked up *Life on the Mississippi*, which had fallen down by the side of the bed. He could hold a book for a short time in his left hand, but he had to put it down to turn over the pages, laboriously, with clumsy fingers, and the effort soon tired him. 'I'll read to you while they finish loading.'

She looked at the book-plate inside the cover, *Ex Libris, Cyrus P. James*, and a strange drawing of engineering equipment sprouting roses. The engineer had strolled over to the steamer while the funnel was being repaired and brought her the book.

'D'you like Mark Twain?' he'd said.

'*Tom Sawyer* and *Huckleberry Finn*, yes, they're old favourites. Not the *Innocents Abroad*, so much.'

'Waal, either you like his Yankee brand of humour or you don't. But I'll guarantee you'll like this one. A skipper told me that most everything he says about the Mississippi goes for your river here. Keep it as long as you like, ma'am. Perhaps your husband would like to read it.'

She took him up to the top deck to meet Brenton and he was courteous and not oppressively sympathetic in his manner. But Teddy Edwards didn't like visitors, even old friends; he was ashamed of his helpless condition, his struggling and thickened speech. Mr James, sensing this, did not stay long.

Turning over the pages, Delie had smiled at the illustrations of those great floating palaces with double funnels and twin boilers. They did not look like Murray paddle-wheelers. Then a paragraph caught her eye:

438

'We noticed that above Duberque the water of the Mississippi was olive-green – rich and beautiful and semi-transparent with the sun on it . . .'

Cut-offs and snags, points and shoals and sandbars, a description of the mirror-like surface at dawn – it was all here. She had taken it to Brenton, promising to read to him as soon as she had time.

Now she opened the book and began to read at random:

'A Mississippi pilot needs a prodigious memory. If he has a tolerably fair memory to start with, the river will develop it to a colossus – but only in the things he is daily drilled in. He needs this memory because the clay banks cave and change, snags hunt up new quarters all the time, sandbars are never at rest, channels are for ever dodging and shirking . . .'

She looked up and caught Brenton's blue eyes, alert and interested, fixed upon her mouth. She began to read Uncle Mumford's diatribe from the wheel-house:

'When there used to be 4000 steamboats and 10,000 acres of barges and rafts, the snags were thicker than bristles on a hog's back; but now, when there's only three dozen steamboats and nary a barge or raft, the Government has snatched out all the snags, and lit up the shores like Broadway, and a boat's as safe on the river as she'd be in Heaven.

'And I reckon by the time there ain't any boats left at all, the Commissions will have the whole thing reorganised, and dredged out, and fenced in and tied up to a degree that will make navigation just simply perfect and absolutely safe and profitable –'

'See! Just . . . same.' Brenton was waving his left hand in his impatience to express himself with his halting tongue. 'Gov'ments everywhere . . . same thing. Locks all be built . . . big dams . . . mouth shut in with barrages . . . plenty water all 'a year round . . . but no boats running. Finished.'

'It was the railway competition, I suppose, that finished them in America?' She leafed through the pages. 'Yes, it says here: "The railroads have killed the steamboat traffic by doing in two or three days what the steamboats consumed a week in doing . . . Mississippi steamboating was born in 1812; in less than sixty years it was dead! A strangely short life for so majestic a creature. Of course it is not absolutely dead; neither is a crippled – "'

Her eyes, leaping ahead in the text, flew wide; she bit her lip. She couldn't read the rest of that sentence.

'Go . . . on. I've read it.'

439

' "N-neither is a crippled octogenarian who could once jump twenty-two feet on level ground; but as contrasted with – with what it was in its prime vigour, the Mississippi may be called dead." '

The last word fell flatly into the silence between them, underscored by the last rattle and rumble of the stone emptying into the barge.

Delie stared at him silently. 'Beware of pity,' she told herself urgently. 'He doesn't want pity . . .'

'Dead! Yes. Be better . . . dead.' His eyes had their old commanding gleam as he looked at her. 'Hand me . . . my . . . rifle. Fetch . . . Hear me?'

'Yes, I hear you, Brenton. But I won't do it. We need you – the children – the boat – and I . . .'

'Huh! Useless!'

'Darling, listen to me! You're better already. You can talk, you've got some feeling back in one hand. You must fight, you've got to fight, for our sakes as well as your own. I didn't think you were a quitter!'

'I'll . . . fight. You'll see. I get out of . . . this bed . . . or die. I won't eat; find some way out. Won't . . . rot like this . . . longer.'

He raised his one good arm in a gesture, at once pathetic and defiant, as if he would haul down the curse of the gods on anyone who tried to stop him; but it fell limply back to his side.

A tap on the cabin door, and the deckhand (the Young Limb, or Limb o' Satan, as Charlie called him) popped his head in.

'Loadin's finished, Missus. Engineer says steam's up.'

'Right. I'm coming.'

She watched him hopping and skipping ahead of her along the deck – he never walked – and marvelled at his bounding energy so early in the morning. Young Brenny and Alex were still in their bunks. The Limb had been up all night, helping the fireman, thoroughly enjoying the race. His round freckled face with its protruding teeth was as cheekily cheerful as ever; and his round felt hat was, as always, jammed tightly down to the top of his ears. She looked downstream, towards Mannum. Early as it was, the town was astir with life. She could see lights in the shops and houses spread up the cliffs like swallows' nests; the punt chugged across the river, ferrying early-shift workers to David Shearer's farm-implement factory downstream; that glow was from the forge at J. G. Arnold's boat-building yards, from whence came a clang of metal.

And somewhere across the river there, Captain Randell's old *Mary Ann* lay in the mud. She had been built here, on these very banks, the first steamer on the Murray. That was just over sixty years ago; and on the Mississippi steamers had lasted less than sixty years! She felt a chill that was not all from the cold morning air.

A pair of whistling eagles circled above the river, against the lightening sky. Their melancholy ascending call was drowned in the noise of steam from the escape valves and a shout from Charlie McBean.

'Eh, you Limb o' Satan, did you tell the Missus we was ready to start?'

'Course I did.'

'All right, Charlie, I'm ready.' She stepped into the wheel-house.

'Cast off the for'ard line there, you Limb.'

The bargemaster and the fireman each stood ready with a long pole to fend them away from the chute. Delie moved the throttle and the paddles began to thrash the water into foam.

> Charlie, Barley, butter an' eggs,
> Sold his wife for two duck eggs,

sang the deckhand raucously.

'You young Limb!' roared Charlie. 'You wait till I catch up with yer.'

SEVENTY-THREE

Another steamer, after all, took the Lake Victoria wool to the Raeburn store at Milang. An opportunity came which Delie could not afford to miss, and which prevented her from visiting the Lakes just then.

The old *Cadell* had taken over the mail-run from Murray Bridge to Morgan, but she found the racing current too much for her engines as it poured through the restricted pass at the Lock works (now pumped out and full of activity again after the flood).

441

So she had tried winching herself upstream by means of a large tree, but her rotten timbers gave way and she pulled her whole stem-post loose.

On the *Cadell* captain's advice, Delie applied for and secured the mail contract for the *Philadelphia*. This meant a regular income, apart from general cargo; but it also meant keeping to a strict schedule because there were trains to be met at either end. It was a triumph for her and for the steamer. His Majesty's mails had not before been carried by a woman on the river.

The construction camp at Blanchetown, between the two termini of her run, had its own mailbag and post office, for there was quite a big temporary village with cabins for eighty men, besides mess-huts and two cottages for the engineer-in-charge and the head clerk.

Sometimes the consulting engineer had last-minute papers or letters, often addressed to Canada, to go in the bag. Delie saw quite a lot of Mr James, who frequently came on board to get his mail and brought a pile of books and magazines for the invalid.

The practical Brenton liked the *Scientific American*s he brought. He had become used to the engineer's visits and no longer shrank from seeing him; but Delie had begun to realise that they were too frequent for her own peace of mind. She had begun to look forward to them with a trembling eagerness which at first she did not trouble to analyse.

Cyrus James was a big man, and he had a habit of walking close up to her when they met, like a barque bearing down on a small skiff, as if he would capture her, conquer her with his mere bulk. She knew that his wife was in Canada and that he was leading a celibate life ill-suited to such a vigorous man, who worked and moved with such energy while speaking with such a gentle drawl. He had big, bony hands with blunt fingers and black hair sprouting from the knuckles, which fascinated and repelled her with their strong masculinity.

When she found herself dreaming about him between visits, she decided that these visits must cease. But she made her decision too late.

He came aboard one evening when some stores were being unloaded at Blanchetown besides the mailbags. They stood together by the saloon table studying Brenton's old chart of the river, debating some point about the cliff and lagoon formation near the site of Lock Three, the next to be built and eighty miles up-river. Cyrus James would not be in charge of construction;

442

as soon as Lock Three was begun he would be returning to Canada.

The long chart was partly unwound on the table in front of them. Delie stood beside it, tracing the inked channel with one finger.

A wide belt outlined her trim waist, between the sensible skirt and the frilled white muslin blouse which was the only really feminine garment she wore these days. Her 'good' clothes were packed away at Mrs Melville's.

Cyrus James stood close behind her, as she was aware with all her nerves. He leant over to look at some point, and casually rested a hand on her shoulder. Then his fingers brushed, very delicately, along the side of her bare neck, beneath the softly turned-up hair. She swayed and a strong shudder went over her. She could not speak.

'You're an enchanting person,' he said softly in her ear. 'Do you know what you've done to me? I can't think of anything else.' His fingers continued to caress her neck. 'Christ! I want you.'

She made an effort and moved away from him, round the other side of the table. 'You'd better go,' she said, but her lips trembled and she hung her head.

'Listen! Listen to me!' He caught her hands across the table, urgently. 'Lift your head! Look at me! I don't mean that I don't love you, honour you, admire you . . . I love you in every way. But I'm not a schoolboy, and you're a woman. Admit it, darling. You need me, you want me too, don't you? Don't you?'

'Yes! . . . No! Please go.' She pulled her hands away.

'All right.' He spoke with sudden calm, as though deciding it was useless to reason with a hysterical child. 'Okay, okay! I'll go. But you're making a mistake. We could be so happy, and how could it harm anyone?'

'What about your wife?'

'It's crazy – I don't know, it makes no difference to my feelings for her, I still love her; but this has just bowled me over.'

'Then I have to be strong for both of us. No! I've been on the other end too often in this sort of situation. I have a fellow-feeling for wives. And it would be treacherous to – to Brenton, when he's helpless, the way he is .   Don't you feel that too? Do you think you're playing a very honourable part?'

He winced a little at that. 'Ah, you're making it all sound planned, hateful. Believe me, I couldn't help myself.'

'All right! I believe you. But please go now.'

She thought she had won, but she had not reckoned with the tenacity which continued to build bridges however often the foundations were swept away, which was pressing on with the completion of the first weir and lock in spite of the worst flood for forty-seven years.

He stepped around the table and caught her in his arms, muttering incoherencies and fastening on her mouth like a man starving. His knee was pressing between her thighs, his hard fingers dug into her breasts, his tongue forced her lips apart. She fought back fiercely, thinking over and over: I must be strong . . . I must be strong. At last she tore herself away, breathless and dishevelled.

She said: 'If you attempt to touch me again I'll call Charlie. Oh, why did this have to happen? Why did I have to be a woman?' She flung herself into a chair, and put her head down on the saloon table, hiding her face.

In a moment she felt a gentle hand on her hair. 'Listen, Delie. For God's sake look up, and listen to me. I'm going now. I'm sorry, really I am – it's just that I'm mad about you, plumb crazy, do you understand? I can't help it!' She didn't look up, but she heard the door close behind him.

That night, lying awake hour after hour in her bunk, staring at the wooden ceiling so close overhead, she fought the same battle over again. Why not? said an insidious voice. Why not, who would know, how could it hurt anyone? Why not give in?

This was a test case and she had to establish a precedent. It was not as though she loved Cyrus James; she liked him, admired him, and found him disturbingly attractive, but that was all. There was no justification, none except the specious one of *carpe diem* – life would not return, and in a hundred years' time it would not matter what she had done. But she could not accept that. Life was given to us once, to make the best of according to our lights; we must behave *as if* everything mattered or the whole thing became a farce.

And there were times, of course, when quite clearly it was a farce . . . but that way lay hedonism or madness. She concentrated instead on the problem of Cyrus James. She could not avoid him entirely, but it would be better not to be alone with him again. She was not sure that she could trust herself and she was certain that she could not trust him.

SEVENTY-FOUR

The Great War, the War to Save Democracy, the War to End War, had finished at last, after dragging on for four incredible years of suffering and destruction. The munition-makers and the steel-barons were richer; the world was poorer by many promising young lives, many young poets who had perished in their prime.

In Australia as in other countries there was a group of returned men to be fitted back into the pattern of civilian life. They had been thrown into the carnage, handed a rifle and a bayonet and instructed to kill without mercy. Now, with blood on their hands and deeds of horror on their minds, they came back to their wives, to gentle children, to polite and stuffy office jobs. Some were eyeless, limbless, disfigured for life; others carried mental scars which did not show on the surface, but crippled them just as surely.

Many returned men could not make the adjustment, especially to city life, and a grateful Government settled them on the land. They were given arid acres of mallee scrub to turn into wheat-farms: tough, tenacious scrub which after burning and rolling still sprang up from the roots which filled the ground like dragons' teeth. When the scrub was conquered, erosion took over, and the topsoil blew away and buried fences in drifts of sand.

The new irrigation areas were surveyed along the Murray and returned men worked at digging channels and ditches and installing pumps.

At last they were settled on blocks of their own to grow fruit for the dried-fruit market. The less tenacious ones went under and drifted to the city again or wandered round the back country as swagmen, while their limestone houses crumbled into white dust. Some built up their holdings and became, if not prosperous, at least self-supporting.

Only one of the Melville boys came back. Jim, the first-born, died in France not long before the Armistice was signed. The unfairness of this end, when he had come safely through three years of slaughter, made his mother bitter. She never mentioned her elder boy and would not let her husband mention him; but her good-natured mouth tightened, and two deep lines appeared from mouth to nose on each side of her compressed lips.

Garry, the younger boy, had a new hardness about the mouth too, though he was young and resilient. He seemed older, but otherwise little changed except for a nervous habit of blinking his eyes slowly once or twice, as if shutting out some sight too terrible to be borne. He had been invalided home and arrived about the same time as the news of Jim's death.

Delie heard of it when she came to the farm to pick up Gordon – now ready to leave school – and to settle Brenny in Gordon's old room. Mr Melville slid down the waterpipe over the cliff, a strained look in his alert blue eyes, and in an almost shamefaced manner told her the news. 'Mum's taking it badly,' he mumbled. 'But I wouldn't say much, if I was you.'

She went in trembling to the farm kitchen – knowing how Mrs Melville must have innocently rejoiced at the news of the Armistice, thinking both her boys had come through – and silently pressed her hand.

The farmer's wife had had a week to get used to the news. She was in fact just beginning to realise that it was true, that Jim would never be coming home – Jim, her first-born, the favourite, who had been named after his father.

She looked at Delie with an air, calm and dry-eyed, of not knowing what the unspoken sympathy was for. She held her head high and her mouth straight; only her capable, freckled hands trembled a little as Delie withdrew her grasp. She rested them on the table to keep them still.

Mrs Melville's hair was the same iron grey, her cheeks, fresh and rosy, seemed to deny the mortal wound her mother's heart had received. But her brown eyes, which used to be bright and clear, had a shadowed look, dark like pools of water when a cloud crosses the sun.

'So you've come to take Gordon back!' she said with all her old vigour. 'I've half a mind to keep him in place of my boy, you know. I'll miss him when he goes back to the boat. He's a very shy kid, but so thoughtful . . . Well, at least you won't lose him the way I lost mine. No more wars.'

'I'm sorry, Mrs Melville. I only heard just now.'

'It's all right, dear. He died to help make the world safe from Germany, in our time anyway. The dirty Huns! I'd shoot the lot

446

of them, or at least fix the men so's they'd never breed again.'

'I can understand your feeling bitter. It was unfair, and the war practically over. . . . But I feel we have to live with the Germans. It's all one world, we're all human beings and they've had their lesson. They'd never start anything again.'

'I wouldn't trust them. Garry says they're fanatics, the officers especially. No, we've got to keep them down.'

'Melvie, Melvie!' Meg came skipping into the kitchen, a basket of eggs over her arm. She stopped short when she saw her mother and rather shyly came over to give her a kiss. She turned away at once.

'Melvie, the bantam's got a nest in the pumpkins. I found it, and it's got four little eggs in it!'

'Yes, dear. Didn't you know your mother was here? Didn't you hear the boat tie up?'

'No, I never; I was in the fowl-house and the chooks were kicking up such a row –'

' "No I didn't", not "no I never", dear,' said Delie; and then wished she hadn't corrected her daughter with her very first words. She couldn't help picking up ungrammatical constructions from other children at school and she would forget them later.

'Well, I didn't. I was s'prised to see you, Mum.'

But were you pleased? thought Delie with a little pang almost of jealousy. Mrs Melville was kindness itself, but was she taking the place of the child's own mother?

She said now with quiet authority: 'Put the eggs on the dresser, Meg, and go and do your hair. Mummy will be thinking you look like a scarecrow.'

'No, she looks lovely to me. Such fine hair! It's like black silk.' Delie stroked it gently, but after a moment Meg moved quietly away.

'Do I have to put on a ribbon?' she said, looking at Mrs Melville.

'Yes, the pink one. And wash your hands. Then you can help me butter the scones.'

Meg dashed away cheerfully. 'She made them,' said Mrs Melville. 'Gordon is carting some water from the dam. He'll be back soon, and we'll have a cup of tea.' She set the big kettle, which always simmered on her wood-range, a little nearer the centre of the stove. Her kitchen was modern and convenient for a country home, with cupboards and gadgets installed by her in-genious and energetic husband. It had muslin curtains and a

447

shining porcelain sink, though they always washed up in a dented tin bowl.

Garry came into the kitchen and Delie shook his hand, looking admiringly at this brown, hard-bitten man who had been a gawky youth when he went away. His bony nose jutted from his lean weather-beaten face, his arms were sinewy beneath his rolled-up shirt-sleeves. This was the type of the Australian Digger. Two fingers of his left hand had been shot away.

He knew that his mother wished it were Jim who had come home; he wished it himself sometimes, as he tried to get used to the quiet of the farm after the great cities – Cairo, Paris, London – of which he'd had a glimpse, and the recurring sick excitement of 'going over the top'.

His mother poured the tea, and he sat at the kitchen table moodily sipping, withdrawn among his memories.

'Garry'll be a real hero to Brenny,' said Delie to Mrs Melville.

'He already is to Meg, I fancy. That child will do anything for him.'

'Brenny will be up in a moment, he's just helping the fireman move a stack of wood. He's a strong lad now, and full of life,' said Delie. 'I hope he'll settle in all right. I'm sure *he* won't be shy.' She bit her lip, wishing she hadn't used that phrase, 'full of life', but Mrs Melville took no notice. 'There's just one thing, I hope you won't let him go sliding down the waterpipe. He's game for anything, game as Ned Kelly, Brenton used to say. But he must go round by the steps till he's bigger.'

'Yes, I'll tell Dad. *I* don't like *him* doing it either, but he's too big to be told. Men! They've given me these grey hairs. Sometimes I wish I'd had all girls. Meg is no trouble and such a comfort. I don't know how I'll ever part with her, I really don't.'

'I suppose I'll have to part with her one day, when she gets married,' said Delie lightly. She didn't quite like Mrs Melville's possessive tone about her children. Perhaps it would be as well to have Meg back on board to live next year. She could do correspondence lessons with Alex, once Brenny had settled in at the farm.

Delie wished she could discuss problems like this with Brenton, but he seemed to take little interest in his children, though he showed some pleasure when Meg came on board to visit him.

She was cheerful and unself-conscious before his disability, unlike Gordon, who shrank sensitively from illness and suffering. Perhaps she would be a nurse, thought Delie, her mind leaping

448

ahead, seeing as it always did now the future in the present, the present embalming the past.

She would never stand in Meg's way if she wanted a career; she believed every girl should have some means of independence. Yet nursing and teaching were no longer the only jobs open to women. The war years, the shortage of labour, had shown that girls were not only *able* to do secretarial work, but were more efficient than boys of the same age.

It was the thin end of the wedge; but equality would only come when there was equal pay for equal work. Already there were some women doctors in Adelaide. Perhaps Meg . . . It would be wonderful if she could take her place in a man's world, throw off the unsought yoke of her womanhood as her mother had been trying to do as long as she could remember! She, too, would have a certificate to show that she was the equal of a man in the work she had chosen. If she wanted to marry, there would be plenty of time later on, when she had her degree.

SEVENTY-FIVE

After the floods had followed pestilence: flies and midges and mosquitoes bred in their millions in the lingering swamps, and tiger-snakes swarmed on the flats; in the settlement of Berri alone, more than a hundred were shot in one day.

And as the flood of war receded, pestilence spread round the earth. As though a miasma rose from the frightful mud where the manhood of so many nations lay rotting, a tiny invisible virus, given the name of Spanish Influenza by the helpless doctors, killed as many people as had died in the war.

It reached Australia by way of the East, in 1919. The hospitals were all full, and dying patients had to be nursed in their homes. Doctors became exhausted by incessant calls.

Delie worried about the children and wanted to have them all under her care. She felt that they were safer on the boat, in the fairly isolated world of the river, than staying at the farm and attending school. Always morbidly aware of death and its impartial appetite for the young as well as the old and infirm, she felt a superstitious fear that one of her sons was marked for sacrifice. 'If one of them must go, let it not be Gordon,' she prayed, thus admitting to herself that her first-born was the dearest, calling inarticulately on whatever fate controlled the future.

It was young Brenny who caught the influenza. The virus must have been incubating in his system already when she called at Waikerie and took him on board. Within a few days he was tossing in a fever, delirious and dangerously ill.

She tied up near Morgan where the local doctor could attend him, away from the wharf and its dues. She sub-leased the mail contract to another steamer and gave up all her time to nursing. She sent Alex back to Mrs Melville.

The doctor said there was nothing he could do but let the disease run its course. Youth and a strong constitution would pull Brenny through, he believed. Devoted nursing was most important.

Delie scarcely slept for the next two weeks. She kept remembering that her own brothers had been no older than this when they died. In the long night watches she began reading Schopenhauer, a dusty, uncut volume she found in a box at the Morgan Institute, *The World As Will and Idea*: 'The form of life is an endless present, however the individuals, the phenomena of the Idea, arise and pass away in Time, like fleeting dreams.'

But philosophy could not console her now, any more than her uncle's fatalist concepts had consoled her for Adam's death long ago, or her aunt's cosy religion for the loss of her family. She got up to fetch cool cloths and bathe Brenny's burning flesh, which seemed to be visibly consumed by the fever. Already his cheeks were hollow. She bent to look into his face, dreading to see there the gentle, faraway look of resignation to an approaching end.

Instead she saw that he was afraid. His blue eyes, bright with fever, usually so fearless and straight-gazing, looked at her in troubled appeal. Dark shadows were marked beneath them, and they seemed sunken in his head.

'Mum, I'm not going to get better, am I?' he said weakly. 'I'm gonner die. I don't wanter. Mum –'

She bathed his brow with firm, gentle hands. Banishing the dread from her own heart, she said: 'Of course you're going to get well. With these things, sometimes you have to get worse before you get better. You're not going to die; I can tell you that right now. When you were little, and you used to get bronchitis badly, I thought sometimes you'd never get better. But you did; and you grew strong and big and you don't think I'm going to let you die now? Why, you've got to help Daddy run the boat, when he's up again and one day you'll run her yourself . . .'

As she talked, at first only to reassure him, a feeling of certainty flowed into her. It was as though, in a flash of second sight, she saw the future: saw Brenny as a young man, strong and handsome, standing in the wheel-house where his father had stood before him. *The form of life is an endless present . . . like the rainbow on the waterfall, it remains constant, while the individual drops fall down to death.*

Meanwhile her voice, her soothing touch, had lulled the child into a shallow, fevered sleep. She started from a reverie to find that he was breathing more deeply, slowly and regularly, and that his face and neck were damp with sweat. The fever had broken: the crisis was past. From that day he slowly convalesced.

Before he was up again, Brenton was stricken with the 'flu. Delie had her hands full, nursing them both; she would not let anyone else go near them, but, hanging a sheet soaked with disinfectant over the door of the cabin where they lay, she tried to isolate the infection. So far Gordon and the rest of the crew had escaped.

She had to be firm with Charlie McBean to keep him away from 'the skipper', but she was afraid the old man would never survive the infection. Without Charlie's ministrations Brenton's beard grew long and thick. When Delie tried clumsily to shave him, he lost his temper, told her she wasn't a nurse's boot-lace and waved her away.

The beard suited him with his long, well-shaped head; it was curly, more gold than silver and gave him the look of an ancient Babylonian king. Brenny thought, as he played patience with an old pack of cards, that he looked like the stern King of Clubs; but as they lay ill in the same room he gradually lost his awe of his father.

Perhaps because he was already in bed when he took ill and so ran no risk of chills, Brenton quickly passed the crisis, but his convalescence was slow. When both were pronounced cured by the doctor, Delie found that she was unutterably tired. The doctor advised her to take a holiday if she didn't want to collapse herself.

Calling at the farm for Meg, she left Gordon and Charlie in

charge of the steamer just out of Waikerie and went down to Adelaide by train. Though she had been within fifty miles of it at Mannum, she had never been to the southern capital.

It was with growing excitement that she looked out at the passing wheatfields, the blond stubble, the sacks of grain already harvested and looking like lumpy brown women. There were miles of open paddocks reminding her of the plains of northern Victoria; but away behind them, like a painted backdrop, was a line of delphinium-coloured hills. Great rounded clouds hung above them in snowy masses, and dropped their shadows on the deep eroded valleys thick with scrub.

The colours sang inside her head: blue and gold, blue and gold, glorious, beautiful gold and blue. She ached for her paints, her canvases locked away in the saloon cupboard, but she knew a week's painting holiday would never satisfy her. Like a drunkard or a drug addict, she could not take small doses of the heady draughts of creation.

Meg's nose was pressed to the window. She had never seen real hills before. 'Look at the mountains, Mummy!' she cried, as they ran down parallel with the gulf and the smoky chimneys of Port Adelaide.

Feeling hot, tired and a little bewildered, Delie emerged with her daughter from the long ramp up to North Terrace. She stood blinking in the brilliant sunlight. There was no smoke in the atmosphere and the buildings shone in pale blocks of light with sharp shadows, like a painting she had seen of a Spanish city. At the end of a wide street was a curve of pale-blue hill, friendly and close.

She hailed a horse-cab, welcoming its slow jog pace while she adjusted her mind to her surroundings. This was not just another Melbourne; it had an atmosphere of its own. The people walked more slowly on the pavements than they did in Melbourne, through the dappling of light and shadow from leafy English trees. Some of them smiled at Meg, the little country girl obviously in town for the first time, twisting round to stare up at the buildings but holding tightly to her mother's hand.

Delie had hesitated to bring Meg to the city with her, but the child was healthy, with plenty of resistance built up by rich farm fare: honey in the comb, clotted cream, milk and cheese and fresh vegetables from the irrigated patch.

It was a delight to have her daughter with her, all to herself, with no demanding household chores to divide her attention,

Mignon, Delie called her sometimes, wishing rather wistfully that she had been slight and pretty as her name; but the child preferred 'Meg', which certainly suited her better.

Intelligence was more important than good looks, Delie told herself. There was not much artistic sensibility in Meg, she found, when she took her to the Art Gallery on North Terrace. So far she liked only pictures with horses in them, or boats and the sea, which fascinated her because she had never seen it.

'Is that the *sea*?' cried Meg. 'Why doesn't it overflow? It's too high up. What holds it in?'

'It only looks like that, dear. That's the horizon-line. It will look lower as we get nearer.'

'But oh, isn't it blue! I never knew water could be so blue, except in pictures. O-oh, sand! It's bigger than the biggest sand-spit I've ever seen.'

They had left the train at the seaside station and walked down to a wide white beach with a cemented foreshore, tumbled sand-hills on each side and banks of brown seaweed like stranded whales. The tide was far out and the glistening, level sand and clear tidal pools stretched almost to the end of the jetty.

Meg had thrown off her shoes while running and went on running till she came to the first pool. She came panting back again, her feet squeaking in the dry, hot sand, to gasp: 'It's clear as glass; I can see all my toes through it; it must be good to drink! Mummy, Mummy, take your shoes off and come and see –' And she was off again.

Delie gathered up Meg's scattered shoes and sat down to remove her own. The sand was silky between her toes and sparkled with tiny grains of mica and of quartz. She closed her eyes and breathed deeply the clean, clear, salty air blowing straight off the sea.

'Tuck your skirt into your drawers, dear, don't get it wet,' she called, but her voice was lazy with well-being. She had been inland for years, wandering the great muddy waterways and sometimes when in Melbourne, years ago, she had gone down to the rather dreary foreshore at St Kilda, a tame suburban beach; but she had forgotten the real sea.

> The sea, the sea! The open sea,
> The fresh, the blue, the ever-free,

sang Meg, jumping up and down in the shallow water and splashing her tucked-up dress. She had just been reading *The Water-Babies*, and remembered how the salmon gave a great skip when they felt the salt water. It stung her legs, rather, but it was beautiful, pure as crystal. She put some to her lips and savoured the briny taste.

Delie stared through half-closed eyes at the blue curve of the bay, unmarked by any ship. Here was the sea, smiling with a wide blue smile of innocent welcome; the same cruel sea which had swallowed up her father and mother, her whole family. She had been saved; why had she been saved? One reason, she mused, was that she was more adventurous, or more impressionable, than her brothers and sisters. She'd had to go up on deck and see the great south land, while the others were snug in their cabins below; and in their cabins they had been trapped and drowned when the ship struck. But there the breakers had raged with the full force of the Southern Ocean. Here they were playful billows, little more than ripples, breaking with a gentle swish about the ankles of her daughter. Her daughter, almost as old as she had been herself when she arrived in this country . . . That thought reminded her of something. She really mustn't put it off any longer.

'Meg, dear,' she said, holding up her ankle-length skirt and paddling among the tender curves of withdrawing waves, 'Meg, dear, I've been meaning to have a talk with you, now you're getting to be a big girl so quickly –'

'Oh, stow it, Mummy,' said Meg, leaping with a little, leaping wave. 'Mrs Melville's told me all that stuff and I've got a book, and anyway most of the girls at school've started already.'

Delie stopped with her mouth open, then smiled at herself! Well! The younger generation was always a step ahead. She remembered how she had shocked Aunt Hester with her knowledge of physiology. But she'd missed girls' school except as an infant and didn't realise that the freemasonry of sex disseminated all acquired information through the group. Meg sounded matter-of-fact; there was no need to worry about her.

In the train going back to the city, Meg kept looking at her brown legs, to which little flakes of dried seaweed clung like flat brown scabs. There was sand stuck to them too, like sugar on a biscuit, and tiny white crystals of salt. Her legs, and the sand sliding inside her shoes, told her it hadn't been a dream.

There was a lady in the compartment with her hair cut in a short bob and Meg frankly stared at her. Delie was fascinated too, but tried to look as if she were not staring; she had never seen a hatless short haircut at such close quarters. She looked in the window-glass at an angle at the young woman's reflection. It really didn't look very nice, not as nice as the pictures she had seen in magazines; but it was a stroke of freedom. Women could cut their hair as well as men! Perhaps she would get hers bobbed in the city and she was certainly going to buy some cigarettes and a holder. She suddenly felt very modern in her new striped fuji dress and big hat.

She didn't get her hair cut, but she had one elating experience before going back to the boat. It was December and she and Meg were revelling in the city shops and wishing they had more money. Then she saw in the paper that Ross Smith and his aeroplane were in Darwin. They had made the first flight across the world from England.

He was expected in Adelaide in a few days' time, by way of Sydney and Melbourne. So they put off their departure for Morgan for a couple of days and waited in the parklands with the expectant crowd, all armed with improvised flags on sticks.

Meg didn't know what to expect; she had seen pictures of flying-machines, of war-time aces in their flimsy-looking craft, but one which had flown all the way from England must be bigger than any of these.

There was a sudden wave of excitement through the crowd, the cry 'There he is!' and she looked up with her mouth open at the little bird-like shape over the eastern hills.

It came quickly closer, she could see the double wings and the letters painted underneath them, G-EAOU, which some newspaper wit had translated as 'God 'Elp All of Us'. She waved her stick with its attached scarf wildly.

The little plane circled the city with droning engine, and then disappeared towards the aerodrome in the north. Meg let her flag trail in the dust. It had been disappointingly small, but she had seen an aeroplane. Wouldn't her brothers be jealous!

Her mother was still staring raptly at the empty sky.

'All the way from England!' she said. 'Do you realise, child, that when I came from England in a sailing ship it took us more than four months? One day it may be possible to fly out in four days. All the letters could go by air and perhaps people will too, instead of going by sea.'

'Oh, Mummy! What an imaginer you are! Aeroplanes aren't big enough to take a lot of people, they'd be too heavy. And it wouldn't be safe.'

'Ships aren't always safe, either,' said her mother.

SEVENTY-SIX

The year was 1920, the flappers' skirts were beginning to creep up towards the knee and, if aeroplanes were still a novelty, motor-cars were common even in the country. Roads, however, were primitive except in the city, and the river was still the main highway into the north.

But in January the water was low and the steamers were tied up all the way from Morgan to the mouth. It was time for the *Philadelphia*'s annual inspection and renewal of her certificate, so Delie decided to have the freeboard built up to eighteen inches and have her certified as 'lake-worthy', in case she should get another offer of wool for Milang.

While the school holidays were on she could have all the children on board, for the crew were paid off, apart from Charlie and the cook. She felt she had got to know her daughter all over again in the time they had spent together in the city. They had shared a room at the hotel and talked each night after the light was out, giggling over little jokes as if they had both been schoolgirls.

Refreshed by her holiday and relieved by Meg of many of her chores for Brenton – for Meg was a born nurse – Delie suddenly found that she had time on her hands. Alex had grown out of babyhood and now that Gordon was home he followed his brother like a shadow.

Delie began to feel like someone who sees a gleam of light at the end of a long, dark tunnel. She went to a locksmith about getting a new key for the locked cupboard.

In her fortieth year she began to paint again. At first, when she rowed off in the dinghy with her painting-box, she felt just the bliss of being alone after years – centuries it seemed – of be_ longing to other people. She was alone with the sun that sparkled gloriously back from the water.

But when she set up her canvas and tried to paint, her hands trembled with excitement and were clumsy with disuse. She fumbled and botched the picture and could have wept with vexation as she scraped it all down again. Yet it was a beginning.

Cyrus James came down to Morgan to catch the train for the city and came aboard, ostensibly to see Brenton. He did not need to be alone with her to destroy all her good resolutions. He had only to look at her across the room, for her memory and her senses to stir. When he had gone she lay awake smoking, one cigarette after another, night after night; fighting her desire for his big, male body and strong hands, for those mad, starving kisses he had forced upon her. Oh, if she could be with him now!

She had to learn to sublimate her deisres, to put all that unused drive into painting. But how could she relax, unwind, when she was taut with longing? Discipline, discipline.

She had a new stimulus to work in the interest of Alastair Raeburn. She wanted to have some worthwhile picture to show him when she saw him again. He had not come back to Morgan and was presumably at Milang with his brother's widow and his aunts. She could imagine him fitting gracefully into that feminine household on the shores of the great lake named after a princess.

And beyond the lakes the river narrowed again, to split into winding channels, the largest flowing past Goolwa; and beyond Goolwa lay the sea. Wasn't it at Murray Bridge – or was it Mannum – that Sturt, its first explorer, saw seagulls?

Here, about Morgan, the country the river flowed through was almost desert and a young explorer had perished just to the northward in the early days. Above the honeycombed cliffs the limestone land was bare, or dotted with wiry mallee. The sparse grasses were withered and brown.

Grey, dun, brown, sand-coloured, indigo with distance, the immense flat plains stretched to the white-hot horizon, level as the sea: while on the low sand-ridges only the scant tobacco bush grew, and the willy-willy rose in strange contorted flowers of red dust.

Yet just below, keeping its ancient course, the river flowed cool and indifferent, ignoring the thirsty land. Translucent, milky-green as a muscatel grape and following its own far purpose, the water was an alien here. Its deep cleft among the barren peneplain was invisible a short distance away; no fringing trees marked the top of the cliffs and, if it had been filled in, there would have been no change in the general landscape.

From the top of the cliffs you could take in with one glance the incredible, impassive flow of green water and the immense plateau, all bare and empty in the clear dry light.

Delie's first painting that she felt at all satisfied with was a simple study of an orange sandhill, bare of all vegetation but a dramatic black-trunked tree.

Meg went back to the farm, feeling older and more sophisticated since she had seen 'the city'. She had suddenly found life more exciting since Garry Melville had come home from the war. Not that he took much notice of her, but that didn't stop her hero-worshipping from a distance.

She had two new dresses, one a floral silk and the other an embroidered linen. Both had come from a city shop and showed off her budding figure. She felt that they were terribly smart. Just to wear one of them gave her new poise and assurance.

Garry was in town with the pick-up truck when she arrived back by steamer, in an old print frock. Before tea she put on the new, yellow linen dress and, after setting the table for Mrs Melville in the dining-alcove of the modern kitchen, she went outside and draped herself artistically against the fence, waiting for the buckboard to come from Waikerie. She heard it before she could see it; then a long cloud of whitish dust, like the exhaust from a rocket, began to spread along the road in the distance, with the buckboard at its head. There were deep ruts worn in the road, exactly the width of a car's wheel-tracks and the tyres ran in these as in the groove of a rail.

The vehicle came abreast and Garry with a wrench of the wheel dragged it out of the ruts and turned towards the gate. Meg moved languidly forward, lifted the loop of chain and swung the gate back, standing on the bottom bar of iron piping and riding with it as it swung. 'Hullo, Meggsie,' he called. 'Thanks, kid. Hop in and I'll drive you round the back.'

Meg fixed the gate closed behind him and, forcing herself not to skip like a schoolgirl, climbed sedately aboard and smoothed the linen skirt down over her knees. Her fluffy black hair had been washed that morning and shone with amber lights.

'What's the matter? You brooding about something?' Garry let in the clutch and swept down the driveway beside the house and round the corner to the sheds at the back, which housed plough and harrow, harness and feed for the horses; the motor vehicle being allowed one small corner and frequently used as a roost by fowls.

'No; why should I be?' She looked sideways at him from dark-fringed blue eyes, bright above the little snub nose. Her plainness was transformed by the subtle attraction of sex, just awakening and becoming aware.

'I dunno; Mum been jawing at you, or something?'

'No; she never does.' She was looking down, intently smoothing a pleat with one finger.

'Well, better get out.' He turned the handle of the door, at the same time giving it an expert bang with one fist, and it reluctantly opened. 'Help us carry some of this stuff, will you?' he said, reaching into the tray and picking up some groceries, piling them in his arms. He turned to hand them to Meg and found her standing obediently beside him; but her eyes were blazing.

He began transferring a bag of flour, two bars of soap, a tin of jam to her arms, when she said bitterly: 'You never notice anything, do you!'

'What's there to notice, for heaven's sake?'

'Can't you *see* I look different? I've been to the city and had my hair cut by a Frenchman called Prevost and stayed at the Hotel Metropole, and I've got a new dress. You're as blind as a bat! You can carry your old things yourself,' and she dashed the pile of groceries to the ground. The tin of jam hit him on the toe. With a roar of rage he grabbed her arm as she turned away.

'Why, you little – !'

He twisted her thin arm while she struggled and panted, so ineffectually that his good humour was restored. 'Go on, hit me why don't you?' he jeered. She brought up her other hand and he grabbed that too, holding her helpless.

'Now say: "I'm sorry I'm such a little spitfire." '

'I won't!' But she was enjoying the struggle, the resistance of his hard muscles, and by now her anger was half-assumed.

He grinned, and twisted harder. 'Say it!'

'I'm . . . sorry. Now let me go, you beast!' As she tried to free her left hand, held in his mutilated one, she saw the stumps of the missing fingers, and all her hostility melted.

'Oh, Garry! Your poor hand. You might have hurt it.'

'Rats! It healed long ago.' He thrust the hand into his pocket, out of sight. She began humbly gathering the scattered things

459

from the ground, while he unpacked the rest. As she went ahead of him to the kitchen door, he said grudgingly: 'It's not a bad dress, all the same. You look good-oh in it.'

Meg gave him a grateful smile over her shoulder.

One result of the war was to provide markets for the Australian dried-fruit crop, all of which was grown along the Murray, for during the war years the whole of the world's supply had come from California or Australia. Two Californians, the Chaffey brothers, had established the first irrigated vineyards at Mildura and these were now flourishing; while Renmark had become a wealthy settlement.

The Murray below the Victorian border was being transformed. Land was mapped out in fifteen-acre blocks and up-to-date pumping machinery lifted the water a hundred and fifty feet to transform the barren scrub. Twenty towns and settlements rose simultaneously in the bush. Gangs of ex-soldiers toiled in the mallee, making roads, scooping channels with primitive horse-scoops, lining them with cement; grading, fencing, ploughing, stacking mallee roots for fuel.

At the end of the first summer there was a big heat wave, the temperature averaging 105° in the shade for a fortnight. The water in the new channels turned stagnant, dead rabbits lay rotting alongside them and mosquitoes bred everywhere. An epidemic of typhoid fever carried away many of those who had escaped the Spanish 'flu. Country doctors, their eyes red from lack of sleep, drove over the rough bush roads and paddle-steamers brought stocks of medicine and disinfectant to the little temporary stores built of hessian.

One steamer even brought the consolations of religion; for the boys of Eton College, away in England, contributing reluctantly to a Foreign Mission scheme, provided a floating Church of England chapel on a paddle-wheeler named the *Etona*. Canon Bussell travelled up and down the river between Morgan and Renmark and every Sunday morning – or any morning when the *Etona* happened to be tied up at a settlement – he gathered a congregation such as was certainly never seen in the mother church in England.

Rabbit-trappers and fishermen, shearers in greasy moleskins, labourers from the irrigation works in old army jackets, all were welcome in the little white-painted chapel on board. While Canon Bussell pumped the foot-pedals of the little organ, they sang the old hymns which some of them had not heard since they were children. They enjoyed the hymn-singing, and for its sake sat patiently through the long sermons when the Canon had recovered his breath after the long organ-pumping.

Further downstream, in the last reaches before the lakes, water was being pumped back into the river. The swamplands in the wide flood-plain on each side of Murray Bridge were being drained, their rich silt exposed for pasture land, and eventually fifty miles of river-flats were to be reclaimed. Milk from the dairy herds established went to a Farmers' Co-operative at Murray Bridge for processing.

At Wall, Pompoota, Jervois, Mobilong, Mypolonga, the ancient sanctuaries of the water-birds were taken from them as the backwaters were drained. Wild duck and black swans, pelicans and shags left for the wide waters of the Goolwa channel and the salty Coorong at the mouth.

Slowly, patiently, with the organised industriousness of ants, men were forcing the great sprawling river into a new pattern. The river flowed on, accepting all the indignities heaped on it by these puny creatures, and quietly bided its time.

SEVENTY-SEVEN

Delie worked long hours in the next months while there was plenty of cargo going; for steamers were once more as busy as bees in a honey-flow, swarming up and down the river to the new works.

She had become thinner and rather haggard and her cheekbones stood out above the hollows of her face; but she still kept by some miracle her soft English complexion, like slightly faded apple-blossom.

Mostly she wore a simple shirtwaist with a straight skirt to her ankles, and in cold weather a man's pullover, and sometimes a belted army jacket over this. She did not own a hat. Her dark hair grew with its old abundance, but through it ran one streak of silver, startling and dramatic in its effect.

Because river-freights were fixed at the same rate whether the

461

steamer discharged at Morgan, two hundred miles from the mouth, or at Goolwa, Delie preferred to get a back-loading consigned to Morgan when she took a load of flour from Murray Bridge, or beer and other essential equipment for the survey party at Lock Three. The down-river freight was usually wheat or wool.

With a load of wool, if she could get alongisde the Morgan wharf early, about 6 a.m., they could have a thousand bales ready to leave on the 2 p.m. train to Adelaide. A hundred bales an hour were discharged by the big steam cranes. The freight was thirty shillings a ton; they were making big money, but the strain was beginning to tell on them all, particularly on old Charlie.

Delie decided that as soon as she had a thousand pounds put by she would sell the barge and re-fit the steamer as a floating store. The new settlements would provide endless customers and there was a big construction camp being established at the Lake Victoria works.

One more load of wool would do it. She was thinking of leaving for Wentworth with a load of flour on the chance of getting a back-loading of wool, but before she left a letter came from Raeburn asking her to pick up the first clip of the season from Lake Victoria Station, and bring it down to his store at Milang. She wired acceptance at once.

The steamer had been passed as seaworthy, but she felt a little nervous. She had never ventured out into such a body of water, and once in the 1917 flood had become lost in a lagoon when she mistook an opening in the trees lining the bank for the main channel. On Lake Alexandrina the shores would perhaps be out of sight and she would have to navigate for the first time.

In the saloon cupboard she found an old chart of the lake, showing the channel close in-shore as the lake opened out below Wellington, then leaving the north-west point and crossing to Milang, half-way down the lake on the western shore. She talked to Captain Wallin of the *Oscar W.*, who was very doubtful if a woman skipper would ever reach Milang in safety.

'You vos too yung, too little,' he admonished her. 'The vind on the lakes, she coom sooden from the south-vest, und vot you do then? You are on a lee shore, rolling in eight-foot waves, und at efery roll your starboard paddle cooms out of the vater und is spinning in the air. You not very careful, you begin to turn in circles.

'Now listen: it iss best you leave at dawn, before the sun is oop. It iss nearly always calm then. If it has been blowing from the south-vest, perhaps you moost vait two days for the vater to go down. If you do not, it is so shallow you vill boomp on the bottom, und then you vill break oop.'

His words seemed to sound in her ears as she passed the old pub on the cliff-top at Wellington, the last town on the river before the Lakes. She had a large map spread on the wheel-house floor and, looking down at it, she traced the straightforward route to Milang across open water, far easier than finding a way through the maze of different channels to Goolwa and the Mouth.

She would follow Captain Wallin's advice, and tie up in the lee of Point Pomander tonight, before the lake widened. Looking up at the sky, she saw low, ragged clouds sweeping wildly from the south-west. The river was sheltered on this side in the lee of the willows, but on the opposite bank she could see their long boughs streaming out horizontally, tossing and writhing like green snakes.

She had no wish to hear the *Philadelphia* 'boomp' on the lake bottom, which was supposed to have a feet-deep layer of fine mud that would swallow a man. There was a dinghy for a life-boat, but she didn't fancy its chances in eight-foot waves. She was scared.

In spite of her anxiety, her heart gave a leap like a salmon when it enters the sea, as the willows suddenly fell away and the water broadened into the wide channel that led from the river into the open lake. For the first time she saw navigation signs ahead – black on the port side, red on the starboard. Mysterious squares and triangles, with gulls and shags roosting upon them, they spoke to her of the open sea.

They passed Beacon 94 just as it was beginning to get dusk and she saw over on the left two ugly snags sticking out of what must be quite shallow water.

Wellington Lodge homestead showed up on the left bank surrounded by palms and poplars and beyond it Low Point only just above the water. Crossing carefully, feeling her way, she made for the Nalpa out-station landing, beside the big stone wool-shed on the opposite shore. Shearing was about to begin and friendly lights showed in the men's huts.

Soon they had ropes out to the solid red-gum piles which had come, Delie reflected, all the way from the forests above Echuca where she had once walked among those giant trees. The barge was made snug to a large willow. The sound of an accordion was borne fitfully on the gusty wind from the direction of the huts.

'Reckon we should stroll over after tea, eh, Charlie?' said the Young Limb, affecting a grown-up drawl. 'Them shearers might 'ave some grog, an' they've certinly got music. No women, though, I s'pose, worse luck.' His freckled face cracked in a toothy grin.

'You Limb o' Satan! What next? Grog an' women! Time enough for that sort o' thing when you're old as me and past rooinin'. You tied that for'ard line proper? No granny knots? It's going to blow like blazes tonight, an' if the wind shifts –'

'Do you think it will, Charlie?' Delie stepped down from the wheel-house, rubbing her shoulders with her arms crossed on her chest. They ached unaccountably; she must have been gripping the wheel too hard in her anxiety at entering unknown waters.

Charlie squinted at the sky from beneath his ragged eyebrows.

'I don't reckon it will, no, unless it swings west. It won't swing north without it goes right round through south and east, so you won't need to worry about the ropes, or bein' banged agin the piles. We're sheltered from the west by them trees.'

'But will it have gone down by tomorrow?'

Charlie spat over the side. 'Dunno. Dunno what she'll do in this part o' the world. I'm a stranger 'ere. I could go over an' chat to them shearers about it –'

'Charlie!' She was looking at him in terrified appeal. He knew what she was thinking. If he once got over there, yarning and drinking . . . it was enough worry to be navigating the lake for the first time, without a drunken engineer into the bargain.

'It's all right, Missus.' He pulled his greasy old cap down over his eyes to hide their sheepish look. 'I don't wanter go. But the Young Limb might pop over and see if 'e can get some fresh bread from their bakehouse. Shearers' cooks makes beaut bread.'

The Limb, waiting only for her nod of agreement, pulled his pudding-basin hat firmly over his ears and was off like a bullet from a gun, bounding from sleeper to sleeper along the little railway that wound through the swampy samphire and brought the bales of wool to the wharf for loading.

Besides the shearing-shed and wool-press and the men's quarters, there was a wool-scouring plant with a big chimney, and built into the side of the fireplace a stone oven which would hold fifteen loaves of bread. The Limb came hopping back with a double loaf under each arm. 'The shearers say it's gonna blow like blazes,' he called cheerfully.

Delie could scarcely eat her meal that night as she sat listening to the roar of wind in the willows and a fainter roar which she took to be the waves beating on the open shore of the lake across the point.

It was no use discussing her worries with Brenton, who showed an almost surly lack of interest in anything connected with running the steamer. She wished, for the first time, that she carried a qualified mate to share her responsibilities. Nominally Brenton was the skipper and she was the mate, but she carried out both duties, snatching a few hours' sleep whenever she could. She was exhausted and could not keep it up much longer; but once this load was successfully delivered she'd go back to quiet store-trading.

In the morning, after a restless night, she was called early. The sky had cleared and the brightest stars were still showing; Venus rising whitely just ahead of the sun, Arcturus yellow and dull in the north-west, and the Cross high overhead. Looking down at the water, she saw that in this sheltered part it had calmed so much that the stars' reflections showed clearly, though distorted.

A zigzag sword of silver pointing towards the boat from the opposite shore was the track of Venus; and, straight below, the two Pointers danced together and apart like a pair of silently clapping hands.

Charlie came to ask if she wanted steam up. She looked at the clear sky, the softly stirring leaves and said, yes, they would leave as soon as it was light. He went to rouse out the fireman, who liked his bunk.

The bargemaster and his assistant were stirring. She heard one of them relieving himself over the side, beyond the tier of wool-bales. The river accepted it all, the warm excrement and the pure light of stars coming across billions of miles of space; and flowed on imperceptibly through the stillness of the lake.

Gordon, who liked the warm galley and had made firm friends with the cook, brought her a cup of strong, steaming tea and a slice of toast which she took to her cabin. He or the Limb often brought her meals to the wheel-house and would take over the wheel under her instructions while she ate. The cook was a blessing she never failed to be thankful for; he was a morose man but an excellent cook. She would rather steer a boat all night than prepare a meal for five critical men.

She went up to the wheel-house as the hidden sun began to glow behind the low hills. As she looked across the narrow neck of land to the open lake beyond, her heart quailed. The water was an ominous olive-green, churned into waves that were capped with dirty white foam. She opened the wheel-house windows and in the westerly breeze could hear the confused roar of their breaking.

But already they had steam up, and the boys were casting off some of the ropes. If she cancelled the order to leave now, they would think she had cold feet. And Charlie, disappointed, would probably go over to the shearers' huts and begin a bender that might last two days.

'Cast off the bow-line!' she called clearly. 'Is the barge untied? Let go that rope there, Gordon, and jump aboard. Stand by with the pole to push her out from the landing – right?' She pushed the engine lever into reverse and put her hand on the throttle. The great paddles churned, bit the water and flung it forward, and the *Philadelphia* edged out, turned and very gently took up the slack on the tow-rope so that the barge obediently followed without a jerk. The bargemaster swore in reluctant admiration. (He didn't really hold with women in the wheel-house.)

Once actually in motion, she forgot her fear in a lift of excitement and began to hum to herself as she picked up her landmarks, the blunt shape of Point Pomander on the right with the lighthouse at its end beginning to show and Low Point away to the left. The engine throbbed with power, chanting 'Onward, onward, onward . . .' She gave a skip in the air with excitement, and banged her head on the low cross-piece of the roof. Charlie came up the wheel-house steps, polishing the cold, red end of his nose with the back of his hand. His greasy cap was pulled low over his ears against the morning breeze.

'Wind 'as dropped overnight,' he remarked, conversationally. 'Them shearers don't know nothink about weather, except rain, when they can say the sheep is wet and take an 'oliday. Hey, you, Limb!' he roared suddenly through the wheel-house window. The Limb o' Satan was sheltering behind a few spare bales for'ard, and looking with lively interest towards the water ahead, now visible against the skyline in a row of ominous rolling ridges. 'Hop in and keep an eye on the water gauge – jump to it!' He pulled the window shut. 'Satan finds work for idle hands to do,' he quoted sententiously.

'The wind has dropped, but the water hasn't gone down much, if at all,' said Delie. 'Look at those waves! And whitecaps too.'

'Paddle-steamers weren't never meant to go out of the river, I say.'

'But Charlie, some of them came into the river under their own steam, all the way from Melbourne. The *Decoy* went to Western Australia and back. If they could go to sea, we can certainly cross twenty-four miles of lake. There used to be so many going in and out in the early days that there was a signal station at the Mouth. Are you scared? Because if so –'

Charlie grinned. 'I don't scare that easy. But *you'll* be turnin' back, I shouldn't wonder.' And he stumped off down the steps.

'You'd better send Gordon up to give me a hand,' she called after him. Delie set her teeth and gripped the spokes with sweating palms. All their lives were in her hands – Brenton's, the children's, the crew's. She doubted if Charlie could swim a stroke.

They rounded the point and she felt the jar of the short, steep waves on the hull: not rhythmical like a deep-sea swell, but abrupt and vicious. The steamer shuddered and heeled to port, while her starboard paddle thrashed in the air half the time. Delie had to hold the wheel hard against her tendency to pivot on the submerged side.

Gordon came up the steps and crossed to the other side of the wheel, holding it up and taking some of the strain. At once she felt more relaxed. He was only a boy, but she felt his calmness and strength.

Just then the sun came out from behind a low bank of cloud and lit up Point McLeay and Point Sturt away across the width of the lake. Where only grey formlessness had been, a bright orange sandhill and something that looked like a square yellow building, but was really a cliff of clay, shone out like a double beacon. Behind were curtains of rain and indigo cloud; red-gold the reed-beds glowed against them, and six black swans flying out of the sun. It was like a promise, like a rainbow after rain. All her anxiety and fear fell away and Delie smiled confidently at Gordon across the wheel-house.

'This is fun, isn't it?' she said, and Gordon laughed with excitement.

'I wish we could take her right out to sea,' he said. His thick, light brown hair was tousled and he obviously hadn't washed

467

that morning, but she forbore to scold him. She looked into his long blue eyes, so like her own, and thought with a rare contentment: 'My son.' They were the words she had said when he was first put into her arms in a Melbourne hospital – could it be sixteen years ago? Brenton's effective life might be finished and she herself was getting old, but life went on.

Across the lake the brief reflection of light faded. They struggled on, buffeted by steep waves, towards the invisible shore.

SEVENTY-EIGHT

Only two other vessels were tied up at the long, curving Milang jetty when the *Philadelphia* arrived after her journey across the lake.

'*Invincible* and *Federal*,' shouted Alex, reading the names of the other steamer and its barge, and dancing with excitement on the top deck at their safe arrival after what had seemed to him as long and perilous a journey as Magellan's crossing of the Pacific. He had never been so far from land before; and now they were to make fast to a real jetty, not a wharf on the riverbank.

The *Waterlily*, an odd-looking vessel like an unfinished schooner, with planks of uneven lengths sticking out from her stern, was just setting off with taut sails for Point McLeay.

The storekeeper, all the children from the local school, the crew of the other steamer and the idlers of the town, including many with dark skins and aboriginal features, had collected to watch the *Philadelphia* and her barge tie up.

Delie, because she was in a new port and felt the stares at a woman in charge in the wheel-house, felt self-conscious, until a hail from the jetty in a well-known voice made her forget her embarrassment.

'Miss Delie! Hi, Missus! Congratulations; you handle her better than a man. Takes a woman to understand a woman.'

'Jim Pearce! What are you doing here?' She came out of the wheel-house as soon as the paddles had stopped thrashing and leaned over the deck-rail.

Dear old Jim, mate of the first *Philadelphia* before she was burnt; Jim who had gone for help when her first child was born on the river-bank.

'Hey, Jim!' she called. 'Come aboard! Teddy will want to see you.' She was so excited that she didn't even notice Mr Raeburn standing a little aloof from the crowd, watching with bright, amused eyes. She had the man's old jacket on, a cap that had been Teddy Edwards's and had seen better days and her hair was coming down. She went down to meet Jim on the lower deck and bring him up to Brenton's cabin.

Jim was captain of the *Invincible* trading between Milang and Meningie, to and fro across the lakes, which was why she had not encountered him earlier on the river.

'You was a bit game, wasn't you, coming acrost there on a day like this? I'd have tied up meself, and waited.' His weather-beaten face was more deeply lined, grained like old leather, the skin of his neck hung in a wrinkled dewlap, and his dark hair was turned to an ivory grey so that his skin seemed browner than ever in contrast. It gave Delie a shock to see him. Jim Pearce with grey hair brought home the passage of time more sharply than the gradual changes in her own appearance. 'What was the hurry?' he asked.

'I had a good reason,' she said in a low voice. 'Charlie McBean is still with us and we were tied up near a shearers' camp.'

'Oh – ah, I see. Good old Charlie, and is he still going strong?'

'Yes, come and see him.'

Jim and Charlie wrung each other's hands and then Jim went up to see Brenton, who became more animated than he'd been for years. They opened a bottle of beer to celebrate the meeting and talked endlessly over old times.

Remembering that she had not seen the consignee nor formally handed over the cargo, Delie went to her cabin and took off the old jacket, put on a fresh blouse of tussore silk and brushed her hair. She coiled it so that the silver streak was less noticeable and dashed a little lavender-water behind her ears – her one luxury.

'And what is all this in aid of?' she asked her reflection sternly, as she looked at the effect in her small mirror. 'Alastair Raeburn is a man, but he is not interested in you and this meeting is purely a business one.'

She picked up a cashmere shawl which had belonged to her Aunt Hester, wrapped it round her shoulders and stepped out on deck.

'Mr Raeburn was 'ere, but he's gone back to the warehouse,' said the bargemaster. 'Told me to tell you he saw you was busy and ast you to come up when you were ready.'

'Oh!' said Delie. 'Thank you.' So he'd seen her in her old outfit, shouting down at Jim like a fishwife! She felt hot at the thought; but she squred her shoulders and stepped briskly along the jetty, between the railway-lines, which led off between two high piles of cut wood stacked ready for steamers. The small line led direct to the dark doorway of the wool-store across the lakeside road. Along the front of this building ran the legend: 'RIVERS MURRAY AND DARLING WOOL', and above this was a balcony with ornate iron-work, apparently belonging to the living-quarters on the first floor.

The cold south-west wind struck her as she crossed the open space and she shivered. It had been silly to take off her warm jacket and put on a silk blouse to venture out of the sheltered wheel-house. Her throat felt dry, as if she had a cold beginning.

Vanity, that was the trouble, though she was forty and her hair was going grey . . .

In Brenton's cabin, with its big window through which the fitful sunshine gleamed from the west when there was a break in the scudding clouds, the two men relaxed in an atmosphere of beer and reminiscence.

After the first shock of seeing each other so changed by time and accident, they realised that the essential being was the same. Teddy Edwards and Jim Pearce had been mates in more senses than the nautical one, they had gone to each other's help in brawls, navigated steamers together through floods and fires and through the great drought of 1902, got drunk together on innumerable occasions and argued over the merits of steamers and skippers. Both had been Echuca men, bred at the 'top end' of the river and both now found themselves at the 'bottom end' with the old joy and verve gone from their lives. No more rivalry between crews from different ends; no more racing a falling river, winching over reefs and warping through rapids, no more girls in the gin shanties of the Darling.

Jim had nine children, who lived ashore at Goolwa with their mother; he didn't like to leave her and go on long trips up-river, though he ran a Sunday passenger trip to Wellington when the weather was fine. His steamer was little more than a glorified lake-ferry, and when the weather kept him tied up he supplemented his income by fishing for mullet and butterfish at Goolwa beach and trapping rabbits for their skins.

All this came out gradually as the beer loosened his tongue.

'Ah, life's not what she used to be, Teddy,' he sighed, wiping the froth from his mouth. 'We don't realise, when we're young, that it don't last.'

'You've got nothing . . . complain of . . . Jim. What about . . . me? You still . . . run your own steamer, active as ever, while I –'

'Yes, old man, I know. I didn't like to speak of it; but I don't know how you've stood it, stuck in bed all the time. A bloke like you, an active, manly bloke, aground in a backwater for the rest of y'r life –'

'Not . . . rest of me life!' With an effort Brenton sat upright, letting the bedclothes fall back. 'Here, take this glass, Jim. Now . . . watch!' Slowly, with infinite struggle, he slewed himself round till his legs hung over the side of the bed and dropped to the floor. He lay panting, lying at an angle. 'See that? Every day – every day I get me feet down, let . . . blood run into them again. They're getting . . . more feeling. And look at this. Hand me . . . them books!'

Jim passed over the two big tomes he indicated, a *Geography of South Australia* and a *History of the Settlement of New South Wales.*

'Delie thinks I'm improving me mind. Know what I use 'em for?' He heaved himself back on the bed, and lying back balanced a book in each big hand. Then he lifted them slowly, slowly, till they were held above him at arm's length. 'Already . . . arms much stronger. I'll show 'em. S'prise – they'll be s'prised. Back in th' wheel-house – nex' year.'

'You beaut, Teddy! You'll show 'em! They can't keep a good man down.'

There was a thump on the door and Charlie McBean came in, minus his cap, which was so much a part of him that he looked unnatural, as though he'd lost the top part of his head. Under his arm was a bottle of whisky. 'Good old Charlie. Come – in!' Brenton dropped the books with a crash and flashed a look of warning at Jim Pearce.

Charlie's faded blue eyes twinkled beneath his wild eyebrows which, now they had turned white, looked like pieces of cotton-wool badly gummed on.

'Thought the beer'd be running low,' he said. 'We'll have a little whisky for a chaser . . . Here's to us, boys!'

471

And soon three voices could be heard, strangely blended, coming from the cabin in what might pass for song:

Another little drink, 'nother little drink—
Another little drink wouldn't do us any harm . . .

Meanwhile Delie had made her way into the dim storeroom, beyond which she saw the great warehouse, stacked almost to the roof with bale after bale of wool, thousands of bales from up-river. It was enormous, like a cathedral, and as dark and silent, while through a window up on the second-floor level a beam of late sunlight shone red-gold as through stained glass.

'Mr Raeburn has gone upstairs,' the storekeeper was saying, when she heard his step and his drawling voice from above.

'Ah, Mrs Edwards! I have been expecting you.'

Small and elegant, carefully dressed to the last detail of his plain tie and polished boots, incongruous in this small lakeside town, he made her feel suddenly shy. She was glad she had put on her best blouse.

'My aunts begged me to bring you up to afternoon tea. They've heard about you, and want to inspect you.'

There was controlled humour in his voice, in the quirk of his left eyebrow and the veiled, mocking, brilliant gaze of his dark eyes. She knew that he was comparing her appearance with that she had presented in the wheel-house and knew that his aunts had expected just some such apparition to arrive for tea – man's cap and all.

She lifted her chin and said clearly: 'Thank you, Mr Raeburn. But we have business to discuss, I think. It's too late to begin unloading today, but – '

He had reached the bottom stair, he ignored his storekeeper and took her cold hand, bending above it and brushing it with his lips.

'You are too beautiful to talk business and I am too much in need of my tea. Shall we go up?'

As he led the way up the stair, she noticed the beautiful carving of the rail and newel-post, and that an old painting of flowers and fruit hung at the first landing, where a strip of red carpet began. She felt as in a dream; she was being escorted into another world, backwards in time, thousands of miles across the sea, to where just such a stair led up to the first-floor drawing-room in her grandfather's house. In all her life in Australia she had never entered such a private home. And outside, the rabbits swarmed among the hedges of prickly pear and the white dusty roads led between swamps where the black snakes bred in hundreds. She looked up and saw at the head of the stairs the gaslight glittering through a crystal chandelier.

SEVENTY-NINE

A confused impression of people, faces, voices . . . far too many people in one room . . . names which refused to register in her brain. 'And these are my aunts, the Misses Raeburn; my sister-in-law, Mrs Henry Raeburn; her son Jamie and little Jessamine. They are having tea with us this afternoon as a special treat. And the children's nurse, Miss Mellership.'

Bewildered and shy, for she'd had few social contacts in the last ten years, and had seen little of her own sex apart from Mrs Melville, Delie found herself seated in a roomful of women. Mr Raeburn's was the only familiar face and him she scarcely knew.

Her eyes flew to the portrait in oils above the mantelpiece – the family's chairs were grouped about the fire in the open hearth – but found no solace there; for one more woman's face looked down at her, with a supercilious stare: heavy-lidded eyes, a strong, fleshy nose and smooth white brow, lips moulded into a disdainful curve.

'And yet another family connection, Mrs Edwards; an ancestress of mine, painted by Lely at the court of Charles the First.'

'A Lely? Truly?'

'Yes. Truly a Lely. Or should I say a really-truly Lely? Either way it's a tongue-twister.'

'But how wonderful! I would like to have a closer look later.' She gazed about, becoming aware that the mantel and fireplace were of marble, the walls papered with a satin stripe in white and green.

'Milk or lemon, Mrs Edwards?' Miss Raeburn, poising the silver teapot, gave her a piercing stare from alert grey eyes, set on each side of a strong, fleshy nose like the one in the portrait. Her mousy-grey hair was piled on top of her head in the fashion of twenty years ago. A bunch of fine lace was pinned at her withered throat with a cairngorm brooch.

'The matriarch!' thought Delie. 'She rules the roost, I fancy, and Mrs Henry, the helpless widow, has never challenged her position. No wonder the other Mrs Raeburn left, if she was a woman of any spirit.'

Aloud she said that she would take milk, that since her years on the Darling she still regarded fresh milk as a luxury; for they'd had only tinned milk or goats' milk when they called at a settlement.

'Have you really been up the Darling, Missus Edwards?' piped young Jamie, big-eyed. 'With your very own paddle-steamer? You don't look a bit like a man. Aunt Allie said –'

'That's enough, Jamie. Little boys should be seen and not heard, unless they want to go and have tea in the nursery. Miss Mellership, would you pass that to Mrs Edwards?'

Delie, taking the frail cup of transparent china, felt afraid it would crumple in her hands. She had been used to swallow her tea from a thick mug brought by a boy to the wheel-house or her cabin. She was handed a plate, a napkin and a buttery crumpet to juggle on her knees, while the disdainful beauty looked down her nose at her from the gilt frame.

She said desperately: 'I saw the words "River Darling Wool" in front of the warehouse. Strange, isn't it, to think that wool from away near the Queensland border should come to this end of Australia, simply because of the arbitrary flowing of water?'

'But it doesn't, any longer; or very rarely. The upper Darling stations all consign by rail from Bourke these days and it goes to the Sydney warehouses. Eventually, I believe, trains will be superseded in their turn by motor-trucks.'

'Or even cargo aeroplanes?' said Delie, thinking of Ross Smith and her feeling when the little plane flew over the hills, that all things were possible to man.

'Aeroplanes! What rubbish!' cried Miss Raeburn briskly. 'Man was never meant to fly.'

'Nevertheless he is doing so, Aunt Alicia.'

'Let him remember the fate of Icarus, and beware.'

'Ross Smith didn't fall into the sea, however,' said Delie, piqued by Miss Raeburn's confident, brook-no-argument manner.

Her hostess's well-marked eyebrows, not yet grey, rose until they met the loops of hair on her forehead. There was a just-audible gasp from Mrs Henry. Delie looked at her and saw that her soft, pretty mouth was slightly open. There was a mole on her cheek and her hair was dark and wavy, parted in the middle over a white forehead. She had tragic-looking, outward-sloping eyebrows, meeting in a peak above her nose.

'Perhaps Mrs Edwards would like another crumpet,' said Miss Janet, the younger aunt, in the silence. Alastair Raeburn's face was buried in his cup and his shoulders shook slightly.

Miss Janet had an anxious look, which Delie later learned was her permanent expression. Her features were worn and faded, her mouth soft and indeterminate. She was like her assertive elder sister only in the soft, mousy-grey pile of her hair.

'Thank you, I won't have any more.'

'Another cup of tea, perhaps?' Miss Raeburn dropped the subject of aeroplanes; her displeasure showed only in her stiffly held back.

'Alastair, pass Mrs Edwards's cup.'

'Yes, please. It's the nicest tea I've drunk in a long time.'

'Do you have a cook on board, Mrs Edwards?' Mrs Henry asked rather breathlessly. 'I'm sure I don't know how you manage.'

'Oh yes; quite a good cook. A man, of course.'

'A *man*!' Miss Janet looked scandalised.

'This tea', Raeburn interposed firmly, 'I import direct from Ceylon. Also coffee from Brazil – rum from Jamaica – spices from the East Indies. You mustn't think that we deal only in prosaic wool.'

'But even wool can be romantic – the sheer quantities of it. A thousand bales! And our load is nothing to what you must sometimes have stored here, and from such tremendous distances – '

'And brought down in face of such tremendous difficulties. There is the romance of it, Mrs Edwards. Do you realise, ladies, that we are entertaining a heroine? She has brought her steamer, single-handed in the wheel-house, all the way from Wentworth – five hundred miles up-river; and has crossed the lake for the first time in a south-westerly. Besides which she is the mother of four – is it? – four children, a skilled and talented painter in oils and the devoted nurse of an invalid husband. I salute your courage, my dear.' And he lifted his tea-cup gallantly.

'Oh, please – !' Delie blushed like a girl, sensing how the feeling in the room was hardening against her.

'Quite a prodigy,' murmured Mrs Henry into her cup.

'Not a very *womanly* occupation,' said Miss Raeburn.

'Surely it would be better to employ a – a captain to run the boat?' suggested Miss Janet.

'Except that he would require a salary,' said Delie. 'And as it is, with the children to educate . . . and I truly believe my husband would die away from the river. Which reminds me, I must go back to him.'

As she stood up to go, making her farewells rather awkwardly, Jamie got up from his stool near the fire and came over to her.

'I like you,' he said frankly. She looked down into the bright dark eyes, wondering if his father had been very like his Uncle Alastair.

'If your mother will let you, you can come and see over the boat tomorrow.'

'Me too,' said Jessie firmly, tossing the dark curls back from her small fire-flushed face.

At the door, Delie suddenly felt hot and faint. Her head was stuffy and her chest felt tight when she breathed. She held on to the banister as Raeburn escorted her down the stairs, and as the cold wind struck her she began to cough.

Gasping, she held out her hand. 'Thank you. Good-bye. Could we leave the papers till tomorrow? I feel a little . . . The room was hot and I have been rather chilled all day.'

'Are you sure you're all right?' He held her hand a moment longer than necessary. 'Tomorrow will be plenty of time. I think I should see you back to the boat.'

'No, please! I'm quite all right in the fresh air. It's only a step, besides.'

She turned and hurried off before he could persuade her. She knew that Brenton and Jim Pearce would be well launched on their celebration by now. She felt a need to keep these two worlds apart. Unconsciously she had slipped back into a manner and a way of speaking which belonged to her life before her marriage. It was not affectation; it was as if that old self, the girl whose soft fingers touched nothing rougher than a pencil, an embroidery-needle or a piano, were still there beneath the skin, to be called out in a moment by a return to the old environment.

She had not disgraced herself, she felt, except by contradicting the formidable Aunt Alicia. She felt that Mr Raeburn was pleased with her and was childishly gratified at the thought.

A ribald song, accompanied by the thumping of bottles on a

table, drifted from the direction of the steamer. She was glad she had come back alone. And after all, she remembered, she had not had a closer look at the Lely, nor had she seen any of Raeburn's own painting. She hoped to be asked to the house again.

EIGHTY

Charlie McBean crawled out of his bunk, screwing up his eyes against the offensive glitter of sun reflected from rippling lake water. He rasped a hand over the white stubble on his chin and groped for his trousers. He blinked his bleary eyes.

A man was getting old, that was the trouble – why, they'd only finished one bottle of whisky last night and then that bit of beer. He had a mouth like the inside of a blackfeller's boot.

Sounds of activity from the galley cheered him a little. Not that he could face food – breakfast eggs – oogh! But a black coffee and the fresh, tangy taste of a raw onion . . .

Old, getting old . . . It was like a refrain in his head this morning, making it ache. He wouldn't get a job on any other steamer these days, he knew. Well, the *Philadelphia* wouldn't get another engineer for the wages he worked for, either.

He went along to the galley and poked his nose in the door. The cook's regard was anything but welcoming.

'Breakfast's not on yet,' he said now, sourly.

'Just came to tell yer, don't cook none for me. I don't feel up to it, some'ow. Any coffee goin'?' he asked brightly, his eyes searching anxiously for the onions. Yes, there were some in the string bag hanging under the end of the sink.

'Help yerself,' said the cook ungraciously.

Charlie picked up the coffee-pot with a hand that shook and poured coffee into a cup without a saucer. He didn't want the cook to hear it rattle. 'That'll do me, thanks. That and an onion.'

'An *onion*?' The cook hadn't been with the *Philadelphia* long enough to have seen Charlie with a hang-over.

'Yairs; and a bit o' bread to take up the juice.'

Charlie took one of the pieces ready sliced for toast and an onion from the bag; but as he picked up the carving knife in his shaky hand, the cook snatched it from him.

'Gimme that, you silly ole bugger, before you cut yer hand orf.' He peeled and sliced the onion expertly and Charlie slapped the raw rings on the bread and folded it over.

'Ah!' he said, breathing the fumes while his eyes watered from their strength. 'That's the stuff to give the troops!' And picking up the coffee-cup in the other hand, he went off, munching.

Delie woke with a headache too – an unusual thing for her – and it didn't seem fair as she had drunk nothing but tea the night before.

She'd had no dinner, but had gone straight to bed feeling hot and shivery, but with a pleasant warm feeling about her heart at Mr Raeburn's tender concern. Even if it was only politeness, it was years since anyone had fussed like that over her health.

And she really did feel ill – she turned over with a groan – all her limbs ached and her throat was sore. She heard the noises of activity in the galley and began to long for a cup of hot coffee. She wanted it with such intensity that she could almost see it on the little table by her bunk, dark brown with just a little top-milk, steam curling from the surface.

As if she had willed him, Gordon put his head in the door. She was so glad to see him that she swallowed the automatic rebuke, 'You haven't done your hair this morning', and instead smiled at him weakly.

'Want a cup of tea, Mum?'

'Oh, darling! Some coffee, if you wouldn't mind . . . black, no, with just a drop of milk. And could you pass me the bottle of aspirin – on the little shelf under the window there. You'd better have a look at Dad too, and see if he wants anything, because I doubt if Charlie's surfaced yet.'

'Alex can. I'll tell him you said so. Are you all right?'

'I feel a bit shivery. I think I've caught a chill.'

'Stay there for now, anyway. I'll bring the coffee.'

As she lay there, already comforted as if the hot coffee were actually inside her, she reflected that life compensated if you were allowed to live long enough. All the anxious care, the endless chores, the night-long vigils by his bed when he was ill, from the time Gordon was a tiny baby; all had led to this moment when he was the comforter and she was comforted. She had even seen families where the natural relationship had been completely reversed by time, so that the parent was treated as a rather tiresome child.

Let me never live so long, she thought, that I become like that, childish and burdensome to my own children!

Her grandfather, she remembered, had been alert and active right up to a day before he died, and she was willing to bet that Miss Alicia Raeburn would be of the same kind. And Brenton, though nearly helpless for so long, was never childish. His sons respected him, were even a little in awe of him, though he could scarcely lift his arm.

'I must get up,' she said aloud, and snuggled further down into the bedclothes.

'A thousand bales in good order and condition.'

Raeburn signed the bill of lading and handed it to her across the table, together with a cheque. She gave him her receipt and felt immensely relieved that the business was over, that she could crawl back into her bunk and close her eyes. A hard, dry cough tore at her chest and involuntarily she put a hand there, where a dull-bladed knife seemed to stab with each breath.

'My dear Mrs Edwards – '

His eyes, wide open, were studying her with unaffected concern.

'It's quite all right. I think perhaps I have caught – a slight chill.' Her voice sounded strange in her own ears, hollow and croaking.

'I shall never forgive myself if you have caught pneumonia through attending to my affairs. You are hot.' He touched her cheek, delicately, with the back of his hand; a clinical gesture.

Her reply was lost in another bout of coughing. Pneumonia! It was a dread word. Her own Grandmother Gordon had died of it, and she remembered, as a child, being taken into the dim room where her grandmother breathed her last: short, gasping breaths with a dreadful bubbling sound in the lungs, as she slowly drowned in her own mucus.

'One moment!' He was rummaging in the desk drawer of his office, which was under the stairs leading up to the main house. He came up with a Centigrade thermometer, an enormous glass tube. He popped it into her mouth before she could protest and, grasping her left wrist firmly, began to feel the pulse with two fingers, checking it with a silver watch on a chain.

His fingers were soft and beautifully manicured, she saw as she looked down, squinting past the big thermometer. She sat perforcedly silent, embarrassed, and felt her pulse rate rapidly going up with agitation. He was silent and abstracted as he counted.

'Hm, hm.' He deftly snatched the thermometer from her mouth, read it and shook it down. His lips moved, making a calculation and he jotted down some figures. 'Yes, just as I thought; quite high. Thirty-nine Centigrade is about 102° Fahrenheit. What on earth are you doing out of bed?'

His manner was so sternly professional that she had to laugh.

'And since when have you been a member of the medical profession? Your bedside manner is almost perfect, but it doesn't fool me. You see, my father was a doctor and you gave yourself away just then. A real doctor never divulges the temperature to the patient. Mystification is his stock-in-trade, Father used to say, as much as it is the African witch-doctor's.'

He smiled, but immediately looked serious again. 'I do know enough of medicine, however, to tell you that, with your temperature and pulse-rate, you should not have been out in today's wind. The sun is deceptive; there is no warmth in it with the south-westerly off the water. You must go back to bed at once.'

'But –'

'Please, Mrs Edwards. You see, I feel responsible.'

'There is no reason why you should,' she said feebly, but at the same time she felt it was delightful having a man to order her about again, to take charge and let her stop thinking for herself. For she was a thoroughly feminine woman, in spite of her theories about the equality of the sexes.

'Where did your father practise – in what part of Australia?'

'No part of Australia. You see, he never reached here . . . in a sense.'

'In a sense?' His lids had dropped a little: how quickly those dark eyes mirrored his moods, whether of humour or scepticism or concern.

'He is buried in Australian soil; he never set foot on it in his life. Our ship was wrecked the night before she was due in Melbourne. All my family were drowned.' After so many years, her voice still trembled as she spoke of it.

'You poor girl! But you must have relatives in England?'

'Oh yes; cousins. My father was an only son, my mother's sister died in Echuca years ago, my uncle more recently. I was –'

A coughing fit interrupted her. He patted her hand and leaped vigorously to his feet. 'Don't talk any more. I'll take you home – that is, to the steamer.'

'The steamer is my home.'

'Of course! Yet somehow I can't believe it. You don't seem to fit into that background, there's such a fineness and delicacy about you. Do you know what I thought yesterday afternoon? I thought how well you fitted into my drawing-room. I should have known that complexion was English.'

He took her arm as they went out into the wide lakeside road, and guided her across to the jetty.

She stopped suddenly, struck by a thought. 'But I haven't seen any of your painting! Where do you work?'

'Oh – upstairs, above the store-room on the top level. It has a skylight.'

'In that dear little circular room on the roof?'

'Yes; it's also an observatory and lookout. I have a telescope there, to give me warning of approaching vessels; I can see the other side of the lake quite clearly. And sometimes at night, I look at the moon or the planets. I will show you when you are well enough.'

'Is there nowhere she could be moved – into a larger room, with more air?'

Drowsily, Delie heard the doctor's voice, somewhat short as though he were irritated by something. This was his third visit in two days; they must imagine she was quite ill. She had just woken from a recurrent nightmare she'd had since a child whenever she had a high fever.

She had to swallow an endless billowing white sausage, which had a subtly revolting taste and smell. It seemed actually to increase in bulk as fast as she ate it, yet she must keep swallowing and swallowing, or it would fill the whole cabin and she would be smothered in its hateful coils. The taste of it was still in her mouth – sickening.

'May I come in?' Raeburn pushed aside the cabin door and joined Gordon and the doctor by the bunk, so that the little cabin was full. 'I would suggest, Doctor, that she be moved across to our house, where my aunts could nurse her properly, in an airy room.

'There is, you realise, no woman on board this vessel apart from Mrs Edwards herself. Her husband is bedridden and there are only a cook and a cabin-boy to look after her besides her son –'

'*Two* sons,' murmured Delie, 'and Charlie McBean.'

'Two schoolboys and a fuddled old man. I think, Doctor –'

'And I agree. No place for sick woman. Damp air rising from the lake. Not enough ventilation. Unhealthy. She must be moved. Well wrapped up, on a stretcher. Hrrmmp!'

This last was a trumpet-peal blown into a handkerchief through his large, fleshy nose; like the word STOP in a telegram, it punctuated the longer pauses in his terse remarks.

'I'm sure it can be arranged immediately. Perhaps you would just have a word with Mr Edwards.'

'Yes. And as for you, young woman' (Delie felt vaguely pleased at this form of address, though she knew it was only relative, the doctor appearing to be well past sixty), 'you must be more careful in future. No skimping meals. No twenty-four hours on duty. Plenty of warm clothes. Hot, nourishing food. Drink stout. But first we must get you ashore, get you better. Hrrmmp!'

'Yes, Doctor,' she said submissively. She wondered how Brenton and the boys would get on without her; but they had managed while she and Meg were away in the city. She was too tired to argue with the doctor. She felt terribly hot and her chest hurt.

'I'll leave a prescription with the chemist. Expectorant mixture . . . aspirin . . . steam tent . . . chest poultice. Miss Janet's an excellent nurse. I'll call in the morning. Good-bye, Mrs – Hrrmmp!'

He picked up his bag and went to see Brenton. He was there rather a long time. Raeburn gave her a reassuring smile and went off to warn his aunts to prepare a sickroom. He knew Aunt Janet would be delighted at the idea of a patient to exercise her skill on. Aunt Alicia – well, he could handle Aunt Alicia.

EIGHTY-ONE

'Pass me the big colander, Meg,' said Mrs Melville, whisking the cauliflower saucepan off the stove. 'You get on and mash the potatoes, will you, dear?'

She lifted the lid and peered into the pot, her firm, ruddy features wreathed in steam. 'That's the girl. This is one of the caulies you grew, isn't it? You should've been a farmer's daughter

482

Meg. It's a real beauty.'

She tipped the real beauty into the colander, where it lay plump and creamy-white, rounded and compact as a cumulus cloud, its stem branching like a tree. The white sauce, rich with butter, dotted with green specks of parsley, was already made and keeping hot at the side of the wood stove.

Meg loved this ritual of the evening meal. It was getting dark outside; the lamplight looked yellow, the sky ink-blue through the top of the big window. The large, light kitchen was aromatic with food cooked to perfection, that subtle scent which tells the experienced cook when vegetables are done without the aid of a testing fork. Tonight she had made the steamed pudding and hoped for a word of praise from Garry. Mrs Melville took a cloth and lifted the hot plates from the oven.

'You can call the men now, Meg.'

Meg went a detour by way of her room, and fluffed up the black floss of her hair with a brush. 'When I am married,' she told her reflection, 'I shall get the dinner all ready and put it in the oven and then go and make myself pretty, and *then* call Ga – I mean, my husband, to come.'

Her reading at the farm consisted almost entirely of women's magazines which Mrs Melville took for the recipes and the fancy-work patterns, but which Meg read from cover to cover: the hints to young wives, the romantic serials, the stories which began with a chance meeting and ended with wedding bells. She had an absurdly distorted view of life and the relationship of the sexes, in spite of the realities of her mother's existence as she had known it for thirteen years; *her* marriage would not be like that.

Her husband would bring her flowers on their anniversary; she would greet him every evening with a pretty ribbon in her hair; and every night, at a suitable interval after dinner, they would retire together to the mysterious, intimate delights of the bed. She was a country child and knew by example as well as theory the strange antics of the beasts in season; but all that was remote from her imagining: herself in filmy chiffon, between the snow-white sheets, yielding to repeated but never palling bliss.

And when a little baby came, they would lean together above the tiny head in the frilled and beribboned cradle. It would be a boy, called Richard, or a girl, called Robina – she couldn't quite make up her mind and sometimes decided on twins, a boy and a girl, to settle the matter. Then he (the indispensable husband) turned towards her: 'She has your lovely hair, darling,' he whispered, and their lips met . . .

'Meg, did you call them?' came Mrs Melville's voice with an edge of impatience. 'The tea's made.'

'Oh, coming,' she sang, and skipped out to the veranda.

Afterwards, as they sat round the table drinking the cups of strong stewed tea which ended every meal, Mrs Melville looked fondly at Meg. The child was quite pretty tonight. If she'd had a daughter, she would have liked one exactly like this.

Delie opened her eyes and fixed them on a spot on the blue-and-silver wallpaper. It was a spot of ink, or a fly sitting there – no, two flies, and now they began to flap their wings.

How silly! Flies didn't have wings that would flap, and it was only one thing, a black bird. It grew as she watched it to the size of a crow. It flapped its black wings lazily, yet did not move from its place between the blue rose and the silver trellis on which it was perching. She wished it would hurry up and fly away, it spoiled the tranquil pattern of silver and blue on which she could have rested her hot, aching eyes.

There were voices from somewhere beyond the trellis . . . Was it a garden where she was lying? She began to concentrate, trying to find out where she was. At once the crow stopped flapping, became quite small and turned into a blowfly on the wallpaper. She was in bed at the Raeburns' house and she was aware once more of the heaviness of her chest, the effort of breathing and a sickening taste in her mouth.

Yes, that was the doctor's voice; had he been to see her already, then?

'High fever, very high. Careful nursing, bathing to get the temperature down. Can rely on you Miss Janet. I would suggest hospital, but too late now to move her . . . Yes. Hrrmmp!'

'I shall do my best, Doctor.'

Delie listened with detachment, as though they were talking of someone who had no connection with her. Nothing mattered as much as she supposed it did; she was ready to leave the world without a struggle, if that was what must be. She did not worry about what would happen to Brenton or the children or the steamer. She saw her life as a drop, less than a drop, a molecule in the enormous river of time. A molecule of H_2O. And with this temperature she would soon evaporate. Her head began to vaporise first, becoming incredibly light. Then her neck and shoulders and soon her heart would be gone, her whole body turned to a wisp of steam . . .

Something cold pressed against her lips which no longer existed.

'Just suck this piece of ice, Mrs Edwards. I'm going to bathe you now to get your temperature down and make you more comfortable.'

There was a long, empty beach where she was walking alone, when a great wave reared up, high above all the others. She turned to run, but it was too late. The wave caught her, lifted her, swept her far up over the sandhills and left her stranded, gasping but conscious, in a bed with a blue silk cover, in a large room with blue-and-silver wallpaper which she remembered seeing somewhere once before. In another life, perhaps?

There was a woman in the basket-chair in the window, crocheting – Aunt Hester! And she still blamed her for Adam's death. She would pretend to be asleep and perhaps she would go away.

But she was too thirsty to sleep. Her mouth was gummed together. With her eyes still closed she made a little whimpering sound in her throat and almost at once felt the cool rim of a glass against her lips, an arm supporting her shoulders. She opened her eyes and saw Miss Janet's worried-looking face.

'Thank you.' She sank back on the pillows, marvelling at her own weakness. She remembered everything, the trip across the lake, her illness and removal.

'You've been delirious,' said Miss Janet with a restrained smile, 'but a good natural sleep has refreshed you. Your eyes are quite clear again. I don't need the thermometer to tell me the fever's gone.' She took out a small lace-edged handkerchief and wiped her lips – a nervous habit, as Delie discovered later, by which Miss Janet seemed to be removing from her mouth any unseemly expression which might be found there.

She poured a dose of strong aniseed-tasting medicine for Delie and then went out, saying she would get some fresh orange juice. Delie lay and looked at the moulded-plaster ceiling, so high above her head after the wood of the cabin roof. There was a white rug on the floor and besides the basket-chair there was an armchair covered in plum-coloured brocade and over the arm of this hung a pink dressing-gown of shining satin. Whose was this lovely room, the silken gown, the white-furred slippers she now saw beside it? Probably the former Mrs Alastair Raeburn's

485

before she went off with the wool-buyer. How could she have left all this behind her? But then Delie remembered the lonely lakeshore, the small country town sixty miles from the nearest city, the cold south-westerly winds sweeping the front of the house, unsheltered by a single tree.

Inside, they might create a corner of the old country, with imported furniture and works of art; but outside the antipodean wind still howled and the natives in from Point McLeay Mission stood on street corners with the lost darkness of an ancient continent in their eyes. The white roads ran east to an empty horizon; and the introduced rabbits, no longer charming bunnies out of a Beatrix Potter story, bred in plague numbers among the prickly pear.

Without children of her own, without resources of the mind and with so many women and servants in the house that she had nothing to do, a woman used to city life could have been savagely bored. The wool-buyer would not have had to be so very attractive. He only had to offer her a life in London. And Raeburn had been often away, at Morgan or Murray Bridge or Goolwa.

A fire was flapping gently in the grate. Small blue flames played over the glowing logs, flickered, went out and were born again. Delie watched them dreamily. What luxury, to have a fire in the bedroom, a thick white rug on the floor and all this space for one person!

When Miss Janet brought her orange juice and later a light meal of chicken broth and jelly, she ate and drank eagerly though her hunger was soon satisfied. It was so pleasant to be waited on, to lie peacefully out of it all, as though she had in fact been swept up by a great wave beyond the restless surge of daily life.

Time had ceased to have its regular pattern. She had just broken her fast after a long sleep and now she found that it was late afternoon, almost evening. The two children came in after they'd had their nursery tea, though warned by Miss Janet not to stay long and tire the patient.

Jamie sidled up to the bed, rather shy, and asked politely how she felt and said he was glad to find her better. The little girl walked with assurance to the brocade chair and, pushing the dressing-gown aside, sat there with her legs sticking out in front of her, regarding Delie gravely.

'What's your name, dear? Jessie, isn't it?'

'My name is Jessamine Raeburn,' said the child primly.

'Jessamine! What a pretty name – like a flower.'

'What's *your* first name?' asked Jamie.

'I'm called Delie, or Del, or Delphine – all sorts of names – and I was christened Philadelphia, after the city in America.'

'And your steamer was called after you, wasn't it? I've been down to see her with Uncle, and the engineer showed us over. He's funny. He was eating an onion when we went on board, just like an apple.'

'Oh!' said Delie.

'I want to go too. Why didden Uncle take me?' asked Jessie in a whining voice, kicking her legs up and down.

'Because you're a girl. Girls can't – '

'Oh yes, girls can', said Delie firmly, smiling at Jessie. 'I did and I was a girl. As soon as I'm strong enough you can come up to the wheel-house with me, Jessamine.'

'See!' said Jessie, making a face at her brother.

'Anyway, Aunt Allie says a woman's place is in the home.'

'Oh, does she!' said Delie to herself, smiling into the blankets.

'But Florence Nightingale didn't stay home,' said Jamie thoughtfully.

'Exactly! I see you have a mind of your own, Jamie.'

His pale face coloured a little with pleasure. He was far too thin, Delie thought, comparing him with her own brown, sturdy boys; and in his eyes was a look of strain and intensity. Probably too much maternal affection. He'd had to take the place of his dead father in her emotional life; and he was sure to be coddled too much in this houseful of women.

Just then his mother came in, approaching the bed rather reluctantly. Her sloping eyebrows looked more helpless than ever.

'My dear Mrs Edwards, I'm so pleased to see you looking better. I haven't been much help with the nursing, I'm afraid. I'm quite hopeless in a sickroom – '

'You are that,' said Miss Janet crisply, coming in with a copper kettle which she stood on the side of the fireplace. 'And you'll have to be getting out in a moment, for I'm going to wash the patient. Both you and the chickabiddies too.'

'Chickabiddies, chickabiddies,' sang Jessie, flinging herself back in the chair.

'I was just coming to get them,' said Mrs Henry plaintively. 'It's nurse's day off and I've been nearly out of my mind. I'll be glad to get them off to bed.'

'Don't want to go to bed.'

487

'You can always send them in here and let me amuse them, as long as I'm to be kept here, said Delie 'I must go back home, of course, as soon as the doctor will let me, but meanwhile . . . They don't worry me in the least.'

'Nevertheless, they must be off now.' Miss Janet efficiently spread a towel on the bed.

For the first time in months, it seemed to her, Delie did her own hair and looked in the hand-mirror which she could just hold in her weak hand. She could not raise her arms to put up her hair, but left it in two long plaits, the ends curling loosely. Miss Janet slipped her into a clean white nightdress buttoning high to the neck, with frills all round the yoke; it was not one of her own.

Looking in the mirror, she was surprised at how bright and clearly blue her eyes were and how thin her face had grown.

'Ye've lovely hair, my dear when it's spread out said Miss Janet, lifting one of the heavy plaits. 'It's so fine and yet so thick and abundant.'

'But I hate this grey streak. I'd like to pull it all out.'

'Nonsense. It looks dignified Better than being pepper-and-salt.' She gathered up the basin, towel and washcloth. 'Now I'll leave you to settle down. Do you want the gas lit?'

'No thank you. I want to watch the sky.'

EIGHTY-TWO

Delie wished her bed had been nearer the window, so that she could look out over the lake. As it was, she could see from this upstairs room only a strip of sky flushed with sunset light, and a beam of ruddy gold which came almost horizontally through the window and shone on the opposite wall.

She lay watching the golden motes that turned and swayed in the light, as on another evening a quarter of a century ago and a thousand miles away upstream. Then, too, she had been in bed, recovering from a slight concussion. There had been this same feeling of unreality, as though the distant noises of activity in the house belonged to another world. Then Adam had come in and had kissed her for the first time.

488

As if she had called him up, she heard a gentle knock and the door opened. A gorgeous figure stepped into the room, treading quietly on the thick rug, and she wondered fleetingly if she were still delirious. Then she saw that it was Alastair Raeburn, looking like a sultan from *The Arabian Nights*.

He was wearing over his suit trousers a dressing-gown of rich white-and-gold brocade, belted with a gold-fringed sash of crimson silk. With his small black beard and dark eyes he looked exotic as a white peacock. She was dazzled and enchanted.

He came up to the bed between her and the window and, lifting her limp hand from the coverlet, brushed the fingers with his lips.

'Thank God you are better. You had us all frightened.'

She smiled gently 'How could I help being better with such wonderful nursing and lapped in luxury as I am? Your family are so kind to me. I've had a visit this afternoon from Mrs Raeburn, from Jamie and Jessamine, and Miss Janet has made me comfortable.'

'No visit from Aunt Alicia?'

'Not from Miss Raeburn, no.'

'She shared the nursing while you were unconscious. She did the night-duty and relieved Aunt Janet.'

'I will thank her as soon as I'm up. And that will be in a day or two, surely.'

'No. Not quite in a day or two.' He stroked the blue coverlet with a fine white hand. 'Your heart has been affected by pneumonia toxins. You are to have two more weeks in bed. And it will be a month before you're strong enough to travel.'

'But I can't! I can't just lie here and the steamer tied up all this time and Brenton and the children – ! I'll speak to the doctor. He doesn't understand.'

'He understands very well. You would be no further use to your family with a permanently damaged heart; you don't want two invalids on board. I'm being brutal. You have no choice.'

'But I can't – ' Tears of agitation and weakness welled in her eyes, and she closed them tightly. He took her hand again.

'You must resign yourself; be thankful you recovered. They would be much worse off if they had lost you. And for myself – I must confess I'm selfishly pleased at the idea of keeping you here.'

She opened tear-blurred eyes and for a moment, seeing his dark eyes bent tenderly upon her, was reminded vividly of her dead cousin. It was as if her life ran in cycles. Once more she found herself in a strange house after coming close to death; this time she had come not from the sea but from the lakes. This was not Adam; but by some form of telepathy she had a distinct impression that he would like to kiss her. Yet he would not, she knew, presume by so much as to sit on the edge of the bed.

To break the tension she said childishly: 'What a lovely gown! It's such gorgeous material.'

'Yes.' He let go of her hand and looked down complacently, smoothing the embroidered stuff over his chest. 'It's a Chinese brocade from Hong Kong. I had it made up in Singapore. There are two others somewhere – a crimson and a turquoise blue. I'll have the blue one sent in to you. It would just go with your eyes, though they are darker – more a lapis lazuli.'

'I – I think Mrs Henry may have lent me –' She indicated the chair over which the pink satin gown was draped, catching the last of the sunlight. He turned, took a step forward and stayed motionless with his back towards her. She saw the rigidity of his whole figure.

'How did this get here?' he asked in a strangled voice. His eyes were half-veiled with their drooping lids as he turned, but even in the dim light she saw the glitter of rage in them.

'I don't know. It was just there when I woke up. And the slippers.'

'These belonged to my wife. I gave orders for her things to be burnt.' He snatched up the gown and slippers and hurled them to the floor.

'Excuse me.' He bowed stiffly and went out.

She heard him stride along the corridor and fling open a door.

'Aunt Alicia! Could I have a word with you in my study, please?'

Some time later, Miss Alicia Raeburn came in with the effect of a cold breeze. 'All in the dark!' she said briskly, rattling the curtains across the windows. 'I'll light the gas for you – or would you rather the bedside lamp?'

'Just the lamp, thank you.'

As the light flared up and Miss Raeburn bent over to adjust the wick before putting the lamp-glass back, Delie saw that there were two brighter spots of colour than usual in her pink cheeks. Over her arm she carried another gown, a much more gorgeous affair than the pink satin one, of turquoise brocade embroidered with gold butterflies.

'I am inclined to think', said Miss Raeburn, 'that pink does not suit you. Also, since this one is quilted, it will be more sensible for someone recovering from pneumonia.' She hung it on the brass rail at the foot of the bed and picked up the other.

'I have my own woollen gown on board. I'll send for it at once, since it seems I'm not to be moved yet. I didn't know I had been so ill or how much I owed to your nursing, yours and Miss Janet's. I would like to thank you.

Miss Raeburn shrugged. 'Please don't mention the nursing, don't thank *me*. Janet did the most of it and anyway I was only doing my duty to the stranger within the gates, as the Bible enjoins.'

'Just like Aunt Hester after I was ill!' thought Delie, who was becoming giddy through the repetition of events. When Miss Raeburn had gone, she lay thinking them over. It was evident that Mr Raeburn's indifference to his wife's desertion had been assumed. He must have been very angry to have made the formidable Miss Alicia meekly remove the other gown.

During the next week, made bold by her growing intimacy with Miss Janet (who was far more approachable than her sister), Delie ventured a question on that long-past scandal.

'Was Mrs Alastair Raeburn very beautiful?' she asked, feeling sure that she had been.

'Well . . not what I'd call just *beautiful*,' said Miss Janet. 'She hadn't the presence or the height - not that a small woman can't be lovely, of course - but she had small features, tiny feet and rather strange green eyes. Kittenish, I would call her. Very pretty with it too. But you can imagine her appealing ways didn't make much impression on Alicia.'

'They didn't get on?'

'They did not. Allie is not an easy person to get on with. And Alastair's wife, for all her soft ways, had claws of steel underneath.'

'Did he - was he very upset when she left? As there were no children, it was perhaps easier to split up.'

'Alastair was hurt in his pride more than his heart. That she could go off with that boor, as he called him - she who had been surrounded by beautiful things and the most delicate attentions - that she could prefer a man from Leeds with a northern accent you could cut with a knife and no appreciation of art or music. He was angrier than I've ever seen him. He burned her pictures –

491

the portrait he'd painted and the studio portrait – and threw her clothes that she'd left when she ran off on the rubbish heap to be burnt.'

'But that was her gown and slippers on the chair?'

'Alicia can't bear waste. I can't think why she wanted you to wear them, though.'

'You think she did it on purpose?'

'Yes, and so does he. She knew it would make him furious. He can't bear to be reminded of her. I just wondered, now . . .'

Miss Janet was looking at her curiously, her rather long face tilted to one side. She took out a handkerchief and quickly wiped her lips, removing at the same time all expression from her withered face.

'Yes? What did you wonder?'

'Oh nothing. Just if perhaps she wanted to remind him of his first marriage for some reason. Alicia is very fond of Jamie,' she added with apparent inconsequence.

Delie was puzzled. Was it perhaps that Miss Raeburn hoped, if he saw her in that gown of painful memory, that he would feel an aversion to her, Delie? But why? And what did it have to do with Miss Raeburn's being fond of Jamie?

'I'm a silly old woman, my dear, letting my imagination run away with me. And yet . . . Allie is gifted with second sight. It's a Scottish trait. Sometimes she knows what's going to happen to people before they know themselves.'

EIGHTY-THREE

Down by the jetty the *Philadelphia* and barge stood idle, her load of wool already taken away on trucks and stacked in the great warehouse on the waterfront. The weather had turned calm and sunny, more like autumn than spring.

Delie had worried unnecessarily about Brenton and the boys. They were getting on very well without her. Brenton had confided in Charlie about his exercises and the engineer helped him each day into a chair, where he sat for a short time with aching, unused back muscles, feeling the blood flow down into his disused limbs.

The boys had a wonderful time exploring the edges of the lake in the dinghy, finding swans' nests among the reeds. They went out early each morning to fish, catching salt-water mullet which were travelling right up into the river, following the brackish water.

Gordon fished more for the pleasure of anchoring out on the glassy lake, with the sun-dazzle on the water and the shoreline reflected below, than from any ardour as a fisherman. Alex was too impatient to fish for long, unless he got a bite straight away. But if one of them caught a fish he was happy. He would sit absorbed, dissecting the fish with a sharp knife, examining the spinal cord, the arrangement of bones as he filleted them, the red frill of the fish's gills and, most marvellous of all, the eye. He had a passionate interest in how all these things worked and how they fitted together, like a wonderfully complex toy.

To Gordon the dead fish with its blood and entrails was disgusting, no longer beautiful or interesting once it had ceased to live and its iridescent colours had faded. He could never bring himself to eat with enjoyment a fish he had caught himself. He liked to catch it, to pit his wits against his prey, but he never liked taking life. When water-spiders got into his cabin he removed them carefully on a piece of bark or paper and let them go, even though he didn't like them. He had an almost Hindu respect for life.

The doctor had come himself to tell Brenton that his wife would be unable to return to the boat for some weeks; he did not tell him that for one day he had despaired of her recovery. He was interested in the big man, the vitality he sensed smouldering under the ash of enforced inertia. He had talked to him on his earlier visit and found an alert intelligence and an iron determination behind the halting speech. The treatment of such handicapped persons was something of a hobby with him, and he was ahead of accepted medical practice in his thinking.

On his second visit he brought Brenton a book by Dr Otto Schmeltzkopf.

'Don't be alarmed by the title,' said Dr Riceman. 'German text – odd-looking alphabet. Hasn't been translated into English yet. It means "Rehabilitation"; deals with the treatment of cases like yours. Illustrations will be some use: show you the latest exercises. Hrrmmpp!'

He blew a trumpet-peal on his nose and put away his handkerchief. 'Now let's see – you've got a bit of feeling in this left leg? And the fingers of the left hand – quite good? H'm, h'rmp! Close the left eye. Now the right. Won't quite close, eh? Vocal cords affected too. You've already overcome that to an extent.'

'Hard – work. But I – can talk.'

'You've stumbled on an important principle: controlled breath. The thing is to swallow air, like a frog; then force it up again and make words with it. It's hard at first; but you've got the idea. Now; how long since you've stood upright?'

'Five – years.'

'Since you sat in a chair?'

'Five hours.'

'So-o! That's how you've kept your legs from withering. I like your spirit.'

'It was get up – or die.'

'Good! You know that – sort of refrain, in *A Tale of Two Cities*, when the old chap is released from prison? "Recalled to life. I do not wish to live." That, to me as a doctor, is a terrible thing. The will to live is far more important than physic. Now look at these diagrams.'

It seemed that Brenton, in lifting the heavy books every day, had anticipated one of the exercises advocated by the Austrian doctor who had written the book. There were many more delicate exercises illustrated, for rehabilitating the muscles controlling the fingers, the eyelids, the jaws.

'Stands to reason,' said Dr Riceman. 'Injured or atrophied muscles can be improved by regular exercise. Look what's done with normal muscles by continuous use: ballet-dancers, acrobats. You don't want to be an acrobat; just to move under your own steam, however slowly. Hrrmmph!'

'That's just it,' said Brenton with intensity. 'Under – my own – steam!'

'You must take these stairs very quietly, Mrs Edwards,' said Raeburn, pausing with her on a landing half-way to the roof-top studio.

Delie too was learning to walk again on feet made of wood with occasional pins and needles of feeling in them. She leaned heavily on his arm; she was already shaky when she reached the first landing. But she had insisted on this expedition. She felt a

494

growing interest in the personality of her host and could not wait any longer to see his work and the place where he worked.

'There are none of your pictures about the house?' she asked. 'Why is that? I've looked carefully since I've been up, but I've seen none.'

'No.' He turned and leaned on the banister, looking down the narrow winding stair they had come up from the first floor. 'I have no illusions about my painting, that's why. As a matter of fact, I have one or two in my room – favourites of my own but still not of a standard I'd care to display publicly.'

'You've never exhibited, then?'

'When I was younger, yes. I was a member of the S.A. Society of Arts and my submissions were always hung. But they didn't satisfy me. I paint now solely for my own pleasure, the pleasure of self-expression.'

'That is the only valid reason for painting, I suppose. Though I think with me there is something more – the desire to create something lasting among the flux of time; something which has its own order imposed from without, as distinct from the utter randomness of life. Art is satisfying for that very reason: it creates pattern and form out of chaos and formlessness.'

'Let's go up and get it over, shall we?' He looked depressed, even his unruly eyebrows seemed flattened and his lids drooped, hiding the expression of his eyes.

'Yes. I'm quite rested now.'

A hinged trapdoor, which was open, led through the floor of the studio. Sunlight spilled down through it on to the yellow wood of the stair. Delie gasped with delight as she emerged into a roof-top world. She had a bird's-eye view all round, for the hexagonal walls were of glass to within two feet of the floor. The floor was bare but for two Persian rugs, their rich colours glowing in the sunlight. There was hardly any other furniture but a divan with a corded velvet cover, two old, comfortable-looking chairs, an easel and a paint-stained table with jars of brushes and boxes of oil colours.

There was a partly worked canvas on the easel, sunset over a sweep of water; and all round the walls at floor-level leaned a series of sea-scapes.

The sea by moonlight, at sunset, at dawn; dark with approaching storm, bright with sunlight, crested with whitecaps . . . the only paintings which were not of the sea were of the lake, or wide Murray billabongs filled with reflections.

She looked about her doubtfully, groping for something to say. What had she expected? Not this. Sophisticated portraiture, perhaps, and genre painting with satirical overtones – not this romantic preoccupation with the moods of the sea, the half-tones of moonlight and dawn. There was not one painting done in the full, rich light of midday.

'Well?' He was looking away from her, down at the lake.

'I am overwhelmed,' she said at last. 'It's so – so unexpected.'

She walked round the walls, giving every picture, even the unfinished sketches, a careful scrutiny.

'I didn't know you had this passion for the sea. Tell me – is this Goolwa Beach?' Sandhills, some tufty grasses and endless rows of waves breaking on a level shore, all was bathed in a coppery light from a red sun hanging low on the horizon. He nodded. 'It's funny; I've had a mental picture of this beach almost all my life, but I've always seen it as cold, cold and white, with a cold blue sea breaking, the sandhills like banks of frozen foam.'

'It *is* like that! The sand's not really white, but the spin-drift blows up the beach on windy days and lies in heaps like snow and the waves break with a cold, inhuman roar. This was painted on the day of the big bush-fire, when there was this strange coppery light on the water. The mouth of the Murray is just beyond sight here, lost in the haze.'

She looked with interest at the point he indicated on the strange beach she had often seen in dreams – miles of uninhabited shore, pounded continuously by the Southern Ocean.

'This is my favourite,' she said at last, pausing again before a small study of a single breaking wave. It reared up against the early light; green, translucent, capped with foam and poised eternally at the moment when its final rush to destruction was begun.

'It's called just *The Wave* and it is a favourite of mine too. I have several times refused to sell it. But your verdict? You were very silent at first.'

'I told you, I was taken aback. I'm immensely interested, also impressed. You are single-minded and energetic; but the sea is a hard mistress, they say.'

'I'm always single-minded and energetic in the pursuit of what interests me.' he said with a deep look. 'You have been warned.'

She did not take that up, but turned to look out of the windows, the vast sweep all round, across the plains and across the lake to the further shore nearly twenty miles away. In front, the jetty and the *Philadelphia* looked small as toys. A steamer was on her way from Point Pomander, trailing a plume of smoke.

'Another load of wool for us,' said Raeburn. 'That's the *Pevensey*, I should think. We'll make sure.'

He pulled a canvas cover off an odd-shaped object by the eastern wall, opened a window and began adjusting the eyepiece of a large telescope.

'This is very handy for advance news of steamers and their loads,' he said. 'Also I can study the moon and the stars at night. That section of the roof slides back and the telescope swings on this mount. The clockwork drive is only for celestial objects; it moves the telescope in time with the earth's rotation so as to keep the object in the field of view.'

'How fascinating! I should love to see Jupiter's moons, and Saturn's rings and the moon's craters – would that be possible?'

'Perfectly possible, if you wait up here until dark. It will be clear tonight. But Saturn won't be up, unfortunately. Meanwhile have a look at the steamer. She's making good time in this calm.'

Delie put one eye to the eyepiece and saw the foreshortened steamboat magically brought up close. The wheel-house window was open and the skipper was discernible behind the wheel, gazing ahead all unconscious of the eye bent upon him from the other side of the lake. She saw someone, deckhand or engineer, come up the steps and speak to him, flinging out an arm. It was like one of the new moving pictures, which she had taken the children to see in the Morgan hall – life-size figures moving and gesticulating and opening their mouths without any accompanying sound. They did not look real.

She turned towards him, smiling. 'Did you look through this thing at me?'

'Yes, I saw you look across the wheel-house and say something to your son and you both laughed. You were well out from the shelter of the point then and waves were coming at you from all directions. I'd expected to see you looking strained or at least anxious. It impressed me very much.'

'As a matter of fact, I was scared. But somehow it had an exhilarating effect. What I said was: "This is fun, isn't it?" And it suddenly was.'

'Gordon's a fine lad. He sat in the room with you until the early hours, one night when you were delirious. I offered to let him sleep here, but he wouldn't go to bed.'

'Yes, he has a sympathetic nature. He reminds me –' and then she found herself telling Alastair Raeburn about her first love, her cousin who had died when he was only nineteen, about Miss Barrett and the farm on the upper reaches of the river and Aunt Hester's hostile attitude and Adam's youthful impatience. 'All so long ago, that sometimes I wonder if that child and myself could possibly be the same person.'

'Yes, it's strange to look back. Dorothy Barrett, eh? How old a woman would she be now?'

'Oh, I don't know – sixty, I suppose. Yes, she must be nearly sixty. How incredible! She was the loveliest person, with the softest brown hair and now I suppose it's grey. We still write to each other about once a year, at Christmas.'

'Barrett, Barrett! Yes, I'm sure that's the name. I had a letter from some English friends, strongly recommending a governess for my niece and nephew – someone they had employed, who was returning to Australia and wanted a position. I wonder, could it be the same person? This woman was not young.'

'It could be. The last time I heard from her she was with a family in Dorset, the Polkinghornes. They – '

'Yes! What a strange thing; it *is* your Miss Barrett. You would recommend her also, I take it?'

'Absolutely; without reservation. Of course it's twenty-five years since I saw her, but her mind is as vigorous as ever, I can tell that from her letters. It would be wonderful if – '

'Then that settles it. Miss Mellership is quite capable, but she is little more than a nanny. I want someone to mould their minds and characters. Young Jamie is already beyond her scope and his mother – frankly, his mother is not a good influence.'

Delie did not reply, being a little embarrassed at this confidence, which confirmed her own judgment of Mrs Henry. She looked again through the eyepiece at the approaching steamer, now showing up clearly in the full level beams of the westering sun.

'I shall have to go down and fix up some business when she ties up', said Alastair 'They won't begin unloading until tomorrow, though. I'll come straight back. Will you stay up here, rather than face those stairs again tonight? I'll have a meal sent up for us.'

'Thank you. I'd love to stay and watch the sun set. What a wonderful place to work in! It makes me feel like a bird on the top of a tree.'

'You won't try to look at the sun through the telescope, will you? You'd be blinded permanently if you did.'

'I won't look through it at all unless you're here.'

'I'll be back soon and we'll have . . . chicken sandwiches, do you think, and a bottle of Sauternes?'

'Perfect.'

He went through the trapdoor, pausing a moment with his head at floor-level. With his satanic eyebrows and pointed black beard, he reminded her a little of Mephistopheles in *Faust*, returning to the deeps of Hell. Then she forgot him, relaxing in the wide sweep of space and air and distant water, feeling at home as an eagle in its eyrie.

She could look down on the *Philadelphia* at the wharf with detachment, though she told herself that those were her sons rowing back in the dinghy and taking a sack of fish on board, that that was her galley from whose chimney the smoke from the stove was issuing and that her husband lay there inside the big window, eating slowly and clumsily with one hand.

She saw a small, ragged figure in a shapeless hat, which could only be the Young Limb, running nimbly along the edge of the deck with a slightly larger figure in hot pursuit – Charlie chasing his pet aversion, no doubt. The Young Limb made a flying leap to the wharf and then turned and made a cheeky gesture at his pursuer.

Delie smiled at the rage silently expressed in Charlie's upflung arms, his cap cast upon the deck and jumped on. It seemed strange not to hear a single swear-word accompanying this violent action, but she was too far away.

When the maid Ethel, a terribly thin girl with a cheerful disposition but no teeth, came up the steps with the tray, she gazed at the dainty sandwiches, the embroidered linen napkins, the crystal goblets, the golden bottle misted with cold, and thought of her first supper on the *Philadelphia*.

From onion omelettes and beer to chicken and Sauternes, it was symbolic of the difference between this and her home. But she had come to like beer and the free-and-easy meals in the wheel-house or under an awning on the deck, with Charlie lifting every forkful to his nose and sniffing it before he ate it – because, he declared, nothing had any taste these days unless he smelt it first; not even a raw onion.

EIGHTY-FOUR

In the *Philadelphia* the cook was slamming pots about on the galley stove. He always made a lot of noise when he was dishing up. He was rather temperamental and when he dropped something – a spoon or a saucepan – he would kick it savagely across the floor.

He was sick to death of cooking fish, but those damn' kids had come back with a great sackful again and there was no ice; he couldn't bear to see them go to waste.

'Hey, youse kids!' he called. 'Come an' get it!'

He usually rang a bell when the meal was ready. This call meant that one of them was to come and get their father's dinner and take it to his cabin. They took it in turn while Delie was away; tonight it was Alex's turn.

He took the tray with its plate of flaky fish, broken up and mixed with mashed potato to make it easy for Brenton to handle, and carried it carefully to the cabin on the top deck. His father was lying with his chin sunk on his broad chest, staring broodingly under his brows at the window.

Brenton didn't like being tied up for so long, it made him feel as if the boat were trapped in a low river, as it had been often in the past; laid up and useless, as he was himself. The lake was still, it didn't flow like the river and without the moving banks outside his cabin he felt that he was beginning to stagnate.

Besides, he missed his wife, far more than he would have done when he was well. Without her he couldn't orientate himself, he felt lost on a wide sea without a compass. She gave continuity to his life, she was the connecting link between what he had been and what he had become.

Charlie was so erratic lately – without the responsibility of running the engine or the steadying influence of the Missus he'd been on an almost continuous bender in Milang. Nearly his whole diet consisted of whisky and beer, raw onions, and bread. His hand was so shaky that Brenton had refused to let him shave him in the mornings any more, so once more he was sprouting a

500

luxuriant beard, not grey like his head but wiry and golden.

Alex's old awe of his father was not quite gone now that he was bedridden, though the tall man was brought down to the child's level and almost a child's dependence. He sat awkwardly on the edge of the bed and said: 'D'you want me to feed you, Dad?'

Brenton made a snorting noise and rolled his eyes angrily.

'What for? I'm perfectly . . . capable . . . feeding myself. What's this pap?' He poked moodily at the contents of the plate with his fork.

'Butterfish, Dad. Salt-water fish – they're good. Gordie and I caught some just now and they're fresh as fresh. I'll butter you some bread.' Brenton shakily lifted the fork with his left hand, spilling some of the food as he did so. 'Dad; d'you reckon you could've swum across the lake? I mean, before you were ill? You were pretty good, weren't you, I mean?'

'What? Twenty-four miles . . . across the lake. Don't be daft, boy.'

'Well, people swim the English Channel, don't they?'

'Yes, they do . . . Well, you wait . . . few years, I might try it yet.'

Alex looked doubtful.

'You wait, son, till I . . . get out . . . this cabin. I'll show you. Why not? I was . . . best swimmer . . . whole length of Murray.'

'But Dad!' Alex looked distressed. 'You'll never get up again will you?'

A surge of blood flowed into Brenton's face, suffusing even his blue eyes. 'Who told you . . . that bloody lie? Who?'

Alex stammered: 'I d-don't know, I thought – and Charlie said – he was crying the other night, when he came home sozzled, something about you never skippering a boat again.'

'Hah! I'll . . . show you something, lad. Hand me . . . that rope. Behind . . . door there. Now . . . tie it . . . end of bed. Firmly, now. No granny-knots. Hand me . . . the end.'

He took the end of rope and wound two turns round his left wrist. Then, feet braced against the bed-end, he pulled himself into a sitting position, pulled harder until his knees bent and he was almost at the bottom of the bed. With his left arm round the upright post, he swivelled round on his buttocks and let his feet slide to the floor. He grasped the post with both arms, and drew himself slowly upright on his trembling legs.

He threw a triumphant glance at his son and sagged back on

the bed, sweat beading his brow.

'How's that, eh? I can stand . . . on me own . . . two feet. Don't tell your mother, mind. Surprise her. I'm getting stronger . . . every week.'

Alex was impressed. 'Gee, Dad! D'you really think you'll be able to swim again?'

'Doctor said . . . swimming's best thing. Less weight . . . in water. But it mustn't be too cold. Next summer – we'll see.'

'Gee!' said Alex again. 'I'd like to be a doctor, and make people walk again.'

For the first time since her illness, Delie began to feel hungry. Once the sun had set and the colour had drained out of the sky and the great reflector of the lake, she waited impatiently in the little roof-top room for Alastair Raeburn's return. Then she heard his step on the stair and first his black satanic eyebrows, then his aquiline nose and pointed beard rose through the trap-door, followed by his dapper figure.

'From the deeps of Hell I come to greet thee!' she murmured to herself, for he was wearing one of his gorgeous dressing-gowns, this time a Japanese silk of Mephistophelean red.

'You are nearly in the dark!' he cried. 'Why didn't you get Ethel to light the lamp? Ah, she's brought our supper, but no ice, the lazy girl. We'll have to drink this before it gets warm.'

'Oh, please don't light it yet! I like to watch the first stars come out.'

'And I like to see what I am eating,' he said imperturbably, fiddling with the wick of a large kerosene lamp with a painted glass shade, like the one she had broken long ago of Aunt Hester's. 'Also, I like to see *you*.'

A faint echo stirred in her mind. Someone had said those words to her once before, but she couldn't recall the context. He soon had the cork out of the bottle and, after tasting a little of the golden wine, he handed her a full glass and filled his own.

'To the future!'

'I'm afraid I seem to be always dwelling on the past.'

'Then you shouldn't be. That's an occupation for the old, whose life is behind them. I have a feeling in my bones that you have a long and interesting future, and that I shall have a part in it.'

'Oh? I don't see –'

'There!' he said delightedly. 'Who ever saw an old woman

blush so charmingly? You're like a girl still: that freshness of complexion, that eagerness of mind which shows in your eyes.' His own dark eyes looked at her ardently, fully open for once.

She looked away and said: 'If you don't mind, I'm terribly hungry. I had the greatest difficulty in restraining myself from falling on those chicken sandwiches before you arrived. I feel as if I hadn't eaten for a month.'

'Poor little thing, you haven't eaten anything solid. I should have ordered a whole chicken; I'm a thoughtless egotist. Just because I prefer a light meal at night. Here, you have them all.'

'No, no!' she protested, laughing. 'I'm not that hungry.'

The light wine was heady enough in her weakened state. It seemed to run through her veins like molten gold, so that she felt shining and warm. She ate two whole sandwiches and the half of the third. By then the brief twilight was over, it was already growing dark, but the lake held the last vestiges of light, as though loath to relinquish such a tranquil day.

She sat looking down at the square of light that marked Brenton's cabin window. 'I hate to think of him lying helpless there,' she said musingly. She had suddenly felt her situation in this little roof-top eyrie, far from the daily worries of existence, to be unreal. 'I must go back tomorrow. He'll be missing me.'

'He's always been a very active man, I imagine, which makes it harder for him,' said Alastair.

'He was the most vital person I've ever known. When he was younger he could do without food or sleep and work a twenty-four hour day and then go swimming for fun at the end of it. And now –' She shrugged.

'Yes.' He sighed sharply. 'Life can be damnably cruel. I don't know if you get any consolation from the stars; I find that when I have an insoluble problem or unbearable thoughts, they calm my mind as nothing else can.'

'Watching the flow of the river has the same effect on me.'

'You mean it makes daily things, small irritations, fall into perspective? Just one of the star cities in the Milky Way, as seen through the telescope, is enough.'

He blew out the lamp and opened a section of the roof.

Starlight rained down on them, the white star Spica stood above, shaking its spear of light.

'That is Virgo overhead: do you know the constellations of the zodiac?'

'Yes; I can orientate by the stars. I started to learn from the captain of the sailing-ship we came out to Australia on when I was still a child. Captain Johannsen . . . He was drowned with the others.'

She saw that twelve-year-old child, thin and eager, her long dark hair whipping in the wind.

'Oh, Captain Johannsen, what is that smell? Is it the flowers?'

'It is the trees, the eucalyptus trees that smell so. Even if ve could not see the land, I vould know Osstralia is there to vindvard.'

'Australia!' Her thin hands gripping the rail, her eyes straining over the dark water at the low loom of coast against the starlit sky: her first glimpse of the promised land.

'Keep watching to the north-east, and you vill see rise Arcturus, a beautiful yellow star . . .'

But clouds had come up swiftly and blotted out the sky, and she had never seen the yellow star rise above the sea. Long, long ago . . .

'Where is Arcturus, is it above the horizon?' she asked now.

'Yes; in Boötes – see – it looks like part of the tail of a great paper kite, flying upside down.'

'May I look?'

'Stars are rather disappointing as telescopic objects; no larger, though their colour is intensified. Wait, I'll get it for you. There it is. You must adjust the eyepiece to suit your own vision.'

He moved aside a little to let her get near the eyepiece, but remained close at her side. The clockwork motor hummed, the deep yellow point of light looked steadfastly into her eye. She felt suddenly the intimacy of their position, alone in the faintly starlit darkness, away on top of the house. They seemed nearer to the sky and the constellations than to the human beings in the rooms below.

'You see?' His voice was low, hushed, as though in deference to the mighty presences of other worlds. 'And now, Jupiter, that will be more rewarding.'

She looked again through the eyepiece and gasped with delight. Jupiter was a luminous ball, faintly striped with colour, and on each side ranged the bracelet of tiny moons, diamond-bright and in a perfect line.

He was so close behind her that she felt his breath on her hair. If she had leant back a little, or turned her face. . . . But she kept close to the instrument, her eye still fixed on that other-worldly vision, until a gentle hand on her shoulder put her aside.

'Now, a star city. This is a globular cluster, about fifty thousand stars all with the same birth. To the naked eye it looks just a faint, fuzzy dot. There, you see, not far from the second Magellanic Cloud? The seeing is good tonight; they look uncountable through the high-power eyepiece. Now look.'

Again that just audible gasp of wonder. A star city, a city of stars. Stars and stars and stars, all encompassed in that one misty dot.

And other wonders: the Tarantula nebula, resolving itself out of a cloud of glowing gas and dark interstellar dust; a double star, green and topaz, seeming as one to the naked eye; the Jewelbox, a handful of garnets, diamonds and rubies strewn near the Southern Cross.

Delie felt her knees begin to tremble with weariness. She was not tired of looking, but she had not spent so long on her feet since getting out of bed and the climb up the stairs had tired her.

She said: 'I think I shall have to sit down now.'

'Oh, my dear, my poor dear! How thoughtless of me. You were so interested and my enthusiasm carried me away.' He was pressing her into a low chair, he sat at her feet and with eyes accustomed to the starlight she saw him gazing earnestly up at her face. 'Amateur astronomers love to get a new victim to show off their wonders to. They begin to feel proprietorial towards the celestial objects, almost as if they had created them. Why didn't you stop me earlier?'

'I didn't want to stop you.'

Still sitting on the floor, he leaned over to turn off the motor and in the silence they heard a swan honking down among the lakeside reeds. He reached up, took her hand and pressed it against his brow. 'You could tell me to do anything, don't you know that? I would lay my life at your . . . foot.'

He released her hand, and lifting one of her feet from the floor, kissed the instep. 'Anything, anything! You have only to command me.'

'But I don't want to tell you to do anything! Just . . not – not to make life more difficult for me, more complicated than it is already.' Her lip trembled. 'I didn't think – I didn't expect this of you. I thought this sort of thing was all behind you. You seem such a collected, self-sufficient person always.'

'Do I?' He had buried his face in her lap and she felt the muscles of his mouth contract in a grimace or a smile. 'That's where you're wrong. . . . I have such a capacity for love and all going to waste. I ask only to give and give; I ask nothing of you

505

in return, only that you should not dislike me –'

'I don't dislike you. But I don't love you, either. So there is no question of giving or receiving.' She felt unreal, this conversation could not be taking place, this could not be Mr Raeburn, abject at her feet. 'Please!' and 'Do get up,' she cried.

His arms tightened convulsively round her, his face remained buried. She was trapped into the age-old maternal gesture of stroking his hair, yet she still felt detached, startled rather than moved.

'That wasn't quite true; of course I want something of you, I want all of you, as any man would. I can't divide myself into flesh and spirit, body and soul. I love you with all of me, I want you with all of me, I worship your mind and your body down to the last hair of your precious little head.'

'Then you won't distress me any further with this nonsense.'

'Nonsense? It's the most sublime sense I've ever spoken. Ah, if I could only get you into bed you would love me a little.'

He was looking up now, his voice was boyish and audacious and she saw the gleam of white teeth between his precise moustache and trim beard.

'Oh! I am going, I'm going at once. I shall go back to the boat this very night.'

'Ah, Delie, you don't need to run away from me. I shan't pester you, I promise.'

Her hands still touched his hair, though unconsciously she had sat more upright, her back very straight and stiff. She felt the thinning patch on top of his head, where the bald spot would begin. This was no boy, to be put off by stern words. 'Single-minded and energetic in pursuit . . .' She believed it; but she felt armoured by her own indifference.

Still, when she went to her room, she sat for long on the side of the bed, her mind so dazed that she could not summon the physical energy to get undressed. The lake water below, stirred by a midnight breeze, lapped in restless ripples on the shore.

She could not pretend to herself that she had been taken by surprise; ever since her illness she had known he was attracted, but she had not been prepared for such depth of feeling, the suppressed passion that vibrated in the tones of his voice. She felt as if she had been walking on the thin crust of a volcano.

Safely back in her usual routine, running the steamer for twelve hours without a break and with little time for thinking about

Alastair Raeburn and his unexpected declaration, Delie found a moment to write to him as he had requested, but she made no reference to what had passed between them.

She wrote of her work, of her plan for running stores to the Department of Works construction camp at Lake Victoria, of painting and the pictures he had shown her.

> You have made me feel tremendously alive; it's as though I'd been half asleep for years. I ask nothing but to lay down my life in front of you, to die like the breaking wave and sink into the sand, if by so doing I can smooth the way a little before your feet.

Alone in the wheel-house, she yielded sometimes to day-dreams of living with Alastair: lapped in the luxury of Eastern silks and the greater luxury of his adoration; shielded from all worries and responsibilities and free to paint all day And then, to discuss her work and its problems with a fellow-artist, and to welcome him to her bed in that beautiful and gracious home beside the lake.

It was the wildest day-dream, and she knew it. Even if she had been free, no life was ever as perfect as that, and unfree as she was, the very idea was treason because of Brenton and the children. They needed her. Did they need her more than Alastair did? That was not the point: her duty lay with them, and duty . . . stern daughter of the voice of God! It was a cold word, giving cold comfort, but generations of upright, dour Presbyterian ancestors stood behind her, nodding glum approval.

EIGHTY-FIVE

'Your mother will be here this afternoon, Meg,' said Mrs Melville. 'Are you going to make a special cake for her?'

'Did you think I'd forgotten?' cried Meg. 'I've been marking on the calendar every day.' She tossed back her straight black hair, a nervous gesture that was habitual with her of late. She was over-thin, with bony shoulders and long legs like a colt though she was not very tall. Her skin was pale, almost colourless, but in her thin uneven face the eyes showed enormous and deeply blue.

Everyone remarked on Meg's beautiful eyes; but to her it seemed that they were underlining the plainness of the rest of her face, her button nose, her straight unmanageable hair.

Mrs Melville looked at her fondly. 'I don't know what your mother will say, you're looking that thin! Without the farm butter and cream there'd surely be nothing of you. You're not strong enough to live that hand-to-mouth life on the boat.'

Meg stopped in the middle of a sliding step across the kitchen.

'Not strong enough? But Melvie' – (for so she had called her foster-mother since she was little) 'I'm perfectly well, you know that!'

Mrs Melville looked obstinate. There was an iron-greyness about her hair, and her mouth set hard as iron.

'You're under-weight and don't forget you're just the age to get TB and go into a decline. I wouldn't sleep a wink if I couldn't see you got your three meals a day and the drink of milk I always bring you in bed. Don't you think you'd better stay with Melvie a year or two yet?'

'Oh, I don't know . . .' Meg was a kind-hearted child and she knew Mrs Melville would be hurt if she didn't agree. But she missed her mother and the boys; if only she could live in both places at once! Then there was Garry; if she lived aboard the boat she'd hardly see him any more.

She said with more enthusiasm: 'I suppose I *could* stay a bit longer, that is if Mummy doesn't need me.'

'I think it would come better from you if you were to suggest it. Your mother knows I want to have you and she must see it's better for your health. Garry would miss you too.'

This was a new idea, suggested by her son's appearing at that moment. He went straight to the cake-tin without looking at either of them and cut himself a slab of fruit cake.

'*Would* you, Garry?' asked Meg, blushing so slightly that Mrs Melville didn't notice it, though she felt as if scarlet banners were waving in each cheek.

'Mm? Would I what?'

'Wouldn't we miss her if she went back to the boat?' put in his mother.

'Yair; like an aching tooth.' He took a large bite of cake.

'Garry!'

He grinned. 'I was only teasing. I'd miss having someone to tease, all right. I like to see you fly into a paddy. And you're not a bad hand at cake-making.'

To the infatuated Meg this was as good as a romantic declaration.

'There! You see?' said Mrs Melville triumphantly. 'And Mr Melville has come to think of you as his own daughter.'

'Help! I hope I'd 've had a better-looking sister than that.'

'Get out of my way, you great lump, I have to make a cake now,' said Meg, pushing him.

'Out of the way yourself, skinny.' (Was ever woman in such fashion wooed?)

'Garry! Get *out*.' After a slight scuffle she ejected him, he allowing himself to be propelled towards the back door.

'Strong, aren't you?' he jeered. 'Little Miss Spitfire.'

Meg was just putting the finishing touches to the cake, squeezing a last pink rose from a funnel of paper, when the *Philadelphia* whistle sounded at the landing. She ran outside, then ran back to take off her floury apron. She took the steep steps down the cliffside two at a time and flew into Delie's arms as she was stepping ashore.

Delie thought she was looking thinner and asked if she was doing too much housework. Oh no, said Meg, she loved it.

How could she tell her mother that she was pining with love for a returned soldier ten years older than herself, a hero who had lost two fingers in the war?

She went in to see her father and kissed his big red face among the golden whiskers. He gathered her thin wrists in his right hand, which had been the weak one, and squeezed until she cried out.

'See? I couldn't do a thing with that hand before. I'll be steering the boat again soon.'

Meg hugged him and ran out to her brothers.

'Coming up to the farm? I made a cake specially.'

'Can't be any good, then,' said Gordon, who already had a fishing-line over the stern.

'Bring us a bit back', said Alex. 'I'm going in for a swim.'

'Me too,' said Brenny, who had just come on board.

Meg took Delie's hand until the path up the cliff became too narrow for them to walk abreast. She thought her mother looked beautiful, even in her old army jacket, which seemed to accentuate her fine features and slender hands. Years later she was to stand in a crowd to welcome Amy Johnston, the lone woman flier from England, and see the same seeming fragility and girlish complexion, combined with a man's determination and grit.

There was a new glow about Delie, a youthful sparkle in her eye; sternly as she had spoken to Alastair, it was lovely to be loved and wanted at her age. 'Heavens! what complications,' she thought rather complacently, remembering her struggle with Cyrus James also.

She remained unaware of the complicated emotions stirring in the daughter by her side: unwilling, perhaps, to admit that Meg was no longer a child.

'I've been thinking about your future, dear,' she said. 'Would you like to study to be a doctor? I think I could manage the fees now. I've established this run to Lake Victoria. Of course, it means years of study.'

'No; I want to be a nurse,' said Meg at once.

'Well, at least you know your own mind. I don't know what Gordon will do. Could you do your training at the Waikerie Hospital? But, anyway, you're miles too young. You can have two years at home –'

'At home?'

'On the boat, of course, with us. You can practise on Daddy. He says you're already a much better nurse than I am. He said I wasn't a nurse's boot-lace.'

'That's because you're impatient, Mummy. Do you think perhaps I could stay here another year, though? Melvie says I'm a bit thin. And they wouldn't take me at the hospital if I was ill. Melvie said something about TB, that you had it once –'

'It was a wrong diagnosis. That's absolute nonsense! She had no right to go frightening you with such tales. Anyway, the doctor recommended the river life and I became perfectly healthy – until I had this last bout of pneumonia. I still have to go slow a bit and I thought you could help me.'

'Of course I'll come if you're not well! But –' The thought of Garry dried up her mouth. 'Perhaps I could come back sometimes.'

'We'll see.' But privately Delie resolved that Meg should be got away from the farm altogether. Mrs Melville had too much influence. Delie remembered her vague uneasiness on that earlier visit at her possessive tone. Meg was her daughter; she didn't want someone else taking the place of mother to her. Soon

510

enough, no doubt, she would have to give her up to some young man.

It was early spring, for they had gone down-river with the first fresh after the exceptionally dry summer that year; and now, walking up to the farmhouse with Meg, Delie passed a late-flowering almond covered in bloom. The almond held out its wide-eyed blossoms with a gesture full of candour and grace. The tree seemed to offer itself, in all its pale, open innocence, to the rough caress of the wind and the sensuous probings of the self-absorbed bees.

EIGHTY-SIX

'Brenton, I want to talk to you; I'm worried about Meg.' How simple if she could thus go to her husband and discuss all her worries, leave the burden on another, stronger pair of shoulders! But Delie felt that it would be useless. His mind was turned inward he had little interest in his children and spent most of his time looking at a queer book in German which she didn't believe he could read and in brooding over his confinement.

Perhaps she was worrying needlessly. She couldn't believe that a court of law would take a child away from its natural mother, especially if the child herself didn't want it. But there was that strange reluctance of Meg's to come away.

Delie stared ahead as Long Reach opened out before the steamer. Round the next bend they would come to the site of Lock Three, where preliminary work was already being carried out. Lock One was nearly completed and soon they would have to pay dues every time they went through.

Later it would be better to make her base for stores at Renmark and avoid the lower river altogether. In this way she would also avoid seeing Cyrus James or Alastair Raeburn either, and this would surely be a good thing.

She regarded the possibility without enthusiasm. In fact, they could probably help her, though Cyrus wouldn't know much about Australian law. She pulled down on the spokes, beginning to cross over where the invisible channel crossed.

It was still hard to believe that Mrs Melville should have turned against her in such a fashion. It almost seemed as if the loss of Jim at the war had unbalanced her a little. It had certainly changed her personality.

She thought of Mrs Melville, a bright flame of colour burning in her cheeks, while she proclaimed that Meg must stay with her; her mouth closing tightly after each word, her jaw obstinately set.

Delie might have been conciliatory and made some compromise if she had not been antagonised by the other woman's manner: telling her that a boat was no fit place to bring up children, that no proper mother would think of taking a delicate child to live on board – and hadn't she lost the baby for that very reason?

It was then that Delie saw red; and she left the farm kitchen without tasting her cup of tea or Meg's cake, while Mrs Melville shouted after her: 'And if you try to get her back I'll take it to the courts! The law won't let you ruin a child's chance in life.'

Meg had gone to call Mr Melville and Garry in to tea, so that she didn't hear this exchange. Delie intercepted her on the way back and asked her to come on board then, at once, and go with them up-river. She needn't stop to pack everything, just get some warm clothes, and they'd buy some more in Renmark. But Meg turned obstinate, too; it happened that Garry had asked her to go spotlight-shooting after foxes that night.

So Delie piloted the boat with a heavy heart, leaving her daughter behind where that woman could influence her mind against her own mother, her own family. She couldn't tie up and wait for Meg to change her mind and she didn't want to order her to come. She had to get through the Lock Three site today, before the coffer-dam was completed, for with the high river it was expected that the by-pass would be almost unnavigable, a race of water sloping like the side of a hill and moving downstream at ten knots.

(Later a government barge was anchored upstream of the race, fitted with a strong winch for helping steamers up through it, or dropping them safely down; but not before the *Avoca* had cracked open down to the waterline while trying to winch through on the sideways pull from a tree.)

In front, a wide vista of park-like flood-plain, grass-covered and dotted with huge trees, spread away on one side of the river, while the other was shut in with yellow honeycombed cliffs more than a hundred feet high. As they came close under the cliffs Delie watched their bow-wave stirring the green grottoes at the base, filled with ferns and mossy growths which grew at the level which was nearly always wet. On top of the cliffs not a speck of green vegetation could be seen; only the barren metal flower of a windmill or the spindly twigs of tobacco bush. Yet further back the irrigation settlements were spreading a film of verdure over the desert.

The *Philadelphia* rounded the next bend and opened up the Lock Three reach. Tents and temporary buildings were dotted on the river-bank, where there was a fairly wide flood-plain below the cliffs on the left-hand side. The coffer-dam was half across the river, and the current raced through the restricted space. At full speed the *Philadelphia* inched through against the force of water and drew in to the left-hand bank.

Delie wanted to speak to Cyrus James about Meg; but she would not see him alone, not alone. She could not trust herself, she would send one of the boys with a message. Gordon and the Young Limb leaped ashore with the ropes and the Limb ran out the gangplank as soon as they were fast.

Charlie let steam go from the escape valves with a hissing roar, called to the fireman to let the fire drop and sauntered out from his engines to stand at the top of the gangplank, with his hand resting on the rail.

He was still leaning there when a red-hot pincers got him by one finger. He raised his hand with a yell, uttering dreadful blasphemies and began to suck his finger frantically. Then he ran down the gangway and bent almost double to examine the ground.

'You Young Limb!' he roared, straightening up and clenching his fists. 'You did it a'purpose.'

'Did what, Charlie?' Delie leaned out of the wheel-house to ask. The Limb prudently kept out of sight.

'Set the gangplank down on a bull-ants' nest, that's what. Blithering blazes, me finger's on fire! Oh, 'elp!'

'Come up and I'll put the blue-bag on it, Charlie. And Gordon, you and the Limb move that gangplank – carefully, now, we don't want a colony of bull-ants on board.'

When she had pacified Charlie and treated the finger, which was already red and swollen about a hard white lump, she found that Cyrus James had already arrived without her sending for him.

'Looks like another blame flood is going to hold us up,' he said cheerfully as he greeted her. 'That means the coffer-dam will fill and we'll have to wait for the water to go down before we can pump it out again.'

'Better a high river than a low river from our point of view,' said Delie, escorting him to Brenton's cabin. 'Eh, Brenton? Isn't that so? We were nearly stuck in the sand below your precious Lock One – there was scarcely four feet of water there – and the rise came just in time.' She spoke volubly, quickly, to cover the sudden breathlessness that had attacked her at his nearness.

'High river's a good river,' said Brenton with some of his old vigour.

'That's all very fine and swell, but we need a few dry years while we get the locks and weirs in, then there won't be any more low rivers. With those and the Hume Dam you'll be able to snap your fingers at droughts. A barrage or rather a series of barrages at the mouth would be ideal. You could stop the whole river flowing for as much as half the year, until the water was coming down again. The whole length one enormous dam!' His grey eyes under their heavy dark brows were shining with an almost fanatical light.

'You engineers!' said Delie. 'You love to tame Nature, to turn rivers out of their courses or dam them up. But this river's too big for you. If you try to fence it in too much, it will just burst everything apart in one almighty flood.'

'No, ma'am; we know how to deal with floods. All the weirs will have moveable trestles; they can be opened, laid flat in the stream when the river is high or hauled right out. Same applies to a barrage.'

'Ever thought ... siltation? You stop natural flow ... channel will silt up. Turn into a ruddy highway for these new motor-trucks.'

'Ah! We've thought of that one, too. We built models of the river and experimented with sand. Training spurs – at Hart's Island, the top of Pyap Reach, Kapunda Island, the Renmark Reach – wherever siltation's likely, we build a barrier half-way across to divert the current and scour out the channel.'

'Encourage ... growth of "sapplins", more likely.'

'More navigational hazards, too,' said Delie.

'They'll all be marked with beacons and lit up at night.'

'Just as Uncle Mumford prophesied!' Delie smiled across at

514

Brenton. 'In *Life on the Mississippi*, you know, how they'd have the river dredged out and tidied up and all lit up like Broadway by the time there weren't any steamers left to take advantage of it. What else can happen, when there's no seaport at the mouth? The railways and trucks will get all the trade in the end.'

'Ah, that's where your government is so short-sighted! Now in America – or even in little Holland – they'd build a canal and seaport at the Murray mouth before breakfast. Here the States are so jealous of each other that it takes for ever to get anything done.'

'At least they've started on the Lake Victoria storage and that's an inter-state thing – the dam in New South Wales, the water for South Australia.'

'Yes, sixty men with horse-scoops! It will take them years. They should have five hundred men there.'

'Transport of stores is the trouble,' said Delie. 'Only a bush track from Wentworth – sometimes under water – and the Rufus is so narrow that only the smallest steamers can go up to the Lake, like the *Philadelphia*. We're making our fortune, did you know?'

Brenton smiled rather sourly. 'She has quite a business head, my wife. Just as well, with a useless hulk for a husband.'

Delie looked uncomfortable and Cyrus smoothly changed the subject, remarking that he would not be seeing much more of them as he was going back to Canada as soon as Lock Three's foundations were down.

'I'll always have a personal interest in the Murray, though. I guess I ought to take a little flask of Murray water for the folks back home, the way they carry bottles of holy water from the Jordan.'

'Rather murky water! However, we drink it all the time.'

'It's good, strong, healthy water, full of mineral salts. Why, it rusts metal a lot quicker than sea-water does; that's why you're always having to clean out your boiler-tubes.'

'And what about our insides?'

'Human beings are not steam-engines.'

'I'm not sure old Charlie hasn't a steam-pump where his heart should be, all the same. He lives and breathes and thinks engines. I believe he'd just die if he had to retire.'

'He should be darn near everlasting, preserved in alcohol. He doesn't believe in drinking Murray water neat, I guess?'

'Who? Youse talking about me? I don't believe in drinkin'

515

water at all,' said Charlie, coming in after a perfunctory knock. 'Terrible stuff, water. Rots yer guts out. Look what it does to me boiler-tubes.'

'Just exactly what I was saying,' said Cyrus James. 'So I've brought you all a present – a bottle of Victorian wine.' He put a magnum of Great Western champagne on the bedside table. 'To celebrate the opening of the first lock.'

Delie gave the bottle to Charlie to put in the cool safe. Then she asked Mr James to step up to the wheel-house and mark the location of Locks Five and Seven on her chart.

'They're the only ones likely to bother us for a while,' she said, leading the way.

She faced him across the width of the big wheel. 'It doesn't matter about the chart; I just wanted to speak to you a moment.'

His eyes widened and he moved towards her, but she held up her hand. 'Please, Cyrus! Just listen to me. I can't turn to Brenton for advice in anything these days, and I want to ask you. It's about my daughter Meg.'

She told him of Mrs Melville's strange attitude, of Meg's apparent reluctance to come back to the boat, her fears that she would lose her daughter altogether. 'What should I do? Isn't there something about possession being nine-tenths of the law? This woman has Meg, she's living in her home and she refuses to give her up. Surely she has no legal right to her?'

'That's hard to say. A mother usually has priority, unless she can be proved to be unfit to bring up the child –'

'That's just it!' Delie flushed. 'She's trying to make out that I'm not fit – because I had some lung trouble once, years ago – and then my last baby . . . died . . . on board. And she says – oh, it's unbelievable! She was always so good to me, taking the children, minding them for me and – and –' She suddenly covered her face with both hands, leaning on the wheel.

'Oh, Delie! I wish I could help you. I wish I had the right! If I were her legal father that woman would not get her away from you. But there's nothing I can do. I can't marry you – worse luck! – and all I can suggest is that you go to the city and get legal advice as soon as possible. The longer she stays there the harder it will be to get her back. She's fond of you still, but you don't know how she's being influenced.'

'You mean I'll have to get a court order, an injunction or something restraining this woman from keeping her?'

'Yes – and I don't think you'll have any trouble getting it, as the child's natural mother. But Meg is old enough to indicate her own wishes in the matter. You think she's not keen to leave?'

'There's some reason I can't understand. She's keeping something from me, I think.'

'At that age it's usually a boy, I guess.'

'Oh no! I don't think – Meg's only a child. And I can't get back for at least a week, I'll have to take this lot of stores up to the Rufus, but as soon as we come down to Morgan I'll go to the city. Thank you, Cyrus dear. You are such a comfort.'

'I wish you'd let me comfort you in other ways,' he said with feeling.

She only smiled at him and slipped out of the wheel-house.

EIGHTY-SEVEN

Meg brushed her hair for the fifth time, and then combed it from underneath to make it fluffy. She was fearfully excited at the prospect of going shooting with Garry; the fear and the excitement made a small hard knot in her stomach. She would be out with him alone in the dark paddocks and anything might happen.

She thought of the ending of one of the *Woman's World* stories; the man was much older than the girl, who had seemed to him a mere child until he suddenly became aware that she was a woman; it had ended with wedding bells.

Underneath her happy excitement a small uneasiness nagged at her. She tried to ignore it, but it persisted – her mother's face when she left this morning, hurt, shocked and angry. Whatever had Melvie said to her? And why did she want Meg to leave this very day? Of course she couldn't go, she must stop at the farm until she had a chance to tell Garry how she loved him.

Three impatient toots came from the back where the buckboard was waiting. She dabbed some eau-de-Cologne on a handkerchief and tucked it in her belt.

'Pooh!' said Garry at once as she climbed aboard. 'What's that stink?'

'You mean my hanky? It's only scent.'

She took it out of her belt and held it under his nose, but he

517

shrank back. 'Hell! It's worse than an old man fox.'

'It's eau-de-Cologne.'

Meg pushed the handkerchief far down the back of the seat. She felt discomfited. All the stories and advertisements said that men were attracted by scent, but Garry seemed to be different.

The guns, not loaded, were lying on the floor, leaving little room for her feet. A large spotlight with a length of flex attached lay on the seat between them, so that she couldn't even sit close to him.

When they came to a gate he waited while Meg got down and opened it. As she fixed the gate in the darkness behind the truck, Meg felt the immensity of the inland night, the starlight raining down on her from a clear and moonless sky. There was a freshness of dew in the air and the night was still and windless. As she climbed in again Garry said he'd seen a fox's hide down near the edge of the swamp in the reeds. They would try there first and she was to hold the spotlight and switch it on when he told her.

'Leave your gun,' he said as they got out. 'I'm not going to be shot by any trigger-happy sheila. You can have a shot later.'

Meekly she followed in his footsteps, like a squaw following a brave. She paid out the long flex behind her as she walked.

Garry had no torch or lantern. They walked easily by the light from the sky as their eyes grew accustomed to it. They wound through scratchy lignum bushes and then Garry stopped, holding up his hand. He silently motioned her forward.

Trembling, she clutched the spotlight to her. There was a rustling in the reeds as the fox broke cover.

'Light!'

She pressed the switch and a blinding beam shot across the flats, lighting up the reeds. The fox dodged the beam, then suddenly ran straight into it. He looked along it and hesitated, pinned by the eyes. In the same instant the rifle cracked deafeningly.

'You got him!' She was triumphant as the fox fell backward and rolled over, limp. But when they came up to it she felt sorry. Blood was coming from its neck. She stroked the fierce pointed muzzle and bushy tail, the rather mangy fur on its back. 'Poor old fox!' she murmured.

'Poor fox my foot! That's the one that killed all the chickens last week, I'll bet. Skin's not worth having.'

He picked up the body and dropped it again with a con

temptuous flick of the wrist.

Meg felt rather let down. The wild animal they had stalked through the night was only this rather pathetic creature, making a small heap at their feet. A leopard or a lion would have suited her mood better.

'All right, let's get back,' said Garry, and led the way. Meg got the flex caught round a bush and he had to come back and untangle it. 'Ruddy women! They're all incompetent,' he remarked, but his teasing voice was like a caress.

When they got back he laid his empty gun on the floor and loaded hers, telling her to hold it carefully and keep it pointed out of the window, while he drove. 'You might get a shot at a rabbit,' he said. 'I don't think we'll see any more foxes.'

They cruised along the top of the cliffs, with the starlit river slipping silently by in its channel two hundred feet below. Suddenly a rabbit shot out from the side of the track and scuttered along in front of the headlights, weaving from side to side but staying in their beam. Garry pulled up.

'Quick! Get him!' he cried.

Meg raised the gun; just then the rabbit stopped and sat up with twitching ears and suddenly she couldn't kill it. She lowered the rifle.

'Hell, what's the matter? He'll get away.' Garry grabbed the rifle from her, but the rabbit had got his wits back and dived off into the darkness. Garry swore.

'I – I just couldn't kill him when he was sitting up looking at me.'

'Ar – women!' said Garry. 'I won't bring you out shooting again.' This feminine weakness was not endearing. When he thought of the men he'd seen shot with no more compunction than if they'd been rabbits: men screaming, with their entrails spilling out; men without faces . . .

'Did I ever tell you about the stew?' he asked.

'Rabbit stew?'

'No, this was on the front and there weren't any rabbits left around there. We had a bit of meat scrounged from somewhere and we were fighting over French farmland, what had been a vegetable patch. I crawled out into no man's land looking for vegetables, ducking into shell-holes when a Very light went up; and I found a few carrots and turnips in the mud and crawled back with them.

'We made a beaut stew; somebody had an onion and he gave

us half of it. We were standing round the cookpot, me and me two mates, sniffing this beaut smell and thinking of the feed, when a shell came over and lobbed fair between us.

'The other two blokes were killed outright, by the blast – it just went their way. I was knocked flat, but I was all right, just a bit dazed. The stew had gone to buggery. And do you know, it was losing the stew upset me most? I was furious with those ruddy Germans. It wasn't till later that I began to miss me mates and sort of realise . . . I'd seen so many men killed.'

Meg sat silent. She was not stupid and she saw the connection.

'I suppose,' she said at last in a small voice, 'you think it's just silly to mind killing a rabbit, after . . . Did you kill many Germans?'

He gave a sharp shrug. 'A good many. The first one's the worst. After that you get hardened. Bayonet fighting's not pretty; you see their eyes as the blade goes in. It's different from lobbing a shell at a distant unit, when you don't see what happens, or what shrapnel does to the men. One of my cobbers was blinded by a shell. A big, husky, hearty chap. I saw him being led to the rear like a baby.'

Unconsciously he was twisting the mutilated fingers on his left hand. Meg put her hand on both of his. She was thrilled that he had begun to tell her something of his war experiences; he would never speak of them at home. 'Tell me how you lost your fingers,' she said.

He flung her away with an oath and started the engine.

'Ar, let's get back,' he said. 'I hate going over all that business.'

Meg sat in her corner of the seat, with silent tears rolling down her cheeks. She had hoped he might kiss her; instead he had drawn his hands away as if a snake had bitten them.

Another rabbit darted across the track. Garry deliberately drove at it and ran it down. There was a small, sickening 'thump' as the wheel hit its body. Meg shuddered, but said nothing.

Back in the farm kitchen, he tried clumsily to make up for his harshness, bustling round making a cup of tea and waiting on her in a way which was most unlike him. He saw the traces of tears on her face and felt a hound and at the same time he felt angry with her for putting him in the wrong.

Still, Meg never harboured a grudge; he had to admit she was a good kid and she was pathetically grateful for the tea and the rough kindness he dispensed with it. When she said good night she held up her face to be kissed, childishly, and almost without thinking he took it between his hands and kissed the awkward red poppy of her mouth, so soft and young, with his hard lips.

To his consternation she gripped him round the neck and kissed him back with fervour. He had to reach behind and unclasp her hands and almost drag her off, while she murmured broken phrases.

'I knew you loved me. I knew you must, because I love you so much, so much, so much . . .'

'For Christ's sake, Meg! Mum'll hear you in a minute. You've only got a crush on me because I'm older and I happen to be around. It's just a stage, you'll grow out of it.'

'No, no, no!' she moaned. 'This is for ever and ever. I love you because you're so good and so brave and – '

'I'm not brave! Will you get that into your head?' In exasperation he began to shout. 'See this wound? This honourable-discharge wound? It was done with my own gun, so I could get out of the bloody war and come home. And me brother stuck it out and got killed. That's your hero for you. A self-inflicted wound!'

'Garry!'

It was Mrs Melville, her hair in long grey plaits, her usually ruddy cheeks white, who leant in the kitchen doorway in her long-sleeved nightgown as if she might fall without support.

'Yes, Mum; you might as well know. It's a relief to tell someone about it. I can't stand this Hero-of-the-Empire stuff much longer.'

Mrs Melville took a tottering step across the kitchen and sank in a chair. 'All right, son,' she said wearily. 'Don't shout; there's no need for your father to know. I'm only glad Jim had enough guts to go on to the end.'

'Jim was worth two of me and he should of come home. But you're stuck with me now.'

'Yes, worse luck!'

Stung, Meg leapt to his defence. 'I don't care, it took courage to pull the trigger against yourself. And you killed lots of Germans first. I'm glad you came home, Garry.'

'Thanks, kid. You'd better get off to bed now. All this is because of that blasted rabbit you wouldn't shoot!' He gave her a thin, twisted smile.

'Yes, run on, Meg dear. I think I'll have a cup of tea, I don't feel as if I could sleep. Is there any left in the pot? You'd better go too, Garry. Perhaps I'll get used to this thing by the morning.'

He shrugged and went slowly to the door, picking up his rifle to clean it.

'Leave the gun!' she cried.

He looked at his mother cynically. 'Why, do you think I'd have the guts to blow my brains out? Don't worry!'

EIGHTY-EIGHT

Lake Victoria construction settlement was like a small town; more civilised than the old survey camp where men lived in tents and had whisky and brawls as their only relaxation.

There were Engineering Department huts fitted with fly-wire screens and a few women braved the distance and the discomfort to join their husbands. There was no doctor, but the wife of the engineer-in-charge was a trained nurse; anyone with an ailment was sure of her sympathy and advice and whatever treatment she could improvise.

Flower gardens grew in front of the huts, clothes-lines blossomed with coloured washing and feminine garments. There were even a few children.

Once a fortnight, the *Philadelphia* came churning up the narrow Rufus to the landing at the entrance to the lake. Her coming was a signal for everyone to drop whatever he was doing as her whistle echoed over the waters.

The shallow lake was usually blue under the cloudless inland sky. Low sandhills of a rich pinkish-orange enclosed it at one end and over these the Darling lilies grew in creamy profusion.

Seeing it again under this sunny aspect, Delie in her troubled state felt unable to paint, as she had thought of doing, a lake scene for Alastair. The landscape was too tranquil, with its muted blues and bleached ochres, for her frame of mind. She wanted to get away to the city and consult a lawyer.

Charlie had already opened up the shutters for the eager crowd. One of the customers was a dog – a curly retriever who belonged to one of the construction camp's labourers. He arrived with a ten-shilling note in an empty tin tied to his collar and a piece of paper on which was scrawled: '1 pkt. plug tobacco (dark), 1 doz matches, ¹1/2 Indian tea. Please put goods and change in tin. Thanks.'

The men all knew Nigger. They said his owner had trained him to retrieve empty bottles from the water and now he had a huge collection in his hut which he hoped to sell one day. Someone had once tried to remove the money from Nigger's tin – 'just for a lark' – and had nearly lost his hand. He wouldn't yield it up except at the floating-store counter.

Delie gingerly took out the note, put the required items and the loose coins in, gave the dog a biscuit and sent him on his way with a pat. He took the biscuit down to the edge of the water to eat before going home.

'He always stops down there a minute to count the change,' said a solemn-faced man known as Larry the Liar, who leant casually on the counter. 'Say, Missus, you haven't brought any of the black stuff, have you? I get me inspiration from Fourpenny Dark.'

'We're not allowed to bring alcohol to the camp, you know that,' said Delie crisply. She also knew that the other steamers were engaged in sly-grogging, one skipper carrying his illicit store in the shells of empty coconuts. The 'Fourpenny Dark' was a villainous black wine, fortified with proof spirit, and was officially banned because it had been the cause of some fatal brawls. She hoped none of the men present could remember how the *Philadelphia* used to engage in running whisky to the survey camp on this very spot, back in the days when Brenton was still in charge.

'Babies' bottles? Yes, I have the latest design, opening at both ends for easy washing,' she told a young woman, weather-beaten and thin, who stood diffidently among the throng of men at the counter. They discussed milk-mixtures and teat-sizes in an undertone. She was really helping women who lived this frontier existence, Delie thought, by bringing the small necessaries of life almost to their doors; and they appreciated having another woman to deal with.

The turnover was excellent and the trade growing. She would soon have enough to put one of the children through medical school. Not Meg – Meg wanted to be a nurse; but perhaps her own financial standing might weigh with the court. And she herself must be without reproach in her private life. Thank goodness she had not yielded to the longing for Cyrus James.

The lawyer leaned back in his leather chair, put his fingers together at the tips and looked at Delie over them.

'Your private life, I take it, is beyond reproach. You are not living apart from your husband, or anything like that?'

'No, but – but he's bedridden, you see, and doesn't take much interest in the children or their welfare.'

'Well, it would be better if you can get him to sign the petition for the child's return. Unless this woman can prove that you are leading an immoral life and are unfit to bring up the child, or that the home influence is likely to corrupt and harm.' He smiled deprecatingly at the absurdity of such a suggestion. He was a man of wide experience, a connoisseur of food and drink and women; and this little thing with the great blue eyes full of trouble appealed even to his cynical heart, hardened by many years' contact with human weakness and fallibility in court.

'Oh no; there's nothing like that,' said Delie, smiling too with relief that she could say so. No one but herself knew how near a thing it had been; in her position a breath of gossip would have been enough to damn her.

'All this other business – your having had tuberculosis, your nomadic life on the river, the fact that your last child died on board, even the fact that the Melvilles are well off and can give your daughter a good home – all this would not influence the court to take a child away from its natural mother, without some other good reason. She has completed her primary education, she has never been a neglected child. The laws regarding child welfare exist to protect children against manifestly unsuitable parents. As far as I can see you have nothing to worry about.'

He smiled urbanely, revealing an excellent set of teeth beneath his moustache, as he escorted her to the door. 'Good-bye, Mrs Edwards. I'll draw up the application to the court for an order restraining this Mrs Melville from influencing your daughter against her parents and requiring her to deliver her person to your care from henceforward.'

'But if the child wants to stay?'

'Fortunately she is still young enough for the court to decide what is best for her. If she were not a minor, of course it would be different.'

Delie went back to her Adelaide hotel, thinking it was as well that kind man didn't know everything. Perhaps she should have told him everything. For there was still one dread at the back of her mind. The doctor at Waikerie Hospital knew, and perhaps Mrs Melville had guessed – and Brenton too – that she was morally responsible for her imbecile baby's death. The doctor had stood by her before and she believed he would again, but she could never feel secure. How our acts haunted the future! 'Action is transitory – a step, a blow . . .' and the effects go on for ever. She remembered the gesture with which she had climbed over the window-sill and shut the window – had she shut the window? – it had been a decisive action, anyway – and so sent Adam to his death. Far, far back along the course of life, some temporary obstruction sent you in an entirely different direction and to a different end.

She thought of the river, too, how the Murray, already flowing on a steady north-westerly course, was checked at one point by some minor movement of the earth's crust and so turned abruptly southward and eventually reached the Southern Ocean, instead of petering out in the sandy wastes of the inland like so many of the westward-flowing rivers. One change of direction and the whole history of this part of the continent was altered.

On the way down-river from the Rufus they had been hailed in a lonely reach by an old 'hatter' living in a bark humpy on a box tree flat. He had reminded Delie a little of Hairy Harry and his simple philosophy; for Scotty, as he was known, did not believe in work. Yet when they pulled in to the bank they had found his camp as neat as a hospital bed: the patch in front of the door swept clean of leaves; empty tins and bottles in a pile at the rear; and drum-nets tidily stacked on the bank.

'Sold a few cod to a passing steamer, so I got some money to spend,' said Scotty. 'Tobacco's all I really need: tobacco an' flour an' tea. They're what I call necessities of life. Women ain't necessities, and neither is beer, though mind you,' he added with a wink, 'I wouldn't sneeze at either, if they was there for the havin'. But slave to keep a wife an' kids? Not Scotty. Lyin' in the sun an' watchin' the river go past – that's my idea of life.'

No doubt it was a heretical attitude to take in this new modern world since the war, with everything speeding up, jazz and motor-cars and aeroplanes and the growing urge to make money, to 'get on', which seemed to emanate from the vigorous young country of the United States. But why? thought Delie. Old Scotty and the most powerful millionaire would come to the same dusty end; and whether covered by a marble mausoleum or a heap of sand on the river-bank, they'd crumble just the same.

To tease him she said: 'But you work at fishing, don't you?'

Scotty shrugged. 'If y' can call it work. I drop in a line and some silly great cod hooks hisself on the end and waits there till I haul him in. Or he swims into a net; *I* don' do nothing to make 'im.'

As they went on down the river, hurrying back for a new load of stores, Delie wondered when she would ever have the sort of life she craved. She suspected that she was a born beachcomber, with a life of endless activity thrust upon her. All she really asked of life was food and shelter, time to think and leisure to paint.

EIGHTY-NINE

When Delie came back from the city to join the boat again at Morgan, Brenton greeted her sitting up in a wheelchair.

The children were delighted with the surprise; they laughed and danced all round her, while Brenton sat smiling with self-conscious pride and pleasure. School holidays were on and Brenny had come down to join them, while Meg remained at the farm.

'You didn't guess, Mummy! Dad's been doing exercises and the doctor at Milang gave him a book and Charlie got the wheelchair.'

'Oh, did you all know about it and didn't tell me?' She kissed Brenton and wiped away a tear. 'It's so wonderful, I can't take it in! I'm so glad for you, Brenton.'

'I didn't want you – to be disappointed – if it didn't come off. Look!'

He spun the wheels with his hands and went shooting across the saloon. 'I can go anywhere – this deck. Charlie says he'll build – ramp up to the wheel-house. Then – '

Delie looked thoughtful. Then he would be able to come back to the wheel-house and really be the skipper once again, no longer in name only.

She suddenly realised that she didn't want her place taken, that she enjoyed her unique position as the river's only woman skipper, and the respect of men like Charlie and Captain Ferguson and Captain Ritchie for her ability and independence. She had been thinking nostalgically of being without responsibilities, free to paint or to laze on deck all day; now the prospect did not please her. Brenton would not be able to steer. She would still be in the wheel-house, working just as long hours, but he would be in command. Already there was a new air of decision about him.

Another thought occurred to her: she could get a reliable first mate to help Brenton and take a cottage on the river-bank, somewhere along the steamer's run, and make a home for Meg. Not even Mrs Melville could say then that she was not providing a suitable home for the child. She never doubted that she would get Meg back, now that she had the court order in her favour, but she knew Mrs Melville's obstinacy. She would try to win Meg back again as soon as she was of age.

Meanwhile, Meg alternated between dizzy happiness and all the pangs of youthful, unrequited love. Garry was touched in spite of himself by her open adoration, but at the same time it embarrassed him and made him uneasy, so that he swung between tenderness and a sudden brusqueness which left Meg bewildered and hurt.

'When are we going out shooting again?' she begged him, having waited at the gate for his return from Waikerie, so that she could get him away from his mother. Mrs Melville had shown an elaborate indifference to him since his revelation, but Meg she watched more closely than before: she had caught the note of hero-worship in her voice in her defence of Garry.

He leaned over now, across Meg's small body and banged shut the door of the truck before replying. His sandy brows were drawn together in a frown of impatience.

'When, Garry? When, when, when?' She put her feet up on the seat and hugged her knees childishly.

'I don't know, Meg; don't nail me,' he said irritably. 'It wasn't such a success last time that you should want to go again.'

'We got a fox.'

'Yes, we got a fox. And Mum got a dose of the bitter truth that she hasn't recovered from yet.'

'It was better for her to know.'

'I'm inclined to think, if you give people the choice, they'd rather *not* know the truth when it's going to hurt them.'

'Well, let's go fishing in the dinghy,' said Meg, changing her point of attack.

'All right – Sunday afternoon then,' said Garry. He felt it would be safer to take Meg out in daylight; she was so intense, and you never knew when the little beggar would make a dead set at you.

On the Sunday afternoon of Meg's outing with Garry, the *Philadelphia* was tied up not more than forty miles away downstream, just below Morgan, waiting to go in to the wharf and load first thing in the morning. The wharfage dues were such that no one tied up unless sure of getting a load handled speedily. Among the other increasing expenses, there would be a toll to pay at every passage through Lock One when it was officially opened in the New Year. Delie was pleased that her present run – from Morgan, just above the first lock, to Lake Victoria – would not mean passing through the lock.

The tolls were to be used for improving the river, building more training spurs, dredging round wharves and financing the Government snagging boat *Industry*, which in the last year had pulled out a thousand snags from the river between Blanchetown and the border.

Gordon was busy mounting his pressed wild flowers in a new interleaved book, and Brenny was with Brenton, supervising Charlie in making a ramp up to the wheel-house for his chair, with a pulley and rope for hauling himself up. Anything mechanical and anything to do with his father attracted Brenny like a magnet.

'Should be worked with steam, be rights,' Charlie was saying, the old fanatical gleam in his fading blue eyes. 'A wire rope from the steam-winch up over the pulley and down agen to the top of the ramp – simple as falling off a log. Now if –'

'If there was no steam up I couldn't get into the wheel-house, that would mean,' said Brenton. 'D'you want to have to get steam up just to drive the flaming wheelchair? No, Charlie; just a hand-winch so I can wind meself up: something really *simple*, I want.'

He gave a vigorous shove to the wheel of the chair and shot across the top deck below the wheel-house, looking up to that three-step-higher elevation as at the Promised Land; like an ambitious cabin-boy dreaming of when he would be himself a skipper. His left arm was now so strong that he actually believed he would be able to steer, where the going was fairly straight. His fingers itched to feel the wooden spokes of the great wheel standing up behind the windows.

Alex had watched for a while until it struck him that neither of his elder brothers was using the dinghy and he could have it all to himself for once. He was excited at the idea, but calmly and methodically he went about gathering what he would need for an exploring expedition. He wasn't going to do a Leichardt or a Burke and Wills, this would be a well-planned and well-equipped journey.

When he had dropped his bundle of food, matches, knife, and billy-can into the dinghy, he went back for his specimen-box and what he called his geologist's hammer, though it was just the same as the one Charlie used for carpentry. Then he cast off quietly and drifted away under the stern, in case Brenny should suddenly decide to come with him. His mother was painting and had scarcely looked up when he said he was taking the dinghy.

She had three apples on a plate in front of a blue cloth, and he supposed she was trying to paint them, but the shapes on the canvas didn't look much like apples to him; they had a thick black line all round them and were sort of square, while the jug which he could see was simply plain white she had painted in just about all the colours of the rainbow. However, he made no comment as he quietly withdrew. Alex was the most tactful of Delie's children.

He pulled downstream, further away from the town and as soon as he was round the first bend he felt alone on the whole river, as alone as Sturt's men in their whaleboat venturing down the unknown stream to the unknown sea.

He went on pulling strongly, exhilarated by the swift movement of the almost empty dinghy aided by the slight current, until he remembered some advice given by his father: never go too far downstream or you may find the current too much for you on the way back. The breeze which had been with him was now in his face; the river had turned completely on itself in a series of bends.

He began looking for caves to explore and pulled into a billabong formed by the cutting-off of a great bend of the river in some former flood. On the far side, the cliffs that formed the real bank of the river were carved and fretted into hollows right to their tops and above them the whistling eagles that nested there were soaring like cinders in the blue sky. Their cries floated down to him, a series of shrill whistles in an ascending scale, ending in a sharp sound like the noise of a ricocheting bullet.

There was a cave high above the waterline, but the cliff was climbable. He tied the dinghy and began to scramble up the rough limestone face, until he was able to pull himself over the edge of the cavern's floor. The floor was not rocky, but thickly strewn with deposits of sand and clay from very high floods in the past.

In a crevice of a big boulder at the mouth of the cave there grew a clump of bluebells, seeming to float on their thin wiry stems like butterflies, blue as the sky; he would take a few back for Gordon's collection.

Alex turned to haul up his billy-can on the rope which he had tied to his foot, with the tea and sugar inside it, the matches, and the corned-beef sandwiches. He tipped out the things and dropped the billy again to the full length of the rope to haul some water. Then he turned to explore.

The cave sloped sharply towards the back, the roof coming down until he could stand only in a crouching position. As the cave went deeper into the cliff it grew darker and mustier. He struck a match, and then another and in its dying sputter saw something on the rock wall; it looked like a white human hand.

Lighting another match he saw the weathered outline of a hand in white clay; beside it some concentric circles and stripes of yellow and red ochre enclosed in a black border. The drawings looked very old. He thought of Tannanobi, the very last of the Pujinook tribe, who had died in Morgan not long before from alcoholic poisoning – 'treated' too often by the white men who regarded him as an interesting relic of a bygone age.

He would have known the meaning of these strange symbolic drawings. Now perhaps there was no one left who could interpret them. Alex wished he had a flash camera or even a pencil and paper. He searched further but found no more drawings, though some, he realised, might have been convered in the passage of time by accumulations of earth on the floor. The cave narrowed into a point and ended.

Searching back below the level of the drawings, he saw a band of sand and charcoal, soft and crumbly, almost at floor level. Near the back of the cave were twisted dead roots of surface shrubs which had forced their way down here in search of water; he broke one off and dug with its sharp point. Charcoal and bits of stone fell out, odd-shaped stones, with curving, shell-shaped fractures and sharp edges. Picking one up, he found his thumb and finger instinctively holding it like a tool. He had discovered a collection of aboriginal stone knives and adzes, scrapers and spear-heads, some half-worked or broken but obviously fashioned by man.

Alex was excited. He thrust the best of them inside the neck of his shirt for carrying, in spite of their sharpness and dirtiness.

He would wash them in the river and find the full beauty of the glassy flints, which must have been brought from many miles away to this sand-and-limestone country.

He poked in the sandy floor of the cave just below the charcoal band, and turned up something white – a thighbone! With a cry he began digging in the half-darkness like a dog, rooting up bones until he had what must be almost a complete skeleton: femur and tibia, finger- and toe-joints, ribs and vertebrae and then the skull with the lower jaw missing.

He squatted there, staring in the dim light at the hollow eye-sockets, the row of square, flat teeth, until suddenly his skin began to prickle. He looked over his shoulder nervously. The small lighted patch of the entrance looked very far away. Abruptly he put the skull back where he'd found it and turned and ran towards the light.

When he was standing there in the sunlight, looking down at the calm billabong and the river with its fringing trees, his panic seemed foolish. He prided himself on having a scientific mind and in fact had always wanted a skeleton of his own to study.

What he needed was to be fortified with food and tea. Resolutely he turned towards the back of the cave again, marched past the silent bones and began breaking off dry roots for his fire.

When it was lit he felt a kind of kinship with that former man back there. He crouched in the cave's entrance above his little fire, with the darkness behind him and an empty world in front, as the Stone Age man must have crouched long ago and wondered and puzzled about death and its mystery and the greater mystery of being alive. His logical mind rejected the resurrection of the flesh; those bones could not be clothed with life again, there were thousands and millions of skeletons scattered through the ancient soil of the earth's crust, in fragments, in solution, in the form of microscopic dust. Not even St Peter could call them into separate being again. No one would really like to live for ever, it would make life pointless. Instead of fixing his mind on a future life, he would prefer to make this life as good as possible.

Already, since the war, they had discovered new treatments, new ways to combat pain and disease and lengthen the useful period of living. They were beginning to realise the interdependence of mind and matter; that a sick mind could waste the body, a physical injury deform the mind.

The living body was the vessel, the lamp, fragile and wonderful, which held the flame of life. To shelter this vessel from all the dangers that beset it, to preserve it as long as possible and keep the individual flame from extinction, was the highest aim of human endeavour, Alex thought.

He decided then and there, looking down at the great flow of water beside which he had been born, that he would be a doctor.

In another dinghy forty miles upstream, Meg sat quietly holding her line and not talking, even though she was bubbling over with happiness and conversation.

Garry had had a few nibbles but had not caught anything, so he was not in a very good temper. A single catfish lay in the bottom of the boat, caught by Meg but landed by Garry.

'Throw the horrid thing back!' she had begged, but he wouldn't. She hated the catfish's slimy, toad-like skin, its revolting rubbery whiskers, and it tasted when cooked, she firmly believed, like baked snake.

'He'll be all right skinned,' said Garry. 'Mum can cook them all right. You just have to be careful of his spines though – they're poisonous.'

'The whole thing looks poisonous to me. I've never liked catfish. Why can't I catch a nice callop?'

'I'd be pleased to catch anything at all,' said Garry, and sank into moody silence.

Meg did land a callop shortly afterwards, a silvery two-pounder, but in spite of her pride she had enough woman's instinct to be sorry and to wish Garry had caught it instead.

'You're better at fishing than you are at shooting,' he said grudgingly.

'Yes I am, aren't I? Well I lived on a boat most of my life and we all used to go fishing with the dinghy or have a set-line over the side as soon as we stopped.'

'Don't you miss the boat, and your people?'

'I only want to stay with you and Melvie,' she said and quoted fervently: ' "Whither thou goest, I will go; and where thou lodgest, I will lodge; thy people shall be my people, and thy God, my God." '

'Don't forget Mother's getting on, she won't last for ever and as soon as I decently can get away I'm off to the city. I'm only stopping to help Dad through the next sowing.'

Meg stared at him, her jaw dropping slightly. She wound in her fishing-line with concentration, her lips trembling.

'Garry!' Unconsciously she clasped her hands in a pleading

gesture, with the rolled-up line on its piece of smooth stick between them. 'Garry, take me with you, won't you? I can't let you go! I can't!'

'For Christ's sake, Meg! You can't come with me.'

'Why not? Why can't you take me? You don't have to marry me, I don't mind. I only want to be where you are, to see you sometimes. You won't even have to speak to me. Why can't I come? I love you, Garry. Why not?'

'Because I don't love you and I never will,' he said, goaded into speaking brutally.

'O-oh!' Meg melted into tears, into heartbroken sobs, her head down on the gunwale, her black fluff of hair hanging over the side.

'Good God, you're only fourteen!'

'So was Juliet.'

'This isn't a play. You're just a romantic schoolgirl, and it's time you woke up to the fact that life isn't a beaut romance, or even a great tragedy – it's just a bloody farce. A shell lands on a cooking-pot; me two cobbers are blown to bits and I'm left alive. Why? Damned if I know. Mum spends the whole war praying that Jim will come back safe and he cops it a month before the Armistice. She's stuck with me and now I'm not even a hero.' He laughed without humour. 'It's funny when you think about it.'

'Garry! Don't be so bitter.' She gulped and wiped her face on her dress.

'I can't help it, Meg. Inside I'm like an old man. That's what the war's done to me. It's not that you're so young, but that I'm so old. I'm just not interested in love and marriage and all that.'

Meg sat crushed and desolate and spoke not a word as she rowed her back to the landing below the cliff. Then, betrayed into tenderness by her woebegone face, he held her for a moment against him as he helped her out of the boat.

Immediately she began to cry again, with her face buried in his shirt-front, and at her tears he stiffened.

Hell, he couldn't stand being wept over, he wished she'd turn off all these waterworks and become the jolly kid of his first arrival. Wearily he passed her a handkerchief and waited for her to compose herself before they climbed the cliff to the farm.

NINETY

The morning song of the sprinklers on the lawns was what Meg remembered most clearly of the following summer, when she came to look back on it in later life.

The chirring of crickets, the whirring of the sprinklers as they turned and the stridulous cries of cicadas perched shrilling on every tree and fencepost, were combined into a summer symphony, a hot, vibrating music.

Delie had bought a small house with a block of land irrigated from the river, some distance out of the town. They had their own small landing-stage of two planks going out into the river and to this they moored their dinghy.

Alex and Meg went to the Renmark High School, catching a bus at the corner of the main road. When Mrs Melville had been forced to return Meg to her mother, Delie decided to make a home for Meg on land, while Brenton ran the steamer with the aid of Charlie McBean and a new mate and his two elder sons.

She had hoped to find in her daughter the first real companion of her own sex she had known since her sisters were drowned; but in this she was disappointed. Meg had always been affectionate on her brief visits home, but now she was remote and self-absorbed.

Meg had been glad enough to come home to lick her wounds, once Garry Melville had gone. He'd left for the city, hinting that he would not be there long before he took a berth on a ship sailing from Port Adelaide.

She wanted to get far away from a place that reminded her unbearably of him at every turn: the living-room where they played card games after dinner, the gate on the Waikerie road where she used to wait for the utility, the picnic spots along the river and the places where they would go shooting and fishing.

In the Melvilles' house, she could not turn a tap or a door-handle without thinking: 'His hand has rested here'. She would lie awake long into the nights, going over in her mind every scene with him she could remember – even the painful ones – and every word he had spoken.

Preoccupied as she was, she found her mother irritating beyond words. Meg, suffering as a woman but being treated as a child, felt herself much older and wiser than Delie, whose aimless muddling in the kitchen filled her with contempt.

She became irritable and snappish and more than a little bossy. Though she always addressed Delie as 'dear', it was in a patronising tone rather than one of affection. Gradually she took over all the housekeeping and cooking, while Delie did the marketing and looked after the garden.

Delie would have liked her daughter to be an artist, but since her talents did not lie in that direction it was pleasant to find her so capable and, she had to admit, so well-trained by Mrs Melville. If only Meg had been more pleasant about it! Delie felt her quick temper rising to meet her daughter's critical attitude, her half-concealed hostility.

If Meg was to remember the summer sounds, it was the fruit Delie would always recall: apricots eaten hot from the tree, squashing into a delicious yellow pulp in the mouth; peaches dripping with juice; loquats like globes of golden wax in which were bedded the satiny brown stones. Muscatel grapes grew over a trellis at the back door and twined about the kitchen window.

Birds came and pierced the translucent globes with their beaks, then the ants and bees followed till each grape was only a hollow skin. To save them Delie tied brown paper bags over the biggest bunches.

She loved the garden, where everything grew with such abundance in the red sandy soil: tomatoes, rock-melons and watermelons with crisp, dark-red flesh; sweet potatoes and maize and butter-beans, and a row of flourishing fruit trees.

She rested like a caravan voyager at an oasis in this fruitful place, before going on into a future which seemed as full of menace as the desert. Brenton might have another stroke; they might lose the steamer; and some said the river-traffic was doomed. So as to put something aside for an emergency, she had taken up art teaching. On three afternoons a week she rowed into Renmark to take a class of enthusiastic amateurs, all women. She found that she quite enjoyed teaching, but it did not leave much time for her own painting.

It seemed strange to her to live in one place after so many years of wandering up and down the rivers, and the row into Renmark stopped her from feeling restless. She did the mar-

535

keting while she was there and rowed back downstream with the current helping her, enjoying the steady rhythm of the oars.

Letters came from Alastair Raeburn, tender, passionate and full of longing, but she refused to let them disturb her tranquil way of life. She had not seen him for more than a year. Cyrus James had returned to Canada and sent her a beautiful set of art books in colour. She was able for the first time to study the work of Braque and Cézanne and the Paris School – a whole new world of which she'd had only a glimpse before.

Delie felt no sympathy with either Cubism or Surrealism, but from each style she learned something and adapted whatever was useful to her individual vision. At times she had a feeling almost of panic – it had come too late, she had lost twenty years when she should have been developing and soon she would be old, or dead; either way it would mean the death of art. If only time would slow to the even pace of her youth! It was speeding up so much that it made her giddy.

In the last ten years so much had happened: the World War and its aftermath, the emancipation of women, the start of harnessing the river; and in her private affairs, Brenton's illness and semi-recovery, his unexpected return to life and the running of the steamer.

Even his voice had become stronger, the sentences came out with little hesitation as he shouted his orders to the deckhands. Two of these were his own sons, but they leaped to do his bidding with as much alacrity as the Young Limb, who openly adored the skipper. Gordon, nearly nineteen, was already training for his Mate's Ticket.

On the first day when Brenton wound himself up into the wheel-house, Delie was standing by to give a hand away from the Morgan wharf; but as soon as they were out in midstream and safely on their way, he made it clear that he could handle the boat himself.

He started with testy criticism of her way of taking the bends. 'Keep in, keep in, you want to cut the point as fine as you can . . . You've got all the current against you, out in midstream like that.'

Delie bit back the reply that leaped to her tongue: that she had worked out her own way of taking the bends, using the swing of the current to save her shoulder-muscles. She quietly brought the *Philadelphia* in close, hoping there was not a hidden sandbank big enough to ground them. Brenton helped by heaving on his side of the wheel.

'Now let me take her,' he whispered. His eyes half-closed, an expression of dreamy joy on his face, he took the wheel for the first time in six years. Propped on an extra cushion in the wheel-chair he could reach almost to the top and with his powerful arms, developed at the expense of his weak and withered lower limbs, he moved the steamer slightly out of line so as to have the pleasure of swinging her back on course.

'Come up, old girl; come up,' he murmured caressingly. 'Up you come, now. Ah, you're still the craft you used to be! Light as a bird and steady as a rock. See how she knows me? See how she responds?' He flashed a glance across the wheel-house at Delie and suddenly, from the reflection of blue sky in tranquil water, or from the new animation within – who knew? – his eyes had come alive again, brilliant and blue-green as the Southern Ocean, charming and compelling as she had known them long ago. She was shaken with an unaccustomed tenderness; the contrast of those young eyes in his ageing face, the grey hair, the flabby cheeks, the roll of flesh about his neck, reminded her sharply of the passage of time, more sharply than her own mirror did.

What a spirit he had – to have fought his way back from help-lessness and invalidism to this half a life, which was surely better than none (and lying useless in a bunk in one room was no life at all). It was still only half a life, as he was well aware; he resented the insentient, useless lower half of his body and all those pleasures of the flesh he had known so well and knew no more.

'I suppose you're glad,' he'd said once in a bitter moment to Delie, 'that I'll . . . never be a man . . . again. No more unwanted babies, eh?' And when she winced and protested, he'd laughed cynically. 'But it cuts both ways, my dear. You were always . . . hot-blooded little thing . . . and now . . . By God, if I thought you were consoling yourself with, with –'

'Brenton, stop tormenting us both! Of course I'm not glad and of course I'm not . . . Oh, I shouldn't even answer you, I won't discuss it.' And she fled away in tears.

The only drawback about Renmark was the friendliness of the people. She longed for more time to herself, none of the days were long enough, even though she always rose with the sun.

After she had been there only a month she was asked to join the Mothers' Club, the Country Women's Association, the Pro-gress Association and the Schools' Committee; and as tactfully as possible had to explain that she had no time for such things

537

The women who asked her couldn't see how she could be busy, with no husband to look after, a daughter old enough to help and a small house. They finished all their housework in a bout of fierce activity every morning by ten o'clock and had the rest of the day for gossiping and good works.

Delie went at her tasks sporadically, sometimes dashing through the washing-up and the bed-making in one burst; but usually she became distracted, she went out to empty the tea-pot after the children had gone to school, and the warm golden morning held her in the garden, weeding or planting or just standing and soaking up the sun like a tree.

Then the sight of the kitchen when she came in, the unwashed dishes and saucepans standing accusingly in the sink, discouraged her so that she wandered away, ostensibly to get a tea-towel from the linen cupboard, and began instead working on a half-finished painting. It was only when increasing hunger told her that the afternoon was well advanced that she would fly to the kitchen to make herself a snack while clearing up before the methodical Meg came home.

Only the bedrooms were always tidy. From living in a small cabin for so long, Delie had learnt to keep things ship-shape, clothes put away and beds neatly made; but dust on the verandas, pieces on the floor – she was not even aware of them until Meg began industriously sweeping up.

'You're an awful muddler, dear,' Meg would say with an indulgent grown-up air. Alex was methodical and neat by nature, even as Gordon and Brenny were naturally untidy; but he could never see any point in making a bed until it was time to get into it. His room was full of labelled boxes of bones, snakes and lizards preserved in bottles and a collection of beetles and butterflies horribly transfixed with pins.

It was a gruesome place. Delie made his bed as quickly as possible and escaped into the perpetual winter sunshine. It was a particularly lovely morning, one day towards the end of the second school term, when she went out into the dew-sparkling garden where a migrant blackbird sang clearly, liquidly as if the dew had filled his throat.

She was weeding the peas, her hands coated with wet red sand, when she heard the click of the gate and saw a neat, bearded figure in a light-coloured suit and a panama hat entering. She stood up with her heart beating chokingly, her hair falling into her eyes, and made a half-move to bolt towards the house; but it was too late.

Alastair had already seen her. She stood there in her old morning frock, while he advanced, smiling rather primly with his lips; but his eyes were all fire and sensibility.

NINETY-ONE

'How did you find where I lived?'

'I knew you were in Renmark and I asked at the Post Office.'

They were seated decorously in the little living-room, conversing politely, Delie plying him with a local wine and a piece of fruit cake, made by Meg. Ignoring the fact of his letters and what had passed between them in that little glass room on the roof at Milang, she tried to keep the atmosphere normal, talked of her painting class, her garden, anything, while he sat smiling at her with an ironically raised eyebrow.

She felt quite breathless and her mouth was so dry that she gulped greedily at the wine, spilling some on the carpet. He continued to watch her; then he suddenly leaned over and, taking her right wrist in a grip of steel, removed the wine-glass with his other hand and set it on a small table.

'Stop it, Delie,' he said. 'What are you trying to do – keep me at arm's length with idle chatter? It won't work, you know.'

She stared into his dark eyes and fell silent. 'I know,' she said in a small voice.

'I haven't seen you for more than a year and you talk to me about broad beans!'

She began to laugh. 'Well, they're certainly a nice neutral subject.'

'Have you forgotten what I wrote to you?'

'No. I wish I could. Your letters frighten me. You idealise me too much! I'm not the wonderful person you carry an image of in your mind, and when you find your swan is only a goose after all –'

He stood up and took her face between his hands, bending her head back to gaze into her eyes. 'What a beautiful face!' he

539

murmured. 'Beauty bred in the bone. When you are an old woman, when you're eighty-two, I shall still love you madly. May I take you out to dinner on your eighty-second birthday?'

'In forty years' time? If we are both here.'

'*You* will live to be a hundred,' he promised confidently.

'Goodness, I hope not! I don't want to be an old thing, I'd rather die.'

'And you will never be an "old thing", you'll always be a woman.'

Suddenly he snatched her up and into his arms, his face resting in the angle of her neck and shoulder; and thus they stood, silent trembling, while his lips moved gently along her throat to her ear.

Delie came to herself first and feebly pushed him away, and sank into a straight-backed chair; so moved and shaken that she could not speak, as if all the breath had been shocked out of her body.

It was ridiculous, it was not possible, she kept telling herself, that Alastair Raeburn could make her feel like this. She had long ago decided that he did not attract her, and here she was unable to think or speak because of his nearness.

'Do your children come home to lunch?' he asked. 'I suppose they go to school in the town.'

The words were commonplace enough, but with the effort of repressing his feelings he looked quite mad, white-faced and burning-eyed.

'No; it's too far to be worth while. They have to go in a bus. Alex seems very bright and is always restless; Meg is much quieter, more grown up in her ways. Sometimes I feel that she is older than I am.'

'You're still a girl in many ways.'

'Meg is always being shocked by my lack of dignity. Sometimes when we're shopping in town on Saturday afternoon, if it's a lovely day and I'm feeling light-hearted I start to sing and she gets very embarrassed. Once I sat down on the kerb and sketched an old woman who was waiting for a bus, and Meg walked away pretending she didn't belong to me. I seem to be out of step with the next generation always. I used to shock the aunt who brought me up, when I was Meg's age.'

'A cuckoo in the nest!'

'Yes. Though sometimes I feel more like a pelican. You know, a clumsy and ungainly bird except in its own element, air or water.'

'I think a phoenix: your element is fire. Your touch burns me, your eyes reduce me to a cinder, I am consumed by the most ardent flame –'

'Alastair, please be serious. We were talking about –'

'About broad beans?'

'Yes. The cultivation of vegetables.'

'I would rather cultivate your affections. I want to grow into your heart, to entwine myself in your arms, to plant myself most deeply –'

'Alastair!'

'Well, I will be good. Show me the rest of your house, what you have been painting.'

She led the way down the little passage which divided the house in the centre. 'This is my workroom, I never have to tidy up in here.' When he had gazed earnestly at the finished and unfinished work, she said rather nervously: 'The kitchen is very untidy, I'm afraid. I just went outside –'

'Never mind the kitchen. I want to see your bedroom.'

At her startled look he smiled wryly. 'It's all right, Delie, didn't I promise not to pester you? I just want to see where you sleep, so that I can imagine you here, among your children and your vegetables and your paintings. So this is your room? I like the white furniture; did you paint the flowers on it? And the plain coloured quilt – no lace, no frills, no meaningless patterns. Yes, it's charming and restful and yet so – virginal.'

'Well, what *did* you expect – rose-coloured satin, gilt furniture and beaded lampshades?'

He laughed. 'Good Lord, no! I can't imagine you anywhere else, now. But do you know, I often go into the spare bedroom at home and imagine you there as you were when you were so ill. So small and fragile in that great bed.'

'Blue-and-silver wallpaper, a white rug on the floor, a chair covered with plum-coloured brocade.'

'And it suited you.'

'No! Much too luxurious.'

'But you should be surrounded by beauty and luxury, because you're so lovely.'

'I would rather be free than weighed down with expensive possessions. I've never managed to keep a piece of jewellery except my wedding-ring. I just shed them like bark from a tree, unconsciously, instinctively. Even love is a burden, it can be a tyranny. I have a dread of any further ties.'

541

'Is that why you keep me at arm's length? Or is it your quaint conscience?'

'Both, probably,' she said repressively. 'Now I shall get you some lunch. Go and pick me some ripe tomatoes while I do something about the chaos in the kitchen.'

He went obediently. They were still sitting at the luncheon-table with a bottle of Renmark wine between them and the remains of Delie's excellent salad, when Meg and Alex came home from school. But when he heard Alex in the distance, Alastair came round the table and kissed her long and silently, as though regretting the lost opportunities of the morning.

NINETY-TWO

Sometimes Delie would look at her children objectively – as creatures fixed in time – and wonder at the age and size they had attained. If every blade of grass was a miracle, intrinsically important in itself, as in Pirandello's story, how much more so was the human individual, grown from a tiny invisible egg to this stature, this complexity and reach of mind! The thought of Meg married, Meg producing a daughter who in turn might produce a daughter, and of the generations which had produced her own identity, made Delie strongly aware of the stream of life, linked like a river from its source to the sea.

She tried to explain this to Alastair on his next visit, but he couldn't share her feeling about the new generation; having no children of his own and feeling no need for that sort of physical immortality, he was rather impatient with her reverence for the mere continuity of life, the family, the human clan. He wanted his own personality to go on for ever and believed that it would, in some supra-physical form.

'I cannot believe that everything ends for me with my death,' he said, 'that a personality, a soul – or whatever you like to call it – has been called into being only to be extinguished again after such a brief span. What we call life may in fact be sleep, a dream to be half-forgotten on waking; and what we call death might be awakening into reality, a deeper reality than we have ever known.'

'But death, the death of the individual, is not really important,' said Delie. 'I believe that each fully lived life adds something to the world consciousness, as every drop adds to the volume of a river, and that every one of us, in certain states, can draw on that stream or pool of consciousness and every one of us can enrich it. I mean that I am a better painter because Rembrandt and Goya lived and were true to art, but not only because they left great paintings in the physical world. It's more than that.'

'You're an a-religious mystic, then. Now *I* believe that "there's a divinity that shapes our ends", and for that reason I feel sure that one day you will be mine. "*Tu deve esser mia.*" '

'What is that?'

'That's what Garibaldi said when he first saw the woman who was to become his wife: "Thou oughtest to be mine!" '

Delie blushed like a girl and looked out of the window. They were drinking their after-lunch coffee in her little living-room, where the sun fell on the faded second-hand carpet in patens of bright gold. She hoped the children would be back soon; she found his voice, tender and caressing, even more disturbing than his nearness.

She sought to lead him back to abstract discussion, knowing how he liked 'descanting on life, poetry, painting, *et cetera*', as he'd said in one letter.

'It's hard to believe in your benign Divinity and the eternal survival of the individual, when he is produced in such appalling quantities. Thousands are dying and being born at this second. It's typical of nature to be prodigal of life and indifferent to the individual. She is only interested in preserving the species. And in twenty million years, astronomers say, the sun will expand and the earth will be engulfed a thousand miles below its surface. Where is mankind then?'

'Perhaps he will have become independent of his physical self, a creature of spirit and fire, at home in the white-hot incandescence of a star. After all, a man and a star are only different forms of energy.'

'Too fantastic,' said Delie.

'Life itself is fantastic. And fantastically beautiful. And all that beauty is concentrated now, for me, in one face; your face. Delie, don't torment us both, let me make you mine. I can give you a home worthy of you, and make a home for your children too, and educate the boys. You said your husband is indifferent to them and he has his steamer which is the most important thing

543

in his life. He doesn't need you as I do, he can't give you love.'

'That isn't fair!' Delie stiffened in her chair, her face stony.

'No, it isn't, that was below the belt; I'm sorry. Forgive me, dear, dearest girl.' He was on his knees beside her now, his arms round her, and on his pale upturned face she saw the glitter of tears. 'Oh, it's terrible to love someone as I love you. I'm completely abject, I think of nothing else, I shed tears in the night like a woman. I try to rationalise my feelings, to analyse them and find why this particular face, with these straight dark brows and these faintly hollow cheeks, should comprise my fate. There's no reason. And there's no escaping it.'

His eyelids were rather red, she noticed, and above the neat black beard his lips were too red, too thin. She felt a faint tremor of repulsion. But in a moment those lips were on hers, the silky springiness of the beard pressed her face, a sensuous tongue delicately explored her mouth. She sank back in her chair with a little moan, all her defences down. The blood thundered in her ears, shutting out all sounds from the world beyond that single chair where they struggled and panted to be closer, to be one, to be lost in each other.

The opening of the door was the first thing she heard with her conscious ears, coinciding with Meg's cheery 'Where are you?' which died in her throat. Delie looked over Alastair's head and saw Meg's eyes, huge, startled, fixed on the tableau in the chair.

In less than a second Delie's point of view had changed, she was looking down on herself from Meg's eyes: her mother crushed into an armchair with a man, not her husband; her clothes rumpled, her hair wild, and on both their faces that bemused, tranced look of passion; she could see it all.

'Meg!'

She struggled to sit up, to push Alastair away. But the door closed quietly and Meg was gone. Alastair got to his feet, but he looked unembarrassed, unaware. He was still tranced. 'That was Meg – she saw us?'

'Yes. Give me a cigarette, please.'

Her hands and lips trembled so that he could scarcely light it for her.

'Now you will have to tell her, and come away with me. It's better so.'

'No! You don't understand. I can't leave Brenton.'

'You've already left him to run the steamer by himself.'

'For a year! And only for Meg's sake. I must go back.'

'Delie! How wonderful you are, and how ardent . . . I would make you love me.'

'I'm afraid I love you already. But please go away now, and don't come back. You must leave Renmark now, at once.'

'But I still have some business to attend to.'

'You must go. I could lose Meg because of you, do you realise that? You must leave at once.'

'I'm sorry, Delie.'

'If you don't go and if Meg leaves, I'll never forgive you.'

'I shall go in two days' time, when I've finished with our agent. In everything else I am your slave, but it would be stupid to rush off like that, with my work unfinished. It's an expensive trip from the Lakes.'

She looked at him, speechless. He was counting the cost in money, when her whole future was involved!

She waited incredulously for him to realise what he had said; but his thin mouth, his arrogant nostrils, were set in a determined expression. No softening was visible there.

'Alastair, I am asking you – '

'I'm sorry, Delie. You need not fear seeing me. I'll keep out of your way.'

'But Meg may see you, she goes in to school, and I have to go to my painting class. If Meg should tell Mrs Melville, that woman will take her back from me, I know. And what will she think of me, her own mother?'

'I think you overrate Meg's innocence, very likely. By her time of life she knows that women have instincts as well as men. She knows what her body is for. Why should she expect you to be a plaster saint?'

But Delie was thinking of herself, not much younger than Meg, coming upon her uncle and the kitchen lubra in the moonlight. Theoretical knowledge was all very well, but the traumatic effect of that peep into the adult world had been profound.

She did not know of Meg's unhappy love for Garry Melville and the erotic fancies she had indulged in, besides the real kisses of an experienced young soldier. She saw herself as the destroyer of a child's glass-walled world.

'Go now, at least,' she said. 'I'll try to explain to her.'

NINETY-THREE

When Alastair had gone, Delie waited like a guilty child for Meg
to speak to her. She lurked in her room expecting a knock on the
door and that Meg would sweep in and accuse her of conduct
unbecoming a mother and announce that she was going back to
Melvie's to live.

In a revulsion of feeling she almost hated Raeburn, the cause
of her shame. She hoped he would go quickly, and that she would
not run into him by accident in the streets before he went.

When at last she had to come out of her room to get the
children's tea, she found that Meg already had the vegetables on
and was quietly playing coon-can with Alex. She looked up
briefly from the end of the kitchen table to say that the oven
was already hot and that the dining-room table was set. Delie,
blessing Meg's thoughtfulness, had only to slip into the oven the
pie made that morning before Alastair arrived. Years ago, it
seemed.

'What sort of pie ?' asked Alex, eyeing it doubtfully, for he had
suddenly developed an aversion to meat.

'Egg and bacon,' said Delie. She looked searchingly at Meg,
who was pale but quite composed, her eyes on her cards. No
trace of tears marred her thin young face with its absurd nose
and intensely blue eyes.

When they'd finished the meal and the children were sitting at
the cleared table doing their homework, Delie prowled restlessly
about. She went outside under the calm stars and listened to the
almost inaudible flow of the river.

The night sky was like a friend, the familiar constellations
shone in their appointed places, the crickets sang under the lawn
as they had sung when she was a child. She had once more that
feeling of being on the very verge of understanding some great
truth about life; but as always it eluded her and she found herself
back in the stream of events, bound to the wheel of her self-
hood.

She turned back towards the house. The fire in the kitchen

range was still going and the smoke streamed away over the roof in a strong breeze. All at once the little compact house set so securely on its block of land was like a steamer sailing uncharted seas under the mysterious light of the stars; the stars themselves were no more than the chance lights of passing ships, sailing on random courses into the unknown; and all was instability and flux.

Giddily she put out her hand towards a trellis and felt the prick of a real thorn from the rose that grew there. Sucking her finger, she went inside and felt normality fall about her like a garment.

Alex finished his homework and began to yawn. There was never any trouble getting him to bed; he would sleep ten hours a night and still be difficult to wake in the morning.

Delie made cocoa for both of them and Alex took his to his room to cool while he got undressed. Delie and Meg were left alone in a constrained silence.

She longed to make some approach to her daughter, some little physical tenderness like touching her hair, but she dreaded to see Meg shrink away from her. Meg drank her cocoa noisily and set down the cup. Delie screwed her courage to the sticking-point. She said with no attempt at lightness: 'Mr Raeburn will not be coming here again. He returns to Milang in a day or two.'

Meg stared at the table; she looked embarrassed. 'I expect you will miss him,' was all she said.

Delie wondered if she had heard her properly, but Meg went on: 'Are you very much in love with him? Of course he's very romantic-looking, although he's so old. And you're beautiful still.'

In the midst of her surprise Delie's mind registered a protest at that youthful judgment; she could not think of Alastair or herself as old.

'I – I – I'm not sure', she stammered. 'He's very impulsive and – and very fond of me. He would like to marry me if that were possible. I don't know what came over me today, but I've been alone so long, and then your father – '

'I know; he's not the man you married, any more. I can just remember him as he was before he got ill, how big and jolly and strong he was and how I used to try and climb up his leg and he would laugh and swing me on to his shoulder. He doesn't seem to care about us any more.'

'I think he does, all the same, and that's why I must go back, just as soon as Alex is through his Leaving Certificate. And of

547

course we'll go back to the boat for the Christmas holidays.'

'Will he write to you, do you think? Raeburn, I mean?'

'Oh! I expect so. We've kept up a correspondence for some time.'

'It's terrible to be far away from someone you love.'

Delie looked at her daughter sharply. 'You read too many romantic books, dear. You can't expect to understand at your age.'

'I understand more than you think, Mother,' said Meg loftily, and gathered up her books. 'Good night, dear. Try to sleep.' She dropped a kiss on Delie's hair in passing to the door.

'Well!' Delie sat at the table feeling as if she had been winded. Then she got up and went to the sideboard, and poured herself a Cognac. 'Well, who would have thought it!' She was as far from understanding her daughter as ever.

When Alastair wrote, he told her that Dorothy Barrett had ar- rived back in Australia and was installed at Milang. Jamie had taken to her at once; he wasn't sure about Jessamine, who was such a feminine little person that she regarded every woman added to the household, of whatever age, as a potential rival.

'Miss Barrett, of course, is longing to see you again,' he wrote. 'She is all you said, a wonderful woman, so wise and calm and with such breadth of mind – just what Jamie needs.

'I was able to give her the latest news about you and Meg, and she will be writing to you herself. She is very anxious to meet your daughter. I suppose she feels it will be like seeing you over again as she used to know you – though I told her that you and Meg are not really alike, except about the eyes.

'Wouldn't it perhaps be possible, before you go back to ship- board life, to spend a holiday down here? Meg would love the lake, and we have room for you both if you'd come – Alex too if he'd like it.

'It would be a rest and a change for you, a joy to Miss Barrett, and I don't need to tell you what it would mean to me to have you under my roof again. You would be well-chaperoned – your old governess, my two aunts, Cecily, the children and the two maids: the house will be full of women.

'Think about it, dearest girl, and do decide to come. Your route can be overland from Adelaide through Strathalbyn, or by train to Meningie and then by paddle-steamer *Jupiter* to Milang

You might enjoy the lake trip more as a passenger than when you last came down.'

Delie thought about it a lot, and the more she thought about it the more she was tempted. She knew that it was unwise to see too much of Alastair in the intimacy of his home, though it seemed unlikely that they would ever be alone.

As she was still wavering, a second letter came from Miss Barrett herself, full of such pleasure at being back in Australia and such wistful and reminiscent affection that Delie longed to see her. She was warmed by Miss Barrett's frank appreciation of Alastair, which bore out her own judgment. 'A man who is truly gentle and of the finest sensibilities, combined with a cultivated mind. We sit up late at night talking about the state of the world and sometimes about you. He is a great admirer of your work, but feels your talents have so far been largely wasted; he is quite angry with you for marrying and having what he calls "all those children!" I tell him that no one has been a worse artist for having led a full life. Your fulfilment as a woman must be reflected in your painting.

'How I hope you will come down here to see us! If not, we must arrange to meet in the city as soon as possible: after all, you are only a hundred and twenty miles from it in one direction, and I fifty miles in the other. And I want to see some of your work. I feel that my life has been justified, in having helped at the unfolding of your budding artistic career.'

Delie looked at the fine, old-fashioned script and tried to imagine Miss Barrett as she would be now, a woman of sixty – would her hair be white? She could not imagine her Miss Barrett so changed by time.

She could not upset the children's school year and she had to be home with Brenton and the boys for Christmas. But by January she and Meg were free to go; in fact it was a little crowded with them all on board.

Brenton made no objections. He was so absorbed with running the steamer again himself that he scarcely seemed to notice them. When Delie tried to tell him about the house at Renmark, the garden and the dinghy and her painting class, he let her run on without interruption but without once replying or asking a question.

Their conversations were quite unconnected; as soon as she stopped speaking he would revert to some problem of his own,

549

saying: 'I wonder how long this water'll last? I'd like to get in another run up to the Rufus before low river. It's the snow-water coming down now, and when that passes I'm afraid she'll drop to blazes.'

'You won't mind if Meg and I stay down at the lake till the end of the holidays?'

'We're putting away a steady hundred a week at present clear profit. It can't last, and that's why I want to keep going ... long's I can.'

'We'll get the train at Morgan tomorrow then.'

NINETY-FOUR

The hands were as Delie remembered them: the almond-shaped nails, pinkly polished, the strong, flexible fingers, the large wrists. Only the skin was wrinkled and the blue veins and moth patches stood out against its whiteness.

Miss Barrett – she could remember so clearly the day she had said good-bye to her, the scene at the station, her parting words, her cool and mannish-looking shepherd's plaid costume, her bright brown hair curling in delicate tendrils on her neck. She had loved Miss Barrett, perhaps more purely and disinterestedly than she had loved anyone else since, and now she felt next to nothing. A nostalgic sentiment, that was all.

She took the strong hand, kissed the withered cheek, looked into the grey eyes flecked with gold, and saw again the firm mouth and sensitive, flaring nostrils; but the skin was flabby under her lips and the bright hair had turned mousy-grey and coarse-looking.

Looking from Miss Barrett to Meg, Meg in the bloom of youth with her fresh complexion and glossy black hair, she felt a dumb protest rising in her soul. Then she thought of herself nearly thirty years ago, the pretty, foolish, ignorant, nervous child of fifteen, living in a world of day-dream and fantasy. No, she would not want to go back.

And if Adam had lived – Adam against whose early death her whole self had cried out in angry rebellion – what would he be by now? A whisky-soaked journalist with thin hair and puffy eyes, perpetually regretting the masterpiece he had never written? Or plump and self-satisfied, smooth-skinned and conventional-minded? What would time have done to Adam, besides destroying his youth and beauty? As long as he remained in her memory, he had cheated time.

'And this is Meg!' Dorothy Barrett took the girl's hand and held it fondly, looking into her eyes. 'I used to think your mother had the most beautiful blue eyes I had ever seen, as a girl; but yours run them a close second.'

Meg was so used to being told how beautiful her mother was as a girl and so convinced of her own plainness that she was conscious of no invidious comparisons. She smiled.

'I would have known you anywhere, Delie,' added Miss Barrett. 'Somehow your expression hasn't changed fundamentally, though I can see of course that you're older and have come to terms with life. And then you haven't put on much weight. She used to look as if a strong puff of wind would blow her away,' she said to Meg.

' "You're so etheweal, Miss Gordon",' quoted Delie. 'Do you remember the young minister? I wonder what happened to him?'

'He's Moderator of the church by now, probably.'

'Oh! To think I might have been Mrs Polson!'

'Really, Mum?' Meg was enchanted. She had hardly imagined her mother had led a real life before she herself was born.

Delie looked curiously at Miss Barrett. 'And you never married? You must have had dozens of proposals.'

'Oh, come! Not dozens!' But she looked pleased and conscious. 'Adam and I were both in love with you.'

'Yes, I know. How long ago it all seems!'

'Long before the war.'

'*Last century!*'

'Heavens, you must be old,' said Meg naïvely.

'I envy you your travelling about the world,' said Delie. 'I've travelled a lot without really going anywhere; like marking time in one place, almost. Though it isn't true that Australia's all the same. "You see one gum tree, you've seen the lot", I heard a passenger on the *Marion* say once. He'd obviously never looked at one.'

'It's so wonderful to be back. The spaciousness when I look across the lake from the upstairs windows and sometimes get a glimpse of the Coorong sandhills! You feel it all out there, the Ninety-Mile Beach, all empty and untouched, and then the

551

Southern Ocean, and beyond that the wastes of the Antarctic, with Scott and his companions frozen into the icy Barrier and nothing beyond but the Pole.'

'Yes; I used to get the same feeling away out west on the Darling. The horizon is more than a horizon. I could feel the emptiness of the Simpson Desert, the sandhills and the gibber plains and the salt lakes, and the lonely perishers on the Birdsville Track. And not just because I *knew*; I think someone set down there without knowing where he was, would feel it too. I've read of travellers in the Sahara feeling the same.'

At tea-time Delie observed Miss Barrett and Miss Raeburn. They were of a like age, Miss Raeburn a little older and of equal firmness of character. When steel struck flint she expected to see sparks fly.

However, they seemed on the best of terms. Miss Alicia and Miss Janet Raeburn were both passionately fond of 'Home', which they had visited once for a finishing tour when they were young women. As someone who had recently seen London, who knew Edinburgh and could talk about the Braemar Games and the Royal Family at first hand, Miss Barrett was a great asset to the tea-table.

'And the heather-r,' trilled Miss Janet. 'The wonderful colour of the heather on the hills. There is nothing like it over here.'

'What about Paterson's Curse?' said Delie. 'I have seen the western plains purple and blue for miles, not a sign of earth showing between the flowers.'

'You mean Salvation Jane, that dreadful weed? It grows on the hills about Adelaide, but it's nothing like the heather. Nothing.'

'And the cool summers,' sighed Miss Alicia. 'If it weren't for the breeze we get from the lake, I don't think I could endure another Australian summer. But when I think of June in England – '

'It rained solidly all last summer. That's partly what decided me to come home,' said Miss Barrett in her deep, humorous voice.

'Home?' Miss Raeburn looked confused. 'Ah, you mean to – er – Australia.'

'Yes, of course. This is my home. I was born here.'

'Well, so were we, but the old country will always be home to us, won't it, Janet?'

'Always, Alicia,' said Janet, wiping her lips nervously with her lace-edged handkerchief.

Alastair, who had been busy with his books downstairs, came in late and sat down between Meg and Miss Barrett. Delie watched anxiously, but could see no hostility on Meg's part; in fact she seemed to like Alastair, while between him and Miss Barrett there had evidently sprung up one of those warm and easy friendships of compatible minds uncomplicated by differences of sex. Miss Barrett, with her deep voice and her solid lace-up shoes, her shirt-waist worn with a silk tie, had perhaps become more masculine with the years; while wasn't there something almost feminine – though not effeminate – about Alastair, with his finely manicured hands, his fastidious ways and his liking for gorgeous dressing-gowns of coloured silk?

'I can see that you are not disappointed in Delie's daughter,' he said, taking a scone and glancing from Miss Barrett to Meg. 'What did I tell you? Though they are not really alike.' Miss Raeburn's mobile eyebrows shot up into her hair at this casual use of Delie's first name.

'Disappointed? I'm delighted,' said Miss Barrett with a warm glance at Meg. 'It's so wonderful to find her the same age as Delie was then – and with those eyes – so that I almost feel as if time had stood still and I were not old after all.'

But Meg did not say, as Delie had on another occasion long ago: 'You're not *old*!' To her Miss Barrett was ancient, a relic from another century. Yet Jamie and Jessamine had found, in the schoolroom, that she seemed younger than their own mother. A life devoted to young people had kept her mind flexible and her outlook youthful.

She had kept up her swimming too, and in the next weeks they all went down to the shallow, rather muddy beach and swam in the warm brackish waters of the lake – Miss Barrett and Delie, who had not swum for years, Meg and Jamie and Jessamine, who was still learning and who did a great deal of screaming and splashing and pretending to be in difficulties.

At night Alastair entertained them in the observatory, or they sat round the carved rosewood table in the drawing-room, playing cards with the children till it was time for them to go to bed.

Miss Raeburn had sensed at once that this was not another Miss Mellership, to be kept politely and firmly in her place. Her sharp intellect appreciated wit and learning in others and she had not so far been crossed in any battle of wills. On the surface, all was harmony.

Miss Barrett was interested in the aborigines sometimes seen about the town, remembering the bark canoes on the river above Echuca and the camp natives who used to come and work on the Jamiesons' farm. She asked about the Point McLeay Mission, and learned there were four hundred aborigines there, of whom only about forty were full-bloods.

There was a regular excursion across the lake in the three-masted schooner *Ada and Clara*. Miss Barrett and Delie arranged an expedition, leaving Meg to mind the two young Raeburns.

They left on a clear morning, using the auxiliary engine, for they headed straight into a 'bald-faced sou'easter', as the local fishermen called it, because it never brought cloud or rain.

After a ten-mile journey they landed at the Point, and Delie followed Miss Barrett – whose long, vigorous strides were un-changed by the years – as she walked about the Mission streets.

Girls stood about outside the huts, holding baby brothers or sisters on their hips, and let the flies crawl unregarded into their smoky dark eyes. Almost without exception they wore bright cotton dresses in plain, vivid colours – red and magenta and yellow and orange – and Delie was reminded of the lubras Minna and Bella long ago in their Christmas finery.

There was a schoolhouse where the younger ones were in school, but it seemed that the girls who were too old for schooling had nothing whatever to do but stand or sit in the sun. There were no jobs for them and little housework could be done in the tiny huts they occupied with their families. They waited – for marriage, or a baby without marriage, whatever might be their fate; but there was a dark hopelessness in their eyes, a knowledge that they had been born into a world which had no place for them.

Sometimes they went out fishing or rowing on the lake, but mostly they squatted by the hut doors and drew idly in the dust, or played knucklebones, or minded the babies for their plump, indolent mothers.

'What is your name?' asked Miss Barrett kindly of one rather handsome girl, with softly waving brown hair which she had evidently taken the trouble to comb. Delie made friends with the baby brother the girl held on her lap, a child with enormous and expressive brown eyes.

The girl looked at her feet.

'Elaine.' Her voice was soft and diffident.

'Just Elaine? What is your father's name?'

'Elaine Paroutja.'

Her name was symbolic of her mixed blood, of the no man's land she occupied: the first name English, with its overtones of Arthurian legend; the second aboriginal, belonging to the old people, the dispossessed, a tribal name now without meaning.

'Wouldn't you like to work, Elaine, instead of just minding your brothers and sisters all day?'

'Work?' She looked vague. 'Ain't no jobs.' Then, with more animation: 'I wisht I never had to leave school. I liked it there. School was good-oh.'

'School was good-oh,' quoted Miss Barrett bitterly as she and Delie walked out. 'That reflects the extent of the education she got there, that poverty of vocabulary. Yet school was everything to her, everything that home is not – not just sitting in the dust all day, waiting for something to happen. Oh, it's shameful! Just when I'd come home, full of love for everything Australian, I find this – this blot.'

'It's conveniently out of the way, you notice,' said Delie. 'On the far side of the lake and sixty miles from the city where most white people, including Members of Parliament, live. These people are only figures in an annual report tabled in Parliament: so many full-bloods, so many half-castes, so many births and deaths. And with relief they notice that the birth-rate is lower than the death-rate; the problem, they fondly think, will solve itself in time.'

'What a solution! Extinction of a race, just as happened in Tasmania. It mustn't be allowed.'

On the voyage home across the lake the sails were run up and the schooner danced along before the sou'easter like a ballerina. Delie sat in the bows and gave herself up to the joy of movement, falling into that tranced state when she seemed to move in harmony with the flow of time. It was with a pang she saw the low shore looming up, the tall chimney of the flourmill and the lakeside buildings taking shape.

Miss Barrett was still depressed, thinking of what she had seen at the Mission. She noticed that the deckhand was an aboriginal boy, and guessed that many of them earned a living thus, or by fishing. There could be no doubt that it was harder for girls.

When the housemaid had removed the sweets dishes from the dining-room that night, and while the family sat eating cheese and fruit under the gas-lamps, she said to Miss Raeburn: 'Have you ever considered employing a native girl from the Mission in

555

the house? Just to help the cook-general in the kitchen? I saw a girl today who would, I believe, be intelligent and willing.'

'Certainly not!' Miss Alicia's eyebrows rose into the loops of hair on her forehead. 'These girls are dirty and very likely diseased. I wouldn't have one handling the food.'

'Quite', agreed Miss Janet, wiping her lips delicately with her napkin.

Miss Barrett gave Delie a look of patient forbearance and said: 'Mrs Edwards will tell you that her aunt – a most fastidious woman – employed lubras straight from the native camp in her kitchen for years. Isn't that right, Delie?'

'Yes, I don't know what Aunt Hester would have done without their help. Of course, it took three of them to do the same work that one energetic white girl would do in the same time; but that was because they regarded all work as a game. They weren't efficient, but they were certainly clean. They spent half their time bathing in the river.'

'And these were not Mission-trained girls, they'd had no schooling whatever,' said Miss Barrett. 'As for disease, you could easily arrange a medical check-up. Also, I should say they bathe far more frequently than the average London housemaid. It is their misfortune to have a brown-pigmented skin whereas ours is pink or red. Many Irish and Spanish peasants are quite as dark.'

'Hmf.' Miss Raeburn gave the irritable jerk of her whole body which signified that she had been contradicted in a favourite prejudice. The strong lines running from her nose to the corners of her mouth deepened.

'Alastair, explain to Miss Barrett, please, that I've already considered her idea at your suggestion years ago and that you agreed with me in the end that it was impracticable.'

Alastair poured himself some more wine before replying. Then he said deliberately: 'I do feel that to take one of the Mission girls into the house would be a great responsibility. They are very likely to be got into trouble by some unscrupulous white man; so that by trying to overcome one evil you may be propagating another.'

Delie thought again of Minna, and wondered if Alastair might be right. Her own uncle had been one of those 'unscrupulous white men' who had set the lubra's feet on the downward path. But was any hell on earth worse than the boredom and hopelessness she had seen on those girls' faces? There was only one form of entertainement free and available to all, and sooner or later they would take it, with or without a marriage ring. And so wise old Nature, utterly careless of the individual's happiness, would see that the race did not die out.

'I don't see that an illegitimate child here or there really matters,' said Miss Barrett obstinately.

Miss Janet gave a small gasp and Miss Raeburn's back stiffened. Mrs Henry, who had taken no part in the conversation but had been carefully segmenting an orange on her plate, looked up with innocent-seeming malice. 'Really, Miss Barrett? You speak from experience of these things?'

Miss Barrett's nostrils quivered. She gave Mrs Henry Raeburn a level stare. 'I speak from common humanity. Have you ever been across to the Mission? Have you seen the hopeless lot of these girls? Have you ever given them a single thought, though they live only ten miles away across the lake? They are your responsibility; every white Australian who has taken their ancient birthright is responsible. Just remember that, when you next see one standing on the street corner in Milang: idle, unwanted and unhappy.'

'The Mission is there to care for them. It's the Government's responsibility.' Mrs Henry looked petulant and remarkably like her daughter Jessamine in a bad mood.

'They are everyone's responsibility, so they are no one's. The Mission sees that they don't starve and that's about all.'

Miss Raeburn cleared her throat loudly and looked significantly down the table. 'I think we have all finished,' she said, and rose and led the way to the drawing-room.

NINETY-FIVE

All round the town, lining the dusty roads that led away from the lake, stood great walls of prickly pear: a cactus that had been imported to the country and planted as a cheap form of fence, but had grown beyond all control. Nothing would eat it, and pieces broken off would root themselves and flourish where they fell.

Here the rabbits had found a natural haven. Born and bred in the heart of a cactus bush, they ventured out only at night. In the summer dusk they could be seen loping about the roads and paddocks in hundreds. Almost their only enemies, apart from men with guns, were the black snakes that lived in the swampy samphire flats; the wheels of passing cars accounted for many.

Meg liked to watch the rabbits playing in the dusk. They reminded her of Garry and, as time swept them further apart, the memory grew distant enough to be sweet as well as painful. Only sometimes, when a sentimental song drifted through a lighted window or on a calm night the lake reminded her of the river brimming between its Waikerie banks, the pain grew real and sharp enough to make her gasp.

Meg was not much given to crying and she despised herself for the way she had become tearful on all the last occasions when she'd seen Garry. Now she never cried, but her face at times had a white, strained look that worried Delie.

Meg, for her part, never dreamed of confiding in her mother. She spent most of her waking hours thinking about Garry. The rest of the time she thought about her mother's relations with Mr Raeburn. She couldn't see how it was going to work out.

The heroines of the books she read were never married, or at least not before the last page or two. If they did happen to be married, to manifestly unsuitable husbands, at the beginning of the book, those encumbrances to romance were always conveniently removed by death. Sometimes the hero was married and it was the unsuitable wife who died, but Meg never felt any real doubt about the happy outcome.

Mr Raeburn's wife was removed, though not dead; and of course she could not wish her own father out of the way. It was all very complicated. Because of her own unhappy experience, she longed for her mother to be happy.

It was in a somewhat ill-assorted household they had come to stay, and they added to its lack of balance; with three spinsters, one widow, and only Jamie for a masculine ally, Raeburn lived in an overwhelmingly feminine atmosphere. Then there was Jessamine – jealous and capricious – and there were the two maids, Flo and Ethel (with their own 'followers' coming to the kitchen door on Friday nights).

Delie had not once seen him alone since they arrived, and this was in a way a relief. She spent much of her time with Miss

Barrett, delighting in a household where everything was run with precision, meals were served punctually and with ceremony, and she hadn't to deal with a morose male cook or a discontented crew complaining about the food.

Sometimes the novelty of it all would overcome her; the lace table-cloth, the shining silver, the massive dinner service with its gilt design; and she would think of meals under the awning on deck, meals snatched in the wheel-house from a tray while navigating a low river.

'I remember once,' she reminisced at breakfast, as she cracked the snowy egg in its silver egg-cup, 'we had a bargemaster who was a vegetarian, and he lived on nothing but eggs. When we ran out miles from any settlement, I put Gordon ashore to walk to a farmhouse and then across the point to pick up the steamer again a mile or two downstream – the river wound so much that it was quite a short walk for him. He got the eggs all right, but when he left the farm by the other gate he got into the bull paddock. The bull chased him to the fence and he flung himself over, right on top of the eggs. He wasn't going back for anyone, he said. He arrived back with two whole eggs and a great deal of scrambled yolk over his face and in his hair. The bargemaster, fortunately, thought it was so funny that he made do with the two eggs until we reached Renmark and didn't complain. Gordon won't go near a farmhouse now.'

'Harrietta laid my egg,' said Jamie. 'I got it from under her yesterday just after she laid it.'

'Where do the eggs come out?' asked Jessamine interestedly.

'They – ' Jamie stopped and looked at Miss Barrett, who said firmly: 'They come out of the oviduct, which is a special organ for reproduction. When Flo is cleaning a fowl next time she will show you how they form – first soft, then firmer, then hard-shelled ones nearest the opening, which is just under the hen's tail.'

'Biology with breakfast!' murmured Miss Alicia Raeburn. 'Spare us the details, pray.'

'I always find it best to answer children's questions as they arise,' said Miss Barrett, tapping her egg sharply with a knife.

'Really, I don't think . . .' said Mrs Henry vaguely.

Delie was tempted to say: 'Then you shouldn't talk', like the rude Hatter in *Alice in Wonderland*, but she held her peace.

While the weather was calm, Alastair took Delie and Meg

rowing on the lake, to show them the old swans' nests among the reeds not far from shore. Black swans sailed about the lake in hundreds and Delie thought they must look like gondolas.

'They do, rather,' he said. 'Because gondolas are black and they have that high curving prow like a bird's neck, though not as graceful as a swan's, and a sort of square beak. Shelley thought they looked like moths that had been hatched out of a coffin as a chrysalis.'

'Tell me about Venice and the paintings in the Accademia, and about Florence and the Raphaels in the Pitti Palace – '

So he told her, talking quietly while he rowed, and Delie drank in every word about Italy as though it had been nectar, and Meg looked into the distance and thought about Garry on a ship, calling perhaps at some exotic Mediterranean port where there were beautiful signorinas.

'My favourite Botticelli is not in the Uffizi, not in Florence at all, but in the little *museo* at Piacenza. And there is a Raphael in the Museo Nazionale at Naples which means more to me than all the others, because it was the first I ever saw – as calm and exquisite and – and *inevitable* as a freshly opened flower.'

'I should love to see Italy.'

'I – ' He looked at Meg, who seemed lost in a dream, and back at Delie. 'I should love to show it to you,' he said in a low voice, warm with feeling. And then, more matter-of-factly: 'You would be so appreciative!'

'I know I'd love it all.'

'And the Italians would love you, because you are beautiful and because you're an artist. I only had to say I was an art student and they let me into the galleries free and couldn't do enough for me.'

'Yes, I would like the Italians.'

'They suck in art and music with their mother's milk. Every bank clerk knows and loves the beautiful monuments and sculptures of his city, and looks with understanding. Here they worship a merino ram, *couchant*, upon a wool cheque.'

'Ah, don't decry the poor old sheep. The wool has provided many cargoes and helped to buy some of the lovely things in your home. If some day they discover a cheap substitute for wool, Australia will be in a shaky position in the world.'

'There will never be a substitute for wool.'

'And yet there's artificial silk.'

'Nothing can take the place of real Chinese brocade. Would you like to borrow the turquoise gown again? It has been kept for you, since you were ill.'

'No, thank you,' said Delie rather primly. 'I have a new dressing-gown of my own, a velvet one.'

'But it's black!' said Meg. 'Why didn't you buy a pretty colour?'

'I like black velvet.'

'It is, I suppose, suitable wear in such a world,' said Alastair. 'As Anatole France said: "The world is a tragedy, by an excellent poet."'

'I don't agree, it's too random altogether. An excellent poet would have ordered events more artistically. That's what we enjoy in a Shakespearean tragedy – the cussedness and cruelty of real life, given form and nobility by an ordering intellect.'

'You're right, as always.' They smiled at each other, the length of the boat apart, and Delie felt nearer to him than ever before. With Meg there she stopped being on guard with him, she relaxed and enjoyed herself, enjoyed arguing with him and feeling his eyes upon her, in an innocent companionship.

Why couldn't it be like that always? she asked her reflection, as she brushed her long hair in front of the mirror that night. She was feeling so happy that she took a long time to get undressed, pausing to smile at herself in the glass, smiling even at the broad grey streak in her hair. She had just slipped on her night-dress when she heard a sound in the passage and there was a gentle tap on her door.

She picked up her velvet dressing-gown and drew it on – her one extravagance, since Alastair had given her a taste for luxurious gowns, it was a medieval-looking garment with enormous sleeves and a sweeping skirt. She wondered if the caller were Miss Barrett, coming for a talk before she went to sleep.

But it was Alastair in his crimson brocade gown, his hair and beard disordered as though he had already been to bed and got up again.

'Alastair! What –'

'Hush, my darling, hush. You wanted me to come, didn't you? I couldn't sleep, I couldn't bear it any longer, thinking of you under my roof, wanting you so much, loving you so much. Are we to waste this precious time in separate rooms? Are we? Are we? You are mine already, in all but this.' And 'this' was his hard male body pressing closer, till she ached with the same longing. She turned so weak that she threw her arms round him for support, but as her head dropped back she saw through half-closed

561

eyes their reflection in the long mirror – scarlet and black, her arms in their velvet sleeves like great black wings wrapped about him: Mephistopheles and a lesser devil, black, black as the pit.

It startled her so that she was about to cry out, when his mouth closed on hers, with warm breath and incoherent words. A strong current was laving her, lifting her, until she was out of her depth, with ho hope of returning to the shore. With a deep sigh she gave herself up to that swirling flood.

NINETY-SIX

'Has anyone seen Jessamine?'

Mrs Henry came into the breakfast-room wearing her outward-sloping eyebrows at a steeper angle than usual. She was in one of her pale, shapeless dresses with some kind of fringed draperies and old-fashioned length of skirt.

Delie, in her striped fuji with its short skirt and sleeveless bodice, felt young and carefree beside her. This morning she had not begun to live with her conscience; she was happy, rested and serene.

'She didn't come in to me to get her shoes buttoned,' said Miss Barrett. 'Delie, you didn't see her, did you? What are you smiling at?'

'I?' Delie coloured slightly. 'Was I smiling? I wasn't conscious of it. No, I haven't seen Jessie. Isn't she with Jamie?'

'No, he's still getting dressed in his room.'

'Meg, you sleep next to her. Did you hear her go out?'

'No, Mummy. I was awake fairly early, but I didn't hear Jessie.'

'Have you asked Alastair?' said Miss Raeburn briskly. 'Perhaps he's taken her for a walk. He had to go down early to meet a steamer.'

'Then he's not back yet. Yes, I expect she's with him.'

Relieved, Mrs Henry took some ham on her plate and a piece of dry toast. She had started to get plump and was on a diet of lean meat.

They had all finished when Alastair came in. Delie felt her

heart begin to thunder in her breast and wished she could escape from the room before they all heard it. Mrs Raeburn asked him about Jessamine.

'She wasn't with me,' said Alastair. 'I went down to the wharf early and I haven't seen her this morning. As a matter of fact I haven't been asleep all night. I walked round the lake and watched the sun rise.' He kept his eyes on Delie's till she trembled and looked down.

'Then where *is* she?' Jessie's mother began to look more distressed and helpless than ever. 'She never misses her breakfast.'

'We'll all go and look for her. She must be somewhere in the garden at the back.' Miss Barrett got up and led the way, and they all followed, leaving only Miss Raeburn to supervise Alastair's breakfast, while Miss Janet was with the maids in the kitchen.

They looked over the gate that led from the yard to the kitchen garden, where dockweed grew high enough to hide a child, and clumps of rhubarb, tall tomato bushes and trailing pumpkin vines made a miniature jungle.

'Jessamine!' Mrs Henry called in a quavering voice.

Meg and Delie looked among the bushes unsuccessfully, and Meg stamped on a stinging-nettle which brushed her ankle. A hen began a noisy clucking in the fowl-house.

'I know!' said Miss Barrett, and led the way towards it.

In the fowl-house young Jessie squatted beside one of the laying-boxes, her head upside down as she peered under the hen which sat there, motionless except for the film of skin that flicked nervously over its hard yellow eye.

Her little face was scarlet with hanging upside down, and her curls brushed the dusty ground.

'Jessamine! What are you *doing*? Didn't you hear us calling, you naughty girl?'

'Yes.' Jessie righted herself for a moment and gave her mother a disgusted glance. 'You'll 'sturb her. Harrietta's laying an egg, an' I want to watch where it comes out.'

'Jessamine!'

'It's all right, Mrs Raeburn.' Miss Barrett's deep voice was firm and cool. 'I'll stay with her until the egg appears. You won't be able to have it for your breakfast, Jessie; they are already cooked and getting cold on the table. You should have told us where you were going.'

'*She'd* have stopped me.'

Cecily Raeburn's face turned a bright pink. 'You will leave that dirty hen and come inside this minute!' she said, gripping Jessie's arm and dragging her away. Miss Barrett compressed her lips and breathed audibly through her nose, but she said nothing until Jessie's screams of rage diminished towards the house.

'I'll get the egg for her,' said Meg, sitting down to wait. As they walked to the house, Miss Barrett said forcefully to Delie: 'Their mother is ruining those children's nerves. Unless Mr Raeburn can give me complete authority over them I can do nothing; I shall have to leave.'

'Oh no, you can't leave!' Delie felt as horrified as when, as a girl, she'd heard Miss Barrett speak of going to another position. 'I'm sure something can be done about it. Why is she like that, do you think? Why does she seem to take a delight in thwarting them?'

Miss Barrett shrugged. 'Frustrated in her own life, so she passes it on to them. Not that she thwarts Jamie exactly; it's just that she fusses him too much. He's not really delicate, but she'll make him so with her incessant coddling. He'd be better away at boarding school.'

'She'd never agree to that!'

'Perhaps you could speak to Mr Raeburn, anyway. I believe he would listen to you. I believe he would do anything for you.'

Delie blushed. She had forgotten that Miss Barrett was a very observant woman, besides a very competent governess. 'All right, I'll speak to him,' she murmured.

'He's a charming man. But underneath the charm there is a quality of steel. I think he will be able to deal with Mrs Henry quite successfully.'

Delie told herself that she had an excuse for going to his room that night, well after Mrs Henry was safely in bed, to speak to him; though there was really no need to get undressed first. But she loved dressing up in the medieval-looking gown that swept the floor. She knotted the black velvet sash firmly about her small waist and went along the passage and tapped at his door.

He drew her into the room and into his arms in the one movement. It was some minutes before she could get her breath back sufficiently to say: 'I wanted to speak to you, I only came –'

'You came, that's all that matters. There's no need for words between us.'

'I came because –'

'Because you wanted to. I was so afraid you wouldn't want to, that I had shocked or hurt you last night. That's why I didn't come to you. It's been so long, it was like the breaking of a drought, but now I want to take time to appreciate you properly, to kiss and value you inch by inch, my sweet girl, my darling.'

It was true, she had been left behind by the wild torrent that had swept him along the night before, but now she was caught up and carried into the vortex, into the still centre of the whirlpool; and there, in peace and joy, she seemed to open every cell of her being to his. She felt like a flower opening to the sun, like the earth opening to the soft rain: blessed, enriched and nourished.

They talked for hours, then, long into the night, in the charmed intimacy of enveloping sheets, like a cocoon woven against the world. He spoke for the first time of his marriage and its breaking-up but he could not speak of his former wife without irony and bitterness.

'She tried to alter me, to make me fit into her preconceived pattern, and I refused to fit,' he said. 'She was so spoiled, she couldn't believe that anyone would refuse her anything, even his immortal soul. I'd had enough of being dominated by women, with the aunts. And now Alicia is trying to get me to marry Cecily.'

'Mrs Henry!'

'Yes; my brother's widow. She seems to think it's my duty.'

'How very Old-Testament!'

'Yes. Alicia is strong on families, and she thinks Jamie needs a father. She's afraid Cecily might marry again and take him away.'

'So *that's* what Miss Janet meant!'

'When?'

'Oh, something she said ages ago when I was ill. But it was about Jamie and his mother I wanted to speak to you.'

She told him what Miss Barrett had said and he promised to speak to his sister-in-law about it, but thought there was little hope of her sending Jamie away to school. 'Unless . . . she had another interest. She really needs a husband. I must try and do some matchmaking.'

'So long as you don't marry her yourself,' said Delie, with a twinge of jealous anxiety.

'Never fear. I doubt if she'd have me, anyway.'

After a while Delie got up and looked at his pictures, two of his own paintings and a reproduction of Botticelli's *Primavera*.

There was the lake at sunset, an impressionist study of calm water full of flakes of coloured light; and a sunrise over a broad channel, dark reeds in the foreground and low purple banks in the middle distance.

'The Goolwa channel, looking upstream past Hindmarsh Island,' he said. Delie looked at it attentively.

'I've never been to Goolwa, but I must go there. Then I will have been the whole length of the river from the Moira Lakes to the mouth.'

'Not quite the mouth, but near enough.'

'How wide, how peaceful it becomes in the lowest reaches.'

'Because it is old. "And calm of mind, all passion spent." Perish the thought! Come back to bed, come quickly.'

When at last she rose to go back to her own room, Delie felt transformed, as a butterfly newly emerged must feel; she had shed the old dry husk of years and spread trembling wings to the light and warmth of love.

But as the door of Alastair's room closed behind her, she froze. Someone bearing a lighted candle was coming along the passage: loops of sandy-grey hair above arched brows and wide grey eyes, a formidable nose with deep lines grooved beside it – Miss Raeburn!

Delie snatched her hand from the painted china door-knob as if it were burning hot and hurried away from the accusing proximity of that door. Of all the people under this roof, Miss Raeburn was the one she would least like to guess her secret.

Her cheeks were flaming as they came abreast; it was impossible that Miss Raeburn should not have seen. Then she noticed something odd about Alastair's aunt. She was walking with a slow, loose stride and holding the candlestick so carelessly that hot wax dripped in a trail of grease along the carpet.

This was so unlike her usual brisk precision that Delie stared at her and saw that both her nose and her cheeks were flushed and that she carried in her other hand a full bottle of brandy.

'Just went along to get some more s'pplies, my dear,' said Miss Raeburn with drunken dignity. 'I always – always keep some in m'room for medic'nal purposes. Goo' night.'

'Good night!' gasped Delie. This was something she would never have believed unless she had seen it for herself. Mrs Henry, perhaps, she might have imagined as a secret drinker, but never Miss Raeburn, the strong, the self-sufficient!

In the morning she looked carefully at Miss Raeburn for signs of a hangover or of trembling hands, but saw none, so that she began to wonder if she had imagined it all. Miss Raeburn seemed quite unconscious or forgetful of their meeting in the early hours.

After breakfast, Alastair summoned Mrs Henry Raeburn to his study, from where she emerged with heightened colour and a suspicion of tears in her indeterminate-looking eyes; and with a weakly venomous look at Miss Barrett, went off to her own room.

At dinner, Delie watched Miss Raeburn again, and noticed that she took several glasses of wine, more in fact than Alastair, and that her nose and cheeks became marked with a network of small red veins; but she was her usual crisp and dignified self. From this Delie deduced that she was accustomed to considerable quantities of drink and that she must have finished the best part of a bottle of brandy in her room to have reached the state in which she'd seen her.

If brandy was disappearing from the household stores at this rate Alastair could hardly be unaware of it – except that his aunt controlled the housekeeping, and she could easily order extra supplies and list them as, say, vinegar, or even medicine. Should she warn him? She felt diffident about it, for in spite of their physical and spiritual intimacy she felt remote from his daily life, his business, his dealings with his family. She had sensed his surprise when she spoke of Mrs Henry and the children; but that had been for her old friend, Miss Barrett. In this more purely personal matter she felt unwilling to intervene.

If Miss Raeburn drank herself into *delirium tremens* he would find out soon enough – if not, it was her own business. She decided to say nothing to anyone; and she did not see her the worse for alcohol again before she left to go back to the boat.

Alastair had now become the centre of her universe, the sun round which her thoughts and feelings revolved. It was enough to be in the same room with him, however many others were present, for joy and contentment to flood her being. When his dark eyes rested caressingly on hers for a moment, it was as if she lay in his arms in his deepest embrace. She could not bear to think of going away.

They walked alone by the lake in the dark before the moon rose, to say good-bye on her last night. In the reflection of starlight from the water she could just make out his face, pale with suffering, his mouth distorted by grief. For once he was wordless, and they parted almost in silence, with a last desperate clinging, at the house door and went to their separate rooms.

She had wanted him to make love to her for the last time out of doors, under the stars, and they had lain in a nest of reeds on the sandy shore. Looking up at the summer constellations strung out across the sky, she had thought vaguely of Adam, and Brenton, and Kevin whom she had almost forgotten, and the man-child she had brought forth on the river-bank, under these same stars. Mysteriously, it was all one, the experiences linked like a river. Here by the still waters she had felt love and peace flow into her, even as the starlight streamed down into the lake.

NINETY-SEVEN

Teddy Edwards was a different man now that he was back in charge of the *Philadelphia*. Though a second person was needed in the wheel-house always, to give assistance at the wheel on the sharper bends, it was he who chose the channel and made the decisions when to take a cut-off like Higgins's or when it was safer to go round by the old river.

He cursed the Department engineers who had placed beacons and spurs half across the river in places, to divert the current and 'scour out the channel'. Like other old skippers, he was convinced that sand and silt would soon encourage a growth of 'sapplins', making a new hazard for navigation. Lock One had been opened early in the year and was already proving a source of revenue to the Government; tolls from four hundred and sixty-five steamers had been collected already. Though the river just below the weir was inclined to be dangerously shallow, its beneficial effect was felt above, where the water was banked up in a still pool right back to Morgan.

The gum trees, now wading many feet deep in a flood that would never go down, looked greener and fresher than ever before; but this was a false flow of vitality before the end, for they were soon to be grey skeletons, drowned by the continuous inundation of their roots.

Though Delie relieved Brenton in the wheel-house and some-times stood by to give a hand, he preferred one of his boys or even the Young Limb; and now that they all lived aboard (except

Alex, who had gone to the city to do his Matriculation course at a boys' boarding school), Meg took over many jobs such as sewing and mending and laundry, leaving Delie with more free time than she'd had in years.

She was painting hard and reading philosophy and aesthetics. As she read Ruskin's *The Stones of Venice* and Baron Corvo's *Desire and Pursuit of the Whole* she dreamed of Italy and of going there with Alastair; she read all Shelley's letters and Mary Shelley's journals and steeped herself in the spirit of the Renaissance in Florence; and her mind took wings and flew across the sea to the fabled shores of the Mediterranean, while her physical self was confined to a ninety-foot boat on a narrow waterway in whose busy centres Art was represented by a pathetic War Memorial statue or a reproduction of *The Menin Gate* in the local Institute.

She was impressed by the sheer randomness of life: beauty unsuspected, the edelweiss blooming on inaccessible ledges; the snowflake's form revealed only by the microscope; the colours hidden in the eternal blackness of the ocean deeps; and the stars on their unimaginable journeys making patterns on the sky at night.

A tiny rod-shaped bacillus could alter the history of the world, by invading the system of a dictator; could deprive the world of a genius, as when Keats died in Rome. And if she were to take the anchor-chain now and wind it round her ankle and jump overboard and so end all her conflict and longing, who would even know in a hundred or so years' time?

It was when her thinking reached this stage that she would shake herself severely and begin on a new canvas just as if it mattered – and soon, by the magic of association, it did matter. The smell of paint, the fascination of colour and texture transported her to a world where the right placing of a brush-stroke meant more than all the troubled history of mankind. It was an escape into a different order of reality.

She began thinking about holding another exhibition, about going to Melbourne again after all these years and trying to take up the threads of her old associations. It seemed fantastically far, another world, almost as far away as Italy.

But before going to Melbourne, she would make one more trip down to Adelaide, and perhaps to Milang – to see Miss Barrett. Alex, the studious one, needed glasses; she meant to take him to a specialist in the city during the school holidays. He had done well at the mid-year exams, and she wanted him to have every chance of getting a bursary for the university, which would help pay for his board in the city as well as fees for the expensive medical course.

She sent a letter to Alastair and collected his reply in Adelaide. He was going to Melbourne on business and asked her to join him there, with such eloquence that a wave of longing swept over her and the distance, five hundred miles, seemed nothing. She longed for wings to fly to him, now, at once, without taking trains and making tedious arrangements.

As soon as Alex had been fitted with glasses, she took him back to Morgan – and found that the steamer had just left for Mildura.

They followed the bumpy coach-road along the route named after Sturt the explorer. She had never travelled this way by land before, driving along the top of the high cliffs with a view from the motor-coach over the wide and barren land, the river lying below in its steep canyon, fringed with unlikely green. Every now and then the road swooped down to river level where the flood-plain spread out, only to climb again till the river disappeared in its folds of limestone or reappeared as a plaque of greenish-blue between yellow walls.

At Waikerie she had looked apprehensively for the Melvilles' buckboard, but did not see it. Later they crossed the river by ferry and Alex got down from the coach to inspect the wheezy single-stroke engine which worked the pulley-wheels and dragged the cumbersome punt along its taut and greasy cable.

The familiar towns all looked different when approached from the land, and Barmera on Lake Bonney, where they stopped for lunch, she had never seen at all; for the big freshwater lake was by-passed by the main river. Here the magnificent red-gums grew right on the sandy beach and small white yachts were reflected in blue water; a scene so strangely peaceful that Delie wished she could have met Alastair here. Suddenly the thought of Melbourne tired her; the crowds, the electric trains, the dressing up and going out to eat.

Was she getting too old for adventures, too used to a quiet life in the outback? But Alastair . . . wherever he was, there was the centre of her being.

Sometime in the night, the rocking train stopped in the desert between Mildura and Melbourne. She pressed her face against the cold glass, sitting on the end of her sleeping-berth, and gazed at a pale moonlit world, empty and still. The engine panted gently, a far-away carriage door banged shut.

She raised the window and put her head out and saw towards the front of the train a small siding, one of those where you waved a red lamp if you wanted them to stop at night to pick you up, or a red flag by day.

Just before they moved on a plover called, a restless, wandering cry uttered on the wing – there must be water near, after all. She felt her flesh prickle and grow cold, that strange shudder of delight and awe which some poems and paintings sent through her. No, she was not too old. The vast, mysterious world called like the plover and she could still hear that call and respond – plover, lover, distance and enchantment . . .

The train arrived soon after dawn and nervously she dabbed powder on her nose and twisted up her hair with trembling fingers. Most of her hairpins were lost. In the train mirror her face looked haggard and lined, only the blue eyes alive in a mask of weariness. She had travelled two hundred extra miles, coming by way of Mildura, and had stopped only long enough to deliver Alex to the steamer and make sure Brenton was not overtired. He had seemed, on the contrary, more vigorous and lively than when she left, though his speech had thickened a little. He propelled himself in the wheelchair all over the top deck, shouted orders and swore vividly. No, he did not need her; or he needed her far less than before.

She stepped out on to the busy platform at Spencer Street and at once saw Alastair waiting, looking the other way. He turned, and came bounding forward with boyish eagerness to meet her; but she felt strange and stiff with him. Her thoughts remained with Brenton and she felt sure Alastair was looking at her with dismay. At seven in the morning, after a restless night, a middle-aged woman in neat but unremarkable clothes was greeting him nervously and making empty conversation.

And he, too, looked small and less significant among the city crowds; she thought of him always lording it and peacocking about his home, or sending tally-clerks rushing about to his orders.

They walked down a long ramp away from the crowd. He took her arm and said quietly: 'I love you', but the words were meaningless.

'Don't!' she cried. 'It's all wrong, don't pretend. I should

571

never have come.' She was near to tears.

'Listen, darling, I overslept, I've not even had a shower or a cup of tea this morning, and I'm scarcely human yet. I just managed to get a taxi and be here in time to meet you in the flesh, but my spirit is lagging on the way. Come and have some breakfast and we'll both feel more like people.'

But in the rather dingy tea-shop she continued to feel a stranger, talking to a man she hardly knew over breakfast. The business of booking in at a hotel was sordid with subterfuge, though she reflected wryly that the hall-clerk was unlikely to suspect any irregularity in such a pair.

In their room they looked ruefully at each other, and at the single beds. 'Coward!' said Delie.

'Yes, I should have demanded a double one, but I didn't dare.'

The room had a grey look, and the noise of traffic drifted up to it. When he took her in his arms Delie said desperately: 'No, let's go out, let's walk in the streets, I need to come alive again.'

The movement of the city exhilarated her; she began to feel she was once more in the metropolis, somewhere near the heart and pulse of things. The sun came out, leaving a few white frothy clouds to romanticise the sky. They walked up Swanston Street and went to the National Gallery.

The Fisherman's Wife was well-hung, in the Twentieth-Century Australian section. Delie looked at it impersonally and was not ashamed, but she felt little interest in the picture now; that phrase of romantic realism was behind her, cast off like the shed skin of a snake, to enable her to expand and grow. She used real forms still as a starting point, but made semi-abstractions from them, patterns of pure colour; and just at present she was fascinated by the use of black.

Strolling with Alastair, listening to his pertinent comments, she began to warm towards him, to feel re-enchantment she had almost ceased to expect. They had luncheon in a small café, but before the second course was over Alastair was looking deep into her eyes across the table, forgetting to eat.

'Let's go back to the hotel,' he said. 'I want to go to bed with you now, and I think it will be wonderful.'

And it was. They dressed as it was getting dark and went out to dinner, and looking at his profile as he sat beside her, touching her knee under the table, she said suddenly with wonder: 'It really is you!'

'Your eyes are so bright!' he said. 'You look ten years younger

572

than you did this morning. Can you explain that?'

'You have done it, only you.'

They went back to their room and rediscovered each other, all they had known already and other new discoveries, scraps of childhood reminiscences and facets of personality; they were travellers in a yet unfamiliar country, delighted with everything because it was still fresh.

It lasted for more than a week, for what seemed months of ordinary existence at a less exalted level, while Delie did not even think of looking up Imogen and her other former friends. Then she said quaintly: 'I have lost the sense of sin, if it is a sin, but I have a superstitious, too-good-to-last feeling. I don't have to go yet, but I'm going tomorrow.'

She was adamant and booked her berth in the train, still feeling supremely happy and invulnerable. Yet when she called at the Post Office where she had told them to send any urgent mail, and was handed the telegram, it was as if she had expected it all along with her subconscious mind.

Alastair saw her off that night with a face of white suffering, but already she was detached from him, called back into her family cares, and eaten up by pangs of remorse. Over and over in the train she took out the hateful yellow slip and read it.

PLEASE COME AT ONCE MURRAY BRIDGE
DADDY IN SERIOUS CONDITION LOVE MEG

Four p.m. on the fifteenth – that was two days ago and she hadn't bothered to call for her mail. She hated herself for leaving Brenton, who perhaps was dead already for all she knew; and for subjecting Meg to the shock and responsibility which her brothers could share but not alleviate.

All night she sat up with her face pressed to the window, staring at the revolving landscape, the gravely curtsying trees.

573

NINETY-EIGHT

At the Murray Bridge Hospital Brenton lay between life and death, neither living nor entirely dead. Standing beside his bed with a stony face, Delie remembered her wild cry of years ago, when she first loved him: 'You mustn't die! You mustn't die!'

He was not aware of her any more; it was no appeal of hers that kept him clinging to the edge of life, like a man on a sheer cliff face, grasping a broken shrub that was slowly pulling out by the roots.

'How – how long?' she had whispered to the doctor, wondering how long she could endure this, knowing that she could never atone, never communicate with him again in this life.

The doctor shrugged very slightly. 'There's no way of telling. It's a final and fatal stroke, but since it was not immediately fatal, he might stay like this for months, even years.'

Even years! He had fought back, he had struggled almost to the top of the cliff again, back to a useful life, and life had knocked him brutally down again. Could he perhaps struggle back once more, back to a limited sensibility?

Impossible, the doctor said. The cells of the brain were damaged irrevocably, no recovery was possible. He would remain in a coma to the end.

Alex had gone back to school; there seemed no point in keeping him home. Meg took over the housekeeping on the boat and mothered all of them, even Delie, who seemed numb and confused so that Meg was almost as worried by her condition as by her father's.

Brenny asked to come with Delie to the hospital once, but he couldn't stand it, the sight of the staring unseeing eyes, the sound of stertorous breathing, the sagging mouth from which life seemed already to have fled so that the sounds might be made by some insentient force that occupied his father's frame.

Delie recognised that force and saluted it bitterly: the life-force, the blind Will expressing itself in the suffering flesh: the burnt child, the aged arthritic, her aunt's gaunt body feeding a host of proliferating cells. She understood that the world was like this, but Brenny was too young; he must not come again to the hospital.

In any case, they would have to leave soon; she could not afford to let the boat stand idle when it could be earning a living for them, especially as the hospital bills were likely to be large. The doctor assured her that there was no point in waiting at Brenton's bedside, as he could never recognise her or be aware of her presence.

Ah, but she should have been there with him when he was struck down, in those first moments when he had perhaps been paralysed, unable to call out, terrified and alone. Meg had not told her much and she did not want to question her; she had been brave and efficient beyond her years, but Delie feared some delayed shock.

Meg and Gordon had met her at the Murray Bridge Station, where most of the passengers, bound for Adelaide, got out to eat a rushed and indigestible breakfast, consuming pale fried eggs in the pallid dawn. They kissed her silently, though not given to such demonstrations in normal times; and in the cab Meg told what had happened.

'Daddy seemed quite well when he went to bed; but in the morning he simply didn't wake up. It was old Charlie who found him. (I'm afraid it's aged Charlie, the shock and everything, I doubt if he'll be able to carry on much longer.) I could see at once that he was in a deep coma, no response to light in the eye, no normal reflexes at all and I rushed ashore and phoned a doctor and he had him removed to the hospital. Then I sent you the telegram. I hated cutting short your holiday – '

'Oh! Don't say that, I'm distressed enough that I didn't get the telegram at once. Not that it would have made any difference, but I feel – I feel that I should have been here. It's too much for you children – ' Her lips trembled so that she could not go on. Gordon pressed her hand.

'Stop it, Mum. It was nothing to do with your being away, and you couldn't have done a thing if you'd come two days earlier.'

They had gone straight to the hospital and then back to the boat. There old Charlie greeted her with moist eyes, the only one of them who shed any tears that day. The children had had time to get over the first shock and Delie was still numb.

'The Skipper, Missus, the poor old Skip. I wish it was me laying there, if it'ud do him any good. It's a bloody shame, if

575

you'll excuse the expression, a bloody shame. 'E's been almost like 'is old self, this last six months.'

'Oh Charlie, I know, and it was you who stuck by us and helped him get his strength back.'

'Not me, Missus. It was sheer guts on his part; 'e wouldn't give in.'

'He won't come back to us, you know, Charlie. It may take a while, but . . . this is the end.'

'The end. I knew it.'

He turned away heavily and the next morning he kept to his bed, saying he didn't feel like getting up and didn't want any breakfast. Meg and Delie nursed him for a week, but when he was no better they called in a doctor, who said simply: 'The old man's failing. Nothing can be done but to ease his end.' A week later Charlie McBean was dead, dying before the extinction of the steamboats, which were his life.

He left only a few pounds, and some faded photographs of early steamers. He had no relatives that Delie knew of. She paid for his funeral at Murray Bridge, and collected the crews of a few boats that were in port, to follow him to his grave.

She spent the few pounds on a display of flowers, though as one cynical fellow-engineer was heard to mutter as he left the cemetery: 'Old Charlie would rather a bottle of good Scotch whisky was poured down there with him, I'll bet.'

Once more Delie was thankful for her sons. She would be able to carry on as skipper and get a more efficient engineer than Charlie. A barge and bargemaster were not necessary for trading, so she would sell the barge to help with the hospital bills, and with the fireman and an extra deckhand they could manage.

In the last months young Brenny had learnt a great deal from his father about navigating and steering and was already far more competent in the wheel-house than the average deck-hand. Soon he would be able to get his Mate's and then his Master's Ticket – Teddy Edwards had been a skipper at twenty-three – and take over altogether. Meg would be willing to cook, but she wanted to be a nurse and must begin her training and there were the fees for Alex's medical course if he failed to get a bursary. Delie felt suddenly terribly weary. She had carried the responsibility for too long and she was tired, almost too tired to go on, to respond with her usual courage. This was her darkest hour. Somewhere below the horizon, still too faint to be seen, glimmered the first rays of approaching dawn.

NINETY-NINE

The last Sunday of September 1927 was the coldest morning anyone could remember. For a thousand miles along the river, throughout the mallee country of Victoria and South Australia and the prosperous fruit-growing centres, the banks glittered like glass in the rising sun. Trees were bearded with white rime, which had settled like snow in the valleys.

After steaming upstream through Lock Three, where the men had to use cloths to handle the metal capstans as they wound the gates open (for nobody owned any gloves), the *Philadelphia* was greeted by a remarkable sight. Here the river was lined with the skeletons of dead gum trees, killed by the rise in the water level above the lock; their dead bark and leaves had fallen away, leaving smooth silvery wood as hard as iron. On this morning the trunks and boughs were coated in crystal, so that when the sun shone behind them they seemed a grove of fairy trees, unreal as something in a pantomime. Delie was enchanted, forgetting how she had hated getting out of her warm bunk when Brenny called her at dawn.

It was not until they reached the first of the fruit-growing settlements further up the river that she realised what this beautiful display had meant to the blockers and orchardists. As the sun grew warmer, the oranges began to blacken on the trees, the apricots withered and the young vines began to wilt. In a few days they were dead, scorched and withered by the cold as by a fire. The fruit harvest was ruined and it would take years for the older vines to recover. Everywhere gloomy faces greeted the steamer as she drew in to the bank, and no one came down with baskets of luscious fruit to sell to the cook. A million-pound harvest had been ruined in a night.

Brenny had brought the *Philadelphia* through the Lock Three chamber in style, steaming full speed into the narrow opening and reversing the paddles to come to a sudden stop. Delie watched him fondly; he was so like his father must have been at that age! He had his Mate's Ticket, and as soon as he had enough time logged would sit for his Master's Certificate. Already he was word-perfect in the theory of river navigation.

Gordon was now a serious young man, fond of what his brothers called 'stuffy 'books. He borrowed all the history and biography he could get from the local institutes and had a regular parcel of books sent each month from the city's Country Lending Service. To Delie's surprise he read all he could get on Napoleon and swallowed biographies of Nelson, the Duke of Wellington, Marlborough and other military and naval heroes, besides more recent ones like Beatty, Earl Haig and Marshal Foch from the last war. He was working, he said, on the theory of military tactics and what made a good general from Alcibiades to the present day. He showed no ambition or interest in a career, either on the river or elsewhere, but pottered about helping the cook in the galley, taking a hand at the wheel on an easy reach and carving little models of paddle-steamers.

Delie hid her disappointment and waited for him to find out in his own good time what he wanted to do. He was still only twenty-four. He had not, fortunately, shown any tendency to get entangled with a girl and as long as he had no family to support he was welcome to live on board. Brenny had an eye for all the girls along the river, but did not show preference for any one. Both brothers were big, brown, handsome lads, but Brenny's bright blue eyes had a mischievous twinkle which Gordon's had not; girls in the street, who pretended not to notice their wicked gleam, turned to look after him when he was safely past.

Meg and Alex were in the city, Meg training at a private hospital, Alex completing a medical course for which he had won bursaries and exhibitions and topped the honours list in the last year's exams.

If only Brenton could have seen them! He would have been proud of his family, most of all of young Brenny with his river skill, acquired or inherited from his father. She thought with more acceptance than before, with gradually lessening bitterness, of the last year of his life, dragged out in the hospital as an insentient thing, uselessly kept alive by the careful ministrations of strangers. She had not been there when he died.

It was as though he had been buried long ago and had been exhumed for the sake of a second funeral, when he was buried at Murray Bridge. She wished he could have lain on the river-bank, but at least he was within sound of the steamers' whistles and the throbbing pant of their engines; but for how much longer? She feared that Brenny was training for a dead-end job, or one that would no longer exist in ten years' time. Good roads were being built into the bush and the motor-trucks and passenger coaches were following them. She noticed that the river skippers who came to the funeral were all much older men, there were no young ones in Brenny's or Gordon's age group.

However, they were still getting plenty of cargo, and were carrying a typical load up-river: ten tons of flour, fourteen bags of bran and pollard, six bags of sugar, twelve bags of oats and nineteen of wheat, half a dozen cases of whisky and a cask of beer, all for one station; besides some heavy farm implements from Shearers' factory at Mannum and several tons of iron rails for the Works Department at Lock Four.

Brenny would not have anything to do with a floating store. He said that sort of stock was all right for women and invalids, but he was a man and was not going to handle embroidery threads and knitting-needles and babies' bottles. He would rather a man's cargo, however awkward to handle: like the famed deck-hand on the Darling who was supposed to have juggled five melons and a piano up the steep banks in one load, and remarked that it was not the weight he minded, but the *awkwardness* of it.

Delie had not seen Alastair again or heard from him for more than a year when Brenton died; for after she returned from Melbourne she had answered his letters coldly and had refused to let him come and see her, punishing herself and him also because of her bad conscience.

In reply to the Murray Bridge papers which she had sent to him and Miss Barrett with their account of the funeral, where Brenton's exploits on the river were recalled and recounted by two retired skippers who remembered them, she had received a rather formal note of condolence.

While praising his delicacy of mind in making no reference to their former relationship or any future renewal of it, in her loneliness she wrote again: a letter in which, if he wanted to, he could read her feeling between the lines.

When his reply came, directed to the *Philadelphia* at Murray Bridge, she took it down in the Reserve to savour it quietly and sat on a bench under one of the ancient red-gums there. She opened the letter and became as still as stone, while her unbelieving eyes remitted to her protesting brain the following message:

'This is just to tell you that Cecily and I were married about a month ago, in fact not long before I had your first message. It had been arranged for some time, as I could see it was for the children's good and, well, it made for peace in the home and I am a man of peace.

'Aunt Alicia, of course, is contented at last, and Jamie has gone away to boarding school where he seems very happy.

'I hope you too may be happy, dear girl, and find time to paint again now that you are more free and those fine boys of yours are big enough to take over the strain of running the boat. If I can help you financially in any way (now don't fly up in arms, I mean it as a business arrangement, an investment for the future, if you like) or with Alex's university fees, *please let me know*. I can certainly put some business in your way in the next wool season, and hope you will bring a load to Milang again and come and visit us.

'Miss Barrett is staying on with Jessamine for the present, and later is going to take a job teaching at the Mission school at Point McLeay. She has already organised a weekly handicraft school for the girls in her spare time.

'Oh, my dear, why didn't you let me come and see you? Your letters were cruel and cold. I thought you had given me up! I felt that I had cast myself down before you, body and soul, and you spurned me with your little foot . . .'

And so you married Cecily! thought Delie, shaken with futile jealousy of that pretty, ineffectual, feminine Mrs Henry who had no doubt been planning this all along; yet mollified a little by the feeling that had at last crept into his impersonal letter.

Well, it was too late now, but she wished her own letter unwritten. As for visiting them in that house! Never, she would never set foot there again.

That was a year ago, and she had not been to Milang since, though Miss Barrett had been on a visit to the steamer and had made a short trip with them, enjoying every moment of it with her undimmed energy and appreciation.

She had stirred things up at Point McLeay and made herself unpopular with the Superintendent, who had been there a great many years and turned out his annual reports mechanically: so mand died, so many born, so many half-castes, so many left school . . . and once they left school, all interest in them ended, except as statistics. She'd had trouble getting a hall or even a small room where the girls could work, and when she got a room there were no cupboards for them to keep their work in and the small children got in and mixed them up and made a mess; but now, by firmness and perseverance, she had things organised.

'But I'll have to be there full time, really to do any good,' she said. 'Mr Raeburn has said I can stay on at the house and go over each day, if I give Jessie her music-lessons and some French on the week-ends for my board. I hope you'll come down to stay again, while I am still there.'

Delie looked obstinate, and said: 'I don't think Mrs Raeburn likes me.'

'Nonsense! And, anyway, what *she* likes doesn't carry so very much weight in that house.'

'It is now her house, however. Besides, Miss Alicia didn't approve of me either.'

'The reason for that is now removed.'

They looked at each other with understanding and Delie saw that Miss Barrett was calculating how much she had been hurt. She abandoned her façade of indifference and asked hopefully how the marriage was going, but received no comfort there.

It had been the wisest thing, Miss Barrett thought; it had probably saved Jamie from some sort of nervous breakdown and everyone in the house was in a much better temper, including Alastair.

'He was lonely, and because his first wife let him down and hurt him in his pride, he was very chary of committing himself again. He has that quick vanity which you find sometimes in small men, which will not let him forgive a slight or lay himself open to receiving one. He and Cecily knew each other well and they have settled down quite comfortably.'

Delie saw that Miss Barrett suspected she had been cold to Alastair, snubbed his first advances and sent him back into his shell of pride, before their relationship had developed very far; for she was far from blind and must have known that some relationship existed, if only to cause Miss Raeburn's hostility.

So that she might continue to think so, she ended by agreeing to make a trip to Milang in the next shearing season, though she was resolved to stay aboard the steamer and invite Miss Barrett to visit her there. 'Though it is Brenny who makes the decisions now,' she added with some pride.

It was now the following September, the snow-water was

coming down and raising the river-levels and wool was piling up at the shearing-sheds all the way to the Darling junction. Churning upstream on this morning of iron frost, the *Philadelphia* broke with the waves from her wake the fragile glass-thin ice along the river's edge.

At Renmark a telegram was waiting for her: Alastair had sent the wire to ask her to call at Avoca Station and bring down a load of wool to the store at Milang.

Delie left it to fate and young Brenny to decide, and Brenny who had never been across the Lakes and had all a riverman's distrust of such large bodies of water, decided that they had plenty of cargo to deliver to the nearer and safer port of Morgan. Delie felt that he had saved her pride, even though it meant that she would not see Alastair again after all.

towards the final shore

And this, O monks, is the noble truth of the cessation of pain; the cessation without a remainder of that craving; abandonment, forsaking, release, non-attachment.

Buddha: *The Sermon in the Deer Park*

ONE HUNDRED

In 1931 the biggest flood since the 1870 one, still recalled by old-timers as the worst ever known, filled the length of the Murray valley. It spread over the natural flood-plain, inundated the pumping-stations, and broke through levee-banks as if they had been walls of brown paper.

There were those who muttered darkly that some people breached the banks on purpose, undermining all the work of conscientious townsmen who had toiled day and night with sand-bags and straw and mud; because some farmers held to the heresy that floods were natural, they cleansed the river, scoured out the channel, and brought deposits of fresh silt to the pasture-lands of the lower reaches. Others muttered against the Government Department of Works, who put in locks and weirs and training-spurs – and now they were even talking of a row of barrages across the mouth – until the river was so hemmed in that it had to burst its banks before the great flow of water could escape from the upper reaches. They were all agreed, at least, that it was somebody's fault; and some even blamed the Roman Catholics who'd held a week of prayer for rain in the dry season that preceded the flood.

Some of the greatest sufferers in each flood, though not in a pecuniary sense, were the shack-dwellers and campers along the low banks below the level of the cliffs, whose homes were inexorably swamped or swept away. Many of them had made permanent homes there, with neat gardens and clothes-lines and all sorts of ingenious devices for raising water from the river.

This year there were more than ever because of the great depression which was sweeping the western world, leaving many thousands of unemployed in each city. A great many of these came to the river and camped there, where it was always possible to get plenty of water and a feed of fish. Mostly they stayed on the outskirts of settlements – like the remaining aborigines – so that they could go in for the weekly dole, the food coupons which gave them flour and sugar and a small ration of tea. The advancing waters were regarded by them with a surly dislike, as one more misfortune heaped on undeserving shoulders.

The *Philadelphia* rescued one group of men who were cut off by the rising waters and unable to get up the high cliff behind their camp. Delie was distressed at their misery and gave them all Brenton's old clothing, but she could not give any of them the job they craved, the feeling of being useful and wanted in a world that seemed to have no use for them: a crazy world, where millions were hungry and food was dumped into the sea or burnt because it was uneconomic to sell it; where the banks closed down their credit and the potential consumers had no money to buy and the wheels of industry ground slowly and more slowly and there was no work.

Delie's sons were fortunate in that they were their own masters and could not be dismissed; they had not that dreadful fear of 'the sack' hanging over them which so many still employed had to suffer.

The two elder boys worked the steamer and Alex was through his medical course and doing 'locums' for country doctors on holiday while he gained experience. He'd had a year as a junior resident in a big hospital, where he had shown a flair for surgery. He thought he would like to specialise as a surgeon later; he wanted to do some post-graduate work overseas, but the Depression stopped all such plans at present. Freights were down, cargoes were scarce, and if living on the boat had not been so cheap it would have been hard for Delie to make ends meet.

Meg was a junior nurse in an Adelaide hospital run by a group of nuns. Her training had been stern and thorough; she had no sooner gone on night duty than she was sent by the sister, alone, to remove the nasal feeding-tube and intravenous saline drip from a patient who had just died in the middle of the night.

There was something strange about night duty, the sleeping by day and waking by night while others slept, the dim corridors and the hospital silent but for the groan of a restless patient, the quiet pad of her own feet as she went on her rounds. At the end of a long spell of night duty she began to feel unreal and found it an effort to go out into the bustling day-time world.

She liked Maternity best, there was always something doing in the Labour Ward in the middle of the night and the babies had to be given drinks of boiled water or supplementary feeds. Only when they lost a mother or a baby she suddenly hated the hospital; but this was rare.

She dreamed of going to the top of her career, of being appointed matron of some big place like the Murray Bridge Hospital, or even a large hospital in the city; but at present she just wanted to nurse. Her legs often ached when she went off duty after twelve hours with only a two-hour break; but her heart was in the work. Even in the theatre when young probationers were fainting right and left, she kept her head. She and Alex had plenty to talk about when they met, and they always talked 'shop'. One day, she thought, she would like to marry a doctor. But she would never love anyone as she had loved Garry Melville.

She was sorry her mother had not married again. Delie was past fifty now, her hair was entirely grey and her face etched deeply with the fine furrows of time; but there was not one line of petulance or temper to be read there. Her teeth were still excellent, so that her smile had much of its old charm.

Meg had started using lipstick when she was off duty; now she felt plain and not properly dressed without it. She had tried to persuade Delie to use some, and to get her hair bobbed, but so far Delie had resisted her. She seemed anxious to forget her sex, though she clung to her long hair; she'd had some trousers made to measure at the time when the hideous fashion of beach pyjamas came in, and because her hips (although her waist had thickened) had not spread very much she looked neat and workman-like in them. Brenny was rather scandalised – he had oddly old-fashioned ideas about women – but Gordon and Meg encouraged her and Gordon quoted instances of women who had worn soldiers' uniform and gone to war, accepted by their comrades as fellow-men.

Meg spent her annual leave each year on the steamer. The year after the flood, she joined tham at Morgan for a trip up to Mildura. Lake Victoria storage works had been completed in 1928, but had been too small to contain the flood. Now the Murray Valley Commission was building a great dam up near Albury, which would be bigger than Sydney Harbour when it was complete, and would hold enough water to keep the Murray flowing for two years. There would be no more great droughts, once the Hume Dam was finished. Lock Seven, just over the Victorian border, had been completed as part of the Lake Victoria works, for it was just at the outlet of the Rufus and could help to back the water up in the lake. Here the *Philadelphia* arrived about mid-morning.

Brenny, in the wheel-house, came steaming into the lock-chamber in his usual style. The Lockmaster was out on the weir, moving the travelling crane which drew the Boulé-type panels out of the water when it was time to let the level drop.

Delie, standing by in the wheel-house in case Brenny needed any help, saw the crane begin to topple. She shouted a warning which was lost in the noise of the steamer and at the same time the Lockmaster saw his danger and tried to run, hampered by the narrowness of the catwalk which limited his escape to one direction.

As in a slow-motion film she saw the heavy crane descending with deliberate calm, the man moving with horrifying slowness from its path.

'Look out!' she screamed uselessly, and Brenny, seeing what was happening, began to swear in quiet and helpless fury. The crane fell, and as the paddles stopped churning they heard the dreadful half-animal groans of a man in agony, while the Lockmaster lay across the catwalk, pinned by one foot.

Delie, sick and trembling, could only cling to the rail while Brenny bounded down the steps, calling for Meg. She fetched the steamer's first-aid box and they joined the two workers who had been winding the capstan to close the lock-chamber, and one of whom had run to fetch a large jack from the bank.

In the box was an ampoule of morphia and a hypodermic which Alex had procured for Delie. She had always feared some terrible and painful accident to one of the crew when they were far from the nearest doctor, for she recalled Brenton's account of how old Captain Tom, the steamer's former owner, had had his leg torn off by the paddle-shaft. It was one of the things that had driven Charlie McBean to drink more and more – the memory of Tom's end and of his own failure to remove the cleat from the shaft.

Meg administered the morphia and sat supporting the man's head while the men from the works and the men from the steamer – even Gordon, who looked green and averted his face – struggled to lever the crane from his crushed foot.

He was quite conscious; he even tried to crack a joke about having timed the accident nicely.

'How's that – for luck?' he gasped as Meg gently lifted his head on to her lap. 'Managed it – just in time – for a pretty girl to turn up and hold me hand.'

'You're luckier than you know,' said Brenny tersely. 'She's a

588

trained nurse and doesn't faint all over the place at the sight of a bit of blood.'

Gordon's ears became rather pink at this, and he turned his head round. Meg thought to spare him, and said:

'Gordon, there are enough men lifting, could you go and get him a drink? Something warm, with sugar in it.' The Lock-master was very pale and his skin felt cold and clammy with shock.

It took some time to free his foot, but he remained conscious, his brown eyes with their fan of wrinkles fixed on Meg's face. He did not cry out, but he gripped her hand harder and harder. As soon as they had him on a stretcher and she saw the mangled foot, the pieces of boot crushed into it, she knew that splints would be useless. It was a job for a surgeon, and the sooner he was in hospital the better the chances of avoiding an amputation.

Lock Seven was in a wild undeveloped corner of New South Wales, not very far above the South Australian border; on all sides was bush, and the Lockmaster got his wages from South Australia, his mail from Victoria, and kept his car on the New South Wales bank. On the Victoria bank there was no road, and on the N.S.W. side there was no hospital nearer than Wentworth. It was decided that the steamer could take him there most com-fortably, for he could lie in a bed instead of being jolted over the rough bush track in an old Model T.

Meg was pleased; it was a busman's holiday for her, but she loved using her nursing skill, and besides there was something about the Lockmaster – a man no longer very young, and with an air of calm self-sufficiency about the mouth, and of humour about the eyes – which appealed to her strongly. Besides, he had been brave, and he had called her a pretty girl. By the time they reached Wentworth she didn't want to let her patient go.

'I'll stay with him and see him settled in the hospital,' she told Brenny and Delie. 'You go on to Mildura and pick me up on the way down. If he has a "special" to nurse him it may be pos-sible to save his foot. I'd hate to think of him on crutches.'

Delie demurred. Some deep mother's instinct warned her that she had better not leave Meg. But Meg had made up her mind and there was no moving her, so the *Philadelphia* went on to Mildura without her.

By the time they reached Mildura the foot had been operated on twice successfully, without need for amputation; by the time they left again the patient was in love with the nurse; and by the time they returned to Wentworth junction, turning once more into the turbid waters of the lower Darling, he had proposed and been accepted.

Delie was surprised and horrified. She had accepted the fact that Meg would marry 'one day', but not yet, and not someone stuck away out in the bush without any proper conveniences, no shop, no doctors in an emergency.

'Exactly, Mother dear, the kind of life that *you* chose,' Gordon pointed out with a smile, backing up Meg's half-defiant happiness.

'I don't even know his name!' wailed Delie. 'What is it? Something queer, beginning with a "G", I think you said.'

'Ogden, dear. Ogden Southwell. It's rather distinguished, I think. And he has a responsible position. And you'll be seeing me every time you go up or down to Lake Victoria or Wentworth or Mildura.'

'But your nursing career!'

'I'll be able to practise on my family as it grows. Do come and meet Ogden, he's sitting up and probably getting a temperature with nervousness, though I told him what a sweetie-pie you are.'

'But I haven't a hat.'

'A hat! Why on earth do you need a hat to confront a prospective son-in-law? Come and I'll put some lipstick on you, and you'll feel a new woman.'

As they swung into the main river again and turned downstream, Delie asked Brenny to let her take the wheel for a while. She wanted to think, to adjust herself to the idea of Meg married. In the wheel-house, alone with the sliding reflections and backward-marching trees, the dance of light on the water and the wild birds that kept flying on and landing just ahead, she examined her own reactions.

Why were they hostile? Meg had a perfect right to get married. She had completed her training and probably could get a job at any time if she needed it. She wanted a husband and a family, and Ogden seemed a nice man and was obviously very much in love with Meg. This was his great recommendation; he appreciated her daughter.

Delie had liked his honest brown eyes, his sharp white smile in his tanned face, and the laughter crinkles etched among the sunburn. He was not going to be crippled and his job was waiting for him; she could really have no objections. None! Only that he wasn't good enough for Meg. She had enough objectivity to smile at her own maternal prejudice. No man would be good enough, that was the trouble. She must just get used to the idea of Meg throwing herself away on some undeserving male. Ogden – what a name! – would do as well as any other.

ONE HUNDRED AND ONE

Miss Barrett wrote that Jessamine had gone off on a girls' 'finishing tour' abroad, with a group of several others chaperoned by a Melbourne lady who knew the Continent well.

'This is something I might do myself if I were younger and more energetic [she wrote]. It would be like rediscovering Europe for oneself, to show it to young receptive minds like Jessie's. Though I fear she has a tendency to be *bored* very easily, something I find hard to understand. I can truly say I have never been bored in my life!

'And life continues to be full of delightful surprises, like Elaine's sister, who has turned out to have a wonderful singing voice and has won a scholarship to the Elder Conservatorium. The aborigines will never be good at competitive commerce, such things are alien to their nature; if they are ever to make their mark and be accorded their rightful place in the community, it will be through prowess in the arts.

'I am still staying with the Raeburns in their very comfortable house which has now become like my own home. In fact, I don't like to leave at present as Miss Janet is very worried. She came to me to tell me her sister drinks and is taking such large quantities of brandy that it must affect her health, though she drinks only at night and her nephew doesn't know about it.

'I don't know what I can do since she won't let me tell Alastair. I've suggested that she speak to the family doctor and get him to treat her sister, but Miss Janet says he will never believe her. He is old, deaf and obstinate, but Miss Raeburn will have no one else. And Mrs Raeburn, of course – it is no use asking her to do anything, she would only look helpless and say it was not her affair. It does not seem, by the way, that she is going to start another family. Perhaps it is wise.'

Delie put down the letter. She was surprised that she still felt the old resentment against Cecily and could even feel a sort of relief that there was no visible result of her union with Alastair. She was not surprised at the news in the first part of the letter; she had wondered that Miss Raeburn's secret was not out long ago.

Ten years had passed since she was last under that roof and she had never returned to Milang. She had seen Miss Barrett several times in the city, once with young Jessie grown into a rather wilful beauty, with beautifully dressed hair and expensive clothes. I could never have lived up to that household, had thought Delie, spreading her feet in her comfortable low-heeled shoes and tucking up a wisp of untidy hair.

Miss Barrett was now seventy, but her handwriting was still firm and clear. She would live to be ninety, most likely, and keep her faculties to the end. It was not possible to imagine her doddering, whatever her age.

It was only a few weeks later when a telegram came from Alastair – catching the steamer, fortunately, at Morgan just as she tied up – asking her to come at once to Milang. She had said she would never set foot in that house again, but this was different. Miss Barrett was seriously ill and asking for her. Delie took the train that day and was in Milang by the following afternoon.

She had not wired what train she was coming on, but took a cab at the station.

'The Raeburn place,' she said to the driver. It was only a step across the road from the station, but she had bags to carry.

He turned and stared at her blankly. 'Where did you say, missus?'

'The Raeburn place. Are you new here, or what?'

'The house and the warehouse was both burnt down, day before yestiddy. Thought everyone knew that.'

Delie felt her jaw drop ridiculously open. She closed it again and said: 'Drive me straight to the hospital – quickly!'

As they turned and went along the lakeside road she stared at the blackened shell of the big stone building. The balcony and the window-frames were gone, the roof had caved in and taken the observatory with it – and all Alastair's paintings, most likely. But he was safe! He had signed the wire.

The windows stared like blank eyes from the desolate ruin

592

which looked hundreds of years old. It was like looking at the mummified corpse of an old friend. She averted her eyes and urged the driver to hurry. He was inclined to stop and tell her about the spectacle of the fire, in which two of the inmates, both women, had been burned to death and one seriously injured. It was the most interesting thing that had happened in Milang for years. Delie felt faint, but she forced herself to ask their names.

'Raeburn, o' course,' said the driver rather impatiently.

'Mrs or Miss?'

'The two ladies of the 'ouse, that's all I know.' Delie flung some money at him and leaped from the cab at the hospital steps.

'Leave my bags at the hotel, please.' (There was only one in the town.) 'Where is Mr Raeburn staying, do you know?'

'I b'lieve 'e's at the hospital in case he's wanted, like.'

Why didn't he give me some warning? thought Delie almost angrily. But perhaps he had feared she would worry more if she knew. She knew nothing, but she dreaded a great deal.

At the hospital she asked first for Miss Barrett. The sister-in-charge looked grave. 'Is it a relative?'

'She has no relatives here. I am her oldest friend. Take me to her, can't you? Mr Raeburn . . .'

'Ah, you are a friend of Mr Raeburn. I belive he's sleeping at the moment, he was sitting up with Miss Barrett all last night; I'll just ask if you can see her. Her condition is serious, you understand; in fact I might say critical.'

'She has been asking for me. I've come two hundred miles to see her, and if you don't hurry I may be too late! Please ask at once.' The sister rustled away and came back quickly.

'The patient is a little easier, and you may see her as long as you don't stay too long. Perhaps you would like to see Mr Raeburn first?'

'As long as there is no urgency –'

'She is in no immediate danger.'

'Then, yes, please.'

Alastair was the same; that was her first impression. She had somehow expected the fact of his marriage to have changed him. He was older of course and much greyer, but he had the same spare figure and the same sleeping fire in his eyes beneath the hooded lids, drooping now with weariness after two nights' vigil at the hospital.

'I felt responsible to you for her,' he explained, as he took both her hands, his eyes going over her face and noting every detail, as a connoisseur might study a beloved painting for signs of damage and decay. 'Ten years . . .' he added half to himself. 'It's a long time, Delie. This is a strange meeting.'

'Yes. Tell me what happened, Alastair. I know nothing, except that there's been this disastrous fire, and that your aunts –'

'It was Aunt Alicia who started it, I'm afraid. I was away in Adelaide. She has apparently been drinking heavily for years, and this night she had a lighted candle in her room and set fire to the curtains; whether in a state of *delirium tremens*, imagining that she was fumigating the room or something (for Janet said she's been complaining of black bugs crawling on the walls) or whether she just fell into a stupor, we don't know. Anyway, the fire started in the middle of the night. Miss Barrett woke first and could have escaped, but she went to Alicia's room and tried to rouse her, but she only roused enough to become obstinate and refuse to move.

'Miss Barrett wasted some time trying to get her out of the room, but by then the stairs were alight. She waited only to get Janet out of her bed in the next room, wrap her in a blanket and bundle her down the stairs; but once safely outside she fainted. Miss Barrett hoped Cecily had woken and escaped, but when she found her unaccounted for she tried to go up the stairs again . . . as I understand . . . just as the whole top storey caved in. Poor Cecily! I pray that she may have been unconscious from the fumes, and simply died in her bed. There was not enough left to tell with certainty.'

'Cecily! Oh, my dear, I thought – ! I'm so sorry.' Dimly, at the back of her mind, she was aware that something wanted thinking out, that this changed everything. But she had no time for it now.

Alastair said sombrely: 'Yes, it was Janet who was saved. I haven't told Jamie and Jessie yet, I dread breaking it to them.'

'Poor children!' Delie beat her hands together. 'Oh, I should have told you, years ago! I knew about Miss Raeburn's drinking bouts. I saw her one night in the corridor, as – as I was leaving your room, and she was holding a candle very carelessly then. And lately Miss Barrett hinted something in one of her letters. All this loss of life – and your beautiful home, your paintings, your Lely –'

He dismissed them with a gesture. 'The world is not much poorer for them. But you have lost something, too. Miss Barrett has no chance of recovering, at her age.'

Delie's eyes were filled with tears, but she held them back.

'Can you take me to her?'

'Yes, she's been asking for you ever since she was conscious. That's why I sent the wire. She has third-degree burns and with their extent it's a wonder she hasn't died already. I believe she's just holding on until she's spoken to you.'

Delie had dreaded what she would see in the hospital room, but the shapeless figure on the bed, an amorphous mass of white cotton dressing through which only the eyes could be seen, seemed to have no relation to her old friend.

Then Miss Barrett spoke, and her deep, vibrating voice which was so much a part of her personality was the same, in spite of the weakness that made her pause between every sentence.

'Hullo, Delie.'

'Oh, Miss Barrett! I came as soon as I had Alastair's wire.'

' "Dorothy", please. We are just becoming contemporaries almost – we would soon have been old women together, if I could have hung on another ten years or so. How old are you now, fifty-five?'

Delie nodded, unable to speak. There was a ghost of the old humorous tone which distressed her more than tears would have done.

'Delie . . . You're just in time, I think. By tomorrow . . . but never mind that. It's strange how things work out; Alastair was away, Janet fainted for the first time in her life . . . I had to decide . . . It was like playing at God . . . I could have gone to her room first, Delie, but I didn't. I knew it was too late when I started to go back, but . . . I had to make the gesture. Otherwise I couldn't have lived with myself . . . Be happy, dear child . . . You deserve it.' Her voice had sunk to a whisper, that disembodied voice coming from the cloud of dressings. 'Alastair . . . he still . . . Ah – !' It was a sigh which sounded like a sigh of content. The eyes filmed over and grew blank and Delie rushed to the bell. Dorothy Barrett was still breathing, but with such shallow, sighing breaths that they were scarcely perceptible. Irreversible shock, thought Delie, dredging up a phrase from one of Meg's nursing handbooks. Two nurses came and bundled her out of the room.

ONE HUNDRED AND TWO

It seemed very strange to be a passenger, not to be able to go into the wheel-house as her right. She paced up and down the deck, avoiding the groups of middle-aged women in hair nets, smiling at the playing children. At each turn round the foredeck she glanced up through the wheel-house windows.

So that was the skipper, that mere boy (as she thought of him), he couldn't be thirty yet, but now, in 1939, her own eldest son was thirty-five – and still drifting, still unable to settle to any definite work in life. It was as though he had been born an artist without any ability for execution.

She realised that this young skipper was just as old as Brenton had been when she first met him, when he'd seemed so adult and assured, after the boys of Echuca, to the shy girl from the farm.

And that girl was I, I, she thought in surprise, looking down at the wrinkles and moth patches on the backs of her hands. How much had happened, how her life had been enriched and complicated and broadened by endless inflowings and contacts!

The widening stream she had become, fuller, deeper and infinitely more complex – and how much more so, again, than the fresh schoolgirl among the mountains of unmelted snow – was already approaching the sea. A few more years . . . she already heard the sound of distant surf on the final shore. Next year she would reach sixty.

An old man came along the deck carrying a bucket. He had a withered dewlap, a pale, wrinkled skin, and faded but alert blue eyes. His hair, though still thick, was quite white. Delie looked at him, seeing herself in a few years when she had faded into the sexlessness of age.

'Are you one of the crew?' she asked with a smile.

'Yairs.' He stopped, holding back his head to look at her, his bony mouth slightly open.

'I wonder if you would remember Teddy Edwards, of the *Philadelphia*? Have you been on the river long?'

'*Teddy Edwards!* Course I remember 'im. Never worked for

'im meself, but knoo he was the fastest skipper on the river. And the best skipper too. The *Philadelphia*: now let me see – '

'She's tied up at Murray Bridge. There's no work for her any more.'

'Ah, all the old steamers is goin'. But the *Melbourne* is still working at Echuca, did yer notice her? And the little *Adelaide* and *Edwards* up here, they'll see me under the sod.'

'My son has been working the *Industry* for the S.A. Government. I'm Mrs Edwards. My husband died, you know. I'm on a sentimental journey back to where my old home was, the Jamiesons' farm.'

'Jamiesons'! Gawd, we used to call there for eggs, must be forty years ago. Nothin' left now – the house was burned down years ago – but you can see the old sheep-pens from the river. We're nearly there now.' He looked at her more closely. 'Did yer say Missus Edwards? Not Teddy's missus?'

'Yes, that's right.'

He was shaking her hand warmly. 'Missus Edwards, eh? Think of that now. I s'pose you remember Echuca in the old days. Ah, she was a great little port. I was on the *Clyde*, y'know, and the *Coorong* – we even went up the Murrumbidgee in them days. Ah, the old days. . . . Everything seems slipping away so fast, some'ow.'

She saw that his faded eyes were bright with easy tears. Inarticulate as he was, he felt the transience of things.

She was back, herself, in the landscape of the past as the steamer rounded the many sharp bends, the steeply sloping points of yellow sand, the clay-ringed banks which the gum trees clutched with wooden hands. There were few big trees left, except those growing in the river-bank. A growth of young 'sapplins' (as Brenton always called them) gave way to a grassy clearing and she saw the weathered wood of the sheep-pens still standing.

Nothing beside remained. There was no sign of houses or outbuildings, of the pine tree she used to climb, the vine-trellis and the almonds. Only a solitary lime tree, surviving by some freak from the old garden, held a few green fruits. Part of her past had disappeared, as it had with the Raeburn wool-store home at Milang in the fire nearly five years ago.

Why hadn't she married Alastair? He had asked her more than once, in spite of his fierce pride, the second time just before he left for London to act as agent for his firm over there.

'It is too late,' she had said, no longer needing to steel herself

597

against him and feeling nothing for him but calm friendship. 'Ten years ago I would have asked nothing more of life. Now I prefer my freedom. Then, when I would have married you, you were not free; now I am no longer the same person.'

'Delie! If one could go back. . . . If I had the chance over again . . . but, as I told you, I felt it was hopeless, and you seemed to have changed towards me. It's not too late. Let me show you –'

But when he would have taken her in his arms she held up her hand firmly, in a denying gesture. Ah, she had grown wiser – or was it harder? – with the years!

'It's no good, Alastair. You are blowing on a dead coal.' She had wondered fleetingly if it had been just the house, the glamour of his background, that she had been in love with. Since the fire she had not felt the same, perhaps because of Dorothy Barrett's last words which had seemed to force her to accept a sacrifice. Poor Dorothy! It was as well she had died, surely, with that decision on her conscience.

And then, when he asked her again, he had been leaving for London to take up a new life and she didn't want to return to England, perhaps for ever. Australia had been her home for nearly fifty years now, and its blue skies and immense distances were part of her blood, as if she had been native here.

Delie looked back as they rounded the bend above where the house had been. All was gone, swept away in the passage of time, with all the people who had lived there, except herself. It existed now only in her mind; and when she was gone, what then remained? It became a drop lost in the river, a fragment of the infinitely complex fabric of life.

The dark red-gums leaned over the river in a familiar pattern and she felt a strange dislocation of time. All was there as it had been: Hester's flower garden, Lige hoeing his 'turmits', Minna lithe and beautiful, Charles whistling as he walked along the banks, Adam wandering absorbed with a book . . . A cold wind seemed to blow down her spine.

The old man's voice recalled her. 'You remember them big red-gum flats? All been cut down for Guv'mint wharves and sleepers for the railways and boat-building and such. They're trying to get them back; the Forestry Commission controls it all now, and you can't cut anything smaller than a' eight-foot butt. It'll take a long time, though. Five hundred years, I'd say. There's hardly a sizeable tree left, except them that's growing right in the river-bank.'

Delie felt glad she had not travelled overland from Moama, through the treeless paddocks and the eroded, sand-drifted higher land where the wild daisies used to grow beneath the Murray pines. Yet she felt the comfort of the river's calm flowing round the familiar bends; this was still unchanged, the eternal, unresting flood which brimmed on for ever.

ONE HUNDRED AND THREE

Meg was in the Wentworth hospital having her second baby and Delie had agreed to stay with Ogden and mind their first child, a girl. She was surprised at the intensity of her feeling for little Vicki, a mercurial child who could wheedle anything out of her father and was close to being spoilt.

Meg thought grandmothers were natural spoilers of babies and they'd had their first real coolness over whether Vicki should be picked up from her pram when she cried. It was then that Delie decided to go away and let Meg have the baby to herself in peace. She was horrified that she'd acted like a typical doting grandma, she who had always declared that she'd had enough babies in her life and certainly didn't intend being a nurse-maid to her grandchildren.

But Vicki . . . A strange feeling had gripped her as she looked down at the small dark head and tightly closed eyes, the tiny fists curled against the cheeks. This was not just another baby of the millions being born every day, but a symbol of the continuity of life.

She saw herself, her own mother, Meg and Meg's daughter as links in an endless chain which stretched back into the beginning of things when the first woman suffered parturition. Or as a bud on the surface of life's great tree, where every female child held within her, miraculously, the seeds of the future. And Vicki was her own private miracle.

Vicki was now five years old and she scarcely knew what rain was. They'd had four very dry years; at the inland site of Lock Seven where she had spent her life, rain was slight even in a good season and the winters were frosty and sunny.

Water there was in plenty, pumped from the river. Meg had a fine vegetable and flower garden, tended by the Lock staff of three men who all seemed to be agricultural enthusiasts with green fingers. The back garden was securely fenced, so that Vicki could not wander away and fall in the river.

It was the one worry of Meg's life; when the weir gates were open and the water cascaded six or eight feet from the upper level to the lower, there was a boiling maelstrom below which no one who fell in would survive. Even the fish were dazed and helpless; pelicans, gathering in great fishing fleets, snapped them up as they floated to the surface.

Otherwise she was perfectly happy in her home. She liked the roar of the weir and the calm glassiness of the reach above; she had spaced her children intelligently, she loved her husband with a steady unagonising love and he thought her the most wonderful woman in the world. She rarely thought of Garry, and when she did it was without the old sharp pain. She was able to practise her nursing on the members of the staff when they fell ill and on Vicki's childish ailments.

It was late September, the sunny winter was over and the sunny spring well advanced when Delie came to her daughter's house. Wild flowers were still out in the bush, bright pink heath and yellow doubletails. She took Vicki for walks, dressed in long linen overalls against the scratchy, prickly bushes and fallen sticks.

Vicki liked blue flowers best, the dark-blue snake-flowers and the sky-blue orchids with yellow eyes, but the hairy spider-orchids frightened her. Delie found a great joy in these expeditions. When she felt Vicki's small soft hand in hers and looked down at her brown curls, as fine as silk straight from the cocoon, she felt a kind of dreamy peace.

As she pointed out the coloured birds, the green and yellow parrots, the red rosellas and sulphur-crested cockatoos, she thought sometimes of Brenton and their first days in the Barmah forest. Brenton, too, lived on in this lively child who danced along beside her. She had his firm and well-cut features, Delie sometimes thought, among the baby softness; she was more like her Uncle Brenny than like her mother, which meant that she was a pretty child. Her cheeks were rosy and her eyes a deep, dark brown.

At five, she was beginning to think for herself and ask searching questions. She had come a long way from the demanding, unthinking infant; she was already aware of death.

After a night of frost, Vicki had picked up a dead orange butterfly with a body of black velvet, its wings stiff and papery.

'They don't really die, Grandma,' she said seriously, ' 'cause they come out of the eggs again in the summer.' (She had kept the eggs and then the caterpillars in a shoe-box the year before and fed them on cotton-bush leaves until she grew tired of it and her mother had to take over.)

Delie was impressed. The child had voiced a profound truth, she thought: that nothing dies, but is only renewed for ever. Except, of course, when a species became extinct; but life, like matter, was indestructible.

But Vicki's ideas of God were primitive and anthropomorphic. 'Is God bigger than the King?' she said. 'Can he have watermelon for breakfast every day?'

Delie thought it best to let the child work things out for herself, as everyone must do in the end unless he was one of the sheep minds, who preferred a doctrine ready-made.

When Delie found a great tear in her best dress, Vicki said innocently that 'a moff must of ate it'.

'No moth was ever that big!' said Delie.

'This was a *god*-moff,' she explained, and when Delie laughed she laughed too, rolling on the floor and kicking with mirth, more for company than because she saw anything funny in what she had said. She liked being with Grandma, who laughed with her whole face, her eyes and her eyebrows and her mouth, and her teeth were nice and white. She was the only person Vicki knew with silver hair who still had a pretty face. Vicki hated old ladies with sharp, hairy chins and yellow teeth. She was sure they were witches and witches troubled her dreams nearly every night. There was one old witch who waited for her in the dream-world, so that often she dreaded going to bed and she always had to have a night-light left on, to help her get quickly back to the other world if she woke in the dark. The witch could not follow her there, across the borders of consciousness; but Vicki was afraid she knew what went on there and she would never 'tell on' the witch when she woke up screaming, whatever dreadful things she had been doing to her; if she did the witch would punish her the next night when she was delivered back into her clutches by sleep.

Delie had insisted on being called 'Grandma'. Once the idea of being a grandmother had horrified her, but she thought the elegant variations invented for children to call their grandparents these days rather foolish: 'Nana' and 'Ganny' and all the rest of it. She had almost ceased to be surprised, now that she was to be made a grandma a second time, that she was actually old enough to be one. She was essentially, she felt, the same Delie who had come to Australia in the early 'nineties, before the invention of the aeroplane or the death of Queen Victoria. She could never take for granted the strangeness of being caught in the current of time.

She was absorbed and content, living in the little island world of the lock and weir; she felt no anxiety for Meg and, when Ogden came home looking quietly happy and announced that they'd had a son, she felt as if she'd known his news already.

She could never be close to her son-in-law. He was likeable enough, a practical, hard-working, easy-going Australian with nothing remarkable about him. They never got past the generalities of life, the small courtesies and exchanges, or discussed anything more intimate than what to have for breakfast; indeed, Delie shied away from even the thought of her daughter's sex life with this pleasant stranger and Meg had never mentioned it. She simply concluded that they got on well because Meg was so obviously happy and fulfilled.

Delie had scarcely bothered to read a paper for weeks, and then, into her little pool of contentment a great rock came crashing. Hitler had at last overstepped himself in Europe and an ultimatum had been issued: if Poland were invaded it would mean war.

Politically innocent, internationally ignorant, Delie could not believe it. She would *not* believe that another war could break out after the dreadful example of the last. No nation, anywhere, could be crazy enough to want it.

She sat with Ogden by the wireless that night, waiting tensely for the BBC news; and then the tired voice of Chamberlain, a defeated man: 'I have to tell you that no such reply has been received; and this means that this country is now at war with Germany.'

Again! 'Never again!' Mrs Melville had said when she lost her son. And all the women who had lost sons had said: 'Never again! It must never happen again!' And it was happening.

She muttered a few words to Ogden – who was saying he supposed he'd be short-staffed now when they called up the younger men – and rushed outside, feeling as if she would choke. For once the sky was clouded; an amorphous mass seemed to press close above her head, for not a star pierced through anywhere. She walked up and down until she was tired, thinking of her sons, feeling glad that Gordon and Brenny were not young, that Alex as a doctor was more valuable than as a soldier. He was now established as a surgeon in the city, regarded as one of the most brilliant of the younger men.

In the morning she rose early – before even Vicki was awake – and ranged far along the river-bank below the weir, where the churning water matched her inner turmoil. The sky was still over-cast, and this was so unusual that she felt a ridiculous, super-stitious idea take hold of her, that all Nature was mourning man's stupidity. As if this corner of Australia represented the whole earth!

Ogden had no wish to go to the war, especially now that he had a son to work for. He'd always been rather shy of girls and he still couldn't believe his luck when he looked at Meg, who had come home from hospital prettier than ever; her complexion milk and roses, her eyes with a look both brilliant and tender.

'Little Mother Meg!' he said, bending over her as she nursed the baby, with the straight dark floss of her hair falling over her eyes.

'Oh, were you brought up on Ethel Turner too? I liked *Seven Little Australians* best; I cried for a week over Judy's death.'

'No, but my sisters were always reading them; and Màry Grant Bruce –'

'Nobody seems to write such lovely books for girls any more. I must get them all for Vicki.'

She removed the nipple and wiped the baby's milky mouth. His eyes were closing drowsily, he was too sleepy to bring up his wind, and that meant he'd probably wake about midnight with a pain, but she hadn't the heart to rouse him. She'd been home a month and they had hardly an undisturbed night.

She laid him down and slipped into bed beside Ogden, leaving the night-light burning.

'Meg! I'm a lucky fellow.' He folded her in his arms, drawing her close and at once she became the child, warm, protected, encompassed by his love and strength; and far away, like drums beginning, she heard the increasing thunder of her blood.

ONE HUNDRED AND FOUR

Peace. There could be nothing more peaceful than the river at dawn, Delie thought. Nothing moved but a web-footed water-mole which ran silently down the bank and slid out into the water, making a small 'V' of ripples with its nose. The water seemed still as a lake, flowing imperceptibly with a glassy surface from which the first rays of the sun shone back through a layer of softly curling steam. It was like an old green serpent basking in the sun.

The light was golden, not the melancholy declining gold of afternoon, but a pale rich promise of warmth to come. War was far away, on the other side of the world; Polish cities were being destroyed, Polish patriots murdered secretly, Polish Jews 'liqui-dated' ruthlessly while the terrible names of Auschwitz and Belsen were still unknown to the world. Here the sun rose in tranquil splendour and the willows trailed their long green hair above their calm reflections.

It was too cold for swimming, with the snow-water beginning to sweep past from the high mountains where it had melted two months ago, in September. She would take the dinghy and row down for the milk and eggs, a job which gave her exercise and pleasure. There was nothing that she *had* to do, nothing at all.

For at last Delie had the life she had longed for: no demands, no distractions, no neighbours, a boat which was tied up but which could be moved to a new setting whenever they felt like it, and all the time in the world. She read and painted, but the old fire was gone. Perhaps she had been wrong and a vegetable existence, or a purely contemplative one, would not have helped her work.

There was no conflict, no tension in her any longer and she had done her best painting when torn by restlessness and dis-content. She had established her style and a genuine Delphine Gordon commanded a ready market; but she knew that what she was turning out now was only a copy of herself; she was not developing.

At sixty, would her useful life be over? Perhaps she would

knit socks for the troops and end her life in good works. She was like so many of the paddle-steamers these days, tied to the bank while their barges lay empty and idle. Only a few passenger steamers were still running, the *Marion* based at Murray Bridge, the *Gem* at Mildura, and the little *Merle* converted to a motor-boat. The *Philadelphia* lay in the sheltered channel between a small green island and the shore, downstream of the Murray Bridge wharf where the *Murrundi* was now moored permanently. (She was the home of Captain Murray Randell, son of the Captain Randell who built the first steamboat, the *Mary Ann*, on the Murray.)

Here the river was broad and straight, no weirs within a hundred miles and green flats on each side where fat cattle grazed. A small jetty, two planks wide, led out through the willows to deep water and here Delie kept the dinghy tied and went for a swim each morning.

There was no crew, only Gordon, who kept the boat painted, pumped water and did all the odd jobs, including most of the cooking. He had decided to read history for an arts degree by correspondence, which would take years and years.

She felt selfishly glad that Gordon was too old to be called up. He was not likely to volunteer, but Brenny . . . He had always been adventurous, and the steamer trade which had provided excitement and a livelihood for his father and for himself as a young man was now almost at a standstill. Paddle-steamers lay rotting at their moorings, empty barges beside them, while trucks and trains and hawkers' vans took the trade which had been theirs.

There was only one area of the river which was busy and that was at Goolwa, where the great barrage works at the mouth were nearing completion. The small steamers that were still active in the 'bottom end' of the river had been busy carting gravel and cement, bringing construction camp huts down from Lake Victoria, besides pumps and pile-driving machinery from the last lock completed. Steel for the coffer-dams arrived by train. *Renmark* and *Rothbury*, *J. G. Arnold* and *Oscar W.* found themselves working again for a while; but the *Industry*, being a Government boat, was still in demand at the works.

Brenny came to dinner with them on the *Philadelphia* when the *Industry* came up to Murray Bridge on business. Delie found to her relief that he showed little interest in the war, but was full of the work at Goolwa.

'This barrage is a tremendous thing,' he said, his eyes shining in the light of the petrol lamp, his fair curls ruffled. (How like his father he is! thought Delie, noting how already his fine-cut features were coarsening, and little red veins appearing in his cheeks.)

'Do you realise there will be nearly *five miles* of weir built across the mouths? Only the Goolwa channel will have a navigable pass and removable stop-logs in the weir section. On one side of the wall will be salt-water and on the other fresh. It will stop the sea-water flowing up into the lakes. D'you remember how we used to catch mullet and butterfish at Milang, Gordie, and save the fresh from flowing away in a drought year?'

'I don't like all this interfering with Nature,' said Gordon. 'History shows that it almost always brings new problems. For one thing, you'll get a growth of reeds along the Goolwa channel and all through the lakes. You'll get fresh-water algae fouling boat-bottoms.'

'You'll always get weed, in fresh or salt.'

'And you'll have a big flood one day, really big, not like the last bad one in 'thirty-one.'

'But haven't I told you the Goolwa weir's movable? And the Tauwitcherie one will lie flat in a strong current, a kind of one-way valve; fresh water can get out, but sea-water can't get in. I tell you, the engineers have it all worked out.'

'Still, the Murray won't like it,' said Delie.

They looked at her as if she had said something peculiar, but perhaps true. She tried to explain what she meant: that it was presumptuous of men to try to control such a huge body of water, however tame it might appear.

'Well, someone's going to have a shot at taming me,' said Brenny facetiously. 'I'm getting married, Mum. You'll like Mavis. She's lived in Goolwa all her life.'

Oh no! thought Delie, and then she thought: It will keep him out of the war.

After Christmas, when she had Vicki to stay on board for a week to give Meg a rest, they moved down to the slip at Goolwa while the *Philadelphia* had her bottom scraped clear of weed. Gordon had kept the upper structure gleaming with paint and Delie made new bright curtains for the cabins and the saloon.

Meg, for some reason, had chosen the name of Charles for her baby; she had never known her Great-Uncle Charles and he was only a relative by marriage, but Delie felt the name ill-omened

Young Charley, however, was almost ridiculously like his father. 'A real little Southwell', as Ogden said proudly, tossing him in his arms.

Delie had looked at the squinting child and failed to see any beauty in him. When he first came home from hospital he was rather sickly, his milk did not agree with him and his face was spotty. But she had felt a great pity for this male scrap of flesh. Just in time for the next war, she thought and wondered with a flash of something like prophecy if it might be a desperate battle for existence here in Australia, against an invasion from the north – the Japanese . . . ? There was all that empty land, and the people living mostly in the coastal cities to the south and east.

She was still sufficiently in love with life to feel that it was worth it; even twenty years of existence were better than none. Afterwards, when the horrors of the prison camps were revealed, she began to wonder. There was evil, evil deeply rooted in human beings – why did every wild animal and bird instinctively flee from man? – and in a war it came to the surface like a foul scum. Already they were fouling streams, polluting the air with coal-dust and petrol fumes, the oceans with oil; burning up the oxygen, cutting down the forests, letting their cities spread like skin cancers over the green countryside, and spawning in ever-growing numbers; like those bacteria which can only thrive at the expense of their host. Oh God, where would it end?

But so far, the war did not seem so bad as the last one, though it was bad enough, no doubt, for the Czechs and the Poles. Then came the fall of France, Italy's 'stab in the back', Belgium's surrender and the British escape from Dunkirk. To Delie it was all remote, until Gordon suddenly announced that he was leaving for the city to enter an officers' training school.

'Perhaps it will all be over by the time I get there, Mum,' he said comfortingly to her white face. 'This is something I *know* I want to do, for the first time in my life. And after the war they'll give me a free university course in any subject I like to choose. I won't be too old.'

'I don't believe it will be over. That's what they said about the last war and this one may go on even longer. Oh Gordon, think! You know nothing of war, you've always hated suffering, you're not soldier-material at all. Let the younger men go. You're thirty-six and by the time it's all over you might be forty and more.'

But he was immovable. Delie did not weep; she had grown

past tears, but that Gordon, gentle Gordon who could never bear to tread on an ant, should be caught up in the killing-machine of war was grotesque. Brenny might have made a soldier, he was made of tougher stuff, less sensitive and more of an extrovert; but he was completely immersed in the life of paddle-steamers and took little interest in the war.

'Little Britain will thrash the Germans like she did before,' he predicted confidently. He was planning to get married in the New Year.

Delie went up to the city to beg Alex to intervene, and persuade Gordon to change his mind; but he refused.

'This will be the making of Gordon, if he survives,' he said. 'There is a softness and a lack of direction in him and I believe he has a deep, suppressed sense of failure. He's never found his true path and perhaps this is it.'

'Gordon will have a terrible time, if he ever gets to the Front. And you, Alex – don't tell me you're going too?'

'No, I think surgeons will be needed more than ever after this war, to patch up airmen and bomb-casualties. I've started to specialise in plastic surgery – skin- and bone-grafting, making new faces out of pieces of thigh-tissue; it's fascinating, you begin to feel like the Creator, though not up to making a complete woman out of a rib.'

ONE HUNDRED AND FIVE

Now that the barrage works were established, a road led right round the elbow of the river after which Goolwa had been named by the natives. Delie walked as far as she could go and then took to the sandhills, where a faint track led upward between wiry grasses higher than her head.

Crickets sang somnolently under the heated ground and the sand sifted into her shoes, burned her feet. She walked warily, looking out for snakes, though the increasing thunder of the surf made her heart beat fast with excitement. She had heard that sound far inland on quiet nights, and since she came to Goolwa she was always conscious of its pervading restless note: sometimes lost in the pauses of the wind, sometimes startlingly loud when there was a steady south-west gale and the water piled up in the channel until it was two or three feet deeper than at the mouth, sloping upwards like a hill.

About to see for the first time the beach of which she had dreamed for half her life, she told herself that of course she must be disappointed. She kept her head down and her eyes in front of her feet, watching the track. Over one sandhill, down into a gully where the roar of the surf grew fainter, and up again to where it sounded louder than before.

A sea-wind buffeted her suddenly and she looked up. Then she sank with a wordless cry on the hot sand.

Blue, incredibly blue, the Southern Ocean stretched away to the shores of the Antarctic. Deep sapphire, lapis lazuli, turquoise near the beach where the water shoaled; and strung round the curving coast like rows of white necklaces, the lines of surf moved endlessly shoreward. Its deep, booming roar was borne to her on the fresh wind; and far to the east she glimpsed the salt-white sandhills of the Coorong.

Delie drank it all in, with her mouth half-open as if actually swallowing great draughts of all that lonely grandeur: that beach which stretched for ninety miles to the south and east where, as far as she could see, not a living creature moved except a group of little sandpipers which seemed blown along the sand, their twinkling legs invisible.

Clumps of froth like soapsuds scudded before the wind and piled against the sandhills in discoloured heaps. She got up and began to trot clumsily seaward, slipping in the soft sand. At the edge of the dunes, out of breath and heated, she looked round quickly and then slipped off her clothes. Almost furtively she crossed the wide smooth slope to the water.

What a fool she would look, an old woman with a flabby chest, bathing naked in the sunlight! But she often used to slip in off the boat without a costume and now she hated the feel of clothing in the water. She dashed in up to her waist, and in a moment was rolled over and over, her ears full of the sound of grinding pebbles and sand, her flesh stinging, her heart pounding as she held her breath interminably.

When she struggled to her feet she was in water up to her knees, and immediately had them knocked from under her by another wave, which in receding tried to drag her out with it. She crawled to safety and lay gasping for breath above the reach of the waves.

Her knees and elbows were raw; she would have more respect for the surf at Goolwa Beach in future, when the wind was in this quarter.

As soon as she was dressed she began to walk briskly towards the mouth, keeping the sea on her right. The wind was cold in her wet hair; she was glad she'd had it cut at last, though it was not very becoming, grey and wispy, but so much easier to look after.

Ahead was a break in the rolling dunes, and there was the mouth of the Murray, the current flowing strong and clear through a deep but narrow channel – a ridiculously small outlet for such a river.

Barker's knoll was gone, washed away in some great storm, and it was said that the whole mouth had moved considerably under the influence of the prevailing south-westerlies. Here, where Sir John Younghusband had perished in the surf while trying to prove that the mouth was navigable, there had afterwards been a signal station and in the early days many paddle-steamers had dodged in and out when wind and tide were right; and many others had been wrecked.

Delie looked across at the terraced bank of sand that seemed so close. Should she attempt the swim? Perhaps it would be a foolish thing to do, for a woman past sixty, but it was the sort of gesture that appealed to her. She still had that romantic, Byronic streak.

And if the current proved too strong and she was washed out into the boiling surf to drown, wouldn't that be a fitting end to her long journeying? From the sea to the mountains, and finally back to the sea . . .

She shook herself impatiently and turned away. Some sensible maternal ancestor overcame the romantic Celt who lived within her breast. She laughed at herself a little; she had no reason to want to die. She had what she had longed for in vain for so many years: solitude and time to be alone with her thoughts, to track down the elusive ideas which are so often lost in the stress of living, as a half-remembered dream is lost in the flood of waking impressions.

No, she was not lonely. She had a small cottage on the river-bank, away from the town and the busy barrage works, which she had found too noisy after her quiet life on the river. Though that, she admitted, was not the real reason for leaving her home of forty years. It was Brenny's marriage which had decided her, the need to leave the young people alone and also the need to get away from Mavis.

'How could he? How could he?' she had thought when he first brought Mavis home. She lived over a shop in the main street of the town; she had never been out of Goolwa in her life and had never opened a book since she left school. Local gossip, local news filled her small mind; her face was thin and narrow and there was a backbiting meanness in some of her comments which suggested a shrew in the making. She was not even attractive, Delie had wailed, talking to Alex over the telephone – for the boys insisted that she should have a telephone if she was going to live alone. Alex had laughed and said the chemistry of attraction was a complicated one and that possibly the well-formed Brenny found something wildly desirable in Mavis's skimpy charms. It was not *that* she had meant; it was that Brenny could want anyone without any mental or spiritual graces. She felt as she had when Brenton went off with that hard-faced girl at the river shanty. And she was forced to admit now that there was a coarseness of fibre in Brenny which was alien to her own nature. She was far happier alone in her cottage, now that Gordon had gone off to the army.

The house was hers and she had legally settled the rights of the *Philadelphia* on the three boys; Meg had taken her share in money when she married. Alex, who had a good income and had not contributed anything to the upkeep for some years, gave his share to the others. That left Brenny in possession and Mavis was busy making it 'homey' with lace curtains, Genoa-velvet sofas, embroidered table-runners and flights of stiff ceramic ducks. At first she had made suggestions, tried to direct Mavis's taste, but at last was glad to give up and leave her in possession. She had never been strongly attached to things.

Now she went up to the sandhills again and lay back on the soft sand, letting her eyes wander along the great lonely curve of beach, disappearing into the haze of white spume and spindrift blown shoreward from the roaring waves.

There was a core of stillness in this unending noise, just as there was a ghost of unrest wafted far inland, on tranquil nights of summer, by the distant sound of the surf. Stillness breathed out from the quiet lakes behind, from the ninety miles of land-locked sea in the Coorong and the endless jumbled sandhills given over to the death-adder and the black snake, to tussock grass and seabirds' cries.

This was the place she had come to find. Like the Old Woman, that legendary lubra of King Charlie's story long ago, who had made the Murray River with her stick and her magic snake, she had come to the end of her journey; this was her spiritual home, this wild and empty shore. In the boom of the surf and the changing phases of the wind she seemed to hear, mindless and eternal, the voice of the Old Woman singing in her sleep.

ONE HUNDRED AND SIX

With a feeling of high adventure, Delie took a plane to go and visit Meg, one which landed at Mildura and from which she would take a bus to Wentworth, where Ogden would meet her in the utility. It was a long way round, but still quicker than travelling all the way by road.

Before leaving she set everything in order, put names and prices on the backs of her last completed paintings (for now that her name was established she had no trouble in selling her pictures to dealers, but preferred to keep them by her as long as possible) and wrote a letter to Gordon.

His letters from training camp were cheerful. He seemed actually to be enjoying military life, as he said all the details of living were decided for you and that left the mind free while the body followed an unthinking routine. He had not seen any fighting yet, but Delie felt illogically sure that he would come safely through the war, just as she was illogically convinced that the plane would crash on her first flight.

They took off before dawn in the grey half-light, while Delie gripped the seat-arms and broke out in a cold sweat, as she mentally took a last farewell of the beautiful earth. Then, incredibly, after the strain of take-off and climb they were effortlessly airborne. She felt herself relax, looking out at a great stratocumulus cloud ahead which caught the light in a glow of softest pink. Then they were in the heart of the cloud, in a glowing pink cotton-wool world with the grey blur of the propellers cutting through it, enclosed in a blue, moving cave of air – miraculous!

She felt her heart shaken with beauty and tears starting to her eyes. At more than sixty! Oh, she was not ready to die yet.

They crossed the river somewhere near Mannum, she thought, pressing so hard against the glass that her forehead hurt. She traced the dark green snake on its sinuous course to the south and the distant pale gleam of the Lakes. When they picked it up again beyond Renmark, the willows had been left behind and there was only the milky jade of the river winding through its flood-plain and on every bend a spit of clean yellow sand.

This was the view the eagles had, when she'd watched them circling high above the steamer on hot afternoons. If only this vibration in the glass would stop, how wonderful flying would be! But already the noise was giving her a headache. She was glad to come down and transfer to a bus.

She had been looking forward particularly to seeing Vicki, but she was not prepared for the beauty of young Charley, who in eighteen months had grown from a rather repulsive scrap to a dimpled, golden-haired perfection, with Ogden's rather ordinary brown eyes transformed by lashes like a film-star's and the finest of pencilled brows.

Delie stopped looking at him with an effort and turned to hug Vicki, who was watching with a jealous alertness. It was easy to guess who was her mother's favourite. Vicki was to start school in the new year, travelling by school bus, and Meg said in an undertone that this would be a relief because she had become rather difficult and something of a 'problem child'; but all her problems had been revealed in that unguarded childish look: was Grandma, too, going to fall for the newcomer's charms?

Delie tucked her hand through her arm, after kissing Meg and Charley, and finally turned her back on them.

'You must come and show me *everything*,' she said to Vicki. They went off happily together. In Vicki's company she regained something of lost childhood, seeing with the eyes that had been hers sixty years ago.

Meg was full of the news of Alex's engagement, to a woman doctor who had gone through her course at the same university, but several years later than he had.

'They will inevitably produce little doctors, I suppose,' said Delie rather dryly. 'I never know in these cases whether it is heredity, example, or parental pressure; though with Alex there may have been an inherited leaning towards medicine from his grandfather. He certainly wasn't influenced by me or his father.'

She was really quite pleased that Alex should marry a woman who was independent, with a career of her own. Why then did she feel this prickle of hostility towards the unknown fiancée? Partly, perhaps, because she dreaded all the fuss, meeting the parents who, she felt sure, would expect a big and fashionable wedding.

Alex was by now an excellent match, a leading surgeon in the city, respected, well-to-do and making a name as a connoisseur of painting. He was in demand as an opener of art-shows, the kind of smart gathering for sherry and gossip which Delie despised. (He had insisted on buying several of her paintings for his waiting-room.)

Delie had shocked Meg and Alex by refusing to buy a hat for the opening, when she had last held a one-man show in Adelaide, and going along in her old flat-heeled shoes, the hair grey and wispy on her blue coat-collar and her hands thrust defensively into her pockets; but the whole rather drab effect had been redeemed, she felt, by a hand-woven silk scarf from India in brilliant, clashing colours.

Now she would be expected to dress up as the bridegroom's mother, in some silly hat with flowers and veiling. She had lived alone too long and social life bored her. She decided to have a convenient illness as soon as the date was fixed. She would send Anne a really nice present to make up for her absence.

During the year the engagement lasted, Alex brought Doctor Anne down to see her a few times and the two of them talked 'shop' a good deal, which Delie preferred to small-talk even when it became technical. Anne spoke rapidly and vivaciously, but she was not a good listener; she liked to hold the floor and Alex was too infatuated to mind. Delie wondered how long after their marriage he would begin to assert himself.

Anne was very fair, plump-faced, with those slightly prominent teeth which give an off-beat charm to some faces. Her figure was sturdy, her hands were large and well-cared-for, with very clean nails cut sensibly short. How would she get on, Delie wondered, with her sister-in-law Mavis, whose dingy talons were disguised with chipped and purplish varnish? Anne's pale, observant blue eyes would notice them at once.

Mavis was not improved by pregnancy and she already had a second baby on the way. Delie began to be bored with the role of grandmother, the fourth was not the same as the first and she did not intend to make her home a crèche for Brenny's children

Firmly and tactfully she had refused to mind little Keith while Mavis was 'under the weather'.

When the news of Pearl Harbor burst upon them, Delie had little idea that it would affect her personally, except that the United States of America coming in would help to shorten the war. Then Gordon wrote to say that he was going north to do a course of training in jungle-fighting in Queensland.

He came home for final leave at Christmas and told her that his unit was going north against the Japanese in their rapid southward march through Malaya. He had done well in the army and had his commission as a lieutenant. Delie looked with unwilling pride at the tall khaki figure – she hated war and the military machine, uniforms and regimentation – but he did look very smart and handsome. She stood on tiptoe to kiss him and stroked the short brown hair at the back of his neck.

She smiled and sighed, thinking of his birth in Melbourne and her foolish pride in her achievement – 'My son'. Millions upon millions of women had achieved the same and millions had seen them go to war.

'I had a sort of feeling about the Japanese,' she said. 'I believe they've been planning this for a long time and they're fanatical and well-trained. Do you think they'll get as far as Australia?'

'Never. We won't let them.'

'But so many of our men are away in the Middle East.'

'They'll have to be brought home. But the Japs will never get to Singapore.'

Delie was touched when he asked for her photograph to take with him, the one taken in Echuca when she was just past twenty. 'I always loved that picture as a kid,' said Gordon. 'I used to think you looked like a princess.'

There was an air of decision about him, his blue eyes had lost their dreamy vagueness, though he hadn't been in the army long enough to have developed a military carriage. It was just Gordon dressed up in a uniform, not Lieutenant Edwards home on final leave, Delie told herself.

She went to the station to see him off, after he had been across to the Public Works Department house now provided for Brenny as married quarters. He there met Mavis and his two nephews for the first time; but 'That Keith's a little tiger', was his only comment.

Delie stood close beside him, biting her lip as she waited for the train to go. All over the world, she told herself, mothers are saying good-bye to their sons as they go to war. You are only one of them. You mustn't cry; Gordon hates a fuss. If only this train would hurry up and go!

At last it went. A khaki arm waved until it was out of sight. Two months later came the fall of Singapore and Gordon disappeared into the limbo of the Japanese advance.

ONE HUNDRED AND SEVEN

One night Delie woke from a vivid dream. She saw a clearing with bright red soil, coconut palms, thatch-roofed huts and a blue sky. In the dream she wondered what she was doing there, when she saw Gordon coming towards her, dressed only in a pair of khaki shorts.

He greeted her casually. 'Did you bring the paints?' he asked.

'Paints? What paints?'

'You know, I asked you to get me some paints of my own.'

'Oh, I forgot! It's so nice to see you again.'

He linked his arm in hers and led her towards a long, low building with open sides. When they got there it turned into a big shop and she bought him a set of oil-paints in a wooden box.

'Gee, thanks, Mum!' he said and suddenly they were back on the *Philadelphia*, the boys were small again and Brenton was saying testily: 'What does he want with paints? That sort of thing is only for girls.'

When she woke the dream was still so real that once again she wondered where she was. What was this strange small room with a big window, through which she could just make out a sloping bank of limestone, some stunted grass? She looked out and saw beyond the road, the strip of samphire flat and shrubs beside the river and then the wide expanse of the Goolwa channel, dark and calm beneath the stars. Shaped like a cross of sacrifice, the Southern Cross hung low above the water and was reflected in sharp white points from its glassy surface. Yet the night was filled with a faint thunder of pounding surf. It was like the muted sound of distant guns. She lay and listened to it, but the sound did not disturb her. She was more than ever certain that Gordon was alive, a prisoner of war somewhere in Malaya. She remembered how she had bought him a box of oil-paints on his twelfth birthday, thinking she detected a promise of talent in his chalk and pencil sketches; but he had not persevered, his interest failing under Brenton's scorn and his brothers' jeers.

When Mavis came to visit her, bringing the two boys whose continuous running about on the bare wooden floors she found hard to bear, she was full of well-meant sympathy over Gordon.

'I think you're so brave,' she said in her thin, nasal voice. 'I'd go stark mad if one of my boys was lost, I would really.'

'Gordon is not lost,' said Delie sharply. 'He is only missing. As soon as the prisoners of war have been traced we will have news of him.'

'Well, I only hope you're right,' said Mavis in a tone which suggested she was wrong.

But the news did come at last, and Delie was right. Captain Gordon Edwards was a prisoner of the Japanese in Changi camp, Singapore. It was the first Delie knew of his promotion.

Meg wrote joyfully about the news and added some of her own. Ogden had been promoted, they were to move to Renmark in South Australia where he was to replace the retiring Lockmaster. He still had a slight limp from his accident, but declared that it was well worthwhile since it had brought him a wife. The children were thriving, Vicki was doing well at school but would have more competition at Renmark, which was a good thing. Ogden sent his love . . .

If only Gordon were free, Delie thought, she would be perfectly content. But no letters came from him, and it was rumoured that no parcels got through.

The war spread south to New Guinea and the ocean named the Pacific became the site of bloody battles. Darwin was bombed and strafed. For the first time Australia heard the sound of enemy fire, though no enemy had set foot on its soil.

The thunder of the Goolwa surf began to sound more than ever like distant guns. Walking by the river's edge, unable to sleep on a night of strong wind that set the river lapping in the reeds (they had grown just as Gordon predicted), Delie saw a late moon rise through sculptured clouds. It was yellow, distorted into the shape of a Japanese paper lantern and against its lurid glow the reeds tossed their curving blades like a thousand Samurai swords.

617

The victorious Ninth Division came home from the Middle East and was thrown almost immediately into the breach; and men who had parched in the desert, washing in a pint of water, ironically greeted the endless rain, the stinking mud and stifling growth of the jungle.

In what came to be known as 'the American occupation', General MacArthur had arrived in Australia with his troops. G.I. uniforms filled the cities, gob-caps lined the wharves and the man-starved girls went wild with delight. So did hotel-keepers, brothel-owners and taxi-drivers who'd never had a chance to acquire so many American dollars before.

Now the flood which seemed to have set inexorably southwards was stemmed, was turned and began to flow in the other direction. Island after island was re-taken by the U.S. Marines and the A.I.F., and the Australians stubbornly pushed the Japanese back to the coast of New Guinea, in the face of fanatical Banzai charges, ambushes and booby-traps.

'The bastards are like mad animals, you can't think of them as men,' said an invalided soldier, gaunt with malaria and dysentery, who had known Gordon in Queensland. 'After a while we were shooting them like mad dogs,' he said. 'We stopped taking prisoners after some of the things they did to our blokes.'

Delie felt a sick fear go through her. Gordon was in the hands of these 'wild beasts'. But there was the Geneva Convention, there were international agreements . . . but did Japan subscribe?

When VE day came in Europe and for many millions the war was over, she planted a Christmas Bush on the river-bank to commemorate it; but for Australians and Americans it was only a stepping-stone to the final victory in the Pacific, now made certain.

For Delie the VP rejoicings, when they came, were hollow; not just that the world now had the atom bomb on its conscience, though she had heard the Bible sententiously quoted to justify it. She felt depressed, uneasy. Yet nothing prepared her for the shock of the news, when the official notification came that Gordon was dead, 'of disease'.

It was only later, when eye-witnesses of his end had been found to give evidence against Japanese war criminals, that she learned he had been ceremoniously beheaded by a Japanese officer, for 'refusing to co-operate'. He had refused to order sick men out to work in the tropic sun, in fact had ordered them not to go and then taken the responsibility himself.

Delie was dazed and unbelieving; she felt she should have known, at the instant of his death, by some perception outside the senses, given to mothers when flesh of their flesh was being destroyed. And perhaps she had had some precognition or warning on the night when the reeds were like swords and she had felt such restlessness and unease.

Meg asked her to go and stay, but she refused; Brenny and Mavis offered to come and live with her, but she refused even more firmly. Alex came down to see her and, alarmed by his mother's apathy and loss of weight – for she said she 'couldn't be bothered' to cook just for herself – insisted that she should get a girl from the town to come in each morning and get her breakfast and midday meal.

Delie sat long hours by the big window and brooded, looking out at the river She went over Gordon's life in her mind, remembering him as a little golden-haired boy afraid of his swimming lessons, fighting with Brenny, learning to read and write on deck in the mornings. How had she failed him? Why had he been a drifter? Finally the war had seemed a solution to him and he had thrown his life away just as surely as if he had jumped from a building. He had scarcely even seen any fighting, but had gone almost straight into prison camp and died there.

As the terrible stories came out, first of the horrors of Belsen and Auschwitz, then of the Burma-Siam railway and the Japanese camps where no Red Cross parcels arrived and men starved on a diet of boiled rice and were driven out to work with their legs eaten to the bone by tropical ulcers – as she read the fearful indictments her mind was curdled with horror and her imaginings of Gordon's suffering, and his pain in seeing the others suffer, kept her awake night after night. For the first time in her life she began to take drugs to make her sleep.

She thought she would like to be back on the *Philadelphia*, in a moving world which always soothed her senses; but Brenny was now running her under contract to the Engineering & Water Supply Department, engaged in dredging and clearing sluicegates in the Pompoota and Wellington area where irrigation by simple gravity-flow was possible. The boat would be full of a male crew and all she could apply for would be a job as cook. No, she must stay in one place, and be thankful for the river at her door, moving and flowing.

From where she lived the barrage was invisible round the bend, though she could watch the ferry chugging across to Hindmarsh

619

Island from the Goolwa landing.

The hull of a barge was rotting just above water on the bank below and further downstream the old *Cadell* lay on the mud, leaning at a dangerous angle into the deep channel. The spokes of her steering-wheel stood out starkly against the sky, for the roof of the wheel-house was gone; but her name still showed up bravely, commemorating the pioneer skipper of the *Lady Augusta*.

Still further towards the town, the proud *Captain Sturt* was aground, her bottom filled with cement so that she could not move. Her big stern paddle-wheel no longer turned; week-end visitors came aboard and enjoyed the novelty of sleeping on a paddle-steamer, for she was now a relic, an anachronism.

Walking between the walls of reeds that grew higher every year, Delie kept a lookout for snakes in the swampy ground on either side. This was the sort of country tiger-snakes liked to haunt. There was a small crescent of grey sand still clear of growth where she used to swim in the mornings.

She looked up towards the lakes, and then back towards the little house which perched on the edge of what was the true bank of the Murray, a hundred yards from where she stood. As she looked her heart almost stopped, for a lean figure in khaki shorts, with brown, scarred legs and an old A.I.F. slouch-hat on the back of his head, was leaning on the gate into her property. She hurried as fast as her short and laboured breathing would let her, noting that the stranger held a leather folder under his arm.

'Good day – Mrs Edwards, is it?' He spoke with a rich Australian drawl, a Queenslander by the sound of him. 'Burns is the name – Mick Burns.'

'Yes, yes – please come in.' Her voice and her hands were trembling as she fumbled at the catch on the gate.

'You knew Gordon, is that it?'

'I was in Changi with him; one of the best blokes I ever knew,' he said simply. They went into the house. Delie began flurriedly trying to get a kettle on, dropping the matches as she tried to light the kerosene stove, spilling the tea-leaves from her shaking hands.

'Let's just have a yarn, shall we, and we can have a cuppa later,' said the man. Mick Burns was thin and hard-bitten, with some extra understanding engraved on a face that underneath was still youthful. She was reminded in some way of Garry Melville, though this man had the bony nose of a hawk, set slightly crooked, which gave a twist of humour to his long face.

'I saw him die,' he said quietly. 'He never flinched. We were

620

all paraded to watch. The Nips were proud of their skill with the sword; it was quick and clean.'

Delie bit her lips and stared out the window.

'Before – before he went, he asked me to try and smuggle some stuff out for him. I couldn't get it out of the camp, but I hid it and here it is. He used to draw and paint a lot, y'know.'

Unbelievingly, Delie received the scraps of paper, the backs of old cartons, the opened-out envelopes, even pieces of wood on which Gordon had worked. They were only sketches, but full of life and feeling – a man helping his mate along, both of them living skeletons with great holes in their legs; a dying man on a stretcher, a corner of the hospital, a portrait of the commandant, small and arrogant – 'All he got was a clip across the mug for doing that one, though the bastard ordered him to do it. He didn't think it was flattering enough,' said Mick Burns. She looked at a view of the camp painted on the back of her own photograph.

'But they're good!' said Delie. 'Where did he get the colours?'

'You'd be surprised. Crushed up weeds for green, white clay, charcoal, ochre from the earth, anything. He was ingenious, old Gordon. His sketches amused the men; sometimes they asked him to do a portrait of them before they died. We hadn't much time for officers up there, on the whole – some of them just bludged and didn't care what happened to the men. But Captain Edwards – he never threw his rank at you – was one of the mob. We all liked him. But this little animal of a commandant hated his guts, because he wouldn't kow-tow. He had it in for him from the beginning.'

Delie stared at the sheaf of paintings and drawings through a blur of tears. They brought home the war for her as nothing else had done. And Gordon *did* have talent, if he'd only used it – was it her fault, had she been too absorbed with her own painting to help him realise it?

She blamed herself, but she saw what she could do for him now. She would paint a series of canvases from these small sketches – the essentials of colour and form were all there – and they would speak for him and his mates and be a cry against war from beyond the grave.

'Let's have that cup of tea, shall we?' she said, and smiled. 'I can never be grateful enough to you for saving these.'

ONE HUNDRED AND EIGHT

Delie was taken out of herself and began painting again with
new vigour. She was now sixty-seven, with only three more years
to her 'allotted span' and she wanted to fill them with work. She
had made a modest name for herself, her paintings hung in every
big gallery in Australia, but she wanted to do something new.
No more heroic figures, huge canvases and wide prospects: a
snake's shed skin beside the road, a burnt stump, a few buttercups
in the cleft of limestone – she could look at these until they
became charged with symbolic meaning and her mind reeled
with the power of that vision. To make others see it too – that
was the labour and the task for which she had been training her
hand and eye for fifty years:

> To see a World in a Grain of Sand,
> And a Heaven in a Wild Flower.

And then, ironically, just when she was beginning to see how
it might be done, she was stricken by an invisible blight, a tiny
floating virus which attacked her weakest point, her chest. 'Virus
pneumonia,' said the doctor, as her temperature soared and her
hands became icy with a cold rigor.

She was taken to hospital semi-conscious, but she did not die.
She believed it was because her will and her spirit were against
death, but the doctors, jabbing needles painfully into her arms,
said it was due to the discovery of penicillin, a mould with
miraculous powers against disease.

Why should a virus destroy, mindlessly, not inimically, and why
should a mould preserve, without volition, this life which was
our most precious possession, she wondered as she convalesced.
Once more she was impressed by the utter randomness of existence. Uncomprehendingly we went through life, surrounded by
worlds unrealised. And time was under all: the tooth that gnawed,
the stream that flowed irreversible and endless.

Delie came back to the cottage on the river-bank, refusing with quiet obstinacy her children's insistence that she should live with them, or have someone to live with her.

'I can get on perfectly well,' she said, 'with Doreen's help, and I must have some time alone every day.' (Doreen was the plump, cheerful girl from the town, with a gap-toothed smile, who came in the mornings and cooked her lunch.)

She did not admit how weak she felt: drained of energy, lethargic, too weak to walk even as far as the river's edge. She looked at the old *Cadell*, clinging precariously to life with her decks canted over the deep channel.

'All the old steamers is goin',' she heard an old man say.

Delie looked at a half-finished canvas she had been working on when she was taken ill. She had tried to go on with it when she was semi-delirious and it had no meaning for her now. She was too tired to begin something new. Her wrists and knees ached and her back began to stoop; the muscles would no longer hold it straight.

After a while she realised that it was not just tiredness, there was something else wrong. Her joints became red and swollen, and the pain was like a continuous toothache. She sent for Alex to come and see her.

He felt her wrists and fingers, the painful, swollen knees and took her temperature; he swore softly.

'Rheumatoid arthritis,' he said, 'in the infective stage. It can go on like this for a year or two.'

'And then I'll be better?'

He looked down. 'You'd rather know, I suppose. I mean, I know what painting means to you, Mum. But by the time the infection dies down, you may be permanently crippled.' Delie looked down at her hands and tried to imagine them twisted and bent until they could no longer hold a brush.

A semi-trained nurse came to look after her, a big, hard-faced, bullying woman whom Delie disliked on sight. But she cooked like an angel and massaged the aching joints with her big hands and brought hot-water-bottles and aspirin just when they were needed, until Delie began to depend on her like a child.

Alex came to say he was going overseas, for post-graduate work at Edinburgh University. He wanted to specialise in plastic surgery on returned airmen, R.A.F. men who'd had half their faces burnt away or were hideously scarred and maimed. Delie brightened up as soon as he came, her eyes, grey with weariness

623

and pain, became blue again and shone with almost their old light. But he noted professionally how they had sunk into their hollows, how thin the cheeks were and the arms she extended to him, the hands with suspicious thickenings at the wrist and knuckles.

She lay most of the day on a couch under the big window, where she could see the river gliding past. She saw almost no one but the nurse, the girl Doreen who still came 'to tidy up', and occasionally Mavis and the children. Brenny was busy converting the *Philadelphia*, putting in a new boiler from another steamer he had bought, with some idea of running trippers across the lakes. Just like his father, she thought . . .

Alex had not brought Anne with him, she had just had a baby and it was a long drive from the city.

'How many grandchildren have I now?' said Delie gaily. 'There are Brenny's four and Meg's two, and this is your second – eight, is it? I can hardly remember all their names. What are you calling him?'

'You should be able to remember it, it's fairly unusual: Alastair.'

'Alastair!' She was silent, staring at him. How much had he known or noticed as a child? 'What made you call him that?'

Alex shrugged. 'It was Anne's idea. She got it from a book.'

Delie lay back on her pillows, lost in a day-dream. 'What a beautiful face!' Alastair was saying. 'You'll still be beautiful, I'll still love you madly when you're eighty-two.' Beautiful! Oh, Alastair, if you could see me now! Her first ball: 'You have no need to wear forget-me-nots, Miss Gordon. Your eyes are far bluer, and no one who has seen them could ever forget them.' And Adam: 'Delie, you're so lovely, so sweet. You are like a white moth –' Then Brenton, and Ben . . .

'It's funny, they all began with A or B,' she said, smiling at Alex, while two great tears formed in her sunken eyes. He smiled and patted her hot hand. Her temperature was up, and her mind was wandering a little.

He left instructions with the local doctor that he was to try every possible cure, including gold injections, and he would bear the cost. He didn't like leaving his mother, but Meg and Brenny were here and her constitution was sound. This thing was an aftermath of the virus pneumonia, he suspected, and Gordon's death had something to do with it, in the queer way these things had of manifesting themselves by physical symptoms, which doctors did not yet understand. He left a prescription for some sedatives with Delie and told her that, with all the new advances of medicine, old-fashioned aspirin would probably help her as much as anything.

Her courage kept her going for a while, but after a year in which she lived with the pain, dozed and woke and dozed and always woke to the same nagging ache, for the first time she longed to die. It was not that the pain was unbearable, she had suffered far worse in her life; but it was unending. If only it would stop for an hour, for a day, if she could wake once and find herself free! But it was like an iron cage in which she seemed bound for the rest of her life.

ONE HUNDRED AND NINE

The small car came bumping along the corrugated limestone road, hesitated, stopped at her gate; went past, came back and turned in, up over the hump that was the true bank of the river and came to rest in the shade of a sugar-gum.

Delie's breath almost stopped. She rarely had visitors and strangers worried her, now that she felt herself to be an unsightly wreck of womanhood. She moved her stiff knees uneasily under the rug. Every morning and every afternoon she got off the couch and walked with her stick once around the house, out of the front door and in at the back, for fortunately there were no steps. And every day she used her hands a little, knitting clumsily at odd scraps of wool or cotton, turning them into pot-holders.

A smart young woman was getting out of the car. She had short, sleek brown hair and slim brown legs without stockings; her sandals were so flimsy that she might as well have been barefoot.

'Nurse!' Delie called in the voice that was now hers, a thin, querulous imitation of what it had been. The semi-trained nurse who lived with her now came in and straightened her rug, picked up her ball of wool; then the back door crashed open and a gay young voice cried:

'Grandma!'

Delie dropped the wool on the floor again and opened her arms.

'Vicki!' she cried, her voice suddenly strong and joyful. 'How did you get – '

'And the trees have grown so much I didn't know the place. Soon you won't be able to see the river.'

Vicki was sitting on the floor, her happy face close to her grandmother's, her brown eyes glowing. 'How did I get here? You'd never guess! I've been transferred from Melbourne, the *Herald* wants me to do a year over here and my first job is to interview my illustrious grandmother!'

'Stop pulling my leg and be serious.'

'I'm not, it is! Don't you know you'll be seventy next week? It's an occasion in Australian art.'

'I'll bet you put them up to it, you wicked child.'

'Well, I did say that Melbourne wanted something and when they teletype it to Melbourne they'll think the idea originated this end. So, shoot!'

'What?'

'Say something, like "What I think of modern art".'

'There's no such thing.'

'Good, that's a beginning. Now – '

In half an hour Vicki had several pages of unreadable scrawl on loose pieces of copy-paper and Delie was wondering uneasily what she had said. She loved to have Vicki near her, she seemed to receive a transfusion of blood from those young veins.

'Let me interview you now,' she said. 'What are you proposing to do after you've finished your cadetship, Miss Southwell? Get married?'

Vicki wrinkled her straight nose. 'Lord, no! I don't intend to get married for ages – if at all.' Delie smiled tolerantly. 'I'm going to the Continent and to London, soon as I can. When I've paid off the car I'll sell it and a girl-friend and I know a cheap boat to Naples and from there we'll hitch-hike round Europe and see England in the spring.'

'England in the spring ... You know, I don't feel any yearning for that, I must have left it too early. But I do envy you Italy. You do that, Vicki.' She put out her hand in what would have been in impulsive gesture, but the bones were too stiff. Vicki's warm young hand met hers half-way. 'You go, whatever happens. Don't get married instead.'

626

'But I've told you –'

'Yes, I know,' said Delie, and smiled the superior smile of age and wisdom. 'You see, I don't want to be a great-grandmother yet. I find very young children tire me out. I don't know which is worse – their yells of distress when they are unhappy, or the terrible noise they make when they're enjoying themselves. Listen!'

She held up a hand for silence and Vicki turned her eyes away. Against the lighted window showed a skinny, twisted claw, the bones contorted until the fingers rested against the wrists, every knuckle bent like the boughs of a wind-writhen tree.

'Listen!' With an effort Delie turned her head, now permanently poked forward on her neck, until she could look out the window. 'Can you hear it?'

Faintly, in the pauses of the southerly breeze, came the low, booming roar of the breakers. 'That is the loudest sound I appreciate these days. Sound that is only just within the bounds of hearing – yet they tell me I am getting deaf. I'm only deaf to voices, because they tire me. Mavis goes on in that loud whine and after a while I can't hear a thing she says. It's just noise.'

'That's one of the compensations of age. You don't have to hear what you don't want to.'

'And how's your mother?'

'Awfully well. She dotes on Charley, of course, a great lump of twelve! You know she's doing some nursing again at the Renmark Hospital, now she's got him more or less off her hands?'

'She's very good about writing to me when I can't reply. Meg was always a good correspondent.' Delie looked down at her hands, lying on the rug. 'I can't hold a paint-brush, much less a pen. I tried for a while with the brushes strapped on my wrists – like Renoir, you know – but I was too clumsy and it made my arms and shoulders ache. Alex told me to keep doing something, so I knit.'

'I'll look him up in London. D'you think he'll ever come back?'

'I hope so, before I die.'

'That won't be for a long time yet, Grandma.'

She looked hard at Vicki. 'I'm afraid you may be right. I've lived too long already, you know. I remember telling myself once that if I couldn't skip when I was seventy I'd be better dead. The aborigines were more realistic: they used to just knock old people on the head, when they couldn't keep up on the march. Much more humane than keeping them alive with drugs – to drag out a useless existence – a half-life with the senses dulled and the blood kept moving with hot-water-bottles and liver injections and vitamin pills. Do you know what it costs to keep each of us alive? Enough to feed a dozen starving babies in Bengal.'

'Your senses aren't dulled, Grandma. You're more lively than half the people who rush round playing tennis, like zombies from the neck up.'

'Ah, my dear, it's you who have brightened me up. Most of the time I'm half asleep, dozing over my memories; and then at night I lie awake and fancy I can hear the river flowing and feel myself dissolving and flowing out to meet the sea –' She did not add that she always kept a light burning beside her bed, as a kind of anchor to normality when she woke in the formless dark, in nameless, unreasoning terror.

'You'd like a cup of tea, I'm sure,' said the nurse heartily, coming in with a tray; and Vicki, who loathed tea, said politely that she would. After the tea her grandmother began to doze; her head fell further forward until it was lolling helplessly to one side; a small dribble of saliva fell from the corner of her wrinkled lips.

With all its animation gone, her face was like a mask of death. The skin lay close to the bone, the outline of skull and cheekbones and jawbones, the thin bridge of the nose, seemed ready to thrust through that covering, fine and dry as crinkled tissue-paper. Her closed eyes had sunk into the eye-sockets; but her eyebrows, still dark with a shadow of their old raven hue, her fine, sharp nostrils told Vicki that this was the same grandmother she remembered, pretty and round-cheeked and laughing, who used to take her for walks through the flowering scrub.

Impulsively she leaned over and touched one of the poor twisted, useless hands; it was ice cold, as though it had died in advance of the rest of the body. She crept away and told the nurse not to wake Mrs Edwards, but to tell her she would be down the following week-end. She let the car run quietly down the slope and out of the gate before starting the engine.

ONE HUNDRED AND TEN

The year of the Great Flood, as it came to be known, was 1956. It began with an announcement in May that the River Darling was unusually high, after torrential rains in Queensland. At Renmark, Ogden removed some stop-logs from the weir to let the level drop. But by the end of the month the reading at the wharf was twenty feet; and it was announced that ferries would probably be put out of action in the lower Murray.

This turned out to be a magnificent under-statement. Within a few days the approaches to the Morgan ferry were under water; a fortnight later Kingston and Walker's Flat were closed and water flowed over Angove's Road at Renmark. The official estimate there was for a maximum of twenty-five feet 'at the most'; but Ogden, looking anxiously at little signs which a life by the river had taught him, predicted twenty-eight feet, which would be disastrous.

By 30 June the Renmark reading stood at twenty-five feet, for the first time since 1931. The official estimate was now raised; water was running down Paringa Street. At Waikerie a dozen families had to be rescued from their homes on the river-flat and a high bank had been built round the pumping station. Lock Five had become an island in an immense sea.

The Darling, not hemmed in by cliffs and levee banks, surged out over the inland plains in a flood seventy miles wide; but still the muddy tide surged into the Murray and met a second flood from the upper reaches. In the lower river the settlers could only wait and watch, while every day the river grew and swelled like a living thing. They knew what was coming, and that nothing could stop it. The Swan Reach storekeeper, just in time, removed as many stores as possible from his shop beside the landing and left for higher ground. At Morgan the railway station went under water.

Now the vanished paddle-steamers began to be missed. The mail-contractor from Wentworth to Renmark, his usual route cut by the flood-waters, had to travel in an enormous arc south

629

of the river, crossing by the railway bridge at Renmark, a journey of four hundred miles.

The water spilled into the main street of Mannum, flowing through the shacks and houses on the riverward side. All along the lower Murray came the slow inexorable rise, as if the water welled up from some underground fountain and would never cease. There was no swirling, destroying torrent.

The Blanchetown Lock was now out of sight and above Waikerie the river spread over the countryside for miles – soon the snow-water from the Murrumbidgee and then from the Victorian highlands would be sweeping down the already glutted Murray.

Renmark was in a state of emergency, with the army helping to fight the flood. Scoops and tractors and bulldozers and hundreds of voluntary workers, with two thousand bags of mud, built up the levee banks and closed the breaches. Tired men patrolled the banks all night, watching for weak patches, flashing their hurricane lanterns and calling by portable radio for help.

The first casualty of the flood was a school friend of Charley Southwell's, who left on his bike to ride across the Paringa Street railway-line and was never seen again. Meg, terrified, lectured Charley about being careful; but she felt that the river had perhaps demanded a human sacrifice and now would be appeased – a fanciful notion she would never have entertained in normal times, for she was a practical person, but long hours of night duty in the strange world of the hospital, now an island completely surrounded by floodwaters, had made her light-headed. The banks built across the lawns were expected to hold a rise of thirty feet; if the river went higher they would have to evacuate the patients.

But in the middle of the night on 11 August the bank broke and the patients were removed by ferry. Men worked frantically to repair the breach, but the bank finally caved in two days later and the Hale Street levees were abandoned in the early hours. The river had won; vines, pumping stations, homes were inundated, but without more loss of life, though one thousand five hundred people had to flee.

By now the figures on all the gauges were submerged and extra sticks had been added. Steady rain began to fall in Renmark and the last bank broke on 22 August. It was the end of a vain fight against a flood too big to be controlled.

Now the drama was removed to the lower river, where the fight still went on to save the rich grazing-flats and the riverside homes. At Berri, Cadell, Murray Bridge and Wellington the banks were built higher and higher, until standing on the swamp side of a levee-bank was a frightening experience – a wall of water ten feet in height towered above, held back by sandbags and mud.

Most of the swamps were defended, hopelessly, but always after the long battle the river won. Quietly, inexorably it rose and rose and, like a giant reptile with an insatiable hunger, it swallowed more and more, until homes and shops and dairy farms, orangeries and vineyards and orchards, all were engulfed by the flood. It rose to the first-floor balcony of the Mannum Hotel, lapping at the words 'Beer and Wines'; it killed the orchard trees and drowned the vines. Haystacks and sheds and dead sheep and cattle and uprooted trees went floating down-river, with a few other nameless shapes which had once been human beings.

Every tree whose top still showed above the water was the home of thousands of living creatures, engaged in a fierce battle for survival like the remaining swamp creatures at the end of a drought; but here conditions were reversed and everything tried to escape the water.

Spiders, scorpions, centipedes and snakes swarmed poisonously on every high point, preying on each other when they could find no other food. Like a war, the turmoil of the flood washed out the hidden evils under the smiling surface of life. Nature's cruel law, 'Eat or be eaten', became more apparent along the whole length of the river valley as the waters reached their peak.

But once the banks had broken, the river seemed to spread out, with a great sigh of triumph, over the wide flat plains about the Lakes. It was shallow, no longer dangerous, and the daily trains to Melbourne ploughed through a foot of water over the line for months, until the crews hardly noticed it. The orchardists went out in rowing-boats to prune the trees beginning to appear above the sinking water; and looking down, one Berri farmer saw his peach trees trying to flower while still submerged. Thousands more were dead and thousands of acres of vineyard were ruined by salt, but life would go on once more.

The *Philadelphia* and Brenny enjoyed the flood, standing by with the *Industry* at Renmark in the worst of the emergency and helping to ferry marooned townspeople when the Paringa bridge closed.

At Goolwa, the old *Captain Sturt* sat gallantly on the bottom, while the flood swirled through her lower decks, wreathing weed and debris round the table-legs. Her owners retired to the top deck which was perfectly dry.

But Delie looked out one morning, when the water was already lapping at the limestone ridge inside her front gate, and saw with a sudden catch of breath that the old *Cadell* was gone at last. Gone! She had slipped over the edge into the deep channel during the night.

She lay thinking about the *Philadelphia* and wondering what her end would be: a quick death, holed and sunk by a hidden snag; burning and sinking in deep water; or rotting slowly on the bank, unwanted and unused? No one but Brenny would keep her going, but she might become a houseboat eventually.

She had followed all the accounts of the flood with great interest, as one by one each of the well-known ports along the river became submerged. She read the paper eagerly every morning, holding it close to her weak eyes. With the self-centredness of the aged, she was not unduly worried by the suffering and loss involved in the flood. 'It's all these banks and barrages,' she muttered. 'I knew the Murray wouldn't like it.'

She read aloud one morning: 'Henry Morgan, aged sixty, was drowned yesterday while trying to save his furniture,' and added: 'Nurse, my bowels didn't work yesterday. You'd better give me a pill.'

Later, she read: 'As the waters go down, houses are collapsing as though trodden on by a giant . . .' 'Trodden on by a giant.' That's good, a very good phrase. Vicki might have written that.'

She began musing about her son far away in England. Alex had been home once to see her, but she found him changed, rather pompous, very much the successful surgeon. ('He's been there too long, and got Pommified,' she said to Brenny. 'Even his voice . . .')

Brenny came to tell her that young Keith was going to swim in the Olympic Games in Melbourne in December, but all she said was: 'Is he, dear? You were pretty good as a youngster, but your father was the best swimmer I've ever seen.' She realised that Brenny was bursting with pride over his son, but to her Keith was too much like his mother to be interesting. She was sure he couldn't swim as well as Brenton did in the old days. Nothing was quite as good as in the old days.

ONE HUNDRED AND ELEVEN

After breakfast the telephone rang, something so unusual that it set Delie's heart beating painfully. 'Who is it? What do they want? she kept calling irritably to the nurse until she hung up.

'Now dear, don't get so excited,' said the nurse equably. 'It was your granddaughter – '

'Vicki! Why didn't you let me speak to her, you fool woman?'

The nurse was used by now to her patients' crankiness and did not let it upset her. 'She's coming down to see you, and show you her new car. She wondered if we might go for a little drive.'

'A drive! I don't know. It takes me so long to get in and out,' muttered Delie. 'I don't know, I suppose we might – '

She went on discussing the idea with herself. While Vicki was driving the sixty miles from the city she came round to the idea and was looking forward to it; in fact she was getting impatient with waiting.

The flood-waters had gone down, leaving a grey scum of silt clinging to fences and tree-trunks, but the river was once more flowing tamely in its bed. Delie herself had reached what seemed to her the incredible age of seventy-nine. She dozed off briefly on her couch – for she insisted on getting up from her bed every day. Once more she was back on the farm a thousand miles upstream, swimming with Miss Barrett in the swift, clear, snow-fed current, and the young blood coursed through her veins. She let her water go and felt its human warmth mingle with the cold current and be swept away . . . It was night, and she was wading into that silky coolness while the stars were reflected on the river's calm breast, and somewhere from the deeps of sky came the far, faint, musical call of the black swans going over.

She woke to find herself lying in a steam and reek of ammonia. She had wet the bed but there was a waterproof sheet beneath her always now. She could still walk with help, and every day in summer she went as far as the edge of the river. She heard a rhythmic beat, becoming louder. Was it her own heart? No, a white superstructure swam into sight, and she heard the gentle chuff of steam. They were in the schoolroom, she and Adam, and the first paddle-steamer they had ever seen was coming past . . .

Suddenly alert, Delie struggled to sit up and looked out at the Goolwa Channel and saw that a real steamer was passing. It was a rare sight these days. She called Miss Bates to look, to help her stand, and watched the ripples of the passing stranger reach the bank.

Just then a smart red roadster appeared in the road, and turned in at her gate. Vicki tooted and waved.

'Look, Grandma!' she called through the window. 'It's a Chevrolet, second-hand but isn't it smart? And it rides beautifully. Are you coming for a drive?'

'Yes, if Miss Bates will only get me ready. I thought you would never get here.'

She had decided where she wanted to be driven; to Victor Harbour, to look at the sea, tame and landlocked, and then to Port Elliott to watch the great southern surges breaking on the granite rocks. 'And I want to have a swim.'

'A swim!' The two younger women stared at her and at each other.

'I've still got my costume. And I want a swim in the sea.'

'In the *sea*!'

'Stop repeating everything I say like a couple of parrots! You heard me – I want to have a last swim in the sea. I'll probably never get out of the house again. You might call it a – a last request.'

'Grandma!' Vicki touched her cold hand with her young, warm one. 'Of course you can have a swim. Can't she, Miss Bates?'

'Well, I wouldn't like to take the responsibility. But if you say so.'

'I do.' She fetched the old, faded navy costume from where it hung on a hook behind the bathroom door. 'Just a dip, of course. You'll find the water too cold to stay in long.' Together they got the poor thin body into the costume, which hung upon her bones.

Dressed in dry clothes and seated on a waterproof cushion in front of the car, with the two younger women each side of her, Delie became quite gay.

'I should have done this before!' she cried. 'It's lovely to be out.' The low shape of Hindmarsh Island across the channel was pale gold with summer grass, and the old limestone buildings, the Customs House and the Court-house, slept in the sun under a pale blue sky. The wide channel reflected the flawless sky and the green of the thick reeds which had grown since the barrage was built. Brenny used to come down and clear them away from her little beach and landing.

It was strange, mused Delie, that she had now lived almost as long as a widow as all the first part of her life up to Brenton's death. Yet lately the years seemed to flow past in a formless mass, as the fence-posts were now whizzing past along the side of the road. Once, when she was a child, a year had seemed to extend forever into a golden mist of distance. Time was all relative. Already this day had stretched beyond its normal span because she was doing something different. She saw her whole life painted in vivid scenes on an opened scroll.

The car stopped. The scroll rolled together, all its pictures lost . . . 'Here we are!' said Miss Bates.

Vicki had driven right on to the grassy verge, the Council lawns beside the sheltered inner beach of the Harbour. It was not allowed, no doubt, but she had simply ignored notices and parked as close as she could get to the smooth, gently sloping, firm sand where the waves broke in a gentle rhythm; withdrew, returned, and withdrew once more.

With some difficulty they got her out of her blouse and skirt and, wrapped in a towelling cloak, down to the water's edge. Nurse Bates took the gown, and Vicki, tucking up her skirt, took Delie's weight as she stepped on her thin white legs into the clear salt water.

It was only a foot deep, but it was delicious, so clean and sparkling. 'Do you know that your mother never saw the sea till she was ten or twelve years old?' said Delie. 'I took her down to Glenelg, I think it was – beautiful white sand –'

'There's a sewage treatment works there now,' said Vicki, 'and the beach is covered with weed and sea-lettuce, and the sand is all washing away.

'I don't want to hear about it. Now let me down gently – on my knees. There! Just leave me like that.'

She turned her faded blue eyes up to the blessed sun. A rocky breakwater beyond prevented her from seeing the horizon. The shallow water was warm, for the tide was coming in over sun-warmed sand. A small wave broke just beyond, slapped against her thighs. Another followed. She felt the sand sucking out beneath her knees as the wave receded. She waited for the next, facing the sea, that old lover: accepting its ancient rhythm, the swing, surge, suck of the waves.

It was life, not death, though the sea meant the end of the river's winding way. Body, identity, memory would be lost, dissolved in the great ocean of the unconscious from which new streams would rise.

Time like an ever-rolling stream, Bears all its sons away . . . That was the hymn they used to sing at home, and long ago she had knelt beside her mother on a little red hassock in Church, and before that, bright and perfect, the moss came out in one piece from between the bricks and lay like a strip of green velvet on her childish palm . . .

The glitter of sun on water turned to a bright vision of snow. Each crystal threw a tiny blue shadow in the level light, and from somewhere near at hand came a faint tinkling sound, ice-clear and musical as a bell. Once more she was high in the Australian Alps where a little stream, just born, moved invisibly beneath the snow; and all the rivers ran towards the sea.

THE BEST PLACE TO BE

by Helen Van Slyke

Sheila Callahan had everything she wanted — comfort, security and a marriage that had lasted for twenty-seven years. Then, one summer afternoon in a Cleveland suburb, everything changed. Suddenly all she has left of her husband is the memory of his overpowering and free-spending ways — she is on her own. But can she face the problems of self-reliance, or will the pressures of her family drag her down? Is it too late to start again — and does she have it in her to do so?

nt devant des égouttoirs pleins de
retenir pour ne pas les envoyer

une queue de cheval huileuse et
nerfs, mais je lui ai parlé du poème
btiliser la moitié d'un concombre

écrivain, hein?» a-t-il demandé. Il
ents de devant cassée et tachée de

u devrais lire Kerouac.

s.» Les hippies sur le retour étaient tou-
de me conseiller de lire Kerouac, mais
jamais été recommandé par quelqu'un
as l'air de s'être brûlé les neurones et
ne plein de toiles d'araignée. J'ai tout de
é la tête, engloutissant une tomate ita-
ux bouchées. Une fois, dans un manuel
ais lu un extrait des voyages de Magellan,
phe décrivant comment, alors qu'ils mou-
im, les membres de son équipage avaient
se nourrissant de fruits, de légumes et de
ui leur étaient absolument étrangers. Pour
ge aux poireaux, salade de roquette, les
émités des pains baguettes.

dit le cuisinier, vas-y mollo avec le gouda.

en guise de matelas. Le moteur roulait au neutre, les ventilateurs soufflaient un air chaud par les bouches d'aération. Je n'avais jamais été aussi heureux.

Pour éviter le froid, j'ai piqué vers le sud sur la I-95, à travers l'Idaho et l'Utah, avant de mettre le cap vers l'est sur la I-70. J'avais collé un calepin au tableau de bord et, en roulant, j'écrivais les étendues désertiques et les plateaux arides, les Rocheuses qui avaient pour compagnie un ciel plus large et plus vaste que ma foi en quoi que ce soit. Il haussait les pics dans sa lumière, en faisait de nouveaux monuments à chaque heure, puis les abandonnait à l'obscurité, raison pour quoi — songeais-je en m'efforçant de trouver le som-meil, les yeux levés vers les rochers escarpés qui se découpaient dans la lunette arrière à la lueur des étoiles — les montagnes, la nuit, sont chose solitaire.

Bercé par les vibrations du moteur, j'essayais d'en-trevoir ma vie. Je distinguais les lignes rouges que tra-çaient sur la carte les autoroutes s'étirant entre les villes comme les fils d'une étoffe déchirée. J'imaginais un livre qui pourrait tout contenir simultanément: plaines et chaînes de montagnes, villes couleur de poussière en retrait des autoroutes et, quelque part tout au bout, la vallée de Colombie-Britannique et ces nuits en Virginie où je partais en cachette sillonner la route en essayant de découvrir ma place sur ce conti-nent usé jusqu'à la corde. J'aurais voulu que tous ceux que je connaissais puissent voir le monde à travers mes yeux, chaque ami, chaque fille que j'avais jamais aimée: le gel étincelant sur les plaines sèches au lever du soleil, ou l'autoroute s'enfonçant entre les collines au contour arrondi avec la parfaite géométrie du désir. Ça me semblait péché d'être témoin de tout cela dans la solitude, une raison de croire en un dieu omniprésent.

Mais la solitude était l'épreuve qu'offrait ce paysage, ma vie ressemblait enfin à un roman de Steinbeck. L'autoroute donnait sur une terre solitaire, la destruction tranquille de maisons fatiguées, des milliers de milles d'une violente alchimie dissolvant un peuple brisé, le distillant jusqu'à ce qu'il ne reste plus que quelques résistants solitaires.

On prétendait que la vie d'écrivain était chaotique, destructrice et aventureuse, et j'avais l'impression qu'en choisissant cela sans cesse, une grande partie de ce que j'étais deviendrait acceptable.

Le message est venu par mon frère : mon père était dans une colère noire, je l'avais insulté, il ne voulait plus jamais m'adresser la parole, je ne devais plus rien attendre de sa part.

J'ai essayé de ne pas y penser. Plus je m'éloignais de sa vie, plus la mienne m'apparaissait nettement. Mais mon départ avait eu quelque chose d'extrême, et avait dû lui rappeler la trahison de ma mère. Je n'étais même pas certain de ce qui m'avait poussé à m'enfuir de la sorte — le désir d'être libre ou la volonté de prouver que j'en étais capable ? En m'efforçant de déterminer s'il l'avait mérité, j'ai songé à la façon dont il avait brisé notre famille. Tout ce qu'il avait construit

périlleuse ? En passa
vaisselle, j'ai dû me
valser par terre.

Le cuisinier ava
me tombait sur les
afin de pouvoir s
anglais.

« Tu veux être
avait une des d
nicotine.

« Ouais.

— Eh ben, t

— Si tu le d
jours en train
il ne m'avait
qui n'avait p
d'avoir le crâ
même hoch
lienne en d
scolaire, j'a
un paragra
raient de fa
survécu er
viandes q
moi : pot
dures ex

« Hé, a

peti
tures
Dicki
d'une
telle d
le chois

Le poè
rence à l'é
prix Pulitz
chose ; il s'
poème était
cal. Il décriva
des fils barbe
n'était pas cla
clôture, les bar
des lambeaux d
rythmes, j'avais é
crier, de dire au c
de continuer à lire
qu'avait éprouvée l'
de sa destruction, qu
le fil dégouttant / br
queté ».

Marmonnant les ve
l'école et roulé jusqu'au
la plonge. Comment est-
pouvais-je écrire la fébril

— Ouais, O.K. » J'ai attrapé la moitié d'une pomme de terre bouillie sur le comptoir et l'ai avalée dans la chambre réfrigérée, accompagnée d'olives noires pigées dans une barquette en plastique.

Le lendemain matin, j'ai demandé à ma professeure d'anglais si je devrais lire *Sur la route*.

« Toi ? a-t-elle dit. Non, tu ne devrais certainement pas lire *Sur la route*. La dernière chose dont tu aies besoin, c'est bien *Sur la route*. »

Je suis donc allé à la bibliothèque emprunter *Sur la route* et *Les clochards célestes*.

Cette fin de semaine là, j'ai lu les deux livres, assis sur le canapé chez un ami, sur la galerie, sous l'arbre, sur la table à pique-nique, me déplaçant souvent comme pour ne pas éveiller les soupçons. J'étais entré dans les pages : l'errance, les nuits de camaraderie, le flirt avec les femmes ; le sentiment d'innocence, l'espoir, la soif d'expériences. Même dans leurs fautes, les personnages restaient purs. Ils vivaient dans l'indéniable flot de l'existence.

Mais ce qui me renversait par-dessus tout, c'était le milieu ouvrier dont Kerouac était issu, la famille canadienne-française de Lowell, au Massachusetts, et la façon dont il s'en était affranchi. Il y avait en lui une attitude d'observateur, un manque de connexion, une absence de racines qui le privaient de force. Je ne pouvais m'empêcher de penser à la vie fracturée de mon père, au vide où il aspirait les autres. Et pourtant, je savais que c'était à cause de lui que j'aimais

Kerouac. Mon père avait vécu des aventures plus débridées, une existence plus désespérée, motivée par une insatisfaction plus grande que tout ce que Kerouac décrivait — un désir que je percevais quand il parlait de son passé, mais dont la source m'échappait. J'avais beau tenter de l'oublier, je savais que les histoires de mon père avaient été les premières à nourrir mon imagination, qu'elles m'avaient donné envie de voyager et que, quand je m'étais moi-même enfui sur la route, ces histoires étaient revenues hanter mes pérégrinations.

Aussitôt que j'ai eu fini les deux livres de Kerouac, j'ai dévoré *Orgueil et préjugés* en quatrième vitesse. Je l'avais emprunté de mauvaise grâce à ma professeure d'anglais afin d'obtenir des crédits supplémentaires, mais le roman m'a surpris. Contrairement à tant d'autres personnages de roman, Elizabeth Bennet semblait pleinement constituée. Sa rébellion émergeait avec fluidité des rouages de la société à laquelle elle appartenait. Je m'imaginais faire sa rencontre, mais sa famille m'aurait probablement engagé pour creuser un fossé, rien de plus. Un insupportable sentiment de solitude m'a broyé les couilles. Kerouac aussi, ai-je compris, aurait rêvé d'elle — il l'aurait aimée farouchement, même si, incapable de trouver sa place, il aurait fini par partir, ou bien elle l'aurait jeté dehors.

Tandis que j'étais en train de lire à la bibliothèque, Charlotte est venue me rejoindre et a poussé un répertoire des universités vers moi.

«As-tu commencé à regarder?» a-t-elle demandé.

Nous avions passé une fête ensemble et nous nous étions rapprochés, bien qu'elle refusât d'être autre chose qu'une amie, ce qui était sans doute sage compte tenu de la trajectoire plutôt erratique de ma vie. Depuis une semaine, elle insistait pour que je soumette une demande d'inscription à au moins une université.

«Choisis-en une. Tous les autres ont fait une demande.

— Nan», ai-je répondu, et je lui ai parlé de Kerouac voyageant sur le toit des wagons de train ou vivant seul dans une tour d'incendie pendant des mois, à écrire des livres.

Elle a levé les yeux au ciel. «Fais une demande, c'est tout. Tu n'es pas obligé d'y aller, mais tu auras le choix.»

Elle avait de longs cheveux auburn et un profil classique, et paraissait beaucoup trop bien pour moi, comme Elizabeth. Rebelle ou pas, Elizabeth aurait désiré qu'un homme possède au moins quelque instruction. Cette idée d'une caste étroite qui m'obligerait à écrire et à penser comme tout le monde m'horripilait, mais j'ai feuilleté le guide.

J'ai fini par dire: «Très bien, celle-là.» C'était l'université la plus étrange que j'avais pu trouver, la plus individualiste, un établissement au Vermont du nom de Marlboro College.

Dans le texte qu'il fallait joindre à la demande, j'ai décrit mon enfance, mon père voleur de banques et ma mère férue de sciences occultes, en exagérant peut-être un brin. Mais je n'avais pas la moindre intention d'y aller. Rien ne pourrait me donner davantage d'énergie que j'en avais déjà. Par moments, je me sentais presque extatique, l'exubérance m'emplissait les poumons à m'en faire éclater les côtes. À d'autres instants, c'était un virus dans mon sang, qui exigeait mouvement et expression. La vitesse à laquelle je gribouillais transformait les mots en hiéroglyphes. Je griffonnais sur des bouts de papier qui jonchaient mon auto, que je devais maintenant pousser avant qu'elle daigne démarrer, l'alternateur ayant rendu l'âme.

Après la fin des cours, j'ouvrais la portière et poussais la voiture, gagnant de la vitesse, après quoi je sautais à l'intérieur, passais en deuxième et lâchais la pédale d'embrayage. Le moteur rugissait et crachotait, et je sortais du stationnement sur les chapeaux de roues. Je conduisais vite, les vitres baissées ; une fois, tandis que je grimpais une longue montée, un coup de vent a emporté plusieurs bouts de papier. L'anxiété que m'a causée cette perte m'a étonné. J'éprouvais un sentiment que je n'avais jamais ressenti pour des êtres humains. J'aurais voulu arrêter et fouiller les broussailles au bord de la route, mais la voiture aurait pu caler et j'aurais été coincé. Enfonçant l'accélérateur, j'ai continué à rouler en pleurant mes vers perdus comme si je comprenais enfin que les gens et les lieux que nommaient ces mots n'étaient plus.

Le besoin, le désir, l'obsession — ce qui me poussait en avant — ne connaissaient pas de repos. Par les matins clairs, la vue des montagnes dans le lointain m'emplissait d'une telle soif que je passais devant l'école sans m'arrêter, pour errer de ville en ville ou bien faire du stop. Au moment de la collation des grades, j'avais pris la mesure de la puissance aliénante de cet élan.

Je vivais au bord d'une rivière sous une tente dôme dénichée dans la remorque à chevaux de ma mère et sous laquelle mon père, mon frère et moi avions déjà campé ; la toile était maintenant couverte de moisissures aux allures de taches de Rorschach. Le terrain appartenait à des amis de ma mère, la berge était isolée. Je me baignais nu et frottais mes vêtements salis par les travaux de construction.

Mes relevés de notes dépareillés s'étant avérés convaincants, j'avais été accepté à l'université, où l'on m'avait même offert une bourse. Les cours commençaient dans deux mois, mais il me semblait impossible d'y aller. Je ne disposais pas de la petite somme que ne couvrait pas l'aide financière, et j'avais des ennuis avec la police du coin, qui m'avait collé une amende pour avoir conduit sans vignette d'inspection, puis sans silencieux, et enfin pour ne pas m'être présenté devant le juge. Mon frère, qui avait mis mon père au courant que j'avais été accepté à l'université, m'avait transmis un message de sa part disant qu'il souhaitait me payer le voyage afin que je lui rende visite. Même si je haïssais mon boulot, il n'était pas question que je cède devant mon père.

J'ai ouvert la portière de ma voiture et me suis assis à l'intérieur. Les vêtements que je portais avaient séché sur une branche d'arbre et étaient aussi raides et rugueux qu'une peau d'animal. Je ne savais que faire. L'idée d'aller à l'université me répugnait, mais qu'y avait-il d'autre ?

Je regardais le ciel, le soleil scintillant à travers les feuilles. J'ai donné un coup de poing dans le pare-brise, qui s'est fendu. Le dommage irréparable a réveillé ma furie, et j'ai arraché le rétroviseur extérieur à coups de pied avant de marteler la portière. Saisissant une cruche en plastique contenant de l'essence, j'en ai aspergé la tente et j'y ai mis le feu. J'ai jeté la plus grande partie de mes possessions dans le brasier. Sans attendre qu'il ait fini de brûler, j'ai fait démarrer la voiture. Le moteur a pétaradé avec un bruit de *lowrider*. J'ai roulé à tombeau ouvert sur le sentier de tracteur qui traversait les bois, parcouru un kilomètre jusqu'à une longue entrée de gravier, puis continué jusqu'à une route de comté menant à l'autoroute. J'ai accéléré jusqu'à en faire trembler la voiture dont les vibrations claquaient à mes oreilles. Après une heure de ce régime, le moteur a émis un boum retentissant et je me suis laissé glisser sur l'accotement.

À l'arrivée de la dépanneuse, j'ai abandonné la voiture d'une signature. Plissant les paupières dans le soleil, je me suis efforcé d'échafauder un plan. Le conducteur de la dépanneuse rigolait ; par la fermeture éclair ouverte de sa salopette, on apercevait la toison noire de sa bedaine de bière sur laquelle il appuyait son bloc-notes pour inscrire son nom sur l'enregistrement.

J'ai fourré mes effets dans mon sac à dos et ai entrepris de me rendre en stop chez un ami habitant dans une commune ratée, communauté faite de déchets de dépotoir dont les murs étaient constitués de pots et de bouteilles enchâssés dans du mortier. Mais je savais que je ne pourrais pas vivre éternellement aux crochets des autres. J'avais fait tant de choses, et rien n'avait changé.

«Deni», a dit mon père quand j'ai fini par lui téléphoner à frais virés.

Combien de fois pourrais-je faire cela — continuer à m'enfuir?

«Où es-tu? a-t-il demandé d'un ton qu'il voulait débonnaire. J'ai entendu dire que tu avais été accepté à l'université.

— Ouais?

— Ouais. Alors, quand est-ce que ça commence?

— Dans deux mois. En septembre.»

Il est resté silencieux un moment. «Deux mois. Tu devrais venir me rendre visite d'abord. Tu vas être occupé quand tu vas commencer, pas vrai?

— Ouais, je ne sais pas. Je serai probablement occupé.»

Nous jouions le jeu. J'accepterais ce qu'il allait proposer, quels que soient les termes. Je ne voyais pas comment je pouvais me rendre à l'université à partir du point où j'étais, avec pour toutes possessions quelques vêtements de rechange et moins de cinquante dollars. Ma mère qui avait déjà peu pour elle-même ne pouvait m'aider. J'avais lutté pour me libérer de toute attache, pour m'éloigner le plus possible, jusqu'aux confins de la vie, et j'en étais là.

Le lendemain, en traversant de nouveau le pays, j'avais l'impression d'avoir trouvé une solution. Tandis que je faisais route vers l'ouest, les plaines s'ouvraient devant moi dans un grand déferlement de lumière, jusqu'à ce que la haute silhouette des Rocheuses dressées vers le ciel, scindant en deux le continent, m'avertisse du changement à venir.

LE DÉLUGE

Les commissures de ses lèvres s'étaient creusées, il avait des pattes d'oie au coin des yeux bien que sa chevelure noire ne présentât pas un fil blanc. Nous étions en train de souper ensemble, mais nous n'avions pas encore abordé les raisons pour lesquelles je m'étais enfui.

«Je me rappelle, une fois, je venais de dévaliser une banque. J'ai acheté une Thunderbird neuve avec l'argent et j'ai décidé de traverser le pays, mais j'ai fait monter un jeune gars en stop. Il n'avait sans doute pas dix-huit ans. On était au Nevada, et je lui ai demandé : "Combien de temps tu crois que ça prendra avant que le moteur explose si je pousse cette auto au maximum?" Il a ri et m'a mis au défi de le faire. J'étais encore pas mal déchaîné à l'époque. Tout ce qu'il me fallait, c'était un défi. Alors j'ai appuyé sur le champignon. On était dans le désert, il faisait chaud. Après environ une heure, le capot s'est soulevé. On aurait dit qu'on avait frappé une autre auto, mais c'était simplement le moteur qui sautait. La vapeur et la fumée giclaient de partout. On était comme ça au bord de la route quand un flic s'est pointé.»

Mon père souriait, et j'ai essayé de deviner ce qui avait pu lui faire penser à cette histoire.

«Ce flic, a-t-il repris, c'était un coriace. On voyait bien qu'il ne croyait pas que le moteur d'une Thunderbird toute neuve pouvait exploser sans raison. Alors il nous a dit: "L'un ou l'autre d'entre vous a-t-il déjà eu des ennuis avec la justice?" Et le gars de dix-huit ans répond: "Ouais." Il jouait au dur et voulait se payer la tête du flic, mais moi j'avais une valise pleine d'argent dans le coffre de l'auto. J'aurais voulu égorger le jeune. Le flic a fini par l'emmener dans sa voiture pour vérifier son dossier et il m'a déposé chez une entreprise de remorquage. Je me suis rendu compte à ce moment-là que je n'étais plus aussi déchaîné qu'avant. J'avais déjà été exactement comme ce garçon, mais j'avais changé.»

Il a hésité. «La jeunesse, c'est un peu ça. Il faut prendre des risques et se mettre les gens à dos.»

J'avais enfin compris. C'était sa façon de dire qu'il comprenait pourquoi j'étais parti. Nous n'aborderions jamais la question directement. Même si je ne m'identifiais pas au garçon et que je me montrais prudent avec la police, je comprenais la joie sauvage qu'il y a à faire rouler une voiture juste pour le plaisir de la voir sauter.

Il a poursuivi : «Au fait, je me disais qu'avant ton départ on devrait aller à la pêche.

— Ouais, peut-être.»

Il a baissé les yeux et a hoché la tête pour lui-même, sachant qu'il ne servait à rien de me rappeler l'enfant que j'avais été ou les choses que j'avais déjà aimées.

Poussé par ses encouragements, je me suis remis au kickboxing. L'entraîneur, un Irlandais de Terre-Neuve aux jambes arquées et dont les joues étaient sillonnées de capillaires éclatés, exhortait ses lutteurs à l'endurance, qu'il illustrait par des histoires de pêcheurs perdus dans le brouillard ou de mineurs prisonniers sous terre qui devaient se résoudre à boire leur propre urine. Dans le sac qu'il portait sur la hanche, il gardait un flacon d'antidouleurs.

«Hé, est-ce que je t'inscris à la compétition? m'a-t-il demandé, même si je n'étais de retour que depuis un mois.

— O.K. Enfin, tu penses que je suis prêt?» J'étais ravi par son enthousiasme, mais il a haussé les épaules et dit : «Pourquoi pas?» avant d'écrire mon nom.

L'été passait trop vite en journées ensoleillées et fraîches. À la mi-août, je n'étais toujours pas décidé. J'étais censé être bientôt au Vermont. Mon père et moi n'avions pas abordé la question de l'université depuis mon arrivée. Il m'avait redonné le VUS et me payait trop bien, me lançant des liasses de billets comme si de rien n'était. Trois ou quatre fois par semaine, nous soupions ensemble.

«Une compétition! s'est-il exclamé en se penchant vers l'avant. C'est quand?

— Dans quelques semaines, je pense.» Je ne voulais pas qu'il y assiste. J'étais heureux qu'il croie en moi, mais je connaissais la vérité. Frapper sur les autres ne me procurait pas de satisfaction particulière, alors que les meilleurs pugilistes de notre gym prenaient plaisir à cogner sur n'importe quoi. Et puis, je travaillais à un roman dystopique, une épopée de désintégration sociale, et souvent, après avoir écrit toute la nuit, j'arrivais à peine à m'entraîner.

«Je pense reporter mon entrée, lui ai-je dit pour changer de sujet.

— Qu'est-ce que ça veut dire?

— Ça veut dire que je retarderais d'une année.

— Retarder quoi?

— L'université.»

Il a haussé les sourcils. «Tu peux faire ça?

— Ouais. Et puis, je n'ai jamais eu l'intention d'y aller. Je peux écrire sans ça.»

Il a hoché la tête d'un air neutre, comme si c'était une conversation de peu d'importance.

«Tu sais, j'ai déjà lu un truc dans le journal sur un écrivain vraiment populaire qui n'était pas allé à l'école. Et puis, tu devrais être boxeur, et il y a cette compétition...

— Je ne serai peut-être même pas prêt, lui ai-je dit. Ce n'est pas une grosse affaire — juste un exercice.»

Il m'a étudié avant de détourner les yeux. Il avait compris et n'allait pas insister, sans doute satisfait maintenant que j'avais abandonné mes projets. Mais je ne l'avais pas fait pour la boxe et, en lui disant, je m'étais senti plein de froideur, malgré moi, comme si je ne pouvais risquer de partager avec lui ne serait-ce que mon incertitude, de crainte qu'il ne veuille m'imposer sa propre vision.

Plongé dans ses réflexions, les yeux au sol, il a repris : «Si tu as l'intention de rester quelque temps, tu voudras probablement un appartement à toi et un boulot qui paie mieux.

— J'imagine, ai-je répondu, surtout pour l'inciter à continuer.

— Je connais un gars qui a un appartement à louer, et il y a un boulot que je pourrais t'obtenir. Ce serait sans doute bien pour toi de faire des choses par toi-même. Tu veux ta liberté, non?»

Au cours des mois précédents, il avait fait allusion au fait que ses magasins battaient de l'aile. Croyait-il qu'il était préférable pour nous deux que je ne travaille pas pour lui, ou était-il en difficulté? J'essayais de voir quels bénéfices il retirerait de cette proposition, mais en vain. Quoi qu'il en soit, j'aimais l'idée d'avoir un appartement à moi, de m'éloigner de lui, de pouvoir lire et écrire tranquille. C'est ainsi que, une semaine plus tard, j'ai déménagé dans cet appartement et commencé le boulot qu'il m'avait trouvé dans une usine de transformation et d'emballage de produits de la mer, un immense rectangle au bord d'un canal juste en périphérie de Vancouver.

Mes journées commençaient à cinq heures du matin. Les bateaux arrivaient lentement, déchargeaient des caisses de morue sous des nuées de mouettes stridentes. Le soleil se levait derrière les portes de livraison tandis que les chariots élévateurs sillonnaient les salles où le poisson était transformé, l'air salin empuanti par des vapeurs de propane.

J'avais eu l'intention de mettre de l'argent de côté pour voyager, mais j'ai eu tôt fait de comprendre mon erreur. Le loyer et le véhicule grugeaient beaucoup d'argent, tandis que le boulot et l'entraînement me laissaient épuisé. La date d'admission à l'université est passée, la température fraîchissait, le soleil cédant la place à la pluie et, pour me prouver que j'avais pris la bonne décision, je me suis acheté un ordinateur d'occasion sur lequel j'écrivais tous les soirs. Plus j'écrivais, plus mes émotions me submergeaient et plus ma faim grandissait. Des scènes insignifiantes — un jeune homme quittant un nouvel ami — étaient pétries de chagrin, comme si j'étais en train de dire adieu à tous ceux que j'avais abandonnés. Mon estomac gargouillait et je vidais le frigo, me précipitant au supermarché à trois heures du matin pour y acheter du jus de pomme et d'orange, des blocs de cheddar, des pots de yogourt aux fraises, des pommes de terre en purée déshydratées, des emballages familiaux de surlonge.

«Qu'est-ce qui s'est passé?» a demandé mon entraî-. neur à la pesée avant la compétition. J'étais trop lourd d'une livre pour la catégorie dans laquelle j'étais inscrit. En voyant mon nom dans la colonne des poids lourds, il a pris le flacon de comprimés dans le sac qu'il portait à la hanche, a fait sauter le bouchon et en a avalé un.

J'avais passé la plus grande partie de la nuit à lire et maintenant j'étais assis, appuyé contre le mur en blocs de béton, en train de finir *Le meilleur des mondes*. Les boxeurs de mon club lançaient des œillades dans ma direction et secouaient la tête.

Quand mon tour est venu de monter dans le ring, un adolescent à la tignasse rousse qui se tenait près de moi m'a dit: «Ah, man, tu es tombé sur le métis. Fais attention à toi.»

Je n'avais pas beaucoup réfléchi au combat. Dès que j'ai eu déposé le livre, je me suis senti désorienté, puis l'indifférence m'a envahi, comme si rien de tout cela n'avait d'importance et que je ne faisais que tirer mon temps. Ce n'est que lorsque je suis monté dans le ring que j'ai senti un pincement d'inquiétude. Me dominant de près d'une tête, mon opposant était moitié chinois et moitié irlandais, si j'en jugeais par son nom de famille. En un instant, il était dans les airs, tournoyant, projetant son talon dans mon ventre. Il m'a asséné des coups répétés tandis que j'essayais de me ressaisir. J'ai calculé le moment où il toucherait terre et l'ai frappé dans les côtes, réussissant à le faire reculer, mais l'un de mes coups de pied a raté la cible et le côté de mon pied a frappé l'os de sa hanche. Une douleur soudaine et intense m'a traversé. J'ai reculé en boitillant, étonné de me trouver là. J'ai ressenti la douleur comme une vérité — j'aurais dû être ailleurs, je me fichais de ce combat —, comme si je ne pouvais apprendre le réel que par le désastre, ou quelque chose s'y apparentant.

«Tu as perdu», a constaté mon père d'une voix dépourvue d'expression, assis à table, les bras croisés. Quand j'avais téléphoné pour lui parler de mon pied, si enflé que j'avais du mal à enfiler mon soulier, il avait insisté pour que nous nous voyions sur-le-champ.

«Je ne sais pas quoi faire pour le boulot», ai-je dit en boitillant jusqu'à une chaise.

Il a braqué les yeux sur moi, voyant l'inquiétude sur mon visage et, pour la première fois depuis mon retour, son regard exprimait le dédain.

Il a craché : «Fais semblant de te blesser. C'est pour ça que je t'ai dit de venir ici plutôt que d'aller chez le docteur.

— Qu'est-ce que tu veux dire? ai-je demandé en m'efforçant de recouvrer mon impassibilité, gêné qu'il me voie dans cet état.

— Ce n'est pas clair? Va travailler lundi et fais semblant de te blesser. Comme ça, tu vas recevoir une allocation pour accident de travail.»

Je prenais de longues et profondes inspirations, me forçant à afficher un air d'indifférence, me disant que rien de tout cela n'avait d'importance, que j'étais capable d'encaisser. Mais quand j'ai repris la parole, l'émotion était revenue.

«Il faut que je passe la fin de semaine comme ça, ai-je dit.

— La belle affaire. Tout ce que tu fais, c'est écrire. Tu n'as pas besoin de marcher.» Il a eu un geste comme pour balayer mes objections du revers de la main, puis m'a expliqué comment frauder la Commission de santé et sécurité au travail. «Tout le monde le fait, a-t-il ajouté comme s'il m'offrait un joint. Je l'ai fait une fois quand je n'étais pas beaucoup plus vieux que toi. Je travaillais sur un site de construction, et je me suis écrabouillé le petit doigt avec une masse.

— Est-ce que ça a fait mal? ai-je demandé dans l'espoir de détourner l'attention de mon cas.

— Évidemment que ça a fait mal. J'essayais de briser l'os. On obtient toujours un congé plus long quand l'os est brisé, mais mon doigt n'a même pas cassé. La peau s'est simplement ouverte. On pouvait voir l'os tout entier. Ça faisait tellement mal que j'étais incapable de me résoudre à le frapper de nouveau.»

J'ai hoché la tête, réfléchissant à ce qu'il suggérait, me disant que c'était sans doute facile, même si je n'avais pas envie de lui obéir. Ça ne me semblait pas nécessaire.

«Mais si je me fais prendre? Les médecins ne peuvent pas savoir de quand date une blessure?

— C'est quoi, l'ostie de problème?» Il s'est penché plus près de moi pour m'examiner durement, relevant les commissures des lèvres. «Ce n'est qu'une égratignure. Avant, tu parlais de dévaliser des banques. Reviens-en.»

La serveuse est arrivée, il s'est reculé sur son siège, a souri, commandé des pâtes et du poulet. Quand elle est repartie en se déhanchant, les menus dans une main, il s'est de nouveau penché au-dessus de la table.

«Juste pour que tu le saches, m'a-t-il dit avec une colère qui exprimait l'étendue de la déception que je lui causais, je ne te ferai pas vivre. Tu veux écrire toute la journée, démerde-toi.»

J'ai haussé les épaules. «Il me reste assez d'argent pour m'en tirer pendant quelque temps.

— Fais un effort, câlice.» Il a agrippé la table comme s'il voulait la renverser. «Tu es mineur. Si tu te fais prendre, ton dossier va être effacé à tes dix-huit ans. Montre-moi que tu as des couilles.»

J'ai hoché la tête en me massant la joue. Ma défaite, le fait que je sois faible et le montre, que je ne sache pas encaisser, tout ça l'horripilait. Et ça m'horripilait aussi.

«Et comment je fais?» ai-je demandé doucement.

Il a secoué la tête. «Tu veux écrire des romans et tu n'es même pas foutu de tromper une bande de crétins. Ça devrait être facile.»

À l'horizon, une barre grise que faisaient onduler des vagues de nuages bas annonçait l'aube.

Je sentais mon sang battre dans mon pied à chaque pas, un coup sourd comme un clou émoussé frappant l'os. Toute la fin de semaine, j'avais écrit tandis que l'ecchymose rouge et noire s'étendait et maintenant, serrant les dents, je traversais le stationnement en m'efforçant de ne pas songer que je m'apprêtais à violer une loi mise en place pour de bonnes raisons. Dans mon roman, la société dystopique était le résultat de la cupidité et de la guerre, et mes actions ne me semblaient pas plus louables. Mais je ne pouvais me défiler maintenant sans donner l'impression que mes paroles n'avaient jamais été autre chose que du vent.

Chassant mes pensées, je me suis décidé. J'ai traversé l'entrepôt vide en n'existant que par mes sens : une bouffée d'air humide, le sifflement des boyaux d'arrosage et le vacarme des chariots de métal sur les drains du plancher, le poids de mes bottes en caoutchouc.

Et puis, brièvement, je me suis retrouvé seul dans le congélateur vaste comme un gymnase, sous les hautes étagères de métal. Bing, un maigre Chinois aux joues tachetées de brun et aux dents orange, était parti chercher le chariot élévateur et je devais empiler des boîtes sur une palette. J'ai jeté un coup d'œil aux alentours puis j'ai tendu les bras, tiré trois boîtes de l'étagère et me suis laissé tomber avec elles. Elles se sont ouvertes sur le béton, les blocs de crevettes congelées s'entrechoquant à l'intérieur. J'ai coincé mon pied entre les lattes de la palette et suis resté étendu à regarder le plafond loin au-dessus de ma tête et à m'efforcer de grimacer, même si je n'éprouvais que résignation, accomplissant cette tâche avec la même indifférence que le reste de mon travail.

« Qu'est-ce qu'il y a ? m'a demandé Bing aussitôt qu'il est descendu du chariot.

— Je me suis tordu le pied », lui ai-je dit en me tâtant la cheville.

Il a ri. « Lève-toi ! » Comme je ne lui obéissais pas, il a plissé le front et répété : « Lève-toi !

— Je ne suis pas capable ! » ai-je répondu en feignant l'inquiétude.

Il est parti au pas de course pour revenir avec le patron, un petit Chinois légèrement voûté qui observait tout avec des yeux aussi fixes et impénétrables que les objectifs d'une caméra de surveillance.

« Tu n'as rien, a-t-il aboyé.

— Non. Je me suis vraiment fait mal au pied.

— Non, tu n'as rien ! » a-t-il répété comme s'il scandait un slogan à une manifestation.

«Je ne suis pas capable de me relever.

— Oui, tu es capable.

— Non, je ne suis pas capable.»

Je pouvais voir qu'il ne me croyait pas, qu'il ne décelait ni choc ni douleur dans mon expression.

Le contremaître, un Canadien français au visage mince et aux yeux brun pâle, s'est avancé devant le petit groupe de ceux qui assistaient à la scène. «Montre-nous ton pied», a-t-il grommelé.

Les employés ont tendu le cou. Un immense Polonais barbu est venu se placer à l'arrière; il parlait de lui-même à la troisième personne et était souvent appelé quand venait le temps de transporter de lourdes charges. «Stan veut voir!» a-t-il annoncé.

Les Chinois devant lui ressemblaient à des enfants souriants aux dents tachées de Kool-Aid.

Avec précaution, j'ai enlevé ma botte de caoutchouc et j'ai ôté les trois paires de chaussettes que j'avais enfilées pour éviter les ampoules. J'avais l'impression que la peau distendue de mon pied allait fendre.

Le petit groupe y est allé de «oh» et de «ah». Ils parlaient chinois tous en même temps, à toute vitesse, montrant du doigt comme si les autres avaient pu rater quelque chose qu'eux-mêmes avaient vu.

Mon pied ressemblait au détail d'une photographie de scène de meurtre sur le bureau d'un détective ou à quelque chose qui pointe sous un drap dans une morgue. Les curieux se sont écartés, Stan s'est avancé et m'a aidé avec une délicatesse surprenante.

Aux urgences, l'anxiété faisait perler la sueur sur mon front. Le médecin verrait tout de suite que la blessure était vieille de deux jours. C'était un type dégingandé à la Al Pacino dont l'haleine empestait la menthe comme le souffle d'un adolescent qui rentre à la maison après avoir fumé en cachette. Il a palpé la peau tendue et émis un sifflement, puis s'est versé des Tic Tac dans la bouche et a failli s'étouffer avec.

«On va te faire passer une radiographie, a-t-il annoncé entre deux mastications. Tu ne pourras pas mettre de poids dessus pendant un moment.»

Les radiographies ne montraient pas d'os cassé, mais il m'a dit que les blessures aux tissus mous étaient parfois pires que les fractures. Je suis rentré en béquilles muni d'un rendez-vous en physiothérapie et bien déterminé à utiliser les prestations de la Commission de santé et sécurité au travail pour terminer mon premier vrai livre. Quand j'ai fait part de ce plan à mon père, au souper, il a baissé les yeux et soupiré.

«J'imagine que tu ne t'entraîneras pas.

— Je ne suis même pas censé marcher.»

Regardant par la fenêtre, il a demandé si je reprendrais l'entraînement quand mon pied serait guéri.

«Je ne sais pas. Je partirai peut-être en voyage, ou bien je vais juste écrire.»

Il a hoché la tête, mais je voyais à son expression qu'il reconnaissait son erreur.

Nuit après nuit, stores baissés, j'échafaudais ma vision de l'avenir, un monde militant purifié par un déluge de feu biblique, anéanti jusqu'à retrouver son état naturel, la civilisation ramenée à un niveau primal, une société matriarcale vivant dans des cavernes.

Je n'avais jamais été aussi heureux. La société oscillait continuellement entre la peur de la perte et le désir de changement, et je m'efforçais de comprendre ce que cela signifiait que de croire en ce monde. Mes méchants ne se préoccupaient que d'eux-mêmes, de leur satisfaction et de leur survie. Quand on croit le monde cruel et égoïste, il est facile de ne vivre que pour soi. Ça me rappelait le parc de maisons mobiles en Virginie, ou bien les moments passés avec Travis et Brad, quand nous complotions pour voler à l'étalage ou berner les autres, pour chaparder tout ce qui nous tombait sous la main. Le monde semblait un endroit primitif, indifférent sinon hostile, prêt à nous écraser, et on se contentait d'y faire notre place, impatients de sauter dans la mêlée, de voir jusqu'où on pouvait aller.

Je me prenais à me demander encore une fois d'où venait mon père, pourquoi il avait rejeté le Québec. Des années plus tôt, il m'avait raconté qu'il travaillait pour faire vivre sa famille quand il était jeune, ne gardant presque rien pour lui. Dans mon roman, le pire personnage se sentait trahi par tous ceux qu'il aimait. Était-ce un accident, ou bien un phénomène universel?

Chaque fois que je retrouvais mon père pour souper, je lui demandais s'il voulait lire ce que j'avais écrit, mais il secouait la tête et répondait: «Je ne lis pas de romans. Je ne connais pas grand-chose là-dedans.» Il demandait si je voulais aller à la pêche avant que la montaison du saumon prenne fin.

«Peut-être plus tard», disais-je.

J'ai fini le roman la veille de mon dix-huitième anniversaire et le lendemain, pour célébrer, je l'ai imprimé et l'ai lu. Peu avant de sortir rejoindre mon père, je l'ai jeté à la poubelle.

«Je vais voyager», lui ai-je annoncé dès que nous avons eu rempli nos assiettes au buffet. J'avais besoin de vivre davantage. Mon livre m'avait paru infantile et faux; il n'était pas marqué au sceau de l'expérience mais fourmillait de grandes idées qui ne m'avaient passionné qu'au moment où je les avais découvertes.

«Quand? a-t-il demandé.

— Peut-être après Noël. Je vais aller en Californie. Un de mes amis de l'école secondaire vit là-bas.»

Il a poussé le contenu de son assiette à coups de fourchette et a soupiré. Je m'attendais à de la rage ou de la dérision, mais il avait perdu le goût de se battre.

«Pourquoi on n'irait pas pêcher une dernière fois?»
a-t-il proposé. Les rides de son visage s'étaient creusées comme sous l'effet du chagrin. «La montaison du
saumon n'est pas encore finie. Autrefois, tu adorais la
pêche. C'était la chose que tu préférais. Tu me sup-
pliais de t'y emmener. On aurait cru que ce serait la
fin du monde si je ne le faisais pas.»

Ce souvenir de moi enfant était saisissant, et j'ai
hoché la tête, triste sans savoir pourquoi. Je ne pensais plus beaucoup à notre passé, ou à quoi que ce
soit hormis mes buts immédiats.

«D'accord, ai-je répondu. C'est une bonne idée. On
peut y aller avant mon départ.»

Il regardait au loin. «Tu sais, je ne regrette pas de
travailler avec les poissons. Ils ont quelque chose
de spécial. J'ai toujours eu cette impression.»

La tendresse que trahissait sa voix m'a surpris, sa
tristesse, et je me suis rappelé ce que les poissons évo-
quaient pour moi quand j'étais enfant, leur mystère.

«Je ne sais pas comment l'expliquer, m'a-t-il dit. Je
ne suis pas écrivain. Je sais seulement que j'ai toujours
aimé l'eau. Quand j'étais jeune, j'étais capable de dire
où il y avait du poisson.

Rendu mal à l'aise par la manière dont il parlait et
souhaitant ramener notre conversation à des aspects
simples et concrets, j'ai demandé : «Pêchais-tu à la
ligne à l'époque?»

Il a baissé les yeux, hésité. «Non, surtout au filet. Plus vieux, j'ai commencé à pêcher à la ligne. Mais ce n'était pas pour l'argent. C'était simplement pour être dans la nature.

— Personne ne pêchait à la ligne quand tu étais petit?

— Bien sûr, mais la plupart d'entre nous utilisaient des filets.» Son regard s'est voilé, se perdant dans le lointain comme lorsqu'il s'apprêtait à raconter une histoire, et j'ai été soulagé de voir le chagrin quitter son visage.

«On avait une petite chaloupe en bois, a-t-il commencé, et je partais avec mon père sur le Saint-Laurent. Je n'oublierai jamais la fois où, alors qu'on venait juste de jeter l'ancre, on a vu deux énormes ailerons fendre l'eau — les plus gros ailerons que j'avais jamais vus. Tous les deux ont tourné au même moment. On aurait dit qu'ils appartenaient au même poisson. Ils fonçaient droit sur nous. C'est dur à croire, mais deux énormes poissons noir et blanc se sont mis à sauter par-dessus la chaloupe. Je portais un chandail des Canadiens rouge et mon père savait que les poissons sont souvent attirés par la couleur rouge. On pouvait même attraper certains poissons juste en attachant une ficelle rouge à un hameçon. Il m'a poussé au fond de la chaloupe et a commencé à donner des coups de rame. Mais aussitôt que j'ai cessé d'être visible, ils sont partis. Ce devait être en 1946, autour de là. Mon père pêchait dans le Saint-Laurent depuis qu'il était enfant, mais il n'avait jamais rien vu de la sorte. Des rumeurs voulaient que le bateau d'un pêcheur disparu plus haut sur la côte avait été rejeté sur le rivage, des dents pointues fichées dans le bois. »

Il a baissé les yeux et transpercé de sa fourchette des morceaux de brocoli frit.

« Un journaliste est venu nous voir après, et le journal a publié un article là-dessus. On nous a dit que les poissons étaient des *épaulards**. Des années plus tard, j'ai vu une photo du même poisson, mais quand je me suis renseigné à leur sujet, le livre disait qu'on en trouvait rarement dans le Saint-Laurent. Une fois, à Stanley Park, j'ai demandé à une femme à l'aquarium, et elle m'a dit qu'il arrivait que les épaulards s'écartent de leur territoire habituel et deviennent agressifs s'ils n'ont pas suffisamment à manger. »

Il a pris une bouchée, et poussé lentement sa nourriture dans son assiette.

Les épaulards m'intéressaient moins que mon grand-père, dont j'ignorais le nom. Quand j'étais enfant, dans les histoires que racontait mon père sur son village, il était toujours question de bagarres, de beuveries et de religion. Je m'imaginais des cabanes penchées et délavées par les éléments vues depuis les vagues d'une mer venteuse, ou bien des hommes à l'église, chacun tenant une chope mousseuse. Mon père avait décrit un bar où, pour un verre, un dur du coin sautait et frappait le plafond bas de ses deux pieds, laissant une trace de bottes noire sur les lattes. Je levais les yeux vers notre propre plafond, essayant de me figurer un moyen de faire la même chose.

J'ai demandé : «Pourquoi tu es parti?

— Quoi?

— Du Québec. Pourquoi tu n'y es jamais retourné?

— Il n'y a rien pour moi là-bas.

— Mais tu y as toujours de la famille, n'est-ce pas?»

Il a fait un geste de la main. «Ça fait trop longtemps que je suis parti.

— Mais justement, pourquoi es-tu parti?

— C'était arriéré. L'Église contrôlait tout. Les curés gardaient les gens dans la pauvreté.

— Tu penses que c'est toujours comme ça?

— Non. Ça a changé. Mais je n'ai rien à retrouver là-bas.»

Je me suis rappelé une chose que j'avais lue à l'époque où je vivais en Virginie. Je devais rédiger un compte rendu pour le cours d'histoire et j'avais choisi le Canada en me disant que ce serait facile. J'avais étudié les *coureurs des bois**, ces trappeurs intrépides qui défiaient les lois réglementant le commerce de la fourrure et vivaient dans la forêt. Le livre expliquait que, comme la population canadienne-française était dans les premiers temps majoritairement composée d'hommes, les mariages avec les Indiennes étaient fréquents.

«Penses-tu qu'on a du sang indien? ai-je demandé.

434

— Quoi?» Il a levé les yeux de la nourriture qu'il triturait plus qu'il ne la mangeait. Quand je lui ai dit ce que j'avais lu, il a laissé tomber : «Je ne crois pas que ce soit vrai.» Il a soulevé son verre d'eau, qu'il a vidé d'un trait avant de reposer le verre embué et de soupirer, la peau de sa gorge pendant tandis qu'il baissait le menton.

«Les vieilles générations, c'était du monde fait fort. Tu ne peux pas comprendre. La vie a été facile pour toi. Quand les hivers étaient durs, les hommes devaient quitter femme et enfants en leur laissant la nourriture et ils prenaient le bois, où ils vivaient avec rien d'autre que leurs fusils et leurs outils. Ils chassaient et trouvaient des moyens de survivre. Comme ça, ils n'enlevaient rien à leur famille.»

J'allais l'interroger sur mon grand-père, mais il regardait derrière moi, au-delà du buffet, plissant les yeux comme s'il essayait de distinguer quelque chose. Je me suis retourné. Au-dessus de la porte de la cuisine, un panneau de plastique montrait un cochon de bande dessinée se vautrant dans la nourriture : *Prenez ce que vous pouvez manger, et mangez ce que vous prenez.*

Il a secoué la tête.

«Qu'est-ce qu'il y a? ai-je demandé.

— Il y avait le même crisse de panneau en prison.» Il a repoussé son assiette en renversant du riz sur la table. «Si les gens paient, ça ne devrait pas être là.»

Sans me regarder, il s'est levé et est parti.

Quand j'avais six ans, à une époque où ses affaires étaient en plein essor, il m'avait dit qu'un homme qui lui devait de l'argent avait accepté de lui donner tout ce que nous désirions dans sa maison.

«Ça va être comme d'aller magasiner sans avoir à payer», nous avait-il expliqué.

Il avait exposé le plan. Nous emporterions des boîtes de carton dans la maison, et mon frère et moi pillerions la chambre du fils de l'homme tandis que mon père se chargerait de la cuisine et du salon. Ma mère avait refusé de venir.

«Ce n'est pas bien», l'avais-je entendue lui dire.

Toutes les maisons de la rue étaient beaucoup plus récentes que la nôtre. Mon père avait frappé fort et tourné la poignée, ouvrant la porte et demandant d'une voix enjouée, comme s'il arrivait chez un bon copain : «Y a quelqu'un?

— Salut, André», avait dit l'homme d'une voix fatiguée. À l'exception d'un duvet couleur carotte, il était chauve, et se tenait le dos voûté, mains dans les poches. «Vas-y. Prends ce que tu veux.»

Mon père avait parcouru la cuisine en déposant quelques casseroles dans sa boîte. Il avait attrapé une lampe et commenté : «Hé, elle est pas mal!» Debout dans un coin, l'homme l'observait. Je sentais une volonté de l'humilier dans la manière dont mon père rejetait ses possessions. Il avait tâté une paire de mitaines de four et émis un bruit nasal pour indiquer qu'elles ne l'intéressaient pas. Il ouvrait des tiroirs et ne prenait pas la peine de les refermer.

«Allez en haut, nous avait dit mon père, à mon frère et moi. Prenez ce que vous voulez.»

J'aurais voulu que ce soit là l'une de nos folles aventures, mais je savais qu'il n'en était rien, qu'il aurait été mal de rire. Mon frère et moi avons monté l'escalier et hésité sur le seuil. Les étagères et le plancher étaient couverts de jouets, et un gros garçon roux au visage plein de taches de son nous barrait la route, les bras croisés.

Il avait crié: «Entrez pas dans ma chambre!» mais son père avait monté les marches quatre à quatre et l'avait saisi par le coude pour le traîner dans le corridor.

Mon frère et moi étions entrés et avions rempli notre boîte de G.I. Joe, de figurines de *La guerre des étoiles,* et des plus récents Gobots. Les trésors dont on chantait les louanges à la télé étaient enfin à notre portée. Nous avions tout pris et étions sortis rejoindre mon père qui empilait des boîtes dans le camion où il avait déjà chargé une table de billard miniature. Le petit garçon était assis dans les marches, le regard lointain, et j'avais compris ce qu'il devait éprouver.

J'avais sorti un Gobot de la boîte et le lui avait tendu.

Il avait étudié la figurine carrée que je tenais à la main avant de planter son regard dans le mien.

«Garde-le, ostie de frog!»

Je ne savais pas ce qu'il voulait dire mais je reconnaissais dans cette insulte une intention plus profonde, plus directe que celle exprimée par un simple sacre.

Des années plus tard, après que ma mère a eu laissé mon père, durant notre première semaine d'école en Virginie, mon institutrice de cinquième année nous avait annoncé que nous allions regarder une vidéo sur le racisme.

Elle avait fait rouler la télé devant la classe et glissé une cassette dans le magnétoscope. Le narrateur racontait l'histoire d'un quartier où anglophones et francophones ne s'aimaient guère. On voyait les vies de deux petits garçons, un de chaque culture, et à un moment le francophone, avec sa bande d'amis, sautait sur l'anglophone et lui volait son argent alors qu'il traversait une ruelle.

«You frog!» disait l'anglophone.

Quand la vidéo s'était terminée, tous les yeux étaient braqués sur moi. Je savais que j'allais avoir des ennuis dès qu'elle avait commencé. Dans une école où Noirs et Blancs se battaient dans les corridors, il semblait étrange que la vidéo traite des rapports entre Canadiens anglais et français. L'institutrice avait voulu montrer aux autres d'où je venais, et maintenant elle me demandait ce que j'en avais pensé. «Ça n'a pas été facile de trouver une vidéo sur le Canada, s'exclamait-elle, mais j'ai finalement réussi!»

Comme je ne répondais pas, elle avait ajouté : «Tu ne veux rien dire?

— Non.»

Plus tard, dans la cour de récréation, un groupe de garçons s'étaient avancés vers moi, les épaules tendues vers l'avant, les poings levés à mi-hauteur, comme s'ils se préparaient à donner des coups.

«Hé, frog!» avait crié l'un d'eux, puis il avait hésité. «Es-tu un frog?

— Non.» J'essayais de penser rapidement. «Les frogs viennent d'ailleurs.

— Oh», avait dit le garçon, dont la déception était manifeste.

Après le souper de mon dix-huitième anniversaire, j'étais incapable d'arrêter de songer aux omissions de mon père. D'où venait-il? Qu'avait-il laissé derrière lui? Je ne voulais plus d'histoires de prison ou de récits sur son ambition de réaliser un gros coup pour pouvoir jeter la somme sur la table de jeu de quelque casino; je voulais entendre ces souvenirs fugaces et voilés de la vie qu'il avait fuie.

L'autoroute sinuait au-delà de nos phares, suivant la montagne. En roulant vers Squamish, il m'a raconté que ma mère et lui avaient déjà vécu là, dans une cabane près de la rivière. Il avait fabriqué des amphétamines et avait défait une couture de sa veste pour y glisser un échantillon. En route vers Vancouver où il devait le livrer, il s'était rendu compte qu'il était suivi par la police. Il s'était arrêté dans un garage, avait peint sa camionnette en vert à la va-vite puis s'était dépêché de rentrer, mais il était tombé sur un barrage routier sur l'autoroute.

«Ce flic, il avait le sens de l'humour. Il m'a demandé si j'avais bu. J'ai dit non, et puis il a dit : "J'aimais mieux votre camionnette en bleu. Passez une bonne journée." S'il ne m'avait pas mis la puce à l'oreille, je n'aurais peut-être pas agi si vite. Il m'a sauvé. J'avais mon labo et deux fusils. Ce soir-là, je suis allé dans le bois et j'ai tout enterré sous un arbre tombé. Le lendemain, la police m'a arrêté. On m'a gardé quelques jours, mais ils n'avaient pas de preuves. Quand ils m'ont relâché, l'officier qui m'a rendu mes effets a commencé à inspecter la boîte. Il s'est mis à palper les coutures de ma veste et je me suis rendu compte que j'avais oublié de sortir les amphétamines. J'ai fait semblant d'être furieux et j'ai crié : "Allez-vous me garder ici encore une journée ? Sacrez-moi patience ! Vous m'avez arrêté pour rien !" Le gars m'a regardé et il a dit : "O.K." Il a tout poussé sur le comptoir et m'a laissé reprendre mes affaires. Il avait été à quelques secondes de trouver les amphétamines.

— Penses-tu qu'on pourrait aller là où tu as enterré les fusils et les déterrer ?» ai-je demandé, fébrile à cette idée — l'équipée aurait marié deux vieilles passions : le crime et l'archéologie.

Il a hoché la tête sans quitter la route des yeux. «Ça fait vingt ans, mais j'avais tout emballé dans du plastique. Je serais peut-être capable de retrouver l'endroit. On pourra regarder plus tard aujourd'hui.»

Jusque-là, il avait le visage plissé de fatigue, la peau lâche, mais il s'est ragaillardi à la perspective de nous voir retrouver ses vieux fusils et son labo.

«Si on est capables de trouver la maison, a-t-il poursuivi, on pourra acheter une pelle à la quincaillerie.»

Nous avons suivi la route de gravier et nous nous sommes garés sur un remblai manifestement aménagé des années plus tôt pour empêcher la rivière en crue d'emporter les routes.

Debout dans la lumière des phares, nous avons fixé nos moulinets et passé les fils dans nos cannes. Il plissait les yeux, prenant son temps pour nouer l'hameçon, finissant bien après moi. En le voyant, je me suis rappelé une nuit au réservoir quand j'étais enfant, ses gestes tandis qu'il passait le fil. Il avait marmonné et tendu le bras par la fenêtre du camion, et les phares s'étaient allumés. Il s'était accroupi devant le pare-chocs, ses mains s'agitant dans le faisceau lumineux, des cicatrices sur les jointures, le bout de ses doigts épaté pinçant, tirant. Debout dans la lumière qui rejaillissait derrière lui, j'avais regardé mes propres mains, les paumes douces, le bout des doigts rose et rond, mes rares cicatrices pâles. Le souvenir m'a étonné par ce qu'il éveillait de sentiment de perte, l'impression que les années qui me séparaient de ce moment avaient été une erreur, que j'aurais dû vivre une autre vie. J'ai pris quelques lentes inspirations et j'ai regardé au loin le temps que l'émotion passe.

Quand il a été prêt, nous avons grimpé le remblai et suivi la berge. Il marchait avec précaution entre les roches et le bois flotté, tête baissée. Quelque chose avait changé en lui, ses gestes étaient plus lents.

«Ça va?» ai-je demandé. J'avais remarqué des flacons de Tylenol dans la camionnette, mais n'y avais pas prêté attention.

«Je me suis battu l'autre jour.

— Quoi?

— Avec un crétin. Un gars… tu l'as déjà rencontré, Tom Alding.

— Lui?» L'homme était grand, pas très charpenté, mais il mesurait plus d'un mètre quatre-vingts et avait l'air solide.

«Ouais. Il a essayé de me vendre du saumon pas frais. Nous étions dans le magasin et j'ai senti un poisson. Je ne sais pas s'il me prenait pour un idiot. J'imagine qu'il avait vraiment besoin d'argent. Je lui ai dit: "Pas question" et il m'a attrapé par le cou et m'a poussé vers l'arrière sur le comptoir. Je me suis fait mal au dos.

— Qu'est-ce que tu as fait?

— Je l'ai cogné. Je l'ai frappé au visage, je l'ai pris par les cheveux et j'ai continué à le frapper jusqu'à ce qu'il ait passé la porte. Alors je lui ai botté le cul et il est tombé en bas de la galerie. Il a eu le culot de dire: "Du calme." Jésus-Christ, le gars me pousse et puis il dit : "Du calme" au beau milieu d'une bagarre. Je suis rentré chercher le bâton de baseball sous la caisse, mais quand je suis ressorti, il s'était sauvé.

— Tu gardes un bâton de baseball sous la caisse ?

— Tu ne savais pas ? J'en ai un dans tous mes magasins. » Après quoi il a serré les dents et dit qu'il avait mal au dos et qu'il était incapable de dormir. Il a annoncé cela sans apitoiement, d'un ton dur, comme s'il était encore aux prises avec l'autre homme.

L'aube éclaircissait le ciel au-dessus de la large rivière dont les eaux, brisées par des rochers, brillaient d'un éclat d'argent comme une longue étoffe ondulant vers les montagnes.

« J'ai cinquante-quatre ans, a-t-il dit en regardant le courant. Je ne devrais pas me battre à mon âge. C'est idiot. Tout ça est idiot. »

J'ai hoché la tête. Je n'aimais pas le voir faible. Cela me remuait d'une façon que je n'aurais su expliquer, mais je savais qu'il me haïrait s'il me surprenait à éprouver de la pitié à son endroit. J'ai compris que si je me permettais de m'inquiéter pour lui, il me serait plus difficile de partir, alors je me suis efforcé de chasser ces pensées de mon esprit et de respirer l'air de la rivière.

Peu à peu, quand nous nous sommes mis à pêcher, ses mouvements sont devenus plus naturels. Ce n'était pas la saison du saumon kéta, aussi nous tentions d'attraper du coho, poisson plus petit et plus rare, dont la chair était beaucoup plus savoureuse. Nous pêchions de temps en temps un gros kéta que nous relâchions, gageant à savoir qui serait le premier à attraper un coho. À la fin de l'après-midi, il s'est mis à crier et à rire et j'ai longé la rive pour le rejoindre.

Les branchies du saumon palpitaient, cherchant l'air. Je me suis agenouillé et j'ai étudié les taches sur le poisson.

«C'est un petit kéta, lui ai-je dit.

— Non. Je travaille avec les poissons à longueur de journée. Tu ne les aimes même pas.

— C'est un kéta, ai-je répété en glissant le doigt le long des écailles. Regarde ici.»

Il a approché le visage, lèvres pincées sous l'effet de la colère. Le saumon ouvrait et fermait la bouche, fouettant sa main de la queue. Il a sorti une paire de lunettes de sa veste.

Sous les lentilles, ses yeux semblaient agrandis, comme des jouets, et clignaient lentement. Il s'est accroupi et a observé le poisson, puis s'est relevé, a replié ses lunettes, qu'il a rangées.

Le saumon se débattait, se noyant dans l'air. Il l'a pris et l'a porté jusqu'à l'eau, où il l'a glissé doucement avant de le relâcher. Puis il s'est rincé les mains et les a secouées pour les sécher. Il m'a dit que nous ferions bien d'aller voir où il avait enterré les fusils pendant qu'il y avait encore assez de lumière.

Nous avons suivi la rivière dans son camion. Les bouches d'aération soufflaient un air tiède et la cabine exhalait l'odeur de sa vie : une senteur animale saumâtre où se mêlaient le chien, le poisson et l'eau de Cologne. Quelques chalets aux fenêtres noires se dressaient dans la forêt, et nous ralentissions devant chacun tandis qu'il l'étudiait, fronçant les sourcils, avant que nous poursuivions notre chemin. Le remblai a bientôt disparu, remplacé par des étendues de pierres éparses le long de la rivière qui brillait, violette, dans le soleil couchant.

Il a pris la route lentement, le regard lointain. Autour de nous les branches nues se tendaient vers le ciel lumineux. Nous étions déjà venus ici quand j'étais enfant, juste lui, mon frère et moi, et avions campé sous la tente dôme que j'avais plus tard fait flamber. Nous nous étions levés à l'aube pour pêcher et, pendant que le soleil se levait, il nous avait dit que nous devrions faire cela chaque automne. J'avais opiné. Pas un d'entre nous n'aurait pu deviner combien nos vies allaient changer.

La nuit tombait. Nous roulions depuis près d'une heure sur des chemins de gravier, nous arrêtant sur des étendues planes où l'eau avait monté par le passé et déraciné les arbres.

Il a garé le camion sur l'accotement.

« Je ne reconnais rien, m'a-t-il dit. Il y a eu une grosse inondation il y a quelques années. Tout est différent maintenant. Même les routes. »

Dès que la serveuse lui a apporté sa bière, il a pris une longue lampée et a soupiré. Il a dit qu'il aurait dû passer sa vie dans la nature.

«C'est tout ce que j'ai jamais vraiment aimé. Tout le reste était de la merde.

— Ce n'est pas vrai. Allons. Tu as vécu. Tu as vraiment vécu.»

Il a haussé les épaules. «Et qu'est-ce que j'ai maintenant, ostie?»

J'ai hésité. «As-tu déjà songé à contacter tes parents?

— Mes parents? a-t-il répété comme s'il n'avait jamais possédé une telle chose.

— Comment ils s'appelaient?»

Il s'est raclé la gorge. «J'ai quitté le Québec pour me donner une nouvelle vie. Il s'est passé trop de temps maintenant. Ça ne rimerait à rien d'y retourner.»

Il a fini sa bière en buvant plus rapidement qu'à son habitude.

«Qu'est-ce que j'irais retrouver là-bas? a-t-il demandé. J'ai lâché l'école en cinquième année. Tous les matins, j'allais arpenter la côte à cheval pour ramasser du bois tombé des barges. Je pêchais ou je travaillais dans les champs, à planter des pommes de terre ou à les ramasser. À seize ans, j'ai commencé à bûcher sur la Côte-Nord. J'étais plus jeune que tu l'es maintenant, et je passais tout l'hiver dans un camp avec des hommes adultes. À ton âge, je travaillais dans des mines d'uranium et sur des gratte-ciel, tout ce que je pouvais trouver.»

Il a commandé une deuxième bière et m'a dit que si son corps était douloureux, c'est qu'il avait trimé trop dur quand il était enfant. «Ça a stoppé ma croissance. Mes épaules me font mal. Tout me fait mal, câlice. On lisait à la lumière des chandelles et maintenant mes crisses d'yeux sont finis. Pourquoi est-ce que je voudrais y retourner? Je travaillais et je leur envoyais mon argent, et ils ne m'ont même pas donné d'instruction.»

Il regardait plus loin que moi, ses pommettes et son front saillants jetant des ombres.

«Je pourrais peut-être écrire tes histoires», ai-je dit, comme si je n'avais rien d'autre à offrir.

Il a pris une gorgée, déposé la bouteille et hoché la tête.

«D'accord. Ça me plairait bien. Mes histoires méritent d'être racontées.

— Oui. Mais je ne sais rien de ton enfance.»

Il a haussé les épaules. «Il y avait le travail. Il y avait quelques bagarres. Il y avait de l'église en masse. J'haïssais l'église. Je me rappelle ma première confession. J'étais tout petit, et quand j'ai dit au curé que je n'avais pas péché, il m'a dit que tout le monde pèche et que c'est un péché de prétendre le contraire. Alors je pouvais avouer mes péchés ou dire des *Ave Maria* pour avoir menti. J'inventais de petits péchés : j'avais été jaloux de mon frère, ou je m'étais fâché contre un ami. Mais c'était de la foutaise. On travaillait. On ne faisait rien d'autre que travailler sur la ferme, et cet ostie de curé-là nous forçait à inventer des péchés. On n'avait pas de jouets. Tout ce qu'on faisait, c'étaient des corvées. On se levait, on nourrissait les animaux, on ramassait du bois ou on travaillait aux champs. Quand est-ce qu'on aurait eu le temps de pécher ? Si ça n'avait pas été de lui, peut-être que je n'aurais jamais commencé à transgresser les règles. »

Il a hésité, hochant la tête pour lui-même, le regard distrait.

« Ma sœur aînée marchait avec moi jusqu'à l'église le matin. C'était un trajet d'environ un demi-kilomètre. La route était juste au-dessus du golfe et il faisait froid. On n'avait pas le droit de déjeuner avant la confession, on allait à l'église à pied, et puis on retournait à la maison avant de marcher jusqu'au village pour l'école. Ma sœur voulait dire ses *Ave Maria* rapidement pour ne pas qu'on soit en retard, mais le curé nous a surpris pendant qu'on s'éclipsait. Il nous a crié après et nous a forcés à rester. Les sœurs à l'école nous frappaient les mains avec une ceinture quand on était en retard. Ça fait qu'on a tous les deux été punis ce jour-là…

« Mais tu sais, cet ostie de curé là, il habitait une grande maison derrière l'église et il avait une femme de charge qui vivait avec lui. C'est comme ça que les gens l'appelaient. Sa femme de charge. Tout le monde savait qu'il la baisait. Mais si une fille allait se confes-

448

ser et disait qu'elle avait couché avec un garçon, il lui criait après si fort que tout le monde pouvait entendre. C'est arrivé à... à des filles que je connaissais. Je voulais le tuer, cet ostie de curé là...»

Il a soupiré. «Ce genre d'histoires là... Tu veux les entendre?

— Ouais.

— Il y en a une que je n'oublierai jamais. Un dimanche, le curé a fait un sermon dénonçant l'adultère. Un homme et une femme du village avaient quitté ceux avec qui ils étaient mariés pour vivre ensemble et le curé nous a dit de prier et d'appeler sur eux les foudres du ciel. Je suis sorti de l'église en douce et j'ai couru jusqu'à leur maison. Je suis allé droit à leur fenêtre. Je n'oublierai jamais ce que j'ai vu. Ils avaient l'air heureux. Il n'y avait pas de foudre. J'attendais qu'elle s'abatte et les consume, et je craignais d'être trop proche de la maison et de brûler moi aussi. Mais comme il n'y avait toujours pas de feu, j'ai compris que l'ostie de curé était un imposteur. Après ça, je n'ai jamais cru un mot de ce qu'il disait.»

Il a fini sa bière. La serveuse nous apportait nos assiettes, et il en a commandé une troisième.

«Tu te rappelles qu'on parlait d'aller habiter dans une caravane et de vivre de la pêche? C'est ça qu'on aurait dû faire. Mes affaires, le crime, tout ça, c'est de la merde.»

Il mangeait lentement, cherchant des morceaux de poulet à l'aide de sa fourchette, puis il s'est interrompu.

«Nos meilleures années ont été dans la vallée», a-t-il dit.

Je ne savais que répondre. Il a regardé au loin pendant un moment, puis a posé les yeux sur moi.

«Promets-moi quelque chose.

— Quoi?

— À ma mort, promets-moi que tu vas faire une chose.

— O.K.» Je ne me souvenais pas de l'avoir jamais vu boire ainsi.

«Promets que tu vas m'enterrer dans les montagnes au bord de la mer.»

J'ai hoché la tête. «Très bien.

— Non. Promets, ostie. J'ai jamais rien demandé à personne et j'ai jamais rien eu, câlice. Alors promets.

— Je promets, ai-je dit, même si je n'avais aucune idée de la façon dont je m'y prendrais pour porter son corps dans les montagnes. De toute manière, pourquoi tu parles de mourir?

— Le monde meurt. Des fois, tu es là et tout va bien, et puis le lendemain tu as perdu ta santé et ton argent et tout le monde se crisse de toi et tu meurs.

— La mort t'inquiète?

— Je fais juste dire que ça arrive. L'argent est toujours un problème. L'économie est merdique. C'est jamais facile. La vie ne va pas en s'améliorant.

— Mais tu es en bonne santé.

— Bien sûr que oui. Ma grand-mère a vécu jusqu'à cent ans. Je vais probablement vivre jusqu'à cent ans moi aussi.» Il m'a regardé, les yeux soudain limpides et sans défense. «Je n'avais jamais pensé à ça. Peut-être que tu seras trop vieux pour grimper dans les montagnes pour m'enterrer. Tu vas être un vieux croûton. Peut-être que je ferais mieux de mourir jeune. Tu pourras me conduire jusqu'à dans les montagnes et m'enterrer à un endroit d'où l'on voit la mer. Ça me plairait, mais il faudrait que tu sois jeune et fort. Je ne pourrais pas attendre d'avoir cent ans.

— C'est probablement illégal», ai-je fait remarquer.

Il a haussé les épaules. «Ouais. Un tas de choses sont illégales si tu te fais prendre. Tu trouveras bien un moyen. Si tu ne peux pas emporter mon corps, prends les cendres. Je ne t'en voudrai pas.

— O.K.

— J'aime pas ces niaiseries de *O.K.*» Il m'a demandé de promettre encore une fois, et je me suis exécuté.

Il a bu une autre bière tandis que nous finissions notre repas en silence. J'avais l'impression de n'avoir jamais vu les choses si clairement, l'étrangeté de ma famille, la difficulté de la comprendre. Il avait été la personne contre qui je m'élevais, celui à qui je me mesurais, dont je m'affranchissais. Je ne savais pas comment le voir faible.

Remarquant que je l'observais, il a plissé les yeux pour me fixer, me faisant savoir qu'il était toujours aux aguets, que je ferais bien de ne pas le voir trop tôt comme une quantité négligeable.

En se levant, il a juré et agrippé la table.

«Je suis trop soûl pour marcher, m'a-t-il dit avec une grimace avant de m'enfoncer son coude dans les côtes. Ouaip, je suis trop soûl pour marcher. On dirait bien qu'il va falloir que je conduise.»

Nous nous sommes vus encore quelques fois avant mon départ. Il racontait des histoires après des soupers tardifs. La neige tombait sur le stationnement, et il fermait presque les yeux en regardant par la fenêtre. Il décrivait l'ennui des camps, un jour où des ours polaires étaient venus errer dans une ville minière, une nuit si froide que ses essieux avaient gelé, même s'il avait pris soin de laisser le moteur tourner pendant qu'il dormait.

«Le crime, disait-il, c'était mieux que tout ce que j'avais connu. Si tu voyais d'où je viens, tu comprendrais. Ça me semblait le seul moyen de m'en sortir.»

Je l'ai déposé chez lui un soir que son camion était au garage. Il a passé la clôture de métal et cinq gros bergers allemands ont traversé la cour pour se rassembler autour de lui, fébriles, levant la tête tandis qu'il les touchait tour à tour sur le museau jusqu'à ce qu'ils se calment. Il est resté immobile à les regarder s'asseoir ou s'allonger à ses pieds.

J'allais bientôt être libre, mais je n'éprouvais plus le besoin de m'enfuir. J'avais simplement soif de l'autoroute, de la liberté et du sentiment d'abandon qu'elle procurait, comme si le divin ne pouvait être atteint qu'en partant, en me perdant dans le pays. Pourtant, alors même que je songeais à cela, je n'arrivais pas à imaginer l'avenir de mon père. De peur de rester, je ne me permettais pas d'éprouver quoi que ce soit ; je me bornais à observer, à voir, à étudier comme pour plus tard, comme si je savais qu'il serait bientôt disparu et que seuls ces souvenirs pourraient m'aider à comprendre. Dans la loyauté muette des grands chiens, dans la manière dont il les apaisait par sa seule présence, je percevais son besoin d'une chose qui jamais ne le quitterait ni ne le trahirait.

Les discours de ma mère sur la destinée me revenaient, ainsi que l'espoir et la nécessaire destruction que je trouvais dans ses paroles. Mais rien dans nos avenirs respectifs ne me semblait aussi parfait que l'avait été notre vie dans la vallée. Debout à la fenêtre, je regardais des chiens caracoler dans les champs, suivis par un homme. Ils s'éloignaient de lui en courant vers un point invisible, bondissant, culbutant les uns par-dessus les autres, puis se précipitaient vers lui tandis qu'il poursuivait son chemin dans les rangées d'arbres du même pas régulier.

Une fois, il m'avait emmené à des pâturages en pente au sommet d'une montagne. Vêtu de son imperméable et de son chapeau de pluie, il arpentait les rangées, taillant les arbres. J'étais resté pelotonné dans la camionnette verte pendant que le brouillard soufflé par le vent l'enveloppait, ne laissant deviner que sa silhouette et le claquement de la machette. Quand il était revenu, ses vêtements étaient trempés. J'avais demandé pourquoi, il m'avait ébouriffé les cheveux et répondu que c'était à cause des nuages. «Quels nuages?» avais-je demandé. Il avait expliqué que ce qui nous entourait n'était pas du brouillard. Plus tard, les nuages s'étaient déchirés et le soleil avait couru sur les arbres et l'herbe humide. En contrebas, la vallée s'était ouverte, ruban vert constellé de taches de couleur, la route et les cours d'eau entrelacés comme des serpents assoupis.

Je suis parti pour la Californie par une claire journée où le soleil brillait sur la neige fondante.

Nous nous sommes retrouvés au garage où je faisais effectuer la mise au point de mon VUS en vue du voyage, et il m'a emmené dîner.

«C'est bien que tu aies la chance de voyager et d'aller à l'université, a-t-il dit en plissant les yeux dans la lumière qui entrait par les larges fenêtres. J'aurais fait pareil si j'avais pu.

— Je pourrai revenir te rendre visite», ai-je dit.

Il a souri et baissé les yeux. «Qui sait? Qui sait, avec cette ostie de vie?

— Non, vraiment, je vais revenir.

— Tu ne le sais pas.» Assis, les épaules creusées vers l'avant, il paraissait fragile.

Tandis qu'il me reconduisait au garage, nous avons suivi une décapotable rouge dans la circulation.

«Regarde-moi ce gars-là, a-t-il dit. Il ne fait pas si chaud.»

Le conducteur blond était sanglé dans un veston, et sa posture alerte lui donnait l'air nerveux. Au milieu de la route à quatre voies se trouvait un large terre-plein; il s'est engagé devant nous dans la voie réservée au virage à gauche. Les voitures dans l'autre direction arrivaient par grappes, et il a laissé passer plusieurs occasions de tourner. À chaque ouverture, il levait la tête et avançait de quelques centimètres. La voiture semblait presque neuve avec sa peinture rouge rutilante et ses pneus d'un noir mat.

«Calvaire, a dit mon père, il ne voit pas qu'il a eu plein d'occasions de tourner?»

La circulation s'est remise en branle, deux nouvelles ouvertures se sont présentées et évanouies. Mon père a baissé sa vitre et s'est penché à l'extérieur.

«Tourne! a-t-il rugi, les tendons de son cou saillant. Tourne, enfant de chienne!»

455

Le conducteur a enfoncé l'accélérateur, une berline arrivant dans l'autre sens a freiné et a embouti son aile, pliant le capot, projetant des éclats de plastique et de verre sur la chaussée.

«Jésus-Christ!» a dit mon père. Il s'est intégré à la circulation et s'est dépêché de s'éloigner. Il m'a jeté un coup d'œil. «Je ne voulais pas dire qu'il devait tourner juste à ce moment-là.»

J'avais le cœur battant en me retournant pour voir les voitures abîmées qui rapetissaient avec la distance, me demandant s'il y avait des blessés. Elles ont disparu hors de vue et nous avons regardé en avant, tous les deux silencieux. Et puis nous nous sommes regardés et nous avons éclaté de rire.

Nous étions encore en train de ricaner et de jurer à mi-voix quand il m'a déposé au garage. Nous nous sommes serré la main et je lui ai dit que je téléphonerais. Il a répondu que je pouvais toujours revenir si je le voulais.

Je me suis contenté de hocher la tête. Il a fait démarrer son moteur et a avancé pour se ranger près de moi.

«Hé, a-t-il dit. Savais-tu que je suis le conducteur numéro un à Vancouver?

— Quoi?

— C'est ce que tout le monde dit. Chaque fois que je conduis, on me dit: "Hé, t'es numéro un" en faisant ce geste.» Il m'a montré sa main, puis a levé son majeur.

Il a ri et enfoncé l'accélérateur, faisant gicler de la gadoue et une bouillie huileuse de sur l'asphalte. Je me suis caché le visage tandis qu'il dérapait pour décrire un demi-cercle. Puis, comme pour signifier que c'était lui qui s'en allait, il s'est engagé dans la circulation à toute allure parmi les voitures qui freinaient et déviaient pour l'éviter, et bientôt son camion a disparu.

5

FAMILLES IMAGINAIRES

Mon père et moi nous sommes peu parlé au cours de l'année qui a suivi. J'ai roulé jusqu'en Californie, où j'ai habité avec un ami et quatre autres jeunes gars dans un appartement de deux chambres à coucher, écrivant quand je le pouvais, travaillant comme intérimaire pour une agence, à rénover une succursale d'un magasin Sears. Nous dormions sur des canapés autour de la télé et escaladions des clôtures la nuit pour aller nous baigner dans des piscines. Mais l'ami s'est brouillé avec moi à cause d'une fille et je suis parti, même si j'aurais quitté les lieux de toute façon, puisque nous avons été expulsés le lendemain.

Quand j'ai raconté cela à mon père au téléphone, il m'a demandé de revenir et de lui donner un coup de main à son magasin. J'ai plutôt mis le cap sur l'est, cherchant du boulot en Utah et au Colorado. J'ai traversé le continent et, en avril, j'étais arrivé en Virginie, où j'ai travaillé sur des chantiers de construction jusqu'au début du premier semestre d'université.

À ce moment-là, j'étais reconnaissant de pouvoir y aller. En me colletant à l'écriture d'un deuxième roman, j'avais constaté combien mes connaissances étaient minces, et à quel point je souhaitais avoir du temps pour étudier. J'adorais les lectures et les discussions. À chaque roman, je me sentais comblé par la langue, qui effaçait les vieux plis que les mots pouvaient prendre, créait des possibilités. J'ai lu *Absalom, Absalom !*, fouillant les méandres de l'identité, l'ambition qui grandissait dans un homme en dissimulant la première impulsion d'un enfant blessé.

Quand je pensais à ce que je pourrais écrire, j'entrevoyais un grand roman de la même façon que mon père aurait pu imaginer un gros coup. Les romans que j'aimais le plus se caractérisaient par une certaine sensibilité à la famille : conversation entre les générations, sagesses partagées et contradictoires, parents et grands-parents enracinant des enfants au regard tourné vers l'avenir. Les romans semblaient le produit de cette tension entre parents et enfants, entre ceux qu'ils aimaient et avec qui ils luttaient. En embrassant ces livres, je me rendais de mieux en mieux compte que je ne connaissais presque rien du passé de mon père. Cette absence, l'obscure histoire qui l'avait façonné, l'empêchait de devenir complet.

Lors de nos rares conversations téléphoniques, je l'interrogeais de nouveau sur sa famille, cherchant à savoir pourquoi il avait rompu les liens avec elle. Comme à son habitude, il éludait mes questions, affirmant que trop de temps avait passé, qu'il n'avait plus rien en commun avec elle. Quand je lui demandais de me parler du Québec, il me répétait à quel point c'était une province arriérée, et comme ses habitants étaient pauvres. Et puis il changeait de sujet pour me parler de son entreprise qui battait de l'aile, et il me demandait de revenir lui prêter main-forte. Mais j'étais heureux, et le désespoir dans sa voix m'incitait à la circonspection.

En lui parlant, je ne savais trop ce que je devais ressentir, comme s'il s'était agi d'un étranger. Ma vie et mes ambitions avaient tellement changé que je ne savais plus où il cadrait dans mon existence. Ce n'est que lorsque j'écrivais que des émotions remontaient à la surface, que je ressentais son absence et m'inquiétais pour lui.

L'été suivant ma première année, j'ai de nouveau travaillé sur des chantiers de construction en Virginie. Nous nous parlions et il me demandait si je voulais venir lui rendre visite, mais je répondais qu'il habitait trop loin. Je craignais de ne pas retourner à l'université. Ma vie avait enfin acquis un équilibre, une cohérence que j'avais peur de mettre en péril.

Le silence s'installait dans les pièces. Par la fenêtre, l'air automnal semblait vaguement sucré par le parfum des feuilles en décomposition. On n'entendait que le pianotement assourdi des dernières phalènes contre les moustiquaires.

Une semaine plus tôt, j'avais emménagé dans un appartement en mansarde sur la route de montagne menant à l'université. Je le louais de deux professeurs, et comme le téléphone ne se rendait pas jusqu'à ma porte, j'ai attendu qu'ils soient partis pour appeler mon père. J'ai regardé les feux arrière de leur voiture disparaître passé la courbe de l'entrée. C'était étrange de songer qu'à quatorze ans je m'étais introduit par effraction dans une maison, mais désormais j'avais une telle soif de cette vie que je me montrais prudent à tous égards. Je ne voulais pas que les professeurs entendent mes conversations, ce bavardage désinvolte autour du crime.

J'ai téléphoné à frais virés. J'avais déjà essayé deux fois cette semaine-là, mais la ligne était occupée. La sonnerie a retenti à plusieurs reprises. J'allais raccrocher quand il a répondu, d'une voix tellement rauque que j'ai eu du mal à le comprendre.

La téléphoniste a donné mon nom, il a accepté les frais, puis demandé : « C'est qui ? »

J'ai répété plus fort.

« Hé, Deni, c'est toi ? » Il a toussé et s'est éclairci la voix.

« Es-tu malade ?

— Un peu.

— Rien de grave ? »

Il a toussé de nouveau. «Juste une minute, j'ai besoin de me racler la gorge.»

Je l'ai entendu déposer le combiné. Au loin, il y a eu le son grêle d'un robinet, et puis sa toux, épaisse et grasse. *Malade* était un mot que mon père n'employait jamais. Une fois, quand j'avais quatre ou cinq ans, ma mère m'avait dit de le laisser tranquille parce qu'il était malade. Il était assis dans son fauteuil, l'air concentré et furieux, comme s'il refusait cette faiblesse.

«Ça va? ai-je demandé quand il a repris le combiné.

— Ouais… Tout va bien. Je me disais bien que tu allais appeler.

— J'ai essayé de téléphoner, mais la ligne était occupée.

— Je laissais le téléphone décroché.

— Quel genre de rhume as-tu?»

Il a semblé près d'échapper le combiné, mais il a simplement répondu : «J'ai été un peu malade ces derniers temps.

— Est-ce que je ferais mieux de te laisser?

— Je viens juste de me lever. Ça me prend un peu de temps à partir», a-t-il répondu, son élocution moins embrouillée.

Il a toussé à quelques reprises, puis respiré bruyamment, sans rien dire, tandis que je parlais au hasard des cours auxquels je m'étais inscrit. Puis il s'est éclairci la voix : «Penses-tu que tu vas vouloir revenir, juste cette fois-ci? Tu pourrais prendre quelques mois de congé.

— Je ne peux pas. Je suis déjà inscrit.»

Distraitement, j'ai éteint la lampe. La maison était plongée dans l'obscurité, seule brillait la lumière de la galerie; les meubles se découpaient en silhouettes indistinctes.

«Comment ça va au marché? ai-je demandé.

— Mal. C'est une nouvelle administration qui gère l'édifice.

— Ça ne devrait pas aider?

— Non, le gérant est un enfant de chienne. Il a augmenté le loyer.» Il a pris une lente inspiration, puis a continué d'une voix faible, m'expliquant que les propriétaires de magasins partaient, s'en allaient sans plus de cérémonie, et que le gérant avait déjà travaillé pour «ce dictateur aux Philippines». «Marcos», a-t-il ajouté sur un ton hésitant.

Il s'est interrompu et a dégluti à quelques reprises; on aurait dit quelqu'un qui replace son dentier. «Je ne suis pas intimidé. Ils exigent trop cher et terrorisent les gens, mais je sais me défendre.

— Vas-tu pouvoir garder le magasin ouvert?»

Il s'est remis à tousser. Son combiné frottait contre sa chemise.

«Désolé pour ça», a-t-il dit. Il avait l'air soûl, son élocution n'était pas claire.

«Tu me parlais du nouveau gérant.

— Ouais. C'est un gars baraqué et le monde a peur de lui, mais ça ne marche pas avec moi. Il veut jouer au plus fin, et je le remets à sa place.» Il a hésité, haletant doucement dans le combiné. «Je commence à en avoir mon voyage de ce maudit magasin. J'imagine que je réfléchis beaucoup au succès ces temps-ci.

— Au succès?» J'ai fait un bruit de gorge pour lui laisser savoir que j'écoutais.

«J'ai réfléchi... j'ai réfléchi au fait que je n'ai pas accompli grand-chose. Je n'aime pas l'échec.» Il a étouffé une quinte de toux, et m'a expliqué qu'il ne pouvait pas franchir la frontière pour ses affaires, ce qui lui nuisait. «Mais c'est bien de te voir aller dans la bonne direction. Je sais que tu vas arriver à quelque chose. On aime tous les deux accomplir des trucs.»

Il avait toujours le souffle court et laborieux. Abruptement, il a dit: «J'imagine que je pense à laisser aller le magasin. Je vais peut-être devoir déclarer faillite encore une fois. Je songe à faire autre chose.

— Qu'est-ce que tu ferais?» ai-je demandé, étonné par la vague irritation qui m'habitait devant la possibilité que ses ennuis puissent me toucher. C'est la seule émotion qui m'est venue, et j'ai compris combien j'étais encore suspicieux.

«Je suis encore en train d'y penser, a-t-il dit.

— Voyager aiderait peut-être, ai-je suggéré, cherchant une solution. Tu pourrais cacher un peu d'argent pour après la faillite.

— Ce serait malhonnête», m'a-t-il dit de sa nouvelle voix.

Je n'ai pas répondu et, après quelques respirations, il a repris: «J'ai eu mes bonnes années. Je suis chez moi à Vancouver… J'aurais pu retourner au Québec il y a vingt, même dix ans, mais aujourd'hui il n'y a plus rien pour moi là-bas.»

Nous sommes restés silencieux tous les deux. Je ne connaissais pas cette voix.

Il a repris: «Et puis, l'argent, ça n'est bon à rien quand tu es mort.

— Es-tu en train de mourir?»

«Non. Bien sûr que non.» Sa colère m'était presque soulagement. «C'est juste une façon de parler. Je parle du moment où ça arrive. Ça ne sert à rien que j'essaie de faire quoi que ce soit d'autre. Il est trop tard. Je n'ai pas d'expérience.»

Comme je ne répondais pas, il a dit qu'il ferait mieux de me laisser aller me coucher puisqu'il était trois heures plus tard sur la côte est. Puis il a hésité. «Penses-tu que tu pourrais me téléphoner plus souvent?

— Bien sûr, ai-je dit, mais il s'est dépêché de changer de sujet.

— Je suis passé devant ton école l'autre jour. Tu sais, celle à Abbotsford. J'ai des clients dans ce coin-là, et je me suis rappelé l'époque où on allait à la pêche. Et puis je me suis mis à penser à l'époque où tu es revenu. Les choses étaient difficiles, je sais, mais tu es revenu. »

Je n'ai pas pipé mot. Il a eu une toux brève et a continué.

« Je devrais te laisser pour que tu puisses te reposer pour l'école. Je veux simplement que tu saches que ce que tu fais, c'est ce qu'il y a de mieux. Si j'avais pu, j'aurais poursuivi mon éducation aussi. J'ai déjà obtenu un diplôme d'études secondaires… quand j'étais en prison. J'imagine que j'en voulais un. Mais il était au nom que j'utilisais quand on m'avait arrêté, alors ça ne compte pas vraiment. »

De nouveau, nous sommes restés silencieux.

« Il doit être tard, a-t-il dit. Tu devrais appeler la fin de semaine pour qu'on puisse parler plus longtemps. »

J'ai froncé les sourcils et fermé les yeux. « C'est la fin de semaine. »

Entre deux inspirations, il a demandé mon numéro de téléphone au cas où il aurait besoin de me joindre. Je le lui ai donné et il a répété chaque chiffre, deux correctement, avant de me faire répéter les deux suivants.

« Je vais t'appeler, a-t-il dit. Je prévois déménager, alors je vais t'appeler quand ce sera fait.

— Quand vas-tu déménager?

— Je n'ai pas encore trouvé l'endroit, mais quelque chose va bien finir par se présenter.

— Pourquoi tu ne restes pas encore un peu où tu es?

— C'est trop cher. »

J'ai demandé où il garderait ses bergers.

Il a hésité. « Ils sont chez un ami. De toute façon, je serais mieux de te laisser. »

J'étais incapable de l'imaginer sans ses chiens. Y avait-il quelque chose qu'il ne me disait pas? Je me suis forcé à parler pour le garder au bout du fil : «Tu sais, je veux écrire tes histoires. J'ai beaucoup pensé à cela. »

Il s'est encore une fois éclairci la voix. «Ce serait correct. Écoute, je ferais mieux de te laisser aller. Ça me fait plaisir d'avoir de tes nouvelles. Ne t'inquiète pas pour moi. Appelle simplement si tu veux parler, O.K.?

— Très bien, ai-je dit. O.K.

— Ça m'a fait plaisir de te parler», m'a-t-il dit d'un ton superficiel, comme si nous avions discuté affaires. Il a raccroché avant que je puisse dire au revoir — c'était une habitude qu'il avait, de raccrocher rapidement.

J'ai tenu le combiné jusqu'à ce qu'il se mette à faire bip-bip, après quoi je l'ai déposé et suis resté assis à me vider l'esprit, refusant de m'en faire pour lui. Je me suis levé et suis sorti, et je suis resté debout dans l'obscurité sous les arbres qui fraîchissaient dans l'air du mois de septembre.

Pour moi, le Québec n'était rien d'autre qu'une liste d'événements : le.voyage de Jacques Cartier remontant le Saint-Laurent en 1534, l'établissement du poste de traite de Samuel de Champlain sur le site de l'actuelle ville de Québec en 1608, la proclamation de 1663 faisant de la Nouvelle-France une colonie royale. On racontait que la Gaspésie, où avait grandi mon père, tenait son nom du micmac *gespeg* : « fin des terres ».

Il lui était arrivé de raconter des histoires sur son village : le jour des élections, des hommes en complet débarquaient et offraient cinq dollars à chaque pêcheur si celui-ci acceptait de les laisser voter à sa place ; ou bien, quand il était petit, son oncle et sa tante de Montréal avaient offert de l'élever et de l'instruire, car ils ne pouvaient pas avoir d'enfants. Il rêvait de jouer au hockey à Montréal, mais son père avait refusé : « *T'es un homme, pis on a besoin de toi*.* »

Mon grand-père avait eu dix enfants, mais il disait que mon père était son as, car il était fier de sa force et de son ardeur au travail. Mon père avait toujours su qu'il refuserait de le laisser partir. Ils se tenaient sur la grève ; la mer, telle que je me l'imaginais, était grise comme le plomb, la côte lointaine à peine plus sombre que le lourd ciel caverneux, comme si le soleil avait brillé moins fort en 1947, ou dans cette région du monde.

Lors de sa visite, l'oncle avait offert à mon père une mince chaînette en métal semblable à un collier. Mon père, qui avait huit ans, l'avait attachée à un bateau en bois qu'il avait traîné dans le bran de scie sur le sol de la grange, en faisant semblant qu'il s'agissait d'un train. Quand la chaînette s'était détachée, il l'avait cherchée, ratissant de ses doigts le bran de scie souillé même là où il n'était pas passé. Il m'a raconté comment il avait de nouveau cherché le lendemain matin, dans la grange obscure, des bandes de lumière filtrant entre les planches. Les cochons s'étaient mis à grogner, croyant qu'il était venu les nourrir.

« La vie était tellement misérable, m'avait-il expliqué, qu'un truc pareil pouvait avoir de l'importance. »

En couchant ces notes sur le papier, j'éprouvais une vague colère, une tension derrière les yeux, tel un début d'épuisement. Comme ces histoires ne parlaient pas de crimes, je ne leur avais accordé aucune importance. Dans un restaurant, il lui était arrivé de mentionner son oncle en passant, et je n'en avais pas fait grand cas. Mais c'était l'une des rares expériences d'enfance qu'il avait racontées, et je me laissais brièvement aller à me demander comment aurait pu être ma vie s'il n'avait pas caché son passé, si j'avais connu sa famille et le lieu où il avait grandi. En essayant d'écrire ses histoires, je sentais son désir confus comme si ç'avait été le mien, le regret d'une occasion ratée, et j'étais sûr que la rage de ce petit garçon l'habitait toujours. Ç'avait été sa première chance de s'enfuir, même si je ne savais toujours pas ce qu'il avait laissé derrière lui.

J'étais assis près de la moustiquaire, le téléphone sur les genoux.

Sa respiration était à peine perceptible. Je lui avais expliqué mon projet de faire un roman de sa vie, mais il me parlait du marché. Il n'était pas d'humeur à raconter des histoires.

«Je suis pas mal fatigué des affaires. Des fois, on finit par en avoir ras le bol de quelque chose. J'en ai ras le bol de travailler tous les jours. On ne devrait pas être forcé de vivre comme ça.

— Qu'est-ce que tu penses faire?

— Il y a beaucoup de choses que je ne t'ai pas dites. Il y a un bout de temps, je me suis blessé. Je suis tombé en bas d'un congélateur et je me suis fait assez mal. J'essayais de réparer une lumière et je suis tombé sur le béton. Depuis ce jour-là, je ne suis plus capable de faire grand-chose. J'ai du mal à soulever quoi que ce soit. Je pense que je me suis esquinté le dos pour de bon. J'oublie que je n'ai plus vingt ans. Je me sens comme si j'étais jeune, mais je suppose que je ne le suis pas.»

J'ai attendu, mais il n'a rien ajouté.

« Tu avais l'air assez mal en point la dernière fois qu'on s'est parlé, ai-je dit en essayant de trouver les mots pour nommer ce que je ressentais. J'étais inquiet. On aurait dit que… que tu n'avais plus envie de vivre. »

Il ne répondait pas, et j'ai écouté le léger frémissement de sa respiration.

« Ne dis rien à personne — même pas à ton frère ou à ta sœur. Je ne voulais pas que vous sachiez. J'ai cru que peut-être vous ne seriez pas capables d'encaisser le coup. Si je te le dis, tu n'en parleras à personne ? »

J'ai dû déglutir en levant le menton avant de pouvoir parler.

« Très bien. Je ne dirai rien.

— Je ne voulais pas te le dire, mais vers la fin de l'été, j'ai décidé de me tuer. Je pense que je le savais depuis un certain temps. J'ai vendu quelques bergers comme chiens de police et j'ai donné ceux qui me restaient. C'était la première fois depuis le pénitencier que je n'avais pas de bergers. Je ne crois pas avoir compris avant ce moment-là que j'allais le faire. »

J'ai gardé les yeux fermés, puis j'ai cligné des paupières et regardé sous l'abat-jour incliné de la lampe qui laissait la lumière déferler. Comment en était-il venu là si rapidement ?

« J'ai acheté de l'héroïne, a-t-il poursuivi. J'avais lu dans le journal que des gens faisaient des overdoses avec de la China White, alors je m'en suis procuré. J'en ai acheté suffisamment pour dix personnes et j'ai tout pris. Ça m'a plongé dans un coma qui a duré plus de deux jours. Quand je me suis réveillé, j'étais tellement malade que j'étais incapable de sortir du lit. J'étais couvert de cloques. Je suis allé chez le médecin ; il m'a dit que nos corps bougent pendant notre sommeil, pour éviter que notre sang se fige. J'imagine que je n'avais pas bougé. J'avais des cloques partout sur les cuisses. Il y en avait une qui recouvrait tout mon talon. J'avais du mal à rester debout.

— C'est à ce moment-là que j'ai appelé ? » Je parlais d'une voix unie, étonné de découvrir combien j'avais l'esprit vide, combien tout me paraissait figé autour de moi.

« J'étais assez malade, a-t-il dit. J'ai passé deux jours dans l'obscurité totale. Ce n'était pas comme de dormir. C'était comme si j'avais été parti. Je pense que j'ai eu peur après. Je ne me souviens plus. Je suis allé chez le docteur et je lui ai raconté. Il m'a prescrit des médicaments.

— Tu les prends toujours ?

— On dirait que ça rend les choses un peu moins pires. »

J'avais la gorge sèche et la poitrine serrée comme si j'avais eu besoin de tousser. D'une voix calme, je lui ai demandé s'il avait l'intention d'essayer de nouveau. Je ne voulais pas qu'il me croie trop faible pour entendre ce qu'il m'avait dit, mais j'étais surpris de mon impavidité, étonné de ne pas éprouver plus de chagrin mais de me sentir simplement vide, imperturbable, vaguement désorienté.

«Je ne sais pas, a-t-il répondu d'une voix lointaine qui réussissait à peine à franchir la distance. Je ne sais pas si ça vaut la peine de risquer qu'il y ait vraiment un Dieu.

— Tu n'as pas abandonné l'idée de Dieu? ai-je demandé, me rendant compte que je paraissais plus étonné par cette révélation que par sa tentative de suicide.

— J'ai abandonné l'Église catholique. Je ne crois pas que Dieu fait partie de l'Église. Des fois, je pense qu'il n'a rien à voir avec elle.

— Vas-tu à la messe?

— Non. J'y suis allé quelques fois, mais il n'y avait rien là pour moi.

— Penses-tu, ai-je commencé, cherchant les mots qui l'amèneraient à reconsidérer ce qu'il m'avait dit, penses-tu que tu peux passer à travers tout ça?

— Pas si je ne veux pas. Les gens de ma famille vivent vieux. Je ne veux pas vivre si vieux, mais j'ai peur de me tuer. J'aurais dû mourir.

— Il n'y a pas autre chose que tu peux faire si le magasin fait long feu? Tu pourrais partir en voyage ou quelque chose du genre.» En prononçant ces paroles, je me sentais lamentable.

«Le magasin, ce n'est qu'une partie du problème. J'en ai marre de travailler à des trucs qui ne donnent rien en retour. C'est trop dur. Ça n'aurait peut-être pas été si pire si les choses avaient tourné autrement. Si je vous avais vus grandir. C'est la seule chose que je changerais. Ta mère n'avait pas le droit de vous emmener comme ça. Elle s'est servi de mon passé pour le faire. Je me rappelle encore quand je l'ai appelée en Virginie. Elle a menacé d'appeler la *po-lice*. C'est comme ça qu'elle l'a dit, comme quelqu'un de là-bas. Ça faisait deux semaines qu'elle était partie. Mais je ne lui en veux pas, plus maintenant. J'ai passé par-dessus ça. J'aurais simplement aimé vous voir grandir.»

Pas un mot n'a été prononcé pendant ce qui m'a semblé une minute. Contre mon oreille, le silence volontaire avait quelque chose de trop intime. Je ne savais pas comment lui parler de cela.

«Je ne suis pas fier des choses que j'ai faites, a-t-il dit. L'autre jour, j'ai lu l'histoire de gars qui avaient dévalisé une banque et ça m'a foutu en colère. Ce genre de personnes là n'apprécient pas la valeur du travail bien fait.

— Pourtant, tu as fait des trucs assez extraordinaires.

— Je ne pense pas que tu peux comprendre. Tu as eu des occasions que je n'ai jamais eues. Si je pouvais, je changerais de place avec toi en une seconde. Mais j'ai raté ma chance. Les choses que j'ai faites dans ma vie allaient contre le monde. Mais tu es sur le bon chemin. Je veux juste que tu saches ça.»

Il s'est arrêté, peut-être pour essayer de voir clair dans ce qu'il venait de me dire.

«Je me suis toujours tellement reconnu en toi. Mais je ne suis pas fier des années que j'ai passées en tôle, et je ne suis pas fier de ce que j'ai fait. Si je pouvais retourner en arrière, je changerais tout. J'ai brisé beaucoup de vies. Je vois le monde autour de moi, et je n'en fais pas partie.

Je me suis rendu compte que j'émettais de petites interjections d'approbation à la fin de ses phrases, mais à ce moment-là j'ai cessé, gagné par la colère. Il fallait que je dise quelque chose pour le faire changer d'idée, mais nous n'avions jamais parlé de la sorte. Je voulais raccrocher. Je voulais déposer le combiné — le reposer sur son socle si doucement et si proprement qu'il ne s'en rendrait pas compte avant que la ligne coupe.

«Tu ne devrais pas avoir honte, me suis-je forcé à dire, la gorge sèche. La plupart des gens n'auraient pas été capables de vivre ta vie.»

Il a hésité. «Peut-être. Je ne sais pas.

— Je veux écrire tes histoires. Voudrais-tu me les raconter?

— Il y a au moins un livre dans ma vie. C'est déjà quelque chose, j'imagine.»

Le silence s'est étiré. Des écureuils grattaient dans les feuilles dehors et se chamaillaient près de la mangeoire à oiseaux. Au loin un chien a aboyé. Je me suis frotté les yeux et j'ai appuyé les doigts sur mes paupières, des phosphènes palpitant le long de la scintillante dentelle des capillaires, la lueur blanche que ma mère avait déjà appelée la lumière de l'âme.

«Qu'est-ce que tu aurais besoin de savoir pour un livre? a-t-il demandé. Par quoi est-ce que je commencerais?

— Par ton enfance.»

Le roman que j'imaginais contiendrait le monde que mon père révélait: une église en pierres grises, des maisons battues par le vent, des filets de pêche tendus sous les toits, les familles, les enfants en file derrière leurs parents le dimanche, des bancs de neige contre les murs, des traces de pas creuses d'un mètre; plus tard, des wagons embourbés jusqu'aux essieux dans le dégel printanier — ou bien le jour où la compagnie d'électricité était venue installer les globes en verre qui brûlaient sans produire ni chaleur ni fumée.

Lui et moi nous sommes parlé régulièrement à partir de ce soir-là. Je l'appelais quand mes logeurs n'étaient pas là, ou bien d'un téléphone sur le campus. Parfois, il s'arrêtait au milieu d'une histoire pour me demander de laisser l'école et de revenir, en répétant qu'il n'avait jamais eu besoin d'instruction. Mais chaque fois que je refusais, il se remettait de mauvaise grâce à décrire son passé.

Enfant, il disait avoir eu conscience des mots — les termes anglais qu'ils utilisaient en français, comme si les pièces d'une auto n'avaient pas de nom dans sa langue. Au magasin, il y avait des étiquettes qui ne voulaient rien dire, n'annonçaient rien, où se lisaient des lettres qui avaient perdu leur place. Il recevait son produit préféré, du lait condensé Eagle Brand, en guise de friandise. «*C'est du vrai Eagle Brand, ça**!» avait même dit l'un de ses frères en parlant de la voiture dans laquelle un touriste américain les avait dépassés sur la route côtière poussiéreuse. Ils avaient tous opiné du bonnet en riant.

Le sentiment de mystère que j'instillais dans ce nouveau monde était le mien. Je le voyais comme par les yeux d'un enfant, chaque détail éclairé par mon désir d'en savoir plus. Mais dans ses mots, je sentais des émotions plus profondes : la loyauté envers ses parents, l'amour et les rivalités entre frères et sœurs, et le désir de s'approprier le monde, de se faire ses propres idées et ses passions, ses propres aventures. J'écrivais pour m'approcher de la lisière de tout cela, voyant non seulement sa famille mais la mienne, le lieu où commençait la route qui menait au loin, et je savais que nous avions commencé à partir bien avant ma naissance.

Par moments, j'étais étonné par ma propre colère qui se levait soudainement comme si elle venait de se libérer et m'emplissait d'une frénésie animale, consumant les heures où j'essayais de dormir, de sorte que je finissais par retourner m'asseoir à mon pupitre.

Dans mon calepin, j'écrivais le Saint-Laurent dans les eaux glaciales duquel je n'avais jamais pêché. J'écrivais des jours en mer sans avoir connu la morsure du froid quand la main s'égare trop loin sur la ligne d'un filet, ne devenant rien d'autre qu'une forme de connaissance, jusqu'à ce qu'on la presse dans sa veste comme pour la faire fondre.

L'un de ses plus vieux souvenirs : debout à la fenêtre, il avait vu un homme traverser le champ, se diriger vers la maison et gravir l'escalier. Reconnaissant le visiteur, il avait appelé sa mère pour lui dire que grand-père était là. Elle avait ouvert la porte, mais il n'y avait personne, que le seuil vide et le vent soufflant sur le pré. Son père vivait sur l'autre rive du Saint-Laurent, à un jour de voile ou à un saut de puce en avion, ce qu'elle avait expliqué à son fils. Mais une heure plus tard, elle avait reçu du village un télégramme annonçant que son père était mort.

Même si mon père était né sur la Côte-Nord, dans un village gouverné par une entreprise de morue de l'île de Jersey, son père avait eu tôt fait de ramener sa famille en Gaspésie, à la ferme ancestrale. Sa mère, qui n'avait jamais tout à fait accepté le nouveau village, lui répétait qu'il valait mieux que cela. Elle confectionnait les vêtements de ses enfants, affirmant que ceux qu'on trouvait dans les magasins étaient de moins bonne qualité.

Pendant qu'elle s'efforçait de faire bonne figure, son mari, un homme costaud au teint foncé qui n'aimait rien tant qu'une bonne bagarre, faisait enfiler des gants de boxe à mon père et à son frère Lucien, qui s'affrontaient dans le salon. «Ça c'est mon as», disait mon grand-père de mon père, attisant la rivalité entre les deux frères.

Mon père avait déjà fait la même chose avec mon frère et moi. J'étais plus grand, mais l'âge jouait en faveur de mon frère et, quand il m'avait frappé, j'avais perdu la boule et m'étais mis à fouetter l'air de mes bras. Lorsque notre mère nous avait ordonné d'arrêter, mon père avait eu l'air abasourdi. Je comprends maintenant, il revoyait son passé.

Du printemps jusqu'à l'automne, mon père travaillait. Il se voyait comme un homme et détestait les hivers, lorsque la côte gelait et que la pêche s'interrompait. Les hommes du village s'engageaient auprès de compagnies forestières et prenaient l'avion vers le nord où ils restaient jusqu'au printemps. Mais mon père restait derrière avec les femmes et les enfants. Les hivers n'étaient que corvées : nourrir les animaux, nettoyer les stalles, rentrer le bois pour le feu.

Le 12 novembre 1953, il avait eu quinze ans. Il fallait en avoir seize pour être embauché par la compagnie forestière, mais il avait menti. Son père l'avait laissé faire, désireux de pouvoir profiter de ce salaire supplémentaire.

L'impatience de mon père grandissait au fil des heures. Il préférait faire n'importe quel travail plutôt que de rester claquemuré dans la petite maison avec sa mère et ses frères et sœurs. Il avait préparé son sac, ses vêtements de travail, ses bottes. Mais, sur la piste de décollage, le curé se tenait debout près du recruteur. Il avait appelé mon père et l'avait fustigé pour avoir menti. C'est lui qui avait enregistré le baptême de mon père dans les archives de l'église, et il avait apporté le certificat de naissance pour en faire foi.

L'avion avait décollé et mon père avait marché le long de la côte, étendue déserte où s'empilaient les plaques de glace. Il avait toujours détesté le curé Félix Jean, qui régnait sur le village comme sur un royaume lui appartenant en propre.

En proie à la rage, il avait regardé par-delà le Saint-Laurent l'horizon déchiqueté. Il était incapable de se résoudre à entrer dans la maison, incapable d'imaginer quelque geste ou action qui auraient pu le satisfaire. .

«Je voulais tellement m'échapper, partir, disait-il au téléphone. J'étais incapable de penser à rien d'autre. Je n'avais aucune idée de ce que je ferais une fois parti. J'avais juste besoin de partir.»

Où donc ces élans habitaient-ils en nous, transmis par le sang ou par les histoires, à travers le regard distant d'un père qui raconte à son fils des endroits lointains? Il me semblait, en entendant ses paroles, que la vie d'un père est la première histoire d'un fils.

Je me suis réveillé dans l'obscurité, sentant que mon esprit avait travaillé pendant mon sommeil.

Il n'était qu'une heure du matin. Je me suis habillé et suis sorti en silence, descendant l'entrée boisée jusqu'à la route d'asphalte. Mon souffle montait en buée pendant que je marchais. La fumée de la cheminée s'élevait à la lueur de la lune, jetant des ombres fugitives sur le chemin. Les étoiles étincelantes semblaient être la source du froid pénétrant, un million de pointes de glace.

Avais-je tant changé depuis l'époque où j'étais enfant? Si je n'étais pas en train de découvrir quelque chose, je me mettais à avoir des fourmis dans les jambes. Peut-être le crime avait-il été le remède qu'avait trouvé mon père à ce mal, comme l'écriture était le mien, ou apprendre sur son passé, lever le voile sur ses secrets. Tout ce que nous vivions n'avait-il pour but que ce frisson qu'on éprouve à se sentir vivant, à se dresser tout entier — intelligence et force — contre quelque chose de si tangible et de si difficile qu'on se sent soi-même pleinement réel?

La forêt donnait sur le terrain de l'université, plongé dans le silence à l'exception du bruit de mes pas. Je suis entré dans le pavillon de services, j'ai allumé la lumière du hall d'entrée et déplié la chaise de métal près du téléphone public.

«Hé, a-t-il dit, et il a accepté les frais. Il est tard chez toi.

— Ouais, je n'étais pas capable de dormir. Je pensais aux histoires que tu m'as racontées.

— Lesquelles?

— Juste des histoires sur ta famille. Je ne comprends toujours pas pourquoi tu n'es jamais retourné là-bas.»

Il a commencé par ne pas répondre puis, de cette façon qui faisait que chaque nouvelle conversation ressemblait à un commencement, il a dit : «Je voulais ma vie à moi. Mon père était fort. C'était un homme imposant et les gens le respectaient. Il travaillait dur et était capable de se battre. Mais c'est tout ce qu'il avait. Quand j'ai eu seize ans, j'ai fini par l'accompagner sur la Côte-Nord. Je me rappelle ses avertissements. Un arbre gelé pouvait fendre en deux et tuer un homme, ou bien durant *la drave**, quand ils faisaient descendre le Saint-Laurent aux billots de bois, les hommes étaient blessés. Mais je voulais juste travailler. Je voulais ne plus être prisonnier de la maison. Je m'en foutais.

«Une nuit, tout avait gelé dur et puis il avait neigé, et au matin nous avons quitté le camp pour la rivière, où on avait amarré un bateau de provisions à la rive. En chemin, nous avons vu un nouveau camp de bûcherons. C'étaient des Anglais. J'étais étonné. Les Anglais possédaient des commerces ou bien ils venaient en touristes, mais je ne les avais jamais vus comme ça. On n'était que quatre, et ils nous ont invités à manger avec eux. La nourriture m'a stupéfié. Ils avaient du bœuf et de la sauce sucrée, des pêches en boîte et une sorte de melon que je n'avais jamais vue. On a mangé tout ce qu'on a pu, et on en a même mis dans nos poches. J'ai remarqué qu'ils riaient. Je n'ai pas compris tout de suite. Je pensais qu'ils étaient contents, mais j'ai fini par me rendre compte qu'ils se payaient notre gueule. »

Il a hésité. «J'étais fier d'être sur la Côte-Nord, mais j'ai compris quelque chose à ce moment-là. J'ai vu que les autres n'avaient aucun respect pour nous. »

Était-ce vraiment pour cela qu'il était parti si loin? Le respect avait toujours été important à ses yeux, mais je ne croyais pas qu'il avait besoin d'abandonner sa famille et sa culture pour devenir quelqu'un d'autre.

Le lendemain matin, j'écrirais ce qu'il m'a raconté ensuite avec des détails bizarres. Son père et lui, ainsi que les deux autres hommes, avaient poursuivi leur chemin jusqu'à la rivière en se frayant un sentier dans la neige fraîche. La terre gelée, drapée entre les arbres, exhalait le calme du Nord. Comme pour briser le silence, l'un des hommes a craché : «*Maudites têtes carrées**! »

Le sentier sinuait le long de la rivière fraîchement recouverte de glace, libérée de la neige par le vent qui avait suivi la tempête, ponctuée de bleu par endroits. Ici et là, de fines congères semblables à des dunes s'élevaient de la surface comme les anneaux d'un serpent qui se déroulent. Le petit bateau avait gelé sur place, plein de sacs. Ils avaient tapé du pied sur la glace. Elle n'était pas épaisse, mais pouvait supporter leur poids, aussi avaient-ils vidé le bateau avec soin et décidé de le libérer pour le tirer sur la rive.

Mon père rêvait toujours de changer de vie, s'imaginant qu'il y parviendrait par le travail, chaque boulot l'éloignant un peu de la maison pour le rapprocher d'une nouvelle vie. Désireux d'employer sa rage à quelque chose, de montrer sa force, il avait pris place près de son père et s'était mis à tirer, étonné de la facilité avec laquelle le bateau s'était soulevé, allant presque jusqu'à lui échapper. La rivière bouillonnait à ses pieds. Il avait eu beau essayer de se souvenir au cours des années, il ne s'est jamais rappelé comment il avait glissé, et même son père à ses côtés ne l'avait pas vu disparaître. Mais il avait mystérieusement senti son absence. Il avait lâché le bateau et s'était mis à courir. L'ombre de son fils miroitait contre le bleu, plus sombre là où le vent avait soufflé fort sur la rivière.

La première décharge avait été trop soudaine pour que mon père puisse la sentir. Puis le froid avait resserré son étau ; des étoiles dans les yeux, il avait senti ses poumons se vider de leur air. S'obligeant à ne pas respirer, il avait essayé de comprendre ce qui était arrivé. Il avait frappé la glace, mais la marque qu'il y avait laissée n'était pas plus grande que le talon de son père au-dessus de sa tête. L'effort l'avait fait caler plus profondément, aussi, cessant de bouger, il s'était laissé glisser le long du ventre de la glace. Il voulait respirer. Dépêche-toi, avait-il songé. Le froid le berçait.

Pour avoir vu son père tirer des filets et des bateaux hors de l'eau et coucher au sol un Clydesdale qui n'avait pas encore été débourré, il savait que les pieds qui martelaient en spirale au-dessus de lui n'étaient pas qu'une vaine tentative pour se donner bonne conscience. Son père n'envisageait pas la possibilité de l'échec tandis qu'il courait, l'ombre de son fils étendue à ses pieds comme si c'était la sienne. La forme sous la glace dégageait un calme absolu, la mort peut-être, jambes molles, paumes si près de la surface qu'au moment où il s'était jeté au sol pour frapper, il pouvait distinguer parfaitement le contour de la main, chacun des doigts.

Dans un rugissement, le ciel s'était soulevé, incliné jusqu'à apparaître à sa vue. Des nuages étaient accrochés à l'horizon, des taches d'encre devant le soleil. Son père avait tiré, avec une telle force que les boutons de son manteau s'étaient éparpillés et avaient gelé debout sur la glace.

«Réveille-toi*!» Son père criait, le secouait et l'avait mis sur ses pieds. Il lui avait donné des claques sur les bras et le dos, le poussant à courir. Mon père avait filé jusqu'au camp, qu'il avait balayé; puis il avait fendu le bois pour le feu, ses vêtements fumant comme si une flamme brûlait en lui. Il avait bourré le poêle en acier, mais quand il avait tendu les mains au-dessus de la grille, son père l'avait de nouveau forcé à bouger. «Dépêche-toi*!» avait-il crié.

Ce soir-là, pendant le souper, mon père avait avalé sa bouchée de pommes de terre et demandé pourquoi son père avait mis tant de temps à lui venir en aide. Les hommes avaient ri en frappant sur la table.

«Mon as», l'avait appelé son père, qui avait expliqué aux autres que son fils était béni. Mais mon père avait toujours la rage au cœur d'avoir eu besoin d'être sauvé, de voir encore son père comme insuffisant — fort, certes, il était célèbre pour sa force sur toute la rive sud, mais cela n'était pas assez. Il était canadien-français, prisonnier de cet univers étriqué gouverné par des curés et qui appartenait aux Anglais. Si les bûcherons anglophones mangeaient si bien, alors de quoi se régalaient les riches?

D'une voix hachée, au téléphone, mon père me racontait ce jour où il avait failli perdre la vie comme s'il s'agissait d'une légende, un mythe d'une puissance ancestrale, et je l'écoutais, devinant son passé, une absence plus grande que sa vie. L'histoire ne pouvait pas être vraie. S'il la racontait ainsi, c'est parce qu'il s'efforçait d'y faire entrer le monde qu'il avait perdu et les sentiments qu'il était incapable d'exprimer.

À la table du camp, tandis qu'il rêvassait, son père s'était vanté de son fils béni, l'enfant qui avait vu le fantôme de son grand-père grimper les marches et incliner son chapeau pour dire au revoir avant de s'évanouir tel un moment de ravissement.

Quand je lui ai dit au revoir, l'horizon avait pâli, infusé d'une lumière violette, et dans l'air d'un gris de perle les rouges et les jaunes vifs des érables commençaient à se détacher nettement, comme s'ils reposaient juste sous la surface de l'eau. Près de la route, des feuilles de molènes gelées s'agglutinaient autour de tiges mortes. J'ai marché sur le chemin, le corps trop plein d'énergie — colère, chagrin, remords.

Il avait parlé pendant des heures, aiguillé par mes questions. De temps en temps, il avait l'air vieux et songeur et je n'étais pas trop convaincu de la chronologie des faits qu'il rapportait, du nombre considérable d'endroits où il avait travaillé, mais je l'interrompais rarement.

Pendant nos silences, je savais que nous nous demandions tous les deux quel avait été le but de sa vie d'excès si ce n'est la joie d'être vivant, en mouvement, en partance vers quelque chose de neuf. Et pourquoi me fallait-il assembler ces morceaux, vivre ce qu'il avait vécu, me laisser aller à éprouver cet abandon, la rage qui nous pousse à chercher une nouvelle existence, les remords de laisser les autres derrière soi? Je revendiquais son passé comme si j'en avais été jaloux, planifiant la façon dont je l'écrirais, la manière dont je m'y prendrais pour qu'il apparaisse clairement. Pourquoi avais-je refusé de lui rendre visite l'été précédent? Je ne pouvais pas retourner là-bas mais je pouvais passer des heures à l'écouter, trouvant dans les mots ce que nous partagions. Et pourtant, à la façon dont il s'efforçait de me garder près de lui avec ses histoires, sa solitude était manifeste.

Le travail, tel qu'il le décrivait, lui avait offert une échappatoire, mais il était loin d'adorer ce qu'il faisait. Dans une mine d'uranium, pour protéger ses poumons, il devait boire deux verres de lait avant de descendre sous terre. La première semaine, il les avait éclusés sans rechigner, mais ne voyait nul plaisir sur les visages d'étain des hommes plus vieux. Les

490

mineurs étaient payés selon la quantité de minerai qu'ils remontaient à la surface, et il courait toute la journée, poussant la brouette le long des rails. Il se vantait de gagner deux ou trois fois plus que quiconque mais, un mois plus tard, une occasionnelle quinte de toux faisait remonter dans sa bouche un épais mucus noir de suie. L'odeur du lait suffisait à lui donner un haut-le-cœur. Repensant à l'oncle qui avait voulu l'adopter, il voyait ce qu'il avait perdu et la rage lui brûlait au cœur, plus forte encore que le jour où son père avait refusé l'offre. Le désir d'une vie meilleure lui déchirait les entrailles.

Il envoyait de l'argent chez lui et rendait visite à sa famille pour Noël, jouant au hockey sur les planchers de la maison avec ses frères cadets. Quand Lucien était là, mon père et lui avaient encore du mal à discuter, tous deux souffrant toujours des blessures de leur rivalité. Leur mère accueillait mon père avec un étalage d'affection, lui embrassait les joues et annonçait à tout le monde combien d'argent il avait fait parvenir à la famille. Ses frères et sœurs plus jeunes bénéficiaient de l'instruction à laquelle il n'avait pas eu droit.

« C'est quoi ton problème ? lui avait demandé mon grand-père.

— Quoi ?

— Ton attitude.

— *C'est rien* * », avait dit mon père, incapable de combler la distance entre eux, de faire taire sa furie et son désir de partir pour ne jamais revenir. Combien de temps allait-il continuer à travailler et à envoyer son argent à sa famille alors que celle-ci ne lui avait rien donné?

Il avait ensuite travaillé sur un gratte-ciel à Montréal. Il aimait le vent en altitude et avait même pu recommencer à boire du lait. Il se moquait de ceux qui avaient peur des hauteurs et courait sur les poutres sans harnais.

Un jour, en croisant un Iroquois sur une poutrelle, il avait marché sur un boulon que quelqu'un avait laissé traîner et s'était foulé la cheville. Il aimait les Iroquois, qui étaient plus courageux que les Blancs; il les imitait quand il plantait son talon sur une poutre et se penchait vers le sol, se maintenant en place par les pieds pour ajuster un rivet. L'homme avait attrapé sa chemise et s'était incliné en arrière afin de faire contrepoids. Ils étaient restés suspendus. Puis l'Iroquois les avait redressés et l'avait lâché.

Mon père avait essayé de se calmer, mais sa rage était revenue, plus puissante qu'avant, en plus de l'impétuosité, du désir de continuer à courir sur les poutrelles, étranger à la peur, sans attaches.

«À quoi ça rime?» avait-il demandé à Martin, un jeune homme avec qui il s'était lié d'amitié. Ils se retrouvaient dans un bar pour boire et discuter de l'avenir, mais la conversation allait rarement plus loin que le travail — des boulots qui étaient peut-être un peu mieux mais pas si différents — ou les filles sans grâce du bar.

«C'était… c'était un job merdique, m'a-t-il dit. Il devait y avoir mieux. Je ne savais pas quoi. J'étais incapable de m'imaginer à quoi pourrait ressembler une autre vie. Je cherchais, c'est tout…»

Sur le gratte-ciel, à la fin de la journée, les plus téméraires couraient jusqu'au coin de l'édifice, agrippaient les rebords évasés et se laissaient glisser, étage après étage, jusqu'à ce que leurs gants soient brûlants et que leurs pieds touchent le sol. Mais le jour de la paie de cette semaine-là, tandis qu'ils couraient en riant, mon père juste derrière Martin, il a vu la jambe du pantalon de son ami accrocher l'extrémité d'un rivet.

C'était peut-être la nouveauté de l'amitié, l'air pur des hauteurs, ou simplement la joie d'être payé, ou de finir une longue journée, le soleil brillant vivement sur l'horizon, leur course agile et trop confiante, et puis le plongeon silencieux, fragile, insignifiant de son ami sur la pierre.

Le lendemain matin, il frappait à coups de masse une poutre coincée quand il s'était mis à transpirer. Il avait asséné encore trois coups puis avait posé sa main sur l'acier, s'était reculé et avait abaissé la masse. La chair de son petit doigt s'était fendue comme la cosse d'un haricot, révélant l'os blanc de l'articulation. Il avait crié, la masse était tombée entre les traverses de métal. Il avait saisi la poutre et avait eu un hoquet. Il avait l'impression qu'il allait fondre en larmes, comme si à ce moment seulement, avec sa douleur, il arrivait à donner une voix à son désespoir. Il aurait souhaité obtenir une meilleure compensation pour un os brisé, mais était incapable de se résoudre à frapper de nouveau.

Pendant quelques semaines, il avait loué une chambre sur le Plateau-Mont-Royal, à Montréal. Il s'asseyait dans l'escalier de secours pour apprendre l'anglais dans un livre. Il avait acheté un lecteur huit pistes et écoutait du rock'n'roll. Il assistait de temps en temps à des matches de boxe, fréquentait les bars et essayait des alcools forts dont les étiquettes étaient aussi étrangères que les logos sur le côté des camions qu'il regardait passer quand il était enfant. Il brandissait son doigt bandé devant lui comme un symbole de noblesse.

Quand il avait été presque à court d'argent et quasiment guéri, il était tombé sur Gaétan, un type aux allures de loup travaillant sur les gratte-ciel et qui avait le don de faire rire les hommes tandis qu'ils se tenaient à soixante mètres dans les airs sur une poutre en I de trente centimètres. Ils avaient parlé de la mauvaise paie et de la mort de Martin. Puis Gaétan avait avoué qu'il avait quitté son emploi et dit qu'il déménageait l'après-midi même. Il avait demandé à mon père de lui donner un coup de main.

«Conduis», avait-il suggéré en le guidant jusque dans une ruelle donnant sur le derrière d'un immeuble d'appartements, où il lui avait dit d'attendre. Mon père s'était demandé comment Gaétan pouvait se permettre d'habiter là ou de posséder une auto si luxueuse ou pourquoi il avait insisté pour qu'ils baissent la capote, quand des vêtements se sont mis à pleuvoir du balcon — robes en soie et complets à fines rayures, puis un petit coffre en bois qui a abîmé le rembourrage, un écrin à bijoux doté d'un miroir qui avait volé en éclats. Des bagues rebondissaient dans le fond de la voiture.

Quand Gaétan avait glissé le long de l'escalier de secours, mon père était furieux. Mais Gaétan était déjà dans l'auto. «*Dépêche-toi**!»

Mon père avait enfoncé l'accélérateur et ils étaient partis sur les chapeaux de roues.

Pendant qu'ils roulaient, Gaétan lui avait montré un disque de Judy Garland. «*Ça, c'est quelque chose**!»

Mon père n'avait pas répondu. Quand il avait atteint l'est de la ville, il s'était garé, était sorti et s'était mis à marcher, insulté d'avoir été utilisé de la sorte. Gaétan l'avait rappelé, lui disant que s'il voulait faire de l'argent pour de vrai, il n'avait qu'à le faire demander au bar.

Mon père avait quitté Montréal, craignant d'être lié au vol. Il avait pris un boulot sur un barrage dans le Nord, où il était resté plusieurs mois. Le dimanche, il ratait la messe pour aller pêcher et, juste avant le coucher du soleil, s'asseyait sur l'échafaudage et fumait en regardant vers l'ouest.

Mais moins d'un mois plus tard, il avait eu un accident. Il travaillait au sommet du barrage, à couler du béton dans des formes de bois près du bord de la structure. Debout sur le bois, il guidait le bec verseur du camion. Le soleil se levait à travers le brouillard et les nuages, parfois jaune pâle ou blanc argenté, à d'autres moments éblouissant. Des tracteurs transportaient de la boue et du roc au pied du barrage. Il avait entendu un craquement et s'était accroché au bois sous ses pieds tandis que la forme sur laquelle il se trouvait se détachait de son socle. La paroi du barrage avait défilé devant lui à toute vitesse et il s'était agrippé au cadre de deux par quatre qui glissait comme un traîneau le long de la falaise de béton, ses clous faisant jaillir une pluie d'étincelles.

Il avait atteint l'eau peu profonde en contrebas, accroupi, le cœur bizarrement calme, l'esprit vide, comme s'il avait été fait pour cela et que rien n'eût été plus naturel. Quand les hommes sur le bord avaient vu qu'il était encore sur ses pieds, ils s'étaient mis à pousser des hourras et il n'avait pas tout de suite compris pourquoi.

Le lendemain matin, il avait fait ses bagages et empoché son dernier chèque de paie. Au bureau de poste, il avait divisé l'argent pour en envoyer la moitié à sa famille. Avec ce qui restait, il était parti en stop vers l'ouest.

Le voyage était chose récente dans ma vie, mais déjà l'émoi du départ me semblait familier. Il y avait la première inspiration prise au début du voyage, les poumons et le cœur qui se dilataient. C'est ce que ses paroles me rappelaient, la liberté de mouvement, la recherche de choses simples — nourriture, endroit où loger — et, par-dessus tout, la réalisation de nous découvrir engourdis, animaux enfermés dans nos propres cages où nous nous nourrissions avec indifférence. Quand on explore, les repas et les lits ne sont pas promis mais gagnés, ils arrivent dans nos vies avec la puissance d'une révélation. Mon père avait traversé le continent, stupéfait de l'infinie diversité de la terre et des gens. Il avait vu l'Amérindien coincé sur une roche au milieu de la rivière et compris qu'il voulait vivre pour lui-même et oublier les morts.

Il avait erré sans but vers l'ouest et puis, comme l'argent était venu à manquer, il avait rebroussé chemin. Il était arrivé à Montréal sans le sou.

« Gaétan m'a présenté à un gars qui m'a appris à ouvrir les coffres-forts. J'étais doué. J'aimais le défi. Percer les coffres-forts, ce n'est pas pour les imbéciles. Ça prend de la concentration. C'était comme un jeu. Je me testais. Je savais que j'étais bon. Mais il ne payait pas beaucoup. On volait mille dollars, il m'en donnait cent. Je voulais partir à mon compte. Je lui ai dit que je ne gagnais pas beaucoup plus que dans les mines. C'est lui qui m'a vendu. »

La nuit où il s'était introduit dans un magasin d'articles de sport, il s'était tapi dans l'embrasure de la porte — rues mouillées, cercles de lumière sous les lampadaires, pas le moindre bruit de pas. Une longue voiture aux ailes fuselées était passée, projetant des gerbes de gouttelettes. Il avait les mains serrées dans les poches, le menton rentré dans son col, le cœur et l'esprit calmes. Il avait commencé à comprendre cette étrangeté qui l'habitait, le fait qu'il ne se trouvait chez lui que dans l'incertitude, en ce lieu où possibilité et danger s'étalent devant vous comme une plaine nue.

Puis il avait expiré, et le son de sa respiration, bruyante dans l'obscurité, l'avait surpris. Il s'était retourné, avait sorti une barre plate de son manteau et forcé la serrure, fendant le chambranle. À l'intérieur, il avait attendu que ses yeux s'ajustent. Il était passé à pas prudents devant des casiers de bâtons de hockey, des étagères de patins à glace et de casques, tous sans couleurs dans l'obscurité. Au fond, il avait exploré à tâtons le battant d'une porte. D'un coup, il avait inséré la barre de métal et y avait imprimé un mouvement de levier. Des éclisses avaient craqué sous ses bottes, les vis avaient roulé sur les lattes inégales du plancher.

Dans la pièce voisine, derrière le pupitre, il avait trouvé le coffre-fort. Alors qu'il s'agenouillait, un éclair de lumière était entré par la porte. Ébloui par la clarté, il avait heurté une étagère. Des balles en étaient tombées et avaient rebondi sur le sol. Chaque fenêtre était une grille brillante où le rouge et le bleu tournoyaient derrière la lumière vive.

Il n'a jamais décrit l'arrestation, uniquement la prison, les détenus qui n'étaient pas plus durs que les hommes de son village, la tension constante, le jaugeage presque sexuel tandis qu'il passait devant les cellules ou frôlait les épaules d'un autre prisonnier. Il haïssait les minces matelas qui sentaient la sueur, la toilette exposée et le lavabo fêlé taché par une fuite d'eau rouillée, le sang sur le rebord après sa première bagarre, quand il y avait frappé la tête d'un homme avant de laisser les cheveux emmêlés glisser de son poing, tirés par le poids du corps ramolli. Il n'avait pas prévu que les détenus allaient expliquer son arrestation, affirmant qu'il avait été piégé, échafaudant des théories en pressant leur cuillère dans leurs pommes de terre tièdes.

«Ça a été mon école», m'a-t-il dit.

Au fil des discussions et des histoires, les détenus lui avaient appris à forcer n'importe quelle serrure, à percer le plus sûr des coffres-forts — ils l'amenaient au-delà de la prison, jusqu'à des bijouteries baignées de la lumière du jour, des banques et, secret par excellence, des voûtes en béton aux barreaux d'acier.

Derrière sa voix, on entendait le son clair de la pluie tombant à verse, un martèlement régulier sur le toit. De l'autre côté de ma fenêtre, sous la lumière de la lune, les premiers flocons de neige tourbillonnaient dans le vent.

«As-tu revu ta famille après ça? ai-je demandé.

— Une seule fois. Une fois après ça. Mais je n'étais plus le même. J'ai compris que je ne pouvais pas rester. Trop de choses avaient changé.»

Il s'est tu un moment, sa respiration à peine audible avec la pluie abondante en bruit de fond.

«Avant, je rêvais de revenir riche. Je me suis rendu compte à quel point ce serait facile. J'avais tout appris en prison. J'ai fait un plan pour me rendre tout droit au sommet. Je ferais un gros coup, je prendrais l'argent et je rentrerais à la maison. Je n'ai jamais pensé à ce que je ferais après.

— Comment ça?

— J'imagine que je savais que je ne reviendrais pas. Je savais que je ne serais jamais satisfait là-bas.

— Y retournerais-tu maintenant?

— Non. Il s'est passé trop de temps.

— Et si on y retournait ensemble?»

Il a hésité. «Ça pourrait être correct. Tous les deux. Ça pourrait être bien.

— Où est-ce qu'ils habitent?» ai-je demandé en m'efforçant d'avoir l'air patient et de masquer la colère et le ressentiment qui me gagnaient de plus en plus souvent.

Mais il restait muet. Je voulais insister, lui dire que c'était mon passé aussi, mais je ne l'ai pas fait. À la pause qu'il ménageait, à la façon dont il se raclait la gorge, je savais qu'il allait me demander de revenir travailler avec lui. Il le faisait souvent. J'aurais dit non, aussi je ne lui ai pas demandé.

REMÈDES POUR LA FAIM

L'anniversaire de mon père était la veille du mien et j'ai décidé d'appeler après minuit pour que ce soit notre anniversaire à tous les deux. Il aimait à trouver des similitudes entre nous et, au cours d'une conversation précédente, m'avait dit que tous les onze ans les chiffres composant nos âges s'inversaient : 15 et 51, 26 et 62, 37 et 73. Il m'avait aussi raconté qu'il était tombé sur un livre d'astrologie dans une librairie et qu'il en avait lu un passage — par simple curiosité, avait-il ajouté, comme pour ne pas avoir l'air ridicule. Il avait remarqué que nous étions un scorpion et un tigre et s'est demandé à voix haute si cela signifiait quelque chose, même s'il avait changé de sujet avant que j'aie pu répondre.

Les feuilles étaient tombées, l'hiver était arrivé tôt, à la radio on prévoyait une légère neige. J'ai poussé la porte du pavillon de services du campus et composé son numéro au téléphone public, mais il n'a pas répondu.

Et s'il allait vraiment se tuer? L'université était-elle si importante? Mais je ne pouvais pas retourner chez lui. Le continent me protégeait de sa vie, même si je me haïssais de penser de la sorte. Mis à part les histoires, rien ne nous unissait, le présent était presque absent de nos conversations, il n'y avait que le passé dans nos paroles, comme si nous pouvions y trouver quelque moyen de combler la distance. J'avais rempli des calepins en prévision du roman que j'espérais construire à partir de sa vie, mais je me demandais ce qu'il avait pu omettre.

«Des fois, je ne sais pas à quoi tout ça rimait, m'avait-il dit un soir. J'essayais de m'en aller, mais je n'ai jamais vraiment su où je voulais arriver. J'étais trop occupé à essayer de m'en aller.»

À d'autres moments il riait en se rappelant la fureur qui l'habitait. Je percevais dans ses paroles la volonté d'accomplir quelque exploit spectaculaire que nul autre ne pouvait réaliser — de poser une action et de dire: «Ça m'appartient. C'est moi qui ai fait ça.» L'élan me semblait véritable, tout comme le désir de faire sa marque sur le monde avant de se demander si cette marque valait la peine d'être faite. Alors même que j'écrivais, j'essayais de comprendre ce que j'espérais trouver, et la raison pour laquelle je composais cet ouvrage.

Une heure plus tard, j'ai rappelé, souhaitant sombrer dans ce fugitif moment de grâce qu'offrait notre fascination partagée pour une vie qui ne refusait rien, qui sanctifiait les motivations lui échappant totalement, dans le but de pouvoir faire pareil, d'écrire avec une égale âpreté.

Je l'ai appelé et rappelé du téléphone public, et n'ai laissé tomber qu'après trois heures du matin, quand est passé ce bref instant qui allait diminuant et que j'avais voulu lui offrir.

Deux ans en prison. Il se sentait comme un parieur qui a perdu la moitié de l'argent qu'il avait en poche, désespéré de regagner ce qu'il croyait lui appartenir. En raison de ces années perdues, son retour à la maison se devait d'être spectaculaire. Il ne pouvait rentrer s'il n'avait rien à faire admirer aux membres de sa famille. Il ne les avait pas appelés et ne voulait pas les voir avant d'être riche. Seul l'argent pouvait justifier son absence.

La prison lui avait montré ce qui fait l'homme, la façon de modeler et de tremper son caractère. Il avait appris à aimer l'adrénaline, à se repaître de l'excitation de la bagarre. Il avait soif du monde — tout ce qu'il prendrait pour lui une fois libre. Cette soif creusait un manque en lui. Il se sentait vidé et avait appris à aimer ce sentiment aussi.

Après la prison, tandis qu'il roulait vers l'ouest et laissait le Québec derrière lui, les plans qu'il avait échafaudés ont commencé à se désagréger. Il était poussé en avant par la rage et un désespoir sans nom.

Il suffisait que quelqu'un le bouscule dans un bar pour qu'il se batte. Il avait commis des vols à main armée, mais l'argent récolté ne lui suffisait jamais. Dans l'intention de se ranger, il avait pris quelques boulots, dans les mines et sur les chantiers de construction, au Yukon et en Alaska, mais ceux-ci n'avaient fait que confirmer ce qu'il pensait : sans le crime, il n'échapperait jamais à l'existence qui était la sienne à la naissance. C'était sa témérité qui le ramenait en prison à répétition, pour des bagarres ou conduite dangereuse.

Après sa libération, il avait obtenu une nouvelle carte d'assurance sociale et un permis de conduire au nom de Gaston Tremblay, après quoi il avait traversé au Montana. Il s'était fait des amis dans des bars et en prison, et ensemble ils avaient dévalisé quelques banques. Soûls, ils entraient dans des boutiques pour touristes à la campagne, leur arme ostensiblement glissée dans leur ceinturon. Ils essayaient des vêtements et des chapeaux, se remplissaient les poches de friandises et de bœuf séché devant le commis, puis sortaient en faisant au revoir du geste. Ils mangeaient leur souper puis s'arrachaient des cheveux de sur la tête, les jetaient dans leur assiette et s'exclamaient : « Pas question que je paie. Il y a des cheveux dans ma nourriture ! » En une occasion, ils avaient affronté la brigade de cuisiniers tout entière avant de prendre leurs jambes à leur cou quand le chef leur avait brandi un couteau de boucher sous le nez.

Ils avaient fini par être arrêtés pour vol et mon père avait passé un an et demi en prison. Les gamins du coin ôtaient les silencieux de leur voiture et faisaient la course devant les murs à la nuit tombée pour réveiller les détenus. Il restait allongé à haïr ces jeunes, et le fait qu'ils ne voyaient en lui qu'un criminel méritant châtiment, qu'ils ignoraient ce qui l'avait amené là, à quoi il cherchait à échapper. Et pourtant il savait qu'à leur place il aurait fait la même chose et en aurait bien rigolé. Sa bêtise et celle des autres lui donnaient mal au cœur, et chaque matin il se réveillait, impatient, de nouveau un enfant dans la maison de son père, comptant les mois avant sa liberté.

Un matin de janvier, alors qu'il marchait en rond dans la cour en fumant avec application, il avait entendu la voix tremblante d'un vieillard annonçant : «Le monde m'appartient. Je vous le dis, il m'appartient au complet.»

Mon père s'était tourné vers le vieil homme qui se tenait debout dans le froid, bras écartés. Il avait secoué la tête. «Non, le monde ne vous appartient pas. Tout, sauf le Québec.»

Au dire de mon père — qui racontait cela avec fierté, comme s'il avait rencontré une vedette —, l'homme était l'un des derniers membres encore vivants de la bande de Karpis-Barker. Il avait travaillé pour Fred Barker et Alvin Karpis, même si, à ce moment-là, quand on l'interrogeait sur ces exploits, il était plutôt enclin à parler de son enfance. «Oh, ces journées passées à pêcher la truite brune au printemps, le printemps tiède!» Il levait des mains décharnées pour montrer la taille du gros poisson qu'avait attrapé son père. Il avait un nez volumineux qu'il heurtait chaque fois qu'il glissait sur la glace, et qui était donc fréquemment bandé. Les gardes comme les durs à cuire l'adoraient, et même le détenu le plus féroce, Joe Yates, qui avait affûté la ferrure rouillée d'une botte pour poignarder l'obèse qui partageait sa cellule, prenait le vieillard par le coude pour l'aider à franchir les plaques de glace. Les gardes avaient conspiré pour lui faire imprimer un faux chéquier, et il passait son temps à faire des achats.

«Combien coûte le Québec? Je vais te l'acheter.

— Cent millions de dollars.»

Le vieil homme avait plissé les lèvres. «Combien de zéros?

— Huit.»

Il avait rempli le chèque maladroitement, l'avait détaché et tendu à mon père.

J'ai ri en entendant cela, et à ce moment j'ai eu l'impression qu'il y avait de l'espoir, que je pouvais recommencer à poser des questions sur sa famille et à parler de retourner la voir. Mais il pensait encore au chèque, et il m'a dit qu'il avait fait une bonne affaire. Il maudissait les catholiques, l'arriération du Québec et, finalement, cette nuit-là, quand il a cessé de parler, je n'avais plus le courage de l'interroger.

Après le Montana, il avait traversé la frontière et de nouveau changé de nom. Il s'efforçait d'aborder le crime de façon calme et professionnelle, mais son caractère fougueux prenait souvent le dessus. Il avait fait quelques vols à Edmonton, mais redoutait que la police soit à ses trousses. Et puis son complice s'était sauvé avec l'argent.

«Cette fois-là, m'a dit mon père, j'ai failli y laisser ma peau. C'est fou comment les choses arrivent — les risques que j'ai pris. On aurait dit que j'étais béni. C'était l'argent d'une petite affaire, mais il suffit que tu laisses un gars se foutre de ta gueule pour que tout le monde te prenne pour une poire. Alors je suis allé chez sa blonde et je lui demandé si elle voulait aller manger quelque chose. C'était l'hiver et il y avait plus de neige que d'habitude. Les bancs de neige bloquaient quasiment le ciel. Aussitôt qu'elle est montée dans la voiture, je me suis mis à rouler au moins à cent soixante à l'heure. Elle me suppliait d'arrêter et je lui ai dit que je le ferais si elle me disait où était son petit copain. Elle a affirmé qu'elle ne savait pas. Elle a juré qu'elle me le dirait si elle le savait. Elle a dit qu'elle haïssait ce mec, et puis elle a balancé des méchancetés à son sujet — elle a dit qu'il avait une petite queue. Des trucs du genre. J'allais arrêter. Rendu là, je la croyais. Au même moment, on est arrivés au sommet d'une petite montée. J'ai à peine eu le temps de voir l'accident sur la route. C'était presque comique. Une de ces voitures funéraires — un corbillard — avait frappé un camion de laitier. Tout ce que j'ai pu faire, c'est de foncer dans le banc de neige. On est rentrés droit dedans, direct dans un champ. La neige était si haute qu'on n'était pas capables d'ouvrir les portières. Le moteur tournait toujours et le chauffage fonctionnait. L'antenne s'était cassée, alors la radio ne marchait pas. La police a mis trois heures pour venir nous chercher. On s'est réconciliés pendant ce temps. On s'entendait plutôt bien. Après, il a fallu aller au poste de police remplir un rapport. Il y avait toujours des tas de photos de criminels recherchés sur le mur, et parmi elles il s'en trouvait une vieille de moi, mais personne n'a eu l'air de s'en rendre compte. »

J'imaginais la peur sur leurs visages tandis que la voiture s'enfonçait dans un bleu de saphir et un calme soudain. Les phares éclairaient encore, un cercle faiblement lumineux luisait devant eux, comme un diamant enfoui quelque part dans la neige. Mon père avait augmenté le chauffage et ajusté les bouches d'aération. Le moteur teuf-teufait, le son semblait émaner de loin au-dessous d'eux.

J'adore cette image : deux êtres prisonniers de la glace, captifs de l'immobilité et de la lumière froide, comme des personnages saisis, rassemblés par un éclair de l'imagination. La mémoire nous tient jusqu'à ce que nous soyons prêts à voir. En racontant, il savait que ses paroles possédaient le charme des chances impossibles, du danger frôlé de près, qu'elles étaient marquées au sceau de la magie et lui rappelaient que sa vie était véritablement sienne.

De retour à Calgary, il a fait un coup avec deux hommes rencontrés en prison. Mais il avait reconnu en eux sa propre témérité, et aurait dû savoir. En s'échappant, ils avaient roulé sur une plaque de glace noire et passé par-dessus un remblai alors que la police était à moins de deux kilomètres derrière eux.

La voiture avait fait des tonneaux. Lorsqu'elle s'était immobilisée, il était dessous, bras et jambes brisés, la poitrine imbibée d'essence. Des véhicules s'étaient rangés sur l'accotement et les conducteurs étaient restés debout à discuter en fumant, malgré que mon père se fût efforcé de remplir ses poumons d'air pour leur dire d'écraser leurs cigarettes. L'un de ses complices s'était frappé la tête sur le tableau de bord avec tant de force qu'il avait été scalpé. Son crâne ensanglanté était exposé et son cuir chevelu pendait derrière sa tête. Pour la première fois de sa vie, mon père avait été soulagé de voir arriver la police. Le juge lui avait imposé une peine plus légère parce que la main de Dieu avait été plus rapide que la justice temporelle.

Le jour où il était sorti de prison, le panier à salade l'avait laissé dans une ruelle. L'agent lui avait donné cinq dollars, après quoi mon père s'était rendu dans un hôtel miteux. Il avait caché de l'argent dans la bouche d'aération au plafond de la chambre qu'il occupait lorsqu'il avait été arrêté, et le même après-midi, il avait acheté d'un fermier un camion sans freins.

Il était prêt à traverser la frontière pour de bon. Quand il avait passé du temps à l'infirmerie de l'hôpital, il avait su que le temps d'un changement était venu. Ce n'était pas la vie dont il avait rêvé : une cellule minuscule ou bien, quand il était en liberté, une chambre d'hôtel minable ou une maison de banlieue décrépite, des vols lui procurant juste assez d'argent pour vivoter. Couché dans son lit, il songeait à l'Amérique, toute proche, comme le battement de cœur d'une femme.

Chaque échec était la promesse d'un nouveau commencement, la preuve que sa volonté était ferme et que rien ne pourrait éteindre le feu qui l'habitait. Était-il motivé par le désir de tout risquer, de tout perdre, d'être dépouillé — de sa langue et de sa culture, de son nom et de sa famille — jusqu'à son essence même, comme s'il pouvait exister une forme d'être aussi absolue et libre que l'âme ? À ce moment seulement, quand tout le reste aurait disparu, il pourrait connaître la métamorphose qui l'obsédait, la possibilité d'entrer dans une autre vie.

Il avait roulé dans le camion sans freins jusqu'à Tijuana. Je connaissais son besoin d'exubérance, de délivrance, l'élan vers la liberté semblable à celui qui pousse vers la fiction, le loisir de se rappeler sa vie comme il l'entendait. Sa voix avait parfois des accents impétueux lorsqu'il s'attardait à certaines descriptions, comme s'il constatait jusqu'où il pouvait aller et se plaisait à tester les limites du possible.

Son trajet vers Tijuana n'était pas autre chose : il avait roulé jusque-là comme d'autres s'étirent. Il s'échauffait en vue d'un changement, d'un nouveau genre de crime, mais il lui fallait d'abord goûter à sa liberté, profiter du ciel vide au-dessus de l'autoroute et voir les multiples formes que pouvait prendre la terre.

Il avait fait une série de braquages le long de la côte ouest et prétendait avoir dévalisé au moins cinquante banques et autant de bijouteries à la pointe du fusil. Voulant se donner un air respectable, il s'était fait refaire le nez afin de réparer les dégâts causés par les bagarres et la prison. Sa vie se déroulait dans le triangle formé par Los Angeles, Las Vegas et Salt Lake City, où sa petite amie était persuadée qu'il était un homme d'affaires souvent sur la route. Pendant tout ce temps, il étudiait les détails du cambriolage d'Hollywood, le gros coup, celui qui allait le libérer et lui permettre de rentrer chez lui la tête haute.

Son imprudence ne l'avait cependant pas quitté : casinos, hôtels — une nuit, ivre, debout sur le capot d'une voiture en mouvement, il était tombé et s'était fracturé le bras. Il avait dévalisé une bijouterie alors que son bras était dans le plâtre mais, une fois de retour dans la voiture, il n'arrivait pas à sortir son arme de sa poche. Il avait demandé à la petite amie de son complice de l'aider, et elle avait accidentellement appuyé sur la détente, trouant son pantalon.

« On a eu de la chance que la balle ne touche pas le réservoir à essence », m'a-t-il dit avant de me décrire un autre vol au cours duquel son complice avait oublié son arme dans une bijouterie après l'avoir déposée afin de remplir son sac. Personne n'avait envie de retourner sur les lieux mais, comme ils se servaient tous des mêmes revolvers, leurs empreintes digitales se trouvaient sur l'arme.

« J'ai eu peur, cette fois-là, en rentrant dans une boutique qu'on venait juste de dévaliser, où il y avait un paquet de monde plutôt furax, avec un de nos revolvers entre les mains. Je suis entré en pointant mon arme, mais ils n'avaient même pas pris celle que nous avions laissée là. Ils se sont tous immédiatement recouchés par terre. »

Il a hésité. « Tu sais, je comprends pourquoi tu veux écrire. Je pige. Je sais pourquoi tu fais ce que tu fais. »

Je me suis simplement raclé la gorge et j'ai hoché la tête, bêtement, comme s'il pouvait me voir, puis il s'est remis à me parler de son gros coup.

« Quand je l'ai fait, je croyais que tout allait être facile. Je croyais que c'était ma porte de sortie. Je ne pouvais pas deviner que mon associé allait faire l'idiot et mettre le feu à l'appartement de surveillance. Lorsque sa blonde et moi sommes arrivés à la maison au Nevada, on a baissé les stores et jeté l'argent sur le plancher du salon. La montagne de liasses de billets arrivait à la hauteur de mes genoux. Je pensais que j'avais fait quelque chose de tellement gros, de tellement parfait que je n'aurais plus jamais à me soucier de quoi que ce soit. Je pensais que j'avais réussi à berner la vie. »

J'essayais de comprendre ce que ça avait à voir avec l'écriture, mais avant que j'aie pu lui demander, sa voix s'est affaiblie.

« Ce n'était pas ce que je croyais. Ces grands rêves ne s'accomplissent pas. Rien n'est aussi facile que ça en a l'air. » Il a hésité et ajouté : « C'est à ce moment-là que j'ai fini par rentrer à la maison. Je savais que la police était à mes trousses et je voulais montrer à ma famille combien j'étais riche. Mais je n'ai pas pu rester. J'étais déjà en cavale. C'est la seule chose que je regrette. Ce que j'ai fait à ma mère. Elle ne méritait pas ça. »

J'avais pris l'habitude de ces contrastes où l'enthousiasme cédait au regret, de la façon qu'il avait de s'exprimer comme un vieillard fatigué de la vie pour ensuite basculer vers la colère, comme s'il faisait de nouveau face aux choix qui s'étaient présentés à lui. Après quoi il avait l'air plein d'espoir, on aurait dit qu'il était encore à planifier son gros coup : LBJ faisait son discours, le camion était garé dans la ruelle, il avait le marteau-piqueur destiné à défoncer la voûte afin qu'il puisse se faufiler à l'intérieur. Mais il avait découvert en tentant de ressortir que le grain du béton pointait vers l'intérieur, accrochant ses vêtements, et il avait dû se déshabiller. Comment s'était-il senti en se tortillant sur les rebords acérés, nu, pour sortir de la voûte — naissance difficile mais pleine de promesses, et non la déception que j'aurais pu imaginer ?

Quand son complice ne s'était pas présenté, il avait su que la police viendrait le chercher. Il avait acheté une Chevy décapotable, des vêtements en soie neufs et des douzaines de cadeaux pour sa famille, puis il avait roulé jusqu'au Québec, traversé le continent et la frontière, passé Montréal, suivi la côte au contour irrégulier jusqu'à la maison, le Saint-Laurent s'élargissant jusqu'à ce qu'il ait du mal à distinguer l'autre rive.

Il avait l'impression de revenir vers quelque région sauvage du bout du monde, et pourtant la sauvagerie qui l'habitait, lui, était plus grande que jamais, et il avait été transformé aussi sûrement qu'un homme qui s'est battu à la guerre.

Je ne crois pas qu'il ait su pourquoi il retournait là-bas, si c'était pour prouver quelque chose ou pour apaiser sa conscience, ou simplement pour que son succès ait des témoins, pour combler ce besoin qu'ont tous les enfants de plaire à leurs parents, de faire étalage de leur force.

Ses frères et sœurs étaient sortis en courant dès qu'il s'était garé.

«*Maman, maman**!» criaient-ils.

Sa mère l'avait embrassé sur les joues. Il n'y avait pas eu de récriminations. Il avait téléphoné au fil des années, et écrit des lettres bourrées de mensonges, mais il y avait eu des silences correspondant au temps passé en prison. Il s'était rendu compte que le sentiment qu'il avait toujours éprouvé, celui d'être son préféré, était juste. Elle lui aurait pardonné n'importe quoi.

Lucien était là, en bottes et pantalons de travail, les bras couverts de tatouages. Lui aussi s'était fait aplatir le nez, et il avait taquiné mon père sur son nouveau nez, lui demandant s'il était devenu une vedette d'Hollywood.

Mon père avait dit non et menti en expliquant qu'il était propriétaire d'une entreprise de transport aux États-Unis.

Lucien avait reniflé d'un air jaloux, le regard incertain. «*Une compagnie de transport*?*» Il s'était essuyé la bouche et avait tourné les talons.

Quelques jours plus tard, mon père avait mené sa mère sur la Côte-Nord rendre visite à ses sœurs qu'elle n'avait pas vues depuis des années. Il avait nolisé un petit avion et, dans l'air printanier, elle avait retrouvé sa famille, les enfants leur tournant autour tandis que lui discutait, debout, avec les hommes, disant peu de choses, se contentant de répéter ses histoires au sujet de son entreprise imaginaire.

À leur retour, Lucien l'avait taquiné sur ses cadeaux, le traitant de «*bon 'tit garçon**». Mon père l'avait ignoré, et Lucien avait évoqué la marine marchande, les bagarres dans les villes portuaires. Il était content que leur père lui ait appris à boxer. Il voulait aller boire, voir de nouveau mon père se battre, mais celui-ci craignait d'attirer l'attention. Il avait prétexté qu'il ne se battait plus, et Lucien s'était contenté de hocher la tête d'un air attentif.

Mon père parlait de la vie aux États-Unis, expliquait qu'il avait choisi de ne pas devenir américain pour éviter d'être conscrit et envoyé au Viêt Nam. Lucien lui avait demandé ce qu'il pensait de la province maintenant que les prêtres avaient perdu leur influence et que le Front de libération du Québec posait des bombes à Montréal. Mais mon père s'était borné à hausser les épaules.

«Tu n'es pas vraiment propriétaire d'une compagnie de transport, hein? avait demandé Lucien.

— Bien sûr que oui», lui avait répondu mon père, puis il s'était éloigné.

Expo 67 avait ouvert ses portes à Montréal, et mon père avait prévu y emmener ses deux plus jeunes frères. La veille, il avait invité son père à faire une balade dans sa décapotable. Ils s'étaient querellés. Il n'a pas dit pourquoi, simplement qu'il n'avait jamais eu d'affection pour son père. Même quand je lui ai posé la question, frustré de tout ce qu'il me cachait, il a refusé de me donner une réponse précise.

«On ne s'est jamais entendus et on n'a jamais eu grand-chose à se dire», m'a-t-il dit avant de continuer son histoire. À Montréal, il était passé devant un poste de police pour voir les photos des criminels recherchés. La sienne y figurait. Il savait qu'il aurait eu tort de s'attarder et pourtant, il ne pouvait s'empêcher de la scruter, écrasé par le poids de ses erreurs. Il ne s'était pas débarrassé de quoi que ce soit, n'était ni léger ni libre. Il ne lui restait plus de frontière à traverser pour recommencer à neuf. Malgré les faux noms et les adresses temporaires, ses crimes l'avaient suivi jusqu'à la maison.

Pendant une grosse chute de neige, je l'ai appelé de chez moi pour lui demander s'il se souvenait de la carte qu'il avait reçue au bureau de poste quand j'étais enfant. Il était resté debout dans le soleil à regarder la carte ornée de fleurs. Je lui avais demandé de quoi il s'agissait et ma mère avait plaisanté, répondant qu'elle venait de son autre famille.

Il ne se rappelait pas la carte, mais sa réponse était étonnante. «C'était peut-être de ma blonde de Salt Lake City. Elle avait un fils.

— Un fils?

— Elle était enceinte quand je suis entré en prison, mais elle ne m'a jamais rendu visite. Elle m'a envoyé des photos. Le garçon te ressemblait beaucoup quand tu étais petit. Mais elle a épousé un autre type et ils ont eu un enfant. J'ai vu une photo des deux garçons. L'autre était vraiment laid. Quoi qu'il en soit, j'ai gardé contact avec elle pendant quelque temps après avoir été déporté. Mais j'ai compris que ça ne servait à rien. L'enfant ne m'avait jamais connu. Il avait un autre père, alors je l'ai laissé vivre sa vie. C'est peut-être elle qui avait envoyé la carte. Je ne sais pas.

— Tu n'as jamais voulu faire sa connaissance?» ai-je demandé en essayant d'accepter cela : j'avais un autre frère. J'ai fermé les yeux sur ma colère.

«Non. Il portait le faux nom que j'utilisais à l'époque», a-t-il répondu, comme si, sous ce nom, il avait été une autre personne, et que par conséquent cet enfant n'était pas son fils. «Mais la femme était pas mal furax. Quand j'étais en prison, elle a découvert qu'elle ne connaissait pas mon vrai nom et elle a changé le nom de l'enfant pour qu'il porte celui de son nouveau mari. Est-ce que ça existe même, un faux nom? Je veux dire, on les invente tous. Ils se valent bien les uns les autres, pas vrai?»

Il était silencieux, comme s'il se rappelait ce qu'il avait ressenti à l'époque. J'ai regardé par la fenêtre, la tempête achevait. Les nuages s'éclaircissaient, la forêt blanche était éclairée par la lune.

« Tu sais, je lisais un article sur les anges l'autre jour », a-t-il poursuivi d'une voix radoucie. Il a résumé un texte où il était question d'un couple de Floride qui avait croisé un mendiant devant leur maison. Celui-ci leur avait demandé de la nourriture ou de l'argent, et ils lui avaient donné un sandwich et vingt dollars. Un mois plus tard, un homme noir aux yeux bleus s'était présenté à leur porte et leur avait remis un billet de loterie gagnant, affirmant qu'ils l'avaient égaré. Ils n'avaient jamais acheté de billets de loterie, ce qu'ils lui avaient dit, mais il leur avait montré que celui-là portait leurs noms inscrits au verso.

J'avais du mal à écouter, je pensais encore au frère, mais il n'y avait là rien à ressentir, pas même de place pour le regret, aussi me suis-je efforcé de prêter l'oreille à son histoire d'anges. Quand il a eu fini, j'ai dit qu'elle me semblait un peu mince.

« C'était dans le journal, a-t-il rétorqué. Ils n'écrivent pas de niaiseries dans le journal. C'est juste des vraies affaires. »

Il a parlé de miracles, de fantômes, de ce jour où, enfant, il avait vu son grand-père. Des années plus tard, après que ma mère nous eut emmenés aux États-Unis, il avait vu son propre père debout au pied de son lit un matin, cheveux et peau si sombres qu'on aurait dit une créature née de l'aube. La lumière filtrait à peine par les fenêtres. C'était son père jeune homme.

«Je l'avais détesté, a-t-il dit, mais à ce moment-là, je me suis senti en paix. J'ai cligné des yeux et il avait disparu.»

J'essayais d'écouter, mais je pensais à autre chose.

«Est-ce qu'André est ton vrai nom?»

Il est resté muet puis s'est éclairci la voix et a dit oui.

Plus tard, quand nous avons raccroché, je suis resté assis, une tension dans ma gorge et ma poitrine. J'étais capable de m'habituer à n'importe quoi, ai-je compris ; le silence de mon logement, la souffrance de ce que je m'efforçais d'accepter. Je commençais à avoir l'esprit encombré, et il m'aurait peut-être été bénéfique de parler à quelqu'un d'autre. J'avais passé trop de temps à étudier et n'avais que peu de contacts avec les autres étudiants. Je ne parlais pas souvent à ma mère, et je m'étais éloigné de mon frère et de ma sœur au fil des années.

J'ai enfilé mes bottes de randonnée et quelques pulls à manches longues et je suis sorti jogger sur un sentier forestier qui n'était guère plus qu'une piste blanche parmi les arbres.

L'air froid me piquait les poumons. J'ai gagné de la vitesse, prenant plaisir à sentir mes pieds glisser et plonger à la recherche d'une prise sur la terre ensevelie. La lune brillait sur les conifères, les rayons blancs sur leurs branches, les érables nus étaient ourlés de neige.

J'ai trouvé un rythme et, en avançant, j'ai vu des douzaines de personnages, des visages sombres ou pleins d'espoir. Qui étaient-ils — les hommes qui lui avaient appris le crime, ou ses complices, sa petite amie, les détenus avec qui il s'était battu, sa famille, Lucien et les autres dont j'ignorais le nom? J'étais furieux contre mon père à cause de tout ce qu'il m'avait caché, et à cause de tout ce que je ne pouvais me résoudre à dire. Je voulais lui en demander plus sur ces visages évanescents, trouver les mots pour les coucher sur le papier, révéler son passé et le rendre humain, lui instiller une profondeur qui va de pair avec la faillibilité et le simple manque.

Après son arrestation à Miami, il avait eu une occasion de s'évader. C'est dans cet espoir qu'il avait refusé de prendre l'avion, préférant traverser le pays dans une voiture de police où les deux agents se relayant au volant avaient l'air plus pitoyables que les détenus à l'arrière. Il y avait mon père et, de temps en temps, un ou deux autres prisonniers qui effectuaient une partie du trajet, transférés d'une prison à l'autre tout comme mon père était ramené en Californie pour pouvoir y subir son procès. Ils mangeaient dans des casse-croûte, utilisaient les toilettes publiques, tout le temps menottés et gardés. Un jour, après le dîner, pendant que l'un des policiers était occupé à régler l'addition, mon père avait subtilisé un trombone qui traînait sur le comptoir près de la caisse.

Sur la banquette arrière de la voiture de patrouille, il était assis au milieu, les détenus à sa droite et à sa gauche tenant chacun le côté d'un journal de façon à ce que tous puissent lire. S'en servant comme d'un écran, il avait entrepris de forcer la serrure de ses menottes. Les prisonniers avaient l'air inquiet mais, avec la radio qui jouait et les fenêtres entrouvertes, mon père avait pu leur souffler que s'ils le dénonçaient, il les tuerait dans leur sommeil. Partageant d'emblée ses ennuis avec la justice, et non dépourvus d'une certaine curiosité envers ce qu'il s'apprêtait à faire, ils étaient restés cois.

Il avait réussi à déverrouiller ses menottes. Alors qu'ils ralentissaient pour traverser une ville du Sud aux hauts trottoirs en bois et aux routes de terre battue, il avait bondi par-dessus le prisonnier près de lui et ouvert la portière. Puis il avait sauté sur le trottoir et s'était mis à courir. La voiture s'était arrêtée en dérapant, les policiers étaient sortis et l'avaient pris en chasse, pointant leur arme mais incapables de tirer parce que mon père courait aussi près des piétons qu'il le pouvait.

Il approchait d'un coin de rue quand un homme lui avait fait un croc-en-jambe, et il était tombé des lattes surélevées, le souffle coupé, incapable de faire autre chose que de regarder le ciel.

«Cet homme-là, a-t-il dit, il a tendu la jambe comme s'il était une sorte de héros.»

La colère dans sa voix était fraîche encore, et il n'avait plus l'air lointain ni vieux. Il n'a pas décrit ce qu'avaient fait les policiers. Il glissait toujours sur sa capture. Une vieille dame avait craché à ses pieds tandis qu'on l'emmenait. «Que Dieu ait pitié de vous», avait-elle prononcé. Cela du moins, il me l'a dit.

Il avait finalement été condamné à sept ans de prison et envoyé dans un pénitencier à Tacoma. Le premier jour, il était allé voir le gardien afin d'obtenir une cellule privée. On lui avait répondu que seuls les meurtriers avaient leur propre cellule.

«Vous voulez que je tue quelqu'un?» avait demandé mon père.

Plus tard, on l'avait amené à une cellule privée à l'étage supérieur.

Au pénitencier, il avait amélioré sa maîtrise de l'anglais et acquis des rudiments d'espagnol. Pour aiguiser sa résolution, il s'imaginait ce qu'il ferait à sa sortie. Il dresserait des chiens. Il aurait une famille et montrerait à pêcher à ses fils. Mais les jours de visite, sa petite amie ne venait jamais. Pour passer le temps, il avait obtenu son diplôme d'études secondaires, et quand le professeur avait expliqué l'expression *tabula rasa* en demandant un exemple, il avait répondu: «Comme mon dossier criminel chaque fois que je change de nom.»

Maintes histoires s'étaient déroulées dans la blême lumière grise du pénitencier. Sans crier gare, un détenu l'avait poignardé à l'épaule, et il avait réussi à briser le bras de l'homme avant que le sien ne s'engourdisse. Il y avait l'histoire de cette bagarre au cours de laquelle il avait fracassé la jambe d'un homme qu'il a racontée de nouveau, comme pour tenter de comprendre cet étrange amalgame de force et d'impuissance, ce qui faisait qu'un captif pouvait en terrasser un autre. L'homme s'était vanté de pouvoir donner une raclée à mon père, aussi celui-ci l'avait suivi dans sa cellule après le dîner, claquant la porte qui s'était verrouillée. Les jointures moites, les coups de pied, les côtes meurtries et brisées, les lèvres fendues étaient monnaie courante en prison et, à la fin, l'homme gisait au sol, se tenant le côté, sa paupière et sa joue enflées masquant une partie de son visage. Il avait voulu ramper sous la couchette pour échapper aux coups. Mon père s'était penché et lui avait saisi la jambe comme s'il s'apprêtait à déplacer un billot. Il l'avait pliée contre le poteau du lit en métal et y avait asséné un coup de pied. Puis il s'était assis sur le siège de toilette tandis que l'homme hurlait et sanglotait sous la couchette. Incapable d'ouvrir la porte de l'intérieur, il avait écouté les gardes arriver en courant.

Le récit qu'il faisait de cet épisode était presque tendre, comme s'il n'arrivait pas à comprendre qu'on puisse faire subir tant de souffrance et d'humiliation à un homme.

On l'avait puni en le mettant au secret pendant deux semaines, dans le Trou, un espace exigu où il pouvait à peine s'étirer. On lui avait enlevé ses vêtements, remplacés par une large salopette. Il n'y avait pas de couchette, seulement une grosse bible à la tranche abîmée qu'il étendait, ouverte, sur le béton humide pour s'en faire un oreiller quand venait le temps de dormir. Une fente dans la porte permettait aux gardes de jeter un coup d'œil à l'intérieur ; une autre, plus grande, près du sol, servait à lui passer du pain et de l'eau.

Il faisait de l'exercice — redressements assis et pompes ; il avait fini par devenir obsédé par le perfectionnement de ses coups de pied, et s'efforçait d'atteindre le plafond. On lui donnait un vrai repas par semaine, le dimanche. Le premier dimanche, quand le gardien avait ouvert la porte pour qu'un second garde apporte le plateau à l'intérieur, mon père était prêt. Il avait effectué son coup de pied parfait, attrapant le dessous du plateau, envoyant valser la nourriture au visage du gardien. L'homme était tombé en arrière et ressorti à quatre pattes tandis que l'autre gardien claquait la porte.

Quelques secondes plus tard, le directeur avait crié par la fente : « Deux semaines de plus ! »

Au pain et à l'eau, mon père avait continué à peaufiner ses coups de pied, plein de rage et affamé tandis qu'il s'étirait ou faisait de l'exercice, ses muscles tendus. Il se bourrait le corps de coups de poing, se penchait en arrière et frappait le plafond en béton de la plante du pied.

« Je ne voulais pas être pathétique, m'a-t-il dit. Je ne voulais pas être reconnaissant et me fourrer toute cette nourriture dans la bouche. Ça avait l'air d'un repas savoureux, et après que j'ai botté le plateau, la cellule embaumait la bonne nourriture. Ça me rendait fou. Mais je ne voulais pas que ces salauds s'imaginent que j'allais les remercier de me nourrir de la sorte. Alors je me suis fait plaisir. J'en ai fait un jeu. Je faisais rien que des pompes, des redressements assis et des étirements. Mon corps n'avait jamais été aussi dur. »

Je connaissais la flamme indomptée dans son regard, la folie joyeuse qui l'avait poussé dans tellement de situations hasardeuses simplement pour qu'il se mette lui-même à l'épreuve, pour qu'il se prouve qu'il pouvait gagner. Il ne voulait pas s'endormir. Il garderait la flamme. Il valait mieux avoir faim.

Le dimanche suivant, quand le gardien avait ouvert la porte, il avait de nouveau donné un coup de pied sur le plateau, plus vite, avec plus de force. Le gardien s'était préparé, mais la nourriture s'était tout de même renversée. Le directeur était revenu au pas de course dans le sous-sol.

« Deux semaines de plus, enfant de chienne », avait-il crié à travers le mince rectangle qui, plusieurs fois par jour, encadrait un œil las et indifférent cerné de rouge.

Mais quelques jours plus tard, on avait renvoyé mon père dans sa cellule, des instances supérieures ayant interprété ses gestes comme une grève de la faim — et personne ne voulait courir le risque qu'il mette sa vie en danger.

Plusieurs mois avaient passé, et il avait appris qu'il allait être déporté vers une prison en Colombie-Britannique, où les contribuables canadiens pourraient nourrir ce criminel qui leur appartenait. Il attendait que les documents de transfert arrivent, mais peu après qu'il eut annoncé son départ aux autres détenus, l'un d'eux avait fait circuler une rumeur voulant qu'il avait l'intention d'assassiner mon père. C'était la première menace de mort qu'il recevait en prison. L'homme bluffait peut-être, essayant de se donner des airs de dur parce qu'il savait que mon père allait partir, mais mon père n'avait tout de même pas le choix. Il m'a confié la règle : si un homme dit qu'il va te tuer, crois-le et tue-le avant. Il était resté assis toute la nuit dans sa cellule à se préparer.

« Je ne voulais pas être obligé de le faire, m'a-t-il dit. J'ai eu de la chance. Mes documents de transfert sont arrivés le lendemain et j'ai été envoyé de Tacoma à Vancouver. S'ils n'étaient pas arrivés, je l'aurais tué. La prison, c'est une question d'honneur. C'est tout ce que tu as. Si quelqu'un dit qu'il va te buter et que tu ne fais rien, tu vas être tué. Quelqu'un va s'en charger. Tu vas devenir une cible. »

Sa voix était sévère, sa respiration bruyante et hachée.

« Tu sais, ces trucs ont toujours hanté mes rêves depuis. J'ai vu beaucoup d'horreurs. J'ai vu ce gars se faire scalper pendant l'accident d'auto. Il a été projeté de la banquette arrière et s'est frappé la tête sur le tableau de bord. Ça lui a arraché le cuir chevelu de sur le crâne. J'imagine que ce qui m'est arrivé était pire encore. J'ai fini sous la voiture. Il n'y avait rien de bon. Rien qui vaille la peine que je m'en souvienne. Le pénitencier était un endroit horrible. Il y avait des hommes qui étaient emprisonnés parce qu'ils avaient violé des femmes et leur avaient arraché les mamelons avec leurs dents. On leur crachait dessus. Ils ne pouvaient pas être laissés avec nous, parce qu'on les aurait tués. Quand on servait la nourriture en file, on crachait sur leur nourriture et sur eux. On continuait à cracher jusqu'à ce qu'ils soient passés. J'étais emprisonné pour des crimes honorables. J'étais respecté.»

Il a cessé de parler, continuant de respirer bruyamment. Je ne pouvais m'empêcher de me demander quelle partie de son passé il choisissait de laisser de côté. Où était la vérité? Il avait passé relativement peu de temps en prison compte tenu de tous les crimes qu'il avait commis. Ma frustration ne faisait que grandir tandis qu'il racontait. J'en avais marre de constater comme il y avait peu de choses que nous pouvions nous dire.

«Les peines n'auraient pas dû être plus longues?» ai-je demandé en essayant de rester calme.

Il a répondu d'une voix rauque: «Non. La plupart des crimes que j'avais commis, personne n'a jamais réussi à prouver que j'en étais responsable. Mais la police veut négocier. Ils ont besoin de clore des affaires. Ils ont accepté de réduire les accusations si je m'avouais coupable de quelques vols et leur fournissais de l'information. Les criminels profitent toujours de la bureaucratie policière de cette manière.

— Est-ce qu'il a fallu que tu leur parles de tes complices?

— Non. Ça n'a jamais été rien de sérieux. Ils voulaient simplement clore des affaires.»

L'intensité de ma colère m'a surpris. C'était à cause de la conversation elle-même, du fait que nous ayons été en train de discuter de cela — de cette façon —, du fait que je n'éprouvais aucune tendresse, n'avais aucun moyen d'exprimer sympathie ou chagrin. Je savais avec une absolue certitude qu'il m'aurait haï si je l'avais fait se sentir faible. À quoi bon toutes ces histoires? Il resterait en vie quelques jours de plus et je pourrais recoller les morceaux de sa vie fracturée, l'écrire simplement pour voir et éprouver tout ce que nous avions perdu? Qu'existait-il d'autre, sinon tester les limites, continuer de partager de folles aventures? J'étais furieux. Même la vérité n'importait pas.

«Alors tu n'as jamais fini par tuer qui que ce soit?» ai-je demandé tranquillement, d'abord incertain de ce que je souhaitais, avant de me rendre compte que j'avais posé la question pour entendre ses remords, pour voir si j'arriverais à lui faire avouer, une fois au moins, tout ce qu'il avait ruiné.

Il n'a pas répondu tout de suite, peut-être étonné que je pose de nouveau la question après si longtemps.

«C'est… c'est compliqué. Des fois, sur un coup, il y a des choses qui arrivent. Mais je ne me suis jamais engagé dans une affaire avec ça en tête. Je n'ai jamais voulu priver quelqu'un de son père. J'en ai fait mon principe…»

J'écoutais, attendant qu'il finisse.

«Je devrais te laisser, a-t-il dit. Il doit être tard chez vous. On se parlera demain. O.K.?

— O.K.», ai-je dit, mais il avait déjà raccroché.

Les pages tournaient et tout à coup j'avais l'impression de comprendre, comme une bouffée d'adrénaline mais, tout aussi soudainement, l'impression s'évanouissait. Je fouillais des phrases qui s'embrouillaient, les pages tournaient de plus en plus vite, l'encre noire des mots coulait sur mon visage comme une pluie.

Le vent frappait les murs, faisait trembler les fenêtres, et je me suis réveillé. On entendait distinctement les glaçons au bord du toit se briser et tomber sur le côté de la maison.

Je suis sorti de mon lit et me suis assis à mon pupitre, où j'ai regardé les pages sombres de mon calepin, leurs contours vides. Quelle proportion de sa vie avait-il inventée? Sa chemise lui collait-elle à la peau, lui piquant le dos, les lacets d'un de ses souliers étaient-ils trop serrés tandis qu'il se dirigeait vers la banque et enfilait son masque? Tous les bruits de l'autre côté de sa fenêtre à la nuit tombée lui avaient-ils fait songer que des hommes épiaient, prêts à désamorcer le monde tel qu'il tournait dans sa tête? Me verrais-je sous la pluie, un bâton de baseball me heurtant la jambe pendant que je marchais — ou un hayon de camionnette encroûté de glace et de sang de poisson tandis que je notais des kilos illégaux, la descente vers l'horizon quand le soleil vidait la nuit, la drainant pour révéler la crasse qui se cachait dessous, le bord de la rivière semblable à une soudure derrière le brouillard, au-delà des arbres —, et trouverais-je quelque forme de rédemption?

Ce n'étaient pas ses histoires de crimes qui me hantaient, mais des images simples: un jour où je l'avais suivi dans les rangées de pins, ses mains à demi ouvertes sur ses jeans tandis qu'il marchait et je lui avais demandé pourquoi il ne pleurait pas ou s'il avait jamais pleuré. Il m'avait dit que je ne devrais pas le faire, et j'avais voulu comprendre comment il était possible de ne pas pleurer quand on était en colère, triste ou blessé. Il s'était arrêté. «Je ne pleure pas. Les hommes ne pleurent pas. J'ai du travail à faire. Retourne à la maison.» Je m'étais empourpré, trop furieux pour parler, les larmes aux yeux, ce qui me gênait et avivait encore ma haine envers lui. J'avais tourné les talons et commencé à m'éloigner mais il avait vu mon visage et m'avait crié de m'arrêter. Il me regardait comme s'il était en proie à la confusion, comme si quelque chose venait juste de lui venir à l'esprit. Il m'avait regardé, le front plissé, les joues relevées. Cherchait-il les mots pour exprimer quelque chose? J'étais resté debout à attendre, et il avait dit: «Je pleurerais s'il t'arrivait quelque chose, alors sois prudent, O.K.?» Et puis il avait souri comme si c'était une blague, et nous avions ri tous les deux. Il avait fait au revoir de la main et je m'étais remis en route vers la maison à travers champs.

Pourquoi ce monde n'avait-il pas duré? Était-ce parce qu'il était incapable de rester en place, ou à cause de la lutte constante dans ses yeux, comme s'il n'était jamais tant lui-même que lorsqu'il s'efforçait d'avoir raison de quelqu'un ou de quelque chose, ou de s'affranchir? Et pourtant il avait essayé, s'était transformé en homme d'affaires, avait ouvert des poissonneries, vendu des arbres de Noël — à une époque, il pouvait même se vanter de posséder la plus vaste plantation d'arbres de Noël du sud de la Colombie-Britannique. Mais il avait toujours l'air d'être sur son départ, mal à l'aise quand il restait où que ce soit, et lorsqu'il racontait des histoires, j'avais l'impression, à son rire ou à l'impatience dans son regard, qu'il revivrait de nouveau bientôt ces aventures.

Nous sommes déjà allés à la pêche au Nicomen Slough, près de l'endroit où je suis né. Il m'avait laissé ramer pour descendre la rivière tandis qu'il fixait les appâts. Puis nous nous étions laissés dériver en pêchant. Le ciel était un champ de gris et le vent faisait tourbillonner l'eau, de petites vagues frappaient la coque de la chaloupe. Quand des aiguilles de pluie glacée s'étaient mises à tomber, il avait ramé. Nous avions dérivé loin, le pont n'était plus qu'une dentelle d'ombre. Je ne croyais pas que nous réussirions à rentrer. Il avait déposé les cannes au fond du bateau et poussait régulièrement sur les rames. Je m'étais pelotonné tandis que le vent nous faisait gicler de l'écume dans les yeux.

Quand il avait chargé la chaloupe dans le camion et l'y avait attachée, nous avions marché jusqu'à un casse-croûte de l'autre côté de l'embarcadère. Il s'était assis sur une banquette et j'étais allé à la salle de bains. Mes doigts engourdis n'arrivaient pas à reboutonner mon jean raide, aussi les avais-je tenus sous l'eau chaude, trop fier pour le lui dire. Quand j'étais sorti, mes mains brûlant de leur sensation retrouvée, deux cafés nous attendaient. Il ne m'avait jamais laissé boire de café. La boisson était d'un léger brun chocolat et, à mon palais, crémeuse et riche. Il m'avait regardé avec fierté, et j'avais eu l'intuition de tout ce qu'il savait, et deviné combien nous étions semblables. La tempête soufflait contre les fenêtres et ses doigts déchiquetaient le rebord d'une serviette de table tandis qu'il fixait quelque chose au-delà de la vitre, dans le lointain.

Il a appelé juste avant minuit, ayant oublié que nous n'étions pas dans le même fuseau horaire. Je me suis excusé auprès de mes propriétaires et j'ai changé de téléphone pour prendre l'appel dans le salon. J'ai demandé s'il allait bien.

«Des fois, je voudrais disparaître, m'a-t-il dit. Je ne veux pas t'embêter avec ça, mais quand ta mère vous a emmenés, j'ai planifié de me suicider. Si je ne l'ai pas fait, c'est que j'avais peur que vous pensiez que j'étais un lâche. Mais tu comprends que ce n'est pas de la lâcheté?»

J'ai dégluti à quelques reprises. Pourquoi me posait-il la question?

«Je comprends.

— En te le disant, j'avais peur de te troubler et que ça interfère avec ton travail scolaire.

— Je veux savoir. C'est important.»

Il s'est raclé la gorge et a demandé, d'un ton presque enfantin : «Tu crois que c'est mal?»

J'aurais voulu voir son visage, lire l'intention dans ses yeux. Comment pouvais-je prendre cette décision — comment lui dire de lâcher prise ou de continuer à souffrir, à attendre?

«Il faut que tu comprennes que ce n'est pas de la lâcheté, ce que je veux faire.

— Je comprends, ai-je répondu, vide d'émotion, détaché.

— J'avais peur de te troubler si je te le disais…

— Je voulais savoir. C'est important.»

J'ai remué les lèvres comme pour parler mais j'ai hésité. Il a soupiré et dit : «Je pensais que tu pourrais peut-être prendre congé pendant quelque temps. Tu pourrais venir ici et me donner un coup de main, et peut-être qu'on pourrait remettre le marché sur pied. À l'été, on pourrait louer un chalet quelque part et aller à la pêche. On pourrait prendre une caravane, juste voyager et pêcher.

— Je ne peux pas faire ça, ai-je répondu trop vite. Écoute, vraiment, je ne peux pas — je ne veux pas travailler à ta poissonnerie. »

J'ai changé le téléphone d'oreille et frotté mon lobe chaud, enfonçant le bout de mes doigts dans la chair comme pour me réveiller. Je voulais lui demander comment il avait cru que sa vie se terminerait après tout ce qu'il avait fait. Mais je n'ai rien dit, et il m'a répondu : « Je comprends. Mais peut-être à l'été…

— Je ne sais pas. Peut-être. » J'aurais voulu m'arrêter et offrir une réponse plus réfléchie, mais j'étais incapable de m'imaginer retourner là-bas. J'aimais ce que j'étais en train de devenir ici. J'avais travaillé tellement fort pour y arriver et je ne voulais pas me retrouver coincé dans la vie qu'il avait créée. Pourtant, j'ai fait taire mes pensées et me suis forcé à garder mon calme afin de poursuivre la conversation. J'ai dit : « J'ai écrit toutes les histoires que tu m'as racontées », mais je n'arrivais pas à lui dire que je voulais en entendre davantage. Il en avait déjà tellement raconté en peu de temps, urgemment, comme si ce n'était qu'une fois qu'il aurait fini qu'il pourrait mourir. Et pourtant je savais que nous ne finirions jamais, que nous n'atteindrions jamais un lieu de véritable échec, ni celui de notre douleur commune. Je voulais être en colère pour ce qu'il était, pour ce qu'il avait été incapable d'être, pour nous, pour notre famille. Pour y arriver, pour croire qu'il avait tort, il me faudrait renoncer à ce qui m'était le plus cher.

« Bien, m'a-t-il dit après une pause, doucement. Ça me plaît, que tu les écrives. »

534

J'ai pensé à tout ce qu'il avait décrit, des voyages qui ne s'enchaînaient jamais tout à fait, et me suis rappelé combien il avait voulu une nouvelle vie. Avait-il appris à vivre pour le seul plaisir de la faim — pour le défi, la victoire, pour la fuite? Cela était-il possible? Faim de l'inatteignable, de ce qu'on n'obtiendra jamais et qui ne nous décevra jamais. Faim de solitude où, quelque acharnement qu'on mette à lutter contre soi-même, on sera toujours victorieux. Faim d'intensité, sensation semblable à l'amande de tous les fruits dépouillés de leurs couleurs et de leurs écorces, rendus semblables, de sorte que ce qui a été perdu peut de nouveau être gagné ailleurs, de sorte que rien n'est désiré pour ce qu'il est mais uniquement pour la grâce d'un fugace instant d'union, de reconnaissance, avant d'être dilapidé et rejeté. Faim de vérité, d'amour, de Dieu, d'une seule chose à laquelle on puisse faire confiance parce qu'elle ne semble pas de ce monde. Faim du parfait plaisir du désir, une faim qui dure depuis si longtemps qu'on ne peut plus y remédier comme on nous dit de le faire, par le recours aux joies simples de la vie.

Il parlait tandis que je transportais le téléphone jusqu'à la fenêtre. La lune éclairait les nuages. Le passé irréel était là, les hivers revenaient, soufflés dans la cour en bourrasques et en flocons.

L'AUTOROUTE LA PLUS LONGUE

Après la fin des cours, cinq mois après sa mort, j'ai roulé jusqu'en Virginie pour travailler dans la construction et me dégeler au soleil.

Je gardais la maison d'un ami, et un soir j'ai rendu visite à ma mère là où elle vivait, non loin des Appalaches. De grosses phalènes au corps épais martelaient les fenêtres de leurs ailes poudreuses, faisant sursauter nos reflets assis à table. L'obscurité étouffante entrait par la porte-moustiquaire, les criquets stridulaient, on entendait dans le lointain la faible écholalie des oiseaux nocturnes.

«Je veux parler d'André, lui ai-je dit.

— Je ne pense plus à lui, a-t-elle répondu. Ça ne donne rien de bon.

— Je veux savoir comment tu le voyais — ce que tu te rappelles.»

Ses yeux étaient bleu pâle, la peau autour légèrement pincée tandis qu'elle examinait ses mains fortes et tannées par le jardinage. Elle en a frotté une le long de son bras. Elle n'avait jamais été une conteuse d'histoires, possédant cette réticence propre aux Écossais, et ce n'était que grâce à des révélations fortuites que j'en étais venu à la comprendre : sa colère contre les États-Unis pendant la guerre du Viêt Nam, la fois où elle avait vu jouer Jimi Hendrix dans le sous-sol d'une université avant qu'il ne soit célèbre, ou son petit ami guatémaltèque dans le District de Columbia pendant les années soixante, un homme appartenant à une puissante famille politique qui souhaitait qu'elle déménage dans son pays. Elle avait manifesté peu de besoin de parler de son passé, aussi devais-je insister si je voulais savoir quelque chose.

Elle a commencé à me relater les faits habituels : que mon père savait vivre de la terre, et lui avait offert la vie dont elle avait envie. Ils avaient voyagé et pêché, leurs libertés se faisant écho, lui libéré de la prison, elle de son éducation protestante. Mais quand il avait renoué contact avec des hommes de son passé, elle s'était mise à avoir peur. Il partait avec eux, et elle préférait ne pas savoir ce qu'il fabriquait. Elle avait l'impression qu'elle pouvait à peine mettre le pied en dehors du chalet. Elle allait à la porte et les horizons sombraient dans le lointain, le ciel était vide, sans couleur, insondable, un vide reflétant sa méfiance et son incertitude.

Quand je l'ai interrogée sur les crimes de mon père, elle a soupiré.

«Bon Dieu, c'est dur de m'avouer à moi-même que j'ai pu être aussi idiote.

— Tu étais jeune, ai-je dit. Et puis, tu ne pouvais pas t'attendre à ça.

— Non. Mais c'est tout de même difficile à accepter.»

J'ai demandé des détails sur son trafic de drogue: les fusils, les amphétamines, le laboratoire.

«Eh bien, il avait des fusils, mais je ne les ai jamais vus. Il me cachait tout. Et il n'avait pas de laboratoire. C'est peut-être comme ça qu'il l'appelait, mais ça ressemblait davantage à une cuisine. Il faisait cuire des trucs sur une plaque chauffante. Pas de doute, c'était une cuisine, rien de sophistiqué.»

Ce n'est que lorsqu'elle est tombée enceinte qu'il a arrêté. Ses grossesses étaient parmi les périodes les plus heureuses de sa vie. Elle adorait la façon dont son corps s'épanouissait. D'autres femmes de sa connaissance se plaignaient, mais elle trouvait la grossesse facile, se sentait vivante et calme, et elle croyait qu'il changerait de vie.

«Il était extrêmement intelligent. C'était parfois stupéfiant d'entendre ses idées. Et dès qu'il s'est lancé en affaires, il a eu du succès. En cinq ou six ans, il était propriétaire de plusieurs poissonneries à Vancouver et dans les environs. Il avait la bosse des affaires et, pour autant que je sache, tout était légal. Je tenais ses livres, et je voyais ce qu'il achetait et vendait. S'il se tramait autre chose, il le cachait bien.

«Je suppose, a-t-elle repris, et elle a hésité, je suppose que lorsque je l'ai laissé j'avais fini par accepter qu'il ne changerait jamais. Il ne serait jamais satisfait. Mais il avait tant de charisme et était tellement persuasif. La majorité de nos amis m'ont critiquée. Personne ne pouvait imaginer qu'il faisait quelque chose de mal. C'est pour ça que je suis restée si longtemps avec lui. Toutes ces années, j'ai cru qu'il serait devenu meilleur, plus doux, parce que c'est l'impression qu'il donnait. Mais on aurait dit qu'il fallait qu'il détruise tout, comme si une partie de lui devait rendre sa vie aussi insupportable que possible, pour qu'il ait quelque chose à combattre. Et même à ce moment-là, il trouvait le moyen de bien paraître aux yeux des autres. Je ne sais pas comment il faisait.

— Je veux retrouver sa famille, lui ai-je dit. Les as-tu déjà rencontrés?

— Non. J'ai déjà parlé à quelques-uns au téléphone une fois, mais on avait du mal à se comprendre parce que je comprenais à peine le français et qu'ils ne parlaient presque pas anglais.

— Pourquoi a-t-il cessé de leur parler?

— Il m'a dit que les familles francophones étaient envahissantes, qu'ils seraient toujours en train de nous rendre visite. C'est la raison qu'il a donnée.» Elle a hésité. «Quand nous nous sommes rencontrés, nous avons traversé le pays en auto. Nous sommes passés par le Québec, juste devant l'endroit où il avait grandi. Il n'arrêtait pas de dire combien c'était arriéré. On s'est arrêtés pour manger dans une roulotte à patates frites le long de la route.» Elle a décrit le Saint-Laurent, la côte venteuse où ils avaient garé la voiture pour marcher sur la berge.

«Il a appelé ses parents quand on a été à environ quatre-vingts kilomètres de chez eux. Il leur a dit qu'il était à Vancouver. Ce soir-là, on a traversé la ville où vivait sa famille et on ne s'est pas arrêtés.»

À l'époque où mes parents se sont rencontrés, il possédait déjà ses bergers allemands, un noir et fauve, l'autre noir avec une marque argentée au poitrail. Il était en libération conditionnelle et vivait dans une roulotte, voyageant et pêchant, dormant à la belle étoile. Il ne pouvait assouvir sa soif de liberté.

Quand il avait évoqué leur rencontre, racontant : «J'ai commandé du jambon et des œufs et puis je suis parti avec elle», je n'avais pas compris ce qui les avait poussés l'un vers l'autre. Mais peut-être existe-t-il des besoins simples, des espaces vides qui doivent être comblés.

À vingt ans, elle avait quitté l'objecteur de conscience avec qui elle s'était enfuie à Vancouver et, comme elle adorait le Canada, elle était restée. Elle avait rencontré mon père et ils avaient voyagé, mais il avait fini par avoir besoin d'argent et avait entrepris de retracer des hommes de son passé. Il avait commencé à fabriquer des amphétamines pour un ami.

«Cet ami…, m'avait-il dit, c'était le type qui s'était brûlé les yeux, celui qui avait mis le feu à l'appartement à Hollywood. Il ne voyait toujours pas très bien. J'avais pitié de lui. C'est lui qui avait eu l'idée, pour les amphés. Il avait les recettes et les ingrédients. J'ai pensé que je pourrais lui donner un coup de main.»

L'histoire ne tenait pas la route. Comment pouvait-il, lui qui avait malmené d'autres hommes, pardonner si facilement? Mais cet ami faisait partie de sa vie depuis des années, avait-il expliqué. Il avait été son complice dans plusieurs coups. Peut-être mon père avait-il reçu une peine réduite en échange de renseignements livrés à la police, et avait-il ainsi une conception différente de ce qu'était la déloyauté.

Il n'avait jamais décrit précisément la période qui avait suivi. Quand ma mère était tombée enceinte, il avait abandonné le crime, ne voulant pas qu'un autre enfant naisse pendant qu'il était en prison. Il avait cru qu'une famille le ferait rester en place et lui apporterait satisfaction. Pour gagner de l'argent, il avait commencé à acheter et à vendre du saumon. Il devait toujours se rapporter à son agent de probation et avait obtenu la permission de rendre visite à son fils aux États-Unis, mais il avait décidé de couper les liens et n'était jamais allé. Il avait appelé sa mère quelques fois au Québec, mais décidé qu'il lui fallait repartir à neuf.

«Je voulais ma vie à moi, m'avait-il dit. Trop de choses avaient changé.»

Mais ses paroles n'avaient pas l'accent de la vérité. C'était la semaine avant les examens. Je me regardais étudier. Je vivais retiré. Tous les jours, je parcourais le chemin à pied jusqu'à l'école et, à l'occasion, je me rendais en ville dans mon camion non assuré, le plus souvent après minuit, pour aller faire des courses au supermarché ouvert vingt-quatre heures. Les rues étaient vides sous les ciels froids de Noël, il y avait des ampoules colorées dans quelques arbres dépouillés de leurs feuilles.

Il était toujours tard quand nous nous parlions, lui d'une voix forte, moi sur le ton du chuchotement. Il m'avait dit que la vie était une blague. Il avait été élevé sans instruction et c'étaient des criminels qui lui avaient montré le chemin à suivre.

«J'ai dévalisé ces banques quand j'étais dans la jeune vingtaine, avait-il dit. J'étais un enfant. Un ostie d'enfant. Je ferais n'importe quoi pour recommencer à zéro. J'aurais voulu pouvoir être toi. Tu as toujours été tellement plein d'espoir.»

J'en avais assez entendu sur le crime, mais si j'avais posé des questions sur sa famille, il m'aurait simplement dit que trop de temps avait passé, qu'il ne servait à rien d'y retourner.

«Pourtant, je n'ai jamais perdu courage, avait-il dit. J'ai toujours eu du cœur au ventre. Je me souviens de la dernière banque que j'ai voulu dévaliser. J'étais avec un gars qui avait fait plusieurs coups. Je l'avais déjà vu faire d'autres braquages. Mais on a fait le tour de l'édifice, et il n'arrivait pas à enfiler son masque. Il n'arrêtait pas de dire : "Pas tout de suite." La dernière fois qu'on est passés devant la porte, il m'a avoué qu'il n'était pas capable d'entrer. Il suait et il tremblait. Il ne savait plus pourquoi il faisait cela. Il m'a dit qu'il voulait juste que sa vie soit simple. On était dans la ruelle, et il a demandé s'il pouvait s'en aller. Voilà comment c'était. Pendant des années tu étais capable de le faire, et puis le courage t'abandonnait.»

Je pense à des chants, à des hommes en prison assoiffés de mouvement, envieux du grondement des trains, du soleil inexorable au-dessus des ouvriers sur la route et des voitures qui passent, des enfants qui regardent ou des épaules nues des filles. L'homme était incapable de supporter la perspective de nuits humides en prison, le soleil en cage dans les fenêtres. Il avait dit qu'il voulait arrêter parce qu'il avait un bébé en chemin, comme mon père, vers qui il s'était tourné parce qu'il le savait fiable. Tous les deux avaient une femme qui les attendait.

Mon père avait hésité, comme s'il cherchait ses mots.

«Je l'ai laissé partir, avait-il fini par dire. Mais je n'ai jamais perdu courage comme ça. J'ai arrêté simplement parce que vous êtes nés. Je voulais une famille et je ne voulais pas retourner en prison.»

En l'entendant, j'avais l'impression qu'il était insatisfait de la vie qu'il avait eue depuis, que la seule chose qu'il avait voulue, une famille, l'avait trahi, et qu'il aurait dû continuer dans le crime. Mais la vérité commençait à m'apparaître. Les vols de banques et de bijouteries avaient été plus faciles pour lui. Il était encore cet enfant craignant d'hiverner dans la maison, d'être enfermé dans une vie normale.

Je voudrais pouvoir l'entendre raconter cela encore une fois, non pas ces histoires de crimes faciles contées dans des restaurants aux lumières tamisées, au milieu de chaises renversées sur les tables, où nous étions les derniers clients, mais la façon dont il avait tenté de décrire son pouvoir quand il avait laissé partir son ami. Il me dépeignait un homme si effrayé, si incertain de ce que le monde lui avait donné, que lorsqu'il s'était arrêté et avait laissé bourdonner les parasites sur la ligne, je n'étais plus sûr de savoir de qui il parlait.

La vallée revient en impressions simples : des taches de lumière sur le plancher de la cuisine, l'ombre des montagnes dehors, l'air frais à travers la porte et notre mère qui nous appelle pour manger, l'odeur du pain brun et les éléments chauds dans le four ouvert. Ou la brume immobile, le sentiment de sécurité au côté de mon père quand nous traversions les champs, les planches gauchies de la clôture, les poteaux dissimulés dans l'herbe jaune.

Les jours passés avec lui sont parmi les plus clairs. J'étudiais son visage tandis qu'il parlait — ses yeux sombres et expressifs, sa grosse barbe. Son haleine sentait le café. Il était toujours en train de prêter de petites sommes d'argent et une fois, debout devant son magasin tandis que la lumière du soleil filtrait parmi les trois pins qu'il avait plantés là, je lui avais demandé pourquoi. Il m'avait dit que ça valait bien un peu d'argent de savoir si l'on pouvait faire confiance à quelqu'un. J'avais apprécié la justesse de l'observation et m'étais mis à prêter des cinq cents à l'école.

Ces années-là, il avait construit des enclos pour les chiens, élevé des clôtures, vendu des arbres et ouvert des magasins. Il n'était pas certain que ce travail lui plaisait, mais les habiletés que lui avait enseignées son père lui étaient vite revenues — le poisson n'était pas si différent sur cette côte, ses doigts manipulaient le couteau d'eux-mêmes, l'amenant de l'autre côté de la poreuse frontière du souvenir. Souvent, on aurait dit qu'il se mettait au défi d'en faire le plus possible, satisfait de l'authenticité de la vie qu'il était en train de bâtir, affirmant sa force, trouvant de nouvelles façons de grandir, de se mettre à l'épreuve.

Un matin, il était sorti de la maison vêtu d'un veston, une mallette à la main. Notre mère était assise dans les marches, à nous regarder jouer. Le vent froissait les feuilles de l'arbre près de la galerie, jetant sur le visage de mon père un entrelacs ombrageux de branches et de lumière. Il avait tiré sur ses manches, elle avait levé les yeux. J'observais, assis sur mon vélo, un pied par terre, et elle avait ri. C'était un rire de plaisir et d'étonnement, mais il avait rougi, avait marché jusqu'au camion, y était monté. Elle aurait voulu vivre dans la nature, mais il désirait devenir l'homme d'affaires dans les histoires qu'il racontait à sa famille, se transformer encore une fois.

«J'aurais peut-être pu retourner au Québec, avait-il dit, si les choses s'étaient passées autrement avec votre mère. J'aurais pu leur montrer ma famille et mon entreprise. Ils auraient compris cela. Mais même à ce moment-là, c'était compliqué…

— Qu'est-ce qui était compliqué? avais-je demandé, sachant maintenant que rien n'aurait jamais été assez bien pour lui.

— J'étais parti depuis longtemps…» Il avait hésité, puis avait repris avec une colère trop grande pour les paroles qu'il prononçait. «Je me rappelle quand je suis retourné, c'était pauvre. Je ne voulais pas faire partie de ce monde-là. Et mon frère, il était toujours en train de se battre. Il avait le nez écrasé. Je voulais vivre ma vie…»

Après le départ de ma mère, il avait passé des semaines au lit, se nourrissant à peine. Il ne se levait que pour aller à la toilette, ou boire de l'eau, ou se remettre à lui téléphoner ainsi qu'à ses parents. Dans un tiroir, il avait trouvé l'adresse d'une médium qu'elle avait consultée, une femme qui lui avait annoncé que Vancouver serait anéanti dans un tremblement de terre. Il avait pris rendez-vous, souhaitant obtenir sa propre prophétie. La femme avait expliqué qu'elle ne pouvait pas parler de ma mère, mais avait prédit que, de ses trois enfants, celui du milieu serait le premier à revenir. Ce ne serait pas avant longtemps. Voilà tout ce qu'elle pouvait dire.

Quand il avait fini par se rendre au centre-ville, il avait les mains qui tremblaient et la nausée lui nouait la gorge. Il avait éraflé deux voitures garées mais ne s'était pas arrêté. Son magasin n'était pas verrouillé et l'endroit était déserté. Il avait mangé une portion de frites, qu'il avait vomie en ouvrant la porte pour découvrir la glace fondue et le poisson en train de pourrir, les vitrines fourmillant de mouches bleues. L'électricité avait été coupée et un liquide rougeâtre et visqueux suintait sous la porte du congélateur-chambre. L'air rance et humide prenait à la gorge, et il était resté juste le temps de vérifier qu'il ne restait pas d'argent dans le tiroir-caisse. Le chariot rouillé d'un clochard était stationné dans la pièce du fond. Des lettres de créanciers s'empilaient sur le sol. Un avis d'expulsion était affiché sur la porte.

Il s'était assis dans la camionnette qu'il avait achetée quelques mois auparavant, alors qu'elle venait juste de sortir sur le marché — parfaite pour les livraisons, avait-il annoncé à tout le monde. Sa mallette en cuir était posée sur le siège du passager et encore une fois il s'était imaginé la remplir de poisson. Il l'aurait apportée à la banque, aurait loué un coffret de sûreté dans lequel il aurait glissé le poisson. Il s'était rendu compte qu'il avait passé des années à se battre contre les banques ou les prisons, essayant d'atteindre quelque chose qui était enfermé ou d'éviter lui-même l'enfermement, dans une prison, une maison ou une vie trop étriquée.

Quand il était rentré chez lui et s'était recouché dans son lit, le téléphone sonnait sans discontinuer. Il avait trop de créanciers et pas d'argent pour les impôts. La vie qu'il s'était bâtie était moins substantielle qu'il ne l'avait cru, et ce qu'il avait fait ensuite cadrait mieux avec sa jeunesse qu'avec ces sept ou huit années de succès relatif. Après avoir entreposé quelques possessions chez un ami, il était retourné à la maison équipé d'essence, de corde et d'un couteau. Il s'était versé l'essence sur la tête, s'était fait une petite incision à la gorge et avait réussi à se ligoter lui-même. Puis il s'était libéré et avait appelé la police. À l'arrivée des policiers, il leur avait dit que des hommes étaient débarqués chez lui, qu'ils lui avaient lié les mains, mis un couteau sur la gorge et l'avaient aspergé d'essence, puis qu'ils avaient menacé de le faire flamber. Il leur avait révélé où il gardait l'argent qu'il avait en réserve, et ils avaient tout pris. Les policiers avaient rempli un rapport pour déclarer les biens volés, que mon père avait envoyé le lendemain, annexé à ses documents d'impôt.

Il avait ensuite glissé dans un sac à dos nourriture, ouvre-boîte et une bouteille de whisky. Ses créanciers allaient le chercher, et il savait que toutes ses possessions seraient saisies. Il avait fait du stop jusqu'à une bretelle d'accès à l'autoroute Transcanadienne. La lune se levait, et c'était l'heure où il rentrait normalement à la maison pour y trouver le confort contre lequel il se débattait. Il n'était pas loin d'un endroit dont il gardait le souvenir, où le large terre-plein était densément boisé et où, juste après la sortie suivante, se trouvait un dépanneur. Il avait attendu qu'il n'y ait plus de phares en vue avant de traverser la chaussée. Le terre-plein faisait soixante mètres de forêt. Il avait planté sa tente dans une ravine confortable, à l'abri du vent. Même le bruit de la circulation semblait lointain. Il avait un bon sac de couchage. Il était tombé un peu de neige, ce qui était préférable à l'humidité.

«Personne ne s'attend à ce que tu disparaisses au milieu du terre-plein d'une des plus longues auto-routes du monde, m'avait-il expliqué. Tes créanciers vont plutôt croire que tu as changé de province ou traversé la frontière.»

Il avait dit que lorsqu'il était en ville, il lui arrivait encore de croiser des hommes qui n'en revenaient pas de le voir. «On te croyait mort. Tu t'es volatilisé!»

Ce soir-là, incapable de trouver le sommeil, il avait pensé à mourir. Il aurait voulu voir sa mère une der-nière fois et lui demander pardon pour les décennies d'absence et les petits-enfants dont elle ne connaissait pas l'existence. Il s'était demandé pour quelle vie il avait été fait, ou s'il n'était pas mieux ainsi, là, tout seul. Il était resté allongé avec sa bouteille de whisky. Son haleine se condensait en gouttelettes d'humidité qui constellaient le toit de toile et gelaient. La neige s'était remise à tomber, étouffant le bruit des camions sur la route.

Mais ce ne serait pas la fin. Il avait rêvé qu'une famille et une entreprise lui permettraient de laisser son ancienne vie derrière lui, même si ma mère me dit encore aujourd'hui qu'il n'avait jamais réussi à changer de la seule manière qui importait — qu'elle l'a laissé justement parce que ce qui faisait qu'il était lui ne pouvait pas changer. C'était trop fort ou trop abîmé, fort de la façon dont les blessures deviennent des forces par l'endurance, de la façon dont les fractures se soudent durement à l'intérieur des os.

Quand il vivait sur le terre-plein, la force qui l'habitait avait dû abandonner un rêve et prendre une autre forme, pas tout à fait neuve, mais toujours à mettre à l'épreuve et à chercher, incapable de ne pas survivre. J'imagine sa tente plantée au milieu des conifères, dans cette large descente de terre rocailleuse, le chant d'un colvert s'élevant en contrebas. J'ai suffisamment voyagé pour connaître les émotions solitaires des nuits d'autoroute, mais je ne peux m'imaginer cette solitude et cette rage. Tandis qu'il était allongé là, des secousses faisaient trembler le sol, causées par des semi-remorques transportant de pleins chargements depuis l'intérieur des terres par l'autoroute qui traversait la vaste nature sauvage du continent, de Vancouver à Québec, reliant les vies qu'il avait abandonnées.

«Je pensais à ma mère, m'avait-il dit. Je l'aimais. J'étais son préféré, et j'avais l'impression que je lui avais fait du mal.

— Tu pourrais y retourner maintenant, avais-je suggéré, hésitant à interrompre son histoire, à le provoquer ou à révéler que ma sympathie s'émoussait.

— Non. Ça fait trop longtemps. Je ne peux pas.

— Comment s'appelait-elle?» ai-je demandé.

Mais il était resté muet, et puis il m'avait dit qu'il était tard, et m'avait souhaité bonne nuit.

Les essuie-glaces suffisaient à peine à chasser la pluie quand je me suis garé près de la cabine téléphonique de la station d'essence. On annonçait une tempête hors du commun : des bourrasques et des précipitations qui se changeraient en neige et en pluie verglaçante après minuit. J'allais bientôt être à la maison. J'avais roulé jusqu'à la bibliothèque de l'Université du Massachusetts pour y faire des recherches, et il ne me restait plus qu'à parcourir la route de la montagne. Les cours avaient pris fin en vue des examens finaux et je n'avais pas parlé à mon père depuis quelques jours, mais la veille au soir il avait laissé un message à mes propriétaires : *ton père a téléphoné.*

J'ai couru sous la pluie jusqu'à la cabine et j'ai appelé à frais virés. La ligne était mauvaise. La voix de la téléphoniste a cédé la place à des grésillements ponctués de bruyants cliquetis. La sonnerie a retenti et j'ai attendu d'entendre son accent, ses *h* tranquilles et ses *r* pesants. Quand il a répondu, il semblait loin.

« Juste une minute », a-t-il dit et, de son côté de la ligne, le silence est tombé. Puis il est revenu, le souffle rauque. « J'ai changé d'idée, m'a-t-il annoncé sans autre forme de préambule. J'ai décidé que je garderais le magasin ouvert. Ça ne sert à rien d'abandonner maintenant. »

J'ai pris une profonde inspiration, pas certain de le croire. « Je suis content de l'apprendre.

— Cet hiver va être dur, mais j'ai déjà connu pire.

— C'est super. Tu m'inquiétais vraiment. J'avais peur de ne plus entendre tes histoires.

552

— Tu sais, a-t-il commencé, quand j'étais petit…»
Sa voix s'est brisée; son assurance l'avait quitté d'un
coup. «La vie était dure. Je veux juste que tu comprennes ça.

— Quoi? Oui. Je comprends ça.

— Je sais que j'ai fait des erreurs, mais je veux juste
que tu comprennes que j'ai été en colère pendant
longtemps. Je pense tout le temps que je ne le suis
plus mais, tu sais, ça ne prend pas grand-chose. Ça ne
prend pas grand-chose et la colère revient. Je pensais
à mon oncle l'autre jour. Si j'étais allé vivre avec lui,
j'aurais pu jouer au hockey. J'aurais pu finir l'école.
Mais mon père avait besoin que je travaille. Point
final. J'étais tellement en colère. Je me souviens, j'ai
épargné chaque sou que j'avais pour m'acheter une
paire de patins à glace rouillés. Mais je n'avais pas de
bâton. C'était débile.»

Il a essayé de rire mais a été secoué par une quinte
de toux sèche.

«Quand j'étais jeune, je pensais que si j'étais né
anglais, tout aurait été pour le mieux. Nous n'avions
rien sauf notre famille et l'Église. Je ne croyais pas à
l'Église, mais je pensais que la famille était la chose la
plus importante dans la vie. Je ne sais pas pourquoi
je haïssais l'une et pas l'autre.» Tout en parlant, il s'arrêtait pour prendre de longues inspirations hachées.
«J'aurais dû haïr les deux. Mais je me disais que j'aurais des enfants un jour et que tout serait différent.
Mais… tu me ressembles beaucoup. Je pense que c'est
vrai, tu n'es pas d'accord?

553

— Par certains aspects, peut-être.

— Par beaucoup d'aspects, je pense. Tu as déjà été sérieusement intéressé par le crime.

— J'aimais les histoires, c'est tout, lui ai-je dit, tout à coup épuisé, ne sachant plus que répondre.

— Je veux que tu fasses mieux que moi. Je ne veux pas que tu gâches ta vie. Si ce n'était pas de toi, je n'aurais jamais reparlé de ces trucs. Tu aurais pu être comme moi, mais ça ne vaut pas la peine.

— Je n'aurais pas été comme toi, ai-je dit en essayant de donner un timbre rassurant à ma voix.

— Tu ne te rappelles pas comment tu étais. Tu aurais été comme moi.

— Mais je ne le serai pas », lui ai-je dit. Ma frustration était revenue, mais lasse, un sentiment qui ressemblait à une capitulation.

« O.K. Eh bien, ne t'en fais pas pour moi. Je vais m'occuper du magasin. Je vais m'occuper de tout ça.

— Tu ne vas pas le laisser aller ? » ai-je demandé tout en sachant que c'est ce qu'il ferait. Mon corps commençait à me faire mal, j'avais les côtes et la gorge douloureuses, la tristesse pesait sur ma poitrine comme le deuil même pressenti fait souffrir, de sorte que la blessure semblerait avoir toujours été là, juste sous la peau.

« Je ne sais pas, a-t-il répondu, la voix enrouée. Je vais m'en occuper. »

La ligne a crépité tandis que la foudre zébrait le ciel.

Il a demandé : « Il y a un orage par chez vous ?

— C'est la première fois que je vois des éclairs depuis des mois. Je doute qu'on en ait beaucoup d'autres.

— Tu ne devrais pas être au téléphone. Tu pourrais recevoir une décharge électrique.

— Ça va aller. »

La pluie a gagné en force.

« Veux-tu me rappeler dans quelques jours ?

— Je vais être débordé ces deux prochaines semaines. J'ai des examens finaux. On peut se parler un moment maintenant. »

Des gouttes de pluie martelaient les vitres de la cabine tandis que des phares passaient sur la route.

Il est resté muet, puis a proposé : « On pourrait louer un chalet à Squamish. C'était sincère, ce que j'ai déjà dit. On pourrait pêcher un peu, et je pourrais conter des histoires.

— Tu sais que je ne peux pas. Je n'aime même plus la pêche maintenant. »

Il parlait doucement. « Ça n'a jamais été pour la pêche. C'était pour être dans les montagnes. C'est agréable d'être sur une rivière, c'est tout. Des fois, on n'attrape rien.

— Je sais.

— Mais tu ne peux pas t'absenter quelques jours?

— Pas maintenant», ai-je répété, sentant ma colère monter, comme si tout ce qui ne pouvait pas être dit, enfermé en moi, s'était mué en rage.

La pluie tombait maintenant bruyamment, de la neige fondue et quelques grêlons frappaient les côtés de la cabine. La ligne a sifflé puis a coupé et, quand sa voix est revenue, je l'entendais avec de l'écho.

«L'orage est violent? a-t-il demandé.

— Ouais.

— Tu sais, si jamais tu as l'intention d'écrire ces trucs, il faudrait que tu les écrives comme ils étaient. Ça me plairait. Ce n'est pas que je sois fier d'avoir été un criminel. Je ne le suis pas. J'aurais donné tout ça pour vous voir grandir.»

La ligne a de nouveau grésillé, et je n'ai pas répondu. Je ne pouvais pas lui dire que dans son cœur il n'avait jamais cessé d'être un criminel, qu'il n'avait jamais abandonné cette destruction et ne s'était jamais permis d'être simplement un père ou un homme ordinaire. Il a parlé et je me suis efforcé de faire taire mes pensées et de l'écouter.

«Mais le crime, a-t-il dit, le crime, ce n'était pas toujours bien. Je ne volais pas parce que ça m'excitait. Ce

556

n'était même pas une chose que je souhaitais faire au départ. Je savais que ça me permettrait de survivre. Ce qui est étrange, c'est que je n'ai jamais pensé à ce qui arrivait aux gens quand je n'étais pas là, à l'exception, peut-être, de ma famille. Mais tu sais, plus tard, je me suis senti coupable à cause de ce type dans la bijouterie. J'ai regretté d'y être allé. Dans le journal, il disait que je mesurais plus dun mètre quatre-vingts et que j'avais les cheveux et les yeux noirs. Il disait qu'il n'avait jamais vu un salopard à l'air plus glacial. Il a fallu que je réfléchisse à ça. C'est une chose de braquer une bijouterie, mais c'en est une autre d'entendre la personne que tu as volée raconter que son magasin avait déjà été dévalisé en présence de sa petite fille, et expliquer qu'il ne voulait pas fermer boutique à cause des criminels. Je ne me rappelle pas tout ce qu'il a dit à notre sujet, mais nous avons ri en le lisant. Plus tard, je me suis demandé comment il se sentait, et s'il allait abattre le prochain qui essaierait de le dévaliser, ou bien mourir pour un sac de bagues. »

Le tonnerre a claqué à travers la terre. Il a soupiré et s'est remis à parler à voix basse, de sorte qu'il me fallait tendre l'oreille pour l'entendre.

« Quand j'ai abandonné le crime, je ne connaissais rien d'autre que le poisson. Je voulais avoir une famille. »

Les bourrasques fouettaient la cabine, la grêle tambourinait sur le toit, noyant sa voix. Des voitures se rangeaient sur l'accotement, feux de détresse clignotants. La ligne coupait, et il a répété quelque chose que je ne suis pas arrivé à comprendre. De l'eau coulait dans le coin des panneaux. Je lui ai crié que je le rappellerais plus tard, mais tout à coup la grêle et le vent se sont tus pour laisser place au grésillement des parasites. À travers la vitre mouillée, j'ai scruté l'obscurité et les phares qui passaient et, sans savoir pourquoi, je me suis rappelé les gestes de ses mains, la nuit, au réservoir, tandis que, debout au-dessus de la rive, il enfilait la soie de la canne à pêche. Il avait passé le bras par la fenêtre du camion, les phares s'étaient allumés et il était allé se tenir dans leur lumière. Ses mains bougeaient dans le faisceau, des cicatrices sur les jointures, le bout des doigts épaté pinçant et tirant le fil.

J'ai fermé les yeux. Nous sommes restés muets, comme si nous attendions de traverser cette accalmie, sans pluie ni vent, comme si la gravité avait cessé de faire effet.

«Je voulais vous voir grandir. Votre mère a été bonne avec vous. Elle vous traitait vraiment bien. Je suis désolé que les choses ne se soient pas passées comme elles auraient dû.»

Sa voix était différente, plus douce, et il parlait plus rapidement. «Tu sais, j'étais là pour te mettre au monde. Je n'oublierai jamais. Tu es né à la maison, mais tu avais le cordon autour du cou. Il a fallu que je souffle dans ta bouche et que j'appuie sur ta poitrine jusqu'à ce que tu commences à respirer. Quand je t'ai pris, tu étais si petit que tu tenais allongé dans mes mains. J'ai su que nous serions très proches l'un de l'autre. J'ai toujours su qu'il y avait quelque chose de particulier à cause de la façon dont je te tenais quand tu as commencé à respirer.»

L'orage gagnait en force puis faiblissait, frappant les fenêtres. La friture hoquetait sur la ligne. J'avais toujours les yeux fermés, et j'ai revu le mouvement lent, étrange, de ses mains, le fil à pêche invisible dans l'obscurité, contre la lumière.

«Tu ne viendras pas me voir, hein? a-t-il demandé.

— Je ne sais pas», ai-je répondu trop vite, regrettant immédiatement de n'avoir pas eu le temps de réfléchir à ma réponse. «Pas tout de suite.

— Je sais. Tu fais ce qu'il faut. Je suis content que tu sois fort. J'ai gâché ma vie, et tu devrais... tu devrais te concentrer sur la tienne. Mais ça va aller?

— Aller? ai-je répété.

— Es-tu sûr de pouvoir vivre avec ça?»

Je n'ai pas répondu, et tandis que nous écoutions le bruit haché de la friture sur la ligne, j'ai pensé à ce que je pourrais lui dire, me suis demandé quelle émotion je pourrais exprimer qui ne serait pas de la force.

«Est-ce que ça va aller? a-t-il répété.

— C'est... c'est ton choix. Je ne peux pas te demander de ne pas le faire.

— Tu peux vivre avec ça?

— Oui, ça va aller.

— C'est pour le mieux», a-t-il dit.

La neige fondue frappait les panneaux, et sa voix semblait lointaine. J'ai frissonné, me rendant compte à quel point j'avais froid.

«Quand je serai mort, a-t-il dit, tu peux contacter ma famille. Ma mère s'appelle Alma. Je suis sûr qu'elle est encore en vie. Je le saurais si elle était morte.» Il a gardé le silence un long moment. «Elle vit dans une ville qui s'appelle Matane, au Québec.

— Matane, ai-je répété.

— Promets-moi que tu n'essaieras pas de la retrouver tant que je suis encore en vie.

— Je te le promets.

— Si tu la contactes, dis-lui que tu es le fils d'Edwin.

— Edwin?

— C'est comme ça qu'ils m'appelaient. C'est elle qui me manque. Je voudrais pouvoir la voir une dernière fois. Je lui ai beaucoup menti, et puis j'ai cessé d'écrire. Je lui envoyais des cartes postales disant que j'étais au Mexique ou en route vers l'Alaska. Une fois, quand je travaillais sur un chantier de bûcherons, j'ai vu un gars se faire écraser sous un arbre. Il a crié et appelé sa mère. Je ne comprenais pas.»

Ni l'un ni l'autre n'avons dit un mot, et j'ai essayé de trouver ce que je pourrais dire, comment je pourrais lui parler autrement, d'une manière qui changerait tout cela.

«Il y a eu une époque, a-t-il repris, où j'aurais pu y retourner. Quand vous étiez petits. Mais c'est trop tard maintenant. Comment est-ce que je pourrais tout expliquer? Qu'est-ce que j'ai fait de ma vie?»

J'ai regardé, à travers la vitre sale de la cabine, les phares embrouillés au-dessus de la route. Quelque chose s'est perdu dans la friture derrière sa voix.

«Écoute, il faut que j'y aille, a-t-il dit. Il faut que j'y aille. Il est tard. Tu devrais aller dormir.»

Il a dit au revoir et raccroché avant que je puisse parler.

Je suis monté dans ma camionnette et me suis engagé sur la route, en prenant mon temps pour gravir la montagne tandis que la pluie tombait en rafales devant les phares. Mon cerveau était muet. J'ai tourné dans mon entrée, je me suis garé, je suis entré dans mon appartement.

Je me suis assis, j'ai touché mon visage de mes mains, les coudes sur les genoux, et j'ai respiré.

ÉPILOGUE

Ce printemps-là, un expert-comptable de Vancouver a téléphoné pour expliquer que mon père devait des dizaines de milliers de dollars en impôts impayés et que le gouvernement s'apprêtait à saisir et à mettre à l'encan ce qu'il pouvait, c'est-à-dire pas grand-chose : deux montres-bracelets. Un mois plus tard, j'ai reçu le reste, une petite boîte de photos portant des auto-collants *Air Mail, Par avion,* accompagnée d'un document de douane précisant : *Valeur nulle.* À l'intérieur se trouvaient des photos entourées d'élastiques bleus, des clichés de notre famille et de lui. C'est tout ce qu'il possédait quand, assis dans l'unique fauteuil de sa maison, il me racontait ses histoires.

Les photos que je préférais le montraient, un éclair de supériorité dans ses yeux noirs, hardi devant l'appareil. Sur l'une d'entre elles, on le voyait, jeune, appuyé sur le coffre d'une vieille camionnette, talon calé contre l'attache-remorque, son corps mince et brun tendu par le rire. Sur une autre, il tenait un bébé. Ses muscles saillaient et le bébé pleurait. Derrière lui, un berger allemand regardait par la fenêtre, sa truffe noire invisible sur la vitre sombre. Et puis, des années plus tard, il prenait la pose devant un arbre de Noël, sa barbe rasée ayant cédé la place à une moustache, le visage sillonné de rides. Il portait un veston gris et une chemise blanche. Il avait la mâchoire relevée, avec une expression pleine de fierté très Vieux Continent, l'air de dire au photographe : Voilà la photo que tu veux.

Cette année-là et la suivante, le silence a bourdonné en moi. J'ai brûlé tout ce que j'avais écrit à l'exception des notes prises lors de nos conversations. J'avais soif d'immobilité, de légèreté — comme si, en perdant tout, je pouvais, ne serait-ce que fugacement, me sentir entier. J'écrivais et j'étudiais, m'efforçant de composer mon père dans un roman. Dans mon besoin d'écrire je reconnaissais son désir de parler — l'urgence de son récit, de nous amener à nous comprendre mutuellement et de rendre le pardon possible. Je voulais savoir ce qui, en lui, avait été capable de guider sa vie, tout comme il s'efforçait de comprendre la vie qu'il avait vécue, et l'existence plus simple qu'il avait désirée mais dont il avait été incapable. Plus j'écrivais, apparaissant de plus en plus nettement, dans mes mots et ma façon de raconter une histoire, plus il s'éloignait. Il m'échappait — le paysage de sa jeunesse, les gens qui avaient contribué à le créer.

Peu à peu, après deux ans et demi, le silence s'est atténué. J'ai commencé à lire souvent en français et à rêver dans cette langue comme je le faisais des années plus tôt. Des souvenirs me sont revenus, des émotions oubliées dans les sons, la langue et la culture que j'avais tenus pour acquis. Je disais *foulard** et le mot recelait un éclair de froid et le délice d'un parent s'agenouillant pour nouer mon écharpe et la rentrer dans mon manteau. Cela ne lui ressemblait pas, mais tandis que je lisais, le son des mots se souvenait pour moi ; mon manuel de grammaire avec des canards sur la couverture, les exercices que nous répétions : *je suis, tu es, il est, nous sommes**.

J'ai écrit la lettre, disant que j'étais le fils d'Edwin, un nom étranger à ma plume :

Chère Alma,

*Je sais que vous ne me connaissez pas et que le contenu de cette lettre va être surprenant et même parfois difficile à lire**...*

Une semaine plus tard, un homme a téléphoné. Sa voix graveleuse était si familière que j'ai eu un moment d'égarement, l'impression de rêver en retrouvant une conversation nocturne deux ans plus tôt. Il m'a dit qu'il était mon oncle et nous avons parlé de mon père et de la famille, de leur bonheur en recevant ma lettre, des questions qu'ils se posaient. Quand j'ai expliqué comment était mort mon père, il a demandé que je n'en parle pas à ma grand-mère. Elle avait plus de quatre-vingt-dix ans et, bien qu'elle fût forte, elle était aussi profondément religieuse ; cette nouvelle l'aurait terrassée. J'ai accepté de dire qu'il avait succombé à un cancer.

Je suis parti pour le Québec, traversant le Maine et le Nouveau-Brunswick puis mettant le cap sur le nord vers le Saint-Laurent, dans un paysage vallonneux de pierres usées par les éléments. Les dernières averses du mois d'août éclataient, poussées par le vent, taches sombres dans un ciel autrement dégagé. Le paysage révélait peu de choses sur ses habitants : rares villages, Lac-des-Aigles ou Saint-Esprit, guère plus qu'une station-service, un dépanneur et quelques maisons le long de la route. La terre montait jusqu'à ce que l'horizon s'affaisse et que, loin en contrebas, le Saint-Laurent s'étale, semblable à une plaine de pierres.

La crainte que j'avais eue — celle de découvrir une famille de bandits — s'est vite évanouie. J'ai d'abord rencontré mon oncle, le plus jeune des enfants, qui était encore petit lorsque mon père était parti. Il était de ma taille, bien vêtu, portait des lunettes, avait les yeux et les cheveux sombres, quelque chose de mon père dans la mâchoire, bien qu'il fût bien différent, comme je l'apprendrais : plus aimable, plus doux. C'était un homme d'affaires accompli, et il m'a présenté à la famille. De temps en temps, il s'interrompait pour dire combien il était heureux, et qu'ils n'avaient jamais su ce qui était arrivé à mon père.

« On est bien contents que tu nous aies écrit. On n'avait pas de nouvelles d'Edwin*. »

Ma grand-mère avait quatre-vingt-dix ans et habitait seule en appartement. Quand je suis entré dans la pièce, son regard ne m'a pas quitté, sondant mon visage alors qu'elle passait rapidement devant les autres. Ses yeux verts étaient attentifs derrière ses lunettes. Elle a agrippé mon bras et m'a étudié.

«*Mon doux, mon doux*, a-t-elle dit, *comme il a l'air d'Edwin**.»

Les quatre jours suivants se sont passés en nombreuses visites, en conversations qui s'étiraient jusqu'au matin, en larmes et en questions. La famille n'avait pas vu mon père depuis 1967, exactement trente ans plus tôt, et la dernière fois qu'il avait téléphoné remontait à 1973 environ. Tous se rappelaient qu'il leur avait annoncé la naissance de mon frère. Une grande photo encadrée de mon père était restée sur la télévision de ma grand-mère pendant des décennies.

Je lui ai demandé comment il était enfant, et elle a réfléchi à la question.

«Il ne pleurait pas, a-t-elle dit, et c'était le seul qui ne chantait pas en travaillant.»

La sœur aînée de mon père m'a montré d'autres photos, dont une de la cabane rudimentaire plantée sur une étendue dénudée de la Côte-Nord où il était né, prise depuis l'eau, devant d'immenses pierres. Et enfin il y avait des photos de l'époque où il était revenu, jeune homme à la mise élégante, le veston rejeté sur le côté, la main sur la hanche, comme un propriétaire terrien prenant la pose pour qu'on fasse son portrait.

En regardant des photos de la famille et de la maison en clin de bois, j'avais du mal à faire le lien entre ce monde et l'homme que j'avais connu. Mon grand-père Thomas était mort des années plus tôt, ainsi que Lucien, le frère de mon père, mais personne n'en parlait beaucoup. Il y avait des histoires que je connaissais déjà, sur le fait que Thomas faisait boxer mon père et Lucien dans le salon.

«C'étaient des durs — ton grand-père, et Edwin et Lucien», m'a dit la femme de mon oncle. Elle a suggéré que j'interroge mon oncle sur Expo 67, la dernière visite de mon père. «Ça l'a troublé, a-t-elle dit. Il n'aime pas en parler.»

Après souper, j'ai posé la question quand mon oncle et moi nous sommes retrouvés seuls. Il a bu sa bière en y réfléchissant.

«Je les ai vus commencer à se bagarrer. Edwin et Lucien. Pas l'un contre l'autre, mais contre tous ceux qui étaient dans le bar. Ça m'a vraiment choqué. Ils m'avaient emmené à l'Expo. J'avais mis mes plus beaux vêtements et je portais une cravate. Un homme a renversé son verre sur le bras d'Edwin sans le faire exprès. Je suis resté figé sur place, incapable de faire un geste. Je n'avais jamais été témoin de tant de violence. Edwin a commencé, et Lucien s'est joint à lui. Ils frappaient tous ceux qui se mettaient sur leur chemin. Ils ont tout cassé. Ils… ils ont détruit des gens.»

Il a eu l'air de considérer ce qu'il venait de dire.

«Tu sais, ton père me téléphonait. J'étais assez jeune à l'époque. Il m'a dit qu'il avait été emprisonné pour avoir accidentellement tué un homme. Il a dit qu'il l'avait battu et que l'homme était tombé et s'était frappé la tête sur le bord du trottoir. Il n'était pas assez vieux pour aller en prison alors on l'avait envoyé dans un centre de détention dans les Prairies. Il m'a dit que c'était ennuyeux.»

Je ne l'ai pas dit à voix haute, mais je me suis demandé si cette histoire était la façon qu'avait trouvée mon père de justifier son absence, de faire en sorte que les années passées en prison semblent accidentelles. C'était peut-être aussi simplement l'une des nombreuses raisons pour lesquelles on l'avait incarcéré.

Nous étions assis tranquilles à table, le reste de la famille regardait la télé dans le salon.

«Comment Lucien est-il mort?» ai-je demandé.

Il m'a regardé, les yeux impassibles derrière la monture d'acier de ses lunettes, comme s'il fallait, pour voir qui j'étais, non pas un examen minutieux mais simplement de la patience.

«*Il s'est suicidé aussi**, a-t-il fini par répondre. C'est pour ça que je ne peux pas dire la vérité à ta grand-mère au sujet de ton père. Savoir qu'un autre de ses fils s'est enlevé la vie, ce serait trop pour elle. Elle a failli tous nous rendre fous en essayant de faire enterrer les cendres de Lucien au cimetière.

Le lendemain, j'ai dîné avec ma tante, qui m'a raconté la dernière visite de mon père. Nous étions assis dans la salle à manger, l'air frais de l'après-midi entrait en coups de vent par la fenêtre ouverte.

«Il conduisait une décapotable, il était habillé de soie et il avait apporté des cadeaux pour tout le monde. Chaque fois qu'on disait quelque chose, il riait et disait que rien n'allait l'arrêter. Il allait monter en flèche. Mais une dispute a éclaté entre ton grand-père et lui. Ils étaient allés faire un tour dans la décapotable neuve d'Edwin. Quand ils sont revenus, ton grand-père est descendu et a craché sur le plancher. Edwin était hors de lui. Personne ne savait ce qui s'était passé. Edwin avait toujours été son préféré. Il était le préféré de tout le monde. C'est lui qui a décidé qu'il nous détestait. Pas nous. On l'aimait. On a toujours souhaité qu'il revienne.»

Peut-être mon père blâmait-il mon grand-père pour leur pauvreté, pour la vie qu'ils menaient. J'essayais de comprendre comment la violence de mon aïeul avait pu façonner ses fils. Ma tante m'a expliqué la rivalité entre les frères, Edwin et Lucien, le désir de chacun de surpasser l'autre, de gagner l'admiration de leur père.

«Lucien nous disait qu'il avait eu de la chance d'apprendre à se battre. Ton *grand-père** faisait enfiler des gants à Edwin et à Lucien, et la famille les regardait se battre. Lucien était beaucoup plus costaud, même s'il était son cadet de deux ans, mais Edwin était rapide. *Il était malin et orgueilleux**. Il trouvait toujours un moyen de l'emporter.

— Et Lucien? Parle-moi de sa mort.»

Elle a hésité. «C'était un homme difficile. Il buvait trop et il était agressif. Il n'avait pas le charme de ton père. Edwin était facile à aimer, et ça a dû être dur pour Lucien.»

Elle a expliqué qu'entre deux voyages dans la marine marchande, Lucien se présentait parfois à sa porte, ivre, pour parler.

«Une fois, il m'a dit qu'il avait vu ton père. Il m'a raconté qu'il l'avait trouvé en prison. Je ne l'ai pas cru. Il a dit qu'Edwin était en prison à Tacoma… *Y était en prison*, qu'il a dit. *Chus allé aux States et je l'ai trouvé**.»

Elle n'aurait accordé foi à personne d'autre, mais Lucien, Edwin et Thomas étaient différents. «Il y avait des hommes dans la famille comme ça, qui pouvaient aller n'importe où, faire n'importe quoi.»

Il lui avait raconté comment il avait trouvé mon père et lui avait dit que tout le monde saurait qu'il était un criminel — qu'il irait le dire à *maman**. Elle avait demandé combien de temps s'était passé depuis. *Plus de cinq ans**, lui avait-il dit.

Mon père avait juré n'avoir jamais reçu la moindre visite en prison. Pourquoi n'avait-il pas mentionné cette rencontre avec Lucien, un frère en retrouvant un autre dans un monde d'impossibilité? Y avait-il eu de bonnes paroles échangées, les vieilles rancunes avaient-elles refait surface plus tard? Ou bien Lucien était-il arrivé désireux de punir mon père de sa dernière et splendide visite à la maison, d'avoir inondé sa famille de cadeaux comme les autres n'auraient jamais pu le faire?

«— *Tout le monde va savoir**», lui avait-il dit.

Que pouvait faire mon père derrière les grillages et le plexiglas? Comment s'étaient-ils dit au revoir? Quand il avait regagné sa cellule, il avait dû croire qu'il ne pourrait jamais retourner à la maison.

Mais Lucien avait ensuite raconté une autre histoire à ma tante, plus étrange, plus récente, datant de cette année-là. Il avait accosté à Vancouver et s'était rendu à un marché populaire du centre-ville, le Granville. Là, il avait vu Edwin derrière l'étal d'une poissonnerie. Edwin avait une grosse barbe et il avait fait semblant qu'il ne connaissait pas Lucien. Il avait prétendu ne pas parler français. Ma tante m'a décrit parfaitement, comme Lucien le lui avait décrit, le Granville Island Market et la boutique que mon père y tenait, ainsi que mon père lui-même, avec sa barbe, comme il apparaissait dans ces années-là.

Mais Lucien n'avait jamais dit ce qu'il savait à sa mère. Quand il avait parlé à ma tante, il était habité par la colère mais aussi par la pitié. Il n'avait pas tout révélé à la famille comme il avait menacé de le faire.

«Ça explique pourquoi ton père a appelé à quelques reprises. Il devait essayer de découvrir ce qu'on savait. Il m'a dit que c'était difficile, qu'il n'avait pas beaucoup d'argent. Normalement, la famille aurait offert de l'aider. Il n'aurait pas eu besoin de le demander. On était comme ça. Mais on l'avait vu tellement riche qu'on ne pouvait pas l'imaginer pauvre. Et il était trop fier pour demander… Ce n'est que maintenant que j'ai vu des photos de ton enfance que je comprends à quel point vous étiez démunis. On aurait aidé. Il aurait dû demander.»

Je me suis souvenu de nos années dans la vallée, où il s'était lancé en affaires et avait trimé sans relâche pour construire une vie. Ses efforts avaient masqué l'amertume de la perte, la volonté d'invalider ce qu'avait pu dire Lucien à la famille. Était-il possible qu'il ait agi contre sa nature et construit cette vie, si semblable, par plusieurs aspects, à celle qu'il avait connue dans son enfance, simplement pour prouver que son frère avait tort?

Quant à Lucien, il n'en avait soufflé mot à personne d'autre que ma tante. Peu après cette conversation, il avait téléphoné de Montréal et elle avait répondu. Il avait demandé à parler à sa mère, qui était attablée pour le souper. Il lui avait dit qu'il l'aimait et s'était tiré une balle dans le cœur.

À quoi avait pensé mon père en voyant Lucien devant son étal au marché Granville? Il devait avoir ouvert ce commerce l'année où Lucien s'était enlevé la vie. Peut-être croyait-il que certaines choses ne se réparent pas. Ou qu'il ne pouvait revenir sur sa décision, fondée sur l'orgueil et la force: disparaître plutôt que de laisser sa famille voir son échec. Mais si Lucien était le seul à être au courant de ses crimes, il ne fait pas de doute qu'il aimait ce grand frère autant que le reste de la famille. Peut-être avait-il voulu dire à mon père qu'il n'avait jamais mis sa menace à exécution.

Aujourd'hui encore, j'essaie de dégager un sens de cela, les deux suicides accomplis chacun en l'absence de l'autre, dans l'ignorance de la solitude et de la souffrance de l'autre — deux frères qui se croisent sans se voir, comme des étrangers.

La nuit, incapable de trouver le sommeil, je réécrivais des brouillons de l'histoire de mon père. Je m'escrimais à lui donner une forme cohérente, à voir d'autres versions de sa vie, à résoudre des questions qu'il avait laissées sans réponse.

Peu à peu, j'en suis venu à comprendre qu'il y avait trop d'affabulations, trop de fantaisie. Je me suis retrouvé à éplucher les strates de fiction. J'avais besoin de distinguer les personnages clairement et me demandais quelle portion de ce que j'écrivais était vraie — non seulement en raison de mes embellissements, mais de ses propres exagérations et de celles de sa famille. Il y avait tant d'événements que je n'arrivais pas à ordonner correctement, tant de faits embrouillés. Il lui arrivait souvent de raconter la même histoire plusieurs fois avec de subtiles différences, selon son humeur, selon la vérité qu'il traquait dans son passé au moment où il en faisait le récit. De ma famille, j'ai appris le mot *agrémenteur,* terme familier pour «conteur», un jeu de mots où *agrémenter* rencontre *menteur*. Je ne m'intéressais pas tellement aux faits derrière ses histoires, aux prisons elles-mêmes, ou aux dossiers de la police. Les souvenirs de fiction ou de fantasmes sont aussi réels que les souvenirs de toute autre expérience. Pourtant, il y avait tant de choses que j'aurais voulu pouvoir lui demander. J'essayais de me rappeler sa voix au téléphone, ses silences tellement intenses que je pouvais entendre le bruissement de chaque feuille tombant sur les fougères gelées de l'autre côté de la fenêtre.

Un après-midi, mon oncle et moi avons roulé le long de la côte battue par les vents jusqu'au sud-ouest de la Gaspésie. Nous nous sommes arrêtés à la vieille ferme où avait grandi mon père, où mon grand-père avait été élevé. Un chemin de terre cahoteux montait à partir de la route principale, les terres en friche s'élevaient en une pente abrupte jusqu'aux champs plus haut. Loin en contrebas se dessinaient ce que mon grand-père appelait *les islets**, quelques crêtes affleurant non loin de la rive, où avaient pêché mon grand-père et son père avant lui. Ma tante m'avait montré l'endroit sur de vieilles photos, des filets tirés du chenal, les poissons éparpillés d'une brillante teinte de gris au milieu des rochers.

À partir de l'emplacement de la ferme dont rien ne subsistait — nulle trace de maison, de fondation ou de grange —, nous avons marché jusqu'aux pierres d'une vieille digue contre laquelle venait frapper le vent régulier du golfe.

Nous avons roulé jusqu'au village voisin, Les Méchins : demeures décrépites dans quelques petites rues près de l'église en pierres qui avait été le théâtre de tant d'histoires, où le curé Jean, ce prêtre que mon père haïssait, avait prêché. Il était mort durant la dernière visite de mon père, en 1967, ce qui pouvait susciter certaines spéculations.

Au cimetière, nous sommes restés un moment devant les tombes de Thomas et de Lucien. J'ai songé à la vitesse à laquelle cette région du monde avait changé, et au fait que le passage d'une génération pouvait faire du plus jeune frère de mon père l'homme d'affaires que lui-même aurait rêvé d'être. Mais je savais que ce n'était pas si simple. Il n'y aurait pas de réponse facile expliquant pourquoi mon père avait choisi sa vie.

Mon oncle a commencé à me dire que je devrais penser à rester, peut-être me trouver un boulot, mais comme je ne répondais pas, il s'est arrêté et nous sommes restés à regarder les pierres tombales. Je savais que je n'avais pas encore satisfait ma faim d'expériences et que bientôt, à ses yeux, je ressemblerais au frère qu'il avait perdu. Au fil de mes voyages, j'en étais venu à reconnaître les passions que je partageais avec mon père : pour le hasard et le plaisir du risque, l'abandon et la solitude, et pour nos faims elles-mêmes, non pas le besoin d'y remédier, mais pour la joie de vivre avec elles, leur façon de nous combler et de nous pousser en avant. Je me suis souvenu d'avoir été un adolescent transporté par les histoires d'aventures de mon père. Je sortais en catimini la nuit et je restais debout au bord de l'autoroute, laissant les poids lourds passer tout près, le vent de leur sillage sur mon visage. Je voulais trouver mon père dans mes propres risques, ressentir tout ce qu'il avait ressenti, atteindre l'obscure frontière d'une autre vie de sorte que, lorsque je reviendrais vers la mienne, elle étincellerait, brillante.

Mon oncle et moi sommes restés à distance de vue de l'église, tous les deux silencieux. La bise du golfe était forte, si implacable que je pouvais m'imaginer un homme devenir fou à force de vivre et de travailler ici. L'espace d'un instant, je me suis penché en arrière dans le vent et l'ai senti me soutenir.

NOTE DE L'AUTEUR

J'ai écrit le premier jet de ce qui deviendrait ces mémoires au mois de mars 1995, à l'âge de vingt ans, trois mois seulement après la mort de mon père. Ne sachant pas exactement quelle histoire je souhaitais raconter, je l'ai rédigé en vitesse au printemps pendant la relâche universitaire. Je n'avais pas encore réfléchi à la distinction entre fiction et mémoires, et à cette époque je parlais plus volontiers d'un roman car je souhaitais être romancier.

Pendant les deux semaines où j'ai couché ce premier jet sur le papier, je ne pouvais m'imaginer que dix-sept années de réécriture s'ensuivraient. Tout en travaillant à un autre roman et à de nombreux projets plus modestes, j'ai réécrit ces mémoires des dizaines de fois, convaincu qu'ils ne seraient jamais publiés, qu'il s'agissait d'une histoire qu'il me fallait écrire pour moi-même. Pendant environ dix de ces années, j'ai sciemment choisi d'en faire un roman, modifiant divers détails tout en conservant les données essentielles. En décidant de réécrire le texte sous la forme de mémoires, j'ai compris comment, en reprenant le récit d'une histoire, quelle qu'elle soit, on la sépare de l'événement originel pour lui donner une vie propre. Après tant d'années à raconter ses propres histoires, mon père a peut-être éprouvé quelque chose de semblable, et j'ai passé des années à creuser à travers les strates, essayant de reconstruire le passé et de trouver ce que je voulais écrire.

On m'a souvent demandé si tout était vrai. Je peins le plus précisément possible les scènes auxquelles j'ai pris part mais, la mémoire continuant d'évoluer dans le temps, il est difficile de mesurer à quel point les années subséquentes ont façonné mon souvenir. Au cours du processus d'édition, la chronologie a parfois connu des modifications, et certains événements ont été rapprochés à des fins de cohérence, ce qui me semblait préférable à l'ajout de détails superflus ou répétitifs. Pour ce qui est des histoires de mon père, il m'en a tant raconté que les transcriptions de n'importe quelle année pourraient faire des milliers de pages. Au fur et à mesure que je vieillissais, il les racontait différemment, révélant ou peut-être ajoutant de petits détails afin de les rendre plus intéressantes à mes yeux. Grâce à sa famille, j'ai pu confirmer une grande partie de ce qu'il m'avait confié sur sa jeunesse, bien qu'il arrive que leurs versions des événements diffèrent. Comme j'en suis venu à m'intéresser moins aux banques qu'il avait dévalisées qu'à l'influence qu'ont eue ces révélations et ces histoires sur moi quand j'étais enfant, je ne me suis pas astreint à vérifier les multiples détails de son dossier criminel. En outre, il a vécu et a été incarcéré sous plusieurs identités, que je ne connais pas toutes. J'ai bien tenté d'obtenir son dossier criminel canadien, mais il faut attendre vingt ans après la mort d'un individu pour y avoir accès. L'une de mes tantes, décédée depuis, m'a dit l'avoir lu des années plus tôt, après avoir réussi à convaincre un ami policier de le lui obtenir. Elle n'a pas voulu dire grand-chose sur le sujet, se contentant de confirmer que mon père avait commis de nombreux crimes et avait été plusieurs fois emprisonné. Au sujet de son dossier, elle a toutefois précisé : « *Il ne faisait rien à moitié**. »

J'ai aussi tenté une approche plus directe que d'écrire au gouvernement, et me suis rendu dans un poste de la Sûreté du Québec muni du certificat de décès de mon père. Les agents en devoir m'ont dit qu'ils n'auraient sans doute rien dans leurs archives, avant de vérifier. Ils ont eu l'air stupéfait. Bien qu'ils aient confirmé l'existence d'un dossier, et le fait que celui-ci était bien rempli, ils ont répété qu'ils ne pouvaient divulguer les renseignements qui y figuraient. Ils m'ont plutôt posé quelques questions, comme s'ils craignaient que je puisse ressembler à mon père, avant de finir par me dire que je devrais m'adresser au gouvernement.

REMERCIEMENTS

Je tiens à remercier les personnes et les institutions suivantes pour l'appui qu'elles m'ont apporté au fil des années : l'Andersen Center de Tower View, la MacDowell Colony, la fondation Edward F. Albee, Ledig House de l'Omni International Arts Center, le programme d'artistes en résidence Jentel, le Conseil des Arts du Canada et le Conseil des arts et des lettres du Québec. Je suis profondément redevable à toute l'équipe de Milkweed Editions, plus particulièrement à Allison Wigen, qui a si méticuleusement coordonné les multiples aspects de la production, et par-dessus tout à Daniel Slager pour son enthousiasme, son appui indéfectible et sa direction éditoriale brillante et rigoureuse.

Composition : Isabelle Tousignant
Correction d'épreuves : Sophie Marcotte
Conception graphique : Antoine Tanguay et Hugues Skene (KX3 Communication)

Éditions Alto
280, rue Saint-Joseph Est, bureau 1
Québec (Québec) G1K 3A9
www.editionsalto.com

ACHEVÉ D'IMPRIMER
CHEZ MARQUIS IMPRIMEUR
EN MARS 2013
POUR LE COMPTE DES ÉDITIONS ALTO

GARANT DES FORÊTS
INTACTES

L'impression de *Remèdes pour la faim* sur papier Rolland Enviro100 Édition
plutôt que sur du papier vierge a permis de sauver l'équivalent de 69 arbres,
d'économiser 260 401 litres d'eau et d'empêcher le rejet de 3 944 kilos
de déchets solides et de 10 253 kilos d'émissions atmosphériques.

EcoLogo°   100 %

Dépôt légal, 2ᵉ trimestre 2013
Bibliothèque et Archives nationales du Québec